THE RISE OF THE SHADOW ACADEMY

THE RISE OF THE SHADOW ACADEMY

HEIRS OF THE FORCE
SHADOW ACADEMY
THE LOST ONES
LIGHTSABERS
DARKEST KNIGHT
JEDI UNDER SIEGE

KEVIN J. ANDERSON
and REBECCA MOESTA

HEIRS OF THE FORCE   Copyright © 1995 by Lucasfilm Ltd.
   Printing History: Boulevard edition/June 1995

SHADOW ACADEMY   ® tm & Copyright © 1995 by Lucasfilm Ltd.
   Printing History: Boulevard edition/September 1994

THE LOST ONES   ® tm & Copyright © 1995 by Lucasfilm Ltd.
   Printing History: Boulevard edition/December 1995

LIGHTSABERS   ® tm & Copyright © 1996 by Lucasfilm Ltd.
   Printing History: Boulevard edition/March 1996

DARKEST KNIGHT   ® tm & Copyright © 1996 by Lucasfilm Ltd.
   Printing History: Boulevard edition/June 1996

JEDI UNDER SIEGE   ® tm & Copyright © 1996 by Lucasfilm Ltd.
   Printing History: Boulevard edition/September 1996

All Rights Reserved.

This book may not be reproduced in whole or in part, by mimeograph or any other means, without permission.

Published by arrangement with:
Boulevard Books
a division of
The Berkley Publishing Group
200 Madison Avenue
New York, NY 10016

ISBN: 1-56865-211-9

Printed in the United States of America.

Contents

HEIRS OF THE FORCE	5
SHADOW ACADEMY	117
THE LOST ONES	245
LIGHTSABERS	361
DARKEST KNIGHT	489
JEDI UNDER SIEGE	601

HEIRS OF THE FORCE

To our parents
—Andrew & Dorothy Anderson
and Louis & Louise Moesta—
who taught us to love books

Acknowledgments

We would like to thank Vonda N. McIntyre for helping to create the kids, Dave Wolverton for his suggestions with Tenel Ka and Dathomir, Lucy Wilson and Sue Rostoni at Lucasfilm for all their ideas and for giving us the opportunity to do this new series, Ginjer Buchanan and Lou Aronica at Berkley for being so enthusiastic about the project, and Brent Lynch, Gregory McNamee, Skip Shayotovich, and the entire STAR WARS FidoNet Echo computer bulletin board for helping out with the jokes. And special thanks to Lil Mitchell for helping with so much of the typing and to Jonathan MacGregor Cowan for Qorl's name.

1

JACEN SOLO HAD stayed at Luke Skywalker's Jedi academy for about a month before he managed to set up his room the way he wanted it.

Within an ancient temple on the jungle moon of Yavin 4, the student quarters were dank and dim, cold every night. But Jacen and his twin sister Jaina had spent days scrubbing the moss-covered stone blocks of their adjoining rooms, adding glowpanels and portable corner-warmers.

The son of Han Solo and Princess Leia stood now in the orangish morning light that spilled through the slit windows in the thick temple walls. Outside in the jungle, large birds shrieked as they fought for their insect breakfasts.

As he did every morning before going to Uncle Luke's lessons, Jacen fed and took stock of all the bizarre and exotic creatures he had collected out in the unexplored jungles on Yavin 4. He liked to gather new pets.

The far wall was stacked with bins and cages, transparent display cages and bubbling aquariums. Many of the containers were ingenious contraptions invented by his mechanically inclined sister. He appreciated Jaina's inventions, though he couldn't understand why she was more interested in the cages themselves than the creatures they contained.

One cage rattled with two clamoring stintarils, tree-dwelling rodents with protruding eyes and long jaws filled with sharp teeth. Stintarils would swarm across the arboreal highways, never slowing down, eating anything that sat still long enough for them to take a bite. Jacen had had a fun time catching these two.

In a damp, transparent enclosure tiny swimming crabs used sticky mud to build complex nests with small towers and curving battlements. In a rounded water bowl pinkish mucous salamanders swam formlessly, diluted and without shape, until they crawled out onto a perching shelf; then they hardened their outer membranes to a soft jellylike form with pseudopods and a mouth, allowing them to hunt among the insects in the weeds.

In another cage strung with thick, tough wires, iridescent blue piranha-beetles crawled around with clacking jaws, constantly trying to chew their way free. Out in the jungle a wild swarm of piranha-beetles could descend with a thin deadly whine. When they set upon their prey, the beetles could turn a large animal to gnawed bones in minutes. Jacen was proud to have the only specimens in captivity in his menagerie.

Often Jacen's most difficult job was not keeping the exotic pets caged but figuring out what they ate. Sometimes they fed on fruit or flowers. Sometimes they devoured fresh meat chunks. Sometimes the larger ones even broke free of their confinement and ate the *other* specimens—much to Jacen's dismay.

Unlike Jacen and Jaina's strict tutors at home on the city-covered planet Coruscant, Luke Skywalker did not depend on a rigorous course of studies. To be a Jedi, Uncle Luke explained, one had to understand many pieces of the whole tapestry of the galaxy, not just a rigid pattern set by other people.

So Jacen was allowed to spend much of his free time tromping through the dense underbrush, pushing jungle weeds and flowers out of the way, collecting beautiful insects, scooping up rare and unusual fungi. He had always had a strange and deep affinity for living creatures, much as his sister had a talent for understanding machinery and gadgets. He could coax the animals with his special Force talent, getting them to come right up to him, where he could study them at his leisure.

Some of the Jedi students—especially spoiled and troublesome Raynar—were not pleased about the small zoo Jacen kept in his room. But Jacen studied the creatures, and took care of them, and learned much from the animals.

From a small cistern Jaina had installed in the wall, Jacen ladled cool water into trays inside the cages. His motion disturbed a family of purple jumping spiders so that they hopped and bounced against the netting of the cage roof.

He ran his fingers along the thin wires and whispered to them. "Calm down. It's all right." The spiders stopped their antics and settled down to drink through their long, hollow fangs.

In another cage, the whisper birds had fallen silent, possibly hungry. Jacen would have to collect some fresh nectar funnels from the vines growing in the stones of the crumbling temple across the river.

It was almost time to go to morning lessons. Jacen tapped the sides of the containers, saying good-bye to his pets. Just before turning to leave, though, he hesitated. He peered into the bottommost container, where the transparent crystal snake usually sat coiled in a bed of dry leaves.

The crystal snake was nearly invisible, and Jacen could see it only by looking at the creature in a certain light. But now, no matter which way he looked, he saw no glitter of glassy scales, no rainbowish curve of light that bent around the transparent creature. Alarmed, he leaned down and discovered that the bottom corner of the cage had been bent upward . . . just enough for a thin serpent to slither out.

"I've got a bad feeling about this," Jacen said, unconsciously echoing the words his father so often used.

The crystal snake was not particularly dangerous—at least Jacen didn't think so. He did know from firsthand experience that the bite of the snake brought a moment of piercing pain, and then the victim fell into a deep sleep. Even though after an hour or so one would wake up and feel no ill effects, this was the sort of hazard someone like Raynar might use to cause trouble and perhaps force Jacen to move his pets to an outside storage module.

And now the crystal snake was loose.

His heart started racing with fear, but he remembered to use one of his uncle Luke's Jedi relaxation techniques to keep himself calm, to help him think more clearly. Jacen knew immediately what he had to do: he would have his sister Jaina help him find the snake before anyone noticed it was gone.

He slipped out into the dim hall, his dark round eyes flicking from side to side to check for anyone who might notice him. Then he ducked into the next rounded stone doorway and stood blinking in the shadows of his sister's room.

One entire wall of Jaina's quarters was filled with neatly stacked containers of spare parts, cyberfuses, electronic circuit loops, and tiny gears taken from dismantled and obsolete droids. She had removed unused power packs and control systems from the old Rebel war room deep in the inner chambers of the temple pyramid.

The ancient temple had once been headquarters for the secret Rebel base hidden in the jungles on this isolated moon, long before the twins had been born. Their mother, Princess Leia, had helped the Rebels defend their base against the Empire's terrible Death Star; their father, Han Solo, had been just a smuggler at the time, but he had rescued Luke Skywalker at the end.

Now, though, most of the old equipment from the empty Rebel

base lay unused and forgotten by the Jedi trainees. Jaina spent her free time tinkering with it, putting the components together in new ways. Her room was crammed with so much large equipment that Jacen barely had enough space to squeeze inside. He looked around, but saw no sign of the escaped crystal snake.

"Jaina?" he said. "Jaina, I need your help!" He looked around the dim room, trying to find his sister. He smelled the sharp, biting odor of scorched fuses, heard the clunk of a heavy tool against metal.

"Just a minute." Jaina's voice echoed hollowly inside the barrel-shaped hulk of corroded machinery that took up half of her quarters. He remembered when the two of them, with the help of their muscular female friend Tenel Ka, had somewhat clumsily used their Force powers to haul the heavy machine along the winding corridors so Jaina could work on it in her room far into the night.

"Hurry!" Jacen said, feeling the urgency grow. Jaina squirmed backward out of an opening in the intake pipe. Her dark brown hair was straight and simple, tied back with a string to keep it away from her narrow face. Smudges of grease made hash marks on her left cheek.

Though her shoulder-length hair was as rich and thick as her mother's, Jaina never wanted to take the time to twist and tangle it into the lovely, convoluted hairstyles for which Princess Leia had been so famous.

Jacen extended his hand to help her to her feet. "My crystal snake's loose again! We have to find it. Have you seen it?"

She took little notice of his words. "No, I've been busy in here. Almost finished, though." She pointed down at the grimy pumping machinery. "When this is all done we'll be able to install it in the river next to the temple. The flowing water can turn the wheels and charge all of our batteries." Her words picked up speed as she began to talk. Once Jaina got started, she loved to explain things.

Jacen tried to interrupt, but could find no pause in her speech. "But, my snake—"

"With phased output jacks we can divert power to the Great Temple, provide all the light we need. With special protein skimmers added on, we could extract algae from the water and process it into food. We could even power all of the academy's communication systems and—"

Jacen stopped her. "Jaina, why are you spending all your time doing this? Don't we have dozens of permanent power cells left over from the old Rebel base?"

She sighed, making him feel as if he had missed some deeply important point. "I'm not building this because it's *useful*," she said. "I'm doing it to see if I *can*. Once I know I can do it, I won't have to waste time anymore wondering whether anything I learn here is useful or not."

Jacen was still not sure he understood. But then, his sister never could grasp his fascination for living creatures. "In the meantime, Jaina, could you help me find my snake? It's loose. I don't know where to look for it."

"All right," Jaina said, brushing her dirty hands on her stained work overall. "If the snake escaped from your room, it probably moved down the corridor."

The two of them stepped out into the long hall. Side by side, they scanned the shadows and listened.

Jacen's room was the last chamber in one of the temple passages leading to a cold, cracked stone wall. But none of the cracks was wide enough for the crystal snake to hide in.

"We'll have to check from room to room," Jaina said.

Jacen nodded. "If something's wrong, we should be able to sense it. Maybe I can use the Force to track the snake, wherever it might be hiding."

They heard the other Jedi students in their quarters dressing, washing up, or maybe just catching a few extra minutes of sleep. Jacen cocked his ears and listened, half-hoping to hear someone scream out loud, because then he would know where the snake had gone.

They slipped from room to room, pausing at closed doors. Jacen touched his fingers to the wood, but he caught no tingling sensation that might indicate his escaped pet.

But when they came to Raynar's half-open door, they immediately sensed something out of the ordinary. Peering inside, the twins spotted the boy sprawled on the polished stone tiles of the floor.

Raynar wore fine garments of purple, gold, and scarlet cloth, the colors of his noble family's house. Despite Uncle Luke's gentle suggestions, Raynar rarely took off his fancy costume, never allowed himself to be seen in drab but comfortable Jedi training clothes.

Raynar's bristly blond hair shone like flecks of gold dust in the morning sunlight spilling into his room through the window slits. His flushed cheeks sagged in and blew out as he snored softly in an awkward position on the cold tile floor.

"Oh, blaster bolts!" Jacen said. "I think we've found my snake."

Jaina slid the door closed and stationed herself by the crack so the crystal snake couldn't get past her.

Jacen knelt beside Raynar's form and let his eyelids flutter closed.

He stretched his fingers into the air, and his knuckles cracked. He let his mind flow, imagining what a snake's thoughts might be like. As usual he felt many things at once through the Force, but he focused down, looking for his snake.

He sensed a slim, languid line of thought, an easily satisfied mind that right now felt cozy and safe. Its only thoughts were *warm, warm . . . sleep, sleep . . .* and *quiet.* The coiled-up crystal snake dozed beneath Raynar in the folds of his purple under-robes.

"Here, Jaina," Jacen whispered. She left the door to crouch beside him. The fabric of her stained overall hissed like another snake as she dropped to her knees.

"I suppose it's directly *under* Raynar's body?"

Jacen nodded. "Yes, where it's warmest."

"That's a problem," Jaina said. "I could roll him over, and you grab the snake."

"No, that would disturb it," Jacen said. "It might bite Raynar again."

Jaina frowned. "He'd sleep through a week's worth of classes."

"Yeah," Jacen said, "but then at least Uncle Luke could finish a lecture without getting interrupted by Raynar's questions."

Jaina giggled. "You've got a point there."

Jacen sensed the coiled snake with his mind, saw it resting peacefully; but just then, as if Raynar had heard them talking about him, the boy snorted and stirred in his sleep.

The snake surged with alarm. Jacen quickly sent out a calming message, using Jedi relaxation techniques Luke had taught him. He sent peaceful thoughts, quieting thoughts, that calmed not only the serpent but Raynar as well.

"Working together, we could use our Jedi powers to lift Raynar up," Jacen suggested. "Then I'll pull the snake out from underneath him."

"Well, what are we waiting for?" Jaina said, looking at her brother with raised eyebrows.

Closing their eyes, the twins concentrated. They touched the fringes of Raynar's colorful robes with their fingertips as they imagined how *light* he could be . . . that he was merely a feather wafting into the air . . . that he weighed nothing at all, and they could make him drift upward. . . .

Jacen held his breath, and the still-snoring Jedi student began to rise from the tiled floor. Raynar's loose garments dangled like curtains underneath him, freeing the sleepy snake.

Suddenly deprived of its warm hiding place, the crystal snake woke up in anger, instinctively wanting to lash out. Jacen sensed it uncoiling and seeking a living target, ready to strike.

"Hold Raynar!" he shouted to Jaina as he flashed forward to snatch the slithering crystal snake. His fingers wrapped around its neck, grasping it behind the compact triangular head. He sent focused calming thoughts into the small reptilian brain, quelling its anger, soothing it.

Jacen's quick movement and release of the Force startled Jaina, and she managed to hold Raynar up for only a second or two. As Jacen worked to calm the serpent, Jaina's grip on the floating boy weakened and finally broke.

Raynar tumbled to the hard stone floor in a pile of arms and legs and garishly colored cloth. The thud of impact was enough to wake him even from a snake-drugged sleep. He sat up with a grunt, blinking his blue eyes and shaking his head.

Jacen continued to calm the invisible snake hidden in his hand. He sent tingling thoughts into its mind until the serpent fizzed with pleasure. Content, it wrapped itself around Jacen's wrist, resting its flat, transparent head on his clenched fist. Even in the best of light it barely shimmered. Its scales were like a thin film of diamonds, its black eyes like two bits of charcoal.

Groggy, Raynar looked at the dark-haired twins standing next to him. He scratched his head in confusion. "Jacen? Jaina? Well, well, well, what are you—hey!" He sat up straighter and shook his left arm as if it had gone numb. Then he glared at Jacen.

"I thought I saw one of your . . . your *creatures* in here, just for a minute. And that's the last thing I remember. Is one of your pets loose?"

Embarrassed, Jacen slid his snake-covered hand behind his back. "No," he said, "I can honestly say that all of my pets are completely accounted for."

Jaina bent down to help the other Jedi boy to his feet. "You must have just fallen asleep, Raynar. You really should have gone to your sleeping pallet if you were so tired." She brushed his clothes off. "Now look, you've got dust all over your pretty robes."

Raynar looked in alarm at the smudges of dust and dirt on his gaudy garments. "Now I'll have to put on a whole new outfit. I can't be seen in public like this!" He brushed his fingers over the cloth in dismay.

"We'll let you get changed then," Jacen said, backing toward the door. "See you at the lecture."

Jacen and Jaina ducked out of Raynar's room. Feeling suddenly bold enough to joke, Jacen waved good-bye with the hand that still carried the invisible crystal snake.

Together, the twins raced back to their quarters so they could put on their own robes in time to hear Luke teach them how to become Jedi Knights.

2

JAINA DUCKED BACK into her quarters to change into fresh clothes as Jacen ran to stash the crystal snake in its cage. She splashed cold water on her face from the new cistern in her bedroom wall.

Her face still damp and tingling, she stepped out into the corridor. "Hurry, or we'll be late," she said as Jacen ran to join her.

Together, the twins dashed to the turbolift, which took them to the upper levels of the pyramid-shaped temple. They entered the echoing space of the grand audience chamber. The air was a bustling hum of other Jedi candidates assembling in the huge room where Luke Skywalker spoke every day.

Shafts of morning light glinted off the polished stone surfaces. The light carried an orange cast reflected from the orange gas giant hanging in the sky—the planet Yavin, around which the small jungle moon orbited.

Dozens of other Jedi trainees of varying ages and species found their places in the rows of stone seats spread out across the long, sloped floor. To Jaina, it looked as if someone had splashed a giant stone down on the stage, sending parallel waves of benches rippling toward the back of the chamber.

A mixture of languages and sounds came to Jaina's ears, along with the rich open-air smell that came from the uncharted jungles outside. She sniffed, but could not identify the different perfumes from flowers in bloom—though Jacen probably knew them all by heart. Right now, she smelled the musty body odors of alien Jedi candidates—matted fur, sunbaked scales, sweet-sour pheromones.

Jacen followed her to a set of empty seats, past two stout, pink-furred beasts that spoke to each other in growls. As she sat on the slick, cool seat, Jaina looked up at the squared-off temple ceilings, at the many different shapes and colors mounted in mosaics of alien patterns.

"Every time we come in here," she said, "I think of those old videoclips of the ceremony where Mother handed out medals to Uncle Luke and Dad. She looked so pretty." She put a hand up to her straight, unstyled hair.

"Yeah, and Dad looked like such a . . . such a pirate," Jacen said.

"Well, he *was* a smuggler in those days," Jaina answered.

She thought of the Rebel soldiers who had survived the attack on the first Death Star, those who had fought against the Empire in the great space battle to destroy the terrible superweapon. Now, more than twenty years later, Luke Skywalker had turned the abandoned base into a training center for Jedi hopefuls, rebuilding the Order of Jedi Knights.

Luke himself had begun training other Jedi back when the twins were barely two years old. Now he often left on his own missions and spent only part of his time at the academy, but it remained open under the direction of other Jedi Knights Luke had trained.

Some of the trainees had virtually no Force potential, content to be mere historians of Jedi lore. Others had great talent, but had not yet begun their full training. It was Luke's philosophy, though, that all potential Jedi could learn from each other. The strong could learn from the weak, the old could learn from the young—and vice versa.

Jacen and Jaina had come to Yavin 4, sent by their mother Leia to be trained for part of the year. Their younger brother Anakin had remained at home back on the capital world of Coruscant, but he would be coming to join them soon.

Off and on during their childhood, Luke Skywalker had helped the children of Han Solo and Princess Leia to learn their powerful talent. Here on Yavin 4 they had nothing to do but study and practice and train and learn—and so far it had been much more interesting than the curriculum the stuffy educational droids had developed for them back on Coruscant.

"Where's Tenel Ka?" Jaina scanned the crowd, but saw no sign of their friend from the planet Dathomir.

"She should be here," Jacen said. "This morning I saw her go out to do her exercises in the jungle."

Tenel Ka was a devoted Jedi who worked hard to attain her dreams. She had little interest in the bookish studies, the histories and the meditations; but she was an excellent athlete who preferred action to thinking. That was a valuable skill for a Jedi, Luke Skywalker had told her—provided Tenel Ka knew when it was appropriate.

Their friend was impatient, hard-driven, and practically humorless. The twins had taken it as a challenge to see if they could make her laugh.

"She'd better hurry," Jacen said as the room began to quiet. "Uncle Luke is going to start soon."

Catching a movement out of the corner of her eye, Jaina looked up at one of the skylights high on a wall of the tall chamber. The lean, supple silhouette of a young girl edged onto the narrow stone windowsill. "Ah, there she is!"

"She must have climbed the temple from the back," Jacen said. "She was always talking about doing that, but I never thought she'd try."

"Plenty of vines over there," Jaina answered logically, as if scaling the enormous ancient monument was something Jedi students did every day.

As they watched, Tenel Ka used a thin leather thong to tie her long rusty-gold hair behind her shoulders to keep it out of her way. Then the muscular girl flexed her arms. She attached a silvery grappling hook to the edge of the stone sill and reeled out a thin fibercord from her utility belt.

Tenel Ka lowered herself like a spider on a web, walking precariously down the long smooth surface of the inner wall.

The other Jedi trainees watched her, some applauding, others just recognizing the girl's skill. She could have used her Jedi powers to speed the descent, but Tenel Ka relied on her body whenever possible and used the Force only as a last resort. She thought it showed weakness to depend too heavily on her special powers.

Tenel Ka made an easy landing on the stone floor, her glistening, scaly boots clicking as she touched down. She flexed her arms again to loosen her muscles, then grasped the thin fibercord. With a snap from the Force she popped her grappling hook up and away from the stone above and neatly caught it in her hand as it fell.

She reeled the fibercord into her belt and turned around with a serious expression on her face, then snapped the thong free from her hair and shook her head to let the reddish tresses fall loose around her shoulders.

Tenel Ka dressed like other women from Dathomir, in a brief athletic outfit made from scarlet and emerald skins of native reptiles. The flexible, lightly armored tunic and shorts left her arms and legs bare. Despite her exposed skin, Tenel Ka never seemed bothered by scratches or insect bites, though she made numerous forays into the jungle.

Jacen waved at her, grinning. She acknowledged him with a nod, made her way over to where the twins were sitting, and slid onto the cool stone bench beside Jacen.

"Greetings," Tenel Ka said gruffly.

"Good morning," Jaina said. She smiled at the Amazonian young woman, who looked back at her with large, cool gray eyes, but did not return her smile—not out of rudeness, but because it wasn't in her nature. Tenel Ka rarely smiled.

Jacen nudged her with his elbow and dropped his voice. "I've got a new one for you, Tenel Ka. I think you'll like it. What do you call the person who brings a rancor its dinner?"

She looked perplexed. "I don't understand."

"It's a joke!" Jacen said. "Come on, guess."

"Ah, a joke," Tenel Ka said, nodding. "You expect me to laugh?"

"You won't be able to stop yourself, once you hear it," Jacen said. "Come on, what do you call the person who brings a rancor its dinner?"

"I don't know," Tenel Ka said. Jaina would have bet a hundred credits that the girl wouldn't even venture a guess.

"The appetizer!" Jacen chuckled.

Jaina groaned, but Tenel Ka's face remained serious. "I will need you to explain why that's funny . . . but I see the lecture is about to start. Tell me some other time."

Jacen rolled his eyes.

Just as Luke Skywalker stepped out onto the speaking platform, a flustered Raynar emerged from the turbolift. Puffing and red-faced, he bustled down the long promenade between seats, trying to find a place where he could sit up front. Jaina noticed the boy now wore an entirely different outfit that was as bright as the one before, and of colors that clashed just as much. He sat down and gazed up at the Jedi Master, obviously wanting to impress the teacher.

Luke Skywalker stood on the raised platform and looked out at his mismatched students. His bright eyes seemed to pierce the crowd. Everyone fell silent, as if a warm blanket had fluttered down over them.

Luke still had the boyish looks that Jaina recalled from the history tapes, but now he carried calm power in his lean form, a thunderstorm bottled up in a diamond-hard gentleness. Through many trials Luke had somehow emerged bright and strong. He had survived to form the cornerstone of the new Jedi Knights that would protect the New Republic from the last vestiges of evil in the galaxy.

"May the Force be with you," Luke said in a soft voice that nevertheless carried the length of the grand audience chamber. The words in the often-repeated phrase sent a tingle across Jaina's skin. Beside her, Jacen flashed a smile. Tenel Ka sat up rigidly, as if in homage.

"As I have told you many times," Luke said, "I don't believe the training of a true Jedi comes from listening to lectures. I want to teach you how to learn action, how to *do* things, not just think about them. 'There is no try,' as Yoda, one of my own Jedi Masters, taught me."

From the front row, in a flash of bright color, Raynar raised his hand, waggling his fingers in the air to get Luke's attention. An audible groan rippled through the chamber; Jacen heaved a heavy sigh, and Jaina waited, wondering what question Raynar would come up with this time.

"Master Skywalker," Raynar said, "I don't understand what you mean by 'There is no try.' You must have tried and failed at some time. No one can always succeed in what they want to do."

Luke looked at the boy with an expression of patience and understanding. Jaina never understood how her uncle could maintain his composure through Raynar's frequent interruptions. She supposed it must be the mark of a true Jedi Master.

"I didn't say that I never fail," Luke said. "No Jedi ever becomes perfect. Sometimes, though, what we *succeed* in doing is not exactly what we *intended* to do. Focus on what you accomplished, rather than on what you merely hoped to do. Or what you failed to do. Yes, recognize what you have lost—but look in a different way to see what you have gained."

Luke folded his hands together and walked with gliding footsteps from one side of the speaking platform to the other. His bright eyes never left Raynar's upraised face, but somehow Luke seemed to look at all of the students, speaking to every one of them.

"Let me give you an example," he said. "A few years ago I had a brilliant trainee named Brakiss. He was a talented student, a voracious learner. He had a great potential for the Force. He seemed kind and helpful, fascinated by everything I had to teach. He was also a great actor."

Luke took a deep breath, facing an unpleasant memory from his past. "You see, once it became known that I had founded an academy to teach Jedi Knights, it's not surprising that the remnants of the Empire would have their own students infiltrate my academy. I managed to catch their first few attempts. They were clumsy and untalented.

"But Brakiss was different. I knew he was an Imperial spy from the moment he stepped off the shuttle and looked around at the jungles on Yavin 4. I could sense it in him, a deep shadow barely hidden by his mask of friendliness and enthusiasm. But in Brakiss I also saw a real talent for the Force. Part of him had been corrupted long ago. He had a deep flaw surrounded by a beautiful exterior.

"But rather than reject him outright, I decided to keep him here, to show him other ways. To heal him. Because if there could be good even in the heart of my father, Darth Vader, there must also be goodness in someone as fresh and new as Brakiss." Luke gazed up at the ceiling, then returned his glance to the audience.

"He stayed here for many months, and I took special interest in teaching him, guiding him, nudging him toward the light side of the Force in every way. He seemed to be turning, softening . . . but Brakiss was colder and more deceptive than even I had suspected. During one part of his training, I sent him on an illusionary quest that would seem real to him, a test that made him face himself. Brakiss had to look inward—to see his very core in a way that no one else could ever see.

"I had hoped the test would heal him, but instead Brakiss lost that battle. Perhaps he was simply not prepared to confront what he saw inside himself. It broke him somehow. He fled from this jungle moon, and I believe he went straight back to the Empire—taking with him everything that I had taught him of the Jedi Way."

Many students in the grand audience chamber gasped. Jaina sat up and looked at her twin brother in alarm. She had never heard this story before.

Raynar again had his hand up, but Luke looked at him with narrowed eyes so full of power that the arrogant student flinched and put his hand back down.

"I know what you're thinking," Luke continued. "That I tried to bring Brakiss back to the light side, and that I failed. But—just as I told you a few moments ago—I was forced to look at how I had succeeded.

"I *did* show Brakiss my compassion. I *did* let him learn the secrets of the light side, uncorrupted by what he had already been taught. And I *did* make him look at himself and realize how broken he was. Once I accomplished that much, the task was no longer mine. The final choice belonged to Brakiss himself. And it still does."

Now he raised his eyes and looked across the gathered Jedi. As Luke's gaze passed over them, Jaina felt an electric thrill, as if an invisible hand had just brushed her.

"To become Jedi," Luke said, "you must face many choices. Some may be simple but troublesome, others may be terrible ordeals. Here at my Jedi academy I can give you tools to use when facing those choices. But I cannot make the choices for you. You must succeed in your own way."

Before Luke could continue, sudden screeching alarms rang out, sounding an emergency.

Artoo-Detoo, the little droid Luke kept near his side, rushed into the grand audience chamber, emitting a loud series of unintelligible electronic whistles and beeps. Luke seemed to understand them, though, and he leaped down from the stage.

"Trouble out on the landing pad!" Luke said, sprinting for the turbolift. He continued to speak to his students as he ran, his robes flapping behind him. "Think about what I've told you and go practice your skills."

The students milled about in confusion, not knowing what to do.

Jacen, Jaina, and Tenel Ka looked at each other, the same thought in each of their minds. "Let's go see what's going on!"

3

JACEN SAW THAT other Jedi students, who now rushed to the winding internal staircases or crowded into the turbolifts, had the same idea.

Tenel Ka, though, leaped to her feet and grabbed Jacen's arm, yanking him off the stone bench. "We can do it faster my way. Jaina, follow!"

Tenel Ka raced back to the stone wall below the skylights, weaving between two short lizardlike students who seemed baffled by the commotion and cheeped to each other in high-pitched voices. Already Tenel Ka had unreeled the lightweight fibercord from her belt and removed the sturdy grappling hook.

"We'll go up the wall, out the skylights, and down the outside," she said, twirling the grappling hook in her hand. The muscles in her arm rippled. At precisely the right moment she released the hook.

Jacen and Jaina helped it with the Force, guiding the hook so that it seated properly in the moss-covered sill. Its sharp durasteel points dug into a crack in the stone blocks and held there.

Tenel Ka grasped the fibercord in both hands, tugged backward, and began to climb up the rope. She dug the toes of her scaled boots against the wall, hauling herself up, somehow finding footing on the polished stone blocks.

Jacen grabbed the rope next, holding it steady as Tenel Ka ascended like a lizard up a sunbaked cliff face. As he climbed, his arms ached. He used the Force when he needed to, raising his body up, catching himself when his feet slipped. He would have preferred to show off his physical prowess, especially with Tenel Ka watching.

At last he pulled his wiry body to the top of the Great Temple, squirming out the windowsill to stand on the broad rough-hewn platform left by the ancient builders.

Jacen reached behind him to grab his sister's arm and pulled her up. The humid air of the jungle clung to the top of the pyramid, making it hot and sticky, unlike the cool mustiness of the temple interior.

Before they could catch their breath, Tenel Ka had retrieved the fibercord and was picking her way rapidly along the narrow stone walkway. Pebbles crumbled under her feet, but she didn't seem the least bit concerned about falling.

"Around to the side," she said, not even panting. "We can get down faster that way."

Tenel Ka ran with light footsteps around the perimeter until she stopped, looking down at the cleared landing field where all ships arrived and departed. She stood stock still, like a warrior confronted with an awesome opponent.

Jacen and Jaina came up behind her and stared in amazement and horror at what they saw down in front of the temple.

A battered supply ship, the *Lightning Rod*, had landed in the jungle clearing. Their normal supply courier and message runner—long-haired old Peckhum—stood transfixed beside the open jaws of his cargo bay. His eyes were wide and white. He looked as if he had screamed himself hoarse, and could now make no sound.

He stared at a huge, unnatural-looking monstrosity that loomed out of the jungle as if ready to attack, snarling at him . . . waiting for Peckhum to make the next move.

"What *is* that thing?" Jaina asked, looking to her brother as if he would know.

Jacen squinted at the behemoth. As enormous as a shuttlecraft, its huge squarish body was covered with shaggy, matted hair tangled with primordial moss. It stood on six cylindrical legs that were like the boles of ancient trees. Its massive triangular head sat like a Star Destroyer on its shoulders, but instead of eyes inset in its skull, it had a cluster of twelve thick, writhing tentacles, each one glistening with a round, unblinking eye. Curved tusks sprouted from its mouth, long and sharp and wicked enough to tear a hole through a sandcrawler.

"It's not like anything I've ever seen in my life," Jacen said.

Tenel Ka glared down at the monster with a grim expression. "Working together, we can fight it," she said. "Follow!" She dashed down the wide-cut stone steps outside the tall temple.

The monster let out a bellow of challenge so loud and so horrendous that it seemed to make the ancient stone blocks tremble. The three young Jedi Knights hurried to the ground level, careful not to slip and fall from the steep steps.

"Help me!" Peckhum cried, his voice tinny with fright.

At the jungle's edge, the hideous monster turned, as if distracted by something. Jacen felt his heart leap, thinking at first that perhaps the wild creature had seen the three of them approaching. But he saw that its attention was fixed instead on another figure walking alone, emerging from the lower levels of the temple pyramid, confidently gliding over the clipped grasses and weeds.

Luke Skywalker wore only his Jedi robe. Jacen expected to see him holding his lightsaber, but both of Luke's hands were empty.

Luke stared at the creature, and the creature stared back with a dozen eyes waving at the ends of tentacles covering its face.

The Jedi Master continued to walk forward, directly toward the monster, as if he were in some sort of trance. He took one step, then another. The beast bristled, but held its ground, bellowing loudly enough to make the trees swish. Jungle birds and creatures fled from the horrifying sound.

While the beast was momentarily distracted, old Peckhum dove to the ground, scuttling on all fours through the open cargo doors of his battered shuttle. Jacen was glad to see the supply runner safe inside the shielded metal walls.

The monster roared upon losing its prey. But Luke spoke in an oddly calm and clear voice that was not at all muffled by the distance. "No, here! Look at me," he said.

Tenel Ka reached the ground by leaping down the last four steps and landing in a crouch. Puffing and red-faced, Jacen and Jaina dashed down beside her, then all three teens stood rigid, watching Luke Skywalker face the jungle beast. They had no weapons of their own.

Suddenly, unexpectedly, old Peckhum charged back out of the open bay doors of the *Lightning Rod*. In his hands he held an old-fashioned blaster rifle. "I'll get him, Master Skywalker! Just stay there." He ducked down and aimed.

But Luke turned to him and motioned with his hand. "No," he said.

The blaster rifle went flying out of Peckhum's grip. The old supply runner stared in astonishment as Luke continued to stroll toward the monster, seemingly without a care in the world.

"This creature means no harm," Luke said, his voice quiet but firm. He never took his eyes off the beast. "It's just frightened and confused. It doesn't know where it is, or why we are here." He drew a deep breath. "There's no need for killing."

Jacen's stomach knotted with unbearable tension as Luke approached the monster. The thing's long eyestalks waved at him, and its six tree-trunk legs took ponderous steps like an Imperial walker.

The beast lowered its triangular head, shaking it from side to side so that the pointed tusks seemed to scratch holes in the air. It let out a strange, soft *blat* of puzzlement.

Jacen hissed with fear, and his sister's entire body clenched. He had used his own talents with the Force to confront many strange animals out in the jungle, but never anything as powerful as this monster, never such a boiling mass of anger and confusion.

But Luke stepped right up to the shaggy, angry thing, within touching distance. The Jedi Master looked incredibly small, yet unafraid.

Beside the battered freighter, Peckhum fell to his knees. The discarded blaster rifle was at hand, but he didn't dare pick up the weapon again. He looked from the monster to Luke, then to the three watching teens—then off into the jungle, as if terrified that another one of the creatures might appear.

Luke stood in front of the nightmarish beast and took a deep breath. He didn't move. The monster held its ground and snorted. Its eyestalks waved unblinking, pointing slitted pupils down at him.

Luke raised his hand, palm out.

The monster snuffled and waited, motionless, its wicked tusks less than a meter away from Luke Skywalker.

The jungle fell silent. The breeze died away. Jacen held his breath. Jaina gripped his hand. Tenel Ka narrowed her cool gray eyes.

The silence seemed so overwhelming that when Luke at last broke the frozen moment, his whisper sounded as loud as a shout.

"Go," Luke told the creature. "There is nothing you need here."

The monster reared up on its hind set of piston legs, its eye tentacles thrashing in a frenzy. Then it let out another high-pitched trumpet before it spun around and crashed off into the thick undergrowth. Branches cracked, trees bent to one side as it plowed a wide path back to the mysterious jungle depths from which it had come.

Like a snapped string, Luke's shoulders slumped with exhaustion. He seemed barely able to keep himself from trembling as Jacen, Jaina, and Tenel Ka rushed toward him, calling his name. "Uncle Luke!"

Luke turned and looked at the three friends with a smile.

Old Peckhum stumbled up, clutching the antiquated blaster rifle. His eyes glittered with unshed tears. "I can't believe you did that, Master Skywalker!" he said. "I thought I was dead for sure, but you faced that monster with no weapons at all."

"I had enough weapons," Luke said with calm conviction. "I had the Force."

"I wish I could do that, Uncle Luke," Jacen said. "That was really something."

"You will be able to do anything you want, Jacen," Luke said. "You have the potential—as long as you have the discipline."

Luke gazed off into the jungle, where they could still hear trees crashing and shrubs snapping as the monster continued to blunder its way through the forest.

"There are many mysterious things in the jungles," Luke said, then he smiled at the twins and Tenel Ka. He nodded toward Peckhum's ship, the *Lightning Rod,* which still sat open, filled with crates and boxes of supplies and equipment.

"I think our friend Mr. Peckhum is having a rough day," Luke said. "He's got a lot more to unload, and he's probably eager to get back up into orbit, where it's safe." He flashed a smile at the old supply runner, who nodded vigorously.

"Why don't you three consider it a Jedi training exercise to help him. Besides, we need to get ready because tomorrow—" He looked at Jacen and Jaina, eyes sparkling. "Your father and Chewbacca are bringing us another Jedi trainee."

"Dad's coming here?" Jaina said with a yelp.

"Hey, why didn't you tell us before?" Jacen added. His heart leaped at the thought of seeing his father again after a full month.

"I wanted it to be a surprise. He's flying in on the *Millennium Falcon,* but he had to stop at Chewbacca's planet first. They've already left Kashyyyk, and they're on their way here."

Filled with excitement, the young Jedi Knights eagerly helped unload Peckhum's supply ship. It was hard work, demanding more concentration and control of their Jedi lifting abilities than they were used to, but they finished in less than an hour. Jaina and Jacen chattered to Tenel Ka about all the adventures Han Solo had experienced. Jaina groaned about how much work it would be to clean up their quarters in time, so they could impress their father.

Finally, the battered old freighter flew off into the misty skies toward the orangish gas-giant planet of Yavin.

Jacen smiled and looked wistfully at the trampled clearing. The next ship to arrive on the landing pad would be the *Millennium Falcon!*

4

"THERE," SAID JAINA, mentally relaxing her hold on a large mass of tangled wires and cables. It came to rest in a more or less contained jumble atop one of the newly tidied stacks of electronic components in her room. "That should do it," she added with a satisfied nod.

"Does that mean we can go to morning meal now?" Jacen said. "You've been at this half the night."

"I want Dad to be impressed." Jaina shrugged.

Jacen laughed. "He never stacks *his* tools this neatly!"

"Guess I did get a little carried away," Jaina replied, matching his grin. "We've still got a few hours before they get here."

Jacen snorted and stood up from the floor, where he'd been sitting next to his sister while they worked. He brushed the dust off his jumpsuit and ran long fingers through his dark brown curls. "Well, how do I look?"

Jaina raised a critical eyebrow at him. "Like someone who's been up all night."

He hurried over to peer anxiously into the small mirror that Jaina had hung above her cistern. She realized that her brother was just as nervous and excited about seeing their father again as she was.

"It's actually not too bad," she assured him. "I think raking the twigs and leaves from your hair really helped. Here, put this on." She pulled a fresh jumpsuit from a chest by her bed. "You'll look more presentable."

When Jacen went into the next room to change, Jaina took his place at the mirror. She wasn't vain, but, as with her room, she preferred to keep her personal appearance neat and clean.

She ran a comb through her straight brown hair and stared at her reflection. Then, with a quick peek over her shoulder to be sure her brother wasn't looking, she pulled back a handful of strands and worked them into a braid. Jaina would never have gone to this much trouble for an ambassador or some silly dignitary—but her father was worth the effort. She hoped Jacen wouldn't notice or comment on it.

Finished, she stepped through her doorway and poked her head into Jacen's room. "All the animals fed?" she asked.

"I took care of that hours ago," he said, emerging in his clean, fresh robe. He heaved a long-suffering sigh. "At least *someone's* had their morning meal."

Jaina gnawed her lip, anxiously scanning the sky for any glimmer that might herald the arrival of the *Millennium Falcon*. She and Jacen stood at the edge of the wide clearing in front of the Jedi academy, where the hideous monster had appeared the day before. The area's short grasses had been trampled down by frequent takeoffs and landings.

Jaina smelled the rich green dampness of the early morning in the jungle that surrounded the clearing. The foliage rustled and sighed in a light breeze that also carried the trills, twitters, and chirps that reminded her of the wide profusion of animal life that inhabited the jungle moon.

Beside her, Jacen shifted impatiently from one foot to the other, a frown of concentration etched across his forehead. Jaina sighed. Why did it seem like everything took forever when you were looking forward to it, and things that you didn't want to happen arrived too soon?

As if sensing her tension, Jacen suddenly turned to her with a mischievous look in his eye. "Hey, Jaina—you know why TIE fighters scream in space?"

She nodded. "Sure, their twin ion engines set up a shock front from the exhaust—"

"No!" Jacen waved his hand in dismissal. "Because they miss their mothership!"

As was expected of her, Jaina groaned, grateful for a chance to get her mind off waiting, even if only for a moment.

Then a comforting hum built and resonated around them, as if the sound of their mounting excitement had suddenly become audible. "Look," she said, pointing at a silver-white speck that had just appeared high above the treetops.

The glimmer disappeared for a few moments and then, with a rush of exhaled breath that she hadn't realized she'd been holding, Jaina saw the *Millennium Falcon* swoop across the sky toward the clearing.

The familiar blunt-nosed oval of their father's ship hovered tantalizingly above their heads for a moment that seemed to stretch to eternity. Then, with a burst of its repulsorlifts, it settled gently onto the ground in front of them. The *Falcon*'s cooling hull buzzed and ticked as the engines died down to a low drone. The scent of ozone tickled Jaina's nostrils.

Jaina knew the shutdown procedures for the Corellian light freighter, but she wished that just for today there was some way to speed things up. When she thought she could wait no longer, the landing ramp of the *Falcon* lowered with a whine-thump.

And then their father bounded down the ramp, gathering the twins into his arms, ruffling their hair, and trying to hug both of them at once, as he had done when they were small children.

Han Solo stepped back to take a good look at his children. "Well!" he said at last, with one of those lopsided grins for which he was so famous. "Except for your mother, I'd say this is the finest welcoming committee I've ever had."

"Dad," Jacen said, rolling his eyes, "we are *not* a committee."

As her father laughed, Jaina took a moment to study him, and was relieved to note that he had not changed in the month that they had been gone from home. He wore soft black trousers and boots that fitted him snugly, an open-necked white shirt, and a dark vest—a comfortable, serviceable set of clothes that he sometimes jokingly referred to as his "working uniform." The battered, familiar shape of the *Millennium Falcon* was unchanged as well.

"How do we look, Dad?" Jaina asked. "Any different?"

"Well, now that you mention it . . ." he said, turning his gaze to each of them in turn. "Jacen, you've grown again—bet you even caught up with your sister. And Jaina," he said with a wicked grin, "if I didn't think you'd throw a hydrospanner at me for saying so, I'd tell you that you're even prettier than you were a month ago."

Jaina blushed and gave an unladylike snort to demonstrate what she thought of such compliments, but secretly she was pleased.

A loud, echoing roar from inside the ship saved her the embarrassment of having to come up with a response. A large form thundered down the boarding ramp. Huge heavily furred arms reached out to grab Jaina and threw her high into the air.

"Chewie!" Jaina shrieked, laughing as the giant Wookiee caught her again on the way down. "I'm not a little kid anymore!" After Chewbacca had repeated this greeting ritual with her brother, Jaina finally said what she and Jacen were thinking. "It's good to see you, Dad, but what brings you to the Jedi academy?"

"Yeah," Jacen added. "Mom didn't send you to check if we had enough clean underwear, did she?"

"Nah, nothing like that," their father assured them with a laugh. "Actually, Chewie and I needed to come out this direction to help my old friend Lando Calrissian open up a new operation."

Jaina had always had a great fondness for Lando, her father's dark and dashing friend, but she also knew him well enough to realize that her adopted "uncle" Lando was always involved in some crackpot moneymaking scheme or another. She held up a hand to stop her father.

"Wait, let me guess. He's—he's starting a new casino on his space station and he needed you to bring him a shipload of sabacc cards."

"No, no, I've got it," Jacen said. "He's opening a new Nerf ranch and he wants you to help him build a corral."

At this Chewbacca threw back his head and bleated with Wookiee laughter.

"Not even close." Han Solo shook his head. "Coruscagem mining deep in the atmosphere of the gas giant." He pointed up to the great orange ball of the planet Yavin in the sky overhead. "He asked us to come and help him set up the operation."

"Oh, blaster bolts!" said Jacen, snapping his fingers. "That was going to be my next guess."

Another faint Wookiee-sounding bellow came from inside the *Millennium Falcon.* Chewbacca turned and strode back up the ramp.

"What was that?" Jaina asked.

"Oh, I forgot to mention," Han said. "When Luke found out we had to come here anyway, he asked us to stop by Chewie's homeworld of Kashyyyk and pick up a new Jedi candidate. He's going to be your fellow student."

As Han spoke, Chewbacca thumped back down the ramp, closely followed by a smaller Wookiee, who was still taller than Jacen or Jaina. The younger Wookiee had thick swirls of ginger-colored fur, with a remarkable swirling black streak as wide as Jaina's hand that ran from just above his left eye up over his head and down to the middle of his back. He wore only a belt woven of some glossy fiber that Jaina could not identify.

"Kids, I'd like you to meet Chewie's nephew Lowbacca. Lowbacca, my kids Jacen and Jaina."

Lowbacca nodded his head and growled a Wookiee greeting. He was thin and lanky, even for a Wookiee, with gangly fur-covered arms and legs. The young Wookiee fidgeted. Chewbacca barked a question to Han and waved one massive arm in the direction of the temple.

"Sure," Han said. "Go ahead—take him to Luke for now. The kids can get to know each other later."

As the two Wookiees headed off to find Luke, Han said, "Wait here, I have something for you," and ducked back into the *Falcon*. He returned in a few moments, his arms laden with a strange assortment of packages and greenery.

"First," he said, tossing each of them a small message disk, "your mother recorded these personal holo letters for you. There's another one from your little brother Anakin. He can't wait to come here himself."

Jaina looked at the glittering message disks, anxious to play them. But she slipped them into one of the pockets of her jumpsuit.

"And now . . ." Han said, holding up a large bouquet of green fronds sprinkled with purple and white star-shaped blossoms. Grinning, he waggled the flowers.

"Oh, Dad, you remembered!"

Jacen ran forward ecstatically. "My stump lizard's favorite food." He took the leafy bundle gratefully and said, "I'll feed 'em to her right away. See you later, Dad." Then he ran off in the direction of the Great Temple.

Jaina stood alone with her father, looking expectantly at the last bulky package he held in his arms. He set it on the weedy ground of the landing clearing and stepped back so that Jaina could pull aside the rags that covered it.

"Great wrapping job, Dad," she said, smiling.

"Hey, it works." Han spread his hands.

Jaina gasped as she removed the coverings, then looked up at her father, who grinned and shrugged nonchalantly. "A hyperdrive unit!" she said.

"It's not in working condition, you understand," he said. "And it's pretty old. I got it off an old Imperial Delta-class shuttle they were dismantling on Coruscant."

Jaina remembered fondly the times she had helped her father tinker with the *Falcon*'s subsystems to keep it running in peak condition—or as close as they could get. "Oh, Dad, you couldn't have picked a better present!" She jumped up and hugged him, wrapping her arms around his dark vest. She could tell that her father was pleased—and maybe even a little embarrassed—by her enthusiasm.

Her father looked down at her and raised one eyebrow. "You know, there's a couple more components on the ship. If you wanted to help me bring 'em out here, your dad could show you how they all go together."

She ran after him into the ship.

5

IT WAS LATE that morning when Jacen and Jaina finally caught up with their father, Chewbacca, and his nephew Lowbacca. The twins, who had spent hours at their respective assigned duties and Jedi training exercises, arrived back at the students' quarters just as they saw the threesome emerge from a formerly empty room.

"Hi!" Jacen called, hurrying up to Lowbacca with his sister in tow. "Are you tired from your trip? If not, I could show you my room. I have some really unusual pets. I collected most of them from the jungles here and Jaina made some cages for them—you should see those cages—and Jaina could show you her room too. She's got all sorts of broken-down equipment that she uses to build things out of." In his enthusiasm, Jacen never even paused to take a breath.

The much taller Lowbacca looked down at the human boy as Jacen rattled on. "Do you like animals? Do you like to build things? Did you bring any pets or equipment with you from Kashyyyk? Do you like—"

His father chuckled into the stream of questions. "There'll be time enough for that later, kid. We spent most of the morning with Luke, and then we got Lowbacca settled in his room. You two want to take him on a tour of the academy, get him familiar with the place? By now, you probably know your way around better than Chewie or I do."

"We'd love to," Jaina answered before their father had finished his sentence.

"We're the perfect tour guides," Jacen added with a confident shrug. "Jaina and I came to the Jedi academy for the first time when we were only two years old." He smiled a cocky, lopsided grin—the one their mother always said made him look just like his father.

Lowbacca gave an interrogative growl. "He asked how many times you've given this tour," Han translated.

"Well," Jacen sputtered, his face reddening slightly, "if you mean in an *official* capacity, as opposed to, er, um . . ." His voice trailed off.

"What he means is," Jaina put in firmly, "this is our first time."

Lowbacca exchanged a glance with his uncle. Chewbacca raised a furred brown arm, indicated the long corridor with a flourish of his hand, and gave a short bark.

"Right," Han said. "Let's go."

The twins led the group down a set of mossy, cracked stairs to the main level and out onto the grassy clearing in front of the Great Temple. Jacen was eager to prove himself a good tour guide and pointed to each squarish level of the gigantic pyramid as he spoke.

"At the very top is an observation deck that gives one of the best views of the big planet Yavin overhead—unless of course you climb one of those huge old Massassi trees in the jungle," he said with a laugh. "The top level of the pyramid has only one enormous room—the grand audience chamber—that can hold thousands of people."

"That's where the Jedi trainees gather when Uncle Luke—I mean Master Skywalker—gives his lessons," Jaina said.

Jacen went on to explain that the lower levels had been remodeled in recent years. The larger level directly below the grand audience chamber housed those who lived at the academy—trainees, academy staff, and Master Skywalker himself—and also contained rooms for storage or meditation, as well as chambers for guests and visiting dignitaries.

The pyramid's huge ground level held the Communications Center, the main computers, meeting areas and offices, and common rooms in which meals were prepped and eaten. It also held the Strategy Center—the chamber that had been known as the War Room in the days when the temple had housed the Alliance's secret base. Underground, and completely invisible from where they stood, was a gigantic hangar bay that stored shuttles, speeders, fighters, and other aircraft.

On two sides of the Great Temple and along the landing area flowed broad rivers, and beyond them lay the lush and mostly unexplored jungles of the fourth moon of Yavin. "The temples were built by the Massassi, a mysterious ancient race. There are actually lots of structures scattered throughout the jungles," Jacen said. "Some of them are just ruins, really—like the Palace of the Woolamander across the river there."

He described the power-generating station next to the main temple, a series of plate-shaped wheels, twice as tall as Jacen himself, standing on edge and connected through the center by a long axle.

"So you see," Jaina said, picking up the narration where her brother had left off, "with the power station, the river, and the jungles, the Jedi academy is fairly self-sufficient. Come on, let's go inside."

The tour concluded at the twins' quarters, where Jacen and Jaina delighted in showing their father and the two Wookiees their respective treasure troves of pets and salvaged bits of machinery. Han Solo beamed with fatherly pride. Lowbacca displayed a gratifying if subdued interest in the creatures in Jacen's menagerie.

When the group moved into his sister's room, Jacen quickly slid the crystal snake he had been showing off back into its cage and hurried after them. By the time he bounded through the door, Lowbacca was already engrossed in an assortment of gadgets and wiring that he had spread out across Jaina's floor. He was far more interested in the electronics than in the wild jungle creatures.

"Do you like working on machines, Chewie—uh, I mean, Lowbacca?" Jaina asked, bending next to the gangly Wookiee.

The hairy creature expressed his fascination with such a long series of grunts, growls, and rumbles that Jacen was at a loss to understand how a simple yes-or-no question could produce such an animated answer.

As usual, their father translated. "First of all, Lowbacca would take it as a great sign of friendship if you would call him Lowie."

Jacen gave a pleased nod. " 'Lowie,' huh? I like that."

"And for the rest . . ." Han continued, "well, I'm not sure I followed it all. The thing he really gets excited about is computers."

Jaina patted the young Wookiee on the shoulder. "We can do a lot of things together, then, Lowie." Chewbacca chuffed in agreement.

But Jaina's forehead furrowed with sudden concern. "Uh, Dad?" she said. "It's obvious that Lowie has studied our language and understands us as well as Chewie does. But we can't understand *him*. After all, it took you years to learn the Wookiee language. How is he going to get by here at the Jedi academy where nobody can understand him?"

Jacen nodded agreement, looking at the young Wookiee. "Who'll translate for us?"

They were interrupted at this point by a triumphant bark from Chewbacca.

"We have just the answer for you," Han said, clapping his hands and rubbing them together. "A little something that See-Threepio and Chewie cooked up."

Chewbacca turned and held out a shiny metallic device for everyone to see. The sidewise-ovoid apparatus was silvery, slightly longer than Lowie's hand and about four fingers thick, flat on the back and rounded on the front. It looked like a face, with two yellow optical sensors unevenly spaced near the top, a more or less triangular protrusion toward the center, and a perforated oblong on the lower portion that Jacen took to be a speaker.

Chewbacca fiddled with something at the back of the device, and the yellow eyes flickered to life. A thin metallic voice, careful and correct, issued from the tiny speaker. "Greetings. I am a Miniaturized Translator Droid—Em Teedee—specializing in human-Wookiee relations. I am fluent in over *six* forms of communication. My primary programmed function is to translate Wookiee speech into other humanoid languages." It paused expectantly and then added, "Might I be of assistance?"

Jacen laughed. "It can't be!"

Jaina gasped. "Sounds just like Threepio!"

"Almost," their father replied, his mouth twisted in wry amusement. He scratched under his collar with one lazy finger. "A little *too much* like Threepio, for my money. But since he did most of the programming on Em Teedee, I couldn't talk him out of it." He shrugged apologetically.

"Why don't you kids try it out during the midday meal? Chewbacca and I still have some business to discuss with Luke, then we'll take off in the *Falcon* later this afternoon. We've got to see Lando at his mining station."

The common room the Jedi trainees used as a mess hall was filled with wooden tables of various heights. The seats—chairs, benches, nests, ledges, cushions, and stools—came in a broad variety of shapes and sizes to accommodate the differing customs and anatomies of human and alien students.

The plantlike members of the Jedi academy had gone outside to the bright sunwashed steps of the Great Temple, where they could soak up light from Yavin's white sun and photosynthesize for nutrients, adding small packets of minerals into their digestive orifices. Inside the mess hall, though, dozens of unusual species sat together eating exotic foods particular to their own kind.

Jacen followed a step behind, still chattering about the old Massassi temples, as Jaina found a table at one end of the large hall that had a chair appropriate for Lowbacca. So far Jacen had been unable to elicit more than a few nods and gestures from the Wookiee, who seemed deep in thought, intent on absorbing the smells, sights, and sounds around him.

Determined to start a real conversation with the new trainee, Jacen cast about in his mind for a good question. *So, Lowie, how much stuff do you need to move in?* Naw, that was a stupid question.

How about, *How old are you?* No, that would get him only a short answer. And anyway, their father had told them that earlier this morning. Lowie was nineteen, barely an adolescent by Wookiee standards. Maybe something like, *How did you know you wanted to become a Jedi?* Yes, that was good.

But before he could pose the question, the solid, muscular form of Tenel Ka swung into the seat next to him, across from Lowbacca.

"New student," she said, acknowledging Lowbacca in the brief, direct way that was so characteristic of her.

"Lowie," Jacen said, "this is our friend Tenel Ka, from the planet of Dathomir."

"And this," Jaina responded, making the introductions for her side of the table, "is Lowbacca, nephew of Chewbacca, from the Wookiee homeworld of Kashyyyk."

Tenel Ka rose formally and inclined her head, tossing her red-gold hair. "Lowbacca of Kashyyyk, I greet you," she said, and resumed her seat. Lowbacca nodded in return and uttered three short growls.

Jacen waited for a moment, looking at the little translator droid clipped to Lowie's belt, but nothing happened.

"Well?" Jaina said expectantly. "You going to translate for us, Em Teedee?"

"Goodness me, Mistress Jaina, I *am* sorry," the tiny droid replied in a flustered, mechanical voice. "Oh, how dreadful! My initial opportunity to perform my primary function for Master Lowbacca, and I've failed him. I assure you, masters and mistresses all, that from now on I will endeavor to make each translation as speedily and as eloquently as possible—"

Lowbacca interrupted the translator droid's self-reproach with a sharp growl.

"Translate?" the little droid replied. "Translate what? Oh! Oh, I see. Yes. Immediately." Em Teedee made a noise that sounded for all the world as if it was clearing its throat, and then began. "Master Lowbacca says, 'May no sun rise upon a day, nor any moon rise upon a night, in which he is not as honored to see you, and to be in your presence, as he is at this very moment.'"

Jaina rolled her eyes. Jacen shook his head in disbelief. But Tenel Ka's face remained expressionless.

From the corner of his eye, Jacen caught sight of the troublesome young student Raynar in his colorful robes, snickering at them from a nearby table. Automated servers carried generous bowls of food from the kitchen and placed them in front of each trainee.

But Jacen's attention was brought back to his own table when Lowie growled down into the optical sensors of the translator droid.

"Well, so what if I *did* embellish a bit?" the droid asked defensively, as a plate of steaming, blood-red meat was placed in front of the Wookiee. "I was only attempting to make you sound more civilized."

Lowbacca's threatening growl left no doubt as to whether he was grateful to the droid.

"Very well," Em Teedee huffed. "Perhaps a better translation of Master Lowbacca's words would have been, 'The sun has never shined so brightly for this humble Wookiee as on this day we meet.'"

Jacen accepted a hot cup of soup that his sister passed across the table to him. He shot a questioning look at Lowie, who growled again at Em Teedee.

"Well, have it your way then," the droid said haughtily, but in a more subdued voice. "But I assure you that my translations were much more refined. *Ahem.* What Master Lowbacca *actually* said was, 'I am pleased to meet you.'"

When the Wookiee finally grunted in satisfaction, Tenel Ka replied gravely, as if she had not heard any of the other translations, "It is a pleasure shared, Lowbacca."

As an automated tray trundled past toward Raynar's nearby table, Tenel Ka reached out and snagged the last jug of fresh juice. She poured the rich ruby liquid into each of their cups and then set the jug with a gentle *thump* on the table before them. She blinked her cool gray eyes and solemnly held out her cup.

"Jacen and Jaina are already my friends. I offer you friendship, Lowbacca of Kashyyyk."

The Wookiee hesitated, unsure of what to do. Jaina pressed a cup into his hand. Jacen raised his and said, "Friendship."

"Friendship," Jaina echoed.

Nodding, Lowie lifted his glass high in the air, threw his head back, and let out a roar that rang through the hall.

The small voice of Em Teedee broke the silence that followed. "Master Lowbacca most emphatically accepts your offer of friendship and extends his own." To everyone's surprise, the Wookiee did not correct the translator.

"Accepted," Tenel Ka said, taking a drink. When everyone had followed suit, she said, "And now we are friends."

"That means you can call him Lowie now," Jaina said.

Tenel Ka considered this for a moment. "I choose to honor him by using his complete name."

At another table, three short reptilian Cha'a sat around a trayful of warm, rocking eggs, staring fixedly at them like the predators they were. When the eggs cracked and opened, the Cha'a lunged for the bright pink furry hatchlings as they emerged fresh from the shells.

Two whistling avian creatures shared a plateful of thin, writhing threads covered with fluffy blue hair—tantalizing ropy caterpillars which they slurped one at a time through their narrow, horny beaks.

As Jacen sat at the table spooning his soup, trying to think of something amusing to say to Tenel Ka, or at least to continue the conversation with Lowie, he caught a glimpse of movement out of the corner of his eye—something slithering toward the table beside them. A glassy glitter. A serpentine flash.

Jacen's heart leaped into his throat. He suddenly wondered if he had fastened the cage of the crystal snake when his father and the Wookiees had finished their tour of his chambers.

"Hey," Raynar said, leaning over the table beside them, his flashy robes so brilliant that they made Jacen's eyes ache. "Would you mind giving our juice jug back?" Raynar used his own Jedi powers to snatch the jug from their table and carry it through the air back toward himself. "Next time please ask before you just take it." He leaned back and crossed his arms over his chest with a self-satisfied expression.

Just then, light fell on the crystal snake, and Jacen saw it with perfect clarity. It reared up on Raynar's lap and hissed at him, its flat triangular head staring the boy right in the face.

Raynar saw it and shrieked, losing his Force concentration. The jug wobbled, then fell, spilling deep red juice all over his bright robes.

Jacen leaped to his feet and jumped for the snake. He had to catch it before it wreaked more havoc. He tackled Raynar, trying to grab the serpent from the other boy's lap. Raynar, thinking he was being attacked from all sides, screamed in terror at the top of his lungs.

As he and Jacen struggled, their entire table toppled over, spilling dark brown pudding, knocking other beverage containers right and left, spraying food on Raynar's companions at the table.

Tenel Ka, not understanding the problem but always ready to defend her friends, jumped into the fray. She picked up Jacen's hot soup and hurled it toward Raynar's companions, who, seeing the attack coming from a new front, decided to retaliate.

A platter of honeyed noodles sailed across the dining hall toward Jaina, but she ducked. The noodles instead splattered and clung to the bristly white fur of a Talz—a bearlike creature that stood up and blatted a musical note of dismay. When Jaina saw the noodles sticking to the alien's white fur, she couldn't stop herself from laughing.

The crystal snake slithered out of Jacen's grasp as Jacen crawled across Raynar's squirming lap. The young Jedi screamed as if he were being murdered, but Jacen scuttled under the dining tables after the serpent. Bumping one of the tables over while grabbing for the snake, he felt smooth, dry scales against his fingertips—but the snake slid through them, and he could not hold on.

Another table was knocked over as Lowie came to help. With a flurry of feathers, the avian creatures squawked and fought over their plateful of squirming, fuzzy blue thread-worms.

More food flew through the air, levitated by Jedi powers, and tossed from one table to another. The Jedi students were laughing, seeing it now as a release from the tension of the grueling studies and deep concentration required of them during their training.

Steamed leaves flew in the faces of the reptilian Cha'a, interrupting their predatory concentration. All three of them stood up and whirled to meet the attack, back-to-back, standing in a three-point formation, hissing and glaring. The milky tan eggs on their eating platter continued to hatch, and the pink fuzzy hatchlings chose that moment to escape.

Lowie let out a stone-rumbling Wookiee roar, and Em Teedee squeaked with a high-pitched alarm. "I can't see a thing, Master Lowbacca! Comestibles are obscuring my optical sensors. Do please clean them off!"

Artoo-Detoo trundled into the dining chamber and let out an electronic wail, but his droid cries were drowned out by the laughter and the tumult of flying food. Before Artoo could wheel around and sound the alarm, a large tray of creamy dessert pastries splattered across his domed top. The astromech droid beat a hasty, whirring retreat.

As the crystal snake slithered toward the cracked stone walls to escape, Jacen desperately plowed forward. He reached out with one hand and grabbed the pointed tail. The serpent rippled around invisibly in a fluid motion, flashing its fangs toward Jacen, ready to bite down on the hand holding it. But Jacen held out his other hand, pointing with his finger and the Force, touching the snake's tiny brain.

"Hey! Don't you dare," he said aloud. Then, as the crystal snake hesitated, Jacen grabbed it around the neck and lifted it into the air. The lower part of its long body whipped and thrashed. Jacen coiled the snake around his arm and sent soothing thoughts into its mind. He stood up, grinning and relieved.

"I got it!" he cried in triumph—just as three overripe fruits splashed against his face and chest, bursting their thin skins and spilling rich purple pulp all over him. Jacen sputtered and then allowed himself to giggle, still maintaining his hold on the crystal snake.

"Stop!" A booming voice enhanced by the Force echoed through the dining hall.

Suddenly everything froze as if time itself had paused. All the flying food hung suspended in the air; each drip of liquid dangled motionless above the tables. All sound ceased, save for that of the trainees' gasps.

Master Luke Skywalker stood in the entrance to the dining hall wearing a stern expression as he surveyed the suspended food fight. Jacen looked at his uncle's expression and thought he saw anger, but also a concealed amusement.

Luke said, "Was this the best and most challenging way you could find to put your powers to use?" He gestured to all the motionless food and seemed very sad for a moment. Then he turned to leave—but not before Jacen noticed a smile spreading across his face.

As he departed, Luke called, "Instead, perhaps you can use your Jedi powers . . . to clean up this mess." He gestured briefly with his right hand, and the suspended food platters, bowls of soup, desserts, fruits, and messy confections were released, tumbling down like an avalanche. Practically everyone was splattered all over again as sticky gobbets sprayed into the air.

Jacen looked at the aftermath of the food war. Still holding the crystal snake, he wiped a smear of frosting from his nose.

The other Jedi students, though subdued, began to chuckle with relief, then set to work cleaning up.

6

THE WARM AFTERNOON sun sparkled in the heavy, moist air as Lowbacca accompanied his uncle and Han Solo back to the *Millennium Falcon*. Beside him the Solo twins chattered gaily, apparently oblivious to the thick jungle heat. He could sense an underlying tension, though: Jacen and Jaina would miss their father every bit as much as he would miss his uncle Chewbacca, his mother, and the rest of his family back on Kashyyyk.

Lowbacca's golden eyes flicked uneasily about the clearing in front of the Great Temple. He was still uncomfortable with wide-open spaces so close to the ground. On the Wookiee homeworld all cities were built high in the tops of the massive intertwining trees, supported by sturdy branches. Even the most courageous of Wookiees seldom ventured to the inhospitable lower levels of the forest—much less all the way to the ground, where dangers abounded.

To Lowbacca, height meant civilization, comfort, safety, home. And although the enormous Massassi trees towered up to twenty times as high as any other plant on Yavin 4, compared with the trees of Kashyyyk they were midgets. Lowbacca wondered if he would ever find a place high enough on this small moon to make him feel at ease.

Lowie was so lost in thought that he was startled to see that they had arrived at the *Falcon*.

"Never have the chance to do a preflight when we're under fire," Han Solo said, "but it's a good idea when we do have the time." Standing at the foot of the entry ramp, he smiled disarmingly at them. "If you kids aren't too busy, Chewie and I could use some help doing the preflight checks."

"Great," Jaina said before anyone else could respond. "I'll take the hyperdrive." She rushed up the ramp, pausing for only a millisecond to brush a kiss on her father's cheek. "Thanks, Dad. You're the best."

Han Solo looked immensely pleased for a long moment before bringing himself back to business with a shake of his head. "So, kid, you got any preferences?" He looked at Lowie, who thought briefly, then rumbled his reply.

Although Han Solo had doubtless understood him very well, the pesky translator droid piped up. "Master Lowbacca wishes to inspect your ship's computer systems in order that he might tell it where to go."

Han Solo gave Chewbacca a sidelong glance. "Thought you said you fixed that thing," he said, indicating Em Teedee. "It needs an attitude adjustment."

Chewbacca shrugged eloquently, gave a menacing growl, and administered emergency repair procedure number one: he held the silvery oval with one huge hand while he shook the little droid until the circuits rattled.

"Oh, dear me! Perhaps I *could* have been a bit more precise," the droid squeaked hastily. "Er . . . Master Lowbacca expresses his desire to perform the preflight checks on your navigational computer."

"Good idea, kid," Han Solo agreed, briskly rubbing his palms together. "Jacen, you take the exterior hull; see if anything's nested in the exterior vents in the last couple of hours. I'll start on the life-support systems. Chewie, you check the cargo bay."

This last was said with a lift of the chin and a twinkle in Han Solo's eye that Lowbacca knew must have meant something to the older Wookiee—but Lowie hadn't a clue. He wondered dispiritedly if he would ever understand humans as well as his uncle did.

The navicomputer was an enjoyable challenge. Lowie ran through all the preflight requirements twice—not because he thought he might have missed something the first time, but because the two places he felt most at home were in the treetops and in front of a computer.

By the time Lowie completed his second run-through, Han Solo had already finished with the life-support systems and was now checking out the ship's emergency power generator. When he saw Lowbacca, Han wiped his hands on a greasy rag, tossed it aside, and held up one finger as if an idea had just come to him. "Why don't you give your uncle a hand in the cargo hold while I finish up here." His roguish grin was even more lopsided than usual.

Lowbacca wondered what the smile meant and why his uncle should still need his help with the cargo. Sometimes humans were very difficult to understand. With a shrug, he headed toward the cargo bay.

"Excuse me, Master Lowbacca," Em Teedee piped up, "but will you be needing my translating services at this time?"

Lowbacca growled a negative.

"Very well, sir," Em Teedee said. "In that case, would you mind if I put myself into a brief shutdown cycle? If you should require my assistance for any reason, please do not hesitate to interrupt my rest cycle."

Lowie assured Em Teedee that the miniature droid would be the first to know if he needed anything from him.

He found his uncle clambering across a mountain of crates and bundles, checking the securing straps. Apparently Lando Calrissian needed a good many supplies for his new mining operation.

Even in the crowded cargo hold, he breathed deeply, enjoying the mix of familiar smells: speeder fuel, machined metal, lubricants, space rations, and Wookiee sweat—enough to make him homesick for the treetop cities of Kashyyyk. He would have little access to speeders or computers while he studied at the Jedi academy—with the exception, of course, of Em Teedee. But perhaps he could console himself occasionally by climbing the jungle trees and thinking of home.

Maybe he would do that after the *Falcon* took off, but for now there was work to do.

Lowie asked his uncle what still needed to be done, and began to check the webbing on a pile of cargo that Chewbacca indicated. The straps and webbing were loose, and so was the cloth that covered the pile—so loose, in fact, that as Lowbacca began to work, the covering slid away entirely. His jaw dropped, and he stepped back to admire what he had accidentally uncovered.

The air speeder, dismantled into large components, was still recognizable. It was an older model, a T-23 skyhopper, with controls similar to the X-wing fighter, but with trihedral wings, and a passenger seat and cramped cargo compartment at the rear of the cockpit. The blue-metallic hull had been battered and stained with age, but the engine mounted between the wings looked in serviceable condition.

He glanced up to find his uncle staring at him expectantly. Then, to his great surprise, Chewbacca asked Lowie what he thought of the craft.

The skyhopper was compact and well constructed. It wouldn't take much to put all the pieces together again. He complimented the vintage speeder's lines and ventured a guess as to its range and maneuverability. Of course, the onboard computer probably needed a system overhaul and the exterior could use a bit of body work, but those were only minor drawbacks. The dings and scars on the hull only served to add character.

With a satisfied growl, Chewbacca spread his arms wide and

shocked Lowie by telling him the T-23 was a going-away gift. The speeder belonged to Lowbacca, if he could assemble it.

Lowbacca stood next to his T-23 in the clearing with Jacen and Jaina and waved good-bye. After a flurry of hugs, exchanged thanks, and last-minute messages, they watched as Han and Chewbacca climbed back aboard the ship.

Now as the *Millennium Falcon* cleared the treetops and angled into the deep blue sky, the three young Jedi trainees continued waving, each lost in thought for a long moment as they gazed after the departing ship.

At last Jaina heaved a sigh. "Well, Lowie," she said, rubbing her hands together with a look of gleeful anticipation as she looked at the battered T-23. "Need any help getting this bucket of bolts up and going?"

Realizing that even though Jaina was younger, she probably had more experience tuning speeder engines than he did, he nodded gratefully.

They spent the next few hours preparing the T-23 for its first flight on Yavin 4. Jacen occupied himself by telling jokes that Lowie didn't understand, or fetching tools for the two enthusiastic mechanics. Jaina smiled as she worked, glad of the rare chance to share what she knew about speeders and engines and T-23s.

When at last they finished and Lowbacca leaned into the cockpit to switch on the engine, the T-23 crackled, sputtered, and roared to life. It lifted off the ground on its lower repulsorlifts, and a bright glow spluttered from the ion afterburners. The three friends let out two cheers and a bellow of triumph.

"Need anyone to take her for a test flight?" Jaina asked hopefully.

Lowie stumbled over a tentative answer. "What Master Lowbacca is trying to say," said Em Teedee, who had long since finished his rest cycle, "is that, as kind as your offer is, he would vastly prefer to pilot the first flight himself."

Lowbacca grunted once.

"And?" the little droid replied. "What do you mean, 'And?' Oh, I see—the other thing you said. But, sir, you didn't mean . . ."

Lowbacca growled emphatically.

"Well, if you insist," Em Teedee said. *"Ahem.* Master Lowbacca also *says* that he would be honored to have you as his passenger, Mistress Jaina. However," he rushed on, "let me assure you that last statement was made with the utmost reluctance."

Lowbacca groaned and hit his forehead with the heel of one hairy hand in a Wookiee expression of complete embarrassment.

"Well, it's certainly the truth," Em Teedee said defensively. "I'm *certain* I didn't get the intonation wrong."

Jaina, who had at first looked disappointed at Lowbacca's reluctance, now seemed amused at his chagrin. "I understand, Lowie," she said. "I'd want to take her out on my own the first time, too. How about giving us a ride tomorrow?"

Relieved that the twins were not upset, Lowbacca loudly agreed, jumped into the cockpit, and strapped himself in. The whine of the engines drowned out Em Teedee's attempt at translating. Lowie raised a hand in salute, waited until Jacen and Jaina were clear, brought the engines to full power, and took off, heading out toward the vast jungle.

The T-23 maneuvered well, and Lowbacca reveled in the feeling of height and freedom as he streaked away. But still he found himself yearning for one more thing, something that he had been thinking of all day.

The trees. Tall, towering, *safe* trees.

Scarcely half an hour later, far away from the Jedi academy and the Great Temple, he landed the T-23 on the sturdy treetops, settling the craft in the uppermost branches of the Massassi trees. The tree canopy was not as high as he was used to. The air was thinner, and the jungle smells, though not unpleasant, were different from those of Kashyyyk. Even so, Lowbacca felt more at peace now than he had at any other moment since landing on Yavin 4.

Jacen had said that the huge orange gas giant overhead was best viewed from a Massassi tree—and the human boy was definitely right. Lowie looked around in all directions—at the sky and the trees, at the crumbling ruins of smaller temples visible through breaks in the canopy. He stared at the languid rivers, at the strange vegetation and animals around him. He sighed with relief. He *could* find a place of contentment and solitude on this moon, a place where he could think of family and home while he studied to be a Jedi.

As the late-afternoon sunlight slanted through the thick branches, a distant glint caught Lowbacca's eye. He wondered what it could be. It was not the color of any vegetation or temple ruins. The light reflected from a shiny and evenly shaped object stuck partway up a tree. Lowie leaned forward, as if that could help him see more clearly. He wished he had brought a pair of macrobinoculars.

Curiosity and wonder struck a spark of excitement in him. He wanted to get closer, but caution intervened. It was getting dark. And after all, if the object was important, wouldn't someone have seen it long ago? Perhaps not. He doubted it could be seen from the jungle floor, and it was unlikely that many students came out and climbed to the top of the canopy, this far away from the Great Temple. He was almost certain that no one knew about this discovery.

Heart pounding, Lowie made a mental note of the shiny object's location. He would come back the very first chance he got—he *had* to find out what it was.

7

"I WONDER WHY Lowie never made it to evening meal," Jacen said. Jaina and Tenel Ka sat next to him in the grand audience chamber, where Luke Skywalker had summoned them all for a special announcement. Dusk light shone like burning metal through the narrow windows overhead, but the clean white glowpanels dispelled shadows in the large, echoing room.

"Maybe he was having too much fun flying his T-23," Jaina whispered. "I probably wouldn't have made it back either."

"Perhaps," Tenel Ka said in a low voice, as if giving the matter serious consideration, "he was not hungry."

Jacen flashed her a look of disbelief. "Hey, a Wookiee not hungry? Hah! And you say *I* make dumb jokes."

Tenel Ka shrugged. "It is a thought."

"Okay, well," Jacen said, "I'm not kidding now—what if something went wrong with the skyhopper? What if Lowie crashed in the jungle?"

"Impossible," Jaina replied. Though she whispered, her tone was clearly firm. "I checked all those systems myself."

Tenel Ka's eyebrows raised a fraction. "Ah. Ah-hah. So because you checked them, the systems could not malfunction?" She nodded, and Jacen could have sworn that he saw the shadow of a smile lurking at the corners of her lips.

"Never mind—there's Lowie," Jacen said with relief, waving his arms to attract their Wookiee friend's attention.

"See?" Jaina said smugly. "Told you nothing could happen."

Jacen pretended not to notice. "You're just in time," he said as the Wookiee joined them. "Master Skywalker should be here anytime now."

No one really knew why this special twilight meeting had been called, but it was fairly unusual. Everyone who lived, worked, or trained at the Jedi academy had arrived, filling the chamber with a hushed excitement.

Jacen whispered, "Where were you, Lowie?"

Lowbacca responded in a low rumble, quieter than any Jacen had ever heard a Wookiee use. Without warning, Em Teedee announced in a clear metallic voice, "Master Lowbacca wishes it known that he had a most successful expedition and—" The translator droid cut off in midsentence as Lowbacca clamped a ginger-furred hand over the droid's mouth speaker.

"Shhh!" Jaina hissed.

"Can't you turn it down?" Jacen whispered.

Curious eyes turned to stare at them from every section of the grand audience chamber. Lowbacca hunched down in his seat with a chagrined look that needed no interpreter. He craned his neck forward to stare at the droid clipped to his webbed belt. He issued a series of soft, sharp mutters.

"Oh! Oh, dear me," Em Teedee replied in an enthusiastic though much quieter voice. "I *do* beg your pardon. I did not fully comprehend that you didn't intend to share your discovery with everyone present."

"Discovery?" Jacen said. "What did you—"

But Master Skywalker chose that moment to make his entrance. A hush fell over the crowd, putting an end to all hope of Jacen satisfying his curiosity before the meeting began. Luke mounted the steps to the wide raised platform, closely followed by a slender woman with flowing silvery-white hair and huge opalescent eyes.

"Thank you for gathering here on such short notice," Luke began. "I received news this morning of a pressing matter that calls me away."

As if from a pebble tossed into a pond, a series of surprised murmurs rippled through the room. Jacen wondered if his uncle's imminent departure had anything to do with the messages brought by his father on the *Falcon*.

The blue eyes that looked out over the audience—kind eyes that seemed wise beyond their years—gave no hint of what the Jedi Master's mission might be.

"I don't know how long I will be gone, so I've asked one of my former students, the Jedi Tionne"—he gestured to the slender, shimmering-eyed woman beside him—"to supervise your training while I'm away. Not only does Tionne know my teachings almost as well as I do, but she has a rich knowledge of Jedi lore and history. As you are about to find out, she's well worth listening to."

This intrigued Jacen. He remembered hearing that she was not a particularly strong Jedi, but from the warm smile that passed between Luke and Tionne, he could tell that they understood each other well, and that Master Skywalker must have complete trust in his former student.

As Luke withdrew from the platform, leaving the students alone with Tionne, the silver-haired Jedi retrieved a curiously shaped stringed instrument from somewhere behind her. It consisted of two resonating boxes, one at either end of a slender fretted neck. The strings stretching across the instrument flared out in a fan pattern at both ends.

Seating herself on a low stool, Tionne began to strum. "I will tell you about a Jedi Master who lived long ago," she said. "This is the ballad of Master Vodo-Siosk Baas."

As she began to sing, Jacen agreed with his uncle: Tionne was indeed worth listening to. Her song rang clear and true. Its pure tones carried easily to the farthest corners of the great hall and transported them all to a time they had never witnessed. The music flowed around them, sweeping them along on currents of excitement and courage and triumph and sacrifice.

She sang of dire events that had taken place four thousand years earlier—how the strange, alien Jedi Master had been destroyed by Exar Kun, one of his own students who had turned to the dark side. Master Vodo had begged the other Jedi Masters not to do battle with Exar Kun, and had tried to reason with him alone—though his gentle hopes had ended in tragedy.

In the silence that followed her song, a flood of insight washed through Jacen as he realized that this Jedi was worth listening to for more than just her voice.

Tionne stood, to a collective sigh from everyone present. Jacen hadn't even realized he'd been holding his breath.

"I trust my first lesson to you hasn't been too painful," she said with a merry twinkle in her pearly eyes. "Tomorrow I will give another lesson, after morning meal."

With that, the evening meeting ended. Some listeners remained seated, transfixed, as if trying to absorb the last trickles of music lingering in the room. Others left singly or in whispering groups, while still others stayed behind to talk with Tionne.

Jacen, Jaina, Tenel Ka, and Lowbacca found themselves free at last to talk. They huddled together and discussed Lowie's find. Em Teedee—carefully modulating his voice to an appropriate, secretive level—provided translations.

They speculated by turns about the strange glinting object that Lowbacca had seen out in the jungle. They came to only one conclusion: at the earliest possible opportunity, they would go out together and investigate.

Tionne's morning ballad fell in a fine musical mist, drenching its listeners with wonder and ancient lore. Jacen sat in the second row with his brandy-colored eyes closed, concentrating on her words, trying to absorb everything the music had to teach him. It was just as well that his eyes were shut, since his view was completely blocked by the colorful bulk of Raynar wearing his finest robes.

As the last notes drained away, Jacen opened his eyes to find his sister staring at him in silent amusement. Neither Lowbacca nor Tenel Ka, who sat beside him, gave any indication that they had noticed Jacen's apparent absorption in the music. Then Tionne spoke, drawing Jacen's attention back to the silver-haired Jedi on the raised platform.

"A Jedi's greatest power comes not from size or from physical strength," she said. "It comes from understanding the Force—from trusting in the Force. As part of your Jedi training you will learn to build your confidence and belief through practice. Without that practice we may not succeed when it is most important. This is true of many skills in life. Listen to a story.

"Once, a young girl lived by a lake. Simply by watching others, she learned much about how to swim. One day when her family was busy, the girl jumped into the deep water. Although she moved her arms and legs as she had seen other swimmers do, she could not keep her head above the water.

"Fortunately a fisherwoman jumped in and rescued her. The woman, a practiced swimmer, had not needed to think about how to swim, but the little girl—who had only learned by watching—did not have the skill even to stay afloat. After they were safely out of the water, the fisherwoman took the girl's hand and said, 'Come to the shallows, child, and I will teach you to swim.'"

Tionne paused as if lost in thought, her pearly eyes glittering. "So it is with the Force. Unless we practice what we learn, and unless we are tested, we never know we can trust in the Force if the need arises. That is why this Jedi academy is also called a *praxeum*. It is a place where we not only learn, but we put the learning to use. As with swimming, the more we practice, the more confidence we have. Eventually, our skill becomes second nature.

"The next several days I would like the beginning and intermediate students to practice one of the most basic skills: using the Force to lift. For today, practice lifting only something small—no bigger than a leaf."

Raynar interrupted in a blustery voice, "How can you expect us to *strengthen* our skills if you take us back to a child's level?"

Jacen rolled his eyes at Raynar's rudeness, but he had to admit that he had been wondering the same thing.

Tionne smiled down at Raynar without annoyance. "A good question. Let me give you an example. If you wanted to strengthen your arms, you might lift many stones one time, or you might lift one stone many times. It is the same with your Jedi skills. For today, practice just as I have asked you. It is not the *only* way to strengthen your skills, but it is *one* way. There are always alternatives. I promise you will learn more than just how to lift a leaf."

Tionne dismissed the students. As they left the grand audience chamber and started down the worn stone stairs, Jaina pulled the other three young Jedi to a halt, her eyes dancing. "Are you thinking what I'm thinking?" she asked.

Jacen, who did not know what she was thinking, nonetheless sensed her excitement and her eagerness to investigate Lowie's mysterious discovery.

Jaina shrugged. "What better place to practice lifting leaves than out in a jungle?"

8

"YOU SURE THIS seat is safe?" Jacen asked as he squeezed himself into the cargo well behind the T-23's passenger seat.

"Of course it is," his sister replied automatically as she climbed into the front. "You like crawling into cramped spaces anyway."

"Only to catch bugs," he grumbled. "There's no cushioning back here."

The cargo well was much too small to accommodate Tenel Ka, who was taller and more solidly built than either of the twins. Jacen would have to settle for the back or be left behind; his sister would take her turn there on the return trip. He squirmed and settled in as the T-23's engines started with a roaring purr.

Lowie called a command over the sound of the warming repulsorlifts. Em Teedee said, "Master Lowbacca requests that you please be certain that your restraints are secure. He is interested in your utmost safety. We shall be departing momentarily."

Lowbacca's voice barked out again, and the droid amended his translation. "Actually, Master Lowbacca *might* have said something closer to, 'Hold on, everyone. Here we go!'"

"Oh, blaster bolts. No crash straps either," Jacen observed as Jaina and Tenel Ka buckled themselves in up front.

The rebuilt T-23 lifted off with a small jerk. The wind howled past the rattling window plates as they picked up height and speed. Jacen felt the thrill of being airborne as the ion afterburners spluttered behind them. Even cramped in the back, he was glad he hadn't stayed behind.

Jacen looked out through the scratched port as Lowbacca let the skyhopper skim just above the treetops, arrowing away from the Jedi academy into unexplored territory. Soon there were nothing but trees as far as Jacen could see through the scratched port, as lush and green as the sky above him was blue.

Though he enjoyed the lovely foliage below him, Jacen's legs began to cramp. By the time the T-23 dove down and came to rest in a small clearing, he could feel the engine vibrations all the way to his teeth.

Up front, Jaina and Tenel Ka unbuckled their restraints and scrambled nimbly out of the T-23. Jacen dragged himself from the cargo well, stretching his stiff legs as he stepped out into the tangled underbrush. He rubbed the seat of his jumpsuit with both hands to get the circulation going again. "I think a leaf is about all I *could* lift right now!"

Lowie rushed to the edge of the clearing, beckoning the others. "Master Lowbacca says the tree holding the artifact is over here," Em Teedee called. "It has several broken branches, so he was able to locate it easily from the air."

Jaina looked in the direction that Lowbacca was pointing. "Well, what are we waiting for?" she said. Tenel Ka marched over to the young Wookiee, as if ready to carve a path through the jungle. Jacen took a long and wistful look at all the strange new plants he saw around him, but followed the others into the deep green shadows.

Lowbacca gestured up into the distant branches of an enormous Massassi tree. The trunk seemed as big around as one of the skyscrapers on city-covered Coruscant, and even the lowest branches were well out of Jacen's reach. But Lowie wanted them to climb up after him!

"Oh," said Jaina, a crestfallen look on her face, "I wouldn't get very far climbing that."

Lowbacca assured them, via Em Teedee, that the climb would be easy for a Wookiee. He offered to go up alone for the first investigation and report his findings so they could decide the next step.

"We can explore down here," Jacen suggested. "We might find some other pieces of . . . of whatever it is." *Or maybe some interesting animals or fungus or insects,* he thought hopefully.

Jaina and Tenel Ka readily agreed. Lowbacca swiped a hairy hand along the thick black streak that ran through the fur above his left eyebrow. He swarmed up the trunk, swung into the lower branches, and soon disappeared from sight.

Jacen's stomach rumbled with hunger, and he hoped that Lowbacca would hurry. The three young Jedi trainees poked around in the underbrush, spiraling out from the T-23 in a wandering search pattern. Taking turns, they practiced their leaf-lifting assignment, fluttering leaves in the shrubbery, lifting dry forest debris from the damp and mossy ground.

* * *

Before long, Lowbacca came crashing back down through the thick branches. He dropped to the ground near them and let out a loud Wookiee cry.

Jaina ran toward him, eager and interested. "Did you find it, Lowie?"

Lowbacca nodded vigorously.

"What was it?" Jaina asked. "Can you describe it?"

"Master Lowbacca believes it to be some sort of solar panel," Em Teedee translated as the Wookiee replied. Then the droid launched into a complete description.

Jaina felt her skin prickle with goose bumps. "Hmmmm," she said. "If I'm right, there should be a lot more to that artifact than what Lowie saw. Let's keep looking."

Tenel Ka dug into a small supply pouch she carried with her and withdrew a pack of carbo-protein biscuits. "Here. Nourishment as we search."

Jacen chomped hungrily on his biscuit. "Just what are we looking for, Jaina?" he asked, speaking around a mouthful of crumbs.

"Scrap metal, machinery, another solar panel." Jaina shaded her eyes, scanning deeper into the thick jungles around them. "We'll keep widening the circle of our search until we find something. What we're looking for shouldn't be too far away."

Jacen retrieved a flask of water from the T-23, took a gulp, and handed it to his sister. Jaina took a few mouthfuls of water and passed the flask on to Lowbacca. Then she set off at a trot for the base of the big tree. Jaina didn't look back to see if the others were following, and bit her lip, feeling a brief pang of guilt.

At times like this Jaina always seemed to assume leadership, just like her mother. But how could she help it? Her parents had raised all three of their children to assess a situation, weigh the alternatives, and make decisions.

"Let's spread out," she said.

"Great!" Jacen said, walking around the massive trunk toward a clump of dense undergrowth.

Jaina smiled, knowing full well that her brother's excitement came not from a desire to find the mysterious artifact, but from the opportunity to explore the jungle and examine its creatures more closely.

She was about to head into the underbrush herself when Lowbacca stopped her with a questioning growl. Em Teedee translated. "Master Lowbacca says—and I personally am inclined to agree with him—that the jungle floor is *not* a safe place to split up. Even to speed up a search."

As impatient as she was to continue looking, Jaina stopped to consider. Tenel Ka caught her eye, placed her hands on her hips, and nodded. "This is a fact."

Jaina gnawed at her lower lip again, thinking, and came to a decision. "All right. We spread out a little bit, but only as far as our line of sight. Good enough?"

The others' murmurs of agreement were interrupted by a loud squawking as a flock of reptile birds took flight from the bushes near where Jacen had been exploring. Jacen emerged from the bushes on his hands and knees, looking startled, but not displeased.

"No big discoveries," he reported, "but I did find this." He held out his palm. In it was a plump, furry gray creature, quivering in a small nest of glossy fibers.

Another animal. Jaina sighed with resignation. She might have guessed.

"Ah. A-hah," Tenel Ka said. Lowbacca bent forward to run a shaggy finger along the tiny creature's back.

"Look, Jaina," Jacen said, turning the fluffy nest in his hand. He pointed to a dull, flat loop of metal that was firmly attached to the mass of fibers.

"A . . . buckle?" Jaina said, finally comprehending.

Her brother nodded. "Like the kind in crash webbing."

"Good work," Tenel Ka said with solemn approval.

"Well, what are we waiting for?" Jaina asked. "Let's keep going."

By midafternoon, though, Jaina began to get discouraged. Jacen, on the other hand, was intrigued by every crawling creature or insect they encountered.

"Do please try to be a bit more cautious!" Jaina could hear Em Teedee saying. "That's the third dent today. And I've lost count of how many scratches I've received while you've been exploring. Now if you would only be more attentive to—"

Em Teedee's admonishments were drowned out as Lowie gave a sharp bark of surprise behind a tangle of vines and branches. "Oh! Oh, my. Mistress Jaina, Master Jacen, Mistress Tenel Ka!" Em Teedee's voice was loud enough to startle not only Jaina but a number of flying and climbing creatures. "Do come quickly. Master Lowbacca has made a discovery."

Needing no further encouragement, all of them rushed to see what Lowbacca had found. Jaina felt her heart pounding in her chest, knowing and dreading what they would find.

They worked quickly, scratching and cutting their hands as they pulled away the thick plant growth from the heap of metallic wreckage. Jaina gasped as they finally exposed it—a rounded, tarnished cockpit large enough only for a single pilot, one squarish black solar panel crisscrossed with support braces. The other panel was missing, stuck up in the tree where Lowie had found it. But still the ship was unmistakable.

A crashed Imperial TIE fighter.

9

"BUT WHY WOULD such a craft be here in the jungles of Yavin 4?" Tenel Ka asked, narrowing her eyes in concern as they worked to remove the debris from the ruined craft. "Is it an Imperial spy ship?"

Jaina shook her head. "Can't be. TIE fighters were short-range ships used by the Empire. They weren't equipped with hyperdrive, so there aren't many ways it could have gotten here."

Jacen cleared his throat. "Well, I *can* think of one way," he said, "but that would make this ship—let's see . . ."

"Over twenty years old . . ." Jaina breathed, finishing his sentence for him.

Lowbacca made a low, questioning noise, and Tenel Ka continued to look perplexed.

Jaina explained. "When the Empire built the first Death Star, it was the most powerful weapon ever made. They tested it by destroying Alderaan, our mother's homeworld. Then they brought it here to Yavin 4, to destroy the Rebel base."

As she spoke, Jaina pulled the last bit of brush away from the top canopy of the TIE fighter and looked inside. There were no bones. She slid into the musty cockpit.

"A lot of Rebel pilots died in one-on-one combat with the TIE fighters that protected the Death Star, and a lot of Imperial fighters were shot down too," Jacen said, picking up the story.

Jaina wrinkled her nose at the mildewy smell, the mold-clogged controls. She ran her fingers over the navigation panels in the cockpit, closing her eyes and wondering what it must have been like twenty-some years ago to be a fighter pilot in the Battle of Yavin 4. She envisioned an enemy fighter swooping toward her in a strafing run, her engine hit, her tiny ship careening out of control. . . .

Jacen's voice broke into her thoughts. "But then in the end, our dad flew cover for Uncle Luke's X-wing fighter while he took his final run. Uncle Luke made the shot that blew up the Death Star."

Tenel Ka nodded gravely, her braided red-gold hair like a wreath around her head. "And why is it called a TIE fighter?" she asked.

Jaina answered, speaking up from the cockpit, "Because it has twin ion engines. T-I-E, see?"

Ducking her head, she wormed her way to the engine access panels at the rear of the cockpit and pried open the tarnished metal plate. A squeaking rodent, disturbed from its hidden nest, scampered away, vanishing through a small hole in the hull.

Jaina tinkered with the engines, checking integrity, noting the rotted hoses and fuel lines. But overall, the primary motivators seemed intact, though she would have to run numerous diagnostics. She had plenty of spare parts in her room.

She stood up slowly in the cockpit and poked her head out again, then ran her callused hands along the side of the crashed TIE fighter. "You know, I think we could do it," Jaina said.

All eyes turned toward her, questioning.

"I think we could fix the TIE fighter."

Her brother stared at her in stunned silence for a moment, then clapped a palm to his forehead. "I've got a bad feeling about this."

As the whine of the T-23 skyhopper faded into the jungle distance, the frightened forest creatures settled back into their routines. They scuttled through the underbrush, chasing each other across the branches, predator and prey. The leaves stirred and flying creatures sent their cries from treetop to treetop, forgetting the intruders entirely.

Far below on the forest floor, the branches of a dense thicket parted. A worn and tattered black glove pushed a thorny twig aside.

The pilot of the crashed TIE fighter emerged from his hiding place into the newly trampled clearing.

"Surrender is betrayal," he muttered to himself, as he had done so many times before. It had become a litany during his years of rugged survival on the isolated jungle moon of Yavin.

The pilot's protective uniform hung in rags from his gaunt frame, worn to tatters and patched with furs from an incredible number of years living alone in the jungle. His left arm, injured during the crash, was drawn up like a twisted claw against his chest. He stepped forward, cracking twigs under his old boots as he made his way to the crash site that was no longer secret. He had camouflaged the wrecked Imperial craft many years ago, hiding it from Rebel eyes. But now, despite all his work, it had been discovered.

"Surrender is betrayal," he said again. He stared down at his fighter, trying to see what damage the Rebel spies had caused.

10

OVER THE NEXT few days, Tionne increased the complexity of the young Jedi trainees' assignments, and the four companions practiced fine-tuning their control of the Force.

Jaina, Jacen, Lowie, and Tenel Ka found excuses to return again and again to the site of the crashed TIE fighter. With Jaina as the driving force, they took on the repair project as a group exercise—but they always managed to work in any assigned practice sessions during their jungle expeditions.

Although the idea was not flattering, Jaina was forced to admit that part of her motivation for this work was her envy of Lowbacca's personal T-23—she wanted her own craft to fly over the treetops. But she was also drawn by the challenge the wrecked TIE fighter represented. Its age and complexity offered a unique opportunity for learning about mechanics, and Jaina could not turn it down.

But the strongest reason for taking on the project—and perhaps the one that kept them all working without complaint—was that it forged a bond among the four friends. They learned to function as a team, to make the most of each person's strengths and to compensate for each other's weaknesses. The strands of their friendships intertwined and wove together in a pattern as simple as it was strong. This bond included even Em Teedee, who learned to make verbal contributions at appropriate times and was gradually accepted as a member of their group.

Jaina spent most of her time overseeing the mechanical repairs, while Lowbacca concentrated on the computer systems. Jacen had ample opportunity to explore and to observe the local wildlife as, officially, he "searched" through the nearby underbrush for broken or missing components; he also made quick supply trips back to the academy in the T-23 for parts that Jaina or Lowbacca needed. Tenel Ka worked with quiet competence on any task that needed doing and was especially valuable in lugging new metal plates to patch large breaches in the TIE hull.

"Hey, Tenel Ka!" Jacen said. "What goes ha-ha-ha . . . *thump!*"

Her gray eyes looked at him, as lustrous as highly polished stones. "I don't know."

"A droid laughing its head off!" Jacen said, then started giggling.

"Ah. A-hah," Tenel Ka said. She considered this for a moment, then added without the slightest trace of mirth, "Yes, that is very funny." She bent back to her work.

From time to time Lowie climbed to the top of the canopy to meditate and absorb the solitude; the young Wookiee enjoyed his time alone, sitting in silence. Tenel Ka occasionally took short breaks to test her athletic skills by running through jungle undergrowth or climbing trees.

But Jaina preferred to stay with the downed TIE fighter, examining it from every angle and imagining possibilities. She considered no bodily position too difficult or undignified to assume while repairing the craft.

Jaina tucked her head under the cockpit control panel, with her stomach supported by the back of the pilot's seat. Her backside was sticking high in the air and her feet were kicking as she worked, when she felt a playful poke on the leg.

She extricated herself from the awkward position. Lowie handed her a datapad into which he had downloaded the schematics and specifications for a TIE fighter, taken from the main information files in the computer center back at the Great Temple. Jaina studied the data and looked over the list of computer parts Lowbacca needed.

"These should be pretty easy for Jacen to find," she said. "I have most of them right in my room."

Em Teedee spoke up. "Master Lowbacca wishes to know which systems you intend to concentrate on next."

Jaina's brow furrowed in judicious concentration. "We've already decided we won't be needing the weapons systems. I think the laser cannons work fine, but I don't intend to hook them up. I suppose the next step might be to work on the power systems. I haven't done much with them yet."

Jacen and Tenel Ka trotted up to join the discussion. "You will need the other solar panel," Tenel Ka said. "Up in the tree."

Jacen cocked an eyebrow at her, using Tenel Ka's own phrase. "This is a fact?" Tenel Ka did not smile, but nodded her approval.

Jacen folded his arms across his chest and looked pleased with himself. "Does anyone remember the assignment Tionne gave us for today?"

"Cooperative lifting with one or more other students," Tenel Ka stated without hesitation.

Jaina clapped her hands and rubbed them together, scrambling out of the cramped cockpit. "Well, then, what are we waiting for?"

The process was much more difficult than they had anticipated, but in the end they managed it. Lowie and Tenel Ka climbed up into the tree to clear away the moss and branches that held the panel in place. Tenel Ka secured it with the thin fibercord from her belt, while Lowbacca added sturdy vines to help support the heavy slab. Jaina and Jacen watched from the lower branches of the tree, craning their necks to see.

"Everyone ready?" Jaina asked. "Okay—now concentrate," she said. She gave them a moment to observe the solar panel glittering in scattered light from the sky. They studied the piece of wreckage, grasping it with their thoughts.

"Now," Jaina said.

With that, four minds pushed upward, nudging. In a gentle, concerted motion they lifted the panel free of the branch where it had rested for decades. The large, flat rectangle wobbled in midair for a moment and then began to slowly descend. Tenel Ka kept her fibercord taut, easing the Force-lightened object down.

Together, they brought it to rest a few branches below where it had been. Tenel Ka and Lowbacca untied the vines and the fibercord from the higher branch, climbed down, and retied the strands to the branch on which the panel now rested.

The process was not perfect. Mental coordination among the four friends proved difficult, and they each lost their grip more than once. But the vines and fibercord held, preventing a disaster.

By the time the exhausted companions brought the panel to the jungle floor and carried it to the crash site, all of them were panting and perspiring from the mental exertion.

Jaina sank down beside the TIE fighter with a weary groan. She flopped backward in the dirt and leaves, not caring for the moment that her hair would become as disheveled and full of twigs as her brother's usually was.

Lowie tossed them each a packet of food from the basket of supplies they brought with them every day. Jaina's packet landed on her stomach, and she rolled onto her side with a mock growl of indignation. As she faced a hole in the side of the broken TIE fighter, a sudden thought occurred to her.

"You know," she said, chin in hands. "I'd be willing to bet there's enough room in there to install a hyperdrive."

"You said that TIE fighters were short-range craft," Tenel Ka said.

Lowie responded with a contemplative sound as he thought this over. Jacen merely moaned at the mention of more work.

"They were *designed* to be short-range," Jaina said. "Never equipped with hyperdrives because the Emperor didn't want to sacrifice the maneuverability."

Jacen snorted. "Or maybe he didn't want any of his fighter pilots making a quick escape."

Jaina turned toward him and grinned. "I guess I never thought of it that way." Her face lit with enthusiasm as she looked at her friends. "But there's nothing to stop us from equipping *this* TIE fighter with a hyperdrive, is there? Dad gave me one to tinker with."

"It is a possibility," Tenel Ka said, without much enthusiasm.

They were all tired, Jaina knew. But her mind raced with the excitement of this new thought. She made a quick decision. "Okay, let's go back to the academy. I want to make some measurements. We'll call it a day."

Jacen sighed with relief. "I think that's been your best suggestion in hours."

Back again the next afternoon, Jacen lay flat on his stomach, his chin resting on one clenched fist as he surveyed the moist ground beneath a tangle of low, thick bushes. He left his feet sticking out from beneath the bushes so that the others could locate him easily should they look up from their work—though there was little chance of that. From behind him he could hear thumping and clinking as Jaina labored to install the hyperdrive in the TIE fighter.

A thick *splat* told him that Tenel Ka and Lowbacca were applying sealant over the hole patch at the base of the reattached solar panel. The others were all busy, leaving Jacen free to hunt for "missing parts" again.

He watched, fascinated, as a leaf-shaped creature that matched the blue-green color of the foliage around him attached itself to a branch. It extended a long mottled brown tongue that flattened against the twig in a perfect camouflage. Jacen could sense the leaf creature's anticipation. Soon a crowd of minute insects, drawn by a smell Jacen could not discern, landed on the "branch" and became stuck fast.

Jacen chuckled and shook his head as the leaf creature retracted its tongue with an audible *fwoookt*.

With nothing interesting to be seen on the ground, he gave the bush a small shake once the leaf creature departed. He was rewarded with a hissing rustle as a dislodged object fell near his elbow. He picked it up.

It was an Imperial insignia.

He turned the metallic object over in his hand, but then he saw a familiar shimmer at the edge of his gaze, and he reflexively grabbed for it. Jacen wriggled backward out of the bushes, stood, and bounded over to the TIE fighter.

"Look what I found!" he crowed. His sister's lower half protruded at an awkward angle from the cockpit, while she was apparently attempting to connect some part of the hyperdrive behind the pilot's seat.

Her muffled voice drifted out to him. "Just a moment. I need a flash heater."

Tenel Ka passed a small tool in from the other side of the open cockpit. She and Lowbacca, wiping sealant from their hands, came around to see what Jacen had discovered.

"A brooch of some sort?" Tenel Ka asked, examining it closely.

Jacen shook his head. "An Imperial insignia. Came off a uniform of some kind."

"There," Jaina said, extracting herself from the cockpit of the TIE fighter and jumping down beside them. "That should do it."

Jacen handed her the insignia, and she nodded absently. "Look what else I found," he said, holding up his left arm, which was wrapped in a glowing shimmer.

Jaina made a sound somewhere between a growl and a laugh, and backed away. "Great. Just what we need—another crystal snake that can get loose."

Jacen used a tactic he knew his sister couldn't resist. "Oh," he said, letting disappointment show. "It's just that you've always been so *good* at designing things—I thought you could come up with a cage that the snakes couldn't escape from. But if you really don't think you can . . ."

He saw Jaina's face light at the challenge, but then her brandy-brown eyes narrowed shrewdly, and he knew that she had caught on. "That," she said, "is a dirty trick. You *know* I could—" She shook her head, sighed in mock exasperation, and seemed to resign herself to the inevitable. "Oh, all right! I'll build you a new cage for your crystal snakes—"

"Thanks," a grinning Jacen cut her off before she could change her mind. "You're the best sister in the whole galaxy!"

Jaina huffed indelicately. "But don't bring this new snake back to your quarters until I have the cage ready."

"Okay," Jacen said, "I'll keep it someplace safe—maybe in the cargo compartment. Can I have the Imperial insignia back, please?" Jaina tossed it to him, and he began to polish it against the sleeve of his jumpsuit. "I wonder if it belonged to the pilot."

Lowbacca looked at the crashed TIE fighter and then back at Jacen and rumbled a question. "Master Lowbacca suggests it is unlikely that the pilot survived the crash, even if his fall was cushioned by the Massassi trees," Em Teedee said.

Tenel Ka looked around the site with unblinking eyes. "No bones."

Jacen shrugged. "After twenty years, that's not surprising. Lots of scavengers in the jungle. I've been assuming he was thrown clear."

Tenel Ka's cool eyes looked troubled, but she nodded. "Perhaps."

The four worked in companionable silence as they attached the final hole patch to the damaged hull. Then, while the other three applied the slow-drying sealant, Jacen hunted around in the underbrush. He knew he shouldn't be out of sight for more than a few seconds, but he had already searched all of the thickets in clear view of the crash site.

Promising himself that he wouldn't be gone long, Jacen pushed through a particularly thick tangle of dense, dark-leaved plants and emerged into a small clearing no wider than his outstretched arms. The dirt was completely devoid of plant life, as if some animal trampled it so often that vegetation no longer grew there. It extended deeper into the jungle—a path! It was narrow, but the hard-packed trail was unmistakable.

Forgetting his earlier promise to stay close, Jacen plunged through the bushes and followed the trail. The grove of Massassi trees was younger, their branches lower to the ground. Perhaps that was why none of the companions had seen this path from up above.

The jungle grew darker around him as he trudged on. The chitters, growls, and screeches of forest animals seemed more menacing.

Just as he began to realize that he was much too far away from the others, he came upon a clearing beside a small stream.

Some creature had built a dam across the stream, diverting some of the water into a depression beside it to form a wide, shallow pool. Against the burn-hollowed trunk of a huge Massassi tree at the water's edge leaned a number of long, fat branches covered with moss and ferns to form a crude shelter—perhaps the lair of the creature whose path Jacen had been following.

Jacen reached out toward the little hovel with his mind, but sensed nothing larger than insects living around it. Skirting the small pond, he approached the low shelter, his heart pounding loudly in his chest. He knew he should be more cautious. But what was this place?

What if the beast that lived here was a predator? What if it returned as he was investigating?

Jacen jumped as he heard a loud *crack*—but it was only a twig snapping under his own foot. He bent forward to look into the branchy opening of the shelter, and gasped at what he saw there.

Fully a third of the Massassi tree's trunk had been hollowed out to form a sturdy, dry cave, tall enough for a man to stand in. A makeshift wooden chair stood beside a low mound of leaves that might have been a bed, partially covered by a ragged piece of cloth. A cache of equipment, vines, fruits, and dried berries lay piled against the back of the cave. Perched atop the pile was a nightmarish black helmet with triangular eyeplates and a breathing mask connected to a pair of rubber hoses that Jacen figured had once been linked with an air tank.

An Imperial TIE fighter pilot's helmet.

Jacen stumbled backward, away from the shelter, his breath coming in shallow gasps. He tripped and fell, and found himself inside a ring of low stones and ashes. A fire pit. He scooped away some of the dirt that covered the pit and felt around with trembling fingers. The ground was still warm.

Jacen jumped to his feet and raced toward the little trail at full speed. He ran along the narrow path, heedless of the branches that slapped his face or the thorns that tore at his jumpsuit, oblivious to the animals he startled from their hiding places. He didn't slow as he approached the bushes that surrounded the crashed TIE fighter.

He burst into the tiny clearing and ran up to the wreck, yelling, "Jaina! Tenel Ka! Lowie! He's here. He's alive. The TIE pilot isn't dead!"

The three of them looked up in astonishment just as Jacen heard a rustling in the bushes behind him. He turned to see a haggard, grizzled-looking man step through the bushes. The stranger's face was deeply lined, and he wore a tattered flight suit. His left arm was bent at an awkward angle, and was wrapped in an armored gauntlet of black leather. But in his glove he held an ugly, old-model blaster. And the weapon was leveled directly at the young Jedi Knights.

"Yes," said the Imperial fighter pilot. "I am very much alive. And you are my prisoners."

11

WHEN THE IMPERIAL TIE pilot turned his eyes from her for a split second, Tenel Ka reacted with lightning speed, just as she had been taught by the warrior women on Dathomir.

"Run!" she shouted to the others, knowing exactly what to do. She turned and bolted for the nearest tangled undergrowth, dodging expected blaster fire.

Tenel Ka reacted so quickly and so smoothly that even her most rigid battle trainers would have been proud of her. Their tactics had been drilled into her:

Confuse the enemy.
Do the unexpected.
Take your opponent by surprise.
Don't waste time hesitating.

Tenel Ka tore through the tangled thorns and blueleaf shrubs, clawing with her hands to clear a path that closed behind her as she moved through the thicket. She gasped and panted, bolting ahead, ignoring the scratches and stinging pain of the thorns against her bare arms and legs. The scaled armor protected her vital parts, but her red-gold hair flew around her, snagging loose leaves and twigs. Branches caught at her braids and yanked strands of her hair out by the roots. She hissed with pain, but clamped her teeth together, plunging ahead.

Why couldn't she hear the others running?

"Get help!" It was Jacen shouting behind her, still in the clearing. Why didn't they run?

Then an explosion of flames ripped into the underbrush just to her left. The TIE pilot was firing his blaster at her! The smell of singed leaves and burnt sap stung her nostrils. Tenel Ka dove to the ground, rolled sideways, then ran at full speed in a different direction. If she gave up now, he would kill her. She had no doubt of that—not anymore.

Intent only on distancing herself from the TIE pilot, she fled, changing directions at random to confuse the enemy. Branches cracked underfoot, and Tenel Ka paid no attention whatsoever to where she ran . . . deeper into the densest jungle of Yavin 4.

Lowbacca hesitated only a fraction of a second longer.

Tenel Ka seemed to evaporate as she shouted "Run!" and ducked into the thick forest.

The TIE pilot whirled and pointed his blaster at the place where Tenel Ka had disappeared, and Lowbacca used the instant of distraction. The young Wookiee let out a bellow of surprise and anger, then instinctively surged up the ancient bole of the nearest Massassi tree, climbing higher, *up*, where it was safe.

He grabbed branches and vines, hauling himself up toward the thick, spicy-smelling canopy. Behind him, the Imperial fighter began shooting wildly. Explosions and bright flames from burning foliage ballooned out from where the blaster bolts struck the branches under Lowie's feet. He smelled the ozone of energy discharge, the steam of disintegrated vegetation.

With Wookiee strength, Lowbacca climbed higher and higher, finally reaching thick, flat branches that allowed him to make his way across the treetops toward where he had landed the T-23.

He had to get help. He had to rescue his friends. Tenel Ka had gotten to safety—or so he hoped—but Jacen and Jaina had not been able to react as quickly or move with such practiced wilderness skills.

"Oh my!" Em Teedee wailed from the clip on his waist. "Where are we going? That person was trying to kill us! Can you imagine that?"

Lowie continued to scramble across the thick branches, loping with great agility, moving farther away from the still-firing pilot.

"Master Lowbacca, answer me!" Em Teedee said, his tinny voice echoing from the speaker-patch. "You can't simply leave me hanging here doing nothing at all, you know."

Lowbacca grunted a reply and kept moving.

"But surely, that's beside the point," Em Teedee quibbled, "since I'm doing everything I can. Just because I have no functional arms or legs doesn't mean I don't *want* to assist you."

The sounds of blaster fire from the clearing below had ceased, and Lowbacca feared that meant Jacen and Jaina were captured—or worse. His thoughts churned it in panic and turmoil. He knew he had to rescue them. But how? He had never done anything like this before. He didn't think Tenel Ka could do it alone, so he had to offer whatever help he could manage.

The branches thinned up ahead, spreading out around the clearing where Lowbacca had settled the T-23. The small ship sat where he had landed it, and he scrambled back down the thick branches, clinging to vines until he reached ground level again. The T-23 was his best chance.

Lowbacca had been so proud of the small craft when his uncle Chewie had given it to him, but now it seemed so small and battered, all but useless against an armed Imperial pilot. He trudged across the weed-covered ground over to the little skyhopper. He would have to use it to make the rescue. He had no better options.

The low, simmering music of insects and jungle creatures filled the air. He could hear no sound of blaster fire, no shouts of challenge or pain. It was quiet. Too quiet. Lowbacca hurried.

"Oh, excellent idea!" Em Teedee said as they approached the T-23. "We're going back to the Jedi academy to get reinforcements, aren't we. That's by far the wisest thing to do, I'm sure."

But Lowie knew it would be too late for the twins by then. He had to do something *now*. He told Em Teedee what he intended to do, and the miniature translating droid squawked in dismay.

"But, Master Lowbacca! The T-23 has no weapons. How can you fly it against that Imperial pilot? He is a professional fighter—and he's desperate!"

Lowie had the same fears as he powered up the T-23's repulsorlift engines. He made an optimistic comment to the translating droid.

"Tricks? What tricks do you have up your sleeve?" Em Teedee said. "Besides, you don't even *have* sleeves."

The craft sounded strong and powerful, thrumming and roaring in the jungle stillness. Lowie smelled the acrid exhaust, and snuffled. His black pilot seat vibrated as the ship prepared to take off.

He would need to do some fancy flying to get the craft through the trees to the crash site—but he had to save his friends, offer whatever help he could. Perhaps his noisy approach would startle the TIE pilot enough to make him flee for cover. And then the twins could jump aboard and make their escape.

Lowbacca nudged the throttles forward and lifted the T-23 off its resting place in the trampled undergrowth. The ion afterburners roared as the small ship arrowed through the forest, dodging branches and hanging moss, heading toward his friends—directly into the path of danger.

Back in the clearing, Jacen and Jaina froze for only a moment, then turned and ran, trying to escape—but the bulk of the almost-repaired TIE fighter got in their way. Jaina grabbed Jacen's arm, and the two of them ran together, frightened but knowing they needed to move, *move.*

The Imperial pilot fired his blaster, shooting twice into the thicket where Tenel Ka had vanished. Burning brush and splintered twigs flew into the air in a cloud. For an instant Jaina thought their young friend from Dathomir had been killed—but then she heard more leaves rustling and branches snapping as Tenel Ka continued her desperate flight.

The TIE pilot fired into the trees next, blasting the lower branches—but Lowbacca had gotten away. The twins ran around the end of the wrecked fighter, and suddenly Jacen stumbled over a rectangular box of hydrospanners, cyberfuses, and other tools they had gathered for the repair of the crashed ship—and fell headlong.

Jaina grabbed her brother's arm, trying to yank him to his feet to run again. The ground screeched with an explosion of blaster fire. Three high-energy bolts ricocheted from the age-stained hull of the crashed ship.

Jaina froze, raising her hands in surrender. They couldn't possibly hide fast enough. Jacen climbed to his feet and stood next to his sister, brushing himself off. The TIE pilot took two steps toward them, encased in battered armor and wearing an expression of icy anger.

"Don't move," he said, "or you will die, Rebel scum."

His black pilot armor was scuffed and worn from his long exile in the jungles. The Imperial's crippled left arm was stiff like a droid's, encased in an armored gauntlet of black leather. He had been severely hurt, but it appeared to be an old injury that had long ago healed, though improperly. The pilot was a hard-bitten old warrior. His eyes were haunted as he stared at Jaina.

"You are my prisoners." He motioned with the old-model blaster pistol that was gripped in his twisted, gloved hand.

"Put down the blaster," Jaina said quietly, soothingly, using everything she knew of Jedi persuasion techniques. "You don't need it." Her uncle Luke had told them how Obi-Wan Kenobi had used Jedi mind tricks to scramble the thoughts of weak-minded Imperials.

"Put down the blaster," she said again in a rich, gentle voice.

Jacen knew exactly what his sister was doing. "Put down the blaster," he repeated.

The two of them said it one more time in an echoing, overlapping voice. They tried to send peaceful thoughts, soothing thoughts into the TIE pilot's mind . . . just as Jacen had done to calm his crystal snake.

The TIE pilot shook his grizzled head and narrowed his haunted eyes. The blaster wavered just a little, dropping down only a notch.

Why isn't it working? Jaina thought desperately. "Put down the blaster," she said again, more insistently. But inside the Imperial fighter's mind she ran up against a wall of thoughts so rigid, so black-and-white, so clear-cut, that it seemed like droid programming.

Suddenly the pilot straightened and glared at them through those bleak, haunted eyes. "Surrender is betrayal," he said, like a memorized lesson.

Jacen, seeing their chance slipping away, reached out with his mind and yanked at the weapon with mental brute force.

"Get the blaster!" he whispered. Jaina helped him tug with the Force, reaching for the old weapon in the pilot's grip. But the armored glove was wrapped so tightly around it that the black gauntlet seemed fastened to the blaster handle. The handgrip of the obsolete weapon caught on the glove, and the TIE pilot grabbed it with his other hand, pointing the barrel directly at the twins.

"Stop with your Jedi tricks," he said coldly. "If you continue to resist I will execute you both."

Knowing that the pilot needed only to depress the firing stud—much more quickly than they could ever mind-wrestle the blaster away from him—Jacen and Jaina let their hands fall to their sides, relaxing and ceasing their struggles.

Just then a buzzing, roaring sound crashed through the canopy above—a wound-up engine noise, growing louder.

"It's Lowie!" Jacen cried.

The T-23 plunged through the branches overhead in a crackling explosion of shattered twigs, plowing toward the crash site at full speed, like a charging bantha.

"What's he trying to do?" Jacen asked, quietly. "He doesn't have any weapons on board!"

"He might distract the pilot," Jaina said. "Give us a chance to escape."

But the armored Imperial soldier stood his ground at the center of the clearing, spreading his legs for balance and assuming a practiced firing stance. He pointed his blaster at the oncoming air speeder, unflinching.

Jaina knew that if the blaster bolt breached the small repulsorlift reactor, the entire vehicle would explode—killing Lowbacca, and perhaps all of them.

Lowbacca brought the T-23 forward as if he meant to ram the TIE pilot. The desperate Imperial soldier aimed at the T-23's engine core and squeezed the firing stud.

"No!" Jaina cried, and *nudged* with her mind at the last instant. Using the Force, she shoved the TIE pilot's arm and knocked his aim off by just a fraction of a degree. The bright blaster bolt screeched out and danced along the metal hull of the repulsorlift pods. The engine casings melted at the side, spilling coolant and fuel. Gray-blue smoke boiled up. The sound of the T-23 became stuttered and sick as its engines faltered.

Lowie pulled up in the pilot's seat, swerving to keep from crashing into the Massassi trees. He could barely fly the badly damaged craft.

"Go, Lowie!" Jacen whispered. "Get out while you can."

"Eject! Before it blows!" Jaina cried.

But Lowbacca somehow managed to gain altitude, spinning around the huge trees and climbing toward the canopy again. His engines smoked, trailing a stream of foul-smelling exhaust that curled the jungle leaves and turned them brown.

"He won't get far," the Imperial pilot said in a raw monotone. "He is as good as dead."

Although the T-23 was out of sight now, far above them in the jungle treetops, Jaina could still hear the engine coughing, failing, and then picking up again as the battered craft limped away. The sounds carried well in the jungle silence. The repulsorlift engine faded in the distance, its ion afterburners popping and sputtering—until finally, there was silence again.

The TIE pilot, his expression still stony, gestured with the blaster pistol. "Come with me, prisoners. If you resist this time, you will die."

12

LOWBACCA WRESTLED WITH the T-23, trying to control its erratic flight as it lurched across the treetops.

Thick, knotted smoke trailed in a stuttering plume from his starboard repulsor engine. Lowie risked a quick glance to his right again to assess the damage. No flames, but the situation was grim enough. The late-afternoon air currents were turbulent and threatened to capsize the skyhopper.

The T-23 jolted and dipped. Once, it bounced against some upraised branches, which scraped like long fingernails against the ship's lower foils and bottom hull, but Lowbacca managed to wrench the T-23 back on course. He was a good pilot; he would make it back to the academy and bring help, no matter what it took. He didn't know what had happened to Tenel Ka—if she was all right, or if the TIE pilot had captured her by now as well. For all he knew, Lowbacca was the only hope for rescue for his three friends.

His heart pounded painfully and his eyes stung from the chemical smoke that leaked into the cockpit. He noticed a sour, noxious smell, and his head began to swim.

"Master Lowbacca," Em Teedee said, "my sensors indicate that significant quantities of fumes have entered the cockpit."

Lowbacca gave a growl of annoyance. Did the little droid think that his sharp sense of smell hadn't picked that up?

"Well, no," Em Teedee rushed on, "it may not be dangerous *yet,* but if we begin to lose airspeed, less smoke will be drawn away. The airborne toxins could reach potentially lethal levels"—the droid raised his volume slightly for emphasis—*"even for a Wookiee."*

The speeder gave a shuddering jolt, scraping against branches again. With grim determination Lowbacca pulled up. The T-23 was even harder to manage now. He wasn't sure how long he could last.

But he *had* to make it. He couldn't leave his friends in danger.

The T-23 shuddered and dipped. Lowbacca wheezed, laboring to pull air into his lungs. As if in response to his effort, the starboard engine coughed and sputtered.

And died.

Using all of his piloting skills, Lowie fought to steady the craft in its wobbling descent. The thick, deceptively soft-looking canopy rushed up at him, and the T-23 came to a crunching halt in a blizzard of leaves and twigs. Like a wounded avian, it lay nestled on the treetops, its right lower wing buried in the foliage. The left engine still chugged, but smoke billowed up from the damaged engine below, pouring into the cockpit now.

Lowbacca's head reeled with the impact, but he knew he had to get out. He fumbled with his crash restraints, trying to unfasten them. His vision was blurred from the acrid smoke, and he gagged at the stench. Confusion made his fingers clumsy.

Finally, with a burst of determination, he yanked on the straps until, loosened by the crash, they tore away. Two of the restraints came free in his hands, and he wriggled out of the remaining webbing.

Still no flames, Lowbacca noted with relief as he scrambled from the cockpit and distanced himself from the smoking T-23. Lowbacca gasped in deep lungfuls of the fresh, humid air of Yavin 4. As he worked his way across the treetops in the gathering dusk, one knee ached from where it had banged against the controls during the crash.

But he had no time to think about that. His first rescue attempt might have failed, but *he* had not failed yet. There were always options. He had to get back to the academy.

In his hurried scramble through the upper branches, Lowbacca did not notice when Em Teedee's clip broke at his waist.

The tiny droid fell with a thin wail into the forest below.

Dusk deepened into the full darkness of the jungle night. Swarms of nocturnal creatures awakened, beginning to hunt—but still Lowbacca pressed on.

Common sense had forced him to travel below the canopy, descending to a level where all of the branches were of a sufficient length and sturdiness to support him as he transferred his agile bulk from one tree to the next. Sometimes when he began to tire, or when his injured knee threatened to give way beneath him, Lowbacca relied on his powerful arms instead, swinging from branch to branch, using his keen Wookiee night vision in the murky shadows.

But he never stopped to rest. He could rest later.

Right now all of his senses were as finely tuned as a medical droid's laser beam. The pads of his feet and his acute sense of smell helped him to avoid decaying patches or slippery growths on the tree branches as he walked. His sharp hearing could distinguish between the sounds of wind through the leaves and the rustling of nocturnal animals as they stalked the jungle heights. For the most part, he managed to stay clear of them.

Lowbacca did not fear the darkness or the jungle. The jungles of Kashyyyk held far greater dangers—and he had faced those and survived. He remembered playing late-night games in the forest with his cousins and friends: races through the upper trees, jumping and swinging competitions, daring expeditions to the dangerous lower regions to test each other's courage, and the usual rites of passage that marked a Wookiee youth's transition into adulthood.

As he pushed through a dense clump of growth, a twig snagged Lowie's webbed belt, and he yanked it free. The feel of the intricately braided strands beneath his fingers reminded him of the night when he had won his belt, of his dangerous rite of passage.

He remembered. . . .

He felt his heart race with excitement as he descended toward the jungle floor that night long ago. Lowie had been down that far only twice before, when he had attended the rites of other friends, as was customary; there was strength in numbers when they sought to harvest the long, silky strands from the center of the deadly syren plant.

But Lowbacca had chosen to go alone, preferring to meet the challenge of the voracious syren plant using his own wits rather than borrowed muscles.

The night on Kashyyyk had been cool and dank. The profusion of screeches, chirps, growls, and croaks had been overwhelming. When he'd reached the lowest branches, Lowie had cinched the strap of his knapsack tighter and began his hunt.

With every sense fully alert, Lowbacca had moved stealthily from branch to branch until he caught the alluring scent of a wild syren plant. With sure instinct he'd followed the distinctive odor, feeling a mixture of anticipation and dread, until he squatted on the branch directly above the plant. He leaned over to study his stationary, but incredibly vicious, quarry.

The huge syren blossom consisted of two glossy oval petals of bright yellow, seamed in the center and supported by a mottled, bloody red stalk, twice as thick around as the sturdy tree limb on which Lowbacca sat. From the center of the open blossom spread a tuft of long white glossy fibers that emitted a broad spectrum of pheromones, scents to attract any unwary creature.

The beauty of the gigantic flower was intentionally deceptive, for any creature lured close enough to touch the sensitive inner flesh of the blossom would trigger the plant's lethal reflexes, and the petal jaws would close over the victim and begin its digestive cycle.

Alone, Lowbacca intended to harvest the glittering strands of the plant from the center of the flower—without springing the trap.

Traditionally, a few strong friends would hold the flower open while the young Wookiee scrambled to the treacherous center of the blossom, harvested the lustrous strands of sweetly scented fiber, and quickly made an escape. But even this assistance was no guarantee. Occasionally young Wookiees still lost limbs as the carnivorous plant clamped down on a slow-moving arm or leg.

Performing the task by himself, though, Lowie had needed to be extra careful. He had removed the knapsack from his hairy back and extracted its contents: a face mask, a sturdy rope, a thin cord, and a collapsible vibroblade. He'd placed the mask over his nose and mouth to filter out the syren's seductive scents. He knew that the pheromones could produce an almost overpowering desire to linger or to touch—and he could afford no mistakes.

Working quickly, enveloped by sinister night sounds, he had fashioned a short length of thin cord into a loose slipknot, then formed a loop to make a sort of seat for himself in the sturdy, longer rope. Passing the free end of the long rope over a branch directly above the syren plant, he'd gathered up the slack in one hand, slid off the limb, and lowered himself with muscular arms.

Lowie had positioned himself as close as he dared to the gently undulating petals of the hungry syren blossom, an arm's length from the tantalizing tuft. He'd gripped the end of the long rope in his strong jaws to hold himself in place and free his hands. Then, using the loop of thin cord to lasso the tuft of precious fibers, he'd pulled himself close enough to slice them loose with his vibroblade. With a triumphant growl he'd jerked his prize toward himself, trapped the bundle against his body with one hairy arm, and stuffed the fiber into his knapsack.

In his excitement, however, the rope had slipped from his teeth. The trailing end uncoiled, dangled precariously, and then brushed one glossy petal of the deadly flower below. With a surge of gut-wrenching terror, Lowbacca had grabbed the tied end of rope and hauled himself upward as the syren's jaws snapped shut. The petals just grazed one foot as they closed with an ominous slurp and a backwash of wind.

He had earned this fiber, Lowie thought, every strand of it, enough to make a special belt, which he always wore afterward.

* * *

Exhaustion sank its claws into every muscle as Lowbacca made his way from one Massassi tree to the next, hour after hour, all through the night.

Distance held no more meaning for him; he had to get to the Jedi academy. He could hear nothing but his own ragged breathing. His injured leg wobbled unsteadily at each step. Fatigue blurred his vision, and twigs and leaves matted his fur. He pushed forward, always forward, arm-leg, arm-leg, hand-foot, hand-foot—

Lowie looked around, confused and disoriented. He had reached for the next branch, but there were no more branches. Raising his head, he looked across the clearing—the landing clearing!—and saw the Great Temple, its majestic tiers outlined in the predawn darkness by flickering torches.

Lowbacca never remembered afterward climbing down out of the tree or crossing the clearing. He noticed only the awesome, welcoming sight of the ancient stone pyramid as he bellowed an alarm. He roared again and again, until a stream of robed figures carrying fresh torches rushed out of the temple and down the steps toward him.

The night and the desperate journey had taken their toll on Lowie. The numbness imposed by his own determination had worn off, and his knee refused to hold him any longer. His gangly legs gave way, and he collapsed to the ground, moaning his message.

When he rolled onto his back, a circle of concerned faces filled his vision. Tionne bent over him and brushed the tangle of matted fur away from his eyes.

"Lowbacca, we were concerned for you!" Tionne said gravely. "Are you hurt?"

Lowie groaned an answer, but Tionne didn't seem to understand. She leaned closer to him, her silvery hair glowing in the torchlight.

"Were Jacen and Jaina with you? And Tenel Ka?" She paused as he tried to moan another answer. "Did something happen?" she persisted. "Can you tell me where they are?"

Lowbacca finally managed to say that the others were in the jungle and needed help. Tionne's brows knitted together in an expression of worry. She blinked her mother-of-pearl eyes. "I'm sorry, Lowbacca. I can't understand a word you're saying."

Lowie reached toward his belt to activate Em Teedee—but he found nothing. The translator droid was gone.

13

TENEL KA RAN through the cool near-darkness of the jungle floor, trying to come up with a plan. She held her bent arms in front of her to protect her eyes and to push obstacles from her path. Branches whipped her face, tore at her hair, and clawed mercilessly at her bare arms and legs.

Her breath came in sharp gasps, not so much from the effort of running—to which she was well accustomed—but from the terror of what she had just experienced. She hoped she had made the right decision. Her pulse pounded in her ears, competing with the symphony of alien noises as the jungle creatures welcomed nightfall. Though she searched her mind, no Jedi calming techniques would come to her.

When the loud squawk of flying creatures sounded directly behind her, Tenel Ka glanced back in alarm. Before she could turn again, she fetched up sharply against the trunk of a Massassi tree. Stunned, she fell back a few paces and sank to the ground, putting one hand to the side of her face to examine her injury.

No blood, she thought as if from a great distance. *Good.* Beneath her fingertips, she felt tenderness and swelling from her cheek to her temple. There would be bruises, of course, and perhaps a royal headache. She cringed at the thought. *Royal.* Although no one could see it, her cheeks heated with a flush of humiliation.

Tenel Ka pulled herself to her feet and took stock of her situation. In her newfound calmness she admitted to herself that she was completely lost. Jacen and Jaina—and by now perhaps even Lowbacca—were counting on her to return with help. She had always prided herself on being strong, loyal, reliable, unswayed by emotion. She had been levelheaded enough during her initial escape, but then she had panicked. She shook off thoughts of her stupid headlong flight.

Well, she thought, pressing her pale lips together into a firm line, *I am back in control now.* She decided to push on until she found a safer place to spend the night. When morning came, she would try to get her bearings again and return to the Jedi academy.

As she trudged along, searching in the fading light of day, the ground began to rise and become more rocky. The trees grew sparser. When she saw a jagged shadow loom out of the darkness ahead of her, she slowed. Ahead was a large outcropping of rough, black stone, long-cooled lava mottled with lichens.

Tenel Ka tilted her head back and looked up, but she could not see how high the rock went; the jungle dimness swallowed it up. Cautiously exploring sideways, she encountered a break in the rock face, a patch of deeper darkness—a small cave. Perhaps she could spend the night here, in this defensible, sheltered place. The opening was no wider than the length of one arm and extended only to shoulder height, forcing her to stoop to explore further. She needed only to find a comfortable, safe place to rest.

She shivered as she hunched down on the sandy, cool floor of the cave. Her every muscle ached, but for now nothing could be done about her pain; she could bear it as well as any warrior. But she had not eaten since midday. She felt in the pouch at her waist, finding one carbo-protein biscuit remaining. As for the cold, she could light a fire with the finger-sized flash heater she carried in another pouch on her belt.

Dropping to her hands and knees, she scrabbled along the ground near the mouth of the cave, searching for twigs, leaves, anything that would burn. Back on Dathomir she'd had plenty of practice in rugged camping and outdoor endurance.

As she thought of the cozy warmth of a fire and a soft bed of leaves, Tenel Ka's spirits rose. The nightmarish events of the afternoon began to settle into perspective. This was an adventure, she assured herself. A test of her will and determination.

When she had collected kindling and some thicker branches, Tenel Ka began to build her fire against the velvety shadows of gathering night. She fumbled in her belt pouches for her flash heater and groaned as she remembered that Jaina had borrowed it that afternoon. She rubbed her cold, bare arms and blew on her hands to warm them.

Tenel Ka thought longingly of the cheery warmth of a crackling fire, of drinking hot, spiced Hapan ale with her parents. A rare smile crossed her lips as she thought of them, Teneniel Djo and Prince Isolder. If she were at home, she would only have to lift a hand to bring a servant of the Royal House of Hapes running to do her bidding. . . .

Tenel Ka grimaced. She had never known poverty or hardship, except by choice. *Well, you chose this, Princess,* she reminded herself savagely. *You wanted to learn to do things for yourself.*

Her father, Isolder of Hapes, had always said that the two years he spent in disguise working as a privateer had done more to prepare him for leadership than any training the royal tutors of Hapes could provide. And her mother, raised on the primitive planet of Dathomir, was proud that her only daughter spent months each year learning the ways of the Singing Mountain Clan and dressing as a warrior woman—a practice that Tenel Ka had enjoyed all the more because it annoyed her scheming Hapan grandmother.

Teneniel Djo had been even more pleased when her daughter had decided to attend the academy and take instruction to become a Jedi. She had enrolled simply as Tenel Ka of Dathomir, not wanting the other trainees to treat her differently because of her royal upbringing.

At the academy, only Master Skywalker—who was an old friend of her mother's, and the man Teneniel Djo most admired—knew Tenel Ka's true background. She had not even told Jacen and Jaina, her closest friends on Yavin 4.

Jacen and Jaina. The twins trusted her. They needed her help now. She shivered in the cave. She had to stay safe for the night and then get back to the academy in the morning to bring reinforcements.

Tenel Ka heard a faint rustling, slapping, and hissing in the darkness behind her. She looked back into the undulating shadows, blinking to clear her eyes. Had the shadows really moved? Perhaps she had been foolish to spend the night in an unexplored cave, but cold and fatigue had overruled her natural caution. She looked up and thought she could discern glossy dark shapes clinging to the ceiling, moving like waves on an inverted black sea.

Don't be a child, she chided herself. She had always tried to show her friends how self-sufficient and reliable she was. Right now, she was cold and bruised and miserable. What would Jacen say if he could see her? He'd probably tell some dumb joke.

Tenel Ka gritted her teeth. She would just have to build a fire without the flash heater, using skills she had been taught on Dathomir.

It took an agonizingly long time for her strong arms to produce enough friction twirling one smooth stick of wood against a flat branch. Finally, she managed to coax forth a glowing ember and a tendril of smoke. Working quickly, she touched a dried leaf to it and blew. A tiny golden flame licked its way up the leaf. With mounting excitement she added another and then another, and then a few twigs.

A gust of wind threatened to extinguish the struggling flame, so she encircled her fire with a tiny earthen berm to protect it. She added more tinder, and soon the snapping blaze was large enough to warm her and cast a comforting circle of light.

Tenel Ka soon realized that the restless sounds of scratching and stirring she had heard earlier had grown louder—much louder.

Suddenly, a shrieking reptilian form plummeted from the ceiling, its leathery wings outstretched. Twin serpentine heads snapped and a scorpion tail lashed, razor-sharp claws outstretched. Tenel Ka raised an arm to protect her face as the thing drove directly at her. Talons raked her arm as she pushed herself backward toward the cave wall. Sharp fangs opened a gash in her bare leg, and she kicked fiercely, striking one of the creature's two heads with her scaled boot. In the flickering light from the tiny fire, Tenel Ka watched in horror as an entire flock of the hideous creatures—each with a wingspan wider than she was tall—dropped from the shadowy recesses of the cave and swarmed toward her.

She struggled for purchase on the sandy cave floor and pushed her feet against the stone wall. Tenel Ka propelled herself toward the mouth of the cave on her hands and knees.

She kicked the embers of her fire at the flapping beasts as she scrambled past, hardly noticing the bits of charred wood and leaf that singed her own legs. One of the reptilian creatures shrieked in pain.

Tenel Ka smiled with grim satisfaction and launched herself through the cave opening, back out into the pitch blackness of the jungle night.

The monsters followed.

14

AT GUNPOINT, THE TIE pilot led his captives back to the clearing with the small, crude shelter where he had lived for some time.

"So this is why you came running," Jaina said to her brother. "You found where he lives." Jacen nodded.

"Silence!" the Imperial soldier said in a brusque voice.

Jaina, her throat tight and dry, swallowed hard and looked around at the small, cleared site in the gathering evening shadows. Beside them a shallow stream trickled past. She couldn't imagine how the TIE pilot had survived all alone, without any human contact, for so many years.

The climate of Yavin 4 was warm and hospitable, placing few demands on the home the TIE pilot had created for himself. He had carved out a large shelter from the bole of a half-burned Massassi tree, in front of which he had lashed a lean-to of split branches. Altogether, it provided him with a simple but comfortable room, like a living cave. Jaina tried to imagine how long it had taken the Imperial, scraping with a sharp implement—possibly a piece of wreckage from his crashed ship—to widen the area under the gnarled overhang.

The TIE pilot had rigged a system of plumbing made from hollow reeds joined together, drawing water from the nearby stream into catch basins inside his hut. He had made rough utensils from wood, forest gourds, and petrified fungus slabs. The man had maintained a lonely existence, unchallenged, simply surviving and waiting for further orders, hoping someone would come to retrieve him—but no one ever had.

The Imperial soldier stopped outside the hut. "On the ground," he said. "Both of you. Hands above your heads."

Jaina looked at Jacen as they lay belly-down on the ground of the clearing. She could think of no way to escape. The TIE pilot went to the thick foliage and rummaged among the branches with his good hand. He wrapped his fingers around some thin, purplish vines that dangled from dazzlingly bright Nebula orchids in the branches above his head. With a jerk he snapped the strands free.

The vine tendrils flopped and writhed in his grip as if they were alive and trying to squirm away. The TIE pilot rapidly used them to lash Jaina's wrists together, then Jacen's. As the deep violet sap leaked from the broken ends of the vines, the plant's thrashing slowed, and the flexible, rubbery vines contracted, tightening into knots that were impossible to break.

Jacen and Jaina looked at each other, their liquid-brown eyes meeting as a host of thoughts gleamed unspoken between them. But they said nothing, afraid to anger their captor.

Marching clumsily through the humid jungle had made them hot and sticky, and Jaina was still covered with grime from her repairs on the TIE fighter's engines. Now the cool jungle evening chilled her perspiration and made her shiver. Her hands tingled and throbbed, as the tight vines cutting into her wrists made her even more miserable.

In the hour or so since their capture, neither of the twins had heard any further sign of Lowie or Tenel Ka. Jaina was afraid that something had happened to them, that her two friends were even now stranded and lost somewhere in the jungle. But then she realized that her own situation was probably a lot more dangerous than theirs.

Without a word, the TIE pilot nudged them to their feet, then over to the large lava-rock boulders near the fire pit he used outside his shelter. They squatted there together. The stone chairs had been polished smooth, their sharp edges chipped away slowly and patiently over the course of years by the lost Imperial.

The last coppery rays of light from the huge orange planet Yavin disappeared, as the rapidly rotating moon covered the jungle with night. Through the densely laced treetops, thick shadows gathered, making the forest floor darker than the deepest night on Jacen and Jaina's glittering home planet of Coruscant.

The Imperial pilot walked over to the splintered chunks of dry, moss-covered wood he had painstakingly gathered, one-armed, and stacked near his shelter. He carried them back and dropped one branch at a time into the fire pit, stacking the wood in formation to make a small campfire.

The pilot withdrew a battered igniter from a storage bin inside his shelter and pointed it at the campfire. Its charge had been nearly depleted, and the silvery nozzle showered only a few hot sparks onto the kindling; but he seemed accustomed to such difficulties. He toiled in silence, never cursing, never complaining, simply focused on the task of getting the campfire lit. And when he succeeded, he showed no satisfaction, no joy.

With the fire finally blazing, the TIE pilot ducked back inside his hut, rummaged in a vine-woven basket, and returned with a large spherical fruit. The fruit was encased in an ugly, warty brown rind. Jaina did not recognize it. It was nothing they ate at the Jedi academy.

Holding it in his injured, gauntleted hand, the pilot used a sharpened stone to split open the rind, then peeled the fruit with his fingers. The flesh inside was pale yellowish-green, speckled with scarlet. He broke the fruit into sections, shuffled over to the two captives, and pushed one of the fruit sections in Jaina's face. "Eat."

She clamped her lips together for a moment, afraid that the Imperial soldier might be trying to poison her. Then she realized that the TIE pilot could have killed either of them at any time—and that she was extremely hungry and thirsty.

Her hands still bound by the drying vine, she leaned forward and opened her mouth to bite into the bright fruit. The explosion of tart citrus-tasting juice proved surprisingly invigorating and delicious. She chewed slowly, savoring the taste, and swallowed.

Jacen also ate his. They nodded their thanks to the TIE pilot, who fixed them with a stony gaze.

Sensing an opening, Jacen asked, "What are you going to do with us, sir?" He tried to rub his chin against his shoulder to wipe off the juice dribbling from his lips.

The TIE pilot stared unnervingly at him for several moments before he turned his face toward the bushes. "Not yet determined."

Jaina's chest muscles constricted. All of this had been an accident, a mistake. From the thick bushes, the TIE pilot had probably watched them tinker with his ruined ship for days. But Jacen's accidental discovery of his primitive shelter had forced him to react.

What could the Imperial soldier do with them? He didn't seem to have many options.

"What's your name?" Jaina asked.

The TIE pilot snapped upright and looked down at the black leather glove covering his twisted arm. He turned slowly toward her, like a droid with worn-out servomotors. "CE3K-1977." He rattled off the numbers as if he had memorized them. Service rank and operating number only.

"Not your number," Jaina persisted. "Your name. I'm Jaina. This is my brother Jacen."

"CE3K-1977," the TIE pilot said again, without emotion.

"Your *name?*" Jaina asked a third time.

Finally her question seemed to perplex him. He looked at the ground, looked at his tattered uniform. His mouth opened and closed several times, but no sound came out, until finally he said in a croaking voice, "Qorl . . . Qorl. My name was Qorl."

"We're staying at the academy in the old temples," Jacen said, wearing a small grin—the kind that always disarmed their mother when she was angry at him. But it didn't seem to be working with the TIE pilot.

"Rebel base," Qorl said.

"No, it's a school now," Jaina said. "Everyone's there to learn. It's not a base any longer. It hasn't been a base for . . . twenty years or so."

"It is a Rebel base," Qorl insisted with such finality that Jaina decided not to pursue the subject any further.

"How did you get here?" she asked, leaning closer on the smooth rock. The campfire crackled between them. "How long have you lived in the jungle?" The tight vines constricting her circulation made her hands numb. She flexed her fingers as she bent toward the fire. The smoke smelled rich and sweet from the fresh jungle wood.

The TIE pilot blinked his pale eyes and stared into the crackling flames. He looked as if he had been transported back in time and was watching a newsloop of his own buried memories.

"Death Star," Qorl said. "I was on the Death Star. We came here to destroy the Rebel base after Grand Moff Tarkin blew up Alderaan. This was our next target."

Jaina felt a pang as she remembered her mother talking of the lovely grass-covered planet Alderaan, the peaceful windsongs and tall towers rising above the plains. Princess Leia's home had been the heart of galactic culture and civilization—until it was wiped out in a single blow by the incredible cruelty of the Empire.

"We must obliterate the Rebels at all costs," Qorl continued. "Rebels cause damage to the Empire."

He recited a litany of what seemed to be memorized phrases, thoughts that had been brainwashed into him. "The Emperor's New Order will save the galaxy. The Rebels want to destroy that dream, and so we must eradicate the Rebels. They are a cancer to peace and stability."

"You were on the Death Star," Jacen prompted. "That was over twenty years ago. What happened?"

Qorl continued to stare deeply into the fire. His scratchy voice was barely more than a whisper. "The Rebels knew we were coming. They fought. They sent their defenses against the battle station. All TIE squadrons were launched.

"I flew with my squadron. All my companions were destroyed by X-wing defensive fire. I was damaged in the cross fire . . . one solar panel out of commission. I spun away from the Death Star, out of control.

"I needed to get back to effect repairs. All comm channels were jammed, filled with dozens of requests for assistance. My orbit was decaying, and I spun toward the fourth moon of Yavin. I kept trying to hail someone on the comm channels. When I finally got through, I was told I would have to wait for rescue. They instructed me to make a good landing if I could—and to wait."

"So you crashed," Jaina said.

"The jungle cushioned my fall. I was thrown out of my craft into the dense brush . . . when one of the solar panels caught and lodged in the trees above. I limped over to my TIE fighter. Stayed as close as I dared, afraid that it might explode. My arm—" He held up his left arm in the black leather gauntlet. "Badly injured, ligaments torn, bones broken.

"I looked up into the sky just in time to see the Death Star blow up. It was like another sun in the sky. Flaming chunks of debris fell through the air. It must have started dozens of forest fires. For weeks, meteor showers were like fireworks as the wreckage rained down onto the moon.

"And I stayed here."

The firelight bathed Qorl's face with a dancing, yellowish glow. The jungle sounds burred in a hypnotic hum all around them. The TIE pilot gave no sign that he realized his two captives were listening. Only his lips moved as he continued his tale.

"I have waited here, and waited, as ordered. No one has come to rescue me."

"But," Jaina said, "all those years! This place has been abandoned for quite some time, but people have been at the Jedi academy for eleven years now. Why haven't you turned yourself in? Don't you realize what's happened in the galaxy since you crashed?"

"Surrender is betrayal!" Qorl snapped, glaring at her as anger flickered across his weathered face.

"But we're not lying," Jacen said. "The war is over. There *is* no more Empire." He took a deep breath and then plunged ahead. "Darth Vader is dead. The Emperor is dead. The New Republic now rules. Only a few remnants of old Imperial holdouts are still buried in the Core Systems at the center of the galaxy."

"I don't believe you," Qorl said flatly.

"If you take us back to the Jedi academy we can prove it. We can show you everything," Jaina said. "Wouldn't you like to go home? Wouldn't you like to be free of this place? We could get your arm treated."

Qorl held up his glove and stared at it. "I used my medi-kit," he said. "I tended it as best I could. It is good enough, although there was much pain . . . for a long time."

"But we've got Jedi healers!" Jaina said. "We've got medical droids. You could be happy again. Why stay here? There's nothing to betray: there is no more Empire."

"Be quiet," Qorl said. "The Empire will always rule. The Emperor is invincible."

"The Emperor is dead," Jacen said.

"The Empire itself can never die," Qorl insisted.

"But if you won't let us take you back to get help, then what do you *want?*" Jaina asked.

Jacen nodded, chiming in. "What are you trying to accomplish?"

"What can we do for you, Qorl?"

The TIE pilot turned away from the campfire to stare at them. His haggard, weather-beaten face held new power and obsession, springing from deep within his mind.

"You will finish repairs to my ship," he said. "And then I shall fly away from this prison moon. I'll return to the Empire as a glorious hero of war. Surrender is betrayal—and I *never* surrendered."

"And what if we won't help you?" Jacen said with all the bravado he could manage. Jaina instantly wanted to kick him for provoking the TIE pilot.

Qorl looked at the young boy, his face coldly expressionless again. "Then you are expendable," he said.

15

IT TOOK EM TEEDEE several moments to recalibrate his sensors after he dropped from Lowbacca's fiber-belt. He had fallen, bouncing, crashing, and bonking through the canopy until he finally came to rest on a dense mat of leafy vines that tied together the lower branches.

"Master Lowbacca, come back!" he said, amplifying his voice circuits to their maximum volume levels. "Don't leave me! Oh, dear. I *knew* that was a bad idea."

He adjusted his optical sensors so he could see better in the dim light of the lower levels. He was surrounded by thickets that were nearly inaccessible to anyone as large as even a young Wookiee.

"Help! Help me!" Em Teedee shouted again. He decided it would be most effective to continue shouting every forty-five seconds, because he calculated that was the minimum amount of time necessary for anyone nearby to come within earshot.

Unable to move and scout out his location, Em Teedee's best guess was that he was still twenty meters above the ground. He hoped that no slight jarring of the branches would cause him to break free and tumble down again. If he fell that far to the ground, he might strike one of the rough lava outcroppings and split open his outer casing. With his circuits spilled across the jungle floor, no one would ever be able to put him back together again in the proper fashion. His circuits buzzed at the thought.

Forty-five seconds had passed. He called out again for help, then waited. He shouted repeatedly for the next hour and eleven minutes, hoping desperately to attract some sort of attention, someone to come rescue him.

But when he finally did attract a curious investigator, Em Teedee wished he had kept his vocal circuits switched off.

A large pack of chattering woolamanders scurried through the lower canopy, stirring up leaves and cracking twigs in their hectic passage. The arboreal creatures were loud and agile, able to clamber from thin branches to thick ones and back again without losing their balance. They seemed to be engaged in a contest to see who could yowl and chatter the loudest in the jungle silence as twilight deepened.

Somehow, over all the ruckus, they managed to hear Em Teedee's cries for help.

Em Teedee knew from his limited database of Yavin 4 that woolamanders were curious, social creatures. Now that they had heard him, they began to search. In only moments, with their sharp, slit-eyed vision, they had spotted the translator droid's shiny outer casing in the jungle shadows. The pack of colorful, hairy creatures swarmed toward him.

"Oh, no," Em Teedee cried. "Not you. Please—I was hoping for someone *else* to rescue me."

The woolamanders came closer, rattling branches, rustling leaves. Their bright purple fur bristled with suspicion and delight.

"Go away! Shoo!" Em Teedee said.

The woolamanders let out a loud, shrieking celebration of their discovery. A large male snatched Em Teedee from his resting place in the vines.

"Put me down," Em Teedee said. "I *insist* that you let go of me at once."

The large male tossed Em Teedee to his mate, who caught the translator droid and turned him over and around, poking at the shiny circles. She dug her grimy finger into the gold circle of his optical sensors.

"That's my eye—get your finger away from it! Now I'm upside down. Straighten me out . . . put me down!"

The female shook and rattled him to see if he would make other noises. When she went to a thick branch and made ready to smash him down on it, as she would crack open a large fruit, Em Teedee set off his automatic alarm sirens, shrieking and whooping at such volume and at such a painful pitch that the female dropped him. He bounced on another leafy branch, then came precariously to rest.

"Help!" Em Teedee wailed.

One of the smaller woolamanders rushed in to snatch him from his resting place. With loud chattering and squeals of delight, the young woolamander dashed along the lower branches, holding his prize high as Em Teedee continued to howl for assistance. The other young woolamanders chased after the youngster, clamoring for the prize.

Em Teedee, in such a panic that he could no longer stand it without overloading his circuits, shut down so he wouldn't have to see what was about to happen to him.

Sometime late in the night he powered back on again to find that he could see nothing: his optical sensors were covered with thick fur.

He detected a gentle motion . . . breathing, snoring. Then the young woolamander stirred in its sleep. It shifted, allowing Em Teedee to discover that the small creature now lay sleeping in the crotch of a tree branch, contentedly hugging his new toy to his fur-covered chest.

Around them, the other family members of the large arboreal group sighed and dozed, resting peacefully. Em Teedee had an impulse to cry out again for help, still hoping that someone might come to rescue him.

All the noisy woolamanders were finally asleep, though, and Em Teedee decided to treasure this moment of peace. He could only hope for something better to happen the next day.

16

DAWN CAME FAST and hot, as the distant white sun climbed around the fuzzy ball of Yavin. Jungle creatures awoke and stirred. The air warmed rapidly, thick with humidity that rose from low hollows where mist had collected in the night.

Jacen and Jaina had slept awkwardly, their hands still tied with the resilient purple vines. Jacen fervently wished he had spent more time practicing delicate and precise Force exercises. He didn't have the skill or the accuracy to nudge and untie the thin knotted vines with his mind.

As soon as there was light enough to work, Qorl emerged from his tree shelter and shook the twins awake. He gave them each sips of cool water from a gourd he dipped in the stream, then used a long stone knife to saw off the vines binding their wrists.

Jacen flexed his fingers and shook out his hands. His nerves tingled and stung with returning circulation.

The Imperial soldier pointed the blaster at them, gesturing for the twins to move. "Back to the TIE fighter," he ordered. "Work."

Jacen and Jaina trudged through the jungle, stumbling through vines and shrubs; the TIE pilot followed directly behind them. They reached the site of the crashed ship, where it lay uncovered and glinting in the early morning light. With a knot forming in his stomach, Jacen saw burned patches from where Qorl had shot his blaster at Tenel Ka and Lowie.

"I know you are nearly finished with repairs," the TIE pilot said. "I have been watching you for days. You will complete them today."

Jaina blinked her brandy-brown eyes and scowled at him. "We can't possibly work that fast, especially with just the two of us. This ship has been crashed for twenty years. We haven't finished cleaning the debris from the sublight intakes. The power converters all need to be rewired."

Jacen watched his sister and knew she was lying.

"Cyberfuses still need to be installed," she continued. "The air-exchange system is clogged; it needs to be—"

Qorl raised the blaster, but did not alter the emotion in his voice. *"Today,"* he repeated. "You will finish today."

"Oh, blaster bolts! I think he means it, Jaina," Jacen muttered. "Show me what I can do to help."

Jaina sighed. "All right. Collect the box of tools you tripped over yesterday. Get the hydrospanner. I'll use my multitool to finish some calibrations here in the engines."

Qorl sat down on a lumpy, lichen-encrusted boulder, using his good hand to brush crawling insects from his legs. The Imperial soldier waited like a droid sentinel, unmoving, watching them work. Jacen tried to ignore him—and the blaster.

Gnats and biting insects swarmed around Jacen's face, attracted by the sweat in his tangled hair. He passed tools to his sister, trying to find the components and equipment Jaina needed as she crawled and rummaged in the TIE fighter's engine compartment.

He could sense Jaina's growing anger and frustration. She couldn't think of a plan. Yes, Jacen supposed, they could simply sabotage the ship repairs—but Qorl would realize what they'd done almost immediately, and he would get even with them. They couldn't risk that.

Now Jacen wished that his sister, in all her excitement, hadn't installed the new hyperdrive unit their dad had given her. He wished that they all hadn't worked so hard, made so much progress. Now it was almost too late.

Jacen brushed a hand across his forehead, blinking sweat away. His stomach growled. He turned to the TIE pilot, sitting nearby on the rock, still pointing the blaster barrel directly at him. The threat was getting tiresome.

"Qorl," he said, intentionally using their captor's real name. "Could we have some water and more fruit? We're hungry. We'll work better if we're not hungry."

Qorl nodded slightly and began to stand up. But then he froze, hesitated, and settled back into his rigid position. "Food and water when you are finished with repairs."

"What?" Jacen said in dismay. "But that could take all day."

"Then you will be hungry and thirsty," Qorl said. The TIE pilot looked somewhat anxious, impatient. "You are stalling. Proceed."

Jacen realized that Qorl might be worried that either Tenel Ka or Lowie had managed to get back to the Jedi academy and summoned help. They were a long distance from the Great Temple, across a treacherous jungle . . . but there was always a chance.

Jaina finished adjusting a cooling system regulator. She twisted a knob; a cold, bright blast of supercooled steam screeched up, making feathers of frost on the exposed metal surface. She stepped back and rubbed a grimy hand across her cheek, leaving a dark stain beneath her liquid-brown eyes.

"Qorl?" she said. "Who are you going to see when you get back?"

"I will report for duty," he said.

"Are you going home? Do you have a family?"

"The Empire is my family." His answer was rapid, automatic.

"But do you have a family that *loves you?*" Jaina asked.

Qorl hesitated for the briefest moment, then gestured threateningly with the blaster. "Get back to work."

Jaina sighed and motioned for her brother to help her. "Come on, Jacen. Take those last packages of surface metal sealant," she said. "We need to reinforce the melt spots on the outer hull." She pointed to three stained and vaporized bull's-eye spots on the TIE fighter's outer plating—damage Qorl himself had caused the day before by firing his blaster at the twins.

With a cushioned hammer, Jaina pounded the bent plates back into position. Jacen dug into the toolbox until he found a packet of animated metal sealant. The special paste would crawl across the damaged area, smooth itself, and then seal down with a bond even stronger than the original hull alloy. Jacen applied one packet of the patch material and listened to it hiss and steam as it coated the burn spot. Jaina fixed the second spot.

The third melted area lay high on the cargo compartment, close to the open transparisteel canopy that protected the cockpit. Jacen took the last pack and crawled atop the small craft. He popped the seal, applied the patch, and waited for the animated sealant to do its work.

As he watched the gooey substance finish its repairs, Jacen heard small creatures stirring around him. He sensed something nearby and, looking down into the cargo space, saw a glimmer of movement, almost transparent, barely noticeable. Jacen's heart leaped. He leaned down, reaching deep into the TIE fighter, and grabbed for it. Hope began to fill him.

"Boy, get out of there!" Qorl yelled. "Come back where I can see you."

Panting, his heart pounding, Jacen pulled himself free. He backed away from the cockpit and jumped to the ground, keeping his hands clearly in sight.

Jaina bent over and whispered to him with concern in her eyes. "What are you doing? What did you find in there?"

Jacen grinned at her, then recovered his expression before Qorl could notice it. "Something that might save us all."

"No more talking," Qorl snapped. "Hurry."

"We're doing the best we can," Jaina replied.

"Not good enough," the pilot said. "Do you need encouragement? If you cannot complete repairs faster, I will shoot your brother. Then you will complete the repairs by yourself."

Both Jacen and Jaina looked at the TIE pilot in shock. "Qorl, you wouldn't do that," Jaina said.

"I received my training from the Empire," Qorl answered. "I will do what is necessary."

Jacen swallowed—he knew the TIE pilot was telling the truth. "Yeah, I'll bet you would," he said.

With a sigh and an expression of disgust, Jaina stood up and tossed the hydrospanner onto a pile of tools on the jungle floor. She brushed her hands down her thighs, wiping grime on the legs of her jumpsuit.

"Never mind," she said. "It's finished. We've done everything we can. The TIE fighter is ready to fly again."

17

INSIDE THE TORCHLIT temples of the Jedi academy, Lowbacca bellowed in confusion and alarm. He waved his lanky, hairy arms to emphasize the urgency of the situation. He didn't know how to make them understand him; he only knew he had to warn them of the TIE fighter, had to get help for Jacen and Jaina and Tenel Ka.

Tionne and the other Jedi candidates around her grew agitated. None of them could speak the Wookiee language. "Lowbacca, we can't understand you," she said. "Where is your translator droid?"

Lowie patted his hip again and made a distressed sound. He'd have never imagined he'd be so upset not to have the jabbering droid at his side.

"Where are Jacen, Jaina, and Tenel Ka?" Tionne asked. "Are they all right?"

Lowbacca bellowed again and gestured out into the jungle, trying to explain everything.

"Was there an accident? Are they hurt?" Tionne asked. Her mother-of-pearl eyes were wide and her silver hair flowed about her as if it were alive. With her long, delicate hands, she clutched Lowie's furred arm.

Her voice had been so calm and silky when she sang Jedi ballads to the gathered students in the grand audience chamber. Now her words had a hard, crystalline edge, the forcefulness of a true Jedi Knight.

Lowbacca tried to think of how to explain, but his growing frustration made it more and more difficult. He had no words they could understand. Yes, he could gesture back toward the jungle—but how to describe a crashed TIE fighter? A surviving Imperial pilot? The twins taken hostage?

The young Jedi Knights had kept their little project completely secret while they were making repairs to the crashed ship. Jaina had wanted the revamped craft to be a surprise she could show off to the other trainees. But now having kept it a secret was working against them. No one could guess what he was talking about; no one knew about the crash site.

He didn't know what had happened to Tenel Ka, either. Had she been killed, or had she somehow escaped? Was she even now lost in the jungles by herself, being stalked by predators? He moaned in dismay.

Unable to restrain himself, Lowie rattled off the whole story in loud Wookiee grunts and roars. Everyone around him grew agitated, unable to decipher a word he was saying. Finally, his frustration got the best of him: Lowie pounded his fists on one of the stone walls and pushed past Tionne and the other Jedi candidates into the cool shadows of the Great Temple.

"Where are you going, Lowbacca?" Tionne called, but he didn't answer her.

Though Lowie was still tired, the others could not catch up with him. With only the slightest limp, his long, muscular legs carried him down the winding corridors of the ancient stone ruin. Breathless, he reached the room that had been the old command center when the temple served as a Rebel base. Luke Skywalker maintained it to keep contact with the rest of the New Republic.

He knew his uncle Chewbacca was still in the Yavin system, near the orange gas giant where Lando Calrissian had set up his orbiting mining facility for Corusca gems. If only Lowie could get in touch with the *Millennium Falcon*, speak to his uncle, he could explain everything directly. Chewbacca—along with Jacen and Jaina's father, Han Solo—would know just what to do.

With a loud sigh of relief, Lowie sank into a chair in front of a console. The station was filled with the only things in the Jedi academy that seemed familiar to him at this moment: the computers and electronic equipment. He knew exactly how to communicate with them.

Lowbacca worked the controls with speed and determination, tapping his clawed fingers over the appropriate buttons. He had already established an open channel to the *Falcon* by the time Tionne and the others caught up with him in the Communications Center.

Tionne immediately realized what he was doing, and she nodded. "Good idea, Lowbacca!" She waited beside the young Wookiee as a sleepy-sounding Han Solo answered the call.

"Yeah, this is Solo. Who's calling? Luke? Is this the Jedi academy?" Lowbacca bleated into the microphone pickup, hoping the human pilot would understand him.

Tionne leaned over next to Lowbacca before he could continue and spoke into the voice pickup. "Something has happened here, General Solo. The twins and Tenel Ka have disappeared, and Lowbacca is trying to tell us what happened. But he can't make us understand him. He's lost his translator droid."

With a roar of surprise, Chewbacca came on the line. Excited, Lowie once again explained everything as fast as he could in the Wookiee language. Chewbacca roared back in outrage, and Han broke in.

"Quiet, old buddy. I heard most of that, but a few of the details were sketchy. Something about a crashed TIE fighter and an Imperial soldier taking them hostage?"

Both Wookiees made loud sounds of agreement.

"Okay, sit tight. We're on our way!" Han said. "We can undock from Lando's station in just a few seconds. We were ready to get out of here anyway. The *Falcon*'ll be there in about two hours—middle of the local morning, I think. Just hold on and get ready to help me fight for the kids!"

Lowie and Chewbacca both bellowed in agreement. Tionne looked at the young Wookiee in amazement. "A TIE fighter! Imperials here? Quick, we must get everyone ready in case they attack."

With a searing white flicker from its aft sublight engines, the *Millennium Falcon* cruised through the deep blue atmosphere toward the ancient Massassi structures. Lowie stood in the open landing area in front of the Great Temple, anxious to see his uncle. He waved his shaggy arms for the ship as it approached.

The bright light of morning grew warmer with each passing minute. The two hours it had taken for the *Millennium Falcon* to leave the Yavin gas giant and approach the jungle moon had seemed the longest of Lowie's life.

Now he stepped back into the shade of the temple as the *Falcon* settled to the ground with hissing bursts of its repulsorlift engines. The landing pads settled and stabilized, and then the boarding ramp came down like an opening mouth.

Chewbacca bounded down the ramp, ducking his hairy head to keep from bumping the low ceiling, and headed toward the temple. Lowie ran to meet him halfway, limping slightly. Han Solo charged out and joined them, his blaster already drawn.

"Ready to rescue the kids? Let's go!" Han said. Tionne and several of the other Jedi candidates hurried out. Han looked around. "Where's Luke? Isn't he back yet?"

"Master Skywalker isn't here," Tionne said. "We have to defend *ourselves.*"

"We'll take care of it," Han said. "Lando gave us some extra weapons, and all our laser cannon banks are charged. Lowie, can you show us where they're being held?"

Lowbacca nodded his shaggy head.

"If there are any more Imperial TIE fighters around," Han said, "the most important thing you can do is guard the Jedi academy, Tionne. This would be their obvious target. The Empire doesn't particularly like the New Republic getting another batch of Jedi Knights."

"We'll be here to defend the academy, General Solo," Tionne said. "You find the children."

"All right, Lowie," Han said. "Let's go—no time to waste."

18

THE ROAR OF twin ion engines shattered the deep stillness of the jungle morning as the TIE fighter returned to life. Birds squawked in terror and fled into the high branches. Dust and dry, crumbling leaves scattered in clouds around the Imperial ship.

Encased in the cockpit, Qorl throttled up the power, slowly, gently, as if feeling it grow at his fingertips. Foul brownish exhaust spat out of the clogged vent ports in the rear of the single-fighter craft. The Imperial ship growled, ready for action again after its long retirement.

The TIE pilot emerged from the cockpit, his battered black helmet in hand, the respirator hoses dangling and disconnected from his empty emergency-oxygen supply. Although the glossy blast goggles had been scratched and worn down during the years of his exile, he carried the helmet proudly, like a trophy.

Qorl was ready to report back to duty.

"Propulsion systems check out," he said. "With the addition of the functional hyperdrive motor you installed, I am now able to cross the galaxy and find the remnants of my Empire. This short-range fighter could not otherwise have taken me there."

"Good work, Jaina," Jacen grumbled. She elbowed him in the ribs, and he fell silent.

"What are you going to do with us, Qorl?" Jaina asked the pilot. "Why go away from here? If you'd just come back with us to the Jedi academy, everything would be all right—the war is over."

"Surrender is betrayal!" Qorl shouted, with a surge of emotion stronger than Jacen had seen in him before. The pilot's hand shook as he pointed the ever-present blaster at them. "Your usefulness to me is at an end," he said, his voice a low threat.

Jacen's stomach clenched with sudden dread. Jaina had hoped to make the TIE fighter her own vehicle so she could joyride just like Lowie did in his revamped T-23. But the small fighter could carry only one person: the pilot. Qorl could never take them along as prisoners, even if he wanted to. Would the pilot remove his last obstacles—the only witnesses to his exile—with clean Imperial efficiency? Would he just shoot them both and then fly off in search of his home?

Jacen desperately tried to send calming thoughts to soothe Qorl, as he so frequently did with his crystal snakes. But it was no use: his mind encountered the rigid wall of brainwashing that had locked Qorl's thoughts into unchangeable patterns.

The TIE pilot looked away, and his temper seemed to lessen. Jacen couldn't tell if that was a result of his Jedi powers or if the Imperial soldier had simply been distracted.

"So what *are* you going to do with us?" Jacen asked.

Qorl glanced back at the twins, his face haggard. He looked very old and drained. "You have helped me a great deal. You were the only . . . company I have had for many years. I will leave you here alone in the jungle."

"You're just going to abandon us?" Jaina asked in disbelief. This time, Jacen elbowed *her* in the ribs. He didn't relish the idea of being stranded in the jungle any more than she did, but several less-appealing possibilities had occurred to him.

"You can survive if you are resourceful," Qorl said. "I know, because I did. Perhaps someone will find you eventually. Hope is your best weapon. It may not take twenty years for *you* to get home."

He pondered for a moment, holding his dark helmet in his hands. Behind him, the repaired TIE fighter continued to purr, as if anxious to fly again. "You are lucky to be here, safe," Qorl finally said. "I will rejoin the Empire. But as my last act here on this cursed jungle moon, I am going to destroy the Rebel base."

"No!" Jacen and Jaina both shouted in unison.

"It's just a school now. It's not a military base," Jacen added.

"Please don't do this!" Jaina said. "Don't attack the Jedi academy."

But Qorl gave no sign that he heard them. He carefully placed the battered old helmet on his shaggy head and tightened down the blast shield.

"Wait!" Jaina cried, her eyes pleading. "They have no weapons in the temples!" She reached out with her mind, trying to touch the pilot, but he aimed his blaster at her and backed away.

Qorl climbed into the cockpit of the TIE fighter, eased himself into the ancient, torn seat in front of the controls, and sealed himself in. The twins rushed forward, pounding on the hull with their fists.

The roar of the engines increased and the repulsorlifts sent out a blast that knocked leaves, pebbles, and jungle debris in all directions.

The TIE fighter hummed, shifted from its overgrown resting place, and began to rise.

Jaina tried one last time to grab the hull plates, but her fingers slid along the smooth metal. Jacen pulled her back as the TIE's engine power increased. The exhaust shrieked through the fighter's cooling systems.

The twins staggered back under the protection of one of the overarching Massassi trees, alone and defenseless in the thick jungles.

Qorl's TIE fighter, which had lain hidden and crippled on the surface of Yavin 4 for more than twenty years, finally rose into the air. Its twin ion engines made the characteristic moaning sound that had struck fear into the hearts of so many Rebel fighters.

With surprisingly skillful maneuvering and a burst of speed, Qorl's fighter climbed up through the forest canopy and soared away toward the Jedi academy.

19

IN THE DARKNESS of the jungle night, Tenel Ka plunged through tangled vines and dense, thorny thickets, hoping that the flying reptiles would not be able to follow. She panted from the exertion; breath burned in her lungs, but she did not cry out.

She could still hear the flap of the reptiles' wide, leathery wings close behind her as they swooped in for the kill with their razor talons. The raucous cries of their hideous twin heads chilled her blood. She remembered hearing that such a beast had almost killed Master Skywalker many years ago. How did the monsters manage to maneuver in the crowded jungle? she wondered. Why couldn't she lose them?

The bushes beside her hissed and rattled, and a stinger tail narrowly missed her arm. One of the winged monsters was directly above her, then. What could she do?

She pushed through a narrower space between two trees and heard a *thump* above her as the flying creature got stuck in the opening between the trees. *Good,* she thought. The rest would have to go around. That would buy her some time.

Tenel Ka pelted across a clearing toward the shadow of what she hoped was another patch of underbrush, but she had misjudged the speed with which the reptilian creatures could navigate the jungle obstacles. She could feel the menacing wind from their wings as one of them swooped down directly in her path.

She sensed, rather than saw, the outstretched claws, and tried to turn aside, but slipped on rotting vegetation and fell hard against a fungus-covered log. She sensed a second pair of claws rip through the air where her stomach had been only moments before. She shuddered as twin heads cried out in rage and frustration above her, tearing at thick, tangled twigs in the brush.

Why couldn't she remember her Jedi calming techniques when she needed them? Why hadn't she practiced harder? She closed her eyes, *sensed*, and rolled to one side as the flying monster drove down for another attack.

The sound of dozens of wings overhead prodded her back into motion. She rolled onto her bare hands and knees, scrambled through some low thornbushes, pushed herself to her feet, and kept running.

Sense, she told herself. *Use the Force.*

Suddenly, she changed direction, as if by reflex. She didn't quite know why she had, for she couldn't see where she was going in the thick night, but she knew she was right. Over and over, she dodged grasping talons and the thrust of stinging tails, until she came to a thick stand of Massassi trees. At her noisy approach, a chorus of squawks and scolding chitters erupted from the trees ahead.

Woolamanders—an entire pack, from the sound of them. She had probably disturbed their communal sleep. Perhaps they would be sufficient distraction.

Tenel Ka crouched low and dove into the shelter of the close-growing trees. Surprisingly, not one of the winged monsters followed. Instead, she heard their cries as they circled above and, deprived of their initial prey, hunted the woolamanders instead. The flying creatures screamed their blood lust, and the voices of the terrified woolamanders became fierce and defiant as the battle raged in the branches far overhead.

Sweat, twigs, leaves, and dirt clung to Tenel Ka's red-gold hair. She shook her head to clear it. She was almost certain that through the racket, she had somehow heard a faint, familiar voice.

"Oh please, *do* be careful. My circuitry is extremely complex and should not under any circumstances be—" The voice cut off a moment later with a tiny wail. Then there was a *thud* as something hard landed beside Tenel Ka's foot.

"Em Teedee, is that you?" she said. She groped around on the ground and picked up the rounded metallic form.

"Oh, Mistress Tenel Ka, it *is* you!" the little droid cried. "I shall be eternally grateful to you for this rescue. Why, you have no idea the ordeal I've been through," he moaned. "The poking, the prodding, the shaking, the tossing. And such a dreadful—"

"My night has been no more enjoyable than yours," Tenel Ka interrupted drily.

"Listen!" Em Teedee said. "Oh, thank goodness! Those dreadful creatures are leaving."

Tenel Ka didn't know whether Em Teedee was referring to the woolamanders or the giant flying reptiles, but she realized that the sounds of the overhead battle were moving farther and farther away through the canopy.

"We must make our escape immediately, Mistress Tenel Ka."

"We can't. We'll have to wait until morning. Can you keep a watch out tonight while I sleep?"

"I'd be delighted to keep a watch for you, Mistress, but *must* we spend the night here?"

"Yes, we must," Tenel Ka snapped, defensive now that the worst danger was over. "I need to wait until daylight so I can climb a tree and find out where we are."

"Oh," said Em Teedee. "But whyever should you want to do something like that?"

Tenel Ka growled, "Because we're lost in the jungle. This is a fact."

"Oh, dear—is *that* all that's bothering you?" Em Teedee said. "Why didn't you say so? After all, I am fluent in six forms of communication *and* I am equipped with all manner of sensors: photo-optical, olfactory, directional, auditory—"

"Directional?" Tenel Ka broke in. "You mean you *know* where we are?"

"Oh, most assuredly, Mistress Tenel Ka. Didn't I just say so?"

She groaned and shook her head. "All right, Em Teedee, let's go. Lead on."

Tenel Ka's spirits were brighter than the twin beams that shone from Em Teedee's eyes and lit her way along the forest floor. As annoying as the little droid could be, she was glad of his company. Em Teedee seemed genuinely interested in hearing all that had happened to her since the TIE fighter pilot had tried to capture them that afternoon. In turn, she found herself enjoying his descriptions of the T-23 crash and his adventures with the woolamanders. She wondered what had happened to Lowbacca, and to the twins.

They stopped only a few times, so that she could drink or check the dressing on her minor wounds. Using rudimentary first-aid supplies she kept in her belt, she had bound up the claw scratches on her arm and the gash on her leg. The wounds throbbed and burned, but did not slow her down. She jogged much of the way, and kept to a fast-paced march even when she needed to rest.

The distant white sun of the Yavin system was bright in the morning sky when Tenel Ka and Em Teedee finally broke through the last stand of trees into the cleared landing area. The sun-warmed stone of the Great Temple glowed like a welcome beacon in the distance.

"Oh, we made it!" Em Teedee said joyfully. Tenel Ka looked

around and saw in the center of the clearing a ship that she recognized well: the *Millennium Falcon*.

Running toward the modified light freighter at full speed were two Wookiees, one large and one smaller, and Jacen and Jaina's father, Han Solo. She guessed immediately what mission they were on and changed her course toward the *Falcon*, waving and shouting as she ran.

Overhead, she heard the bone-chilling howl of a fast-approaching TIE fighter. She put on another burst of speed toward the ship.

But Solo and the Wookiees did not see her. In their hurry to rescue Jacen and Jaina, the three scrambled up the ramp of the *Falcon*. They must have kept the engines idling to keep them warm, she figured, for she could hear their whine.

Tenel Ka wanted to help rescue the twins; she couldn't let them down again. "Call them, Em Teedee," she said, pouring on a last burst of speed, though her legs already trembled with exhaustion.

Em Teedee mused, "Am I to take it that you wish to communicate with them?"

"This is a fact."

"Certainly, Mistress. I would be delighted, but what shall—"

"Just *do* it!" She gritted her teeth and sprinted as fast as she could.

Suddenly Em Teedee's voice boomed at top volume through the clearing. "Attention, *Millennium Falcon*. Please delay departure momentarily to take on two additional passengers."

Tenel Ka didn't even mind the ringing in her ears when she saw the ramp of the *Millennium Falcon* lower. At full tilt, she ran up the ramp.

"Okay," she gasped, collapsing to the floor in the crew compartment. "Let's go!"

Han Solo and the two Wookiees looked at her in amazement for an instant, but no one needed any further urging. Even as she spoke, the hatches sealed, and with a surge of defiance the *Millennium Falcon* took off.

20

QORL FLEW HIS single fighter at top speed over the thick jungle canopy. The rushing air of Yavin 4 screamed around the TIE fighter's rounded pilot compartment and the rectangular solar arrays. He remembered his days as a trainee. He had been an excellent pilot—one of the best in his squadron—soaring through mock battles and enforcing the Emperor's unbending will.

Air currents buffeted him, and the pilot reveled in the sensation of flight. He had not forgotten, not even after so many years. The vibrating power that pulsed through the fighter's engines, along with a sense of freedom and liberation after so long an exile, buoyed him.

Qorl watched the knotted green crowns of Massassi trees flowing beneath him in the storm of his ship's passage. With his thickly gloved, badly healed arm, he found it difficult to control the Imperial craft—but he was a fighter pilot. He was a *great* pilot. He had managed to land his ship, despite grievous engine damage, under heavy enemy fire. He had survived undetected in hostile territory for two decades.

Now, flying low over the trees to avoid notice from any possible defenses at the Rebel base, Qorl felt his memories, his ingrained skill, come flooding back to him.

The Empire is my family. The Rebels wish to destroy the New Order. The Rebels must be eliminated—ELIMINATED!

His greatest advantage was surprise. This attack would come out of nowhere. The Rebels would be expecting nothing. He would streak in with all weapons blazing. He would level the Rebel base structures, blast them into rubble. He would kill all those who had conspired to blow up the Death Star, who had killed Darth Vader and Grand Moff Tarkin. He, a single soldier, would secure vengeance for the entire Empire.

There! Qorl squinted through the scratched goggles of his blast helmet. Protruding from a clearing in the dense jungle, a towering stone temple rose up—a ziggurat, the squarish pyramid that served as the main structure of the base.

Qorl roared low over the facilities of the old Rebel stronghold. A wide, sluggish river sliced through the jungle near the site of the temples. On the opposite side of the brownish-green current lay other crumbling ruins, but they seemed uninhabited. Then he noticed a large power-generating station next to the towering ziggurat and knew for certain that he had not been wrong: this base was still used as a military installation.

As he brought the TIE fighter in on his first attack run, Qorl saw that the jungle had been cleared to make a large landing area in front of the Great Temple. On the flat field he saw only one ship—disk-shaped, with twin prongs in front.

Qorl didn't immediately recognize the make or model of the lone ship below. It was some kind of light freighter, not a Rebel X-wing or any of the familiar battleships he had learned about during his rigorous combat training.

On the ground, several people ran toward the ship, sprinting away from the stone pyramid. Scrambling to battle stations perhaps? His lip curled in a snarl. He would take care of them.

He flicked the buttons on his control panel, powering up the TIE fighter's weapons systems. Before he could align the victims in his targeting cross, though, all the small figures below managed to climb aboard the light freighter. Its boarding ramp drew up, preparing for launch.

He dismissed the light freighter as a possible target—for now, at least. It was probable, Qorl realized, that the Rebels kept a large force of more powerful fighters in an underground hangar bay. If so, his first task was to prevent those craft from launching—even if only by damaging the doors enough to keep the ships trapped inside.

He decided his best strategy would be to continue his straight-line course and fire with full-power laser cannons on the main structure of the Great Temple. He would blow the entire building to rubble—perhaps causing it to collapse internally, thus eliminating the Rebels and destroying all their equipment inside.

Then he could swoop around and take care of the single light freighter, even if it managed to get up off the ground. His third target would be the power-generating station.

With the Rebels completely paralyzed by his lightning attack, he would swing back for the last time. He would charge up his laser cannons again and go for the kill, mopping up anything he had missed the first time.

From start to finish, it would take only a few minutes to bring the Rebels to their knees.

Qorl centered the Great Temple in his targeting cross, aiming at the apex of the squared-off pyramid, with its thin banks of skylights and ancient vine-covered sculptures. The TIE fighter zoomed in.

He grasped the firing stick with his good hand. At exactly the right moment he depressed the firing buttons, letting an expression of anticipation light his normally emotionless face.

Nothing.

He squeezed the button again and again—*and nothing happened!* The weapons systems did not respond.

Qorl flicked on the backups as he spun the TIE fighter in the air, barreling down again on his target. Over and over he tried to fire, but the laser cannons were completely dead. His eyes swept the diagnostic panels, but all the readings seemed normal.

With his gloved hand Qorl pounded on the instrumentation panel, as if that would fix anything—and with old Imperial equipment, sometimes it did. But not this time.

He frantically worked with the controls, digging under the panels to restart the weapons systems even as he flew on. He reached down and felt around his seat, searching for anything he could use to jump-start the malfunctioning laser cannons.

Qorl caught the glimmer out of the corner of his eye, reflected against the dark goggles of his helmet. He glanced down and noticed something *moving* . . . sinuous, barely seen, glittering and transparent.

The crystal snake reared up right beside him, its triangular head showing up as a faint rainbow in the glow from the cockpit lights. Qorl, who had seen plenty of the reptilian creatures during his exile on Yavin 4, spotted it immediately and reacted.

He let out a startled cry and tried to brush the snake away. It lunged and bit down as he reached out with his crippled arm to block it. The crystal snake dug its spearlike fangs into the thick leather of Qorl's gauntlet, but was unable to penetrate all the way to his skin.

As he flung his hand back and forth, Qorl could feel the heavy weight of the crystal snake writhing, snapping, though he could see almost nothing at all.

He let the TIE fighter fly itself as he reached with his good hand to grab the long body of the serpent just behind its head. He ripped the fangs free and stuffed the thrashing creature into the cockpit jettison chute. With a cry of disgust he ejected the snake into the air, where it fell toward the treetops of the jungle moon, disappearing instantly in the bright sunlight.

He wrestled for control of his weaponless vessel. The Jedi twins must have done something in their repairs.

He managed to stabilize his erratic flight—but before he could decide on a new course, bright streaks from an enemy laser cannon sizzled through the air, bolts of energy that ionized the atmosphere around Qorl's TIE fighter.

He yanked at the control stick with his good arm, and his fighter lurched into a starboard spin. The Rebel light freighter had taken to the air and was flying after Qorl like a furious bird of prey. And *its* weapons worked just fine.

Qorl punched in full power to the twin ion engines and decided that his only chance for now was to try to escape.

In the heart of the jungle, next to Qorl's primitive dwelling, Jacen and Jaina sat beside each other, deep in concentration. They reached out with the Force to see what was going on back at the Jedi academy. Their powers were only sufficient to bring them shadowy images, distant echoes of thoughts . . . but it was enough.

"He didn't know I never fixed the weapons systems . . . but then, he never asked. I managed to jury-rig the readouts so they would look normal," Jaina said at last. "He can fly, but his ship is defenseless."

"Yes, and I think the crystal snake must have distracted Qorl somehow," Jacen said. "I wonder what happened to it." They smiled at each other.

"I suppose our next step," Jacen said, squinting up at the morning light that filtered through the trees, "is to figure out how to get back home."

Jaina pushed a tangle of her usually straight brown hair back from her face and took a deep breath. "Agreed," she said, then clapped her hands and rubbed them together. "So what are we waiting for?"

21

"HANG ON!" HAN SOLO yelled.

As the *Millennium Falcon* lifted off from the trampled landing area in front of the ancient temple, Tenel Ka struggled to a seat beside Lowbacca and strapped herself in.

"That TIE fighter's coming in, and it looks mean," Han said as he and his Wookiee copilot frantically set switches and calibrated the weapons targeting systems. "Hope Tionne managed to get all the Jedi trainees to safety."

Their seats tilted back as the *Falcon* angled up into the air, its sublight thrusters roaring behind it. The Imperial TIE fighter broke through the sky overhead like a yowling battering ram.

Han Solo looked grim as he gripped the controls. His jaw was set, his shoulders rigid. At the moment he had no way of knowing whether his children were safe, or if this Imperial enemy had killed them both, just as the pilot had tried to blast Lowbacca and Tenel Ka.

Tenel Ka wished she could give him some reassurance, but she knew nothing herself. Still panting with exhaustion from her long run through the jungle, she adjusted the restraints across the reptilian armor on her chest. At her side Em Teedee's thin, warbly voice spoke up. "I beg your pardon, Mistress Tenel Ka, but I can't see a thing! Your crash webbing has blocked my optical sensors."

When Tenel Ka freed the flat, silvery device from its restraints, Em Teedee let out what sounded like a sigh of relief. "Ah, yes, much better. Now I can see perfectly. Oh, dear!" he said in alarm. "I didn't want you to rescue me from that dreadful jungle just so we could all be blown up chasing that TIE fighter."

Lowbacca grunted and looked over at the small translating droid with obvious surprise and relief.

"This is yours, Lowbacca," Tenel Ka said. "I found it in the jungle." She handed Em Teedee to the young Wookiee, who accepted the little droid gratefully, bleating his thanks.

Han Solo spun the *Falcon* around in a tight arc, its engines rumbling behind them as they pursued the TIE fighter. "He's coming in on an attack run," Han said. "But he's not firing his weapons for some reason."

Through the cockpit windows, Tenel Ka watched as the TIE fighter she had helped to repair zoomed low over the Great Temple, seemingly bent on destruction—but its laser cannons did not fire.

"I'm going to get his attention, Chewie," Han said. "You open a comm channel. That guy did something to my kids—and I want to find out where they are."

Chewbacca growled and reached with his long hairy arm to toggle a few switches on the *Millennium Falcon*'s control panel.

Han fired two warning shots. Bolts of brilliant light streaked past the squarish planar wings of the Imperial craft—bracketing it, but doing no damage.

"Attention, TIE pilot," Han said. "You're going nowhere if I don't find out where . . ." He paused. ". . . the two young Jedi Knights are. You're in the middle of my targeting cross, so your choices are simple: surrender, or we blow you out of the sky."

A gruff voice came back over the comm systems. "Surrender is betrayal," the pilot said, then broke the connection.

The TIE fighter zoomed upward on an impossibly steep trajectory, climbing into the air above the dense green treetops. Then the Imperial ship wheeled about in an evasive maneuver.

"All right," Han said, his anger evident. "This old ship has taken on plenty of TIE fighters in its day. We can take on one more. Punch it, Chewie."

The *Falcon* lunged forward in another burst of speed as Chewbacca worked the controls.

Em Teedee wailed, "Oh, no! I can't watch. Somebody cover my optical sensors."

Han spared a second to glance back at the droid, and found Lowbacca cradling Em Teedee in his lap. "Just like having See-Threepio with us again. I think we may need to adjust that programming."

"Oh, dear," Em Teedee said.

In the back Lowbacca grumbled a suggestion, which his uncle seconded loudly.

"Good idea," Han said. "Let's try the tractor beam first. Maybe—just maybe—we can bring that ship to the ground without destroying it. That way we can get some information. If we say 'Please,' he might be a little more cooperative."

Chewbacca worked the *Falcon*'s tractor beam generator, casting out the invisible beam like a force-field net to grab the Imperial ship.

The TIE fighter lurched and jerked to one side as the tractor beam snagged a partial hold—but the pilot alternated bursts from his twin ion engines and tore free, spinning upward in a tight corkscrew that made Han whistle with reluctant admiration.

"This guy's good," he said. "After him, Chewie! Full speed."

The TIE fighter, as if seeing it as his one chance for escape, darted back down toward the rough greenery of Massassi trees. It dodged jagged branches that thrust up like blackened witches' fingers where lightning and forest fires had burned the jungle, dipped down to trace the winding courses of rivers, and streaked over lush canyons—all with the *Millennium Falcon* following in hot pursuit.

If it were only a matter of speed, the *Falcon*'s more powerful engines could have outrun the TIE fighter and brought it down, but the small ship's maneuverability among the dangerous treetops gave the Imperial pilot a definite advantage.

Han Solo, however, had greater determination. "What have you done with my kids?" he yelled into the comm channel.

It was obvious he expected no answer, but to everyone's surprise, the pilot spoke back in a calculating voice. "They are your children, pilot? They were alive when I left them—but the jungle is a dangerous place. There's no telling if they will last long enough for you to rescue them."

Tenel Ka marveled at the brilliant strategy. "It's a trick," she said. "He wants you to break off the pursuit."

"I know," Han said, glancing back at her. His face was ashen. "But what if it's true?"

The TIE pilot used Han's brief hesitation to take his last best chance for escape: arrowing upward and bolting straight toward space. The twin ion engines roared through the thinning atmosphere.

Chewbacca yelped in reaction. Without waiting for Han to give the order, the Wookiee copilot pushed the accelerators to maximum. The *Falcon*, white heat rippling from its rear sublight engines, zoomed after the TIE fighter.

The acceleration slammed Tenel Ka back against her seat, and she grimaced as the tug of additional gravities stretched her skin. She squeezed her eyes shut. Beside her, Lowbacca grunted with the strain, but Han and Chewie seemed accustomed to putting such stress on their bodies.

The bright, milky-blue sky grew darker, turning a deep purplish color around them as they soared upward. The stars shone out as the

Falcon pulled into the night of space. The blurry sphere of the great orange gas giant Yavin filled most of their cockpit windows.

The TIE fighter zigzagged to throw off pursuit, shifting course at random intervals and burning a great deal of energy.

"Maybe we can still wound his ship and pull him in," Han said, his voice strained.

Chewbacca piloted the *Falcon* as Han controlled the weapons systems. "I can't get a target lock," Han said.

The TIE fighter zoomed above the green jewel of the jungle moon.

Arching around in a tight orbit, the *Falcon* clung to it, following closely. Han fired repeatedly with his laser cannons—but the scarlet bolts missed.

Han pounded his fist on the control panel. "Hold still for a minute!" he shouted.

Then, as if obliging, the TIE fighter paused in the middle of the weapons system's aim-point grid. The target lock flashed brightly, and Han gave a whoop of excitement.

"Gotcha!" he said, and depressed both sets of firing studs.

But at the last possible instant, the lone TIE fighter shot forward with a blaze of astonishing speed, becoming a molten metal point of light. It dwindled in the sudden distance, screaming forward with instant lightspeed—and plunged into hyperspace with a silent bang.

"It's not my fault," Han Solo said, gaping at the vanished target. He let his shaking hands fall away from the firing controls. "A TIE fighter doesn't have lightspeed engines! It's a short-range ship."

Lowbacca grumbled an explanation, and Tenel Ka nodded.

"Jaina did *what?*" Han said in disbelief. "But that hyperdrive was for her to tinker with, not to install. She's got a lot of explaining to do when I see her—" He broke off, suddenly realizing where the twins were.

"Forget the TIE fighter. Let's go get the twins!" he said.

He changed the *Falcon*'s course and arrowed straight back down to the emerald-green sphere of the jungle moon of Yavin.

22

BACK AT THE tiny jungle clearing where the wreck of the TIE fighter had rested for two decades, Jacen and Jaina decided that their best chance for rescue lay in climbing to the treetops—no matter how difficult it might be. From that height, they could spot any incoming ships and set up some sort of signal.

Before leaving, they scrounged at the crash site and at Qorl's old encampment for whatever they could possibly find useful, then stuffed it in their packs. Their Jedi training had taught them to be resourceful.

Remembering how they had used the Force to help them scale the Great Temple with Tenel Ka, the twins found a Massassi tree with plenty of densely interwoven branches and hanging vines. They stared upward, then at each other, before beginning the long, sweaty climb. Jacen and Jaina were scratched up and aching and smeared with forest debris by the time they made it to the top—but to their surprise, they felt invigorated by their accomplishment.

Up in the canopy in a thick nest of tangled branches, they tried to light a leafy fire to send a beacon of smoke into the sky. Jacen collected leaves and twigs and piled them onto a curved piece of plasteel left over from their repairs on the TIE fighter.

Jaina had brought Tenel Ka's flash heater, but the charge was low. When the finger-sized unit sputtered and flashed, sending out a few last sparks, she took the back panel off and used her multitool to tinker with the circuits. By pumping up the power output, she produced one last flash that set the pile of fresh branches on fire.

The lush green leaves burned slowly, and the fire would not gain enough heat to become a bright blaze. But, as they had hoped, a satisfying gray-blue smoke curled upward, a clear signal for anyone who was looking.

Even so, they couldn't be certain that anyone would know where to look. Unless Lowbacca or Tenel Ka had managed to get back to the academy, no one would have any idea where to begin a search.

"Guess it might be a good idea next time if we let someone know where we're going and what we're doing, huh?" Jaina said, staring up at the discouragingly empty blueness.

"Probably," Jacen agreed, settling himself beside her on the branches. Sweat ran down his face as he rested his chin on his grimy hands. "Want to hear another joke?"

"No," Jaina answered firmly. She wiped her damp forehead with the sleeve of her now-ragged jumpsuit, and continued scanning the skies. She shifted beside him, feeling the breeze and listening to the whisper of millions of leaves.

Jacen fed more leaves to the fire.

Suddenly, Jaina sat up straight. "Look!" she said, pointing up. A white starpoint grew brighter, glittering silver. Ripples of sound from a sonic boom echoed like thunder across the sky of Yavin 4. "It's a ship."

Jacen closed his liquid-brown eyes and smiled. Then the twins blinked and looked at each other. "The *Falcon,*" they said in unison.

"Can Dad sense us?" Jacen asked.

"I don't think so," Jaina said. "At least not with the Force. But wait . . ." She closed her eyes again, reaching out with what she knew of Jedi powers. "Lowie's with him!"

"And Tenel Ka, too," Jacen said. "They're all right!"

Jaina laughed with relief. "Did you expect any less from a young Jedi Knight?"

The *Falcon* must have spotted their smoke, and now headed toward them. High in the branches, the twins stood and waved. As it approached, the blaster-scarred light freighter seemed the most beautiful machine they had ever seen.

The big ship hovered over them with a gust of its repulsorlifts. Branches blew away beneath them, but Jacen and Jaina held their positions, reaching upward as the bottom access hatch of the *Falcon* popped open.

Chewbacca's hairy arm dangled down, grabbing Jacen's hands and pulling him up into the ship as if he were a piece of lightweight luggage. A moment later, Lowie's ginger-furred arms reached out to help Jaina up.

Han scrambled from the cockpit, rushing to scoop up both of his children in a big hug. "You're alive—you're not hurt!" he said, looking them over with anxious relief. "Sorry I'm late."

"It's all right," Jacen answered. "We knew you'd come."

Tenel Ka and Lowie also greeted the twins, with hugs all around and enthusiastic thumps on the back.

"Oh, hooray!" Em Teedee's tinny voice chimed in. "This *is* cause for a celebration."

"Let's get back to the Jedi academy first; I'm sure everyone's been worried about us," Han said. "I think we need to tell about a few adventures."

A few days later, after the *Falcon* carried the T-23 back from where it had crashed in the treetops, Lowbacca and Jaina worked in the shadow-draped courtyard of the Great Temple, tinkering with the damaged skyhopper. Jaina poked her grease-smeared face up out of the engine compartment and looked around.

She watched as Jacen scurried across the landing field out front, low to the ground, trying to catch an eight-legged lizard crab he wanted to add to his collection. Leaves and broken blades of grass were tangled in his tousled hair, as usual. The creature darted left and right, trying to find a hiding place among the close-cropped weeds of the landing field.

Spying a large shady spot, the lizard crab scuttled for shelter out of reach under the T-23. Jaina giggled as Jacen pulled up short just in time to keep from banging his head against the skyhopper's hull.

With a shrug, he leaned against the craft and brushed the dirt from his jumpsuit. "Oh well," he said, grinning. "Next time."

"As long as you're just standing there, could you please hand me a hydrospanner?" Jaina said.

Jacen bent and rummaged in the tool kit on the grass, then handed the tool up.

"You concentrate on the onboard computer systems, Lowie," Jaina said, discussing repair strategies. "That's what you're best at." At the Wookiee's growl of agreement, she added, "Don't worry about these engines. I'll have them running again in no time."

"Mind if I join you?" a calm voice said from behind her.

"Uncle Luke!" Jaina cried, jumping up and turning toward him. "When did you get back?"

"Only this morning," Luke Skywalker said, looking admiringly at the vehicle. "Could you use any help? I'm pretty good with these little air speeders, you know." He smiled as if savoring a fond memory. "I had a ship a little like this once . . . my own T-16 skyhopper when I was growing up on—"

Just then, Tenel Ka emerged from the large lower door of the Great

Temple. The cool underlevels had once stored the Rebel base's X-wing fighters.

"Excuse me for a moment," Luke said, and turned to raise his hand in a warm greeting. He strode over to Tenel Ka and spoke to her for a long while as if she were an old friend. Being with the great Jedi Master caused the young girl from Dathomir to look uncharacteristically intimidated.

"Well, what are we waiting for?" Jaina asked the others. She opened an inner access panel with her multitool and began running diagnostics on the T-23's engines. Jacen surreptitiously scanned the cropped grass and weeds, looking for another specimen to catch.

Lowbacca snared a tangle of wires from the cockpit control panels and began sorting them by color and function. He murmured to himself as he worked, and Jacen could hear Em Teedee start to speak. At a *clunk* of something metal hitting the floor plates, Jacen stuck his head into the T-23. Lowbacca had accidentally dropped Em Teedee from his belt again.

The miniature translating droid began scolding the young Wookiee at high volume. "Really, Master Lowbacca, do try to be careful! You've dropped me again, and that's simply careless. How would you like it if *your* head detached and kept falling on the ground? I am an extremely valuable piece of equipment and you ought to take better care of me. If my circuits become damaged I won't be able to translate, and then where will you be? I can't believe—"

With a grunt, Lowbacca switched off Em Teedee, and then made a satisfied sound.

Jacen looked up to see Jaina staring at the deep blue sky. He followed her gaze and knew exactly what she was thinking. "Do you suppose Qorl ever made it back home?"

"If he does, I wonder if he'll find what he expects when he gets there," she answered. "He would have been better off staying with us."

When they noticed Luke Skywalker and Tenel Ka strolling back toward the T-23, Lowie and Jaina climbed out of the dismantled cockpit to stand next to Jacen.

Luke looked at the battered air speeder and ran his fingertips over its smooth hull. "Back on Tatooine I used to roar through Beggar's Canyon in my own T-16, chasing down womp rats."

Jacen and Jaina looked at their uncle, amazed and unable to imagine the introspective Jedi Master as a hotshot daredevil pilot.

Luke's lips curved in a wistful smile. "That was a whole different life from now." He turned to the young Jedi Knights. "When you get this thing fixed, I'd like to go for a ride with you. If that's all right."

They looked at him in astonishment. Lowie muttered something indecipherable and cleared his throat nervously.

"I hope you're fitting in here, Lowbacca," Luke said, nodding toward the young Wookiee. "I know it's difficult to go away from home and stay in a strange place, but I see you've made some new friends."

He looked at the others. "I'm proud of you all," Luke said. "You did a fine job under very trying circumstances, even when I wasn't here to guide you. You have a lot of potential—but becoming a Jedi Knight takes a great deal of hard work and practice."

The students nodded. "This is a fact," Tenel Ka said solemnly.

"You're young, and there are many things you could do with your lives," Luke said. "Are you certain you still want to become Jedi Knights?"

Their enthusiastic shouts rang out in unison. Lowbacca's loud bellow was so emphatic that even with Em Teedee switched off, none of the others needed a translation.

SHADOW ACADEMY

To our brothers and sisters—

Mark—who has been my hero since childhood. A true Jedi Knight, always ready to race to the rescue

Cindy—who always watched out for me. You showed me that effort and determination will get you what wishing and waiting will not

Diane—who broadened my horizons. Thanks for forcing me to watch every monster-and-hero movie ever made

Scott—who tolerated all the books I read to him. Thanks for telling me in May of 1977 that there was a movie I just had to go see—*Star Wars*

Rebecca Moesta

and *Laura*—for never fighting with me, always understanding (just kidding!), and providing a wealth of experiences for me to draw upon in my writing

Kevin J. Anderson

Acknowledgments

We would like to thank Lil Mitchell for her tireless typing and for urging us to bring her each chapter faster and faster, Dave Wolverton for his input on Dathomir, Lucy Wilson and Sue Rostoni at Lucasfilm for their unwavering support, Ginjer Buchanan and Lou Aronica at Berkley/Boulevard for their continuing enthusiasm, Jonathan MacGregor Cowan for being our test audience . . . and Skip Shayotovich, Roland Zarate, Gregory McNamee, and the entire *Star Wars* ImagiNet Echo computer bulletin board for helping out with the jokes.

1

JACEN GRASPED THE lightsaber, feeling its comforting weight against his sweaty palms. His scalp tingled beneath its unruly tangle of brown curls as he sensed the approach of his enemy. Closer, closer . . . He drew in a slow breath and reached with one finger that trembled ever so slightly to press the button on the handle.

With a buzzing hiss, the cold metal handle sprang to life, transforming into a sword of glowing energy. The deadly lightsaber pulsed and vibrated in his hands like a living thing.

With a mixture of fear and excitement, Jacen's wiry frame tensed for the attack. His liquid-brown eyes fluttered shut for a moment as he visualized his opponent.

Without warning, he heard the hum of a lightsaber slice down from above.

Jacen whirled just in time and caught the blow with his own lightsaber. The deep red of his opponent's weapon throbbed with power, filling his vision as the two glowing blades warred for dominance.

Jacen knew he was far outmatched in size and strength, that he would need all of his wits to get out of this encounter alive. His arms ached with the strain of holding off the blow, so he took advantage of his smaller size, spinning under his opponent's arm and dancing out of reach.

The attacker advanced toward him, but Jacen knew better than to let him get that close again. The ruby glow flashed toward him, and he was ready. He parried the blow and then swept sideways with his own blade before dodging backward and blocking the next thrust.

Attack and counterattack. Thrust. Parry. Block. Lightsabers sizzled and hissed as they clashed again and again.

Though the room was cool and dank, perspiration ran down Jacen's face and into his eyes, nearly blinding him. He saw the arc of red light barely in time and ducked to avoid it. A cocky lopsided grin sprang to his lips, and he realized he was enjoying himself. Stone chips flew around him as the deadly ruby blade gouged the low ceiling just over his head.

Jacen's grin faded as he tried to take a step backward and felt cold stone blocks press into his shoulder blades. He parried another thrust, sprang sideways, and fetched up against another stone wall.

He was cornered. An icy fist of fear clenched his stomach, and Jacen dropped to one knee, flinging up his blade to ward off the next blow. A sound like thunder echoed through the chamber. . . .

Jacen opened his eyes and looked up to see his uncle Luke standing in the doorway, clearing his throat. Startled, Jacen fumbled to turn off the lightsaber and accidentally dropped the extinguished handle to the flagstones with a clatter.

The sandy-haired, black-robed Jedi Master strode into the private room that served as both his office and his meditation chamber at the Jedi academy. He held his hand out toward the lightsaber, and the weapon sprang to his palm as if magnetized.

Jacen gulped as Master Luke Skywalker fixed him with a solemn gaze. "I'm sorry, Uncle Luke," Jacen said, his words coming out in a tumbling rush. "I came here to ask you for your help, and when you weren't here, I decided to wait, and then I saw your lightsaber just lying on your desk, and I know you said I'm not ready yet, but I didn't see how it could hurt to just practice a little. So I picked it up, and I guess I just got carried away and—"

Luke held up one hand, palm outward, as if to forestall further explanation. "The weapon of the Jedi shouldn't be taken up lightly," he said.

Jacen felt his cheeks flush at the gentle rebuke. "But I *know* I could learn to use a lightsaber," he said, defensive. "I'm old enough, and I'm tall enough, and I've been practicing in my room with a piece of pipe I got from Jaina—I'm sure I could do it."

Luke seemed to consider this for a moment before shaking his head slowly. "There'll be time enough for that when you are ready."

"But I'm ready *now*," Jacen protested.

"Not yet," Luke said, smiling sadly. "The time will come soon enough."

Jacen groaned with impatience. It was always *later*, always *Some other time*, always *Maybe when you're older*. He sighed. "You're the teacher. I'm the student, so I have to listen, I guess."

Luke smiled and shook his head. "Ah. Be careful—don't assume a teacher is always right, without question. You have to think for yourself. Sometimes we teachers make mistakes, too. But in this case, I am right: You're not yet ready for a lightsaber.

"Believe me, I know what it's like to wait," Luke continued. "But patience can be as strong an ally as any weapon." Then his eyes twinkled. "Don't you have more important things to be worrying about right now than imaginary lightsaber battles—like getting ready for your trip? Don't your pets need to be fed?"

"I'm all packed, and I'll feed the animals just before we leave," Jacen said, thinking of the menagerie of pets he had collected since coming to the jungle moon. "But the trip *is* what I came here to talk to you about."

Luke raised his eyebrows. "Yes?"

"I—I was hoping you could talk to Tenel Ka and convince her to come with us to see Lando Calrissian's mining station."

Luke's brows drew together, and he chose his words carefully. "Why is it important to change her mind?"

"Because Jaina and Lowbacca and I are all going," Jacen said, "and . . . and it just won't be the same without her," he finished lamely.

Luke's face relaxed, and his eyes sparkled with humor. "It's not so easy to change the mind of a Force-wielding warrior from Dathomir, you know," he said.

"But it doesn't make sense that she wants to stay behind," Jacen exclaimed. "She made up some dumb excuse that it would be boring—said she was sure Corusca gems weren't any more beautiful than rainbow gems from Gallinore, and she's seen plenty of those. But she didn't *sound* bored; she sounded worried or nervous."

"We must think for ourselves," Luke said, "and sometimes that means we have to make difficult or unpopular decisions." Luke put an arm around Jacen's shoulders and led him toward the door. "Go feed your pets now. Have a safe journey to GemDiver Station—and rest assured, Tenel Ka has good reasons."

Tenel Ka woke with a start, shivering and drenched with perspiration in the cool, stone-walled chamber. Sunset-copper hair hung across her vision in tangles that had once been orderly braids. Her bedsheets were twisted about her legs as if she had been running in her sleep.

Then she remembered the dream. She *had* been running. Running from black-cloaked shadowy figures with purple-splotched faces. Muddled memories of stories her mother had told her as a child swirled through her sleep-fogged brain. She had never seen those terrifying forms before, but she knew what they were—witches from Dathomir who had drawn on the dark side of the Force to work all manner of evil.

The Nightsisters.

But the last of the Nightsisters had been destroyed or disbanded long before Tenel Ka had even been born. Why should she dream of them now? The only Force-wielders left on Dathomir used the powers of the light side.

Why these nightmares? Why now?

She squeezed her eyes shut and flopped back on her bed with a grunt as she realized what day it was. This was the day that her grandmother, Matriarch of the Hapan Royal Household, was sending an ambassador to visit Tenel Ka, heir to the Royal Throne of Hapes. And she didn't want her friends to know she was a princess. . . .

Ambassador Yfra. Tenel Ka shuddered as she thought of her iron-willed grandmother and her ambassadors, women who would lie or even kill to preserve their power—although her grandmother no longer ruled Hapes. Tenel Ka shook her head in wry amusement. The impending visit must be why she had dreamt of the Nightsisters.

Although the inhabitants of her mother's primitive planet of Dathomir and her father's plush homeworld of Hapes were light-years apart, the parallels between the Hapan politicians and the Nightsisters of Dathomir were obvious: All were power-hungry women who would stop at nothing to keep the power they craved.

Tenel Ka levered herself into a sitting position. She did not relish the idea of meeting with Ambassador Yfra. In fact, the only positive thought she could muster about it was that her friends would not be here to observe it. At least Jacen, Jaina, and Lowbacca would be far away on Lando Calrissian's GemDiver Station before the ambassador ever arrived. They would not be here to wonder why their friend, who claimed to be a simple warrior from Dathomir, was being visited by a royal ambassador from the House of Hapes. And Tenel Ka was not ready yet to explain that to them.

Well, she couldn't stay in bed any longer. She would have to get up and face whatever the day had to offer her. The meeting was unavoidable. "This," she muttered, flinging aside the covers and standing, "is a fact."

Jaina and Lowbacca sat in the center of Jaina's student quarters surrounded by a holographic map of the Yavin system.

"That ought to do it," she said. Her straight shoulder-length hair swung forward like a curtain, partially veiling her face, as she hunched over to scrutinize the input pad for her holoprojector. She had built the projector herself, piecing it together from her private stock of used electronic modules, components, cables, and other odds and ends that she kept neatly organized in a bank of bins and drawers that filled one wall of her quarters.

"Pretty impressive, huh, Lowie?" Jaina asked, flashing a lopsided grin at the ginger-furred young Wookiee. She pointed at the luminescent sphere drifting above their heads that represented the gas-giant planet of Yavin.

Lowbacca pointed to the image of a small green moon that hovered just above his left shoulder, in orbit around the big orange planet. He gave an interrogative growl.

"Ahem," the miniature translator droid Em Teedee said from the clip on Lowie's belt, as if clearing its throat. Em Teedee was roughly oval in shape, rounded in the front and flat on the back, with irregularly spaced optical sensors and a wide speaker grill at the center. "Master Lowbacca wishes to know," the miniature droid went on, "if the sphere he indicated represents the moon Yavin 4, where we are now."

"Right," said Jaina. "The gas planet Yavin has more than a dozen moons, but I haven't managed to program them all in yet. What I mainly wanted to see," she continued, "was the trajectory we're going to follow when Lando takes us to his gem-mining station in the upper atmosphere of Yavin."

Lowie growled a comment, and Jaina waited impatiently while the prissy translator droid interpreted for her.

"Of course it's a *bit* dangerous," she responded, rolling her brown eyes in exasperation, "but not much. And this is too good an opportunity to pass up. Lando's going to let us help with some of the mining operations, not just watch," Jaina said, pointing to a spot just above the glowing surface of Yavin.

Lowbacca reached for the holoprojector's input pad and pressed a few buttons. In a moment a tiny metallic-looking object appeared near the surface: GemDiver Station.

"Show-off," Jaina said, chuckling at the speed with which Lowie had programmed the holo map. "Tell you what, from now on I build 'em, you program 'em—fair enough?"

Lowie pretended to preen, rumbling his agreement as he smoothed his hand along the black streak that ran through his fur from his forehead down his back.

Just then Jacen bounded through the door. "They're here," he said breathlessly. "I mean *almost* here. They're on approach. I was in the control room and I heard that the *Lady Luck* was coming in." Twin pairs of eyes—each the color of Corellian brandy—met in a mixture of excitement and anticipation.

"Well, then," Jaina said, "what are we waiting for?"

Jaina watched with admiration as Lando Calrissian strode down the ramp of the *Lady Luck,* an emerald-green cape billowing out behind him and a broad smile on his dark, handsome face. His frequent companion, the bald cyborg assistant Lobot, followed him down the gangplank and stood stiffly at his side.

Lando greeted Jaina with a gallant kiss on the hand before turning with a formal bow to her twin brother Jacen and Lowie. Next, he clapped the shoulder of Luke Skywalker, who had come to meet the *Lady Luck,* his barrel-shaped droid Artoo-Detoo following close behind him.

"Take good care of them, Lando," Luke said. "No unnecessary risks, okay?" Artoo added a few beeps and whistles of his own.

Lando looked at Luke, pretending to take offense. "Hey, you know I wouldn't let these kids do anything I didn't think was a safe bet."

Luke grinned and gave Lando's shoulder an affectionate slap. "That's what I'm afraid of."

"You're just worried that once they see my GemDiver Station they'll be so impressed they won't want to come back to your Jedi academy," Lando joked.

Then, with a flourish of his cape, Lando Calrissian motioned Lowie and Jacen up the ramp. He turned to Jaina. "And what can I do to make this field trip more interesting and rewarding for you, young lady?" he asked, offering her his arm to escort her into the ship.

"The first thing you can do," she said, accepting his arm with an enthusiastic smile, "is tell me all about the *Lady Luck*'s engines. . . ."

2

THE *LADY LUCK* left the jewel-green jungle moon behind as Lando Calrissian and his trusted companion Lobot piloted them across space toward the gaseous ball of Yavin.

"You kids should enjoy this," Lando said. "I don't think you've seen anything quite like Corusca mining before."

As the *Lady Luck* approached the giant planet, the orbiting industrial station came into view. Lando's Corusca-mining facility, GemDiver Station, was a symphony of running lights and transmitting grids surrounded by dozens of automated defensive satellites. The security satellites homed in on the *Lady Luck,* powering up weapons as the ship approached. But when Lando keyed in an access authorization code, the satellites acknowledged his signal, then turned back to their robotic perimeter search for intruders and pirates.

"Can't have too much security," he said, "not when you're dealing with something as valuable as these Corusca gems."

Lobot, the bald, computer-enhanced human, continued his cool surveillance of the controls. Lights on the mechanical apparatus implanted on the back of Lobot's skull flashed and blinked as he studied the guidance grid and compass. Piloting smoothly, Lobot brought the *Lady Luck* into the main docking bay on GemDiver Station.

"I'm glad Luke let you come up here," Lando said, glancing back at Jacen, Jaina, and Lowie. "You can't learn everything about the universe just by sitting in the jungle and lifting rocks off the ground with your mind." He flashed a grin. "You need to broaden your horizons—learn about the way commerce works in the New Republic. That'll give you some useful knowledge, in case your lightsabers ever fail."

"We don't have lightsabers yet," Jacen said dejectedly.

"Then you might as well learn something useful in the meantime," Lando answered. Seeing Jacen's frustration, he added, "You know, your uncle Luke is concerned about your safety. He can be pretty cautious, but I trust his judgment. Don't worry, you'll get that lightsaber eventually. I bet if you just relax and stop thinking about it, you'll be practicing with a lightsaber before you know it." That said, he helped Lobot finish the landing check as the *Lady Luck* settled down in the empty bay.

Stepping out of the ship, Lando beamed and showed off his station, making enthusiastic gestures. With Lobot trailing silently behind, Lando led the three young Jedi Knights to a transparisteel viewing window that looked out at the tempestuous orangish soup of the gas giant.

Jacen pressed close to the broad window, peering down at the knotted storm systems that chained through the clouds. From this distance Yavin looked deceptively gentle in pastel yellows and whites and oranges. But he knew that even in the upper atmosphere, the winds had crushing strength, and the pressure farther down was enough to squash a ship down to a fistful of atoms.

Beside him, Jaina studied the weather patterns analytically. Lowie stood between the twins, his lanky form towering over them. He growled with amazement.

"I think it's most impressive," Em Teedee said from the clip on Lowie's belt. "And Master Lowbacca thinks so too."

GemDiver Station orbited just at the fringe of Yavin's outer atmosphere. The station's inclined orbit took it high above the planet and then dipped down to graze the gaseous levels so that Lando's Corusca gem miners could delve into the planet's deep, swirling currents.

Lando tapped his fingertip against the transparisteel window. "Far down where the atmosphere ends, the metallic core scrapes against the liquefied air. Pressures are great enough to crush elements together into extremely rare quantum crystals called Corusca gems."

Jacen perked up. "Can we see one?"

Lando thought for a moment, then nodded. "Sure. We've got a shipment ready to go out," he said. "Follow me."

With his emerald cape flowing behind him, Lando strode down the scrubbed-clean corridors. Jacen stared at the metal bulkheads, the chambers, the computer-lined offices.

The walls were smooth plasteel plates painted in soft colors and embroidered with glowing optical tubes in a variety of designs. In the background Jacen heard the faint whispering noises of forests, oceans, rivers. The soothing colors and gentle sounds made GemDiver Station an attractive place, comfortable and pleasant—not at all what he had expected.

As they approached a set of large armored doors, Lando tapped buttons in his wristlink and turned to Lobot. "Request access to security level."

Lobot mumbled something into a microphone at his collar. The sealed metal doors hissed, then slid aside to reveal an airlock chamber, the far side of which was an insulated portal providing access to open space. Four armored, conical projectiles lay on a rack; each module was only about a meter long and bristled with self-targeting lasers.

"These are the automated cargo pods," Lando said. "Because Corusca gems are so valuable, we have to take extra security precautions."

Several multiarmed droids worked busily beside the first cargo pod, an open module padded with thick insulation. The droids' copper exoskeletons gleamed, as if newly polished.

"They're packing up our next shipment. Let's take a look," Lando said.

The companions peered into the small opening of the cargo pod, where a nimble-fingered copper droid had packed four Corusca gems, each no larger than Jacen's thumbnail. Lando reached in and plucked out one of the gems.

The droid flailed its multiple hands in the air. "Excuse me, excuse me!" it said. "Please do not touch the gems. Excuse me!"

"It's all right," Lando said. "It's me, Lando Calrissian."

The copper droid's flailing ceased abruptly. "Oh! Apologies, sir," it said.

Lando shook his head. "I've got to get those optical sensors replaced."

He held the Corusca gem between thumb and forefinger; it glinted like liquid fire in his grasp. It did more than just reflect light from the glowpanels on the ceiling—the Corusca gem seemed to contain its own miniature furnace, its trapped light bouncing around inside the crystalline facets for ages until by sheer probability some of the photons found their way out.

"Corusca gems have been found in no other place in the galaxy," Lando said, "only the core of Yavin. Of course, prospectors keep searching other gas-giant planets, but for now my mining station is where all Corusca gems come from. A long time ago the Empire had a sanctioned station here. It went bankrupt pretty quickly without Imperial price supports, though. Corusca mining is a hazardous job, you know, with a high investment right from the start—but it's really paying off for me."

He let Jacen, Jaina, and Lowie hold the gem and marvel at its beauty. "Corusca gems are the hardest substance known," he said. "They can slice through transparisteel like a laser goes through Sullustan jam."

The nervous packing droid plucked the gem from Lowbacca's hairy hand and replaced it in the cargo pod, packing extra sealant around the stones before it closed the access port. The droid engaged a sequence of controls on the back of the cargo pod, and the bristling spines of self-targeting lasers raised themselves up to their armed position.

"Cargo pod ready for launch," the copper droid said. "Please leave the launching bay."

Lando ushered the three kids out of the room, and the heavy metal doors sealed behind him as the droids scurried about their tasks. "Over here. We can watch through the outer port," he said. "This cargo pod is a hyperspace projectile targeted to my broker on Borgo Prime, who distributes the Corusca gems for a percentage of the profits."

They pressed together at a thick round window that looked away from the planet out into space. As they watched, the cargo pod shot out of the launching bay, then hovered to reorient itself and adjust its coordinates. The bright light of its thrusters traced a line across the blackness of space.

Satellites around GemDiver Station rotated as their sensors tracked the pod, aiming their own weapons; but the cargo pod apparently sent the proper ID signals, and the defensive satellites left it alone. Then, in a blur of motion, the pod streaked forward, flashing into hyperspace with a wealth of Corusca gems in its belly.

"Hey, Lando, can we help you do some of the gem mining?" Jacen asked.

"Yes, we'd like to see how it's done," Jaina added.

"I don't know . . . ," Lando said. "It's tough work, and a little risky."

"So is training to be a Jedi Knight," Jaina pointed out, "as we've already seen. Don't you think learning is worth a bit of risk?"

Lowbacca growled a comment.

"What do you mean you're willing to take the risk?" Em Teedee said. "Dear me, I believe Master Calrissian was actually emphasizing the hazards in the hope that you would *not* want to go."

"Well, we'd like to go anyway," Jacen piped up.

Lando held up a hand, grinning as if he had just thought of something—though Jacen could sense that he had been planning it all along. "Well, maybe it *is* time I got back to doing some real work around here instead of all this management stuff. All right, I'll take you down myself."

To Jacen, the Submersible Mining Environment looked like a large diving bell. Its hull was thickly armored, a dull gray with oily smears of color that reflected weirdly in the lights. The hatch appeared thick and durable enough to withstand turbolaser fire.

"This is called the *Fast Hand*," Lando said, "a little ship we designed exclusively for going to the greatest depths of Yavin 4. It's gone almost all the way to the core, where we can reach the biggest Corusca stones." He ran his fingers over the oily hull plating.

"The *Fast Hand* is covered with a fine skin of quantum armor," Lando said, awe apparent in his voice, "a little something developed by the Empire. But we turned the military applications to our own uses—the ultimate in commercial spinoff technology." Lando sounded as if he were giving a speech to a board of directors, and then he remembered his audience. "Well, never mind. The armor on this baby is strong enough to withstand even the pressures deep in Yavin's core. We'll be lowered down, connected to GemDiver Station by an energy tether—like an unbreakable magnetic rope."

"Not even the storms can snap it?" Jaina asked.

Lando spread his hands wide, dismissing her concern. "We might get jostled around a bit, but . . ." He laughed. "The seats are padded. We'll be okay."

Lowbacca stooped, but still banged his head on the low doorway as he climbed into the diving bell. Jacen and Jaina jumped in after him. As Lando followed them into the *Fast Hand*, he pulled the hatch shut.

He rapped his knuckles against the inside wall with a metallic thump. "Safe and sound," he said, then settled into the cushioned seat in front of the piloting controls. Jacen strapped into the copilot's chair beside him, while Jaina and Lowie took the rear seats. Thick, square windows covered the walls and floor, giving them a view no matter which way they looked.

"Oh my, isn't this exciting?" Em Teedee said. Lowie grunted in agreement.

3

LANDO KEYED IN some instructions on the control panel. "I'm telling Lobot we're ready for departure."

Red lights flashed on the bay walls, signaling the *Fast Hand*'s status as it prepared for release into Yavin's atmosphere. Three technicians trotted out of the room, and the airlock doors sealed behind them.

"Hang on," Lando said.

The floor beneath the *Fast Hand* slid away. Jacen's stomach lurched as the armored diving bell fell from GemDiver Station, down into the swirling fury of gases. Lowie yelped in sudden astonishment. Jacen's pulse raced. Jaina gripped the arms of her seat.

The *Fast Hand* hurtled downward, but soon Jacen sensed their descent stabilizing, slowing, becoming more controlled.

"I can feel the energy tether holding us," Jaina said.

Jacen reached out with his Jedi senses and detected a shimmering cool thread that connected them to the orbiting station high above. Eager and interested, he unclasped his crash restraints and looked out the nearest windowport as the roiling clouds rushed closer, slamming toward them.

Jacen saw a fleet of tiny ships like agricultural drones skimming across the tops of the rising gases. The small ships hauled a glowing golden web behind them, like a faint net dragged through the clouds.

"What are those?" Jaina asked, curious as always about how things worked.

"Contractors of mine," Lando said. "Corusca fishermen. They take a fleet of skiffs along the cloud tops, trailing an energy seine behind them. As they fly through the clouds, the energy differential in the net reacts to the presence of tiny Corusca stones. They pick up only smaller stones and Corusca dust. It may not seem like much, but it's still quite valuable and worth the effort.

"I help support their operation, and they give me a percentage of their catch. But the larger Corusca gems are deeper down. The great pressures near the core always made it impossible to mine those big gemstones, but with this new quantum armor, we can take the *Fast Hand* all the way down."

"Well, what are we waiting for?" Jaina asked.

"Right. Let's go," Jacen said, rubbing his hands together. Then he flashed a mischievous grin. "Hey, Lando, I heard two droids talking the other day. The first one said, 'Well, did you beat the Wookiee at sabacc?' and the second one said—"

"—'Yes, but it cost me an arm and a leg,'" Lando finished. "That's an old joke, kid."

Jacen frowned at first, then giggled. "Maybe that's why Tenel Ka didn't laugh at it."

Jaina looked at her brother. "I don't think that's the reason she didn't laugh."

The diving bell continued its descent. Lando plied the controls, unreeling the energy tether. As the dense organic mists and colored aerosols folded around them, the winds became gentle fingers drumming against the walls, growing louder and more insistent.

The storm systems increased in fury. Bolts of blue lightning shot across the murky sky as far as Jacen could see. Static electricity crawled over the outer hull like jagged caterpillars, sparking and snapping against the connecting point of the energy tether.

Lowie uttered a long and concerned-sounding sentence in Wookiee language, and his translator droid piped up. "A good question, Master Lowbacca. What *does* happen if the energy tether is severed? How would we get back?"

"Oh, we've got life-support supplies aboard," Lando said, waving his hand again. "We could survive quite a while down here until a rescue mission was mounted from GemDiver Station. We have communications and energy backups—but it won't happen, don't worry."

As if to disagree with him, an unexpected gust of wind slapped them sideways so that Jacen tumbled from his seat. He pulled himself back up and sheepishly refastened his crash webbing.

Suddenly the *Fast Hand* seemed to snap free from its connecting line. They dropped like a cannonball, plunging and plunging for a full ten seconds. Lowie yowled, and Jacen and Jaina cried out. Lando pumped up the energy levels until finally he managed to reconnect the tether.

"See? No problem," he said with a nonchalant grin, but Jacen could see the beads of sweat on Lando's forehead. "You all might want to tighten your crash webbing, though," he said. "These storms make for some hefty turbulence in the lower atmosphere. That's what stirs up the interface level and gives the Corusca gems a nudge. Once we get a little lower, we'll start hunting."

"I'd like to try my hand at it," Jaina said.

"I'll let you each have a turn at the controls, but I should warn you that Corusca gems are very rare, even down here. Don't expect to find anything."

Jacen asked, "If we're at the controls and we find a Corusca gem, can we keep it?"

Lando smiled indulgently. "Well, I suppose . . . but we can't spend a lot of time down here looking for gems."

"Oh, we won't," Jacen said. "But it's still good to have some incentive."

Lando laughed. "Just like your father," he said. Jacen smiled, thinking of all the times Lando Calrissian and Han Solo had worked with each other—or in competition against each other—over the years of their long friendship.

Lando looked at his controls again and opened up more window panels on the floor so they could see the murky gases beneath them, supercharged with energy.

"This is probably good enough," Lando said. "Let's start fishing." He glanced at the chronometer on his wrist. "We really need to head back up soon." He swallowed, and Jacen sensed just how nervous Lando really was to be down this far. Daredevil gem hunters willing to risk their lives for the fabulously expensive Corusca stones usually did all the deep dives.

The *Fast Hand* had gone so far into the planetary atmosphere that by now the winds were dark around them, so dense that even light from Yavin's sun could not penetrate. Lando clicked on the diving bell's spotlights, and cones of creamy light struggled against the battering storms and whirling gases.

"I'm going to deploy our trolling cables," Lando said. "They're electromagnetic ropes that dangle down to catch flying Corusca gems whipped up by the storms. You can each have only a few minutes, because we need to get back up to the station. These storm systems are getting worse."

The storms hadn't seemed to be getting worse at all to Jacen; they had been bad enough to begin with. But the tension apparent on Lando's face made Jacen want to end their expedition quickly as well.

"Lowbacca, why don't you try first?" Lando suggested. "Come up front and take the controls."

The young Wookiee crouched in a seat that was far too small for him and rested his hands on the multiple joysticks of the controls. He directed the dangling, sizzling energy cables that trailed out like magnetic tentacles through the stormy atmosphere.

Jacen unbuckled his crash webbing again and crawled along the floor to peer through the square portholes. He could see the yellow magnetic whips that extended from the *Fast Hand* raking through the gaseous clouds, but catching nothing.

After a few moments, Lowie groaned in frustration. Em Teedee said, "Master Lowbacca wishes to offer someone else a turn." Lowie relinquished the controls to Jaina, who sat down with focused concentration, the tip of her tongue wedged between her lips at the corner of her mouth. Her eyes, golden-brown pools that stared into nothingness, fell half-closed as she worked the controls. Jacen watched the energy lines writhe below, sifting through the clouds, searching.

"Now, don't get disappointed," Lando said. "I told you it's still hard work to find even one gem. They're quite rare. If they weren't, they wouldn't be so valuable."

Jaina continued to search for a few minutes longer, then gave up. Jacen climbed to his feet and came forward, struggling to keep his balance in the gale-force winds. He caught the arm of the chair and pulled himself into it, letting his hands wrap around the controls.

As he tugged on the joysticks he could feel the response from the lashing energy cables, groping about like nimble fingers sifting through sand to find gold. He reached out with his mind, concentrating as Jaina had, using what he knew of Jedi powers to search for the precious gems. He didn't know what a Corusca stone would *feel* like, but he expected he would know if he encountered one. The whirling clouds seemed empty, thick with useless gases and crushed debris, nothing of interest.

His twin sister sat behind him, and he could feel her hoping for his success. Just as he was about to give up, Jacen suddenly felt a flash, a glint in his mind. He nudged the joysticks sideways, stretching out the long electrical fingers, searching, extending them as far as they would reach. With one lightning tip he scratched through the clouds, stretching, *stretching* . . . and finally he snagged the glimmer in his mind.

The control panels lit up. "I got one!" he cried.

Lando looked as shocked as anyone else. "You did!" he said. "Okay, let's bring it in fast. Time to go."

Lando took over and reeled the magnetic tentacles back into the *Fast Hand,* pulling in the catch. As he stabilized the energy tether again, Lando opened a small access port in the floor and pulled up a durasteel cargo box rimed with frost. He withdrew an irregular but beautiful Corusca gem, larger than the one he had shown them earlier. It flashed with trapped fire.

Breathlessly, Jacen took it from Lando, cradling it in the palms of his hands. "Look what I got!" he said.

Jaina and Lowie offered their congratulations. Lando, knowing he had promised to give the prize to the kids, shook his head in grudging admiration. "Keep that safe, Jacen," Lando said. "That's enough to buy half a city block on Coruscant, I bet."

"It's worth *that* much?" Jacen ran his fingers along the smooth, incredibly hard surface of the gem. "What if I lose it?" he said.

"Put it in your boot," Jaina said. "You know you never lose things there."

"I will," Jacen agreed. "I think I'll give it to mother for her next birthday."

Lando slapped his forehead. "Even Han never gave Leia something that valuable! Almost makes me wish I had a couple of kids," he muttered. "All right, let's head back up."

As if to encourage him, another fist of wind slammed the side of the *Fast Hand* and sent them spinning. Jacen fumbled with his Corusca gem, nearly dropped it on the floor, then caught it again and clutched it in his fist. He immediately tucked it into his boot, where he wouldn't have to worry about it falling out.

His forehead still furrowed with anxiety, Lando Calrissian reeled in the energy tether, hauling the *Fast Hand* back toward the safer levels of Yavin's atmosphere.

The storms tossed them around. Once they heard a loud *spang* against the quantum-armored hull. Lando yelped and looked over at the wall. "Another one! Jaina, get over there and check that seal," he said.

"What happened?" Jacen asked.

On her knees, Jaina scuttled over to check. "Looks like it's okay," she said.

"What was it?" Jacen insisted. He saw the tiniest dent on the inside, but sensed no leaking atmosphere.

"We just got hit by a Corusca gem thrown at high speed by these winds. It's like a projectile weapon striking us, and only the quantum armor saved us. I can't believe this luck." Lando shook his head. "I spend hours and hours looking for those gems on my own and come up empty-handed. But when I bring you down here, Jacen snatches one right away, and then we get hit by another as we're heading back up top."

Lowie bellowed a comment, and Em Teedee said, "I fervently agree with Master Lowbacca: Let's hope we don't encounter any more of them."

Lightning bolts flashed around the hull, sparking blue light into the murky clouds. But as they rose higher toward the safety of GemDiver Station, the storm winds grew calmer, less insistent. Lando relaxed visibly.

When they finally rose back into the glittering GemDiver Station, and the floor sealed beneath them, Lando heaved a sigh of relief and slumped down in the pilot's chair.

The pressure bay refilled with atmosphere, and Lando flicked the controls to unseal the armored hatch. "There. We're back safe and sound," he said, climbing out on unsteady legs. "I think that's enough adventures for now. How about we relax and get something to eat?"

Lando had barely finished making the suggestion, though, when the sudden wailing of station alarms screeched across the intercom systems.

"Now what is it?" Lando asked. "What's going on?"

The three young Jedi Knights jumped out of the *Fast Hand* and followed Lando as he ran to a comm station on the wall. "This is Lando Calrissian. Give me a status update."

"An unidentified fleet just appeared out of hyperspace," came the tense voice of a station security chief. "They refuse our hails and are heading toward GemDiver Station at great speed, intent unknown." The voice clicked off.

Jacen and Jaina ran toward one of the viewports and looked out into the darkness of space. Then Jacen saw the ships, like a swarm of meteors, streaking in their direction. Somehow he sensed they were powering on their weapons—up to no good. He gulped.

"Looks like an Imperial fleet to me," Jaina said.

4

LANDO RUSHED TOWARD the control bridge of GemDiver Station. "Come on, kids. Follow me!" he shouted.

Jaina took the lead while Lowie and Jacen followed at a run. Lowie's long Wookiee legs nearly made him plow over Lando in his haste. "Oh, *do* be careful, Lowbacca!" Em Teedee called.

Taking a turbolift to the upper observation tower, they bustled onto the control bridge, a cylindrical turret that protruded above the main armored body of GemDiver Station. Narrow rectangular windows encircled the control room, allowing a full view in all directions. The glowing diagnostic screens directly below each viewport flashed alarm warnings. Lando's armed guards ran about, strapping additional weapons to their belts, preparing to defend the station.

"We are under attack, sir," Lobot murmured in his quiet, difficult-to-hear voice. The cyborg was a blur of motion, hands darting from keyboard to keyboard, eyes scanning the screens around him and silently assessing details. The lights on the computer implants at the sides of his head flashed like fireworks.

Lando scanned the narrow observation ports and saw the fleet of ships coming in from deep space. "Do you think they're pirates?" he asked. Then to the twins and Lowie, he said reassuringly, "Don't worry. We've got station security on alert. These people don't have a chance against our defenses."

Jaina studied one of the diagnostic screens, pursing her lips. She shook her head. "Not just pirates," she said, recognizing some of the ships by the ellipsoid shape of their main body, engine turrets swept back like jagged wings on top and bottom. "Imperial craft. The four on the outside are Skipray blastboats, each fully equipped with three ion cannons, proton torpedo launcher, concussion missiles, and two fire-linked laser cannons."

Lando seemed startled. "Yeah, that's right."

She looked calmly up at his surprised expression. "Dad had me study a lot of ships. Believe me, these're more than even your security systems could hope to fight."

Lando clapped a hand to his forehead and groaned. "That's not just a pirate fleet, that's an armada! What's the big ship in the middle? I don't recognize it."

In her mind Jaina ran through mechanical specifications of all the ship designs she had learned from her father—but right now she was at a loss.

"Some kind of modified assault shuttle, maybe?" Jaina said. Through the magnification on the screens they stared as the ships came relentlessly in. "But I don't understand that contraption in the bow."

The mysterious assault shuttle had a strange device mounted at its front end, circular and jagged, like the wide-open mouth of a fanged underwater predator.

"Send a distress signal," Lando said to Lobot. "Full spectrum. Make sure *everybody* knows we're under attack here."

With maddening computer-enhanced calm, Lobot shook his bald head. "I've already tried. We're jammed, sir—can't punch a signal through their screens."

"Well, what do they want?" Lando asked in exasperation.

"They've made no demands," Lobot replied. "They refuse to answer our hails. We do not know what they're after."

Jaina stared out the window at the incoming ships and felt cold inside. She shuddered. Jacen squeezed her hand, his forehead wrinkled with anxiety. They had realized the same thing.

"I've got a bad feeling about this," Jacen said. "It's . . . *us* they want, isn't it?"

"Yeah, I can feel it," Jaina said, her voice barely above a whisper. Lowie nodded his shaggy head and groaned in agreement.

"What do you kids mean?" Lando looked at them with disbelief in his large brown eyes. "They *must* be after our Corusca gems—it's the only thing that makes sense."

Jaina shook her head, but Lando was too busy to pay further attention. The four flanking blastboats angled out from the central assault shuttle toward the defensive satellites surrounding GemDiver Station.

"Have you removed the fail-safes from the targeting systems?" Lando asked.

Lobot nodded. "Systems ready to fire," he murmured. High-powered lasers from the defensive satellites lanced out toward the blastboats, but the small satellites could not generate enough power to penetrate the heavy Imperial armor.

Each Skipray blastboat targeted one of the small satellites and unleashed a crackling blur from its ion cannons. The defensive satellites powered up, preparing to fire again, but then all the lights went dead.

"The ion cannons fried the circuits," Lobot announced in his calm voice. "All satellites are off-line."

The Skiprays came in for another strike and fired with laser cannons, this time blasting the defensive satellites into molten metal vapor.

"We've still got the station's armor," Lando said, but now his trembling voice betrayed his lack of confidence.

The modified assault shuttle in the middle of the armada homed in on one of the lower space doors. From the bottom decks of the station came a loud *thump* and *clang* as something large and heavy struck the outer hull—and stayed.

"What are they doing?" Lando asked.

"The modified assault shuttle has attached itself to the outer wall of GemDiver Station," Lobot reported.

"Where?"

The bald cyborg checked readings. "One of the equipment bays. I think they're trying to force their way in."

Lando waved his hand in dismissal. "Well, they can knock but they can't come in." He smiled nervously. "Just keep all the airlocks sealed. Our station armor should hold."

"Excuse me," Jaina said, "but I may have figured out what that modification is. I think they plan to bore through the station walls. The jagged things we saw looked like teeth—so I'm guessing they cut through metal."

"Not *this* metal." Lando shook his head. "The station wall is double-armored. Nothing could cut through it."

Jacen spoke up. "I thought you said Corusca gems could cut through anything."

Lando shook his head again. "Sure, but that would take a whole shipment of industrial-grade Corusca gems." Then he stopped, eyes widening. "Well, uh, we *have* shipped some industrial-grade gems since we upgraded our operations."

He picked up a comlink and spoke into it. "This is Lando Calrissian. All security details go to lower equipment bay number"—he leaned over Lobot's shoulder to look at the screen—"number thirty-four. Full armor and weapons. We're about to be boarded by hostile forces."

Lando took a blaster pistol from the sealed armory case inside the bridge deck. He turned to Lobot. *"Nobody* boards my station without my permission." He started down the corridor, calling over his shoulder as he ran. "You kids find a safe place, and stay there!"

So of course the young Jedi Knights followed him.

Station guards in padded, dark blue uniforms sprinted from corridor intersections. The pastel colors and nature sounds of GemDiver Station seemed oddly out of place, no longer soothing amid the chaos of defensive preparations and the turmoil of screeching alarms.

By the time they reached lower equipment bay 34, a squad of station guards had already set up their position behind storage containers and supply modules, blaster rifles drawn and aimed at the wall.

Jaina heard a whining, gnawing sound that made her teeth vibrate. A circular section of the outer wall glowed, and she could imagine the assault shuttle on the other side, linked to GemDiver Station like a huge battle-ready brine-eel, chewing its way through the station armor.

A bright white line appeared in the circle as a Corusca tooth bit through the thick plate. Jaina hoped belatedly that the attacking ship's seal against the station was airtight.

One of Lando's station guards, keyed up with overwhelming tension, let off two shots from his blaster rifle. The bolts spanged against the wall and left a discolored blotch on the inner hull, but the jaws of the boring machine continued to chew through the plates.

In a flash, with a puff of steam and the *crump* of small, shaped explosives, a large disk of the outer hull fell forward into the equipment bay.

Lando's security forces started firing immediately, even before the smoke cleared; but the enemy on the other side did not pause either. Dozens of white-armored Imperial stormtroopers boiled through the hole like a hive of frenzied lizard-ants that Jacen had once kept in his collection of exotic pets. The stormtroopers fired as they charged—using only the curving blue arcs of stun beams, Jaina was relieved to see.

Four stormtroopers went down with smoking holes in their white armor; but more and more poured out of the assault shuttle. The air in the equipment bay was crisscrossed with bright weapons fire.

Looming behind the armed stormtroopers, cloaked in shadows and rising smoke, stood a tall and sinister woman dressed in a black cape with spines on each shoulder. She had flowing ebony hair like the wings of a bird of prey. Despite her growing terror, Jaina saw that the woman's eyes were a striking color, like the violet of iridescent jungle flowers on Yavin 4. Jaina felt her heart clench as if hands of ice had wrapped around it.

The ominous dark woman stepped through the smoldering hole in the wall of GemDiver Station, oblivious to the weapons fire. A faint electric-blue corona of static lightning clung around her like the powerful discharges that had zapped the *Fast Hand* in the atmospheric storms of Yavin.

"Remember—don't harm the children," the woman shouted. Her voice was slow and heavy, but razor-sharp menace edged every word.

At the mention of the children, Lando whirled to see that the twins and Lowie had followed him. "What are you doing here?" he said. "Come on, we've got to get you to safety!" He waved his blaster pistol toward the entryway. Then, as if in afterthought, he turned and fired three more times, catching one of the white-armored stormtroopers full in the chest.

Jacen and Jaina bolted down the corridor. Lowie, needing no further encouragement, bellowed as he ran along.

Lando came charging after. "I guess you were right," he said, panting. "For some reason they *are* after you."

"I'm just a simple droid," Em Teedee wailed. "I certainly hope they don't want me."

A series of muffled explosions erupted behind them, and a shockwave of heat rippled through the station's metal corridors, making the kids stumble.

Lando caught his balance and steadied Jaina. "Turn right," he gasped. "Up here."

They ran. More blaster fire followed them, then a third explosion. Lando clenched his teeth. "This has *not* been a good day," he grumbled.

"I most heartily concur," Em Teedee chimed from Lowie's waist.

"Here! In the shipping chamber." Lando gestured for the three others to stop outside the barricaded door of the launching room where they had seen the cargo pods and the droids packing Corusca gems for automated shipment.

He punched in an access code, but Lando's fingers were trembling. A red light blinked. "ACCESS DENIED." Lando hissed something, then rekeyed the number. This time the light winked green, and the heavy triple doors sighed open. Inside, the two copper-plated droids continued packing the hyperpods. "Excuse me," one droid said, sounding flustered, "would you please discontinue those explosions? The vibrations make it much more difficult for us to process."

Lando ignored the droids as he pushed the kids inside. "We can't get you away from here—those blastboats would come after you before you knew it—but this is the safest place on the station. I'll stand outside and guard the door." He gripped his blaster pistol, feigning confidence.

Lowie growled, obviously wanting to fight; but before Jacen or Jaina could say anything, Lando slapped the emergency panel. The thick doors clanged shut, locking them inside the chamber.

Jacen placed his ear against the thick door and listened, but he could hear only the muffled noises of battle. Lowie, his ginger-colored fur standing on end with battle-readiness, kneaded his big knuckles. Jaina looked around the room for anything to help them fight.

Jacen yelled to the droids, "Hey, is there an armory in here? Do you have any weapons?"

The droids interrupted their packing and swiveled smooth copper heads toward him, optical sensors glowing. "Please do not disturb us, sir," they said, then resumed their tasks. "We have essential work to do."

Outside the door, the sound of gunfire suddenly increased. Jaina pulled Jacen back from the door as she heard Lando shout. The door vibrated with the impact of energy bolts, then everything went quiet. Jaina waited, backing away and looking into her twin brother's brandy-brown eyes. They both swallowed. Lowbacca let out a thin sound like a whimper. The multiarmed droids continued working, undisturbed.

A shower of sparks ran around part of the door as heavy-duty lasers cut into it, slicing away a section.

"D'you suppose you could invent some sort of weapon for us in the next few seconds?" Jacen said.

Jaina racked her brain for inspiration, but her inventiveness failed her.

The door split open, melted and smoking. The security breach set off yet another alarm, but the sounds were pitiful and superfluous in the already-overwhelming noise of the battle for GemDiver Station.

Stormtroopers muscled their way in.

The two packing droids trundled indignantly toward the stormtroopers. "Intruder alert," one of the droids said. "Warning. No unauthorized entry is permitted. You must return to—"

In response, the stormtroopers fired with all their weapons, blasting both copper droids into shards of smoking components that clattered and sparked on the floor.

Jaina saw Lando sprawled unconscious on the floor outside the door, his green cape pooled around him, his right arm extended forward, still grasping the blaster pistol.

The towering dark woman strode in, her violet eyes flashing at the three companions. The stormtroopers leveled blaster pistols at Jacen, Jaina, and Lowbacca.

"Wait!" Jaina said. "What do you want?"

"Do not let them manipulate your minds," the dark woman shouted to the stormtroopers. "Stun them!"

Before Jaina could say anything else, bright blue arcs shot toward her and the others, and they were overcome by a wave of unconsciousness.

Jaina fell into blackness.

5

ON YAVIN 4 TENEL Ka paced the ramparts of the Great Temple that housed Luke Skywalker's Jedi academy. As befitted a warrior of Dathomir, she wore scaled armor that shone as if it had just been polished . . . which it had. Her red-gold hair was caught up in a multitude of ceremonial braids, each decorated with feathers or beads. Her cool gray eyes scanned the leaden skies for any sign of the ship that would bring the dreaded ambassador from her grandmother.

Wind whipped the ornamented braids about her face, and Tenel Ka pushed them away in annoyance. The humid air felt oppressive, charged with menace. Yavin's dry season had ended.

She sensed an uncomfortable tingling in the depths of her mind that told her something was about to happen, as if lightning were about to strike. She sighed. Her grandmother's messengers and diplomats could be as lethal as lightning. . . .

They were not above killing an enemy, or even a friend, to ensure that the successor to the throne of Hapes was the one they most desired to have in power. It was rumored that her grandmother's assassins had murdered Tenel Ka's own uncle, brother to her father, Prince Isolder.

She started in surprise as a raindrop, warm as blood, landed with a splat on her bare arm. Although the air was not cold, she shivered.

Her feelings toward her grandmother were complex: she both admired and despised the older woman. Tenel Ka preferred to dress in the lizard-skin armor of the warrior women of Dathomir, like her mother, rather than in the fine web-silks of the Royal House of the Hapes Cluster.

So far, Tenel Ka had managed to tread a fine line between pleasing and annoying her grandmother. She knew that if she stepped over that line too far, assassins might someday pay her a visit. . . .

A branch of lightning crackled across the ominous sky, followed by a boom of thunder. Atop the temple, Tenel Ka paced like a caged animal, her agitation increasing as she stalked along the edge of the pyramid and wondered why Ambassador Yfra did not come. So great was her turmoil that she didn't even notice that Luke Skywalker had joined her on the observation deck until he stood directly in front of her.

The Jedi Master placed both of his hands on her shoulders and looked into her eyes. Peace and warmth flowed from him, and Tenel Ka felt herself begin to relax. "There's a message in the Comm Center for you," he said quietly. "Would you like me to be present while you speak with the ambassador?"

Tenel Ka could not suppress a shudder of revulsion as she thought of her grandmother's thin-lipped emissary. "Your presence would"—she paused for a moment, searching for words—"honor me, Master Skywalker."

Tenel Ka stood erect, holding her head high as she faced her grandmother's ambassador in the Comm Center viewscreen—an image that for all its apparent cruelty still held traces of proud beauty. Ambassador Yfra's hair and eyes were the color of polished pewter.

"Our meetings on Coruscant took longer than we anticipated, young one," Yfra was saying in a voice that indicated she was not used to being questioned. "Therefore, our meeting with you must be postponed for two days."

Tenel Ka gave no outward sign of her discomposure, but her heart sank. Jacen, Jaina, and Lowbacca were due back long before then. She sent a pleading glance to Luke.

The Jedi Master stepped forward and spoke in a soft voice. "Perhaps I could bring the Princess of Hapes to meet with you on Coruscant?" he offered.

Ambassador Yfra smiled in what Tenel Ka knew was meant to be a kindly fashion, but there was no kindness or conciliation in her eyes. "I have specific orders to observe the heir of Hapes in her place of study."

Tenel Ka opened her mouth to speak, but was spared the necessity when an emergency beacon flashed next to the screen. Luke reacted instantly. "Ambassador Yfra, we have a priority override communication coming in. Please wait," he said, switching the channel before the ambassador had a chance to reply.

The dark face of Lando Calrissian appeared, his handsome features marred by a worried frown. Confusion haunted his bleary eyes. His hair and clothes were disheveled, and warning sirens whooped in the background.

"Luke, buddy," he rasped, "I'm not sure exactly what happened. They . . . fried our security satellites, boarded the station . . . must've stunned us. We're okay, but—" Lando's troubled eyes closed and his jaw tightened, "Jacen, Jaina, and Lowbacca are gone. They've been kidnapped."

Luke drew in a deep breath. Tenel Ka guessed he was using a Jedi calming technique, but with less success than usual. His body appeared relaxed, but his clear blue eyes carried a laser-sharp look. One hand was clenched into a fist at his side. "Who did this?" he asked, his voice terse.

Lando shook his head. "We don't know who has the kids or why, but I've got all my best people working on it. It was someone connected with the Empire, though—that's for sure."

"I'll be there within the hour," Luke said, reaching for the comlink.

"Wait," Tenel Ka said. "These are my friends. I know how they think. I know what they would do. I cannot cower here while they are in danger. Please. I must go with you."

Luke nodded. "Your presence would . . . honor me," he answered, echoing her earlier words. His eyes went back to Lando's image. *"We'll* be there within the hour," he amended, then switched back to the ambassador's comm frequency.

Ambassador Yfra's mouth was open as if she were prepared to protest such rude treatment, but Luke spoke first. "I'm sorry to keep you waiting, Ambassador, but an emergency has come up. It requires both my presence and that of the princess. I'm afraid we must postpone any plans to meet with you until this situation is resolved. Please convey our respectful greetings to the Royal House of Hapes." With a slight bow, he snapped off the comm channel.

Even though she was worried about her friends, a feeling of satisfaction bubbled up within Tenel Ka at the deftness with which Master Skywalker had handled Ambassador Yfra.

Luke looked at Tenel Ka. "I'm sure the ambassador isn't used to being postponed with so little explanation, but we have more important things to do right now."

Tenel Ka nodded emphatically. "This is a fact."

Tenel Ka tried to be impartial and unemotional as Master Skywalker expertly guided the shuttle toward GemDiver Station. She needed to remain unruffled and alert, to search for any clue that might help them recover the three young Jedi—the best friends she'd ever had.

The multicolored lights of the station winked as the docking-bay doors slid open and Luke brought the shuttle in for a landing. At any other time Tenel Ka might have noted her surroundings, the artistry and craftsmanship that had gone into the station's construction—but the moment the shuttle doors opened, she was assailed by a sense of lingering violence and darkness. Of *wrongness*.

Harried and disheveled, Lando Calrissian met them at the shuttle. Motioning for Luke and Tenel Ka to follow, he led them to the sealed shipping bay where the final struggle had occurred.

Tenel Ka swept the chamber with her eyes, noting the blaster burns on the walls and ceiling of the outer corridor, the congealed rivulets of molten plasteel, the shards of broken metal. Then she watched as Luke sank down on one knee, placed both hands against the floor, and let his eyes flutter closed.

"Yes, it happened here," he murmured. He took a few deep breaths, then fixed Lando with the piercing blueness of his gaze. "Don't blame yourself," he said. "You fought well."

Lando's face was filled with regret, and he shook his head. "But it wasn't enough, buddy. I couldn't save them." A note of anger and self-reproach crept into his voice. "I was too busy trying to defend my station—thinking they were pirates come to steal my Corusca gems. I didn't even realize they were after the kids until it was too late."

Luke neither condemned nor pardoned Lando, Tenel Ka noticed. He simply listened.

At last Lando spoke again in a quiet voice. "If there's anything you need to help find them—my station, a ship, a crew . . . anything at all—"

Lando's offer of help was cut short by the arrival of his assistant Lobot, whose computer headset flashed with an ever-changing array of lights. "We finished patching the hull breach in lower equipment bay thirty-four," he said without preamble.

Lando turned to Luke and Tenel Ka, his forehead creasing into an indignant scowl. "They sliced us open like a disposable can of emergency rations."

The bald cyborg nodded in corroboration. "Their equipment was specially designed to remove a section of hull."

Lando continued, "The only thing I know of sharp enough to slice through durasteel that quickly is—"

"Corusca gems," Luke finished for him.

"Industrial grade," Lobot added.

"Right," Lando said morosely. "They used *our own gems* against us."

"Rare and expensive," Lobot said. "Not just anyone could purchase them."

Tenel Ka saw Luke's eyes light with sudden hope. "Can you tell us where your shipments of such gems were sold?"

Lando shrugged. "Like my friend said, industrial-grade gems are fairly rare. We've made only two shipments since our operation opened." He sent a questioning glance at his cyborg assistant.

Lobot pressed a panel on the back of his head and cocked it to one side as if listening to a voice no one else could hear. A moment later he nodded. "Both shipments were sold through our broker on Borgo Prime."

"Can you find out who he sold them to?" Luke asked.

"I doubt it," Lando said. "Gem brokers are pretty skittish. They pay a good percentage, but they're secretive—afraid that if we know who their customers are, we won't need the middlemen anymore."

"Then we must go to Borgo Prime and find out ourselves," Tenel Ka said with fierce determination.

Luke sent her a warm smile, then turned back to Lando. "What is Borgo Prime anyway?"

"An asteroid spaceport and trade center. It's also a hangout for merchants, thieves, murderers, smugglers . . . the dregs of the galaxy." Lando flashed Luke a grin. "A lot like Mos Eisley on Tatooine. You'll feel right at home."

Tenel Ka waited in silence as Master Skywalker faced the screen in GemDiver Station's Communications Center.

Han Solo stood with one arm around his wife, Leia, who was supported on the other side by Lowie's uncle, Chewbacca.

Tenel Ka studied the images on the screen and decided that at this moment Leia Organa Solo looked more like a concerned mother than a powerful politician.

"But Luke, they're *our* children," she was saying. "We can't simply stand by and do nothing if they're in danger."

"Not on your life!" Han said.

"Of course not," Luke agreed quietly. "But as the New Republic's chief of state, you can't afford to put yourself in that same danger. Mobilize your forces. Start an investigation. Send out spies and probe droids. But stay there and act as a central clearinghouse for information."

"All right, Luke," Leia said. "We'll work from Coruscant for now, but once we've done everything we can from here, we'll go looking for them ourselves."

"I'll come get you in the *Falcon*," Han said.

"Give me ten standard days first," Luke said. "I have a lead I'm going to follow right now before the trail gets cold. We need to get going. We'll keep you informed of our progress."

"We?" Han asked. "Is Lando going with you?"

"No," Luke replied. "The heir of Hapes will honor me with her company," he said, gesturing to Tenel Ka.

"We are grateful for your assistance," Leia said formally.

Tenel Ka nodded toward the screen with a brief, stiff bow. "Jacen, Jaina, and Lowbacca have a greater call on me than honor," she said. "They have my friendship."

Leia's face softened. "Then I owe you my gratitude as a mother as well." Chewbacca rumbled what Tenel Ka could only interpret as an agreement.

"Don't worry, we'll find them," Luke said, his voice filled with urgency. "But we need to leave now."

Han lifted his chin and smiled at Luke. "Okay, get going, kid."

Just before the communications link was broken, Leia spoke again. "And may the Force be with you."

6

JAINA CAME BACK to consciousness with Lowie shaking her shoulders. The lanky Wookiee moaned plaintively until she groaned and woke up, blinking her eyes.

A rush of unpleasant sensations flooded through her: queasy stomach, pounding head, aching joints—aftereffects of the stormtroopers' stun beams. The human body wasn't designed to be knocked out with a blast of energy. Her ears hummed, too, but her instincts told her that the sounds were real—the rumbling vibrations of a big ship in hyperdrive.

Uncertain about whether she dared risk a more vertical position, Jaina cautiously turned her head. She saw that she, Jacen, and Lowbacca were together in a small, nondescript room. Jaina took a deep breath, scratched her straight brown hair, and ran her hands down her grease-smeared jumpsuit to make sure everything was still intact.

Suddenly recalling the attack on GemDiver Station, Jaina sat up so quickly that a fresh wave of nausea washed over her and pain exploded at her temples. She gasped, then forced herself to relax and let some of the pain drain away. "Where are we?" she asked.

Jacen was already sitting up on a narrow pallet, rubbing his brandy-brown eyes and running long fingers through his tousled hair. He wore a look of confusion, and Jaina sensed deep turmoil coming from her brother. "Not a clue," he said.

Lowbacca also made a dismayed, questioning sound.

"Least we're all together," Jaina said. "And they didn't put binders on us." She held up her hands, surprised that the Imperials had not separated their prisoners and tied them up. Water and a food tray lay in an alcove by the wall. From the looks of it, Lowie had already sampled some of the fruit.

"Hey, I wonder what happened to everyone at GemDiver Station. What do you suppose they did to Lando?" Jacen asked.

Jaina shrugged, still feeling queasy. "Saw him lying unconscious just before they stunned us. But I don't think they planned to kill him. They weren't looking for Corusca gems, either. Seems like they only wanted *the three of us.*"

"Yeah . . . kinda makes you feel valuable, huh?" Jacen agreed glumly. Lowie growled.

Jaina stood up and stretched, feeling better as she moved. "Guess I'm okay, though. How about you two?"

Jacen smiled reassuringly, and Lowie nodded his shaggy head. The streak of black fur that swept over his eyebrows bristled with uneasiness. He smoothed the fur back and grunted.

It was then that Jaina noticed something else wrong. She looked down at the Wookiee's waist, but the miniaturized translating droid was no longer there.

"Lowie! What happened to Em Teedee?"

Lowie made a strange, sad sound and patted his waist.

"Imperials must've taken it from him," Jaina said. "What do they want?"

"Oh, just to take over the galaxy, cause a bunch of problems . . . hurt a lot of people—you know, the usual," Jacen answered flippantly. He went over to the flat metal door. "Hmmmm . . . it's probably locked, but there's no harm in trying," he said, tapping the controls with his fingers.

To Jaina's surprise, the door hummed sideways to reveal a guard standing at attention just outside. A stormtrooper in a skull-like white helmet turned to face them.

"Whoa!" Jacen cried, then he lowered his voice. "Well, at least the door opens."

"Maybe they just can't figure out how to lock the door," Jaina said. "Remember how clunky and unreliable Imperial technology is." She let sarcasm seep into her voice for the guard's benefit. "And you know how lousy stormtrooper armor is. Probably couldn't even stop a water blaster."

"Just walk past him," Jacen suggested in a stage whisper, seeing that the stormtrooper hadn't moved. "Maybe he won't stop us."

The stormtrooper shouldered his blaster rifle. "Wait here." The filtered voice coming through the white helmet was flat, but somehow menacing. The guard spoke quietly into his helmet comlink, then shut the three young Jedi Knights in their cell again.

They sat in anxious silence for a moment. "We could tell jokes," Jacen suggested.

Before Jaina could think of an appropriate answer, the cell door whisked open again. This time, beside the stormtrooper stood the towering, sinister woman from the assault on GemDiver Station. Jaina took a quick breath.

The tall woman's black hair flowed like waves of darkness down her shoulders, and her ebony cape sparkled with bits of polished gems, swirling around her like a starry night sky. Her violet eyes blazed in a face so pale it seemed carved from polished bone. Her lips were a dark wine color, as if she had just eaten an overripe fruit. The woman was beautiful—in a cruel sort of way.

"So, Jedi Knights, you are awake at last," she snapped. Her voice was deep and thick, without the hissing edge Jaina had expected. "I must begin by saying how *disappointed* I am in you. I had hoped for more resistance from such powerful students already trained in the Force. Your Jedi defenses were pitiful! But we shall change that. You will be taught new ways. Effective ways."

The woman spun on one heel, and her black cloak swept around her like trailing smoke. "Follow me," she said, and stepped into the corridor.

"No," Jaina responded. "Who do you think you are? Why have you brought us here against our will?"

"I said *follow!*" the woman repeated. When they made no move to comply, she pointed her polished nails at them and twitched her fingers.

Suddenly, it felt as if a resilient invisible cord had wrapped around Jaina's throat. The woman crooked her finger, yanking at Jaina as if she were a pet on a leash. Jaina lurched as the invisible rope hauled her out of the cell.

Lowbacca and Jacen strained against similar bonds of Force, the Wookiee yowling his defiance. Despite their struggles, all three children were dragged on Force leashes tripping and stumbling into the corridor.

"I can do this all the way to the bridge, if you like," the woman said, her deep red lips curved into a mocking smile. "Or, you can save your energies for more productive resistance later."

"All right," Jaina croaked, sensing that this woman had dark Jedi powers she could not match—at least not yet.

When the Force bonds dropped away, the companions stood gasping and trembling. They looked at each other in angry humiliation, knowing they were beaten.

Jaina was the first to recover. Swallowing hard, she stood straight, put her chin in the air, and followed the woman in black. Her brother and Lowie fell in behind Jaina. "Who are you?" Jaina asked after a while.

The woman paused in midstep, as if considering, then answered. "My name is Tamith Kai. I am from a new order of Nightsisters."

"Nightsisters? You mean like on Dathomir?" Jacen asked.

Jaina remembered the stories their friend Tenel Ka told when it was her turn to scare them before they practiced Jedi calming techniques—stories of the horrible evil women who had once twisted civilization on her world.

Tamith Kai looked at Jacen, her wine-dark lips set in something between a scowl and a smile. "You've heard of us? Good. My planet is rich in Force-wielders, and the Empire has helped to bring us back. Now perhaps you'll realize you can't resist. Cooperation, on the other hand, will be rewarded."

"We won't cooperate with you," Jaina challenged.

"Yes, yes," Tamith Kai said, as if bored. "All in good time."

"Hey, where are you taking us?" Jacen asked, walking quickly to keep pace with his sister. Lowie strode behind them, grumbling and fumbling at his waist as if he actually missed Em Teedee.

"You'll see soon enough," the Nightsister said. "We are almost ready to leave hyperspace."

All four of them stepped onto a lift platform that carried them up a level and opened out onto the bridge of the fleeing ship. The single pilot sat with his back to them in a padded high-backed chair, hunched over the controls. Ahead, through the bridge viewports Jaina could see the swirling colors of hyperspace.

The pilot reached out with his right hand and grabbed a lever as a countdown trickled to zero. Then he yanked the lever, and hyperspace suddenly unfolded, washing away into the star-studded darkness of normal space.

"We're near the Core Systems," Jaina said immediately, looking out at the rich starfields and the streamers of interstellar gas clotted together near the center of the galaxy.

The crowded Core Systems were the last bastions of Imperial power; not even New Republic forces had been able to flush them out completely. But they had arrived nowhere close to any system. They found themselves merely hanging, out in the middle of the star-strewn blackness.

"We have reached our destination, Tamith Kai," the pilot said, swiveling in his tall chair.

Jaina's heart leaped as she recognized the weary, hard-bitten face and iron-gray hair of the former TIE pilot who had been stranded on Yavin 4 for so many years.

"Qorl!" Jacen exclaimed.

Lowie roared in anger.

Qorl had attacked them in the jungles when the young Jedi Knights had found his crashed TIE fighter and tried to fix it. The Imperial pilot had shot at Lowie and Tenel Ka, who had managed to escape into the undergrowth, but Qorl had taken Jacen and Jaina prisoner.

"Greetings, young friends. I never did thank you for fixing my ship and allowing me to return to my Empire."

"You betrayed us!" Jaina cried, feeling a surge of anger toward the brainwashed man. While being held captive, the twins had befriended Qorl, exchanging stories with him around the campfire. Jaina had felt sure the TIE pilot was softening, realizing that the ways of the Empire were filled with lies. But in the end, Qorl's military conditioning had been too strong.

"I returned as any soldier would and gave my report," Qorl said in a dull voice. "These people accepted me and . . . reindoctrinated me. I told them of your existence—powerful young Jedi Knights just waiting to be trained to serve the Empire."

"Never," Jaina and Jacen snapped in unison, and Lowbacca agreed with a roar.

Tamith Kai looked down at them mockingly. Standing beside Qorl, the dark-haired woman seemed even taller than before, more intimidating than ever. "Your anger is good," she said. "Fuel it. Let it grow. We will use it when your training begins. But for now . . . we have reached our destination."

Lowie gave a growl of disbelief.

Jaina looked out the front viewports, trying to calm herself. Master Skywalker had said that giving in to anger was a path to the dark side of the Force. She must not lash out, she knew; she must think of some other way to fight back.

"We're in the middle of empty space," Jaina said. "What is there for us to see?"

"Space is not always empty," Tamith Kai said. Her thick voice held a singsong quality, as if her mind was thinking of something else. "Reality is not always what it seems."

At his station Qorl verified the coordinates, then punched in a security code. "Transmitting now," he said.

Tamith Kai turned her sharp violet eyes toward the young Jedi Knights. "You are about to begin a new phase of your lives," she said, pointing to the viewscreens. "Behold."

Space shimmered like a blanket of invisibility peeling away. Suddenly a space station hung in front of them, torus-shaped, like a donut. Weapons emplacements ringed the station's entire perimeter, pointing in all directions, making it look like a spiked disciplinary collar for some ferocious beast. Tall observation towers rose like pinnacles on one side of the station.

Jaina swallowed hard.

"Cloaking device off," Qorl announced.

"Take a good look," Tamith Kai said, but she did not glance at the viewscreens. Her eyes glittered with violet fervor at the children. "Here you'll be trained as Dark Jedi . . . for the Empire."

Qorl spoke up, reminding her. "We must commence docking immediately and reactivate the invisibility shielding."

The Nightsister nodded but did not seem to hear, never taking her eyes off the young Jedi Knights. "Welcome to the Shadow Academy," she whispered.

7

TENEL KA SLID a hand under the crash webbing of the copilot's seat and scratched at the rough-woven, unfamiliar material of her disguise. She wished for the dozenth time that she could wear her comfortable reptilian armor, which was as supple as it was protective and never irritated her skin.

She had been silent, intimidated, through most of the journey to Borgo Prime, unable to bring herself to speak. Beside her sat Master Skywalker—the most famous and revered Jedi in the entire galaxy—calmly and competently piloting the *Off Chance,* an old blockade runner Lando had won in a sabacc game and claimed he no longer needed.

Tenel Ka's grandmother had insisted that the girl's royal training include diplomacy and correct methods of addressing individuals of any rank, species, age, or gender. Though not loquacious, Tenel Ka was also not shy; yet somehow, alone with the impressive Jedi Master in the confines of their tiny cockpit, she could find nothing to say. She tried to think, but her sluggish mind would not cooperate. Weariness clung to her like the sweat-damp clothing she wore. She squirmed in her seat and tried to suppress a nervous yawn.

Luke glanced over at her, a smile at the corners of his mouth. "Tired?"

"Not much sleep," Tenel Ka answered, embarrassed that he had noticed her fatigue. "Bad dreams."

Luke's blue eyes narrowed for a moment, as if he was searching for a memory, but then he shook his head. "I haven't been sleeping well either—but, tired or not, we can't afford to make mistakes. Let's go over our cover story again. Tell me who you are."

"We are traders from Randon. We will avoid using names. But, if we must, you are Iltar and I am your ward-cousin Beknit. We trade in archaeological treasures. We are not above breaking the law to make a profit. We have come from a secret archaeological dig on . . ." She paused for a moment, searching her brain for the name of the planet.

"Ossus," Luke supplied.

"Ah. Aha," Tenel Ka said. "Ossus." She took a deep breath while she etched the name into her mind, then she continued. "On *Ossus*, we discovered a treasure vault, secured with an Old Republic seal. The treasure chamber is set deep into rock and plated with armor so thick that no blaster or laser can pierce it.

"We dare not blast the surrounding rock for fear of destroying the treasure. We've come to Borgo Prime in search of industrial-grade Corusca gems to slice through the armor and open the treasure vault. We are ready to pay handsomely for the right type of gems."

Tenel Ka watched with interest as the dull, lumpy asteroid of Borgo Prime loomed in their forward viewports. The rock had been hollowed out, honeycombed in ages past by generations of asteroid miners who sought one type of mineral, then another as market conditions changed. But more than a century ago, Borgo Prime had been stripped clean of even the least-desirable ore—leaving a spongelike network of interlocked caves, fully equipped with all the life-support systems and transportation airlocks the miners had needed. It had been a simple matter to convert the played-out mine into a bustling spaceport.

Luke transmitted the standard request for clearance to land and received it without difficulty.

"We've been cleared for docking bay ninety-four," Luke said. "Are you ready, uh, Beknit?"

Tenel Ka nodded matter-of-factly. "Of course, Iltar."

Luke studied her for a moment, earnest concern filling his face. "It could be rough down there, you know. You heard what Lando said: Borgo Prime is filled with people who have no conscience—thieves, murderers, creatures who would just as soon kill you as greet you."

"Ah. Aha," Tenel Ka said, raising an eyebrow. "Sounds like a visit to my grandmother's court on Hapes."

The two Randoni traders, "Iltar" and his ward-cousin "Beknit," left their blockade runner in the dockyard cavern behind an immense hangar door and walked along the causeway that joined Borgo Prime's largest space dock to its business district deep in the core of the asteroid.

In spite of her many rehearsals, Tenel Ka found it difficult to remember that she was supposed to be an experienced trader, used to frequenting such spaceports. She gawked openly at the tall rows of prefabricated dwellings welded up and down the inner walls and all the garish flashing lights of the alien businesses in separate atmosphere domes around them.

This place was so different from the primitive, untamed world of Dathomir. Even Hapes with its serene and stately cities—some of them larger than this entire asteroid—bore no resemblance to the spaceport's seedy, gaudily lit establishments, that hummed with a life of their own. Overhead, through the clear arching plasteel that covered a rift in the ceiling, the stars and space were all but obscured by Borgo Prime's glaring lights.

Luke paused beside Tenel Ka, letting her collect her thoughts. "You've never been anyplace like this, have you?" he asked.

She shook her head and started to walk again, searching for words to describe the unsettling emotions. "I feel . . . foolish. Out of place." She scuffed her toes along a causeway surface that was paved with colorful, glowing advertisements.

She paused to read an ad, then another. The first one announced in phosphorescent script that flared into light as she stepped near it,

>BORGO LANDING
>SPACE DOCKS BY THE HOUR OR BY THE MONTH.

The next one said simply

>INFO TO GO
>DISCREET INQUIRIES OF ALL SORTS
>COMPLETELY CONFIDENTIAL.

Tenel Ka shook her head. "I do not understand this place," she said. "It both revolts and . . . entices me at the same time."

"You don't have to go through with this, you know," Luke said. "I could handle it myself."

It was completely true, Tenel Ka realized—an uncomfortable thought. She tossed her head and ran a nervous hand over her hair, which she wore loose, in Randoni style, so that it flowed down her back in a cascade of red-gold ripples like a sun-dappled stream. She tried to look confident, but icy fingers of doubt prodded her mind. "I will do what I must to rescue my friends," she said, her voice as brisk and businesslike as she could make it. "Where is this nest or hive that Lando told us to find?"

Luke pointed to another lighted ad at their feet. "I think we just found it," he said with a pleased expression.

Shanko's Hive
Fine Drinks and Entertainment
All Species, All Ages.

The flat image showed an insectoid barkeeper proffering a dozen drinks with its multijointed, chitinous arms. A row of blinking beacon lights set into the walkway indicated the direction of the "hive."

A sudden bout of stage fright assailed Tenel Ka, but she knew how important it was for them to stay in character. She straightened her clothing, cleared her throat, and looked at Luke. "You must be very thirsty after your long journey, Iltar," she said.

"Yes. Thank you, Beknit," he answered smoothly. "I could use a drink." Then he leaned toward her and asked in a lower voice, "Are you *sure* you want to do this?"

Tenel Ka nodded firmly. "I'm ready for anything."

"I did not expect an establishment quite so large on an asteroid of this size," Tenel Ka said, tilting back her head to look at the rounded ripples of Shanko's cone-shaped Hive, a gray-green edifice sealed in its own atmosphere field. The edifice rose at least a quarter kilometer above the inner floor of Borgo Prime.

Feathery wings of fear and uncertainty fluttered in her stomach, and she paused to draw in a deep breath. To Tenel Ka's great chagrin, a subtle spark of amusement danced in Master Skywalker's eyes. "You know what waits for us in there, don't you?" he asked.

"Thieves," she answered.

"Murderers," he added.

"Liars, scum, smugglers, traitors . . ." Her voice trailed off.

"Almost like family back on Hapes?" he asked with a gentle, teasing smile.

As heir to the Royal Throne of Hapes, Tenel Ka had faced trained assassins, as had her father, Prince Isolder, before her. If she could do that, surely she could handle a little spaceport cantina.

"Thank you," she said, taking the arm he offered. "I am ready now."

Luke slid a pass chit into a small slot in the door. "Let's try to keep a low profile." The door slid open.

The first thing that caught Tenel Ka's eye when she stepped through the door was the insectoid bartender, Shanko, who stood over three meters high.

The room was filled with indescribable odors she could not begin to identify—not actually pleasant, but not quite offensive either. Particulates hung in the air from a multitude of burning objects: pipes, candles, incense, chunks of peat in blazing bog-pits, even clothing or fur from the occasional customer who got too close to one of the fires.

Without speaking, Luke gestured with his chin toward the bar. Even if he had spoken aloud, Tenel Ka could not have heard him above the noise of at least half a dozen different bands playing hit tunes from as many different systems.

Fortunately, they had decided before entering where they should start their inquiries. Knowing that on Randon the female ward-cousin was highly honored—mainly for her potential inheritance—and was always served first, Tenel Ka stepped up to the bar to place her order.

"Welcome travelersssss," Shanko said, folding three pairs of multijointed arms and bowing until his antennaed head nearly touched the bar.

"Your hospitality is as welcome as the prospect of refreshment," Tenel Ka replied.

"Sssso, you have been well ssschooled," Shanko said. "Are you perhapsss a sssscholar? A diplomat?"

"She is my ward-cousin," Luke put in smoothly.

"Then it iss *indeed* an honor to ssserve you," Shanko said, raising himself to his full three-meter height.

"I would like a Randoni Yellow Plague," Tenel Ka said without hesitation. "Chilled. Make it a double."

"And I would like a Remote Terminator," Luke said.

The covering membranes of the bartender's multifaceted eyes nictated twice in surprise. "Not often requesssted. A ssstrong drink, iss it not?" He seemed flustered for a moment, then made a gurgling buzz deep in his thorax that Tenel Ka could only interpret as a laugh. "Will that be preprogrammed or randomizzzed?"

"Randomized, of course," Luke replied.

"Ah, a rissssk taker," Shanko said, tapping two forelegs on the bartop in approval.

Then his arms became a blur of motion as he pulled levers and pushed buttons, filling cups and vials, mixing their drinks in less time than it had taken to order them.

"There is no profit without risk," Luke said, accepting his drink from one of Shanko's many hands.

Tenel Ka leaned forward and lowered her voice. "We seek information," she said, drawing out a small string of Corusca gems that she had kept hidden under the rough material of her robe until then.

Shanko nodded in understanding. "We have the finesssst information brokerss in the Sssector. There iss even a Hutt." He gestured toward an area to the right of the bar. "If you do not find what you sssseek here," he said with obvious pride, "it isss not to be found on Borgo Prime."

They thanked Shanko and headed in the direction he had indicated. The music of the bands faded slightly as they pushed into the milling throng of patrons, each imbibing its favorite form of refreshment. The crowd was so thick, Tenel Ka could not see where they were going.

Beside her, Luke paused and closed his eyes. "A Hutt information broker, huh?" he mused aloud. "They're the best you can get."

Tenel Ka felt a slight tingle as she watched him reach out with the Force to touch the minds around him, searching. She searched, too, but with her gray eyes open. A quick glance revealed nothing of interest. She looked up the open center of the hive's cone and at the curving stairways that climbed its ridged sides, which—judging from the signs on the walls—led to gambling rooms and lodgings.

Luke opened his eyes. "Okay, I have him." He took Tenel Ka's arm and pushed his way through the crowd. They passed a bank of stim lights, where a cluster of photosensitive customers wriggled and bounded to silent strobing "music."

They found the Huttese information broker ensconced behind a low table near the wall of the hive. A small Ranat with gray-brown fur stood at the Hutt's elbow, whiskers twitching. The Hutt was thin by Huttese standards and could not have had much status on his homeworld. Perhaps that was why he did business on Borgo Prime, Tenel Ka thought.

"We have come for information, and we are prepared to pay for it," Luke said without preamble.

The Hutt picked up a small datapad that lay on the table in front of him and punched a few buttons.

"What are your names?" he asked.

"What is *your* name?" Tenel Ka asked, raising her chin slightly.

The Hutt's eyes narrowed to slits, and Tenel Ka had the impression that the broker was revising his opinion of them. "Of course," he said. "Such things are unimportant."

Luke shrugged. "And all information has its price."

"Of course," the Hutt repeated. "Please sit down and tell me what you need."

Luke sat on a repulsorbench, adjusted the height, and motioned for Tenel Ka to sit beside him, next to a planter holding a tall, leafy shrub. Luke took a long gulp from the drink in his hand, but when Tenel Ka raised her cup to her lips, he sent her a warning look. When the Hutt bent to confer with his Ranat assistant for a moment, Luke took the opportunity to whisper, "That drink could knock you from here to the Outer Rim."

"Ah," Tenel Ka said. "Aha." She set the drink down with a small *thunk*.

When the Ranat scurried off on whatever business the Hutt had assigned it, Luke and Tenel Ka began telling their fictional tale, carefully offering only as much information as they thought was needed.

As they rambled on, taking turns embellishing the details, the other patrons in the hive supplied the usual chaos of a busy, seedy bar. Several different blaster battles rang out from dim areas, while huge armored bouncer droids trundled in to bash heads together and eject any customers who did not pay for the messes they made.

A group of smugglers played a reckless game of rocket darts, missing the prominent target on the wall and launching one of the small flaming missiles into the side of a fluffy, white-furred Talz. The creature roared in pain and surprise as his fur ignited, then took out his misery on the drunken Ithorian sitting next to him.

Large customers tried to eat smaller customers, and the bands kept playing, and Shanko kept mixing drinks. The Hutt information broker was distracted by none of it.

As they spoke, Luke continued to sip his drink and Tenel Ka cast about for a way to dispose of hers. When the Ranat returned and conferred again with the Hutt, Tenel Ka reached over to the planter beside her chair and dumped half of her drink into it.

It was only after the stalk began to shudder violently and the leaves curled up that Tenel Ka realized that the shrub was not a decoration but a plant-alien customer! She whispered an apology and turned back just as the Ranat hurried off with the Hutt's datapad and a new assignment.

The Ranat came back in a moment, followed by a heavily bearded man who walked with a limp.

"This Ranat here said 'no names,' and that's fine with me," the bearded man said, sitting down at the table. "Ranat tells me yer in the market for an industrial-grade Corusca gem? Ain't no one else can arrange that fer ya. Industrial-grade gems . . . sooner er later they hafta come through me."

"Are you the purchasing agent, then?" Tenel Ka said without thinking.

The bearded man snorted. "How 'bout we jes say I'm a middleman."

Again, Luke explained as briefly as possible about the treasure vault on Ossus, and before long they had struck a deal to purchase one industrial-grade Corusca gem.

That done, Luke probed the middleman for information about who else might have bought industrial-grade gems. The man's eyes grew wary and distrustful. "No names—that's the bargain," he said stoutly.

Tenel Ka pulled off another string of the fine Corusca gems that hung around her neck and placed them on the table beside the payment she and Luke had already made for the large gem.

"Surely you understand our caution," Luke said. "We must know if there is anyone capable of stealing our treasure from us."

The middleman picked up the string of gems and looked them over carefully. "Can't tell ya much," he said in a low voice. "Last shipment o' big industrial gems, one person bought 'em all. Big order."

"Can you describe their ships, tell us what planet they came from?" Luke pressed.

The bearded middleman still did not look up. "Not much, actually. Never saw the ship she came on. All I know's she called herself a . . . a lady of the evenin' . . . er a daughter of darkness, er somethin' like that."

Tenel Ka caught her breath, and she felt Luke stiffen beside her. "You mean a—a *Nightsister?*" Tenel Ka asked with a quaver in her voice.

"Yeah, that was it! A Nightsister," the middleman said. "Goofy name."

Luke's eyes met Tenel Ka's and held.

"Thank you, gentlemen," Luke said slowly. "If you're right, I'm afraid this 'Nightsister' may have taken some of our valuables already."

8

JACEN STOOD BEHIND Qorl's pilot chair, biting his lip. The Nightsister Tamith Kai loomed over them, powerful and threatening. He flashed a glance at Jaina, but he didn't think they could do anything to resist.

Not yet anyway.

Docking doors on the ring of the Shadow Academy eased open in the silence of space, exposing a dark cavernous bay rimmed with flashing yellow lights to guide Qorl's ship in. The Imperial pilot worked the controls with grim proficiency, and Jacen noticed that his damaged left arm—which had never properly healed when his TIE fighter had crashed on Yavin 4—was now bulkier, encased in black leather from the shoulder down, wrapped with straps and battery packs.

"Qorl, what happened to your arm?" Jacen asked. "Did they heal it for you, like we promised we'd do at the Jedi academy?"

Qorl diverted his attention from the docking maneuvers, turning his haunted pale eyes toward the boy. "They did not heal it," Qorl said. "They *replaced* it. I now have a droid arm, which is better than my old one. Stronger, capable of more tasks." He bent his leather-bound arm.

Jacen caught the faint whirring of servomotors. His stomach clenched in sick revulsion. "They didn't have to do that," Jacen said. "We could have healed you in a bacta tank, or a medical droid could have tended you. At worst you would have been fitted with a biomechanical prosthetic that looks just like a real arm—even my uncle has one of those. There was no need to give you a droid arm."

Qorl's face was stony, and he turned his attention back to piloting his craft. "Nevertheless, it is done. My arm is better now, stronger."

The Imperial ship drifted into the docking bay, and lines of pulsing lights continued to illuminate the reflective metal walls. A transparisteel-encased observation bay with angular windows protruded from the inner wall above. Jacen could see small figures running diagnostics, working systems to guide Qorl's ship in.

The ship settled down with barely a bump. The docking-bay doors closed behind them, sealing the prisoners inside the sinister Shadow Academy.

Tamith Kai spoke into the comm channel. "Engage cloaking device," she said, her deep voice as irresistible and compelling as a tractor beam.

Though Jacen could see or feel nothing different, he knew that the large space station had suddenly vanished, leaving the illusion of nothing but empty space, where no one would ever find them.

Flanked by a stormtrooper escort, Tamith Kai ushered the children down the boarding ramp, away from the assault ship that had kidnapped them from GemDiver Station. She took them across the bay, toward a broad scarlet door that slid open as they approached.

On the other side stood a young-looking man dressed in flowing silvery robes. His smooth skin and silken blond hair seemed to glow. He was one of the most *beautiful* humans Jacen had ever seen—perfectly formed, like a holo simulation of an ideal man, or a sculptor's masterpiece chiseled out of alabaster. A contingent of stormtroopers stood behind him, blaster rifles resting on their shoulders.

"Welcome, new recruits," he said in a gentle voice that carried undertones of music. "I am Brakiss, leader of the Shadow Academy."

Jacen heard his sister gasp and couldn't restrain his own exclamation. "Brakiss?" he said. "Blaster bolts! We've heard about you. You were an Imperial spy planted at Master Skywalker's academy, trying to steal our training methods."

Brakiss smiled as if inwardly amused.

"That's right," Jaina continued excitedly. "Master Skywalker figured out who you were, but when he tried to turn you to the light side—to *save* you—you couldn't face the ugliness inside yourself."

Brakiss's smile never faltered. "Ah, so that's how he tells it? Master Skywalker and I did not agree on the . . . particulars of training in the Force. But he had at least one good idea: He was correct to bring back the Jedi Knights. He realized that the Jedi were the preservers and protectors of the Old Republic. They unified the decaying old government and kept it alive long after it should have dissolved into anarchy.

"And now that there is anarchy among the remnants of the Imperial forces, *we* need such a unifying force. We have already found a powerful new leader, a great one"—Brakiss smiled—"but we also need our own group of Dark Jedi Knights, Imperial Jedi, who will cement our factions together and give us the will to defeat the wicked and unlawful government of the New Republic and bring about the Second Imperium."

"Hey, our *mother* leads the New Republic!" Jacen objected. "She's not wicked. And she doesn't torture people, or kidnap them, either."

Brakiss said, "It all depends on your perspective."

"Who's this new leader, anyway?" Jaina interrupted. "Haven't you tried to find a single leader before—and ended up with everyone fighting to run what's left of the Empire? It won't work."

"Silence," Tamith Kai said, her voice thick with menace. "You will not ask questions; you will receive indoctrination. You will be trained as powerful warriors to fight in the service of the Empire."

"I don't think so," Jacen said defiantly.

His sister's face flushed with anger. "We won't cooperate with you. You can't steal us away and just expect us to be diligent little students for you. Master Skywalker and our parents will comb the galaxy to find us. They *will* find us, and then you'll be sorry."

Behind them, Lowie snarled and spread his long arms as if longing to tear something limb from limb, as his uncle Chewbacca was rumored to do whenever he lost a hologame.

The stormtroopers suddenly trained their rifles on the infuriated Wookiee.

"Hey, don't shoot him!" Jacen said, moving between the stormtrooper and Lowie.

Jaina spoke up in an authoritative tone that took Jacen by surprise. "What have you done with Em Teedee, Lowie's translator droid? He needs to communicate—unless of course all of these stormtroopers can somehow speak the Wookiee language?"

"He will be given his little droid back," Tamith Kai said, "as soon as it has undergone . . . suitable reprogramming."

Brakiss clapped his hands at the troopers. "We will go to their quarters now," he said. "Their training must begin soon. The Second Imperium has a great need for Dark Jedi Knights."

"You'll never turn us," Jaina said. "You're wasting your time."

Brakiss looked at her, smiled indulgently, and stood in silence for a long moment. "You may find that your mind will change," he said. "Why don't we wait and see."

The stormtroopers formed an armed escort around them as they marched along the clanking metal deck plates.

The Shadow Academy was not comfortable and soft like Lando's

GemDiver Station. The walls were not painted with pastel colors; there were no soothing strains of music or nature sounds over the loudspeaker systems, only harsh status reports and chronometer tones that chimed every quarter hour. Stenciled labels marked the doors. Occasional computer terminals mounted to the walls displayed maps of the station and complicated simulations in progress.

"This is an austere station," Tamith Kai said as Jacen stared at the cold, heartless walls. "We don't bother with luxury accommodations like your jungle academy. However, we have made sure that you each have a private chamber so you can conduct your meditation exercises, practice your assignments, and concentrate on developing your Force skills."

"No!" Jaina said.

"We'd rather stay together," Jacen added.

Lowbacca roared in agreement.

Tamith Kai came to an abrupt stop and looked down at them. "I did not *ask* your preference!" she said, her violet eyes blazing. "You will do as you are told."

They reached an intersection of corridors, and here they split into three groups. Brakiss led the cluster of stormtroopers that surrounded Jaina, taking them down a corridor to the right. A larger group of guards, tense and with weapons at the ready, helped Tamith Kai to escort Lowbacca. The remaining guards closed around Jacen and led him off to the left.

"Wait!" Jacen cried, and turned to look at his twin sister for what felt to him like the last time. Jaina stared back at him, her brandy-brown eyes wide with anxiety, but when she bravely lifted her chin, Jacen felt a surge of courage himself. They would find some way out of this.

The guards hustled him down a long corridor until they stopped at one door in a line of identical-seeming doors. Student chambers, he thought.

The door whisked open, and the stormtroopers herded Jacen into a small cubicle, bare-walled and uncomfortable. He saw no speaker panel on the wall, no controls, nothing that would let him communicate with anybody.

"I'm staying in here?" he said in disbelief.

"Yes," the lead stormtrooper said.

"But what if I need something? How am I supposed to call out?" Jacen said.

The trooper turned his skull-like plasteel mask to look directly at him. "Then you will *endure* until someone comes for you." The stormtroopers stepped back, and the door shut behind Jacen, closing him in, weaponless and alone.

Then, to make things worse, all the lights went out.

9

TENEL KA WOKE to pitch-darkness, cramped and confined, surrounded by a dull vibration. Her heart drummed a rapid cadence, and perspiration prickled her skin. An urgency, a feeling that something was terribly wrong, nudged the back of her mind. She tried to sit up and bumped her head—hard—against the unyielding bottom of the bunk above her. Stifling an exclamation of annoyance, she remembered that she was aboard the *Off Chance*. She relaxed slightly—but only slightly.

When they had finished with the Hutt information broker on Borgo Prime, Luke and Tenel Ka decided their best hope for finding Jacen, Jaina, and Lowbacca lay in going directly to Dathomir, homeworld of the original Nightsisters. Their only clue was the mysterious Nightsister, and they had to find out who she was and whether she had the twins and Lowbacca.

Luke had urged Tenel Ka to get some sleep while they made their journey. It was the first opportunity she had had to rest since her friends had been kidnapped, and Tenel Ka gratefully accepted.

And so she had slept, sealed away from light and sound, in one of the berths aboard the *Off Chance,* but her rest had again been disturbed by shadowy dreams. She touched a switch by her head and winced as bright cabin light flooded the sleeping cubicle. She rolled onto her stomach, swung her legs over the side of the bunk, and dropped a meter and a half to the floor of the cabin. Shaking back her tumble of loose red-gold hair, Tenel Ka stretched to her full height and noted with pleasure the freedom of movement that her tough, supple lizard-hide armor afforded her. She was glad to be dressed as a warrior again.

The uneasy feeling left by her dream persisted as Tenel Ka made her way to the cockpit and lowered herself into the copilot's seat next to Luke. She gazed through the front viewport at the swirling colors that indicated the *Off Chance* was traveling through hyperspace.

Luke looked up from the controls. "Did you get some sleep?"

"This is a fact." She fastened the crash webbing around her, then grabbed a thick clump of her hair and began plaiting it into a braid, adding a few feathers and beads that she kept in a pouch attached to her belt.

"But you didn't sleep *well?*"

She blinked at this, somehow surprised that he had noticed. "This is also a fact."

Luke did not reply. He simply waited, and with growing discomfort she realized he was waiting for her to explain.

"I . . . had a dream," she said. "It is not important."

His intense blue eyes searched her face. When he spoke, it was in a low voice. "I feel fear in you."

She grimaced and shrugged. "It is a dream I have had before."

His eyelids fluttered shut briefly, and he tilted his head as he might have done had he been studying her with his eyes open. ". . . the Nightsisters?" he said at last.

"Yes. It is childish," she admitted as color rushed to her cheeks, staining them with embarrassment.

"Strange . . . I dreamt about them, too," Luke said.

Tenel Ka looked at him in disbelief. "I used to think they were just a story that mothers and grandmothers on Dathomir told to scare children. But the Nightsisters were all destroyed. How could there be any left?"

"The people of Dathomir are often strong in the Force, and it would not be difficult for someone else to train them in the ways of evil," he said. He leaned back in the pilot's seat and stared out at hyperspace as if summoning an old memory. "In fact, many years ago—before you were born—I traveled to Dathomir searching for Jacen and Jaina's parents, Han and Leia. That was when I met your mother and father, and we all joined forces to defeat the last of the Nightsisters."

Tenel Ka looked at him curiously. This was a part of the story her parents spoke little about. "My mother thinks very highly of you," she said, hoping he would elaborate.

Luke slid her a teasing glance. "But did she ever tell you how we met? That she *captured* me?"

"You don't mean—" Tenel Ka began. "She couldn't have expected . . ."

Luke chuckled at her discomfiture. "This is a fact."

"Oh, Master Skywalker!" Tenel Ka gasped in chagrin at the very idea of Luke submitting to the primitive marriage customs she had always viewed as quaint and provincial. On Dathomir, a woman selected and captured the man she wanted to marry. Her mother, Teneniel Djo, had done *that* to Luke Skywalker?

It brought a renewed flush of embarrassment to her face to realize that her mother had captured the greatest Jedi Master in the galaxy and had expected him to marry her and father her children. Then, all at once, the situation struck her as so ridiculous that she let loose with what was, for her, a rare sound indeed—a giggle.

"My mother has always taught me to have respect for Jedi, and most of all for you, Master Skywalker, but . . . please do not be offended"—she gasped, tears of mirth rising to her eyes—"I am certainly glad she did not succeed."

Luke, still smiling, reached over and gave her shoulder an understanding squeeze. "So am I. Your parents belonged together."

"I love my father, you know," Tenel Ka said, sobering, "and my mother."

"And yet you've never told your friends who your real parents are," Luke said. "Why?"

Tenel Ka squirmed uncomfortably in her crash restraints, which suddenly felt too confining. She had often mulled this problem over, and had come to the same decision again and again. "It is difficult to explain," she said. "I am not ashamed of my parents, if that is what you think. I am proud that my mother is strong in the Force and that she, a warrior from Dathomir, now rules the entire Hapes Cluster. And I am proud of my father and what he managed to become, despite the way he was raised—despite the one who raised him."

Luke nodded sagely. "Your grandmother?"

"Yes," Tenel Ka gritted. "Of *that* part of my family, I am not proud. My grandmother is power-hungry. She manipulates. I am not sure she even knows how to love." She felt a bleak bewilderment as she turned to look at Luke. "Yet my father is loving and wise. He is not like her."

"No, he isn't," Luke said. "Long ago your father Isolder did something difficult and very brave. Realizing that your grandmother loved power so much she was willing to kill anyone who threatened her, he rejected her teaching. She is a strong, proud woman, but her lessons were poisonous. He chose instead to value and honor life wherever he found it. Your father's difficult decision was the right one."

Tenel Ka nodded. Her thoughts were bitter. "My lineage is tainted by generations of bloodthirsty, power-hungry tyrants. I am not *proud* that I was born to the royal family of Hapes," she spat. "I do not wish my friends to know that I am heir to the throne, because I have done nothing to earn it, choose it, or deserve it."

Luke's face was thoughtful. "Jacen and Jaina would understand that. Their mother is one of the most powerful women in the galaxy."

Tenel Ka shook her head violently. "Before I tell them, I must prove to myself that I am not like my ancestors. I choose to take pride only in what *I* accomplish, first through my own strength, and then through the Force—never through inherited political power. My parents are very proud that I have decided to become a Jedi."

"I understand," Luke said. "You've chosen a difficult path." He smiled at her warmly. "It is a good start for a Jedi."

10

THE NEXT DAY, Jaina's joy at seeing her brother again was overshadowed by Tamith Kai's presence and the fact that they were each being shepherded down the corridor by a pair of well-armed stormtroopers.

When Jacen broke away from his guards just long enough to give her a quick hug, she spoke her words in a whispered burst. "I've got a plan. I need your help."

Rough, armored hands pulled the brother and sister apart. One of the armor-clad guards leveled his blaster pistol at the twins and motioned them to move on.

Jaina smiled in wry amusement. Even with Tamith Kai present, Brakiss still wasn't certain of their cooperation. The stormtroopers were here to ensure that they caused no trouble.

A slight nod of Jacen's head told Jaina that he understood her words. "Want to hear a joke?" he asked brightly, purposely changing the subject.

"Sure," Jaina answered with feigned innocence.

Jacen cleared his throat. "How many stormtroopers does it take to change a glowpanel?"

Jaina cringed inwardly. Her brother certainly was brave—or perhaps foolhardy. Nonetheless, she took the bait. "I don't know, how many stormtroopers *does* it take to change a glowpanel?"

One of the guards stepped ahead of Jaina and stopped at the door to a lecture room in which she could see dozens of people seated. She guessed they were probably the other Shadow Academy trainees. The guard with the blaster pistol gestured for them to enter.

"It takes two stormtroopers to change a glowpanel," Jacen said in a voice loud enough for everyone to hear. "One stormtrooper to change it, and the other one to shoot him and take credit for all the work."

Jaina tried unsuccessfully to suppress a snort of laughter. Tamith Kai glared violet daggers at Jacen.

Jacen squirmed under her angry regard and muttered, "I can tell *you're* from Dathomir. Your people aren't exactly known for their sense of humor."

As her two guards took her arms in a bruising grip, Jaina was forced to admit that her brother's small act of bravado had released something inside her, had shown her that her mind—at least for now—was still free, that she still had choices.

She was dragged into the meeting room, where her guards shoved her into a sitting position at one end of a narrow, backless bench. Jacen's guards seated him on the opposite side of the room—no doubt to punish him for his joke. Jaina was delighted to see that Lowie sat less than a meter away from her, with only one student between them. He roared a greeting at her and Jacen.

The other students were all human, clean-cut, and wearing dark uniforms. They seemed eager to learn, glad to be at the Shadow Academy, genuine Imperial youth. She had seen people like this before. She, Jacen, and Lowie might be the only ones resisting the training, she knew.

Jaina frowned when she saw that Em Teedee was still not at Lowie's belt. That would make communication difficult. She wondered what her uncle Luke would do in such a situation. She sat up straight, cleared her mind, and sent a gentle thought probing in Lowie's direction. She did not feel any pain from him. He was unharmed—of that she was certain—but she did sense tension, confusion, and simmering frustration. She tried to send him soothing thoughts. She wasn't sure how much got through, but when Lowie briefly reached a furry hand around to touch her shoulder, she knew he understood.

Jaina wondered if she dared speak openly to her Wookiee friend. She would have to find out what the student next to her was like first. He was about her age, and a little taller. Like all the willing students, he wore a tight, sleek-fitting charcoal jumpsuit beneath a flowing robe of purest black. He had blond hair and moss-green eyes, and he glanced at her without any particular recognition or interest.

She sent her thought probe toward the young man, but caught nothing beyond elusive snatches that blared fleetingly in her mind, like disconnected notes from an orchestra tuning its instruments.

"Why are we here?" Jaina asked in a voice just above a whisper.

"Because we are here," he replied, aloof and a bit defensive. "Because Master Brakiss wishes us to be here." He looked at her with suspicion, as if she had proved herself mentally deficient. "Are we not all here to learn the ways of the Force from Master Brakiss?"

Before Jaina could reply, Brakiss himself strode into the chamber.

The silence in the room was instant and complete. Not a cough or a syllable challenged his compelling presence. Brakiss let his piercing eyes rove across the faces of the gathered students. When his eyes met hers, Jaina felt an inexplicable chill creep down her spine.

Without preamble, he began to teach.

"The Force is an energy that surrounds all living things. It flows through us. It flows from us."

As his voice streamed around the students, Jaina felt her mind begin to relax. This wasn't so bad after all. All of it was true. The power in Brakiss's voice urged action, demanded agreement. Jaina saw the heads of many of the students nodding. She nodded too.

Jaina could not remember the words as Brakiss led them smoothly, logically from one concept to another. All she remembered were the thoughts, the feelings, the *rightness* of it all.

Then suddenly, for some reason—perhaps it was the light touch of a furry hand on her back—the words came into focus again, began to penetrate the complacent fog of unquestioning agreement that had blanketed her mind.

"You each have the tools inside you to master yourselves, and to master the Force," the tranquil, confident voice said. "And to draw on the strength of the Force, you must learn to draw on what is strongest in you: strong emotions, deep desires, fear, aggression, hate, anger."

A resounding *No!* rang through Jaina's mind, and she shook her head to clear it. "That . . . can't be true," she whispered. "It's not true."

The student next to Jaina flicked his eyes at her with a look of disdain. "Of *course* it's true," he said, as if using indisputable logic. "Master Brakiss said it, so it must be true."

"What makes you so sure?" Jaina hissed. "Can't you see that he has a hold on your mind? You should get away from this place and start thinking for yourself."

"I don't *wish* to leave," he said, his expression implacable. "I wish to study with Master Brakiss and become a Jedi."

Jaina seethed at his stubbornness. "Have you even thought about this? You can't just blindly accept whatever he says without bothering to think about it. What if he's wrong?"

"He is the *teacher.*" The student's moss-green eyes blinked at her as if her question made no sense. He stood abruptly, begging Brakiss's attention.

Jaina took the opportunity to lean behind him and whisper to Lowie. "I've got a plan! In a couple of days, I'll need you to knock out all the station's power. Be ready." As she sat back up, her mind finally registered the fact that the stubborn blond student was addressing Brakiss.

"—is trying to convince your other students that they should not believe you, that you do not have the true teachings of the Force. And therefore I suggest that this—this *girl* is not a worthy pupil for you, Master Brakiss."

Brakiss's beautiful, piercing eyes narrowed and came to rest on Jaina. She felt the press of his powerful mind against hers. She tried to resist.

"You are new here," he said. "You do not know our ways. Listen to my teachings, then make your judgment. Decide for yourself. But do not encourage others to disbelieve me *ever* again."

In unison, the students murmured their agreement—with three exceptions.

"At this academy we do not learn only one side of the Force," Brakiss went on, resuming his lecture, though his comments seemed directed primarily toward Jacen, Jaina, and Lowie. "This is not a school of darkness. I call this a Shadow Academy, for what does life create by its very nature, if not shadows? And it is only through using the full range of your emotions and desires—the light *and* the dark— that you will become truly strong in the Force and fulfill your destiny. The light side by itself offers only limited power. But when the light is blended with the dark, and you work within the shadows, then you achieve your full potential. Use the strength of the dark side."

Jaina looked across at Jacen, who was slowly shaking his head. Close beside her, Lowie growled deep in his throat. Unable to contain herself any longer, Jaina stood. "That's not right," she said. "The dark side doesn't make you any stronger. It's faster, easier, more seductive. It's also more tenacious. Just as the light side brings freedom, the dark side brings only bondage. Once you enslave yourself to the dark side of the Force, you may never escape."

A collective gasp went up, but no one said a word as Jaina and Brakiss faced each other over the students' heads. Brakiss was silent for a long moment, his mind pressing down on hers with suffocating weight.

With a mental heave Jaina flung aside the influence of his mind on hers and challenged him, her eyes filled with pride, her thoughts free.

At last, Brakiss shook his head sadly. "I did not wish to make an example of you. But you leave me no choice. You have chosen to pit your puny light-side powers against my own. I gave you one warning. You will not receive another."

With that, Brakiss lifted one hand slightly, almost as if to wave a fond farewell. Blue fire danced from his fingertips and surrounded Jaina in a haze of bright agony.

Brakiss's calm cruelty against Jaina launched Lowbacca into an unbridled rage. Unable to control himself, he leaped from his cramped seat, knocking over the blond student. He howled at the top of his lungs and bared long Wookiee fangs. Ginger-colored fur stuck out in all directions as he yanked up the bench he had been sitting on and raised it over his head.

Alerted by the disturbance, the guards charged into the room, their stun pistols drawn, looking for the source of the chaos—and the enraged Wookiee was not difficult to find.

Lowie threw the bench at the incoming stormtroopers. His blow knocked the first cluster of guards backward into each other, tumbling them down like children's blocks. Five more stormtroopers tripped over their fallen companions but still managed to wade into the room.

The other Shadow Academy trainees added to the uproar, trying to shout Lowie down. The Wookiee just roared back at them. From the podium, Brakiss urged everyone to be calm, but no one listened.

Another door whisked open, and a new contingent of stormtroopers rushed in from the far side of the room.

Jacen dashed to his unconscious sister's side and cradled her head and shoulders in his lap. With relief, he sensed that she was not seriously injured from the Force blast. She groaned and blinked her brandy-brown eyes, trying to fight her way back to consciousness.

"Jaina," he called. "Jaina, snap out of it!"

"All right . . . I am," she said, struggling to sit up. Then she seemed suddenly to notice the brawl that Lowie had started on her behalf.

The second set of stormtroopers drew their stun pistols as Lowie yanked a bench out from under another Shadow Academy student, sending her to the floor. The student squealed in outrage. Lowie ignored her and raised the bench to throw at the incoming stormtroopers.

They pointed their stun pistols and fired—but the beam caught the front of the bench, doing no damage. Lowie tossed it, and the troopers scrambled out of the way as the bench crashed against the side wall. Lowbacca ducked to pick up something else to throw—and just as he did, the first set of stormtroopers on the other side of the room, finally climbing back to their feet, fired their stun pistols.

Glowing blue arcs shot over Lowie's back, missing him and striking full against three of the second set of troopers on the other side, stunning them. They sprawled senseless on the floor in a clattering tumble of white plasteel armor.

"Cease this disturbance!" Brakiss shouted. His normally smooth features had lost their serene composure.

One of the stormtroopers in the first group took two steps forward and aimed his stun pistol directly at Lowie's back as the Wookiee stood up, presenting an easy target.

Jacen watched and—in the moment before the stormtrooper could fire—used his greatest strength with the Force to grasp the trooper's blaster and wrench it halfway around, twisting it in the white-gloved hand so that when the guard squeezed the firing button, the barrel was pointed toward his own chest. The stun beam splashed out, knocking the trooper to the ground, unconscious.

"Lowie, I'm all right," Jaina called, picking herself up and climbing to her feet. "Look, I'm all right!"

More stormtroopers rushed in from both sides of the room, weapons drawn.

"Lowie, calm down," Jacen said.

Lowbacca looked from side to side, fingers spread, arms ready to tear something apart, until he saw he was clearly outnumbered.

Brakiss stood with his fingers outstretched. A shimmering power curled between them, ready to be unleashed.

"We don't want to damage you," Brakiss said, filled with savage intensity, "but you must learn discipline." The master of the Shadow Academy looked to the stormtroopers. "Return them to their quarters, and keep them separated! We have great work to do here and cannot be distracted by unchanneled displays of temper."

Then Brakiss adjusted his handsome features until he looked calm and soothing again. He raised his eyebrows in admiration toward Lowie. "I am pleased to see the strength in your anger, young Wookiee. That is something we must develop. You have great potential."

White-armored guards crushed Lowie's hairy arms in their unfeeling grip. The stormtroopers marched the three young Jedi Knights out into the corridor and toward their cells.

11

DATHOMIR SPARKLED LIKE a rich topaz jewel, welcoming Tenel Ka as Luke piloted the *Off Chance* down into the atmosphere. Anticipation tingled through her. Regardless of the unhappy circumstances that brought them here, Tenel Ka could not help the feeling of pleasure and joy that throbbed through her veins with every beat of her heart. *Home-home. Home-home.*

Turbulence buffeted the blockade runner as they descended. Luke studied the displays on the navigation console and adjusted their course from time to time.

"It's been a long time since I made a visit to the Singing Mountain Clan," Luke said. "I don't remember exactly how to get there. I think I can get us close, but unless you happen to know the coordinates—"

Tenel Ka rattled off the numbers before he could finish his thought. At the same time, she leaned forward and entered the coordinates into the navicomp.

"I come here often," she explained. "It is my second home in the galaxy, but it is the first home of my heart."

"Yes," Luke said, "I can understand that."

As the *Off Chance* carried them to the home of the Singing Mountain Clan, they passed over shining oceans, lush forests, vast deserts, rolling hills, and wide fertile plains. Tenel Ka felt strength and energy flow through her, as if the very atmosphere of the planet had the power to recharge her.

"Look," Luke said, pointing down at a herd of blue-skinned reptiles racing at incredible speed across a plain.

"Blue Mountain people," Tenel Ka said. "They migrate every dawn and every dusk."

Luke nodded. "One of them gave me a ride once."

"That is a rare honor, Master Skywalker," she said. "Not even I have had that opportunity."

* * *

The pale pink sun was high above the horizon by the time they reached the wide, bowl-shaped valley of the Singing Mountain Clan, Tenel Ka's second home. A green and brown patchwork of fields and orchards spread beneath them in the pinkish sunlight. Small clusters of thatched huts dotted the valley, and morning cooking fires glimmered here and there.

Luke pointed to the stone fortress built into the side of the cliff wall that rose high above the valley floor. "Does Augwynne Djo still rule here?"

"Yes. My great-grandmother."

"Good. We'll go directly to her then. I'd prefer to tell only a few people why we are here and keep our presence as secret as possible," he said, then he brought the *Off Chance* to a smooth landing on the valley floor beside the fortress.

"That should not be difficult," Tenel Ka replied. "My people do not speak unnecessarily."

Luke chuckled. "I can believe that."

Tenel Ka paused halfway up the steep path that led to the fortress. She was not at all fatigued; she was simply savoring the moment.

Luke, who had been following behind her with unwavering steps, halted without a word and waited for her to continue. He did not seem the least bit winded, his breathing slow and regular—no small feat considering the rapid pace Tenel Ka set.

The longer she knew Master Skywalker, the more she admired him, and the better she understood why her mother—who did not often speak highly of any man except her husband, Isolder—had always held Luke Skywalker in high esteem.

Tenel Ka drew in a deep breath. The air was delicious, but not just from the mouthwatering odors of roasting meat and vegetables that wafted from the cooking fires. It was late summer in the valley, and the warm breeze was redolent with the scents of ripening fruit, golden grasses, and early harvest. Despite the intermingled odors of the lizard pens and the herd of domesticated rancors, there was a freshness to the air that lifted her heart.

Tenel Ka set off again as if there was not a moment to lose. Finally, she stood before the gate of the fortress, where she announced herself as a member of the clan.

The gates were thrown open and Tenel Ka's clan sisters welcomed her with warm embraces and low murmurs of greeting. All were dressed in lizard-skin tunics of various colors, like the one Tenel Ka wore. Some wore elaborate helmets, while others simply wore their hair in decorated braids.

One clan sister with black hair that fell to her waist drew the two travelers inside. "Augwynne told us you would come," she said. Her expression was grave, but Tenel Ka could see the smile that lit her eyes.

"Our mission is urgent," Tenel Ka stated, not bothering to greet the woman. "We *must* see Augwynne alone at once." She had never used such a tone of command in Master Skywalker's presence before, but she knew her clan sister would not be offended. At times like this, pleasantries were an unnecessary luxury among her people.

The woman inclined her head slightly. "Augwynne has guessed this much. She waits for you in the war room."

The ancient woman stood as they entered the room. "Welcome, Jedi Skywalker. And welcome great-granddaughter Tenel Ka Chume Ta' Djo." She embraced each of them in turn.

Tenel Ka groaned. "Please," she said, "do not use my full name. And do *not* send word that we are here."

Luke interrupted. "We're following a trail that has led us from Yavin to Borgo Prime to Dathomir. Our need for information has brought us to you."

Tenel Ka took a deep breath and searched for words. She looked directly at her great-grandmother. Augwynne's wrinkle-nested eyes were attentive, cautious. "We are searching for the Nightsisters. Do any remain on Dathomir?"

Augwynne's heavy sigh told Tenel Ka that they had come to the right place. The old woman fixed her gaze on Luke. "They are not Nightsisters as you and I knew them," she said. "Not wizened crones with discolored skin, who rotted from the nightspells they spoke." She shook her head. "No, they are a newly formed order of Nightsisters, young and fair, and allied with the Empire." She lifted a finger to stroke Tenel Ka's cheek. "Their evil is subtle. They tame and ride rancors as we do. They dress as warriors, if they choose. They are not even all women . . . but they *are* the children of darkness. They are dangerous, with new goals. Do not seek them out."

"We must," Tenel Ka said simply. "It is our best hope for rescuing my closest friends."

Augwynne gave her great-granddaughter a measuring look. "You pledged friendship with these people you must rescue?"

Tenel Ka nodded. "With full ceremony."

"Then we have no other choice," Augwynne said with finality. "You must present your case before the Council of Sisters."

12

BRAKISS HAD A private office on the Shadow Academy, a place where he could go for solitude and contemplation.

Now, as he pondered, he stared at the brilliant images surrounding him on the walls: a waterfall of scarlet lava on the molten planet Nkllon; an exploding sun that spewed arcs of stellar fire in the Denarii Nova; the still-blazing core of the Cauldron Nebula, where seven giant stars had all gone supernova at once; and a vista of the broken shards of Alderaan, destroyed by the Empire's first Death Star more than twenty years before.

Brakiss recognized great beauty in the violence of the universe, in the unbridled power provided by the galaxy or unleashed by human ingenuity.

Standing alone and in silence, Brakiss used Force techniques to meditate and absorb these cosmic catastrophes, crystallizing the strength within himself. Through the dark side, he knew how to make the Force bend to his will. The power stored within the galaxy was his to use. When he captured it and held it with his heart, Brakiss could maintain his calm exterior and not be prone to violence, as his fellow instructor Tamith Kai so often was.

Brakiss eased back in his padded chair, letting his breath flow slowly out. The synthetic leather squeaked as his body rubbed against it, and the warmers inside the chair brought the temperature to a relaxing level. The cushions conformed themselves to his body to give him the greatest comfort.

Tamith Kai refused such indulgences outright. She was a hard woman, insisting on privation and adversity to hone her skills for the Empire that had recognized her potential and taken her from the bleak planet Dathomir. Brakiss, however, found that he could *think* better when he was at ease. He could plan, mull over possibilities.

Brakiss switched on the recording pad on his desktop and called up the day's records. He would have to make a report and ship it in an armored hyperdrone to their powerful new Imperial leader, hidden deep in the Core Systems.

It had been some time since the encampment he founded in the Great Canyon on Dathomir had provided any strong new students, but the three talented young trainees kidnapped from Skywalker's Jedi academy were another story, worth the risk of stealing them. Brakiss could sense it.

But their focus was all wrong. Master Skywalker had taught them too much and in the wrong ways. They didn't know how to turn their anger into a sharpened spearpoint for a larger weapon. They contemplated too much. They were too calm, too passive—except for the Wookiee. Brakiss needed to train those three. He and Tamith Kai would employ their separate specialties to work on them.

Brakiss drummed his fingertips on the slick surface of his desk. Occasionally, he felt twinges of sadness for having left the Yavin 4 training center. He had learned much there, though his own mission for the Empire was always uppermost in his mind.

Long ago, the Empire had selected Brakiss because of his untapped Jedi ability. He had undergone rigorous training and conditioning so that he could spy on Skywalker's academy, gathering precious information. No one was supposed to know he was a scout, planted there to learn techniques that he could teach to the Second Imperium. The new Imperial leader had insisted on developing his own Dark Jedi, a symbol that those faithful to the Empire could rally around.

Somehow, though, Master Skywalker had immediately seen through the deception. He had realized Brakiss's true identity. But unlike previous clumsy and unpracticed spies who had come to Yavin 4 with the same mission, Brakiss had not been expelled outright. Skywalker had shown little patience for those others—but apparently he had seen real potential in Brakiss.

Master Skywalker had begun working on him, openly teaching him those things he most needed to learn. Brakiss did have a great talent with the Force, and Master Skywalker had shown him how to use it. But Skywalker had repeatedly tried to contaminate Brakiss with the light side, with the platitudes and peaceful ways of the New Republic. Brakiss shuddered at the thought.

Finally, in a private and supremely important test, Master Skywalker had taken Brakiss on a mental journey within himself—not allowing him to look outward through the rivers of the Force, but turning the dark student inside to see his own heart, so he could observe the truth about what he himself was made of.

Brakiss had opened a trapdoor and fallen into a pit filled with his self-deception and the potential cruelties that the Empire could force him to carry out. Master Skywalker stood beside him, forcing him to look—and keep looking—even as Brakiss scrambled to escape from himself, not wanting to face the lies of his own existence.

But the Imperial conditioning ran too deep. His mind was too far lost in service to the Empire, and Brakiss had nearly gone insane from that ordeal. He had run from Master Skywalker, taking his ship and fleeing into the depths of space.

He had remained alone for a long time before finally returning to the embrace of the Second Imperium, where he put his expertise to work . . . just as it had been planned from the beginning.

Brakiss was handsome, perfectly formed, not at all corrupted as the Emperor had appeared in his last days, when the dark side had devoured him from within. Brakiss tried to deny that corruption—to comfort himself with his outer appearance—but he could not escape the ugliness in the darkness of his heart.

He knew his place in the Empire would be reborn, and he had learned to be content with that service. His greatest triumph was his Shadow Academy, where he could oversee the new Dark Jedi being trained: dozens of students, some with little or no talent at all, but others with the potential for true greatness, like Darth Vader himself.

Of course, the new Imperial leader also recognized the danger in creating such a powerful group of Dark Jedi. Knights who had fallen to the dark side were bound to have ambitions of their own, tempted by the power they themselves controlled. It was Brakiss's job to keep them in line.

But the great leader had his own protective measures. The entire Shadow Academy was filled with self-destructive devices: hundreds, if not thousands, of chain-reaction explosives. If Brakiss did not succeed in creating his troop of Dark Jedi, or if the new trainees somehow staged a revolt against the Second Imperium, the Imperial leader would trigger the station's self-destruct sequences. Brakiss and all the Dark Jedi would be destroyed in a flash.

A hostage to darkness, Brakiss was never allowed to leave the Shadow Academy. By order of the great leader, he would remain there, confined, until he and all his trainees had proven themselves.

Brakiss found that sitting on a huge bomb made it difficult to concentrate. But he had great confidence in his own abilities and in Tamith Kai's. Without that confidence he could never have become a Jedi in the first place—and he would never have dared to touch the teachings of the dark side. But he *had* learned those ways, and he had grown strong.

He would turn these new students. He was sure he could do it.

Brakiss smiled as he finished the report encapsulating his plans. The lanky Wookiee's anger was something to take advantage of, and Tamith Kai was the best at that. The new Nightsister was a born tormentor, and she carried out her duties extremely well. Brakiss would let her train Lowbacca.

He, on the other hand, would work with the twins, the grandchildren of Darth Vader. They were too calm, too well trained, and resisted in subtle ways that would prove far more difficult to deal with.

For them, he had other methods. First, he had to find out what Jacen and Jaina *really wanted*—and he would give it to them.

From that point on, they would be his.

13

THE SHADOW ACADEMY'S training chamber stood large and empty, a yawning, vacant space walled off on all sides. The doors sealed behind Jacen, imprisoning him with Brakiss, leaving him to face whatever the teacher had in store. The walls were a flat gray, studded with a grid of computer sensors. Jacen saw no controls, no way out.

He looked up at the beautiful man, who stood in silvery robes watching Jacen with a calm, patient smile.

Brakiss reached into his shimmering robes and withdrew a black cylinder about half the length of Jacen's forearm. It had three power buttons and a series of widely spaced grooves for fingerholds.

A lightsaber.

"You will need this for today's training," Brakiss said, broadening his smile. "Take it. It's yours."

Jacen's eyes widened. His hand reached forward, but he drew back, trying to hide his eagerness. "What do I have to do for it?" he asked warily.

"Nothing," Brakiss answered. "Just *use* it, that's all."

Jacen swallowed and did not meet Brakiss's eyes, afraid to show how he longed to have his own lightsaber. But he didn't want to have it in this place, under these circumstances. "Hey, I'm not supposed to," he said. "I haven't completed my training. Master Skywalker and I had this discussion just a few days ago."

"Nonsense," Brakiss said. "Master Skywalker is holding you back unnecessarily. You already know how to use one of these. Go ahead."

Brakiss extended the lightsaber handle to Jacen, moving it closer, tantalizing him. "Here at the Shadow Academy we feel that lightsaber skills are among the *first* talents a Jedi should develop, because strong, able warriors are always needed. If a Jedi Knight is not ready to fight for a cause, then what good is he?"

Brakiss pressed the lightsaber into Jacen's hands, and Jacen instinctively curled his fingers around it. The weapon felt at the same time heavy with responsibility and light with power. The finger grooves were widely spaced for his young hand, but he would grow accustomed to it.

Jacen touched the power button, and with a *snap-hiss* a sapphire beam crackled out, indigo at the core but electric blue on the fringes. He flicked the blade from side to side, and the molten energy sliced through the air, trailing a faint smell of ozone. He slashed back again.

Brakiss folded his hands together. "Good," he said.

Jacen whirled and held the lightsaber up. "Hey, what's to stop me from just cutting you down right here, Brakiss? You're evil. You've kidnapped us. You're training enemies of the New Republic."

Brakiss laughed—not a mocking laugh, but simply an expression of wry amusement. "You won't kill me, young Jedi," he said. "You would not cut down an unarmed opponent. Cold-blooded murder is not part of the training Master Skywalker gives his young trainees . . . unless he has changed his curriculum since I left Yavin 4?"

Brakiss's alabaster-smooth face seemed exquisitely serene, but he raised his pale eyebrows. "Of course if you do let loose your anger," he said, "and slice me in half, you will have taken a significant first step down the dark path. Even though I won't be here to see the benefits, the Empire will no doubt use your abilities to great advantage."

"That's enough," Jacen said, switching off the lightsaber.

"You're right," Brakiss agreed. "No more talk. This is a training center."

"What are you going to do to me?" Jacen said, holding up the lightsaber handle, alert and ready to switch it on again.

"Just practice, my dear boy," Brakiss said, easing toward the door. "This room can project holo-remotes, imaginary enemies for you to fight, to help you hone your skill with your new weapon. Your lightsaber."

"If they're just holo-remotes, why should I fight at all?" Jacen said defiantly. "Why should I cooperate?"

Brakiss crossed his arms over his chest. "I'm inclined to ask you to indulge me, but I doubt you would do that—at least not yet. So let us put it another way." His voice took on a sudden hard edge, as sharp as razor crystal. "The holo-remotes will be monster warriors. But how do you know I won't slip in an actual creature to fight against you? You would never know the difference, the holo-remotes are so realistic. And if you stand there and refuse to fight, a real enemy might just remove your head from your shoulders.

"Of course, I probably won't do that in the first session. Probably not. Or maybe I will, to show you I'm sincere. You'll be here a long time training in the dark side. You never know when I might lose patience with you."

Brakiss stepped out of the training chamber, and the metal doors shut behind him with a clang.

Alone in the dimly lit chamber with its flat gray walls, Jacen waited, tense. Except for his breathing and his heartbeat, the room was completely silent, as if it swallowed all noise. He shifted, felt the hard Corusca gem still hidden in his boot. He took comfort in the fact that the Imperials had not found it and taken it away from him, but he didn't know how it could help him now.

Jacen turned the lightsaber handle in his hands, trying to decide what he should do. Intellectually, he was certain Brakiss was bluffing, that the man would never send in a real murderous monster. But a part of Jacen's heart wasn't so sure, and the slight twinge of doubt made him uneasy.

Then the air shimmered. Jacen heard a grinding sound and whirled to look behind him. A door he had not noticed before crawled open to reveal a shadowy dungeon from which something large and shambling scraped forward, dragging sharp claws along the floor.

Jacen's hobby back at home had been studying strange and unusual animals and plants. He had pored over the records of known alien races, memorizing them all—but still it took him a few moments to recognize the hideous monster that was now emerging from its cell.

It was an Abyssin, a one-eyed monster with greenish-tan skin, broad shoulders, and long, powerful arms that hung near the ground and ended in claws that could shred trees.

The cyclopean creature plodded out of its cell, growled, and looked around with its one eye. The Abyssin seemed to be in pain, and the only thing it saw—and therefore its only target—was young Jacen, armed with his lightsaber.

The Abyssin roared, but Jacen stood firm. He held up his free hand, palm outward, trying to use the soothing Force techniques that had proven so successful when he'd tamed new animals as his pets.

"Calm down," he said. "Calm down, I don't want to hurt you. I'm not with these people."

But the Abyssin didn't want to be calmed, and stalked forward, swinging its long arms like clawed pendulums. Of course, Jacen realized, if the monster was really just a hologram, then his Jedi techniques would be irrelevant.

The Abyssin pulled out a long, wicked club that had been strapped against its back. The club looked like a gnarled branch with spikes on one end, with a far longer reach than the lightsaber's. The one-eyed monster could pound Jacen and never be touched by the Jedi blade.

"Blaster bolts!" Jacen muttered under his breath. He flicked on the lightsaber, feeling the power of the energy blade that pulsed in front of him with a blinding blue glow.

The Abyssin blinked its single large eye, then charged forward, its fang-filled mouth wide open. The creature swung its spiked club like a battering ram.

Jacen slashed in front of himself with the lightsaber defensively, instinctively. The glowing blade sliced off the tip of the club as easily as if it were a piece of soft cheese. The spiked end clanged on the metal floor.

The monster looked at the smoking end of its club for just a second, then howled and charged again. Jacen was ready this time—his heart pounding, adrenaline flowing, attuned to the Force and focused on his enemy.

The Abyssin hammered down with the club, too close for Jacen to strike with the lightsaber. He dodged to the side, and the creature swung again, this time with a raking handful of claws.

Jacen made a dive for the floor and rolled, holding the lightsaber at arm's length to keep from harming himself with the deadly blade.

The Abyssin pounced on him, thrusting with the thick end of the club. But Jacen lay on his back and held the lightsaber up, twisting his wrists to slash the remainder of the club down to a smoldering stump in the monster's hands, then rolled sideways to dodge the heavy wood as it fell to the floor.

The Abyssin tossed away the useless stump and yowled again, then lunged to grab Jacen from the floor. But Jacen held the lightsaber in front of himself, pushing it forward like a spear. The glowing tip plunged into the descending monster's broad chest, scorching through until it disintegrated the Abyssin's heart.

With a loud and fading shriek of pain, the creature slumped and fell forward. Jacen winced, knowing he would be crushed by the brute—but in midair the cyclops flickered and dissolved into static, then nothingness, as the hologram projectors shut down.

Gasping and sweating, Jacen turned off the lightsaber. The hissing energy beam was swallowed into the handle with a descending *thwoop*. He stood up and brushed himself off.

As the door opened again, Jacen whirled, ready to face another hideous enemy. But only Brakiss stood there, quietly applauding.

"Very good, my young Jedi," Brakiss said. "That wasn't so bad now, was it? You show great potential. All you need is the opportunity to practice."

14

LOWIE CROUCHED ATOP the sleeping platform in his own cell, back pressed to the corner, shaggy knees drawn up to his chest. He wallowed in abject misery and self-recrimination; occasionally he let out a groan.

How could he have been so stupid? He had let the riptide of Brakiss's teaching draw him further and further into his sea of anger until he had been immersed in it, swept away by its current.

Jacen had not given in. And seductive as Brakiss's teachings were—Lowie refused to think of him as *Master* Brakiss—Jaina had not succumbed to them either; she had merely stood up and spoken for what she believed.

A growl of self-reproach rumbled deep in his throat. He alone, who had always prided himself on his thoughtfulness—on his dedication to studying, to learning, to understanding—had allowed himself to be influenced by the poisonous teachings. He would have to be more careful in the future. Resist, block out the words.

If Jacen and Jaina could stay strong, then so could Lowie. Jaina had not given up. She said she had a plan, and he would need to be ready to do his part when the time came to escape. Lowie drew comfort from the thought of his friends' strength. He *could* resist giving in to his anger. He pounded a furry fist against the wall at his side and bellowed his defiance. He *would* resist.

As if in response to his challenge, the door slid open and two stormtroopers stepped in, followed by Tamith Kai. Lowie wrinkled his nose, noting something else that had entered his room uninvited: the unpleasant smell that hung about them, an odor of darkness. The stormtroopers each carried an activated stun wand, and Lowie guessed that they expected him to cause further trouble.

"You will stand," Tamith Kai said.

Lowie wondered whether he dared resist. A prod from one of the stormtroopers' stun wands answered the question for him.

Tamith Kai's violet gaze raked up and down Lowie for a moment, and then she blew out a short breath, as if about to start a difficult task that she had set herself.

"You are not yet skilled in the ways of the Force," she said, not unkindly, "yet you have the capacity for great anger." She nodded with approval. "This is your greatest strength. I will teach you now to draw upon that anger, to bring forth your full power in the Force. You will be surprised at how it will accelerate your learning."

She turned to the stormtroopers. "Remove his belt."

Lowie put a protective hand to the glossy braids that encircled his waist and crossed over his shoulder. He had risked his life to acquire these fibers from the syren plant as part of his rites of passage into Wookiee adulthood; then he had painstakingly woven them into a belt that symbolized his independence and self-reliance.

He opened his mouth to snarl an angry objection but stopped short, realizing that this was exactly the response Tamith Kai hoped for—to goad him into anger. He would not be so easily fooled this time. He stood, resolute and passive, while the stormtroopers removed the precious belt.

She motioned for him to precede her from the room. One of the stormtroopers administered an encouraging prod. Tamith Kai's smile mocked Lowie. "Yes, young Wookiee," she said, "your anger shall be your greatest strength."

They led him to a large, unfurnished chamber. Bright orange and red light glared down from unfiltered glowpanels set into the ceiling. The chilled air stank of metal and sweat. When the door slid shut with a hiss and a clang, Lowie looked around. He was completely alone.

Lowbacca stood waiting for what seemed like hours, alert, prepared for whatever Tamith Kai might use to provoke him. His golden eyes roved the blank walls with suspicion.

Nothing happened.

As he waited, the lights in the room seemed to glow brighter, the air to turn colder. Finally, he sat down with his back pressed to one wall, still wary, still watching.

Nothing.

After a long time, Lowie straightened up with a jerk, realizing that he had been about to doze off. He eyed the walls again, looking for any changes, and found himself wishing for even the annoying Em Teedee to keep him awake—and to keep him company.

* * *

Sound exploded in Lowie's head, high-pitched and excruciating, awakening him from a fitful sleep. Garish lights flashed overhead, blinding in their intensity. Lowie sprang to his feet.

Trying to focus his eyes, he looked around for the source of the siren and pressed his hands over his ears, groaning in pain. But he could not block out the sound that sliced into his brain as a laser would slice into soft wood.

Without warning, all sound ceased, leaving a vacuum of silence. The glowpanels stabilized, returning to their former level of brightness.

Tamith Kai's face appeared behind a broad transparisteel panel in the wall that Lowie had not noticed before. Still groggy from his interrupted sleep, Lowie threw himself against the panel in frustration. Tamith Kai's pleased chuckle sobered him instantly. "A fine start," she said.

Lowie backed into the center of the room and sat down, wrapping his long hairy arms around his legs, afraid to make any further response lest he lose his temper again.

Her taunting voice echoed through the empty chamber. "Oh, we are *far* from finished with our lesson, Wookiee. You will stand."

Lowie pressed his forehead to his knees, refusing to look at her, refusing to move.

"Ah," the voice continued, "perhaps it is for the best. The fire of your anger will burn brighter the more fuel I add."

The high-pitched sound drilled into his brain again, and flashing lights assaulted his eyes. Lowie concentrated, focused his mind inside himself. He mutely endured.

The lights and sound ceased as a heavy black object fell from an access hatch onto the floor beside him. Deep in concentration, Lowie didn't flinch, but he looked up to see what it was.

"This is a sonic generator," Tamith Kai's rich, deep voice announced. "It produces the lovely music you've been enjoying today." An undercurrent of cruel amusement rippled through her words. "It also contains the high-intensity strobe relay for the glowpanels. To complete your lesson for the day, all you need do is destroy the sonic generator."

Lowie looked at the boxy object: it measured less than a meter to a side, was made of a dull burnished metal with rounded edges and corners, and had no handholds whatsoever. He reached for it.

"Rest assured," Tamith Kai's voice came again, "even a full-grown Wookiee cannot lift it without using the Force."

Lowie tried to heft the object, found that she was correct. He closed his eyes and concentrated, drawing on the Force, and tried again. The generator hardly budged. Lowie shook his head in confusion. The weight itself, or the object's size, should not have mattered, he told himself. Perhaps, he reasoned, he was just too tired. Or perhaps Tamith Kai was using the Force to hold it down.

"Think, my young Jedi," Tamith Kai chided. "You cannot expect to lift the heaviest object with your weakest muscles."

Lights flashed again, and a dagger of sound pierced his ears. But only for a moment.

"Do not keep your anger pent up," Tamith Kai's voice continued as if there had been no interruption. "You must use it . . . release it. Only then can you set yourself free."

Lowie recognized what she was doing, and the knowledge gave him strength. He closed his eyes, drew a deep breath, and concentrated, prepared to resist the lights and sound.

But he was not prepared for what followed.

From all sides, jets of icy water exploded from the walls, buffeting him with bruising force. He was drenched and shivering, but still the high-pressure streams pummeled him, invaded him. The prying liquid forced itself up under his eyelids, inside his ears and mouth, and streamed down his body, chilling him to the bone.

As unexpectedly as it had begun, the watery attack ended. Shuddering convulsively from the cold, Lowie looked down to find himself ankle-deep in water that was barely warmer than glacial runoff. Anger welled up within him, but he suppressed it, let it flow out of him as the water had streamed down his body. He tried instead to shift the sonic generator again, but to no avail.

As if Lowie's effort had triggered it, the sonic generator began a fresh assault on his senses, strobing the glowpanels and flooding the room with high-pitched wailing until Lowie feared he would drown in it.

Instead, he concentrated on thoughts of his friends Jacen and Jaina. He would be strong.

When the generator paused, more fists of freezing water pounded him again from all sides.

How long these tortures alternated, Lowie could not say. After a time, it seemed his life had always been a litany of lights, sound, water, lights, sound, water . . .

And still he did not give in to his anger.

By the time Tamith Kai spoke to him again, he was curled into a tight, freezing ball of soggy misery, perched directly on the sonic generator in an effort to bring feeling back to his numb legs and feet.

"You have the power within you to end your ordeal," her voice said with mock pity. "Alas, young Jedi, fortitude is only admirable when it gains you something."

Lowie did not raise his head or acknowledge her words.

"You cannot help yourself in this way. You cannot help your friends. Your friends have already learned the truth of my words," she went on.

Lowie's head snapped up, and he voiced a growl of disbelief.

"Ah, but it is true," she said, a note of encouragement in her voice. "Would you like to see them?"

Before he could utter a bark of agreement, a pair of holographic images spun in the air before his eyes. One showed Jacen wielding a lightsaber, a look of fierce enjoyment lighting his young features. In the other Jaina used the Force to toss aside heavy objects, her head thrown back with a challenging grin.

Lowie reached toward the luminescent images with a yelp of stunned disbelief—and fell face-first into the icy water that covered the floor. He hauled himself back to his feet, and the sonic generator resumed its torturous whine.

From deep within him, horror mixed with rage and a sense of betrayal, fanning the embers that had smoldered for so long. Flames of anger sprang up inside him, warming him with their undeniable heat, rising higher and higher until they burst from his throat in a howl of fury.

And he knew no more.

Lowie woke to restful darkness back in his own cell. The room was warm, and he lay on his sleeping platform covered with a soft blanket. His muscles ached, but he felt well rested. He moved a hand to his waist and found that he was once again wearing his webbed belt.

The voice of Tamith Kai spoke next to him. Lowie was not surprised to find the tall, dark-haired Nightsister standing beside him. In the dim light of the cell's glowpanels he saw that she held an irregularly shaped metal object.

"You have done well, young Wookiee," she said.

Lowie gave a sad moan as the memory of what he had done flooded back to him.

"With your anger you succeeded beyond my highest expectations," Tamith Kai said, looking at him with obvious pride. "As a reward, I've brought you back your droid."

Lowie's mind faltered with confusion. Should he feel *proud* of what he had done? Should he be ashamed? He received Em Teedee from

Tamith Kai's hands with relief and clipped the little droid to its accustomed place at his belt.

"You will make a fine Jedi," Tamith Kai said. She smiled conspiratorially. "After you unleashed your anger, we were unable even to repair the sonic generator, as we have every time before." And then she swept out of the room, leaving him to his thoughts.

Lowie stood and groaned as his muscles refused to cooperate, and he slumped back onto the sleeping platform.

"Well, if you ask my opinion," Em Teedee's thin voice piped up, "you caused a great deal of your own pain through your needless resistance."

Lowbacca growled a surprised reply.

"Who asked *me?*" Em Teedee said. "Well, I really don't know why you should be so upset. After all, you're here at the Shadow Academy to learn. Why, you're very fortunate that they've taken such an interest in you.

"The Imperials are very perceptive, you know. So perceptive, in fact, that they saw my own potential and have included me in their plans. I am most honored."

With an uncomfortable suspicion, Lowie barked a question.

"Wrong with me?" Em Teedee asked. "Why, nothing. Quite the contrary. As an expression of their complete confidence in me, Brakiss and Tamith Kai have had my programming enhanced. I feel much better now than I ever have. I am to be an integral part of your instruction here. You must realize that they have only your best interests at heart. The Empire is your friend."

Lowie made a thoughtful sound as if accepting Em Teedee's words—and reached down to switch the little droid off.

His head had suddenly become clear. Em Teedee's words had crystallized something in his mind. He might have given in, but he had not given up. And if he knew anything about Jacen and Jaina, the same was true for them—at least that's what he would have to hope.

15

IT WAS MIDAFTERNOON by the time Tenel Ka returned. She found Master Skywalker quietly contemplating in the small slave's quarters Augwynne Djo had offered him to keep him away from curious eyes during the meeting.

"I've spoken with the Council of Sisters," she said. Waves of afternoon heat rippled up the cliffside to the fortress of the Singing Mountain Clan, giving the air a flat, burnt smell. "They expect visitors to come at dusk. At that time all of our questions will be answered."

"Then we wait," Master Skywalker said, looking at her with his intense blue eyes. "It is one of the most difficult things to do—especially at such an urgent time, when we don't know what's happened to Jacen or Jaina or Lowbacca. But if waiting gets us answers where action would not . . . then waiting"—he smiled—"is the action we must choose."

Like a good guest, Tenel Ka busied herself with minor duties to help the Singing Mountain Clan as the hours crawled slowly by.

The sun swung toward the horizon and dusk. Low clouds in the otherwise clear air burned pink and orange, scattering leftover rays into the heated atmosphere. Clicking insects and scuttling lizards began to move about as their world cooled with evening, adding faint rustling noises to the day's silence.

On the lower tier of cliff dwellings, looking down upon the baked rocky plain, Tenel Ka and Master Skywalker watched the lengthening shadows cast by sunset across the desert. Compared with the bright reptilian hides Tenel Ka wore, Master Skywalker's brown robes seemed drab and nondescript—but she knew the strength and skill he harbored within himself.

Tenel Ka noticed something dark and large moving across the plain. She perked up and squinted her gray eyes, studying the creature as it came closer. Some large beast bearing a rider—no, two riders.

Master Skywalker nodded. "Yes, I see it. A rancor carrying two." Tenel Ka squinted again, then realized that Luke was enhancing his vision with the Force, sensing as well as seeing.

Others from the Singing Mountain Clan came to their open adobe windows and stood on the cliff balconies, gazing down in nervous anticipation.

The rancor plodded forward, slow but unstoppable. Tenel Ka could clearly see the hulking monstrosity, whose knobby, tan-gray body seemed nothing more than a vehicle loaded with ferocious fangs and claws. A tall, muscular woman rode in front; behind her sat a dark-haired young man with thick eyebrows, wearing a cloak of silver-shot black, just like the woman's.

"She's a Nightsister," said Tenel Ka. "I can feel it."

Master Skywalker nodded. "Yes, but this new breed seems well trained and even more dangerous. Something is happening here. I can feel we're on the right track."

"But—what is that . . . man doing with her?" Tenel Ka asked. "No ruler on Dathomir would treat a man as her equal."

"Well," Luke said, "perhaps things really *have* changed."

Below, the Nightsister rider pulled the enormous rancor to a halt. The clawed, lumpy-headed beast hissed and reared up, dragging its knobby knuckles across the baked hardpan. The Nightsister dismounted, and her black-robed companion slid down beside her. They stood between two towering bronze rocks that thrust up from the sands.

"Hear me, worthy people!" the woman called up the cliffs. Her shout echoed along the rocks, reflecting her words and making her voice seem louder and broader. Tenel Ka wondered how the dark woman could speak so forcefully. She felt the Nightsister's tug on her imagination even as she stood and listened.

"She's using a Force trick," Master Skywalker said, "pulling on your emotions, making you interested in what she's about to say."

Tenel Ka nodded. A cool breeze stirred up by the rapidly changing temperatures of evening whipped her red-gold hair about her face.

"Once again, we come to seek others interested in what we have to offer. Yes, we know that long ago evil Nightsisters ruled Dathomir with an iron hand and a cruel will. They were bad people—but that doesn't mean their training was completely wrong, that everything they knew about power is to be despised.

"I am Vonnda Ra, and this is my companion Vilas. Yes—a male. I can sense you are shocked and surprised, but you should not be. From other allies, we have learned that this power we call . . . *the Force* dwells in all things, male and female. Not only can the Sisters use it for their own benefit, but males—Brothers—can also wield such strength."

Many of the people in the cliff dwellings stirred.

"I sense your disbelief," Vonnda Ra said, "but I assure you it is true."

Tenel Ka whispered to Master Skywalker. "I have seen many things in the last few years," she said, "and I believe I know how other societies work—but I fear that some of the more conservative clans on Dathomir are not quite ready to accept such measures of equality."

Master Skywalker nodded, but pursed his lips gravely. "There's nothing in Jedi teachings that favors either male or female—or even human, for that matter. Your people have only been deceiving themselves."

Far below, Vonnda Ra stood beside her tamed rancor and shouted up. "Vilas, my best male student, will demonstrate for you one small thing he has learned, something that will amaze you."

Dark-haired Vilas removed his spangled black cloak and draped it on the patched whuffa-hide saddle across the rancor's back. He began to concentrate, standing off to himself in the flat, baked dirt between the stone columns, his arms at his side, hands clenched into fists.

Even from this far up the cliff, Tenel Ka could hear Vilas humming. Beneath their bushy brows, his eyes were squeezed shut. His black hair began to rise, flickering with static electricity. He rippled with a growing power.

Up in the purple sky, stars had just begun to shine through, bright white lights against the darkening backdrop of the almost-faded sunset. Clouds started to gather, faint wisps at first, like corded shadows across the sky that knotted and drew together. Tenel Ka stood back as the breeze picked up and became colder.

"We are always searching for new trainees," Vonnda Ra shouted up to the gathered crowd. The Singing Mountain people clustered forward to their windows and balconies.

"If any of you would like to learn the ways of the Force, to do what Vilas and I can do—whether you be male or female, noble-born or slave—come join us. Our settlement is at the bottom of the Great Canyon, only three days' journey from here by foot.

"We cannot guarantee that we will choose you, but we will test your abilities. Any we find with the right kind of talent, we will adopt as our own. We will teach you to be an important part in the machine of the universe. Your future can be bright, if you are with us."

As Vonnda Ra finished, an ear-shattering peal of thunder drowned out her last words. Violent blue lightning danced in great forks that skittered across the sky.

Vilas had climbed one of the bronze rock pinnacles, scrambling up, light-footed, as if someone were drawing him up on cables. Now he stood on the flat weathered rock, arms raised. Static electricity swirled like a whirlpool around him as the gathering thunderstorm coalesced at his bidding.

More lightning flickered around the desertscape, striking solitary boulders on the flat plain and sending up showers of dust and sparks. The storm thickened, slashing at them with cold wind. Tenel Ka blinked back stinging tears as her hair thrashed around her.

Vilas stood atop his pinnacle of rock, commanding the storm. The clouds thickened, turning the sky black.

Tenel Ka looked down the cliff face and saw that beside the lone rancor, Vonnda Ra also held her hands outstretched, palms up, fingers spread, calling the storm. Lightning came down across the desert. The rancor snorted and reared, but did not run.

"Come to the Great Canyon," Vonnda Ra shouted above the screaming wind. "If you want to touch power such as this, come to the Great Canyon."

Vilas sprang down from the stone pinnacle and landed with ease on the windswept desert sands next to the rearing rancor. He and Vonnda Ra scrambled onto the patched saddle.

Vonnda Ra grabbed the creature's reins and yanked it about. The clawed monster loped off into the distance as the storm continued to rage around the cliffs.

Tenel Ka stared after, trying to keep her eyes on the dwindling silhouette of the monster and its two riders. "So now we know. . . ." she said. "What shall we do?"

Luke put his hand on her shoulder, and she could sense his confidence. "We go to this Great Canyon and offer ourselves as candidates," he said. "They *are* looking for new people to train. And now we're sure we're on the right track. Jacen, Jaina, and Lowbacca might be there already."

Tenel Ka bit her lip and nodded. "This is a fact."

16

JAINA LEFT THE lightsaber switched off and pushed it back toward Brakiss, but he wouldn't take it.

"I won't play your games," Jaina insisted.

"We do not *play* at the Shadow Academy," Brakiss said. "But we do practice. Important training for a Jedi."

"Fighting stupid holographic monsters? I won't do it anymore. I've done too much for you already. You may as well just take us home, because we'll never serve your Shadow Academy."

Brakiss spread his hands. "Ah, but you're getting so good with the lightsaber," he said, as if reasoning with a recalcitrant child. "Try it one more time. I'll give you a worthy opponent, someone a bit more challenging to fight."

"Why should I?" Jaina said. "I don't *owe* you anything. I want to see my brother. I want to see Lowie."

"You will see them soon enough."

"I won't fight unless you promise I can see them."

Brakiss sighed. "Very well. I promise to let you see each other again, during classes. But only"—he held up one finger—"if you agree not to cause more disturbances."

Jaina pressed her mouth into a grim line. For now, this was the best she could hope to accomplish. "Agreed."

Then Brakiss said, his tone disturbingly encouraging, "Think of it this way—the more training you undergo, the better chance you'll have if ever you fight against me. Consider it . . . training for your eventual escape, hmmm?"

She found the calm smile maddening on his smooth, handsome face.

"There will be another change in our session this morning. As you fight, you will be shrouded in a holographic disguise. It will not hinder your movements, but you may find it a bit distracting. You must learn to fight wearing this three-dimensional mask: for the good of the

Empire, we may occasionally need to deploy our Dark Jedi in disguise."

Jaina held the lightsaber in front of her. "All right, I'll fight this one training session—then you have to let me see my brother and Lowie."

"That was our agreement," Brakiss answered. "I'll go arrange it now. Meanwhile, good luck." He slipped back out the doorway, and it sealed shut.

The flat gray walls flickered, and Jaina saw shadows wrap themselves around her—not enough to blind her, just a blur. She realized it must be the holographic costume.

On the other side of the room an imaginary wooden door groaned open, and Jaina rolled her eyes. Just a corny illusion, as everything else had been. Jaina was not amused. Her only challenge was trying to figure out how the equipment on the station worked. Someday she would foil the Shadow Academy, bring its systems crashing down. For now, she would play along with Brakiss, and eventually she would find a way to turn the head teacher's schemes against him.

Her new opponent stepped out of the barred dungeon doorway—a tall, looming figure wrapped completely in black. The black plasteel mask echoed and hissed as Darth Vader breathed through his respirator.

Startled, she caught her breath, instinctively flicking on her lightsaber. Brakiss wasn't playing fair! This went beyond any of the other illusions he had sent against her before. Darth Vader had been killed before the twins were even born, but the Dark Lord of the Sith had been her grandfather; she knew all about him.

Vader's lightsaber was a deep pulsing red, like fresh blood, glowing with light from within. Jaina felt both anger and dismay rise within her, and she stepped forward to confront him. Her holographic costume swirled around her, but she didn't let it distract her.

Jaina hated the evil acts Darth Vader had performed during his alliance with the Emperor—but she also loved the *idea* of what her grandfather Anakin Skywalker could have been, the good man he had become in his last moments when he turned against the Emperor and ended his reign of terror.

Whether it was her own fear or something deeper, Jaina sensed a great uneasiness in the training chamber, a pulsating dread that slowed her movements.

Darth Vader took advantage of her shocked hesitation. He came toward her, scarlet lightsaber sizzling. His breathing echoed all around her. Vader slashed with the weapon, and Jaina countered with her own beam, producing a shower of sparks as the energy blades crossed and struck.

They struck again and again. Thrusting. Parrying. Attacking. Defending.

Jaina swung, trying to land a blow on Darth Vader's chest armor, but the Dark Lord brought his own beam up to crash against hers. She backed away as he attacked with greater strength, slashing, striking with his lightsaber. The shrieks of electrical discharge nearly deafened her. But as Jaina began to falter, she pretended Vader was Brakiss or Tamith Kai—the ones who had kidnapped her and brought all of them to this school of darkness—and was able to defend herself with renewed strength, this time pushing Vader back.

She struck blow after blow. The lightsabers clashed, but Darth Vader seemed to draw strength from Jaina's fury. They fought on for a long time, neither gaining the upper hand. Jaina lost track of how many minutes or hours passed.

They stood with lightsabers crossed and electric arcs flying around them, pressing against each other, straining with all their might. But Vader could not defeat her, and she could not defeat him. They were equally matched.

She gritted her teeth and strained, her breathing heavy, her lungs burning cold. She gasped, but would not let up. Vader also did not stop.

"Enough!" Brakiss's voice came over the intercom.

The training room's holographic simulation faded, leaving her standing in the flat gray room, her lightsaber still crossed with her opponent's. Only now she could see who her adversary really was.

Jacen.

In the control room, looking down at the displayed images from the simulation chamber, Brakiss tapped his fingers together. With great pleasure, he watched the twins battle each other.

Wearing his dark Imperial uniform, Qorl stood beside him, observing the activity. The monitor showed none of the holographic disguises, just the twins fighting, battling to the death—and not even knowing it! Their lightsabers crossed and locked, neither twin overpowering the other.

Qorl remained silent for a long moment, fidgeting with restrained anxiety. Finally he said, "Isn't this dangerous, Brakiss? With one slip, those children could kill each other. You would lose two of your best trainees at the Shadow Academy."

"I doubt I'll lose them," Brakiss said, dismissing the thought with a wave. "But if one kills the other, then we will know which is the stronger fighter. That is the one we must concentrate our training on."

"But what a waste," Qorl said. "Why would you do this? What is the point?"

Brakiss turned to the old TIE pilot, allowing just a trace of anger to show on his perfect face. "The point is to obtain and develop the strongest fighters for the Empire. The most talented Dark Jedi."

"No matter what the cost?" Qorl said.

"Cost is of no consequence," Brakiss replied. "These young twins are simply tools to be used—as you are, as we *all* are."

Qorl frowned and watched the continuing battle. "Are you saying the twins are expendable?"

"They are ingredients . . . components to be installed in a great machine. If they do not meet our stringent testing requirements, they are no good to us.

"But perhaps you're right," Brakiss said, finally conceding. "They have both fought well and demonstrated their skills with the lightsaber. Now to make a real impact on them."

He turned on the comm. "Enough!" he said, and disabled the holographic disguise generator.

The twins cried out, then sprang apart, astonished to discover they'd been fighting each other.

After a few moments Brakiss switched off the intercom, not wanting to listen to the children's outraged cries anymore. He shrugged and smiled at Qorl. "I did promise to let her see her brother. I don't know why she should be so upset."

Qorl turned away and walked toward the exit, so Brakiss would not see the depth of his uncertainty. The harsh treatment of Jacen and Jaina disturbed him, affecting him against his wishes.

"Their training is coming along quite nicely," Brakiss said as Qorl reached the door. "I am pleased with their progress. They will become great Dark Jedi in our service."

Qorl made a noncommittal reply as he slipped out and closed the door behind him.

17

TENEL KA AND Luke rode astride a young rancor that had not yet been marked to show ownership by any particular clan.

The night air was warm and still heavy with moisture from the unnatural storm Vonnda Ra and her student Vilas had called up. Dathomir's two moons floated in and out of wispy clouds, shedding a diffuse pearly light on their path.

Tenel Ka sat in front of Luke on the whuffa-hide saddle, guiding the rancor steadily in the direction of the Great Canyon. She was a good rider, and she knew it. She had to admit that it felt good to demonstrate to Master Skywalker that she was an expert at something.

A light breeze rustled the leaves of the low bushes around them, so that when Luke leaned forward to whisper in her ear, Tenel Ka hardly heard him at first. "I had to kill a rancor once," he said. "It was a shame—they're such fine creatures."

"Even so," Tenel Ka answered, "they are dangerous to those who are not their friends."

Luke was silent for a while. "I've fought many battles," he said at last, "and yes, I have had to kill. But I've learned from the light side of the Force that it's better to do everything in my power first to . . . *turn* a situation—"

"But surely," Tenel Ka interrupted, "a Nightsister—or anyone else seduced by the dark side—would not hesitate to kill *you.*"

"Exactly!" Luke's soft exclamation took her by surprise. "Now you begin to understand," he said. "Those who use the light side do not believe the same things as those who use the dark side. But we can only *demonstrate* our differences by acting on our beliefs. Otherwise . . . we're not so different after all."

"Ah. Aha," Tenel Ka said. "Just as *I* struggle to show that I am different from my grandmother on Hapes. . . ." Her voice trailed off. "Yes, I see now."

* * * *

In spite of the darkness, their surefooted rancor picked its way steadily down the steep path that led to the floor of the Great Canyon. During their descent, they spotted a cluster of more than a dozen campfires, and knew that they had found the Nightsisters' encampment.

By the time they reached the canyon floor, both Luke and Tenel Ka were sore and aching and weary. The air was cool, with a light mist hovering close to the ground, and they were both glad of the warm cloaks that Augwynne had pressed on them during their rushed preparations for departure. She had given them each a change of clothes appropriate to their cover story, along with a bag of provisions. Then she had hugged Tenel Ka fiercely. "Daughter of my daughter's daughter," she said, "go in safety. The thoughts of the Singing Mountain Clan are with you." She turned to Luke. "And may the Force be with you."

Augwynne had released Tenel Ka and spoke again to her. "I am proud of what you do for your friends. You are a true warrior woman of our clan. Always remember our most sacred rule from the Book of Laws: 'Never concede to evil.' "

Now, as they drew closer to that evil, Tenel Ka shivered and pulled her cloak more tightly about her. She wondered if they would find Lowbacca, Jacen, and Jaina at the camp of the Nightsisters, or if that would only be an intermediate step in their search. Could the Nightsisters be training them in the dark ways of the Force? Tenel Ka let her eyes drift shut and cast about with her mind, but she sensed no trace of her three friends.

As if understanding the direction of her thoughts, Luke leaned forward again. "If we don't find them here, the Force will guide us. We are close . . . I feel it."

An ululating cry rang out from the canyon rocks above them. Tenel Ka started in surprise. "A scout sounding the alarm," she said, irritated with herself for having been caught off guard.

"Good," Luke replied. "Then they know we're here."

Tenel Ka hesitated at first, uncertain of whether it was safe to continue, and then urged the young rancor forward. She looked up at the sky, which had lightened from black to predawn grayness, reminding her again of how much time had passed since her friends had been captured.

Rounding the next bend in the trail, the rancor came to an abrupt stop. Tenel Ka looked at the path ahead of her and saw that their way was blocked by three full-grown rancors, each bearing a rider, dressed much as Vonnda Ra and Vilas had been earlier that evening.

The pressure of Luke's hand at her waist was a warning, but she already knew. Even in the dimness she could see that each of the riders held an Imperial blaster aimed directly at them.

Tenel Ka had been raised to take command, and though she rarely exercised that power, it did come naturally. She sat up straighter in the saddle and held one arm high. "Sisters and brothers of the Great Canyon Clan," she said, "we have heard your message as far away as the Misty Falls Clan and have traveled here to join you. We are not without skill in the Force, and we wish to learn your ways, to use *all* of the Force and to become strong."

Leaving the rancors at the well-provisioned stockade, Tenel Ka and Luke followed the guards toward the center of camp. She was surprised to see two Imperial AT-ST scout walkers clanking like mechanical birds around the perimeter on guard duty, near the penned rancors.

Passing between boldly colored tents made of water-repellent lizard hides, Tenel Ka noted roughly ten women and at least as many men going about their early-morning business in eerie silence, as if the warm ground mists swirling up to their knees muffled all sound. She saw no children at all in the encampment, heard no baby's cries, no sounds of young ones playing. In fact, she saw very few in the Great Canyon Clan who were even as young as she was.

Though she had known what to expect, it amazed Tenel Ka that men came and went here as freely as the women, apparently slaves to no one. She wondered if it really was possible on Dathomir that these men and women now thought of each other as equals.

At the center of camp, they came at last to an enormous patchwork pavilion that floated on the mist like a barbaric island made of furs and lizard hides sewn together. It was held up at the center and the corners by spears, three meters long and as thick around as Tenel Ka's wrists.

One of the Nightsisters raised a tent flap and motioned them inside. They entered, but the Sister did not follow. The flap dropped shut behind them, sealing out the wraithlike mists and the morning light. Waiting for her eyes to adjust, Tenel Ka tried to sense her friends; she still found no trace, but the light touch of Master Skywalker's hand on her arm reassured her.

At the center of the tent a tiny pinpoint of light suddenly flared into a bright flame, and Tenel Ka saw that it came from an oil lamp fashioned out of the inverted skull of a mountain lizard. Beside the lamp, on a wide platform covered with furs and cushions made from the hides of a variety of wild beasts, an imposing woman reclined in a massive chair made from a stuffed rancor head. The woman beckoned them forward into the flickering circle of light.

Without so much as a greeting, Vonnda Ra asked, "What is your business here?"

Tenel Ka, who had recognized the dark-haired woman instantly, said, "I have come to join the Nightsisters, and I have brought my slave with me."

"What have you to offer us?" Vonnda Ra looked mildly interested, but not impressed. "Many come wishing to join us, but they are weak. Women seek us out because their powers are small or they have no status in their clans. Men come here because they have never had power, and our teachings offer them freedom—but they usually have even less to offer. What do you have?"

Vonnda Ra's hand reached out and pointed to the lizard skull filled with burning oil. "Can you do this?" The lamp floated straight upward toward the peak of the tent, casting an ever-wider but dimmer circle of light, and then settled slowly back down onto the platform beside Vonnda Ra.

Tenel Ka nodded. "I have had some training." Deciding against using any theatrical gestures or words, she half-closed her eyes in concentration and grasped the lamp with her mind. She had never enjoyed showing off her skill with the Force, using it only when absolutely necessary, but this performance was not for herself. She would probably never see Jacen and Jaina and Lowbacca again if she could not show these Nightsisters her true potential.

She drew in a deep breath, let it out again. Without a sound the lamp glided off the platform and high into the air over their heads. Tenel Ka thought about the flame, feeding it with her mind and making it brighter, brighter, until its warm radiance reached even to the darkest corners of the pavilion. Then she sent the lamp sailing around the outer edges of the tent; it made the complete circle so quickly that she heard Vonnda Ra gasp with amazement. Through her half-closed eyes Tenel Ka watched the dark-haired woman sit up, one hand outstretched, palm up, as if to ask a question.

Tenel Ka brought the lamp in closer for another circle, and then another, smaller and closer to the central tent post, until at last it spun around the center pole in a dizzy downward spiral, still glowing brightly—all in a matter of a few seconds. Last, Tenel Ka brought the spinning lamp lightly to rest in Vonnda Ra's outstretched hand.

The Nightsister gave a gleeful chuckle. "You are welcome here, Sister," she said. "What is your name?"

Tenel Ka threw her head back. "My name—*our names*—no longer have any meaning for us. We discarded them when we left our clan."

"Come here," Vonnda Ra ordered. When Tenel Ka did as she was told, the Nightsister stood and took the young girl's chin in her fingers and looked deep into her eyes. "Yes," she said with a satisfied nod. "You have much anger in you. Are you willing to go elsewhere to learn? To a place of instruction among the stars?"

Tenel Ka's heart leaped. Perhaps *this* was where Jacen, Jaina, and Lowbacca had been taken. "Wherever your finest teachers are, that is where I wish to go," she replied.

"But you must leave your slave behind. We will have little use for him," Vonnda Ra said.

"No!"

Vonnda Ra sighed. "What if I were to tell you that men rarely have any talent, and that we have never trained one this old? He would only distract you from what you must learn. There is little hope of teaching him. If you knew all this, then what would you say?"

"Then I would say . . . ," Tenel Ka replied, leveling her best cool gray stare at Vonnda Ra, "that you are a fool."

Vonnda Ra's eyes went wide with surprise, but Tenel Ka did not stop. "This man has watched and learned the ways of the Force since before I was born. Not many—*not many who still live*—have seen his power. But I have seen it."

Vonnda Ra abruptly turned her skeptical gaze toward Luke. "If you can lift this," she said, pointing to her lizard-skull lamp, *"and* bring as much light to this tent as she did"—she nodded toward Tenel Ka— "then you shall accompany her."

The Nightsister looked at Luke and then back down at the lamp. When it did not move, a small contemptuous smile flickered at the corners of her mouth. Then something large and dark floated between them and blocked her view. The flame from the oil lamp brightened, and the massive rancor-head chair grinned at her, its lifeless eyes glowing with reflected light. Then the head lifted and glided around the perimeter of the tent like a shuttlecraft.

Tenel Ka could see Master Skywalker standing with arms crossed over his chest, one knee bent in an apparently relaxed posture, his head cocked to one side, smiling at Vonnda Ra as he sent the rancor head whizzing about the pavilion.

"Since you asked," he said, "I will give you light." Suddenly, in a blur of motion, the stuffed rancor head shot upward with the speed of blaster fire. It disappeared through the ceiling of the tent, leaving a gaping hole in its wake, through which the bright morning sunlight streamed.

Vonnda Ra looked more than a little nervous as she stepped forward and took Luke's chin in her hands. For more than a minute she gazed transfixed into his eyes. "Yes," she hissed at last. "Yes, you understand the dark side."

She backed away from him as if in awe, stared up at the rent in the ceiling of her pavilion, then looked back at Luke and Tenel Ka. "We expect an Imperial supply shuttle at dawn tomorrow," she said. "When it leaves this planet, the two of you must be on it."

18

JACEN, JAINA, AND Lowbacca were at first surprised and delighted that they would be together for the next exercise—but the grim expressions on Brakiss and Tamith Kai soon soured their pleasure. Obviously, Jacen thought, the two Shadow Academy instructors had something difficult and dangerous in mind.

"Because you must move forward in your training," Brakiss said, motioning outward to represent progress, "we have designed exercises to present greater and greater challenges for your abilities."

Lowie groaned in dismay.

"For this next test, the three of you must work *together*. Each trainee must learn to act in concert with others to assist our cause. There are times when we must be unified to provide appropriate service to the Second Imperium."

Em Teedee parroted from his place at Lowie's waist, "Oh, most certainly—appropriate service to the Empire."

Lowie growled at the translating droid to be quiet.

"You needn't take that tone with me! I am simply reinforcing the things you need to know," the reprogrammed Em Teedee replied, miffed.

The three companions found themselves in a new room this time, smaller, more claustrophobic, with numerous round hatches built into the walls on every side.

Tamith Kai went to a control panel in one corner and tapped in a series of commands with her long-nailed fingers. Four of the metal hatches slid open, and spherical remotes floated out on repulsorfields.

The remotes were metal balls studded with tiny lasers. They reminded Jacen of the defensive satellites that had been unable to stop the Imperial blastboats from invading GemDiver Station. He felt uneasy, wondering if the floating drones would start firing at them.

"These remotes are your protection," Tamith Kai said. "That is, if the Wookiee can operate them correctly."

Lowie growled a question. "Oh, do be patient, Lowbacca," Em Teedee said. "I'm sure she'll explain everything in good time. She's quite good at this, you know."

Brakiss gestured to the remaining hatches on the wall. "These will open at random," he said, "and they will hurl objects at you."

Brakiss reached into the folds of his silvery robe and withdrew a pair of polished wooden sticks, each about the length of Jacen's arm. He handed them to the twins.

"These are your only weapons: these sticks—and the Force. If the Force is your ally, you have a powerful weapon."

"We know that already," Jaina snapped.

"Good," Brakiss said, his intensely calm smile still in place. "Then you won't object to the other restrictions we place on you." From his sleeve he pulled out two long, black strips of cloth. "You'll be blindfolded. You must use the Force to detect the objects coming at you."

Jacen felt his heart sink.

"When the objects fly at you, you must either nudge them aside with the Force or strike them with the wooden sticks." He shrugged. "That is all. A simple enough game."

Tamith Kai took up the explanation. "The Wookiee will be in an observation chamber, working to protect you as well. He'll have full control of the computer to run these four remotes. They have powerful enough lasers to disintegrate any of the projectiles. Of course, if he misses, and the laser strikes you instead, he could cause serious injury."

"So"—Brakiss rubbed his hands together, a look of anticipation on his beautiful face—"you have your own weapons, and the Wookiee has the remotes. The three of you must work together to keep yourselves alive."

Jacen swallowed nervously. Jaina lifted her chin and scowled at the two teachers. Lowie bristled, clenching and unclenching his hairy hands.

"Let me point out," Tamith Kai said, her voice thick and powerful, "that these are *not* holograms. These are real threats, and if one strikes you, you will feel real pain."

"Just what kind of objects are these, anyway?" Jacen asked. "What're you going to throw at us?"

"There will be three levels to your test," Brakiss answered. "During the first stage we will throw hard balls at you. They may sting, but will cause no permanent damage. In the second round, as the test speeds up, we will throw rocks, which could break bones and cause serious injury."

Tamith Kai's deep red lips wore a broad smile, as if she were savoring some pleasant thought. "The third round will involve *knives.*"

Jaina sucked in a shaky breath.

"Glad you have such faith in our abilities," Jacen grumbled.

"I will be greatly disappointed if you are both killed," Brakiss told them, his expression earnest.

"Hey, so will we," Jacen said.

"I think *he'll* get over it before we will," Jaina added in a low voice.

Jacen shifted his weight on his feet and covered a wince as he stepped down on the hard Corusca gem in his boot. He had kept it hidden there, not knowing what else to do with it—but right now the last thing he wanted was to feel the sharp gemstone under his heel and be distracted. He wiggled his foot until the gem was tucked comfortably off to the side.

Brakiss snugged the blindfold over Jacen's eyes, and everything went black. "The Wookiee will do what he can to protect you."

Jacen gripped the hard stick in his hands and considered dealing the Dark Jedi teacher a good whack on the kneecaps, then claiming he had become disoriented by the blindfold and it was an accident. But he decided that such an act would only buy them trouble, and they needed their energy for other purposes.

"Good luck," Brakiss said, unseen, close to his ear.

Jacen didn't respond, and he heard Tamith Kai chuckle as they led Lowie out of the chamber. The Wookiee moaned, but Em Teedee's tinny voice snapped back, "Now, Lowbacca, complaining will do you very little good. You must learn to be brave and dedicated, as I am."

Jacen, standing in blackness with nothing to hold on to but his stick, heard the doors hiss shut behind them. "You ready for this, Jaina?" he asked.

"What kind of question is that?" she said.

The room remained silent around them. He could hear himself breathe, his heart pounding in his ears. He sensed Jaina beside him, heard the rustle of her clothes as she moved.

"Might be better if we stand back-to-back," she suggested, "cover each other as much as we can."

They pressed themselves shoulder-to-shoulder and listened and waited. Soon they heard a hum of machinery, a quiet, grinding sound, as one of the metal portholes slid open. Jacen reached out with the Force to see through the blindfold, to detect where the projectile would come from.

Then, with a sudden *whump* of compressed air, one of the objects shot at them like a cannonball. Using his senses, Jacen whirled, swinging the stick like a bat. He tried to smack the ball out of the way, but it struck him on the shoulder. It was hard, and it stung.

"Ow!" he yelped. Then a second ball shot out. He heard the sizzle of the remotes firing, but then Jaina also cried out behind him—not so much in pain as in startled embarrassment.

He tried to visualize where the next missile would come from. The noises came faster now. He heard another metal porthole hissing open, another hard ball shooting toward him. He swung the wooden stick, and this time grazed it with the edge. He felt a surge of triumph, but realized that he had hit the ball more through blind luck than any skill with the Force.

Another hiss of a porthole, another ball, and another, coming from a different direction. Under Lowie's control, the remotes shot tiny blasts at the flying balls. Jacen heard an impact and thought perhaps Lowie had struck one of the targets. He hoped the lanky Wookiee wouldn't misfire.

Brakiss had instructed them to use anger to increase their control over the Force; as another ball hit Jacen in the ribs, the stinging impact did make him want to lash out in retaliation. But Jacen also remembered his uncle Luke's lessons: a Jedi knows the Force best when he is calm and passive, when he lets it flow *through* him rather than trying to twist it to his own purposes.

Jacen heard a loud crack of wood as his sister struck one of the hard balls. "Gotcha!" she cried.

As he let his mind open up, Jacen saw a small, bright blur through the blindfolded darkness; and he *knew* the next ball would come from that direction. He used the Force to nudge it out of the way, and the ball swung wide, smacking the wall instead. Then he saw another bright blur, then another, and another, as more projectiles came, faster and faster!

He used the Force. He swung the wooden stick, trying to keep up with the flying balls. He sensed that Jaina was also doing better, and that the laser bolts from Lowie's remotes seemed to be striking their targets more often. But with the sheer number of projectiles, Lowie had to miss occasionally.

Something hard and rough struck Jacen on the right arm just at the elbow, and the wave of blazing pain took his breath away. His arm went numb, and Jacen shifted the stick to his left hand, realizing that the test had reached its second stage—they were being bombarded with sharp stones.

* * *

In the observation chamber, Lowbacca worked frantically at his computer controls, guiding the four defensive drones. He fired their lasers and vaporized a few targets. But then the projectile launches picked up speed, and Lowie knew he didn't dare misfire—because if he struck one of the twins with a laser, it would do at least as much damage as one of the stones.

He missed another one, and a rock hit Jaina on the thigh. He saw her blindfolded face crumple in a wince of sudden agony. Jaina's knees buckled, and she nearly went down; but she managed to keep her balance somehow, swinging automatically with the stick and deflecting another stone that came straight at her head.

More sharp rocks hurtled toward the twins, launched with deadly speed. Lowie began shooting all the remotes at once—targeting, firing, targeting, firing. He had already slagged one of the portholes so it could no longer launch stones. But despite his best efforts, he missed again, and this time a rock struck Jacen in the side.

The twins were both hurt now, badly bruised and reeling, though they kept fighting as best they could. Lowie groaned a quiet apology and kept working at the computer controls.

Em Teedee spoke in a sharp, pestering voice. "Need I point out, Lowbacca, that the Empire will be quite disappointed if you don't perform to the best of your abilities in this test?"

Lowie didn't waste energy telling the translating droid to be quiet. He worked the complex controls, calling up programming, reassigning parameters, hammering instructions with his left hand, controlling the remotes with his right hand, using everything he knew about computers. Lowie had a desperate plan—but his attempt absorbed part of his concentration. In his moment of distraction more and more of the hard rocks got through to pummel the Jedi twins. But Lowie had no choice, if he was to make his plan come off.

He sensed that in order to demonstrate their power, the teachers at the Shadow Academy were willing to risk hurting their students. As long as they were left with the strongest trainees, they didn't care if someone actually got killed during the exercises. Lowie's only hope was to bring it all down.

He glanced up, tossing ginger-colored fur out of his eyes, as the stones kept flying.

Jacen was on his knees now, dazedly swinging one-handed with the stick. His right arm hung limp at his side. Lowie saw that both of his friends were battered and bruised, and that still the rocks fired at them without mercy.

After a moment's pause, something changed—and long metal knives began flying out.

Lowie worked close to panic, but forced his concentration on the computer. It was his only hope. Jacen and Jaina's only hope.

The twins used their Force abilities to deflect the incoming blades into the walls, where they left long white scars on the metal. Another knife launched out. And another.

Frantically keying in more commands on the control terminal, Lowie let the floating remotes fall silent. He had one last idea. One last chance.

"Master Lowbacca," Em Teedee scolded, "just what do you think—"

Lowie punched in a command string that he hoped would bypass all other informational sequences, then executed it.

Five portholes opened at once, each ready to launch its deadly knife blade—

Suddenly, the entire training room shut down. The lights winked out. The porthole doors slammed shut. Everything went dark.

With a heavy groan of relief, Lowie slumped back in his chair, running a broad hand over the black streak of fur above his eyebrow. At last he had managed to crash the murderous testing routine.

"Oh, Lowbacca!" Em Teedee wailed. "Dear me, you've really botched everything up! Have you any idea how much trouble it will be to fix this mess?"

Lowie smiled, showing fangs, and purred in contentment.

Brakiss and Tamith Kai charged into the observation room. The Nightsister, her black cloak swirling around her like a storm cloud, was furious. Her violet eyes looked ready to shoot lightning bolts. "What have you done?" Tamith Kai demanded.

Brakiss raised his eyebrows, an expression of proud amusement on his face. "The Wookiee has done exactly what I told him to do," Brakiss said. "He defended his two friends. We didn't tell him he had to follow our rules. It seems he accomplished the objective admirably."

Tamith Kai's wine-dark lips formed a sour expression. "You *condone* this, Brakiss?" she said.

"It shows initiative," he said. "Learning to find innovative solutions is an important skill. Lowbacca here will be a fine addition to the defenders of the Empire."

Lowie roared at the insult.

"Oh, Lowbacca, I'm so proud of you!" Em Teedee said.

Stormtroopers brought out Jacen and Jaina, who stumbled as they walked, obviously hurt. Their clothes were ragged and torn. Scrapes and bruises covered their faces, arms, and legs. Blood oozed from a dozen minor cuts, and the twins blinked their brandy-brown eyes in the bright lights of the observation room.

Brakiss commended both of them for their efforts. "A very good test," he said. "You young Jedi Knights continue to impress me. Master Skywalker must be doing a good job selecting his candidates."

"Better candidates than *you'll* ever get," Jaina said, finding the strength to defy him despite her injuries.

"Indeed," Brakiss agreed. "That's why we decided to take some of those that he has already selected. You three were only the first we obtained from the Jedi academy. You've shown such potential that we are now ready to kidnap another group from Yavin 4. From there, we'll have all the Jedi students we could possibly use."

Lowie growled. Jacen and Jaina looked at each other aghast, then at their Wookiee friend. Even without using the Force, the three companions knew they all shared the same urgent thought.

They had to do something—and soon.

19

TENEL KA USED a Jedi relaxation technique, hoping to quell her nervousness before Vonnda Ra could pick up on it. Waiting beside her at the strip of packed dirt the Nightsisters used for a landing field, Luke looked serene, but Tenel Ka caught a trace of curiosity and excitement in him, as if he were embarking on a great adventure.

"There," said Vonnda Ra, stretching an arm toward the horizon where a glimmer of silver flickered. As Tenel Ka watched, the streamlined metallic shape grew rapidly larger.

"You are most fortunate," Vilas said, striding up behind them. Vonnda Ra sent him a questioning look, and he shrugged. "I felt *her* presence, and I could not help but come to greet her." He indicated the approaching craft. "One of our most accomplished young sisters, Garowyn herself, will escort you to your new place of training."

Tenel Ka guessed that Garowyn must also come from Dathomir, since the name was common enough here. Another Nightsister then. *How could so many Nightsisters have come together so quickly?* she wondered. It was not yet two decades since Luke and her parents had eradicated the old Nightsisters, yet here again was a growing enclave of both women *and* men who had been seduced by the dark side of the Force, lured by its promises of power. The Empire had been here as well, seeking new allies.

Tenel Ka gritted her teeth. Were her people truly so weak? Or was the temptation of great power, once tasted, too strong to resist? She renewed her resolve: She would *not* use the Force unless her own physical powers were inadequate for the situation. She didn't like easy solutions.

Tenel Ka stifled her feelings as a compact, shiny ship settled with effortless precision not far from where they stood. Although she knew it belonged to the Nightsisters—or to whomever had kidnapped Jacen and Jaina and Lowbacca—she marveled at its construction.

The ship was not large, probably built to carry a dozen people, but its lines were clean and smooth, almost inviting Tenel Ka to run her hand along its side. No carbon scoring stained the hull; its surface bore no pits, dents, or evidence of the meteorites commonly encountered in space and atmosphere. The overall design seemed vaguely Imperial, but Tenel Ka could not identify it as any type of craft she had ever seen before.

She heard a low whistle from Luke and a murmured question, as if he were talking to himself. "Quantum armor?"

"Exactly," Vilas said, sounding pleased.

As an entry ramp extended from the sleek underbelly of the small craft, Vonnda Ra stepped forward to greet the woman who emerged, clasping both of her hands in welcome. When the woman stepped off the ramp, Tenel Ka saw that she was half a meter shorter than Vonnda Ra. Though petite, the newcomer was powerfully built. Long, light brown hair streaked with bronze fell to her waist, secured with just enough braids and thongs to keep it out of her way, as befitted a warrior woman of Dathomir.

Without further ado, the woman pilot broke away from Vonnda Ra and came to stand before Luke and Tenel Ka. Her hazel eyes assessed each of them critically. "You are new recruits?"

Before Tenel Ka could answer, Vilas broke in, as if desperately eager to talk to the pilot. "You'll find that they have remarkable potential, Captain Garowyn."

Tenel Ka heard tension and hope—and longing—in his voice. She wondered if Vilas could be secretly in love with Garowyn. Her features were refined, and her creamy-brown skin was set off to perfection by her tight-fitting red lizard-skin armor. The black knee-length cape she wore open at the front seemed to be her only outward concession to the fact that she was a Nightsister, and Tenel Ka guessed from the haughty set of her mouth and her shrewd eyes that Garowyn did not often make concessions.

"Vilas, busy yourself unloading the supplies," Garowyn said dismissively. "I will test these two myself." Vilas cringed and shuffled dispiritedly over to unload the ship, but Garowyn did not notice. She threw Luke and Tenel Ka a challenging look and directed a question at them. "What do you think of my ship, the *Shadow Chaser?*"

"It's beautiful. I've never seen anything like it," Luke replied softly.

"This is a fact," Tenel Ka said in a reverent voice.

"Yes, this is a fact," Garowyn said, apparently satisfied. "The *Shadow Chaser* is state-of-the-art. At the moment she's the only one of her kind." Then, seeming to forget that Vonnda Ra and Vilas even existed, she said, "I do not wish to waste time. Come aboard. When the hold is empty we will get under way."

With that, she turned smartly and headed for the ship. Luke and Tenel Ka followed.

As the *Shadow Chaser* accelerated into hyperspace and the twinkling lights in the forward viewscreen elongated into starlines, Tenel Ka watched Garowyn set her automatic controls and stand up from the pilot seat.

"Our journey will take two standard days," Garowyn said, moving past them and out of the cockpit. "I may as well acquaint you with my ship. No expense was spared for the *Shadow Chaser.*"

She showed them the food- and waste-processing systems, the hyperdrive engines, the sleeping cubicles . . . but most of it was a blur to Tenel Ka.

"And these"—Garowyn pointed toward several hatches at the back of the cabin—"are the escape pods. Each is large enough to carry only one passenger, and is equipped with a homing beacon that broadcasts its location on a signature frequency that can only be decoded at the Shadow Academy, where you will learn your true potential."

With that, Garowyn resumed the tour, but Tenel Ka flashed an alarmed glance at Master Skywalker, who met her gaze with equal concern. Her mind whirled at the idea that another Jedi academy existed, an academy for learning the dark powers of the Force. A *Shadow Academy.*

Garowyn decided to test them thoroughly. She questioned Luke and Tenel Ka by turns about their familiarity with the Force. Luke was vague in his answers, but Garowyn—perhaps because she was from Dathomir and considered men to be of little importance—concentrated her efforts on finding out more about Tenel Ka.

When Garowyn asked what experience she had, Tenel Ka answered truthfully. "I have used the Force, and I believe that I am strong. However," she added, her voice growing hard, "I will not rely on the Force so much that I become weak. If there is anything I can do under my own power, I will not use the Force to do it."

Garowyn laughed at that, a harsh, cynical laugh that grated in Tenel Ka's ears. "We will change your mind without too much difficulty," she said. "Why else would you come to us for training?"

Tenel Ka considered this for a moment and phrased her reply carefully. "I have no greater desire than to learn the ways of the Force," she said at last.

Garowyn nodded, as if that closed the issue, and turned to Luke. "I refuse to conduct lightsaber drills aboard the *Shadow Chaser,* but we shall see soon enough how well you sense my intentions using the Force." She picked up a stun staff in each hand and tossed one of them to Luke. Luke stretched out his arm, fumbled slightly, but caught the staff before it touched the floor.

And so it went for most of the day.

Tenel Ka did the best she could at each stage of the testing, but she could see that Luke was holding back, not revealing the full extent of his power—she had observed Master Skywalker enough to know this.

After seeing him weaken or fail in several of the tests, however, a thread of worry began to weave through her mind. What if Master Skywalker had fallen ill? What if he couldn't use his powers? Or what if—it hurt to even think it—what if he had been wrong, after all? What if the dark side really *was* stronger? If so, she and Master Skywalker did not stand a chance of rescuing Jacen, Jaina, and Lowbacca.

Tenel Ka felt weak and drained by the time she had lifted her tenth object to satisfy Garowyn's sense of completeness. The titanium block wobbled and shook as she lowered it to the floor of the cabin.

Garowyn gave a derisive chuckle. "Your pride in self-sufficiency is your weakness." With that, she closed her hazel eyes, flung her head back, and stretched an arm out toward Tenel Ka.

Tenel Ka felt the hair on her scalp and her skin prickle as if lightning were about to strike. Her stomach churned, and she felt giddy and disoriented. She bent her legs to sit but found nothing to support her. She was floating a meter above the cabin floor. Tenel Ka stifled a gasp of outrage and attempted to use her mind to wrench herself free.

Garowyn's creamy-brown face was furrowed with cruel lines of deep concentration. "Yes," she said in a guttural, triumphant voice, "try to resist me. Use your anger."

Realizing that this was exactly what she *had* been doing, Tenel Ka went limp. As she did so, Garowyn lost her grip slightly, and Tenel Ka wobbled in midair. *So,* she mused, *the Nightsister is not as strong as she thinks she is.*

Then, pretending to struggle again to hide what she was doing, she removed the fibercord and grappling hook that she carried at her waist and looked around for an anchor point. She soon found something that would work perfectly: the wheel on an escape pod's pressure hatch.

Garowyn was still amusing herself with Tenel Ka's "struggles" when, with a practiced flick of her wrist, Tenel Ka flung out her line;

the grappling hook caught securely on its intended target. Before the Nightsister could notice, Tenel Ka went completely limp again. When Garowyn's grasp wavered again, Tenel Ka jerked on the line and wrenched herself free, falling to the floor and landing painfully on her rear.

She looked up to see Garowyn's petite form towering over her. But instead of an angry rebuke, all she heard from the Nightsister was a short, sharp bark of amazed laughter.

Garowyn reached out a hand to help Tenel Ka up. "Your pride has served you this time, but it may be your downfall yet," she said.

"That is often true of pride," Luke said quietly, seeming to agree. His eyes assessed the Nightsister. "I believe I could do that."

Garowyn's lips twisted in a derisive smile. "What? You think you could fall on your—?"

"No," Luke cut in. "I believe I could lift a person."

"So?" Garowyn chortled, as if rising to a challenge. "Do your best."

She crossed her arms over her chest, and her hazel eyes dared Luke to move her. Suddenly, her eyes grew wide with astonishment and confusion as her feet drifted off the floor and she rose a full meter and a half into the air.

"I can see that it is time to teach *you* the power of the dark side as well," she snapped haughtily. She closed her eyes and wrenched with all her might.

Tenel Ka sensed that Luke loosened his grip—but only partially. Garowyn still floated above the deck, but he allowed the force of her movement to turn her around and send her into a dizzying spin.

Then, never taking his eyes from the twirling Nightsister, Luke said, "Tenel Ka, if you would be so kind as to open that first escape pod."

She understood his intention immediately, and moved to do as he asked. Within moments they had the gyrating, disoriented Nightsister deposited and sealed within the pod. Tenel Ka's hand hovered above the automatic jettison switch. Luke nodded.

With great satisfaction, she triggered the launch. With a *whoosh* and a *thump,* the escape pod containing Garowyn shot out into deep space.

"Master Skywalker," Tenel Ka said, her face serious, "I believe I now understand how it might be possible, as you said, to . . . *turn* a situation."

Luke looked at her, blinked once in amazement, and laughed. "Tenel Ka," he said, "I believe you just made a joke. Jacen would be proud of you."

* * *

Later that day, when they dropped out of hyperspace and the autopilot alerted them that they were about to arrive at their destination, Luke and Tenel Ka sat in the cockpit looking vainly for a planet, a space station, *anything* on which they might land.

But they saw nothing.

Tenel Ka turned to Luke in confusion. "Could the autopilot have malfunctioned?" she asked. "Did we have the wrong coordinates?"

"No," he said, seeming calm and self-assured. "We must wait."

Then, as if a curtain had suddenly been drawn aside, they saw it: a space station. *A Shadow Academy,* Tenel Ka reminded herself. A spiked torus spinning in space, protected by exterior gun emplacements and crowned with several tall observation towers.

"It must have been cloaked," Luke said.

As they approached the Shadow Academy, docking-bay doors opened automatically, and Luke placed a reassuring hand on Tenel Ka's shoulder.

"The dark side is *not* stronger," he said.

Tenel Ka let out a long breath, and some of her tension drained away with it.

"This is a fact," she whispered.

20

DURING THE SHADOW Academy's sleep period, all students were locked in their individual chambers and told to rest and meditate, to recharge their energies for further strenuous exercises. It was just part of the Imperial rules, and most students followed them without question.

Jacen sat alone in his small cubicle, bruised and aching from the training ordeal. He dampened one of his socks and used it to soothe the many cuts and scrapes he had received from the sharp rocks and knives.

He and Jaina had requested simple pain relievers, but Tamith Kai had flatly refused, insisting that the aches would serve to toughen them up. Each twinge of pain was supposed to remind them of their failure to deflect a ball or stone. He used what he knew of the Force to dull the worst of the pain, but it still hurt.

Jacen sat cross-legged, trying furiously to figure out some escape before Brakiss launched another raid on Yavin 4 to grab more of Uncle Luke's trainees.

His sister Jaina was always best at making complicated plans. She understood how things worked, how pieces fit together. Jacen, on the other hand, who liked to live in the moment and enjoy what he was doing, was a bit more disorganized. He managed to get things done—but not always in the same order he had originally planned.

Maybe the most important step was to free Jaina and Lowie. After that, they could decide what to do next. Of course, the biggest question was *how* Jacen could free them all from their cells.

Then he remembered his Corusca gem.

Jacen nearly laughed out loud—why hadn't he thought of it before? He grabbed for his left boot, shook it, and was startled to hear nothing. Then he recalled he had put the stone in his other boot. He picked it up and dumped the precious jewel into his cupped hand. Smooth on one side, with sharp edges and facets on the other, the

Corusca gem glowed with internal fire—trapped light from when it had formed deep in Yavin's core ages ago.

Lando Calrissian had said a Corusca gem could slice through transparisteel as easily as a laser through Sullustan jam. But then, Lando said a lot of things that couldn't entirely be believed. Jacen hoped this wasn't one of them.

Jacen held the jewel between his thumb and his first two fingers and went to the sealed door. When Tamith Kai and her Imperial forces had stormed GemDiver Station, they had used a large machine fitted with industrial-grade Corusca gems to cut through the armored walls. Surely Jacen's little gem could cut through a thin wall plate....

He ran his fingers along the smooth metal near where the door sealed. Jacen wished he understood machinery and electronics like his sister did, but he would do his best.

He didn't think that he could cut through the whole door using only the strength in his fingers, but Jacen knew where the control panel was. Perhaps he could peel back this side of the plate, get to the wires, and somehow trigger the door to open—though he hadn't the slightest idea how to do it. Still, he took the gem, found where the control box should be, and probed lightly with the Force. He sensed a power source here, tangled controls. This was it.

Jacen drew a generous rectangle with the gem, easily scratching a thin white line in the metal plate. *A good start,* he thought.

Pressing harder this time, Jacen retraced the rectangle, feeling the sharp edge of the gem gouging deeper into the metal. After his third effort, his fingers hurt, but he could see that he had made a substantial cut through the plate. His pulse raced, and excitement gave him new energy. He forgot all about his aches and pains.

One side cut through and bent inward. Jacen gasped. *Almost there.* He sawed away at the long side of the rectangle. With a *clink,* the metal parted. The last two sides were easier, and he sliced through them quickly.

The metal rectangle slipped from Jacen's sore fingers and fell to the floor with a loud clatter. "Oh, blaster bolts!" he muttered. He was sure the other Shadow Academy students would wake up and that stormtroopers would come running.

But outside, the halls remained utterly silent, as if a cloth gag were bound around the station, muffling all sound. Everyone remained locked in their quarters. Only a few guards wandered the halls at night.

Jacen was safe for the time being. He peered into the hole he had cut, looking with dismay at the mass of wires and circuits that controlled the door. *Okay, what would Jaina do?* he wondered. He closed his eyes and let his mind open up, tracing the lines of the wires and circuits. Some ran to communications systems, or computer terminals mounted at regular intervals along the corridors, or lights, or thermostats. Some ran to alarms, and others . . . connected to the door mechanism!

Jacen took a steadying breath. *Now, what to do with those wires?* He probably needed to cross them, but in a particular way. There was nothing to do but try it.

With aching fingers, Jacen disconnected one of the wires in the cluster he had isolated and touched it to another, careful that the exposed, electrified ends didn't touch his bare skin. A little spark flashed, and the lights in his room flickered—but nothing else happened. He tried with the second wire and got no response at all.

Jacen hoped he wasn't setting off silent alarms in the guard stations. He sighed. What if none of this worked? Well, he reasoned, then he might have to slice directly through the door after all. He shook his stinging fingers, anticipating the pain. First, he decided, he would try the last set of wires.

As if sensing Jacen's impending despair, the door slid quietly open when he touched the wires together.

Jacen laughed aloud and looked out into the empty corridor. He glanced from side to side, but saw only a string of sealed, featureless doors. Glowpanels lit the metallic corridors at half illumination, conserving power during the academy's sleep period.

The door controls looked much easier from the outside, and he didn't think he would have any trouble freeing Jaina and Lowie—once he found them.

It proved less difficult than Jacen had feared. He had seen the corridors down which the guards usually led Jaina and Lowie, so he went in that direction, calling with his mind. *Jaina will be the easiest,* he thought. He tiptoed along, afraid that at any moment stormtroopers would come marching around the corner.

But the Shadow Academy remained silent and asleep.

Jaina, he thought. *Jaina!*

Jacen walked along, listening at each of the doors. He didn't want to cause too much of a disturbance, because the Dark Jedi students might sound an alarm if they noticed him.

At the seventh door he found her. Jacen sensed his sister, awake and excited, knowing he was out there. He worked the controls until her door slid open. Jaina burst out, hugging him. "I've been expecting you," she said.

"Used my Corusca gem," he explained, pointing toward his boot, where he had stashed the stone again.

Jaina nodded, as if she had known all along what her brother would do.

"We've got to find Lowie and free him, too," Jacen said.

"Of course," Jaina agreed. "We'll escape and warn Uncle Luke before Brakiss makes his raid on the Jedi academy."

"Right," Jacen said with a lopsided grin. "Uh, since I got us this far, I was hoping *you* could figure out the rest of the plan."

Jaina beamed at him as if he had paid her the highest compliment she could imagine. "Already have," she said. "What are we waiting for?"

They managed to find Lowie, who was excited to see them, and Em Teedee, who was not. "I feel obligated to warn you that I simply must sound an alarm," the translating droid said. "My duty is to the Empire now and it's my responsibility—"

Jaina gave the little droid a rap with her knuckles. "If you make so much as a peep," she said, "we'll rewire your vocal circuits so that you talk backwards and they'll toss you in the scrap heap."

"You wouldn't!" Em Teedee said in a huff.

"Wanna bet?" Jaina asked in a dangerously sweet voice.

Jacen stood next to her and glared at the miniaturized translating droid. Lowie added his own threatening growl.

"Oh, all right, all right," Em Teedee said. "But I submit to this only under stringent protest. The Empire is, after all, our friend."

Jaina snorted. "No it isn't. Think we may need to arrange for a complete brain wipe when we get you back to Yavin 4."

"Oh, dear me," Em Teedee said.

Jaina looked around, casting her gaze from one end of the silent corridor to the other. She rubbed her hands together and bit her lower lip, considering options. "All right, this is the plan." She pointed to one of the corridor terminals.

"Lowie," she said, "can you use that computer to slice into the main station controls? I need you to drop the Shadow Academy's cloaking device and also seal all the doors so that no one gets out of their quarters. No sense inviting trouble for ourselves."

Lowie made a sound of optimistic agreement.

"Lowbacca, you aren't capable of accomplishing all of that," Em Teedee said, "and I'm certain you know it." Lowie growled at him.

"If we can all get to the shuttle bay," Jaina continued, "I think I can pilot one of the ships out of here. I've trained in simulators for various craft, and you know I was ready to fly that TIE fighter before Qorl took it."

Lowie tapped the keyboard of the computer terminal with his long hairy fingers. He hunched low to stare at the screen, which was not mounted for someone of Wookiee stature. Lowie called up the screens he needed, showing the status of the Shadow Academy's shuttle bay.

"Perfect," Jaina said. "A new ship just came in, still powered up and ready to go. We'll take that one, as soon as Lowie locks everyone in their rooms."

Lowbacca grunted in agreement and kept working, but he soon encountered an impenetrable wall of security passwords. He groaned in frustration.

"Well, there now, you see?" Em Teedee said. "I told you you couldn't do it by yourself."

Lowie growled, but Jaina brightened as an idea struck her. "He's right," she said. "But Em Teedee was reprogrammed by the Empire. Why not plug him into the main computer and let *him* get through for us?" She plucked the small translating droid from the clip at Lowbacca's waist and began opening Em Teedee's back access panel.

"I most certainly will not," Em Teedee said. "I simply couldn't. It would be disloyal to the Empire and completely inappropriate for me to—"

Lowie made a threatening sound, and Em Teedee fell silent.

Working rapidly, with nimble fingers, Jaina pulled wires, electrical leads, and input jacks from the droid's head case and plugged them into appropriate ports on the Shadow Academy's computer terminal.

"Oh, my," Em Teedee said. "Ah, this is much better. I can see so many things! I feel as if my brain is full to overflowing. A wealth of information awaits me—"

"The passwords, Em Teedee," Jaina said, reaching toward the recalcitrant droid.

"Oh, dear me, yes. Of course—the passwords!" Em Teedee said hastily. "But I remind you, I really shouldn't."

"Just do it," Jaina snapped.

"Ah, yes, here it is. But don't blame me if the whole lot of stormtroopers comes after you."

The screen winked, displaying the files Lowbacca had been trying to access. Jacen and Jaina sighed with relief, and Lowie made a pleased sound. His ginger-furred fingers were a blur as he descended rapidly through menu after menu, finally penetrating all the way into the station computer's main core.

With two swift commands Lowie shut down the Shadow Academy's cloaking device. Then, with a resounding *clunk* that echoed throughout the station, he closed and sealed every door except those the three of them would need to escape. He yowled in triumph.

Belatedly, the station alarms went off, screeching and grating with a harsh, piercing sound, unpleasant as only Imperial engineers could make it.

Lowie unplugged Em Teedee. "There, I tried to warn you," the silvery droid said. "But you wouldn't listen, would you?"

21

BRAKISS SAT CONTEMPLATING in his dim office, long after the other workers had retired for the night. He reveled in the dramatic images on his walls: galactic disasters in progress, the fury of the universe unleashed like a storm around him—with Brakiss as its calm center, able to touch those immense forces but not be affected by them.

Brakiss had just written up the plans for a swift attack on Yavin 4 so that he could steal more of Master Skywalker's Jedi students. He had sent the encoded message deep into the Core Systems to the great Imperial leader, who had immediately approved his plans. The leader was eager to get more ready-chosen Jedi students to train as dark warriors.

The assault would occur in the next few days, while Skywalker was no doubt still reeling from the loss of the twins and the Wookiee, perhaps even away from Yavin 4 looking for them. Tamith Kai would go along for the assault. She needed the outlet to vent her anger, to drain some of the rage she kept bottled within herself. That way she could be more effective.

Brakiss stood and looked at the blindingly bright image of the Denarii Nova, two suns pouring fire onto each other. Something was bothering him. He couldn't quite put his finger on it. The day had gone routinely. The three young Jedi Knights were doing even better than he'd expected. But still Brakiss had a bad feeling, a low-level uneasiness.

He walked slowly out of his chambers, his silvery robes flickering around him like candlelight. He let the door of his office remain open as he turned to scrutinize the empty corridor. Everything was quiet, just as it should have been.

Brakiss frowned, decided he must be imagining things, and turned back toward his office. But before he could get there, the door slammed shut of its own accord. Brakiss found himself trapped outside his office.

Up and down the corridor the few open doors also sealed themselves. He heard clicking sounds as locking mechanisms engaged all around the station.

Automatic alarms shrieked. Brakiss would not tolerate such an interruption in his routine. Someone would be punished for this. He held the storm inside himself and strode down the halls, intent on squashing the disturbance.

Jacen, Jaina, and Lowie rushed into the docking bay, tense and ready to fight their way out of the Shadow Academy.

A gleaming Imperial shuttle of unusual design sat in the middle of the brightly lit landing pad, still going through its shutdown procedures. Other TIE fighters and Skipray blastboats stood locked down and in various stages of maintenance. The alarms continued their deafening racket.

Jacen saw movement in the shuttle and frantically gestured for the others to duck down, just in time to see two figures emerge from the entry ramp. One of the figures crouched and drew a lightsaber.

"Uncle Luke!" Jaina cried, springing to her feet.

The second figure, a fierce-looking girl, whirled, ready to attack. Her braided red-gold hair swept like a burst of flame across her gray eyes.

"And Tenel Ka!" Jacen said. "Hey, am I glad to see you!"

Lowie bellowed a delighted welcome.

"Well, it certainly is a relief to see familiar faces in the midst of all this infernal racket," Em Teedee said.

"All right, kids," Luke Skywalker said, "we came to rescue you—but since you managed to get yourselves this far, I guess we're ready to go. Right now."

Jaina issued a brisk report. "We managed to shut down the cloaking device, Uncle Luke. Sealed most of the doors on the station. Won't be many people coming after us, but we should get out of here as soon as we can."

"How will we get the sealed space doors open again?" Tenel Ka said, looking over her broad shoulders. "It will be difficult to open them without help from someone inside. Is this not a fact?"

Lowie answered her with an extended series of growls and snorts. He waved his lanky arms.

Em Teedee, his chrome back plate still rattling loose behind him, scolded, "No, you can*not* do it yourself, Lowbacca. You're getting delusions of grandeur again. It was *I* who helped bring down the Shadow Academy's defenses and . . . oh—oh dear, what have I done?"

"Maybe I can help," Jaina said. "Let's get into the shuttle cockpit. We'll try it from there."

Up in the control center for the docking bay, Qorl stood amazed as the unexpected alarms continued.

He watched the three young Jedi Knights rush into the large room below. The *Shadow Chaser* had just returned from a supply run to Dathomir, and a sandy-haired man emerged with a tough-looking young lady. Qorl recognized her as one of the Jedi students who had worked on his crashed TIE fighter back in the jungle.

As soon as the alarms sounded, Qorl knew that Jacen, Jaina, and Lowbacca were somehow behind the disturbance. The other Dark Jedi students were pleased to have an opportunity to increase their powers and appreciated their training; but Qorl had been certain these three would cause trouble—especially since Brakiss and Tamith Kai seemed determined to injure or kill them.

Qorl had been gravely disturbed at the supposed duel to the death between the holographically disguised brother and sister. He also knew the dangerous testing routine with flying stones and knives had already been responsible for the deaths of half a dozen promising Shadow Academy trainees.

He didn't agree with Brakiss's tactics, but Qorl was just a pilot; no one listened to his point of view, no matter how certain he was. Yet Qorl served his Empire, and he had to do what he knew was right.

He opened the comm channel and gruffly reported. "Master Brakiss, Tamith Kai—anyone who can hear me. The prisoners are attempting to escape. They are currently in the main docking bay. I believe they intend to steal the *Shadow Chaser*. All of my defenses are down because of computer failure. If you can offer assistance, please come to the main docking bay immediately."

Tamith Kai's violet eyes snapped open, and she leaped from her hard, uncomfortable bunk at the first sound of alarm. She came instantly awake, her mind burning with demands to know what was going on. Someone was threatening the Shadow Academy.

The Nightsister threw on her black cloak, which swirled around her with glittering silvery lines, like the trails of stars during a launch into hyperspace. She reached the door to her quarters, but it would not open. She pounded on it, punched the override controls, but the locking mechanisms remained engaged.

"Let me out!" she snarled. Tamith Kai worked the controls once more, again with no success. Her rage built within her. Something was happening, something terrible—and she knew the three kidnapped trainees were behind it all! They had caused more trouble than they were worth. The Shadow Academy could find so many other willing trainees in all the worlds of the galaxy that regardless of the talent of these three, their potential for disaster was too great.

She would destroy them once and for all, and then the Shadow Academy could settle back into its smooth, regular routine, with Tamith Kai dominating and Brakiss running the details. Then she could be happy again.

Her fingers coiled, and a smoky black electricity curled between them. "Out!" she roared. "I must get out!" Tamith Kai slashed with both of her hands in an opening gesture as she cried her command.

With an explosion of power, the doors bent backward, folding down in a burst of smoke and sparks from the sheared-off wiring in the controls. Then using her bare hands, she tore one of the heavy metal plates completely out of its tracks and tossed it with a loud *clonngg!* onto the floor. Tamith Kai stormed out, her eyes shimmering like violet lava.

Qorl's message came over the hall comm systems, and Tamith Kai did not let her anger slacken for an instant. *The docking bay.* She strode forward at high speed.

While Jacen, Jaina, and Lowie scrambled aboard the *Shadow Chaser,* Luke remained outside with Tenel Ka. He glanced back and shouted to the twins. "I need to know about this place. There's something familiar and . . . very wrong here."

"Yes," Jaina said. "Uncle Luke, the person running the Shadow Academy is—"

But Luke had become distracted—fascinated, really. He suddenly stood up straighter, his eyebrows drawing together. "Wait," he said. "I sense something. A presence I haven't felt in a long time."

He walked slowly across the bay and drew his lightsaber again, feeling a storm in the Force, a deadly conflict. As if in a trance, Luke strode toward one of the sealed red doors that led deeper into the academy station.

"Hey, Uncle Luke!" Jacen cried, but Luke held up a hand for the boy to wait.

They needed to escape soon—it was their only chance. They had to seize the moment. But Luke also had to *see,* had to know. Behind him, he heard the weapons systems of the *Shadow Chaser* powering up. The ship's external laser cannon turrets raised and locked into firing position.

When the red door slid open ahead of him, Luke Skywalker stood transfixed. He stared at the sculpture-handsome face of his former student.

"Brakiss!" he whispered in a voice that carried across the docking bay, even above the chaos of shrieking alarms.

Brakiss stood where he was with a faint smile. "Ah, Master Skywalker. So good of you to come. I thought I sensed you here on my station. Are you impressed at how well I have done for myself?"

Luke held his lightsaber out in front of him, but Brakiss remained outside in the corridor and did not step across the threshold.

"Oh, come now," Brakiss said with a dismissive wave, "if you intended to kill me, you should have done it when I was a weak trainee. You knew I was an Imperial agent even then."

"I wanted to give you the chance to save yourself," Luke said.

"Always the optimist," Brakiss replied in an airy tone.

Luke felt cold inside. He didn't want to fight Brakiss, especially not now. They had little time. But didn't he have to confront his former student somehow—resolve their conflict?

They had to go *now.* He needed to escape with the kids before the Shadow Academy managed to get its defenses back on-line again.

Brakiss held out his soft, empty hands. "Come and get me, Master Skywalker—or are you a coward? Would your precious light side allow you to attack an unarmed man?"

"The Force is my ally, Brakiss," Luke said. "And you have learned to use it to your own ends. You are never unarmed, any more than I am."

"All right, have it your way," Brakiss said. He brushed the fabric of his shimmering robe and made ready to step forward. His eyes blazed now, as if he held the fury of the universe within him, ready to unleash it from his fingertips.

Just then, an explosion of hot energy streaked past Luke's head from behind and melted the door controls. With a second blast from the *Shadow Chaser*'s laser cannon, the controls were completely fried. The heavy metal plates slammed back into place, sealing Brakiss and Luke apart from each other.

"Uncle Luke, come on!" Jaina yelled from the ship. "We have to go."

Luke shuddered with stunned relief, turned, and sprinted back toward the shuttle. He knew it wasn't over between him and Brakiss; but that would have to wait for another time.

Jaina and Lowie and Em Teedee linked into the *Shadow Chaser*'s computers, trying to open the station's huge space door from within. While they worked, Tenel Ka raced around the docking bay, sealing all of the red doorways, making sure that none would open. The ominous man in the silvery robes had stalled Luke, and they couldn't afford another skirmish like that. Tenel Ka had to seal the doors, just in case a contingent of stormtroopers made its way to the docking bay.

Luke climbed into the shuttle. Tenel Ka sealed another metal door, then ran to the last one. Just as her fingers touched the controls, though, the door slid open. A tall, dark woman loomed in front of Tenel Ka, crackling with angry energy and ready to attack.

Tenel Ka looked up and instantly knew what this person was. "A Nightsister!" she hissed.

The dark woman glared down at her with a similar flash of recognition. "And you are from Dathomir, girl! I claim you. You are a fitting replacement for the three I am about to destroy."

Tenel Ka stood in front of the Nightsister, her arms and legs spread like a barrier. "You will have to get through me first."

The dark woman laughed. "If you insist." She struck with the Force, an invisible blow that nearly knocked Tenel Ka sideways—but the young woman deflected it and stood strong, lips clamping together in determination.

The Nightsister drew herself taller in surprise, looking like a black bird of prey. "Ah, so you are already familiar with the Force. That will make it easier for me to train you, to turn you."

Tenel Ka remained tense and rigid, glaring at her opponent. "This is not a fact. And I will not let you harm my friends."

The Nightsister seemed to snap as her anger came free of its delicate cage. "Then I won't hesitate to destroy you as well!" Her black robes rippled like a thunderstorm. Locking her violet gaze on Tenel Ka, she raised her clawed hands, fingers outspread, glossy dark hair crackling with static as her body charged with electrical power.

Tenel Ka stood directly in front of her, unflinching, as the dark Force built to a climax within the Nightsister.

Without warning, Tenel Ka lashed out with her foot, putting all of the strength of her muscular, athletic legs behind the kick. The sharp toe of her hard, scaled boot struck the Nightsister's unarmored kneecap. Tenel Ka distinctly heard the *crunch* of a breaking bone and tearing muscles as her blow struck home. The Nightsister shrieked and fell to the ground, writhing in agony.

Calm and self-satisfied, Tenel Ka stared down at her with cool gray eyes. "I never use the Force unless I have to," she said. "Sometimes old-fashioned methods are just as effective."

Leaving the Nightsister moaning on the floor, Tenel Ka jogged back toward the *Shadow Chaser*, where Luke was gesturing for her to hurry. She climbed aboard, and the ship doors sealed.

Alarms continued to sound, their clamor muffled inside the cockpit of the *Shadow Chaser*. Luke piloted the vehicle, raising it off the floor on its repulsorfields. Jaina and Lowie still worked desperately to open the heavy space doors.

With a loud *crrummp*, two sets of the red metal doors blasted open. Smoke from detonators curled out, and white-armored stormtroopers charged in, blasting at the shuttle.

"You'd better get that space door open," Luke said. "Soon."

Lowie yowled. "We're trying!" Jaina said, keying in a new command string, working even more furiously.

More stormtroopers came through. Blaster fire sprayed across the room. They could hear the splatter and boom of impacts. But the *Shadow Chaser*'s armor held.

"We've got company," Luke said, staring at the sealed bay doors. "We're out of time."

"I can't get the—," Jaina began, and suddenly the heavy doors cracked open, spreading wide for the *Shadow Chaser*. The atmosphere-containment field shimmered in front of the star-strewn blackness, but now the shuttle could launch into open space.

"Well, what are we waiting for?" Jaina said, trying to cover her confusion.

"Let's go!" Luke shouted, and punched the accelerators.

Everyone grabbed the arms of their seats as the launch threw them back. The *Shadow Chaser* roared away from the Imperial station, leaving the huge, spiked structure uncloaked in space behind them.

Luke heaved a loud sigh of relief as he punched the escape coordinates into the navicomputer. "Let's get back to Yavin 4," he said.

None of the young Jedi Knights objected, and they surged into hyperspace.

"Good work, Jaina and Lowie," Luke finally said. "I didn't think you'd ever get that docking-bay door open."

Lowbacca mumbled something unintelligible, and Jaina fidgeted.

"Uh, Uncle Luke," she said, "I kind of hate to mention this, but—we *didn't* get the door open."

Luke shrugged, not wanting to quibble. "Well, we owe our thanks to whoever did it."

Qorl stood by the docking-bay controls, watching the *Shadow Chaser* disappear. The escape left absolute turmoil in its wake as the Shadow Academy scrambled to regroup. Qorl touched the space door controls, smiled faintly to himself, and then closed the doors. He would, of course, never tell Brakiss or Tamith Kai.

Brakiss came into the control room next to Qorl, exhausted and troubled. "Is our cloaking shield up yet? We must get it working. The Rebels will no doubt send attack fleets in search of us. We'll have to relocate. That's why this station was designed to be mobile."

Brakiss drummed his fingertips on one of the control panels. "I don't know what I'm going to say to our great Imperial leader. He can trigger this station's self-destruct sequence at any time, if he's displeased."

Qorl nodded grimly. "Perhaps he won't be quite that displeased . . . this time."

Brakiss looked at him. "We can only hope."

Tamith Kai limped into the control chamber, utterly outraged. Her eyes still glowed with violet fire, and her hands were set in clawed curves, as if she wanted to shred hull plates with her fingernails. "So they've escaped! You let them get away?"

Brakiss looked at her mildly. "I didn't *let* them do anything, Tamith Kai. I don't see what more we could have done. Our duty now is to get away and plan our next step—because you can be sure there will be another opportunity."

Qorl powered up the station engines, and they began moving the Shadow Academy to a new hiding place.

22

JACEN AND JAINA crowded together, pushing closer to the transmission area in the Jedi academy's Comm Center as the image of Han and Leia came into focus. The twins cried out their greetings.

Han Solo laughed in delight. "Looks like I didn't have to come after you kids in the *Falcon* after all!"

"And I didn't have to mobilize the whole New Republic to rescue you." Leia beamed. "We got Luke's report yesterday. The scouts I had out searching for you kids are already looking for the Shadow Academy." In the background, Chewbacca roared a message in the Wookiee language to Lowie, who responded in kind.

In the Comm Center, Luke Skywalker stood next to Artoo-Detoo, letting the excited young Jedi Knights talk. Jacen's words tumbled out in a rush. "Lando Calrissian says something like this can never happen again. He's already working with his assistant Lobot to come up with refinements to GemDiver Station's security. I think he's even going to use Corusca gems somehow."

Luke spoke up. "Yes, but I doubt the Shadow Academy will come here again to look for new trainees. We know what Brakiss is up to now—I suspect he'll go somewhere else for potential new Dark Jedi."

"But we brought the Shadow Academy's best ship back with us," Jaina said. "And you should see the design. State-of-the-art. Not like any of the models in the manuals, Dad!"

Luke put a hand on her shoulder. "We need to offer it to the New Republic, Jaina. It isn't ours—"

Han interrupted. "Hey, Luke, you need us to send some mechanics over to check out the ship, try to figure out its design?"

Luke shrugged. "Go right ahead if you want, but I've got a skilled mechanic and an electronics specialist right here on Yavin 4, ready to start on the project right away—Jaina and Lowie."

Leia flashed a bright, warm smile. "All right, Luke. We'll send our engineers to study it, but you keep the ship there. Use it when you need to. You earned it rescuing Jacen, Jaina, and Lowie. Besides, you're an important part of the New Republic. We'll all feel better knowing you've got a safe, fast ship when you go running off across the galaxy—and don't tell me you've forgotten how to fly a fast ship!"

Luke gave an embarrassed chuckle. "No, I haven't forgotten—but I could still use the practice."

Jaina and Lowbacca sat in her quarters, tinkering with the holographic projector, making a coarse schematic of their new ship, the *Shadow Chaser*. The schematic was not as accurate as the one they had made of Lowie's T-23 skyhopper, but they would refine it as they learned more about the Imperial ship.

Lowie roared as the hologram lost its focus.

"Master Lowbacca says that he most fervently hopes a comet will crash into the vacation home of the designer of this subsystem," said Em Teedee from the clip on Lowie's belt.

Lowie growled down at the miniature translator droid. Em Teedee had been completely purged of his corrupted Imperial programming, and the irritating little droid was now back to his normal self.

"Well, how am *I* supposed to know that you don't wish me to translate Wookiee epithets?" the little droid said defensively. "Although you must admit, I certainly captured the feeling well. Why, think of all the idioms I have to parse during a single—"

Lowie switched Em Teedee off with a satisfied grunt.

Tenel Ka entered the Comm Center, feeling well rested. No nightmares had plagued her since her return to Yavin 4. She wondered what would happen now that a new order of Nightsisters had appeared on Dathomir, joining forces with the Empire, but at least they did not haunt her dreams.

Tenel Ka made contact with the Hapan Royal Household; she spoke to her parents, assured them that she was unharmed, and passed along greetings from the Singing Mountain Clan. Then, steeling herself for a set of imperious orders, she asked to speak with her grandmother, the Royal Matriarch.

When her grandmother's face appeared on the screen behind its customary half veil, her eyes carried a smile and something else Tenel Ka wasn't sure she could read—surprise?

"Thank you for remembering to call. My sources tell me I should be very proud of you," the Matriarch said, with what seemed to be genuine pleasure. "I'm sorry that my ambassador wasn't able to visit you.

Now, I'm afraid the meeting will be delayed indefinitely. I was forced to send Yfra on an urgent errand to the Duros system."

Tenel Ka's mouth opened, but she could not think of a response.

"But you'll forgive a concerned grandmother if she tries to find a way to look out for her granddaughter from a distance, won't you? One or two unobtrusive guards in a nearby system, perhaps? I think that might be the best thing for both of us."

The image of her grandmother leaned forward to turn off the communication link, but just as the connection broke the Matriarch whispered, "Besides, I have a feeling you weren't terribly disappointed to miss Ambassador Yfra."

"This," Tenel Ka muttered, "is a fact." And she realized it was the first time in years that she had agreed with her grandmother.

Jacen stood atop the Great Temple on Yavin 4, waiting for Master Skywalker. In the aftermath of the morning's rainstorm, reflected orange light from the giant planet pierced the gray clouds overhead and gilded their edges with a warm glow. The light breeze ruffled his hair and spattered him with an occasional raindrop.

As much as he dreaded the reprimand Uncle Luke was almost certain to deliver, Jacen was glad to be back on the jungle moon. In the day since their return from the Shadow Academy, the Jedi Master had already spoken privately with Jaina and with Lowie. Though he had no idea what Luke had said to either of them, both had been quiet and reserved afterward.

And now it was his turn.

Jacen sensed Master Skywalker's presence even without seeing him as Luke came to stand quietly next to him. For a long time, neither said a word, as if by mutual agreement. Gradually Jacen relaxed. He was ready for anything the Jedi Master had to say to him.

Almost anything.

"Take this," Luke said, pressing a metallic cylinder into Jacen's hands. "Show me what you learned."

Surprised, Jacen looked down at Luke's lightsaber. The weapon was solid and heavy, its handle warm as his own skin. He hefted it, studied it, ran a finger along the ridges of its grip up to the ignition stud. His eyes closed. In his mind, he could hear the hum of the lightsaber, feel its pulsing rhythm as the weapon sliced through the air. . . .

Jacen opened his eyes and squared his shoulders. "This is what I learned," he said, handing the lightsaber back to the Jedi Master without igniting it. "You were right: I'm not ready. The weapon of the Jedi is not to be taken up lightly."

"Even so, you learned to use it. Didn't Brakiss teach you?"

Jacen nodded. "I'm physically capable. I know how to fight an opponent with it—but I'm not sure I'm ready mentally. Maybe I'm not mature enough emotionally."

"You didn't enjoy the fighting as much as you had thought you would?" Luke raised his eyebrows.

"Yes. No. Well, yes—I learned some things. . . . I'm just not sure they were the *right* things. A lightsaber isn't just some impressive tool to dazzle and amaze your friends. It's such a big responsibility. One mistake could get an innocent person killed."

Luke nodded, his blue eyes twinkling with understanding. "It sometimes feels like too great a responsibility, even to me. But the Force guides us as we fight. Not simply how to defeat our enemies—but also to know when *not* to defeat them."

Their eyes locked. "Even if what our enemies teach or do is evil?" Jacen said.

Luke Skywalker's gaze did not waver. "No one is completely evil. Or completely good." He flashed a rueful smile. "At least nobody *I've* ever met."

"But Brakiss—" Jacen began.

"Brakiss passes the teachings of the dark side on to his students. You heard him teach. But a teacher is not always right. And because you thought for yourself, you knew not to believe him." Master Skywalker nodded approvingly.

Jacen thought this over. "Brakiss let me do what I wanted to do more than anything else: practice with a lightsaber. But I couldn't trust him. He was hoping to turn me to the dark side, to use me for the Empire. I *do* trust you, though. You were right about the lightsaber, and I'll wait until you think I'm ready."

Luke looked up toward the clouds, which were breaking up, letting more and more light through. "With the Shadow Academy out there, and the young Dark Jedi that Brakiss is training, I'm afraid that time will come all too soon."

THE LOST ONES

To our editor Ginjer Buchanan,
for her support and enthusiasm,
which made this entire project possible
in the first place, and for extending the series
to let us tell the whole story
. . . and for just being a really neat person.

Acknowledgments

To Lillie E. Mitchell, for her fast and furious typing; Jonathan MacGregor Cowan, for being our test reader and providing youthful excitement; Karen Haber and Robert Silverberg, for allowing us to mangle their monickers (sort of); Sue Rostoni and Lucy Wilson at Lucasfilm Licensing, for their sharp eyes and helpful suggestions . . . and Norys Davila at Walt Disney World Celebrity Programs, for having such a nifty first name we couldn't resist using it.

1

AS THE JEWEL-GREEN moon of Yavin 4 dwindled behind them in the *Millennium Falcon*'s rear viewscreens, Jaina Solo gave a happy sigh. "Excited to be going back home, Jacen?" she asked, looking into the liquid brown eyes of her twin brother.

Jacen ran long fingers through his tousled brown curls. "Never thought I'd say it," he admitted, "but a month on Coruscant with Mom and Dad and our kid brother does sound kind of nice."

"Must be a sign of maturity," Jaina teased.

"Who, *me?*" Jacen said, pretending to take offense. "Nah." Then, as if to disprove her theory, he flashed a lopsided grin that made him look like a younger version of their father, Han Solo. "Want to hear a joke?"

Jaina rolled her eyes and tucked a strand of straight brown hair behind one ear to keep it away from her face. "Don't suppose you'd take no for an answer?" Then pretending to have a brilliant idea, she snapped her fingers. "Say, why don't you go up to the cockpit and tell it to Tenel Ka instead?"

She knew full well that the young warrior woman, one of their closest friends at the Jedi academy, had never even smiled—much less laughed—at Jacen's jokes, though he tried daily to coax a chuckle from her.

"I want you to be a test audience first," he said. "Then I'll go try it on Lowie—wherever he is. He's got a pretty good sense of humor for a Wookiee."

"Shouldn't be too hard to find him," Jaina said. "The *Falcon*'s not *that* big, and you can be pretty sure he's somewhere near a computer."

"Hey, you're just trying to distract me from telling my joke," Jacen said. "You ready?"

Jaina heaved a long-suffering sisterly sigh. "All right, what's the joke?"

"Okay, how long does Uncle Luke need to sleep?"

She gave a puzzled frown. "You got me."

"One Jedi *night!*" He laughed out loud, proud of his joke.

Jaina gave a melodramatic groan. "I don't think even Lowie will laugh at that one."

Jacen looked crestfallen. "I thought it was one of my best jokes so far. I made it up myself." Then his face brightened. "Hey, I wonder if Zekk is still hanging around back on Coruscant. *He* always laughed at my jokes."

Jaina smiled at the mention of their mischievous friend, a street urchin who had been taken in and cared for by old Peckhum, the man who brought supplies to the Jedi academy. A couple of years older than the twins, Zekk had proven to be a resourceful scamp, despite his disadvantaged life. Jaina would sit and listen to Zekk for hours as he regaled her with stories of his childhood on Ennth and how, when the colony had been devastated by a natural disaster, he had escaped on the next supply ship.

Jaina had to admire Zekk's determination. The wild dark-haired boy never did anything unless he wanted to. In fact, when the captain of the rescue ship had suggested that Zekk might be better off in an orphanage or a foster home, Zekk had jumped ship to another outbound freighter at the very next stop and stowed away on it. From then on he had traveled from planet to planet, sometimes working as a cabin boy, sometimes stowing away, until one day he had met old Peckhum, who was on his way to Coruscant. Though both were independent, somehow a friendship had formed, and they had been together ever since.

"Okay, Zekk might laugh at your joke," Jaina agreed at last. "He has a strange sense of humor."

Leaving the Jedi academy far behind on Yavin 4, Jaina and Jacen watched the viewscreen in silence as the stars stretched into starlines and the *Millennium Falcon* flew into hyperspace, taking them toward Coruscant. Toward home.

Sitting at the hologame table in the rec area, Jacen studied the board. He racked his brains for a strategy to counter Lowie's previous gambit.

"It is your turn," Tenel Ka pointed out, her voice low and matter-of-fact.

Jacen had been hoping to impress his friends by winning a game or two, but he found it hard to concentrate with Tenel Ka beside him. She crossed her bare arms over her reptile-skin tunic, watching his every move. Her reddish-gold hair, tamed into numerous braids, dangled wildly around her head and shoulders every time she spoke or shifted position.

Across the table, Jaina stood behind Lowie and conferred with the ginger-furred Wookiee in a whisper, pointing from one holographic gamepiece to another. The tiny wriggling figures on the table seemed impatient for Jacen to make his next move. A thin film of perspiration formed on his forehead and upper lip. Jacen knew he didn't stand a chance against the computer whiz—especially not while Jaina was helping Lowie.

"We'll be coming out of hyperspace in about five standard minutes," Han Solo announced from the cockpit. "You kids ready?"

"Hey, Dad, can we try some target practice?" Jacen leaped to his feet, glad for the interruption. Finally, something he was good at!

Jacen loved this game their father had devised for them. Whenever he brought them back to Coruscant in the *Millennium Falcon,* Han let the twins sit in the two gun wells. As the ship approached orbit, Jacen and Jaina scanned for floating chunks of metal and debris left over from the space battles that had raged over Coruscant years before, during the overthrow of the Empire.

"We hardly ever find enough debris for both of us to shoot at," Jaina grumbled.

"Oh yeah?" Jacen said, giving her his most challenging smile. "You're just worried because last time I hit something and you didn't. I'm *sure* we're going to find some wreckage to shoot at today. I have a *good* feeling about this." He shrugged once. "But if you're just not up to it . . ."

Jaina's eyes narrowed as she accepted his challenge. A smile tugged at one corner of her mouth. "What are we waiting for?" she said. With that, she dashed toward one of the gun wells, leaving Jacen to scramble to the other. Tenel Ka followed him, while Lowie loped after Jaina, eager to help.

Behind them, the blurry monstrous figures on the hologame table hunkered down and waited for somebody to make a move.

Jacen settled into the overlarge seat of the bottom gun well. He strapped in and leaned forward to take the laser-cannon firing controls as Tenel Ka dropped into place beside him. Her granite-gray eyes narrowed, intent on the weaponry. "Watch that screen there," Jacen said. "Help me get a target. There's plenty of debris left, but it's all pretty small."

"Even small, such wreckage could be deadly to incoming ships," Tenel Ka said.

"This is a fact," Jacen answered with a grin, echoing his friend's often-used phrase. "That's why we clear it out every chance we get." Loud explosions sounded from the other gun well as Jaina began firing her quad lasers. Jacen heard a loud Wookiee roar of encouragement.

"Hey, how did she target so fast?" he said.

"Honing in," Tenel Ka said, pointing at glowing lines on the tracking screen.

"Oh! Well, I could fire too—if I was paying attention," Jacen said. He swung the four-barreled weapon into position, then watched the targeting cross move closer and closer. Maybe it was an old shielding plate from a blown-up Star Destroyer, or an empty cargo pod dumped by a fleeing smuggler. He tracked in closer. . . .

"Stay on target," Tenel Ka said. "Stay on target . . . fire!"

Jacen reacted instantly, squeezing the firing buttons, and all four laser cannons shot focused beams that vaporized the hunk of debris. "Yahoo!" he yelled. A similar whoop of delight came from the other gun well.

"It would appear that Jaina also hit her target," Tenel Ka said.

"Don't get cocky, kids," Han shouted good-naturedly from the cockpit. His copilot Chewbacca roared agreement.

"Just making the galaxy safe for peaceful navigation, Dad," Jacen called.

"We're at a tie," Jaina said. "We need one more shot each. Please, Dad?"

"You twins are always at a tie," Han answered. "If I let you keep shooting until one of you scores and the other doesn't, we'll be circling the solar system for years. Come on back up to the cockpit. We're almost home."

As the *Millennium Falcon* settled onto a clear rooftop, Lowbacca unbuckled his crash restraints and groaned. The landing on Coruscant had been smooth, and he had enjoyed his time optimizing the *Falcon*'s computers—but he was anxious to get back into the open air. Even city air, as long as he could be high enough off the ground.

By the time Lowie reached the ship's exit ramp, Jacen and Jaina had managed to unfasten their crash webbing too. The twins sped past him down the ramp and into the waiting arms of their mother. Leia Organa Solo, the New Republic's Chief of State, stood on the landing platform with her younger son, Anakin Solo, and the golden protocol droid See-Threepio.

Lowie adjusted the miniaturized translating droid, Em Teedee, at his hip and made his way down the ramp, watching the close family scene with a certain amount of envy. Dark-haired Anakin hovered beside his two older siblings, asking occasional questions, his ice-blue eyes taking in everything. Leia, her long brown hair arranged in intricate coils, looked at all three of her children with obvious pride and affection. When Han Solo came out to join the reunion, the family erupted in another joyous burst of kisses and hugs and hair ruffling.

Lowie missed his family on Kashyyyk.

Jaina said, "Thanks for letting us bring our friends home with us for the visit, Mom."

"Your friends are always welcome here," their mother replied. She stepped forward to greet Lowie with a warm smile, then bowed briefly to Tenel Ka, who had followed him down the ramp. "We're very honored to have you all here. Please, treat the palace as if it were your own home."

Though Lowie didn't say a word, Em Teedee spoke up at his waist, chiming in with a delighted voice. "Ah, See-Threepio! My counterpart, my predecessor, my . . . *mentor!* I have many things to upload to you. You'll be most distressed to hear about some of the adventures I've had since Chewbacca first delivered me to the Jedi academy—"

"To be sure! A pleasure to see you again, Em Teedee," Threepio said. "I doubt, however, that your tribulations are anything compared to the heavy diplomatic responsibilities *I* have to bear here on Coruscant. You simply couldn't believe how easily offended some of these outworld ambassadors can be!"

As the two droids chattered along in near-identical voices, Lowie rolled his large Wookiee eyes. Chewbacca, having finished the *Falcon*'s shutdown procedures, came out to join his nephew just as Lowie handed Em Teedee over to See-Threepio so that the two could reminisce as "family" for a while.

Lowie heaved a small sigh, thinking of his homeworld of Kashyyyk, his parents, and his younger sister. His uncle placed a sympathetic hand on his hairy shoulder. Perhaps Chewbacca sensed Lowie's homesickness, because he immediately launched into a description in Wookiee language of the room he had picked for his nephew to sleep in—one of the highest rooms in the Imperial Palace. Though Lowie would see no treetops from his window, Chewbacca assured him that the heights were indeed breathtaking, which should make him feel comfortable and secure. Chewie had also seen to it that the room was furnished with trees and hammocks and lush green jungle plants.

It wasn't as good as visiting home, Chewbacca said, but it was a great place for a vacation.

* * *

Tenel Ka stared at the opulent room chosen for her by Leia Organa Solo. The furniture was beautifully carved, and the draperies and bed coverings were of the finest quality. The mattress looked soft and luxurious.

It felt like home in the Fountain Palace on Hapes. Tenel Ka shuddered. She was a princess of Hapes, since her father, the son of the former queen, a powerful matriarch, now ruled the Hapes cluster with his Dathomiran wife. But Tenel Ka had kept this fact hidden from her friends at the Jedi academy, preferring instead to follow her mother's heritage from wild Dathomir. This palace was a bit *too* much like home on the Hapes central world—and Tenel Ka was uncomfortable with such amenities right now.

"Ah," she said. "Aha."

Striding to the bed, she yanked the covers off and pulled the pad onto the polished stone floor. She squatted down on it and nodded with satisfaction. The room no longer seemed as posh and fluffy—therefore, it was much more comfortable, not to mention much more suitable for a tough warrior woman. This was a fact.

2

AS SHE TRIED to sleep, Jaina thought of how different Coruscant was from the thick jungles of Yavin 4. The planet-wide capital city bustled with an intensity and energy that filtered into every aspect of daily life. Unlike the tiny moon, which managed to still itself in the quiet hours before dawn, the New Republic's central world stayed awake all the time.

Her brother Jacen blinked his bleary brown eyes as he joined her in the dining area the next morning. Tenel Ka and Lowbacca had risen early and, already at work on their morning meals, greeted the twins as they arrived. The golden protocol droid See-Threepio hurried about, making sure the guests had a fine eating experience.

Lowie ate steaming pieces of heated (but still raw) red meat from a gold-etched plate frilled with sculptured loops; Threepio had used the best diplomatic tableware and the choicest garnishes. The Wookiee youth, however, seemed to have trouble avoiding the decorative sprigs and delicate flowers that adorned the bloody meal. Tenel Ka, using a small dagger to poke at her plate, speared a piece of fruit.

"Ah, good morning, Mistress Jaina, Master Jacen," Threepio said. "Such a pleasure to have you home with us again."

Jaina glanced at the holographic window that stretched across the wall of the room—actually an image transmitted from one of the towers elsewhere in the great city. Because their mother was the important Chief of State, their family quarters were protected deep within the palace, without any real windows to the outside. Jaina knew that many other diplomats around the city were looking out their own false windows at the same projected image.

"Thanks, Threepio," Jacen said. "We've been looking forward to this vacation. Uncle Luke has been teaching us some terrific Jedi skills, but it can be exhausting."

The droid tapped his gold-plated hands together. "I am delighted to hear it, Master Jacen. Although I am naturally quite busy tutoring young Master Anakin, I have taken the liberty of setting up a fine curriculum of studies for you while you remain here on Coruscant. Your guests are more than welcome to attend classes as well. Oh, it will be just like old times!"

"Classes!" Jacen interrupted as he plopped down in a chair and began to shovel breakfast into his mouth. "You're joking, right?"

"Oh, no, Master Jacen," Threepio said sternly. "You mustn't neglect your studies."

"Sorry, Threepio," Jaina said, "but we have other plans today."

Before the droid could advance his argument any further, the twins' mother came into the room. "Good morning, kids," Leia said.

Jaina smiled at her mother. Princess Leia looked as beautiful as in the old picture Jaina had seen from the Rebellion. Since that time, Leia had taken on extremely heavy political duties and devoted most of her waking hours—along with quite a few of those she should have spent sleeping—to untangling knots in the threads of diplomacy.

"What are you doing today, Mom?" Jaina asked.

Leia sighed and rolled her dark brown eyes in an expression that Jaina often unconsciously imitated. "I have a meeting with the Howler Tree People of Bendone . . . they speak a very strange language and need a team of translators. It'll take me all morning long just to hold a conversation." She closed her eyes and rubbed her fingertips at her temples. "And their ultrasonic voices give me a headache!" Leia drew a deep breath and forced a smile. "But it's part of the job. We have to keep the New Republic strong. There are always threats from the outside."

"This is a fact," Tenel Ka said gruffly. "We have seen the threat of the Shadow Academy and the Second Imperium firsthand." Lowbacca growled, clearly remembering the dark and difficult time he and the twins had experienced aboard the cloaked Imperial training station.

"Hey, I've got something that'll cheer you up, Mom," Jacen said, reaching into his pocket. "A present I kept for you."

He held out the glittering corusca gem he had snagged while using Lando Calrissian's gem-mining machinery deep in the stormy atmosphere of the gas-giant Yavin.

Leia looked down at it, blinking in amazement. "Jacen, that's a corusca gem! Is this the one you found at GemDiver Station?"

He shrugged and looked pleased. "Yeah—and I used it to cut my way free from my cell in the Shadow Academy. Would you like to have it?"

Leia's expression showed how deeply moved she was, but she closed her son's fingers around the valuable gem. "Just having you offer it to me is a very special gift," she said. "But I don't really need any more jewels or treasures. I'd like you to keep it—find a special use for it. I'm sure you'll think of something."

Jacen flushed with embarrassment, then turned an even deeper red when she gave him a big hug.

Han Solo came into the cozy dining area from the family's living quarters, freshly washed and wide awake. "So kids, what's up for you today?"

Jaina ran to give her father a hug. "Hi, Dad! We're going to spend some time catching up with our friend Zekk."

"That scruffy-looking teenaged junk hunter?" Han asked with a faint smile.

"He's *not* scruffy-looking!" Jaina said defensively.

"Hey, just kidding," Han said.

"Just make sure you don't get into trouble," Leia said.

"Trouble?" Jacen said, blinking his eyes in feigned innocence. "Us?"

Leia nodded. "Keep in mind that we're having a special diplomatic banquet tomorrow night. I don't want to have you stuck with a medical droid because of a sprained ankle—or worse."

Threepio interrupted as he tried to herd dark-haired Anakin off to a quiet room. "I do wish you'd let me keep them here to continue their studies, Mistress Leia. It would be ever so much safer." Anakin looked dejected that he couldn't go out on an adventure with his older brother and sister.

Em Teedee spoke up from Lowbacca's waist. "Well, you need have no fear for their safety, my conscientious colleague. I shall personally see to it that they behave with the utmost caution. You can count on me."

Lowbacca growled a comment, and Jaina didn't think the Wookiee was agreeing with the little translator droid.

In the open air Jaina waited next to Lowbacca, Tenel Ka, and Jacen as they stood in one of Coruscant's busy tourism information centers, a deck that jutted from the grandiose pyramid-shaped palace. Dignitaries and sightseers from across the galaxy came to the capital world to spend their credits visiting parks, museums, odd sculptures, and structures erected by ancient alien artisans.

A boxy brochure droid floated along on its repulsorlifts, babbling in an enthusiastic mechanical voice. It cheerfully listed the most wonderful sights to see, recommended eating establishments catering to various biochemistries, and gave instructions on how to arrange tours for all body types, atmosphere requirements, and languages.

Jaina fidgeted as she studied the bustling crowd—white-robed ambassadors, busy droids, and exotic creatures leashed to other strange creatures. She couldn't tell which were the masters and which the pets.

"So where is he?" Jacen said, putting his hands on his hips. His hair was tousled and his face flushed as he scanned the crowd for a familiar face.

The four young Jedi Knights stood under a sculpture of a gargoyle that broadcast shuttle arrival times from a speaker mounted in its stone mouth. Gazing up at the cloud-frothed sky, Jaina watched the silvery shapes of shuttles descending from orbit. She tried to amuse herself by identifying the vehicle types as they passed, but all the while she wondered what had delayed their friend Zekk. She checked her chronometer again and saw he was only about two standard minutes late. She was just anxious to see him.

Suddenly, a figure dropped directly in front of her from the gargoyle statue overhead—a wiry youth with shoulder-length hair one shade lighter than black. He wore a broad grin on his narrow face, and his sparkling green eyes, wide with delight, showed a darker corona surrounding the emerald irises. "Hi, guys!"

Jaina gasped, but Tenel Ka reacted with dizzying speed. In the fraction of a second following Zekk's landing, the warrior girl whipped out her fibercord rope and snapped a lasso around him, pulling the strand tight.

"Hey!" the boy cried. "Is this the way Jedi Knights greet people?"

Jacen laughed and slapped Tenel Ka on the back. "Good one!" he said. "Tenel Ka, meet our friend Zekk."

Tenel Ka blinked once. "It is a pleasure."

The wiry boy struggled against the restraining cords. "Likewise," he said sheepishly. "Now, if you wouldn't mind untying me?"

Tenel Ka flicked her wrist to release the fibercord.

While Zekk indignantly brushed himself off, Jaina introduced their Wookiee friend Lowbacca. Jaina grinned as she watched Zekk. Though the older boy had a slight build, he was tough as blaster-proof armor. Under the smudges of dirt and grime on his cheeks, she thought, he was probably rather nice-looking—but then, *she* wasn't one to talk about smudges on the face, was she?

Recovering himself, Zekk raised his eyebrows and flashed a roguish smile. "I've been waiting for you guys," he said. "We've got plenty of stuff to see and do . . . and I need your help to salvage something."

"Where are we headed?" Jacen asked.

Zekk grinned. "Someplace we're not supposed to go—of course."

Jaina laughed. "Well then, what are we waiting for?"

Jacen looked out at the sprawling city and thought of all the places he had yet to explore.

Coruscant had been the government world not only of the New Republic, but also of the Empire, and of the Old Republic before that. Skyscrapers covered virtually every open space, built higher and higher as the centuries passed and new governments moved in. The tallest buildings were kilometers high. Many had been destroyed during the bloody battles of the Rebellion and had recently been rebuilt by huge construction droids. Other parts of the planetwide city remained a jumble of decay and wreckage, their abandoned lower levels and piled garbage forgotten over the years.

The buildings were so high that the gaps between them formed sheer canyons that vanished to a point in the dark depths where sunlight never penetrated. Catwalks and pedestrian tubes linked the buildings, weaving them together into a giant maze. The lower forty or fifty floors were generally restricted from normal traffic; only refugees and daring big-game hunters in search of monstrous urban scavenger beasts were willing to risk venturing into the shadowy underworld.

Like a native guide, Zekk led the four friends down connecting elevators, slide tubes, and rusty metal stairs, and across the catwalks from one building to another. Jacen followed, exhilarated. He wasn't sure he knew exactly where they were anymore, but he loved to explore new places, never knowing what sort of interesting plants or creatures he might find.

The skyscraper walls rose like glass-and-metal cliff faces, with only a narrow wedge of daylight shining from above. As Zekk took the companions farther down, the buildings seemed broader, the walls rougher. Mushy blobs of fungus grew from cracks in the massive construction blocks; fringed lichens, some glowing with phosphorescent light, caked the walls. Lowbacca looked decidedly uneasy, and Jacen remembered that the lanky Wookiee had grown up on Kashyyyk, where the deep forest underworld was an extremely dangerous place.

High overhead Jacen could hear the cries of sleek winged creatures—predatory hawk-bats that lived in the city on Coruscant. The breeze picked up, carrying with it heavy, warm scents of rotting garbage from far below. His stomach grew queasy, but he pressed on.

Zekk didn't seem to notice. Tenel Ka, Lowie, and Jaina hurried behind them.

They proceeded across a roofed-in walkway where many of the transparisteel ceiling panels had been smashed out, leaving only a wire reinforcement mesh that whistled in the breezes. Jacen noted etched symbols along the walls, all of them vaguely threatening. Some reminded Jacen of curved knives and fanged mouths, but the most common design showed a sharp triangle surrounding a targeting cross. It looked to Jacen like the tip of an arrow heading straight between his eyes.

"Hey, Zekk, what's that design?" He pointed to the triangular symbol.

Frowning, Zekk glanced around them in all directions and then whispered, "It means we have to be very quiet down here and move as fast as we can. We don't want to go into any of these buildings."

"But why not?" Jacen asked.

"The Lost Ones," Zekk said. "It's a gang. They live down here—kids who ran away from home or were abandoned by their parents because they were so much trouble. Nasty types, mostly."

"Let's hope they stay lost," Jaina said.

Zekk glanced up, his forehead creased with troubled thoughts. "The Lost Ones might even be looking at us right now, but they've never managed to catch me yet," he said. "It's like a game between us."

"How have you managed to get away from them all the time?" Jaina whispered.

"I'm just good at it. Like I'm a good scavenger," Zekk answered, sounding cocky. "I may not be in training as a Jedi Knight, but I make do with what skills I've got. Just streetwise, I guess. But," he continued, "even though I have kind of an . . . understanding with them, I'd rather not push it. Especially not while I'm with the twin children of the Chief of State."

"This is a fact," Tenel Ka said grimly. She kept her hands close to her utility belt in case she needed to draw a weapon.

Zekk quickly ushered them through dilapidated corridors that were heavily decorated with the gang symbols. Jacen saw signs of recent habitation, wrappers from prepackaged food, bright metallic spots where salvaged equipment had been torn away from its housings.

At last they moved on to deeper levels. They all breathed more easily, although Zekk confessed even he had not fully explored this far down. "I think it's a shortcut," he said. "I need your help so I can recover something very valuable." He raised his dark eyebrows. "I think you'll like it—particularly you, Jacen."

Zekk made his living by scavenging: salvaging lost equipment, removing scraps of precious metal from abandoned dwellings. He found lost treasures to sell to inventors, spare parts to repair obsolete machines, trinkets that could be turned into souvenirs. He seemed to have a real skill for finding items that other scavengers had missed over the centuries, somehow knowing where to look, sometimes in the unlikeliest of places.

They descended an outer staircase, slick with damp moss from moisture trickling down the walls. Jacen had to squint just to see the steps. As they turned the corner of the building, Zekk stopped in surprise. In the dim light reflected from far above, Jacen could see a strange jumble protruding from the side of the building—smashed construction bricks, naked durasteel girders . . . and a crashed transport shuttle. From the drooping algae and fungus growing on its outer hull, the damaged shuttle appeared to have been there a long time.

"Wow!" Zekk said. "I didn't even know this was here." He hurried forward, edging his way along the damaged walkway. "I don't believe it. The salvage hasn't even been picked over. See—I'm lucky again!"

"That's an Old Republic craft," Jaina said. "At least seventy years old. They haven't used those in . . . I can't even remember. What a find!"

Tenel Ka and Lowie held the creaking ship steady as Zekk scrambled inside to look around. He poked into storage compartments, looking for valuables. "Plenty of components are still intact. Engine still looks good," he called. "Whoa, and here's the driver. I guess his parking permit ran out."

Jacen came up behind him to see a tattered skeleton strapped into the cockpit.

"Oh, do be careful," Em Teedee said from Lowbacca's waist. "Abandoned vehicles can be terribly dangerous—and you might get dirty as well."

"Was this what you wished to show us, Zekk?" Tenel Ka said.

The older boy stood, bumping his head on a bent girder that ran along the shuttle's ceiling. "No, no, this is a new discovery. I'll have to spend a lot more time down here." He grinned. Engine grease smudged his face, and his hands were grimy from digging through compartments. "I can get this stuff later. I need your help for something different. Let's go."

Zekk scrambled out of the shuttle wreckage and grasped the rusted handrail on the rickety walkway. He looked around to get his bearings, making certain he wouldn't forget the location of this prize. The skull of the unlucky pilot stared out at them through empty eye sockets.

"Looks like you really do know this place like the back of your hand," Jacen commented as Zekk led them elsewhere.

"I've had plenty of practice," Zekk said. "*Some* of us don't take regular trips off planet and go to diplomatic functions all the time. I have to amuse myself with what I can find."

It was midmorning by the time they reached Zekk's destination. The dark-haired boy rubbed his hands together in anticipation, and pointed far below. "Down there—can you see it?"

Jacen looked down, *down* over a ledge to see a rusted construction crawler latched to a wall about ten meters away . . . completely out of reach. The construction crawler was a cranelike mechanical apparatus that had once ridden tracks along the side of the building, scouring the walls clean, effecting repairs, applying duracrete sealant—but this contraption had frozen up and begun to decay at least a century ago. Its interlinked rusted braces were clogged with fuzzy growths of moss and fungus.

Jacen squinted again, wondering why the other boy meant to salvage parts from such an old machine—but then he saw the bushy mass, a tangle of uprooted wires and cables woven together, bristling with insulation material, torn strips of cloth, and plastic. It looked almost like a . . .

"It's a hawk-bat's nest," Zekk said. "Four eggs inside. I can see them from here, but I can't get down there by myself. If I can snatch even one of those eggs, I could sell it for enough credits to live on for a month."

"And you want *us* to help you get it?" Jaina asked.

"That's the idea," Zekk said. "Your friend Tenel Ka there has a pretty strong rope—as I found out! And some of you look like good climbers, especially that Wookiee."

Em Teedee shrilled, "Oh no, Lowbacca. You simply can*not* climb down there! I absolutely forbid it." Lowie hadn't looked too eager at first, but the translating droid's admonishment only served to convince him otherwise. The Wookiee growled an agreement to Zekk's plan.

Tenel Ka attached her grappling hook to the side of the walkway. "I am a strong climber," she said. "This is a fact."

Zekk rubbed his hands together with delight. "Excellent."

"Let me get the eggs," Jacen said, eager to touch the smooth, warm shells, to study the nest configuration. "I've always wanted to see one up close." This was such a rare opportunity. Hawk-bats were common in the deep alleyways of Coruscant, but they were horrendously difficult to capture alive.

Pulling the fibercord taut, Tenel Ka wrapped her hands around it and began lowering herself to the old construction crawler. Jacen had seen her descend the walls of the Great Temple on Yavin 4, but now he watched with renewed amazement as she walked backward down the side of the building, relying only on the strength of her supple arms and muscular legs.

Jacen admired the girl from Dathomir—but he wished he could make her laugh. He had been telling Tenel Ka his best jokes for as long as he had known her, but he still hadn't managed to coax even the smallest smile from her. She seemed not to have a sense of humor, but he would keep trying.

Tenel Ka reached the construction crawler and anchored the fibercord, gesturing with her arm to summon him down. Jacen wrapped the cord around himself and started down the slick wall, trying to imitate Tenel Ka. He used the Force to keep his balance, nudging his feet when necessary, and soon found himself standing beside Tenel Ka on the teetering platform.

"Piece of cake," he panted, brushing his hands together.

"No thank you," Tenel Ka said. "I am not hungry."

Jacen chuckled, but he knew the warrior girl didn't even realize she had made a joke.

Lowie slid down the fibercord with ease, while Em Teedee wailed all the way. "Oh, I can't watch! I'd rather switch off my optical sensors."

When they all stood on the creaking platform, Jacen bent over, straining to reach the tangled nest just below. "I'm going to climb down there," he said. "I'll pass the eggs up."

Before anyone could argue, he dropped between two thin girders, holding a crossbar to reach the piping brace that supported the odd nest. The eggs were brown, mottled with green, camouflaged as knobs of masonry covered with pale lichen. Each was about the size of Jacen's outspread hand; when he touched the warm shells, the texture was hard and rough, like rock. With the Force, he could sense the growing baby creature inside. Perhaps he could use the Force to levitate the prize up to his friends.

He smiled, tingly with wonder as he hefted one of the eggs. It wasn't heavy at all. As he touched a second egg, though, he heard a shrill shriek from above, coming closer.

Tenel Ka shouted a warning. "Look out, Jacen!"

Jacen looked up and saw the sleek form of the mother hawk-bat, swooping down at him and screaming in fury, metallic claws extended, wings studded with spikes. The hawk-bat's wingspan was about two meters. Its head consisted mostly of a horny beak with sharp ivory teeth, ready to tear a victim to shreds.

"Uh-oh," Jacen said.

Lowie bellowed in alarm. Tenel Ka grabbed for a throwing knife—but Jacen knew he couldn't wait for help.

The creature dove toward him like a missile, and Jacen closed his eyes to reach out with the Force. His special talent had always been with animals. He could communicate with them, sense their feelings and express his own to them. "It's all right," he whispered. "I'm sorry we were invading your nest. *Calm.* It's all right. *Peace.*"

The hawk-bat pulled up from her dive and clutched one of the corroded lower crossbars with durasteel-hard claws. Jacen could hear the squeaking sound as the claws scraped rust off the metal, but he maintained his calm.

"We didn't mean to hurt your babies," he said. "We won't take them all. I need only one, and I promise you it'll be delivered to a fine and safe place . . . a beautiful zoo where it will be raised and cared for and admired by millions of people from across the galaxy."

The hawk-bat hissed and pushed her hard beak closer to Jacen, blowing foul breath from between sharp teeth. He knew the hawk-bat was extremely skeptical, but Jacen projected images of a bright aviary, a place where the young hawk-bat would be fed delicacies all its life, where it could fly freely, yet never need to fear other predators or starvation . . . or being shot at by gang members. Jacen snatched the last vision—blurred figures of young humans shooting as she hunted between tall buildings—from the mother's mind.

This last fear convinced the mother, and she flapped her spiked leathery wings, backing away from the nest and leaving Jacen safe . . . for the moment. He grinned up at his friends.

Tenel Ka stood poised, dagger in hand, ready to jump down and fight. Jacen felt a pleasant warm glow to think that she was willing to defend him. He took the hawk-bat egg he was holding and used the Force to carefully levitate it into Jaina's hands. She cradled it, then handed it to Zekk.

"What did you do?" Zekk called.

"I made a deal with the hawk-bat," he said. "Let's go."

"But what about those other eggs?" Zekk said, holding his treasure with great amazement.

"You only get one," Jacen answered. "That was the deal. Now we'd better get out of here—and hurry." He scrambled up to join Lowie and Tenel Ka.

Lowie climbed the fibercord first, racing up the side of the building to the upper ledge. Jacen urged the others to greater speed, and finally, when they were all standing back on the walkway, Zekk said, "I thought you made a deal with the mother. Why do we have to hurry?"

Jacen continued to hustle them out of sight of the construction crawler. "Because hawk-bats have extremely short memories."

3

AS THE FIVE companions left the hawk-bat's nest behind, Jaina stuck close to Zekk. She watched the dark-haired boy move instinctively, hurrying through the maze of upper and lower walkways and cross-connecting bridges as he made a beeline back to his living quarters. The green-eyed boy beamed with self-congratulatory pride at the precious egg he held, as if it were a trophy he had hoped to win for a long time.

"Peckhum is going to be so pleased!" Zekk crowed, looking from Jaina to Jacen. "He'll know just what to do with it. He's got a line on everyone who's looking for anything." He glanced sidelong at Jacen again. "Don't worry about it. We'll find a good home for this baby, just like you promised, Jacen. It shouldn't be too hard for a professional zoologist to incubate this egg until it hatches."

Tenel Ka cleared her throat and said ominously, *"If* we bring the egg back intact."

Jaina suddenly noticed that they had returned to the abandoned levels emblazoned with gang graffiti. *The Lost Ones.*

The sharp corners of the cross in a triangle symbol seemed brighter now, as if freshly painted. Jaina wondered if the gang members could have marked their territory afresh in the short time since the young Jedi Knights had passed through. If the gang members kept such a careful eye out for everything, they might have spotted the five companions already.

Maybe they were watching from hidden, shadowy corners right now. . . .

Tenel Ka tensed and pulled out a small throwing knife, looking from side to side. She seemed alert, ready to spring at the first sign of danger, but Jaina didn't feel safe. With her Jedi senses, she felt a tingle down her spine.

"If the Lost Ones are so tough and powerful, how come we've

never heard of them before?" Jacen looked around nervously in the creaking, musty buildings.

"Because you never come down here," Zekk answered. "Whenever we get together, you either have me come to the Imperial Palace or we meet in the safe upper levels. I'll bet your parents would blow their thrusters if they knew where we were right now."

"We can take care of ourselves," Tenel Ka said defensively, flashing her tiny dagger.

"Dear me, I shouldn't be so certain about that, if I were you," Em Teedee replied from Lowie's waist. The young Wookiee groaned.

Zekk smiled thinly. "Down here you can see how *I* live every day. I don't have anyone to wash my hands for me or cook my meals, you know. And I don't have the luxury of worrying about how to amuse myself. Every day is a search—I'm just lucky I have a special knack for finding things."

Jaina was surprised to hear a hint of resentment behind her friend's words. "Zekk, if you needed anything, you should have just asked. We could have found you new quarters, given you credits to spend—"

"Who said I wanted that?" he responded through clenched teeth. "I don't need charity. I've got my freedom here. I can do whatever I want. Besides, it's more satisfying to live by my own wits than to be pampered and coddled all the time."

Em Teedee piped up, "Well really, Master Zekk! It might interest you to learn that not *everyone* minds being pampered and coddled." Jaina ignored the translating droid and wondered if Zekk really meant what he said.

"Nothing personal," Zekk said with shrug. He looked up at the cross-in-triangle symbol. "Being a gang member doesn't impress me either. Their leader Norys—who's our age—is a big bully who likes to throw his weight around. I can run my way through the lower levels better than any of the Lost Ones, so he's been after me to join for a long time. He'd love to have me as his right-hand man, but I'm too independent for that. I work for myself."

They stood at the entrance to a sheer-walled building, near one end of a dilapidated covered walkway that extended to an adjacent skyscraper. More threatening gang symbols marked the inside walls. Half of the windows were broken, and confined breezes whispered through the walkway like voices warning them to go back.

Zekk looked behind him. "This building we're in is the headquarters of the Lost Ones. We're taking a pretty big risk being here." His emerald eyes sparkled. "Kind of exciting, isn't it?"

The building was large and dark, filled with cavernous spaces of empty meeting chambers, offices, and abandoned supply rooms. Jaina wondered if any record or blueprint of this ancient building still existed in the vast computer archives of the Imperial Information Center.

"I don't think you have to worry about Norys, though," Zekk said, raising his voice. "He talks big, but his ambitions are definitely low. He has no interest in becoming anything more than the biggest bully in a run-down section of a single building on an average planet in a big galaxy." Zekk's voice sounded taunting. "He'll never go anywhere, because his dreams are small."

Just then ceiling panels smashed down from above them, and a dozen wiry young men and women dropped to the floor. They looked scuffed and dirty, with hard, lean faces; each held an interesting cobbled-together weapon scavenged from sharp pieces of scrap.

"You trying to annoy me, trash collector?" the biggest burly young man said. His face was broad and dark, his eyes close-set, his teeth crooked as he ground his jaws together and spread his lips in a sneer.

"It's not polite to eavesdrop, Norys," Zekk said.

Then the gang leader's eyes fixed on the precious hawk-bat egg that Zekk cradled close to his chest. "What has the little trash collector found?" Norys said. "Hey, everybody! Looks like we're gonna have fresh eggs for morning meal."

Lowbacca growled loudly enough to startle the Lost Ones, baring his long Wookiee fangs. Zekk looked suddenly nervous, as if the valuable hawk-bat egg made him vulnerable in new ways.

"What do you want the egg for?" Jacen said.

"He only wants it because *I* want it," Zekk said. "He'll probably smash it, not knowing what it's worth."

Tenel Ka now held a throwing dagger at the ready in each hand. The Lost Ones looked at her and Lowie, then at the three seemingly easier targets of Zekk and the twins.

"In a case like this," Zekk said, moving slowly, extending the mottled egg gradually, as if reluctant to surrender it to the brawny gang member, "the most sensible idea is to . . . *run!*"

He whirled and dashed onto the rickety walkway. The vibration of his running knocked loose a broken wall plate, which dropped silently into the murky depths below. The young Jedi Knights reacted quickly and scrambled after their friend onto the covered bridge.

The gang members howled and gave pursuit, clattering their crude weapons against the walls.

Out in the middle of the dilapidated walkway Zekk suddenly pulled to a stop as a gang member—an angry young woman who looked even tougher than Tenel Ka—appeared from the opposite building and stood ominously at the far entrance.

"We're trapped," Jaina said with a hard gulp. This did not seem like a good place for a standoff.

Zekk looked back and forth, as if seeking inspiration in the middle of the swaying bridge. The cold wind sighed through the broken windows and gaps in the flooring. "Just to be fair," he said, crossing his arms with feigned good humor, "I'll let you guys solve this one. Got any ideas?"

Jaina tried to think of something she could do with what Uncle Luke had taught them at the Jedi academy. With uninterrupted concentration she could manipulate objects with the Force, but she couldn't think of any way her fledgling powers could help them escape.

Norys strode forward, his chest puffed with confidence. "Now give me that egg, trash collector, and maybe we won't throw you over the edge!"

Just then a screeching sound came from above, a blood-curdling animal shriek. A predator's heavy shadow swept like a dark blanket over the cracked windows of the walkway.

With another loud scream, the mother hawk-bat struck the side windows, smashing against the wire mesh that barely held the frames in place. She spat and hissed, her sharp beak ripping at the wires, her forked tongue thrashing as she dug her claws in, trying to get at Norys. The gang leader staggered backward with a surprised yelp.

Zekk protected the egg again, holding it to his chest. At the same time, Lowie—focusing on the lone woman guarding the opposite end of the walkway—let out a ferocious roar and charged forward.

"Oh, my!" Em Teedee squeaked. "Would anyone object if I switched off my optical sensors again so I don't have to watch?"

Distracted by the attacking hawk-bat and startled by the snarling battering ram of Wookiee fur, the gang member backed off and leaped aside.

"Well, what are we waiting for?" Jaina cried. Zekk ducked low to protect the hawk-bat egg as he ran after her. Jacen followed them, while Tenel Ka turned once to threaten the Lost Ones with her throwing daggers before bringing up the rear, sprinting along on her muscular legs.

Seeing them escape, the mother hawk-bat shrieked one more time, then flew off, as if satisfied.

Zekk kept running while Norys yelled after them. "We'll catch you next time, trash collector. Do you hear me?" he shouted. "You'll join our gang—one way or another."

Zekk didn't respond as he led the young Jedi Knights through a maze of stairwells, slides, and lifts in the lower levels, climbing up to rickety catwalks, then higher to lighted levels. He was panting, but his flushed face wore a grin of exhilaration. Triumphant, Zekk cradled the hawk-bat egg close to his body.

"I thought you said hawk-bats had short-term memories," he gasped.

Jacen shrugged and looked sheepish. "Aren't you glad I was wrong?"

"Yes," Jaina said. "We all are."

"Come on," Zekk said. "Let's get this egg back home."

4

VORACIOUSLY HUNGRY AFTER their adventure, the four young Jedi Knights followed Zekk back to where he made his home. Since much of Coruscant's population had fled the capital world during the devastating battles of the Rebellion, many of the midlevel apartments had been left empty but still serviceable. People scraped out a decent existence there without being forced to live in squalor far below at the bottom levels.

For years, Zekk had shared quarters with old Peckhum. The thin, gray-haired man had no particular career, but spent his days doing odd jobs such as transporting cargo in his battered ship, the *Lightning Rod,* or performing whatever duties the New Republic required. Zekk and the old supply runner got along well and helped each other as if they were family, providing mutual support, company, and a place to stay.

Zekk led the companions through dim corridors on the way to his apartment. At the entrance Jaina saw that Peckhum had installed a new messaging center beside the door so that visitors could leave videonotes if no one was home.

"We can kick back here for a while," Zekk said, tucking the hawk-bat egg into the crook of his elbow as his nimble fingers punched in an access code.

The metal door slid aside to reveal a paradise of junk—rooms stacked high with salvaged items, partially restored antiques, and strange gadgets whose original use had long since been forgotten. A small sapphire-feathered bird flitted around inside, but Jaina couldn't tell if the creature was a pet or just some stray that had wandered in to look for nesting materials.

A grizzled old man stood up from a rickety table where he had been poring over manifest files on a scuffed datapad. He had lank gray hair, a leathery face, and a broad smile—and he very much needed a shave.

"Ah, Zekk, you're back." He looked past the teenager. "And you've brought guests. Hello, my young Jedi friends."

Zekk sealed the door behind them, and Jacen immediately began trying to catch the bird, while Tenel Ka poked around suspiciously in the stacked cases and gadgets, as if attempting to uncover traps. Lowie sniffed at a cluttered jumble of electronic equipment.

Zekk beamed proudly as he held out the mottled hawk-bat egg. "Look at this prize!" he said. "How much do you think we can get for it?"

Peckhum nodded with enthusiasm as he held out his hands to take the egg gently in his grasp. "More than a hundred credits, I'd guess. Plenty of zoos and biological establishments are begging for a specimen like this."

Jacen said sternly, "Just make sure it goes to a good home. I made promises to its mother."

Peckhum laughed, shaking his head. "I'll never understand you Jedi Knights. But I don't suppose that'll be too difficult," he said. "In fact, I think I'll even talk to your mother—I heard a rumor that the Chief of State was looking for some unusual zoological specimens."

Jacen blinked his eyes in astonishment. *"Our* mom wanted to collect weird animals? She could have just asked me. . . ."

Peckhum shrugged. "I didn't ask *why* she wanted it. I think it's for some sort of diplomatic gift. And I think this egg, with the proper incubating apparatus, might just do the trick!"

Jaina found a place to sit down, perching herself on a stack of recycled blankets that Peckhum no doubt intended to sell to some alien merchant. Zekk hurried off to prepare a quick lunch. "Last time we saw you, Peckhum," Jaina said conversationally, "you were cornered by a jungle monster on Yavin 4."

Peckhum laughed nervously at the memory. "I haven't been that scared in a dozen years!" he said. "Let's hope your jungle moon gets a little more civilized."

"Are you making another supply run to the Jedi academy soon?" Jacen asked.

"No, I've been assigned to riding the mirrors up in Coruscant orbit," Peckhum said. "It's a lonely job, but the pay is good—and somebody's got to do it. Besides, it's relaxing . . . if you look at it that way."

Because so much of the surface of Coruscant was covered by cities, engineers had long ago found ways to make even the cold northern and southern latitudes more habitable. By focusing sunlight from huge orbiting mirrors, they could direct enough warmth to thaw land as far north as the arctic, so that millions upon millions could live even in Coruscant's less hospitable areas.

Jaina understood the engineering difficulties of operating the huge automated mirrors, of making sure that the beams of directed sunlight shone down on appropriate areas. The job was not unlike the ancient task of running a lighthouse on an ocean world, where people worked alone, ready for emergencies that rarely came.

"Such an austere assignment would provide a good environment for contemplation," Tenel Ka pointed out.

"It does that, all right," Peckhum said. "I just wish conditions weren't so . . . basic."

"What makes the mirror station so uncomfortable?" Jaina asked. "Don't you have entertainment systems and food-processing units up there?"

Peckhum snorted. "According to the design, yes. But they're all malfunctioning. The mirror stations were set up long ago, even before the Emperor took over. During the Imperial years, riding the mirror station was a punishment assigned to stormtroopers who had disobeyed orders.

"Nowadays, the food-prep units, entertainment systems, temperature control systems—even the communication systems—all fritz out randomly. No repair tech is willing to go up and give the whole station an overhaul. The New Republic has so much other business that I'm afraid getting spiffy holovideo reception for the mirror station just isn't high on anyone's priority list."

Jaina pursed her lips and placed her chin in her hands. "Those symptoms you described sound familiar," she said. "Could be you need a new central multitasking unit. That might fix everything all at once."

Peckhum switched off his datapad and tucked it into a satchel hanging from the seat. "Don't I know it! But those units are expensive and hard to come by. I've requested a new system five times, and it's always been turned down. 'The resources of the New Republic are allocated according to greatest need,'" he said, as if quoting from a report. "My comfort isn't a great enough need." He scratched his stubbled chin. "Oh well, I'll survive. It's a job. Last month I used some of my own credits to get a hand-held holoplayer to take up with me. It'll do."

Zekk came out of the kitchen area balancing a stack of self-heating ration cans in his arms. "I know where we can get a central multitasking unit!" He pressed his chin against the top can in the stack to hold them all in position. "Remember that old shuttle we found? Models like that had lots of subsystems. They must have had units to run everything."

"Sure did," Jaina said, nodding vigorously. "Those outdated passenger shuttles all had central multitasking units. They were cumbersome, but they worked."

Peckhum grinned, then frowned. "Well, I'm leaving tomorrow morning, and I'm not sure how I'd install one of those units myself, even if you did get it."

Zekk waved his hand in dismissal. "Relax, Peckhum—I'll get one for you by the time you return. I promise."

Jaina piped up, seeing an opportunity. "And maybe next time you go up to the mirror station, we could go along and help install it." Lowbacca bellowed his interest in the project as well.

Peckhum's eyes widened with surprised delight. "Well, I suppose that might work after all. Let's celebrate by eating lunch."

The old man swept unsorted debris from a low table, clearing a spot for Zekk to set down the stacked cans of food. The dark-haired boy studied them and passed out rations to everyone. Warm steam curled up from open lids as thermal units heated the contents.

Jaina sniffed at hers suspiciously, and Jacen poked into the goo, while Tenel Ka studied the label seriously. Lowie gave a doubtful growl.

"You needn't complain, Master Lowbacca," Em Teedee said. "I'm certain it's quite nutritious. See? The label bears the Imperial stamp of approval."

Zekk held up one of the cans. "These are old stormtrooper rations. We found an entire cache in one of the lower buildings. They don't taste like much, but they have all our nutritional requirements."

Tenel Ka dug in, grunting with satisfaction. "Quite acceptable," she said.

Jaina stirred the grayish puttylike substance, smiled as Zekk dug in, then took a small bite herself. It didn't taste bad. In fact, it didn't taste like *anything,* so she ate courteously. When they had finished, She stood up, meeting Zekk's emerald-green gaze. "Want to join *us* for a meal next time?"

Zekk brightened. "Fine with me. When?"

"Well," Jaina said, biting her lower lip and considering, "since Peckhum is leaving you all alone, why don't you come to the Imperial Palace tomorrow night? We're taking a holiday with my parents in the morning, but we're having some sort of special banquet in the evening. Banquets are usually pretty boring, but I'm sure we could get you invited."

"Really?" Zekk said.

"Sure," Jaina answered.

"That's right," Jacen agreed. "We'll probably give Threepio the time of his life tending to us."

5

FAT SNOWFLAKES FELL in skirling patterns of white against white. There was ice and snow as far as the eye could see on the frozen mountains of Coruscant's polar ice caps. Jaina's exhaled breath produced small puffs of fog in front of her face. Her nose and throat tingled with cold as she inhaled, reveling in the feeling. The crisp air was fresh and clean and delicious.

The tauntaun beneath her, however, smelled *bad*. The creature was supposed to be well behaved, but Jaina didn't think the Bothan stable manager at the polar corrals spent any more time training the wild arctic animals than he did bathing them.

The tauntaun was a white-furred reptile with curved horns jutting from its head. It ran on muscular three-toed hind legs designed to crunch across the snow at high speed. The animals were native to the ice world of Hoth, where the Rebel Alliance had long ago established a secret base. In recent years, though, an enterprising stable manager had transported a few of the beasts to Coruscant's ice caps, intending to offer tauntaun riding as an activity for winter-sports enthusiasts who came to the north pole. But the tauntauns had become surly and stubborn after being transplanted from their home, and Jaina couldn't see how riding one was supposed to be fun.

Her tauntaun fought the bit in its mouth as she tried to make it keep pace with Jacen and his mount. Anakin stayed closer to their father, who hung back next to Leia. Han Solo had claimed to be an expert rider of the uncooperative tauntauns, but Jaina giggled as she watched her father experience plenty of difficulty as they raced across the snows.

The part Jaina enjoyed most was just being able to spend a few hours away from the bustling city with her family, so they could be kids and their parents could be parents—if only for a little while.

Lowie had already made plans with his uncle Chewbacca, and See-

THE LOST ONES

Threepio had offered to spend the day showing Tenel Ka the finest obstacle courses and training facilities that Coruscant had to offer.

Before long, she and Jacen and their friends would have to return to the Jedi academy to continue their training, and Han and Leia would get back to their work building the New Republic.

For now, though, they were on vacation.

"Race you," Jacen called, hunching over his tauntaun.

Jaina took up the challenge instantly. "Well then, what are we waiting for?" She leaned forward and jabbed her heels into the side of the snow lizard.

But just as Jacen whooped his own challenge, his tauntaun stopped dead in its tracks and refused to go a centimeter farther.

Jaina's mount lurched forward at full speed, but she wasn't able to gloat over her victory in the race, because she had as much trouble getting her tauntaun to *stop* as Jacen had getting his to move.

"More soup?" Leia asked, huddling next to the thermal container on the snow.

Jaina shook her head. "Don't think I could eat another bite, Mom."

"Hey, I'd love some more," Jacen said.

"Me too," Anakin chimed in.

"Make that three hungry Solo men," Han Solo added with a lopsided grin, handing his soup cup to Leia. "Never could resist one of your packed lunches."

"Yeah, I can push food-prep buttons better than anyone you know," Leia said wryly.

Jaina sighed with contentment, glad just to relax. After the tauntaun riding, they had spent hours turbo-skiing, having snowball fights, and building cities in the snow. Now, seated on a thick slab of heat-reflective insulfoam, Jaina spread her arms wide, catching snowflakes on her gloved hands. "I wish we could do this more often," she said.

"Maybe we should," her mother replied.

Anakin slurped the last of his soup. "I'll be coming to the Jedi academy again soon," he said. "We can have more meals together then."

"Oh, that reminds me," Leia said. "Don't forget, I'm hosting a very important banquet tonight for the new ambassador from Karnak Alpha."

"Where's Karnak Alpha?" Jacen asked. "I don't think I've ever heard of it."

"Out beyond the Hapes Cluster near the Core Systems," his mother answered.

"Aren't there still some Imperial strongholds in the Core Systems?" asked Jaina.

"Sure are," Han Solo replied. "That's why your mother thinks this dinner is so important. You'll have to be on your best behavior."

Jacen groaned. "If it's so important, how come *we* have to be there?"

Leia smiled warmly. "I'd like you to meet the ambassador. Children play a very special part in the society of Karnak Alpha. They are seen as great treasures that grow richer every day. In Karnak society, the more children you have, the more status and honor you gain. Their government even has a children's council."

"Blaster bolts!" Jacen said. "I almost forgot. We invited Zekk over for evening meal tonight."

"Can he come to the banquet too, Mom?" Jaina asked.

Leia looked flustered, an expression Jaina did not often see on her mother's face. "Zekk? Your young friend from the streets?"

"Aren't you always saying that everyone is valuable, no matter what their background is?" Jaina put in, a little defensively.

"Yeeeesss . . . ," Leia said, drawing the word out.

"Please? If you say yes, I'll even let you braid my hair," Jaina offered hopefully. She glanced at her brothers, looking for support, and saw Anakin's face take on that peculiar measuring look it always did when he was solving a problem.

"If they value children so much, won't the ambassador be happy to have another kid join us?" Anakin said.

Leia's face cleared. "Yes, of course—that's right. Your friend Zekk is more than welcome to come. In fact, we'll invite Lowie and Tenel Ka too."

Jaina laughed with relief. "Great! I'll let them know as soon as we get back."

Jacen finished his soup and stood up. "Do we have to leave right away?"

Han consulted his chronometer. "No, we've got an hour or two yet."

"Well, in that case," Jacen said, "I'll race you all to those hills!"

Everyone laughed and dove for their turbo-skis.

6

AT THE APPOINTED hour that evening, Zekk arrived at the enormous palace and was ushered inside. New Republic guards checked his name against the approved-visitor list and let him proceed into the elegant corridors, with their high vaulted ceilings. Although he knew his way to Jacen and Jaina's quarters, the uniformed soldiers insisted on "escorting" him, which Zekk found somewhat intimidating.

His new formal clothes were stiff and exceedingly uncomfortable, but he knew that this dinner was an important occasion. He silently vowed not to embarrass anyone. He especially didn't want to disappoint the twins.

Before old Peckhum had departed for his lonely mirror-station duties, he'd helped Zekk select a few items of formal clothing, and the young man had also gone out trading, bartering some of his best trinkets and artifacts for a particularly slick jacket. Now he felt like a dandy as he rode the turbolift up to the higher levels and wound his way through the maze of corridors to the Chief of State's quarters.

The protocol droid See-Threepio met Zekk at the doorway and hustled him inside, dismissing the soldier escort. "Ah, there you are, young Master Zekk. We must hurry—you're late! We have preparations to make."

Zekk tugged at his uncomfortable formal suit. "What do you mean 'preparations'? I'm all ready, I'm dressed . . . what more could you want?"

Threepio tsked through his mouth speaker and brushed the front of Zekk's shirt. "Dear me. These clothes are indeed fine and they are most . . . *interesting.* According to my files they were quite fashionable some decades ago. Quite an historical find, I should say."

Zekk felt a stab of disappointment. He had worked so hard, doing his absolute best to prepare for this special event—and in the space of a few seconds the prissy droid had dismissed all of his efforts.

Leia Organa Solo hurried out of the back room, her dark eyes widening as she saw him. "Oh . . . uh, hello Zekk. Glad you could make it." Her gaze seemed to dissect Zekk; he clenched his teeth and tried not to show any embarrassment, though he was sure his cheeks were flushed crimson. His fine suit now seemed as ridiculous to him as a clown's costume.

"I hope I'm not being too much of bother," he stammered. "I didn't mean for Jaina and Jacen to invite me—"

"Don't worry about it," Leia said quickly and smiled. "The ambassador from Karnak Alpha has brought her own brood of children. So please relax. Just do the best you can."

Threepio returned with a kit of grooming implements. "First, we'll comb your hair, young Master Zekk. Everything must be presentable. This is a matter of diplomatic pride for the New Republic, though I do wish I could have located those old files about the customs on Karnak Alpha. The place seems to have been forgotten by my protocol programmers." He fussed over Zekk's hair. "Dear me, you could certainly use a trim! Hmmmm, I wonder if we have time . . ."

Jaina and Jacen came out to greet their friend as he stood soundlessly enduring the golden droid's overattentive ministrations. Jacen's hair seemed awkwardly straight, his face scrubbed so clean that Zekk barely recognized the boy. "Hello, Zekk!" Jaina cried with sincere delight, but when she noticed his outfit she covered her mouth to stifle a giggle. He felt his cheeks burning with fresh shame.

When Zekk struggled against the buzzing device, Threepio said sternly, "I *am* a protocol droid, you know, fully trained in grooming techniques." Zekk didn't argue, but winced as Threepio cleared a snag in his dark hair.

"I'm not sure this is such a good idea," Zekk said. "I don't know anything about diplomacy. I don't know any manners or etiquette."

Jaina laughed. "That's not important. Just use your common sense and watch what the rest of us do. It's a big diplomatic banquet, and you have to follow all sorts of boring ceremonies—but the food's good. You'll enjoy it."

Zekk didn't point out that it was easy for Jaina to say such things, since she had been brought up in this high political society and trained in the proper responses for so many years that such actions were second nature to her. Zekk, though, had no such instruction. This whole dinner was going to be a disaster, he just knew it.

See-Threepio finally gave up on his attempts to comb out Zekk's hair and shook his gleaming head in exasperation. "Oh, dear. I have a bad feeling about this," he sighed. Zekk couldn't argue with him.

* * *

Tenel Ka followed the group as they filed toward the formal dining chamber, conscious of her every movement. This was an important diplomatic function, and she had been well tutored by her harsh grandmother in the plush courts of the Hapes Cluster. Tenel Ka was a royal princess, after all, the heir apparent to an entire cluster; but she avoided such nonsense and spent as much time as possible training instead on her mother's austere world of Dathomir. Tenel Ka's Hapan grandmother strongly disapproved of the path that the princess had chosen to follow, but Tenel Ka had a mind of her own—as she frequently demonstrated.

Now she strode behind Jacen, Jaina, and Zekk, walking next to Lowbacca and the silent younger boy Anakin, as they hurried to the dining chamber. She wore a short, tight-fitting sheath of colorful reptilian hides, freshly oiled and polished so that they gleamed with her every movement. Her muscular arms and legs were bare, but she wore a flowing cape of deep forest green over her shoulders.

Tenel Ka had spent many months at the Jedi academy in the primitive jungles of Yavin 4, and before that she had lived in the cliff cities of the Singing Mountain Clan. It had been a long time since she'd been spoiled with luxuries, but she viewed the formal evening meal with the Karnak ambassador as another challenge to face.

Lowbacca had been shampooed and dried, his fur neatly combed so that he seemed much thinner than usual without his swirling hair sticking out in all directions. The black streak that swept back above his eyebrow had been slicked down, giving him a dashing appearance . . . for a Wookiee.

See-Threepio strutted ahead of Leia and Han as if he were an escort. New Republic guards stood beside the entrance to the great dining hall and swung the doors wide as they approached. Clasping Han Solo's arm, Leia walked in, regal in her fine white robes. Though small of stature, the Chief of State seemed full of energy and confidence, like a battery overcharged with power. Tenel Ka admired her.

Their timing was exactly right. As they passed into the dining hall from one end, the opposite entrance opened, and the ambassador from Karnak Alpha entered, followed by her train of eight children.

The ambassador was a haystack of tan hair, a mound of fur that grew so long that it obscured every other feature of her body. Not even the ambassador's eyes were visible peeping out from between the strands, as she scuttled forward on feet also hidden by her flowing tresses. The ambassador took her place at the head of the table beside the seat reserved for the Chief of State. Leia sat down, with her husband next to her.

The ambassador's children, all eight of them, were miniature versions of her, heaps of hair that bustled to their seats. The girls' fur was knotted into colorful ribbons, while the boys jingled with bells tied to strands of hair. All of them seemed well-groomed and impeccably behaved as they took their seats along one side of the table.

Tenel Ka was glad she had thought to braid colorful ribbons into her own red-gold hair. She had seen natives of Karnak Alpha during her time at the royal court of Hapes. The hairy creatures were shy and had some unusual customs, but they were relatively easygoing.

Tenel Ka sat beside Lowbacca, while Jacen and Jaina took their dark-haired friend Zekk to the front end of the long polished table. Their little brother Anakin, with his eerie ice-blue eyes, seemed content to sit anywhere they directed him, quietly waiting for his place between Lowbacca and Jacen.

See-Threepio moved up and down the line, fussing over items and reveling in his position. This type of duty was, after all, what a protocol droid was programmed for—not for bravery or adventure, but for intricate diplomatic functions.

In front of each gleaming plate sat a crystalline vase containing a cluster of fresh, rich-smelling greens, exotic plants taken from some of Coruscant's botanical gardens—interesting specimens that formed a lovely bouquet for each honored visitor.

Before the start of the meal, Leia gave a carefully rehearsed speech, welcoming the ambassador and expressing her wish for a long and fruitful relationship based on commerce, mutual respect, and support. She whispered to Threepio, and the droid disappeared into an alcove, only to reemerge a moment later carrying a small package. Tenel Ka immediately recognized an incubator sheath wrapped around a smooth ovoid object.

"Hey, that's the hawk-bat egg we rescued!" Jacen said, unable to stop himself.

Leia smiled and nodded. "Yes, and I suppose the ambassador may appreciate the gift even more, now that she knows it was found by the very children she is dining with."

The Karnak ambassador trembled with excitement, her long hair jiggling, as Leia explained. "Madam Ambassador, we know very little about your culture—but we do know that you have a great love for unusual zoological specimens. We have heard reports of your magnificent holographic dioramas and huge alternate-environment zoos where the animals don't even realize they are in a cage. As a diplomatic gift to you and your people, we present to you this rare and precious hawk-bat egg, one of the most difficult-to-catch creatures native to Imperial City. Very few of them are in captivity."

Delighted, the Karnak Alpha ambassador cooed. "This will surely be a wonderful addition to our rarities."

"But you have to take special care of it," Jacen chided. "I promised its mother personally!"

The hairy ambassador didn't seem to find the comment at all strange. "I give you my solemn promise." Then the ambassador responded with her own rehearsed speech, her mouth moving somewhere between the strands of fur as she echoed the sentiments Leia had expressed.

Meanwhile, her children, little wriggling piles of hair, sat impatient and hungry for the meal, while Jacen, Jaina, and the other young Jedi Knights similarly felt their stomachs growling. Han Solo squirmed restlessly beside Leia in his formal clothes, as if chafing under his stiff collar and his medals of military service. Tenel Ka felt sympathy for him.

See-Threepio came into the room, strutting beside a trundle droid that carried a beaten silver tray of ornate plates piled high with scrumptious-looking cuisine, beautifully garnished and displayed. Out of normal political courtesy, the golden droid marched toward the head of the table while Leia and the Karnak ambassador made the appropriate appreciative sounds, showing how impressed they were with the exquisite food.

Tenel Ka watched See-Threepio move directly toward the ambassador, picking up one of the larger plates from the trundle droid's tray. She knew instantly that Threepio meant to offer the first meal to the ambassador—which was a terribly rude thing to do, according to Karnak custom.

In one quick, fluid motion she sprang to her feet and called across the table. "Excuse me, See-Threepio," she said. "If you would allow me?" She hurried to one end of the table as the droid stopped, completely at a loss as to what to do. One by one, Tenel Ka removed the plates from the tray and reverently set them in front of each of the ambassador's children, starting with the smallest—and presumably the youngest—furball.

Princess Leia looked at Tenel Ka, surprised but reserving judgment. The Karnak ambassador made a motion that must have been a bow of her head. "Why, thank you, young lady. You do us a great honor. This is an unexpected observance of our customs."

Tenel Ka nudged See-Threepio and moved him around to the other side of the table, where she tapped Anakin on the shoulder. She handed the boy a plate, then whispered into his ear. Anakin—without argument or question—stood up, dutifully moved down the table, and presented the next plate of food to the Karnak ambassador.

The ambassador chirped with surprise. "I am most honored, Chief of State," she said to Leia, "that you would choose your youngest to serve me."

"I—thank you," Leia said, uncertain of what else to say.

Tenel Ka stood behind Leia, nodding. Her braided red-gold hair fell forward. "Yes, Ambassador," she said. "We wished to show you honor by respecting the customs of Karnak Alpha—that a young member of the household provides for the guest's children, before a child of the host family serves the most honored adult guest."

"I am most pleased," the ambassador said. "We shall have a simple time making diplomatic treaties, if all members of the New Republic are so considerate of our customs."

Trembling with relief that she had averted what could have been a social gaffe for the Chief of State, Tenel Ka sat back down, while Jacen bent toward her, his brandy-brown eyes wide with astonishment. "How did you know that?" he said in a low whisper.

Tenel Ka shrugged beneath her reptilian armor. "It is . . . just something I learned," she said, and then fell silent, reluctant to reveal her royal upbringing, even to a good friend.

Even though Zekk sat back and remained quiet, he still felt uncomfortable. The meal tasted delicious, but each time he moved he was afraid that one of his gestures might offend someone or cause a diplomatic incident.

Threepio served the rest of the meals, and Zekk fell to eating with quiet attention, savoring the delicious food . . . though it was far richer than what he was accustomed to.

The salad in the crystal bowl in front of him was crunchy and strange—some of the leaves bitter, others stringy—but he had eaten far worse in his days of scavenging the streets. He had roasted rock slugs and eaten sliced duracrete fungus. These greens at least were fresh, and he relished them.

The conversation around the table seemed to be empty polite chit-chat, and Zekk, feeling like an irrelevant guest, did his best to participate. He pushed aside the empty crystal bowl. "Delicious salad," he said. "I don't believe I've ever had greens like that." That sounded good, a complimentary but neutral statement—enough to show willingness to take part in the dinner conversation, yet nothing anyone could fault him for.

Suddenly he felt all eyes turned toward him. He looked down to see if he had spilled something down the front of his out-of-style jacket.

Jacen seemed full of disbelief. Tenel Ka made no sign that she had even heard Zekk's comment. Jaina nudged Zekk with her elbow in a teasing way. "That wasn't a *salad,*" she whispered. "That's the *bouquet.* You weren't supposed to eat it."

Zekk listened in horror, but kept his face a careful mask.

See-Threepio spoke up from behind them. "Now then, Mistress Jaina, many plants *are* edible, including all of those within the bouquet. I'm certain there's been no harm—"

From the far end of the table Princess Leia cleared her throat. "I'm glad you liked the salad, Zekk," she said in a voice loud enough for everyone to hear, and pulled her crystal dish toward her. She selected a frilly purple-green leaf and stuffed it in her mouth, munching contentedly. Han Solo looked at his wife as if she had gone crazy, then jerked as if he had been kicked under the table. He too began to eat his bouquet. Jaina followed suit, and soon everyone at the table had devoured their "salads."

Zekk was mortified, though he tried not to show it. His manners were laughable, his clothing was outdated, and he had embarrassed everyone by eating something he should have known was a decoration. He wished he had never been invited to this banquet.

He endured the rest of the evening in simmering silence until the Karnak ambassador and her entourage of furball children finally departed, accompanied by the Chief of State and her husband.

When New Republic escorts came to return them to their rooms, Zekk decided to take the first opportunity to escape.

"Don't worry about tonight, Zekk," Jaina said in an understanding voice. "You're our friend. That's all that matters."

Zekk felt stung by her comment, by the fact that she had even needed to say such a thing. He didn't belong here. That truth was etched in burning letters in his brain. He should have known better, but he had pretended that he could fit in with such high-class friends.

When he slipped out the back door of the main dining hall, fully intending to walk too fast for even the rigid escorts to keep up with him, Jaina tried to stop him. "Wait!" she called. "We're still going to meet tomorrow, right? We promised to help you get that central multitasking unit for Peckhum."

Zekk didn't particularly want to go home, but he certainly couldn't stay. He hurried out into the corridors without answering Jaina.

7

LATER THAT NIGHT, the bulk space cruiser *Adamant* lurched into the Coruscant system, heavily guarded by New Republic warships. The number of assault fighters bristling with turbolaser cannons that clustered around the supply cruiser hinted at the military importance of the cargo it carried.

Standing ready on the cruiser's command bridge, Admiral Ackbar remained tense despite the additional precautions that had been taken. The *Adamant* approached a docking zone near the Coruscant space stations, precisely according to schedule. The assault fighters powered down their weapons and split off as each squadron signaled farewell to the admiral, commander of the New Republic Fleet.

"Thanks for the escort," Ackbar said into the comm unit. "Coruscant security will take over from here." He switched off and paced the bridge. It had been a long haul, but the New Republic badly needed the modern hyperdrive cores and turbolaser battery emplacements his ship carried in its armored holds. The *Adamant* would deliver the components to the Kuat Drive Yards, where they would be installed in a new fleet of battleships. Ackbar had been charged with making a formal inspection tour—and he always relished the chance to be aboard a fine military ship.

Though the main threat from the evil Empire had ended, trouble still flared up in the non-allied systems. The fragile government, led by Chief of State Leia Organa Solo, had to be ready at all times with a force strong enough to ward off attacks from known or unknown enemies.

"Coruscant Central acknowledges our arrival," said the helmsman.

Admiral Ackbar nodded. "It'll be good to take some rest and recreation downside," he said, turning to the helmsman and staring with his round, fishy eyes. "Ever been to Coruscant for a furlough before, Lieutenant?"

The young man nodded. "Yes, sir. Several times. I know where there's this little rooftop cantina, a rotating restaurant that lets you look out across the whole city. They've got a keyboard player with ten tentacles. Boy, you should hear the music she makes!"

Admiral Ackbar chuckled just as the tactical officer turned from her station, her normally pale skin flushed as she shouted an alarm. "Admiral! An unidentified fleet just appeared off our starboard bow. Range is less than fifty kilometers and closing fast. They appear to be in an attack formation."

Ackbar whirled to look out the front viewports. "Attack formation?" he said. "But we're in the Coruscant protected zone, one of the most heavily guarded areas in the galaxy. Who could possibly attack us?" He saw the incoming fleet as it soared in like birds of prey, appearing out of nowhere. In the same moment, he felt the stunning blows from their ion cannons, which immediately crippled the *Adamant*'s defensive systems.

"Battlestations!" he cried in his gravelly voice as another thundering blow slammed into the side of the *Adamant*.

"Minor outer hull breach," the operations officer shouted. "Loss of pressure. Emergency bulkhead doors have closed."

"Transmit a distress signal," Ackbar yelled. "Request immediate assistance from Coruscant security. Now!"

"All weapons systems off-line," the tactical officer reported. "We can't even fire a shot. Engines are still undamaged, though—almost as if our attackers are trying *not* to target them."

"They want to steal this ship," Ackbar said as the cold realization struck him. "And its cargo."

The communications officer had begun transmitting a distress signal, but the round-faced young man looked up almost immediately, his cheeks pale. "Sir, communication systems are nonfunctional. We can't even request help."

Admiral Ackbar swallowed. Coruscant would note the attack and respond within minutes—but by then, he knew, it would be too late.

The enemy ships closed in.

The modified assault shuttle zeroed in on its target. At his controls the former TIE pilot Qorl guided the attack. He wore a black skull-like helmet that sealed against his skin and recirculated breathable air. The dark goggles covering his eyes transmitted important tactical data to his retinas.

He positioned the shuttle's circular cutting "mouth" attachment against the armor plating of the Rebel supply cruiser. The name *Adamant* had been stenciled on the side . . . *Adamant*, which meant impenetrable, unyielding. Qorl grunted to himself. The exceedingly tough cutting teeth were made from industrial-grade Corusca gems and could slice through any known substance. The Shadow Academy's takeover troops would be in control of the ship within moments.

Qorl punched an important-looking red button on the controls. It set the Corusca blades spinning, chewing, until the attachment had sliced out a large circle in the *Adamant*'s hull, opening a hole into the supply cruiser.

Qorl clenched the black-gloved hand of his bulky droid arm into a fist. His own arm had been crippled when his TIE fighter crashed on the jungle moon of Yavin 4, but Imperial engineers had replaced the twisted limb with a more powerful droid attachment. His strength had increased, though he could not feel anything with his new mechanical fingers.

Eager stormtroopers assembled in the boarding tube, holding their blaster rifles ready. Qorl knew that the supply cruiser's main defenses had been on the escort ships, the fourteen heavily armed corvettes, E-wings, and X-wings that had flanked the *Adamant* on its trip to Coruscant. The Rebels had become complacent at their capital world, though, and they had let their defenses lapse for just a moment. Qorl, lurking in his invisible hiding place, had seized that moment to strike.

"Airtight seal complete," a stormtrooper captain reported.

"Very well," Qorl said, standing from his command chair. "Begin the assault. We must be away from here within five standard minutes. We have no time for errors."

The sealed hatch of the boarding tube popped open, and the stormtroopers charged in, firing at anything that moved using only stun beams. They had no particular desire to avoid killing the *Adamant*'s crew, but deadly blaster bolts might cause irreparable damage to the bridge's control systems.

Some of the Rebel crew had taken shelter behind consoles. They fired at the stormtroopers, releasing wild bursts of energy. One trooper went down, a smoking hole in his white chest armor, making a gurgling sound that ended with a burst of static over his comm system.

Qorl marched in, holding a blaster pistol in his droid hand. The stormtroopers fired repeatedly. The Rebel helmsman went down, flying backwards as bolts of blue energy knocked him aside. A tactical officer screamed a challenge as she leaped from her position, shooting four times in quick succession. She killed two stormtroopers before she, too, was stunned.

Qorl strode forward, intent on the *Adamant*'s helm. He needed to get this ship moving soon. The dark goggles of his TIE helmet allowed little peripheral vision, and as he passed the command station, the Rebel commanding officer—a fish-faced Calamarian—leaped up and tackled him. Qorl's blaster pistol clattered to the floor.

The officer wrestled with Qorl, fighting with flipper hands, but the TIE pilot drove his powerful droid fist into the face of the alien, knocking him out cold. Qorl retrieved his blaster pistol and climbed to his feet, brushing off his black uniform.

A stormtrooper captain marched up to him smartly. "The bridge is secure, sir. Ready to move out."

Qorl sat down in the *Adamant*'s command chair. "Very well." He sealed his helmet and his padded suit for total containment, which would protect him from the rapid decompression when the assault ship detached itself from the hull. He hesitated. "Stuff these Rebels into an escape pod, and launch it."

"Save them, sir?" the trooper asked, perplexed. "We don't have much time."

"Then be quick about it!" Qorl snapped. Conflicting emotions warred within him. These were the enemy, and he had sworn to fight them—but the crew on this ship had battled valiantly, and he couldn't stomach letting them die as they lay there unconscious.

The stormtroopers paused for only a second, then hustled as they dragged the limp forms to the bridge escape pod and unceremoniously dumped them inside the defenseless craft. The stormtrooper captain sealed the hatch and punched the pod's external launch control. With a hiss from explosive bolts and a gush of compressed gases, the escape pod shot away.

Qorl studied the *Adamant*'s tactical station. Rebel defensive forces were finally on their way, streaking up out of orbit and heading toward the besieged supply ship. "Go!" he said to the troopers. "Take the assault shuttle and escape. I will meet you back at the base."

The stormtroopers hurried to the shark-mouthed assault shuttle and sealed the boarding hatch. Qorl braced himself as the modified ship detached itself, letting the contained atmosphere rush out of the bridge through the gaping hole, to space.

Secure in his suit, Qorl powered up all the engines. He fed in preprogrammed coordinates, and the *Adamant* lurched into motion. As the Rebel fleet zoomed in, Qorl followed his Imperial ships, carrying with him an incredible treasure that would help the Second Imperium gain its rightful place of military superiority.

The base was very close indeed.

* * *

Admiral Ackbar returned to consciousness, and found himself crammed with his crew inside an escape pod that whirled out of control through space. His head ached, and he felt as if a space mine had exploded inside his skull. His crew members groaned and stirred, coming awake. For some reason their lives had been spared. He wriggled his way over to one of the tiny viewports so he could watch for rescue craft.

As the escape pod spun about in a nauseating spiral, Admiral Ackbar saw his own ship from the outside. The hijacked space cruiser *Adamant* lumbered into motion and picked up speed as the Imperial fighters streaked ahead of it.

New Republic reinforcements headed on a direct path to recapture the precious weapons and supplies—but already Ackbar could see that the Imperial ships would be long gone by the time those reinforcements arrived.

Ackbar watched the *Adamant* vanish before the Coruscant ships came close enough to fire a shot. He wished he could just fall back into unconsciousness, but the splitting pain in his skull kept him wide awake.

8

AS ZEKK HURRIED through the night streets of Imperial City, heading away from the palace, he took back stairways and crossed alley catwalks, wanting to see no one. Overhead, blinking lights from shuttles taxiing across the atmosphere fought through a blurring mist of condensed moisture from roof exhaust vents. The city's myriad lights and its sprawling landscape of skyscrapers extending beyond the horizon taunted him with the knowledge that, despite the millions upon millions of inhabitants, he was totally alone.

After the evening's miserable escapades, he felt as if a marquee droid was hovering over his head, broadcasting to everyone that Zekk was a clumsy fool, an embarrassment to his friends. What had he been thinking—trying to fit in with important society, mingling with ambassadors and diplomats, making friends with the children of the Chief of State? Who was *he* to spend time with such people?

He looked at his feet for something to kick, finally spotted an empty beverage container, and lashed out with his boot, a boot he had spent time polishing so he would look good in front of his so-called friends. The container clattered and bounced against a duracrete wall, but to Zekk's frustration it refused to break.

He kept his gaze turned downward, to the shadows and the clusters of garbage in the gutter. He shuffled aimlessly, wandering the back streets, not caring where he might end up. The lower world of Coruscant was his home. He knew it well, and he could survive here—which was good, because it looked as if he would be stuck in this gloomy place for the rest of his life. There was no hope, no chance for advancement. He simply wasn't the equal of those people who could look forward to a bright future—people like Jaina and Jacen.

Zekk was a nobody.

He saw a group of merchants closing up their kiosks for the night, chatting cordially with the New Republic guards who patrolled the streets. Zekk didn't want to go near them, didn't want any company whatsoever. He slipped into a public turbolift and punched a button at random, descending nineteen floors and emerging in a dimmer section of the city.

Old Peckhum had already gone up to the mirror station on his tour of duty, so even Zekk's home would be empty and uninviting. He'd have to spend the night alone, trying to keep amused with games or entertainment systems . . . but nothing sounded at all interesting.

He could wander around for as long as he liked, so he decided to enjoy it. No one would tell him to go to bed, no one would admonish him for going places where he wasn't allowed, no one would breathe down his neck.

He smiled thinly. *He* had a freedom Jaina and Jacen didn't have. When they were out exploring and having fun, the twins constantly checked their chronometers, making sure they would be back home at the appointed time, never making allowances for unexpected circumstances. They certainly didn't want to give their protocol droid a burned worry circuit by not following their explicit orders. The twins were prisoners to their own schedules.

What did it matter if Zekk didn't know all the manners a life in the diplomatic court required? *Who cared* if he didn't understand which eating implement to use, or what the appropriate phrase of gratitude was when speaking to an insectoid ambassador? He snorted with derision. He wouldn't want to live like Jaina and Jacen. No way!

As he wandered along the abandoned corridors, purposely scuffing his toes against the floor plates, he paid no attention to the thickening shadows, to the oppressive silence that surrounded him. He sniffed and clenched his teeth in remembered humiliation. He didn't care about any of that. Zekk was his own person, independent—just the way he liked it.

Overhead, the glowpanels flickered intermittently; those at the far end of the corridor had completely burned out. A skittering sound in the ceiling ducts signaled the passage of a large and clumsy rodent. Ahead he heard another rustling sound, something even bigger.

Zekk looked up with a gasp to see a tall figure, darker than the inky shadows, step out in front of him. "Well, what have we here?" a syrupy voice said, deep and powerful.

The figure stepped closer, and Zekk could see a tall woman with eyes that flashed a burning violet. She wore a glittering black cloak with shoulder spines like defensive armor. Long black hair flowed around her like wire-thin snakes. Her skin was pale, her lips a deep crimson. She tried to smile, but the expression looked foreign on her face.

"Greetings, young sir," she said, her voice oozing persuasion. "I require a moment of your time." When she stepped more fully into the light, Zekk noticed that the woman walked with a pronounced limp.

"I don't think so . . . ," he said, backing up and turning around just as two sinister figures emerged from the side corridors: a compact woman with light brown skin and wavy bronze hair and a shadow-faced young man with dark bushy eyebrows.

"Just one moment of your time, boy. Vilas and Garowyn here will make sure you don't do anything foolish," the dangerous-looking woman said. She limped closer to him. "I am Tamith Kai, and we need to perform a test on you. It won't hurt a bit." Zekk thought he detected a tone of disappointment in her voice.

The young man Vilas and the short, bronze-haired woman grabbed him from behind. Instantly, Zekk struggled, thrashing and shouting out loud. The strangers didn't seem bothered by how much noise he made, and Zekk knew with a sinking certainty that cries for help were not at all uncommon in these abandoned levels—although brave rescuers were.

Zekk tried to yank his arms free from the clawlike grasp of his captors, but to no avail. Tamith Kai withdrew a strange device from the black folds of her cape. Unraveling wires connected to a pair of flat crystalline paddles, she switched on an additional power grid. A high-pitched hum vibrated through the machine case.

"Leave me alone!" Zekk lashed backward with his foot, hoping to deliver a sharp blow to sensitive shins.

"Be careful," Tamith Kai said to her colleagues with a meaningful scowl. "Some of them can be dangerous when they kick."

She leaned closer and waved the humming crystal paddles around his body, scanning him. His heart pounding with fear, Zekk gritted his teeth and squeezed his emerald eyes shut. To his surprise, he felt no tingling energy; no burning analytical beam sliced through his skin.

Tamith Kai withdrew, and Garowyn and Vilas leaned over Zekk's bony shoulders to observe the readings. Still struggling, Zekk caught a glimpse of the glowing image, a colorful aura projected in a micro-hologram.

"Hmmm, surprising," Tamith Kai said. "Look at the power he has."

"A good find," Garowyn agreed. "Quite fortunate."

"Not fortunate for me!" Zekk snapped. "What do you want?"

"You'll be coming with us," Tamith Kai said. Her tone was filled with confidence, as if she didn't care about his objections.

"I'm not going *anywhere* with you!" Zekk shouted. "No matter what you found, I won't—"

"Oh, just stun him," Tamith Kai said impatiently, turning about on her stiff leg and limping back down the shadow-shrouded corridor. "He'll be easier to carry that way."

Vilas released his grip on the boy's arms, and Zekk tried to run, knowing this was his last chance . . . but arcs of blue fire looped out, engulfing him and slamming him down into unconsciousness.

9

JAINA STARED MOROSELY at her brothers. She bit her lip, wondering what their mother would say when she got back from seeing the Karnak Alpha ambassador to her quarters. She hoped Leia wasn't too upset with Zekk.

Jacen paced the living area, muttering to himself. "Blaster bolts!" he said with a dramatic gesture. "Can you believe Zekk thinking the bouquet was a salad? It's a good thing Tenel Ka was there to head off that other problem. We still probably made a terrible impression on the ambassador."

"I don't think it turned out so badly," Anakin said from where he sat on a large cushion near the door. "Mom will handle it. You'll see."

Jaina groaned. "Zekk probably feels terrible."

"We'll see him in the morning," Jacen said, "when we help him look for that central multitasking unit. We can apologize to him then."

The door to their quarters swished open and Leia walked in wearing a bemused expression. After a moment of anxious silence, all three of her children spoke at once.

"I'm sorry, Mom. It's all my fault," Jaina blurted.

"Was the ambassador very angry?" Jacen asked.

"Where's Dad?" Anakin said.

The barrage of questions snapped Leia out of her daze. "Nothing to be sorry for, Jaina," she said, giving her daughter a hug. "The ambassador says I've got three wonderful children, and they have charming friends." She stooped to smooth back Anakin's straight dark hair. "And to answer *your* question, your father had begun discussing hyperspace trade routes to Karnak Alpha with the ambassador, and decided to stay for some business that was even more important."

Jaina blinked in surprise at this unexpected turn of events and sat down at one end of a long, cushioned repulsorseat. Leia sat down beside her, and Jacen settled next to his mother on the other end of the seat. Leia adjusted the repulsorseat's controls to a gentle rocking motion. Anakin dragged his floor cushion over to sit beside them, quiet and attentive.

Leia smiled down at her children. "The ambassador was certainly impressed by the number of young people we had invited to meet her at the dinner. She also said that any adult who was willing to break with her own social traditions just to make a child feel more comfortable should have no problem negotiating an alliance with Karnak Alpha. I'm glad you twins were here with us, rather than at the Jedi academy."

"That's great, Mom," said Jaina, snuggling deeper into the cushions.

"I learned something very important about myself tonight," Leia continued. "As your father and I walked the ambassador and her children back to their quarters, I realized that *my* kids were more important to me than any ambassador. When we got to their quarters, the ambassador said she was ready to discuss her planet's alliance with the New Republic. That's when I amazed even myself. I said I'd be happy to talk with her about it in the morning—but that for right now I needed to be with my children."

Jaina gave a low whistle. Her mother was always so wrapped up in her duties as Chief of State, such a response seemed inconceivable. "You didn't!"

Leia chuckled. "Yes I did, and you know what she said?" She sounded a bit surprised. "She said in that case she no longer had any doubts that we could form an alliance. Everything is all set."

"If everything's all set, why didn't Dad come back with you?" Anakin asked. "What other important business was there?"

"He offered to stay behind," Leia said, raising her eyebrows, "and tell the ambassador's children one of your favorite bedtime stories. Can you guess which one?"

Jacen, Jaina, and Anakin all murmured in unison, "The Little Lost Bantha Cub."

"Then you'll have to tell us a story, too, Mom," Anakin said in a sleepy voice.

So she did.

10

THE NEXT MORNING, as they found their way through the streets, Jacen had an uneasy prickly feeling at the back of his neck, as if a trail of mermyns were crawling along his skin. Something felt wrong, but he couldn't quite put his finger on what it was. "Blaster bolts," he muttered.

For some reason they all seemed a bit jumpy today. Jaina had taken the lead, since she was most familiar with the way to Zekk's quarters. Jacen, on the other hand, always got lost. Tenel Ka followed Jaina in silence, her shoulders squared, her back rigid, while Jacen and Lowie brought up the rear.

They trooped through the ancient cramped alleyways of metal and stone. The lights were too dim in this area, and the air tasted of rusting metal and decay. Even the odors were unfamiliar and, to Wookiees at least—judging by the wrinkling of Lowie's nose—none too pleasant.

"Here we are," Jaina said, rounding a sharp corner into an even narrower passageway. She stopped at a low doorway and pressed the signal button. The indicator light flashed red, denying them access. Jaina bit her lower lip. "That's strange. Zekk said yesterday that he'd clear us for access."

"Perhaps he is more upset than we expected," Tenel Ka suggested.

"Maybe," Jaina agreed, "but not likely. Zekk doesn't break promises. We've had disagreements before, but . . ." Her voice trailed off.

When Lowbacca rumbled a comment, Em Teedee translated. "Master Lowbacca wonders if Master Zekk might not simply have stepped out for a morning constitutional. Or perhaps he decided to procure comestibles for morning meal."

"Yeah, that would be better than those stormtrooper rations he gave us last time," Jacen pointed out, feeling his stomach gurgle with distaste at the thought.

"He knew we were coming," Jaina said. "He should have been here."

"Let's wait for a while," Jacen suggested, sitting with crossed legs on the floor. "He'll probably turn up in a few minutes with some wild story."

"That would be just like him," Jaina agreed.

Jacen, knowing his sister was still worried, tried to sound as confident as possible. "He'll be back any minute—you'll see. In the meantime," he suggested brightly, "I've got some new jokes, if anybody wants to hear them."

The twins entertained the other young Jedi Knights with stories of Zekk's past adventures. Jacen told about the time Zekk climbed forty-two stories down an abandoned turbolift shaft because he saw something glittery and reflective by the glow of his pulsed-laser spotlight. Imagining treasures that grew more and more extravagant with each level he descended, Zekk discovered in the end that the shining object was merely a discarded foil wrapping stuck to the ooze dripping along the shaft wall.

Jaina shared a story about how Zekk reprogrammed a personal translating device for a group of snide reptilian tourists who had shoved him out of line for free samples of a new food product. Zekk changed their translator so that every time the reptilian tourists asked for directions to eating establishments or museums, they were instead guided to seedy gambling parlors or garbage-reprocessing stations.

"How simply dreadful!" Em Teedee commented.

Minutes crept by and became an hour, and still their friend did not return.

At last Jaina stood. "Something's wrong," she said, biting her lower lip. "Zekk's not coming."

Lowie growled and Em Teedee translated, "Master Lowbacca suggests that perhaps Master Zekk requires a certain amount of time to overcome his embarrassment. I don't suppose I'll ever understand human behavior," he added.

"Maybe," Jaina said, her face troubled and unconvinced.

"Hey, why don't we leave a videonote," Jacen suggested. "We'll try again tomorrow. How long can he stay mad at us?"

But the next day Zekk was still nowhere to be found. Jacen pressed the access request button beside Zekk's front door, but again there was no response. Old Peckhum would be returning from the mirror station soon, and he would come home to an empty apartment.

"I think it's time to start looking for Zekk," Jacen said, staring at the blank infopanel.

"Agreed," Tenel Ka said.

"Well then," Jaina said, rubbing her hands together briskly, "what are we waiting for? And if we still can't find him, we'll talk to Mom."

Leia Organa Solo seemed preoccupied and concerned as they entered her private office. Leia smiled at them and brushed a stray hair out of Jaina's eyes. "I'm glad you're here, kids. I wanted to show you something."

Before Jacen or Jaina could tell her about Zekk, Leia played a grainy long-range videoclip that showed Imperial attack vessels striking a New Republic military supply cruiser in space near Coruscant.

"That looks like the ship that kidnapped us from Lando's GemDiver Station!" Jaina cried.

Lowbacca growled in agreement.

Leia nodded. "I thought so, from your description—and now I can confirm it to Admiral Ackbar. This attack came two nights ago. We may have a real threat on our hands, right here on the capital world."

Jaina watched the videoclip again and frowned. "Something else isn't right about those images. I'm trying to figure out what. . . ."

Leia returned to her desk. "Admiral Ackbar and a handful of tactical experts are analyzing the footage, and they might want to ask you some questions. We're stepping up security against the very real possibility that we may see another Imperial attack."

After that news, when Jacen poured out the story of Zekk's disappearance, Leia didn't seem overly concerned. She let her gaze drift across all four of the young Jedi Knights standing in her office. "All right, let me ask you this: Who knows the city better, the four of you . . . or Zekk?"

"Well, Zekk does," Jacen answered in a hesitant voice. "But—"

"And if Zekk is upset and hiding somewhere," Leia continued, "is it any wonder that you haven't been able to find him?"

"But he wouldn't do that," Jaina objected. "He promised us."

"Well then," Leia said in a calm, reasonable voice, "maybe he's found that central multitasking unit already and Peckhum shuttled him up to the mirror station."

"But he would have left us a message." Jaina set her mouth in a stubborn line.

"She's right, Mom," Jacen spoke up. "Zekk may seem like a scamp, but he always does what he says he's going to do."

Leia swept her children with a skeptical look. "How many years have we known Zekk?"

Jaina shrugged. "About five, but what—"

"And in those years," Leia went on, "how many times has he just disappeared on some adventure, only to reappear about a month later?"

Jacen cleared his throat and shifted uncomfortably. "Um, maybe half a dozen times."

"There. You see?" Leia said, as if that closed the matter.

"But those other times," Jacen pointed out, "we didn't have plans to spend the day with him."

Leia sighed. "And those other times he wasn't upset over an embarrassing diplomatic dinner, either. Look, he's older than you are, and legally he can come and go as he pleases. But even if we knew for certain that he was missing—which we don't—there's very little we could do about it. The galaxy is a big place. Who knows where he might be?

"People turn up missing all the time, and we simply don't have the resources to look for everybody. Just this week I've had reports of at least three other teenagers missing in Imperial City alone. Why don't you wait and talk to Peckhum when he gets back tomorrow? Maybe he'll have some ideas." She herded them out of the room so she could get back to work.

"Right now I've got to get ready for my next meeting with the Karnak Alphan ambassador. And then I have to see the Howler Tree People again for a musical ceremony this afternoon. . . ." She rubbed her temples as if in anticipation of a headache. "I really do love my job—uh, most of it at least."

As they left Leia's office, Jacen groaned. "Mom doesn't believe there's even a problem."

"Then I guess we'll have to keep searching on our own," Jaina said.

Lowie growled agreement.

"It's all up to us," Jacen said, pounding a determined fist into his palm.

"This is a fact," said Tenel Ka.

11

AFTER WHAT SEEMED like an eternity, Zekk fought his way back to consciousness. He felt as if a million volts had shot through his body, short-circuiting half of his nerves and leaving his muscles tingly and twitching.

His head ached. The hard metal floor beneath his body oozed a cruel chill. The harsh white light hurt his eyes.

When he sat up, he had to blink away sparkling, colored spots. Waiting for his vision to focus, Zekk finally realized there was nothing to *see*—only blank, whitish-gray walls. He found a small speaker grille and the vent for an air-circulation system, but nothing else. He couldn't even find the door.

Zekk knew he must be in some kind of cell. He remembered struggling with the evil-looking people who had captured him in the lower city—a black-haired woman with violet eyes using a strange scanning device, and a dark young man who had stunned him. . . .

"Hey!" he yelled. His voice sounded rough and hoarse. "Hey! Where am I?" He got to his feet, swaying from dizziness, and made his way to the nearest wall. He hammered on the metal plates, shouting for attention. He worked his way around the small room, but found no door crack.

He stumbled to the speaker and shouted into it. "Somebody tell me what's going on. You have no right to take me prisoner!"

But in spite of his brave words, Zekk knew things that Jaina and Jacen, raised within the protective confines of the law and guarded by security forces all their lives, had never understood. Zekk knew that his "rights" wouldn't be protected if someone had the power to take them away. No one would fight for *him*. No one would send military fleets to rescue *him*. If Zekk disappeared, there would be no public outcry. Few people would even notice.

"Hey!" he shouted again, kicking at the wall. "Why am I a prisoner? Why do you want *me?*"

He whirled as he heard a whishing sound on the opposite side of the room. A smooth door slid aside to reveal a powerful-looking man flanked by stormtroopers. The man was tall and wore silvery robes. His hair was blond and neat, his face gentle and complacent. His exceedingly handsome features looked as finely made as a sculpture. The man's very presence exuded an aura of peace and calm.

"Aren't you overreacting a bit?" the man said. His rich voice hummed with power and charisma. "We came as soon as we realized you were awake. You could have hurt yourself by pounding so hard on the walls."

Zekk did not allow himself to relax. "I want to know why I'm here," he said. "Let me go. My friends will be looking for me."

"No they won't." The man shook his head. "We have enough information about you to know that. But don't worry."

"Don't worry?" Zekk sputtered. "How can you say—" He stopped short, as the man's words struck home. No, his friends wouldn't be looking for him, would they? He doubted Jaina and Jacen would want to be seen with him after the debacle of the diplomatic banquet. "What do you mean?" he asked in a subdued voice.

The man in the silvery robes gestured to the guards. The stormtroopers waited outside as the man entered the cell alone, sealing the door behind him. "I see they put you in our . . . least extravagant living quarters." He sighed. "We'll find you a more comfortable room as soon as possible."

"Who are you?" Zekk said, still not letting his guard down. "Why did you stun me?"

"My name is Brakiss, and I apologize for the . . . enthusiasm of my colleague Tamith Kai. But I do believe she authorized the use of force only because of your struggles. If you had cooperated, it could have been a much more pleasant experience."

"I didn't know being kidnapped was supposed to be 'pleasant,' " Zekk snarled.

"Kidnapped?" Brakiss said in feigned alarm. "Let's not jump to conclusions until we've got the full story."

"Then explain it to me," Zekk said.

"All right." Brakiss smiled. "Would you like any refreshments? Something warm to drink?"

"Just tell me what's going on," Zekk said.

Brakiss pressed his hands together. His silvery robes flickered around him like rippling water under a cloudy sky. "I have some news for you—good news, I hope you'll agree, although it may come as something of a shock."

"What?" Zekk asked, frowning skeptically.

"Are you aware that you have Jedi potential?"

Zekk's green eyes widened. "Jedi—me? I think you've got the wrong person."

Brakiss grinned. "Fairly *strong* potential. We were surprised ourselves. Didn't your friends Jacen and Jaina tell you? Weren't you aware?"

"I don't have any Jedi potential," Zekk mumbled. "I couldn't have anything like that."

"And why not?" Brakiss asked, raising his eyebrows. He seemed so reasonable. He waited for Zekk to answer, and finally the boy looked down at his hands.

"Because I . . . I'm just a street kid. I'm a nobody. Jedi Knights are great protectors of the New Republic. They're powerful and . . ."

Brakiss nodded impatiently. "Yes they are—but the *potential* to be a Jedi has nothing to do with where you live or how you were raised. The Force knows no economic boundaries. Luke Skywalker himself was just the foster son of a moisture farmer.

"Why shouldn't a poor kid like you have just as much Jedi ability as, for instance, a politician's twin children who live in luxury with all their needs cared for? In fact," Brakiss said in a lower voice, "it could be that because your life has been so tough, your true potential as a Jedi has been honed even sharper than the potential of those pampered little brats."

"They're not brats," Zekk retorted. "They're my friends."

Brakiss dismissed his comment with a casual wave. "Whatever."

"How come I never knew about this? How come I never . . . felt anything?" Zekk asked. He realized suddenly what Tamith Kai had been scanning for with her strange electronic device.

Brakiss rocked back on his heels. "You might not know you had any Force talent if no one ever trained you. It's a simple enough thing to measure, though. If Jacen and Jaina were such close friends, I'm shocked to think that they never *bothered* to test you. Isn't it true that Master Skywalker is desperately on the lookout for more Jedi Knights?"

Zekk nodded uncomfortably.

"Well, if that's so," Brakiss continued, "why didn't they test everyone around them? Why would they just dismiss you out of hand, Zekk? I think they've shortchanged you; they probably never even *imagined* that a street kid, a lowborn scamp, would be worthy of Jedi training, no matter what his innate potential."

"That isn't it," Zekk muttered, but his words carried no strength.

"Have it your way." Brakiss shrugged.

Zekk looked away, though the featureless walls of the cell gave him nothing else to stare at. He waved a hand around to indicate the cold, close cell. "What is this place?" he asked, trying to change the subject.

"This place is the Shadow Academy," Brakiss said, and Zekk was startled to recognize the name of the hidden station where Jaina and Jacen had been held against their will. "I am in charge of training new Jedi for the Second Imperium. I use different methods than Master Skywalker follows at his Yavin 4 training center." Brakiss frowned sympathetically. "But then you wouldn't know, would you? Your friends never took you there." His voice turned up in a question. "Did they? Even for a visit?"

Zekk shook his head.

"Well, *I* am training new Jedi, powerful warriors to help bring back the glory and order of a new Empire. The Rebel Alliance is a criminal movement. You wouldn't understand that, because you're too young to remember what it was like under Emperor Palpatine."

"I hate the Empire!" Zekk said.

"No you don't," Brakiss assured him. "Your friends have *told* you to hate the Empire, but you never witnessed any of it firsthand. You've only seen their version of history. You realize, of course, that whichever government is in charge always makes the defeated enemy look like a monster. I will tell you the truth. The Empire had very little political chaos. Every person had opportunities. There were no gangs running wild through the streets of Coruscant. Everyone had a task to do, and they did it willingly.

"Besides, what does galactic politics have to do with you, young Zekk? You've never been concerned with such things. Would your life really change if the Chief of State were replaced by a different politician in a different Empire? If you work with us, on the other hand, your life could be much improved."

Zekk shook his head, clamping his teeth together. "I won't betray my friends," he growled.

"Your friends," Brakiss said. "Oh, yes . . . the ones who never tested you for Jedi potential, the ones who only come to visit you when it fits into their social schedule. They're going to leave you behind, you know, as they find more 'important' work to do. They'll forget about you so fast you won't have time to blink."

"No," Zekk whispered. "No they won't."

"Tell me, what does the future hold for you?" Brakiss continued, his voice persuasive. "Certainly, you've made friends that move in rich and important circles—but will you ever be a part of that? Be honest with yourself."

Zekk didn't answer, though he knew the truth deep in his heart.

"You'll be scavenging for the rest of your years, selling trinkets to earn enough credits for your next meal. Do you really have any chance for power or glory or importance of your *own?*"

Again, Zekk refused to answer. Brakiss leaned forward, his beautifully chiseled features radiating kindness and concern. "I'm offering you that chance, boy. Are you brave enough to take it?"

Zekk searched for the strength to resist, focused on a thread of anger. "The same chance you offered to Jaina and Jacen? They told me how you kidnapped them, brought them to the Shadow Academy, and tortured them."

"Tortured them?" Brakiss laughed and shook his blond head. "I suppose after being pampered all their lives, a bit of hard work might *seem* like torture. I offered to train them to become powerful Jedi—I admit it was a mistake. We wanted young Jedi Knights to train, but the candidates we invited were too high-profile. The risk was greater than we had anticipated, and it called too much attention to our academy.

"So I decided to change my plan. As I told you, the Force moves as strongly within the less-fortunate as in those who are rich and powerful. Your social status doesn't concern *me* in the least, Zekk—only your talent and your willingness to develop it. Tamith Kai and I have decided to search among the lower levels of society for people whose potential is just as great as in those among the higher levels, and yet whose disappearance won't cause such a stir. People with the incentive to work with us."

Zekk scowled, but Brakiss's eyes blazed. "If you join us, I guarantee you the name of Zekk will never be ignored or forgotten."

The cell door opened again, and a stormtrooper held out a tray with steaming beverages and delicious-looking pastries. "Let's have a snack while we keep talking," Brakiss said. "I trust most of your questions have been answered, but feel free to ask anything else you wish."

Zekk realized that he was voraciously hungry, and he took three of the pastries, licking his lips as he ate them. He had never tasted anything so wonderful in his life.

The implications of Brakiss's words terrified him, but the questions about his future bubbled to the surface again and again in his mind. Although Zekk didn't want to admit it, he could not shake the feeling that Brakiss and his promises made a lot of sense.

* * *

As Brakiss sealed the door behind him on his way out, he turned to the stormtrooper guards in the hall. "See that the boy gets a nicer room," he said. "I don't think we'll have much trouble with him."

The master of the Shadow Academy glided down the corridor as the old TIE pilot marched up to report. Qorl was still in his black armored suit and cradled his skull-like helmet in his powerful droid arm. "The captured Rebel cruiser *Adamant* is now enclosed within our shields, Lord Brakiss," he said. "Its weaponry is being off-loaded even as we speak."

Brakiss smiled broadly. "Excellent. Was it as big a shipment as we expected?"

Qorl nodded. "Affirmative, sir. The hyperdrive cores and turbolaser batteries will enable us to virtually double the Second Imperium's military strength. It was a wise move to strike now."

Brakiss folded his hands together, letting his flowing silvery sleeves swallow them up. "Most excellent. Everything is proceeding as planned. I will report to our Great Leader and tell him the good news. Before long, the Empire will shine again—and these Rebels can do nothing to prevent it."

12

"SHUTTLE *MOON DASH,* this is Coruscant Control Tower One. You are cleared to leave spacedock. Bay doors opening in Gamma Section."

Captain Narek-Ag opened her main comm channel. "Thank you, Tower One. This is shuttle *Moon Dash,* heading for Gamma bay doors with a full load of cargo." She switched off the comm unit and grinned conspiratorially at her copilot, Trebor. "A few more good payloads like this," she said, "and I may just ask you to marry me." Her hazel eyes held a teasing look.

Trebor grinned back, accustomed to his captain's sense of humor. "Keep making good business deals like this one, and I may just accept."

With the ease born of long practice, Narek guided her shuttle out of its docking bay in one of Coruscant's orbiting space stations. "Coordinates locked in?" she asked.

"Locked in and confirmed," her copilot answered the moment she finished speaking.

Narek chuckled as her shuttle streaked away from the spacedock. Accelerating through the inner Coruscant system, she calibrated their hyperspace path for Bespin, the next planet on their run. "You know, for a small-time operation—"

"—we're not half bad," Trebor finished for her.

"Not half bad," she echoed with a satisfied nod. "Calculating hyperspace path."

"Almost ready," Trebor said. "If we hurry, there might be enough time to deliver this cargo to Cloud City and still arrange for a second payload on the return trip. That would double our profit for this run."

A pleased smile spread across Narek's face. She flicked her auburn hair to one side. "I love it when you think like a businessman."

"Business*person,*" Trebor corrected. "Approaching top acceleration. Prepare for jump to lightspeed."

Suddenly the *Moon Dash* lurched as if it had slammed into an impenetrable barrier. The tiny craft ricocheted, spinning uncontrollably. Alarms whooped and bright warning lights flashed across the control console.

"What was that?" Narek demanded, shaking her head to clear the blurry spots from her vision. She stared out the viewport at empty space.

"I don't know!" Trebor said. "Nothing showed up on the sensors. Nothing showed up on the sensors! It's supposed to be clear space!"

"Well, it's the *hardest* piece of clear space I've ever encountered," Narek-Ag shot back. "Damage report!"

"Not sure. Can you get us stabilized?" her copilot asked. "Okay, looks like we got a lower hull rupture. Awww, there goes all our cargo! Engines running beyond the red lines." He swallowed. "We are in deep trouble, lady."

Then, as if to emphasize Trebor's assessment, a shower of sparks erupted from the main guidance console. *Moon Dash* careened out of control.

"Emergency, Coruscant One! This is shuttle *Moon Dash*. We've struck unknown space debris," Trebor yelled into the comm unit. A burst of static from the speaker grille was accompanied by a squeal of feedback and another spray of sparks.

Narek-Ag coughed and tried to wave away the smoke. She flicked a pair of switches. "Aft-thrusters not responding," she said in a terse voice. "Still scanning the area—there's *nothing*. What did we smash into?"

"News ain't any better from where I sit," Trebor said. "Can't get much worse."

"It can't, huh? Well, it just did," Narek said with a hard gulp. "I guess I'd better ask you to marry me after all."

Trebor caught sight of the readout that had grabbed his captain's attention. He groaned aloud. An unstoppable chain reaction had begun to build inside their engine chambers like an avalanche of deadly energy. Within seconds, the *Moon Dash* would explode like a small supernova.

"Always wanted to get married out among the stars," he said. Tears stung his eyes. Probably from the acrid smoke, he thought. "Never had a better offer." He placed his hand over hers. "I accept . . . but I have to say that your timing stinks."

She squeezed his hand, then looked down at the panels. "Uh-oh! Hyperdrive engines are going crit—"

In space, the *Moon Dash* erupted in a silent shower of molten metal and flaming gases, fading to black.

Jaina paced the main living area of her family's quarters in the Imperial Palace like a caged jungle creature she had seen once in the Holographic Zoo for Extinct Animals. She hated inactivity. She wanted to *do* something.

Jacen and Tenel Ka had gone out again to look for Zekk, taking along See-Threepio and Anakin, while Lowie was off working with his uncle Chewbacca. When Jacen had pointed out that it would be a good idea for someone to stay behind in case Zekk or Peckhum tried to reach them, Jaina had reluctantly agreed to be the one.

She had finally broken down and tried to contact old Peckhum up in the mirror station, though he was due to return home that day. At his station holo panel, Peckhum had answered right away, but as she started to explain that Zekk had disappeared, the old man's fuzzy image quickly deteriorated. His response was all but drowned out by static. ". . . can't understand your . . . not receivi . . . transmission . . . returning tonight . . ."

The station's central multitasking unit was getting progressively worse, and communication wouldn't be possible until she saw Peckhum face-to-face.

By the time her mother came home for midday meal, Jaina was ready to scream from just sitting around. She was eager to talk, but Leia's face seemed tired and careworn, and Jaina decided it was best not to intrude on her mother's thoughts. She brought Leia a warm lunch from the processing station and sat down to eat beside her in silence.

A few minutes later Han Solo dashed in and rushed over to his wife. "I came as soon as I got your message. What is it?"

A grateful smile lifted the corners of Leia's mouth as she looked at her husband. "I need to get your opinion on something," she said. "Do you have time to sit down and eat with us?"

Han flashed her a roguish grin. "Midday meal with the two most beautiful women in the galaxy? Of course I've got time. What happened? Another disaster like the Imperial attack?" He helped himself to a bowl of warm Corellian stew.

"A disaster all right." Leia took a deep breath. "A shuttle blew up this morning just as it was leaving orbit."

Jaina looked up in surprise, but her father nodded. "Yeah, I heard about it an hour ago."

Leia's brows drew together in a frown of concentration. "No one seems to know what happened. What could have caused something like that?"

"Poor maintenance?" Jaina suggested. "Engine overload?"

Leia looked troubled again. "Coruscant One picked up a transmission just before the *Moon Dash* exploded. The captain seemed to think they'd run into something."

Han's eyebrows shot up. "Still in outer orbit, you mean? Any other ships around that weren't cleared for takeoff?"

"Noooo . . ." Leia said slowly.

"A space mine deliberately planted there? Or a piece of debris?"

Jaina's ears perked up. "We ran into a lot of debris on our way home this time, didn't we, Dad?"

Leia grimaced. "I was afraid of that. The Commissioner of Trade has taken this personally. He says that all the leftover wreckage in orbit over Coruscant has always been an accident waiting to happen. He insists that we give higher priority to plotting safer space lanes. We've mapped out some of the bigger pieces, but I think quite a few chunks escaped our surveys—and we haven't had time to check it. Some of that wreckage has been up there in orbit for decades."

Han pursed his lips. "These accidents are pretty rare, Leia. Let's not overreact."

"According to the *Moon Dash*'s transmissions, they never saw what hit them—and it wasn't on any map. The Commissioner considers this an important safety issue. I have to agree—in the wake of this accident, we need to do something about it."

"How much work would it be to map the orbits of the larger pieces of wreckage?" Han asked.

"Quite a bit. And time-consuming, too." Leia pinched the bridge of her nose as if she had suddenly been assailed by another headache. "I'm not even sure the New Republic has resources to commit to a project like that—"

"Maybe I could help," Jaina interrupted, fixing her interest on an idea that would take her mind off Zekk. "After all, Uncle Luke said we were supposed to choose a study project while we're away from the academy. Lowie and I could map the debris for you. It sounds like fun."

Jaina looked from the datapad to the computer screen, then at the holographic simulation. "Okay, this is the next trajectory, Lowie." She stretched, trying to loosen the knotted muscles in her shoulders, then rubbed her bleary eyes, but her vision did not clear. They had been at the task for hours. She couldn't imagine why she had ever thought it would be fun.

The lanky Wookiee carefully programmed the orbit she had indicated, and another glowing streak appeared on the holomap. Jaina groaned. "This may be an important job, but I sure thought it would be more interesting."

Lowie grumbled a reply, and Em Teedee translated. "Master Lowbacca maintains that—although plotting swarms of orbital debris never *should* have seemed an interesting project in the first place—schoolwork is rarely interesting. This job, at least, carries a certain amount of urgency." Lowie growled another comment. "Furthermore, he points out that the project is only approximately twelve percent complete, and he will be most gratified when it is finished."

Jaina sighed wearily and ran her hands through her straight brown hair. "Well then," she said, "what are we waiting for?"

13

PECKHUM SHIFTED THE strap of the travel duffel to his other shoulder as he trudged away from the *Lightning Rod*'s low-rent docking station, where many smugglers and con artists also parked their ships. It was good to be back in the city, if only because the equipment *worked* in his apartment, which was more than he could say about the facilities aboard the mirror station.

Despite his heavy pack, the grizzled old man slid through the broad streets and narrow alleyways with unconscious ease, muttering to himself as he went. " 'You'll just have to make do, Peckhum.' 'We've got procurement problems, Peckhum.' 'New equipment is expensive, Peckhum.' 'Central multitasking units don't grow on starflower vines, Peckhum.' " Scratching at his chin stubble with one hand, he continued to rant, as used to talking to himself as he was to talking to Zekk.

He growled. "You'd think they'd at least wait till I got off my ship to tell me the news. 'We tried to reach you, Peckhum, but we couldn't get through.' Serves 'em right, since they haven't fixed my comm system!" He shifted his duffel again. " 'Your replacement was reassigned to an additional security detail due to the recent Imperial attack, Peckhum. We need you back at the station tomorrow, Peckhum.' Hah!"

He stomped ahead, hardly noticing the cheery merchants, the wide-eyed tourists, the self-absorbed civil servants. "I just wish the administrator in charge of the mirror station would stop sitting in his comfy office down here and go up for a field trip. Feed him some of the swill the food-prep units have been putting out and see how much *he* likes it! See how well *he'd* 'make do.' "

Peckhum turned a corner and made his way down the corridor toward his home. "If I waited for those bureaucrats to get something done, why, the whole station would fall apart." Then he smiled at the thought of Zekk's promise of a new central multitasking unit. "Sometimes you just gotta do things for yourself . . . with a little help from your friends."

Peckhum looked up with satisfaction to find himself at his door. He keyed in the unlocking code, and the door slid open with a *whoosh* of escaping air. The air smelled stale and musty, as if it had been recycled over and over again for days. He'd have to remind Zekk to let in some fresh air now and then.

He tossed his duffel inside the front entryway, as the door sealed itself behind him. No friendly voice rang out to greet him. "Hey, Zekk!" he called. The apartment seemed oppressively silent, so he raised his voice a bit. "After three days of breathing from bad tanks on the mirror station, even *this* air smells good, but . . ." He paused. There was no response. "Zekk?"

He looked around the cluttered main living area, then searched the food-prep chamber, Zekk's bedroom, even the refresher unit. All empty.

A concerned frown crinkled Peckhum's forehead. Zekk rarely went out when he knew Peckhum was returning from a job—especially not when he had promised to deliver a piece of scavenged equipment. But Peckhum saw no sign of the central multitasking unit. He would need it before the next morning's trip back up to the station.

He scratched his cheeks again and thought for a moment. Then he relaxed. "Of course," he said to himself, "the Solo kids."

Zekk's friends Jacen and Jaina would be on Coruscant for only a few weeks. They were probably all out somewhere, enjoying themselves, telling tall tales of their adventures on other planets. Glancing back, he noticed the winking light on the infopanel beside the front door. That meant some messages hadn't been picked up yet. Probably just Zekk letting him know where he and his friends were, Peckhum thought.

There were three messages in all. Peckhum reviewed them. The first message showed the image of Jaina and Jacen Solo, standing with the other two young Jedi Knights.

"Hey, Zekk," Jacen said in his characteristically good-humored voice. "We came to go on the scavenger hunt with you for that unit Peckhum needs. It was this morning, wasn't it? We'll come by again tomorrow morning. Let us know if there's a change of plans."

As the next message played, Jaina Solo appeared, her hair straight and her expression concerned. "Zekk, it's us. Are you all right? We've been looking for you everywhere! I'm sorry if you still feel bad about the other night—it's okay, really. Can you call us when you get home?"

The final message showed Jaina again, her face anxious and drawn. She spoke slowly, as if each of her words stuck in her throat. "Zekk, are you upset about anything? We're all really . . . sorry if we said anything to make you feel uncomfortable at the banquet. If you've already found that central multitasking unit and you don't want to take us scavenger hunting with you right now, we'll understand. Please talk to us, if you get this message."

As Peckhum listened, his stomach contracted with dread. Something had to be wrong. He looked around again, seeing no signs that the boy had planned to leave. No messages. No notes.

That was unlike Zekk. He was more reliable than that. Others might brush him off as a young scoundrel or a street urchin, but Zekk knew his responsibilities well and always met them. He had promised Peckhum a new central multitasking unit, knowing how important it was to the mirror station. If Zekk told him he was going to do something, the boy did it. Always.

Sure, Zekk was an orphan, a joker, a teller of tall tales, an adventurer—but he had always been a good friend, and he had always been completely reliable.

Almost before he knew it, his decision was made. Stopping only to leave a brief videomessage for Zekk on the infopanel, just in case the boy came back, he headed out the door toward the palace.

"Hey, am I glad to see you!" Jacen said, opening the door to find Peckhum standing there bedraggled and distraught. "Do you know where Zekk is? Have you seen him? Have you heard from him?"

Peckhum's face gave Jacen his answer. "I was hoping maybe you'd have some news for *me*," the old spacer said.

Suddenly remembering his manners, Jacen gestured Peckhum inside. "Uh, sorry. Come on in. I'll get Jaina and the others."

His sister and Lowie were at work plotting orbital debris patterns in their holo simulation, while Tenel Ka polished the weapons at her belt.

"Hey," Jacen said, "Peckhum's here, and he says he doesn't know where Zekk is either."

His sister's intent expression turned to one of concern. Lowie scrambled to his feet and pulled Jaina to hers. Back in the living area, all five of them reviewed a map of Imperial City, bending over a projection while Tenel Ka indicated several highlighted blocks of skyscrapers. "We have searched this area near your home," she told Peckhum.

Jacen crowded next to the image. "And we went to some of the places Zekk took us when we were scavenger hunting," he added. "The ones we could find our way back to, that is."

Peckhum nodded, scratching at his stubble, a distracted look on his face.

"Anakin and Threepio even went to a couple of the places that Zekk had talked about—didn't find anything," Jaina said. "We'd hoped you could offer us some other suggestions about where to look."

Lowie rumbled a comment, and Em Teedee said, "Master Lowbacca wishes to point out that our lack of familiarity with the, shall we say, 'less savory' aspects of Imperial City is, perhaps, an impediment to our search." The Wookiee growled at this overblown translation, but made no further comment.

"He's right, you know," Jaina said. "We really only know the good parts of the city."

Tenel Ka added, "And we were not absolutely certain until now that Zekk was missing. Your observations make it more definite."

"Hey, now that Peckhum's back, and we know for sure that Zekk's missing," Jacen said, "we can report his disappearance to security."

Peckhum looked up sharply. "No, not security. Zekk wouldn't want that."

"But he's missing," Jaina pleaded. "We *have* to find him."

Jacen was surprised to see tears spring to his sister's eyes.

"Yes," Peckhum agreed, "but Zekk has had a few . . . 'misunderstandings' with security before, and he wouldn't thank us for calling them in. Don't worry, though—I can probably think of a lot of places you wouldn't have known to check."

"Well," Jacen said reluctantly, "that means we'll have to keep searching by ourselves then, but your ideas will be a big help, Peckhum. I guess it's still up to us."

"Zekk is a tough kid," Peckhum pointed out with forced optimism. "He's been through a lot, and he can take care of himself." Then his voice dropped. "I sure hope he's all right."

14

INSIDE HIS PLUSH new quarters at the Shadow Academy, Zekk awoke feeling oddly refreshed and exhilarated. He had slept deeply and well, as if he had somehow needed recharging. He wondered if Brakiss had placed some sort of drug in his food. Even if that was the case, he thought, it was worth it, because he had never felt so alive or so enthusiastic.

He tried to stop thinking positively, tried to summon up some anger at being kidnapped and dragged off to the Imperial station. But Zekk could not deny that he was being treated with more respect than he had ever experienced before. He gradually began to think of this place as his *room* rather than as a *cell*.

He showered until his body tingled with warmth and cleanliness, then spent altogether more time getting ready than he should have. He didn't care, though. Let Brakiss wait. It would serve him right. Zekk didn't want to be here, no matter how much attention the leader of the Shadow Academy paid him.

He was concerned about old Peckhum and knew that his friend must be wild with worry for him by now. He was pretty sure that Jacen and Jaina would also have sounded the alarm. But Zekk guessed that Brakiss knew how to deal with that. Zekk just had to bide his time until he could come up with a plan.

While he showered, someone had taken his tattered clothes and replaced them with a new padded suit and polished leather armor, a sleek uniform that looked dark and dashing. He looked around for his old outfit, not wanting to accept more of the Second Imperium's hospitality than necessary, but he found nothing else to wear—and the fine new clothes fit perfectly. . . .

Zekk tried his door, expecting to find it sealed, and was surprised when it slid open at his command. He stepped out to find Brakiss waiting in the corridor. The calm man's silvery robes pooled around him, as if knit from shimmering shadows.

A smile crossed Brakiss's sculpture-perfect face. "Ah, young Zekk—are you ready to begin your training?"

"Not really," Zekk muttered, "but I don't suppose it makes any difference."

"It makes a difference," Brakiss said. "It means I haven't explained well enough just what I can do for you. But if you'll open a chink in the wall of your resistance—just to listen—perhaps you will be convinced."

"And what if I'm not convinced?" Zekk said with more defiance than he felt.

Brakiss shrugged. "Then I will have failed. What more can I say?"

Zekk didn't press the point, wondering if he would be killed if he didn't fall in with the plans of the Second Imperium.

"Come to my office," Brakiss said, and led the boy down the curving, smooth-walled corridors. They seemed to be alone, but Zekk noticed armed stormtroopers standing in doorways at rigid attention, ready to offer assistance if Brakiss encountered any problems. Zekk stifled a smile at the mere thought of *him* posing a threat to Brakiss.

The Academy leader's private chamber seemed as dark as space. The walls were made of black transparisteel, projecting images of cataclysmic astronomical events: flaming solar flares, collapsing stars, gushing lava fields. Zekk looked around in awe. These violent and dangerous images showed a harsher edge to the universe than the galactic tourism kiosks on Coruscant had.

"Sit down," Brakiss said in his calm, unemotional voice. Zekk, listening for any implied threat, realized that at this point resistance would be futile. He decided to save his struggles for later, when they might count for more.

Brakiss took his place behind his long polished desk, reached into a hidden drawer, and withdrew a small cylindrical flare stick. Gripping both ends in his fine, pale hands, he unscrewed the cylinder in the middle. When the two metal halves came apart, a brilliant blue-green flame spouted upward, shimmering and flickering, but giving off little heat. The cold fire, mirrored on the office walls, threw its washed-out light against the images of astronomical disasters.

"What are you doing?" Zekk asked.

On his desk Brakiss balanced the two halves of the flare stick against each other, forming a triangle. The pale flame curled upward, strong and steady.

"Look at the flame," Brakiss said. "This is an example of what you can do with your Force abilities. Manipulating fire is a simple thing, a good first test. You'll see what I mean if you try. Watch."

Brakiss crooked one finger, and his gaze took on a faraway look. The bright fire began to dance, swaying back and forth, writhing as if it were alive. It grew taller and thinner, a mere tendril, then spread out to become a sphere, like a small glowing sun.

"Once you've mastered the simple things," Brakiss said, "you can try more amusing effects." He stretched the flame as if it were a rubber sheet, creating a contorted face with flashing eyes and gaping mouth. The face melted into the image of a dragon snapping its long head back and forth, then metamorphosed into a flickering portrait of Zekk himself, drawn in blue-green fire.

Zekk stared in fascination. He wondered if Jacen or Jaina could do anything like this.

Brakiss released his control and let the flame return to a small bright point glimmering on the flare stick. "Now you try it, Zekk. Just concentrate. Feel the fire, like flowing water, like paint. Use fingers in your mind to draw it into different shapes. Swirl it around. You'll get the feel of it."

Zekk leaned forward eagerly, then stopped himself. "Why should I cooperate? I'm not going to do any favors for the Second Imperium or the Shadow Academy—or for you."

Brakiss folded his smooth hands and smiled again. "I wouldn't want you to do it for me. Or for a government or institution you know little about. I'm asking you to do this for *yourself*. Haven't you always wanted to develop your skills, your talents? You have a rare ability. Why not take advantage of this opportunity—especially you, a person whose life has had, if I may say, too few advantages. Even if you return to your old life afterward, won't you be better off if you can use the Force, rather than relying on what you once thought of as a 'knack' for finding valuable objects?"

Brakiss leaned forward. "You are independent, Zekk. I see that. We're looking for independent people—people who can make their own decisions, who can succeed no matter how much their so-called friends expect them to fail. You have your chance, here, now. If you aren't interested in bettering yourself, if you don't bother to make the attempt, then you fail before you've even begun." The words were sharp, reprimanding, but they struck home.

"All right, I'll try it," Zekk said. "But don't expect much."

He squinted his green eyes and concentrated on the flame. Although he didn't know what he was doing, he tried different things, various ways of thinking. He stared directly at the flame, then saw it out of the corner of his eye, tried to imagine moving it, nudging it with invisible fingers of thought. He didn't know what he did or how to describe it—but the flame jumped!

"Good," Brakiss said. "Now try again."

Zekk concentrated, retracing the mental path he had taken before, and found it with less effort this time. The flame wavered, bent to one side, then jumped and stretched longer in the other direction. "I can do it!"

Brakiss reached forward and snapped the flare stick together again, extinguishing the flame. Immediately, Zekk felt a sharp disappointment. "Wait! Let me try it one more time."

"No," Brakiss said with a smile that was not unkind. "Not too much at once. Come with me to the docking bay. I need to show you something else."

Zekk licked his lips, feeling *hungry* somehow, and followed Brakiss, trying to squelch his impatience to try again with the flame. His appetite had now been whetted—and part of him suspected that was exactly what the leader of the Shadow Academy had intended. . . .

Inside the hangar bay Qorl and a regiment of stormtroopers worked to unload the precious cargo they had stolen from the Rebel cruiser *Adamant*. Brakiss came in leading Zekk, who stared at all the ships stationed at the Shadow Academy.

"I wish I could show you our finest small ship, the *Shadow Chaser*," Brakiss said with a look of regret, "but Luke Skywalker took it when he charged in here to capture our trainees Jacen, Jaina, and Lowbacca."

Zekk scowled, but refrained from telling Brakiss that it served the Shadow Academy right, since they had kidnapped the three young Jedi first, for their own ends. He looked away.

Up in the control room overlooking the cavernous docking bay, the black-haired Tamith Kai stood watching the activities through slitted violet eyes. Beside her were two dark allies from Dathomir, Vilas and Garowyn. Zekk flinched, his lips curling downward in anger as he noted that these were the ones who had stunned him and taken him from Imperial City.

"Pay them no mind," Brakiss said with a dismissive gesture. "They're jealous because of the attention I'm paying you."

Zekk felt a surprising flood of warmth and wondered if the comment was true, or just something Brakiss had said to make him feel more special.

One of the stormtroopers stopped in front of them and saluted. "I have an update for you, sir," he said to Brakiss. "Our repairs on the upper docking tower are almost complete. We should have it fully functional in two days."

"Good," Brakiss said, looking relieved. He explained to Zekk, "I still find it difficult to believe that a Rebel supply shuttle could have been so unfortunately clumsy as to smash right into the cloaked Shadow Academy! These Rebels cause damage even when they're not looking!"

Qorl hefted one of the small weapons cores from a sealed crate. Zekk guessed from the melted, blackened craters around the control panel that the stormtroopers must have used blasters to break the cyberlocks. The hyperdrive core was long and cylindrical, with yellows and oranges pulsing through translucent tubes where condensed spin-sealed tibanna gas had been charged to power the drives.

"These are fine new models, Lord Brakiss," the old TIE pilot said. "We can use them to power our weapons systems, or we can convert more of our fighters to lightspeed attack vessels, like my own former TIE fighter."

Brakiss nodded. "We must let our leader make that decision, but he will be greatly pleased to see this new increase in our military capabilities. Be careful with those components, though," he said sternly. "Make sure that not a single one gets damaged. We cannot afford to squander resources in the Second Imperium's quest to regain its rightful power."

Qorl nodded and turned away.

"You see, Zekk," Brakiss said, knitting his pale eyebrows together, "we are truly the underdogs in this struggle. Although our movement is small and somewhat hopeless—we know we're right. We are forced to fight for what is ours against a blundering New Republic that continually seeks to rewrite history and force its chaotic ways upon us all.

"We believe that can only lead to galactic anarchy, with everyone following their own ways, invading one another's territories, disturbing people, neither caring nor respecting the rule of order."

Zekk placed his hands on his leather-clad hips. "Okay, but what about freedom? I like being able to do what I want to do."

"We believe in freedom in the Second Imperium—truly we do," Brakis said with great sincerity. "But there's a point at which *too much* freedom causes damage. The races of the galaxy need a road map, a framework of order and control, so they can go about their business and not destroy the dreams of others in their own pursuits.

"You are independent, Zekk. You know what you're doing. But think about all those aimless people displaced by the changes in the galaxy, beings who have nowhere to go, no dreams to follow, no goals

... and no one to tell them what to do. You can help to change that."

Zekk wanted to disagree, wanted to refute Brakiss's words, but he couldn't think of anything to say. He clamped his lips together. Even if he couldn't come up with any good arguments against what Brakiss said, he refused to agree openly.

"No need to give me your answer yet," Brakiss said in a patient voice. Then he withdrew the flare stick from the pocket of his robe. "Take as long as you need to think about what I've said. I'll show you back to your quarters now."

He handed the flare stick to Zekk, who took it eagerly.

"Spend some time playing with this, if you'd like." Brakiss smiled. "And then we'll talk again."

15

JAINA SPREAD HER hands in confusion as Peckhum began to describe some of the places where Zekk might have gone. They could spend months combing the underworld of Coruscant, even years, and still never find the dark-haired boy—especially if Zekk didn't want to be found.

"Hang on a second," she interrupted. "Aren't you going to be with us during the search?"

Peckhum shook his head. "New emergency schedule, thanks to that Imperial attack on the *Adamant*. I have to go right back up to the mirror station tomorrow. Thing is, I'm not sure how to keep the systems running without some major repairs. Now even my comm units are down. Fat lot of good I'd be if Coruscant Central calls a red alert. I sure wish I'd gotten that replacement multitasking unit Zekk promised."

Jaina felt a wash of indignant defensiveness on the young man's behalf. "You know Zekk would've brought it to you if he could."

Peckhum looked back at her with a mixture of surprise and amusement. "I won't argue with that," he said, "but I can't keep my mirror station running unless something gets fixed—pronto."

Lowie spoke through Em Teedee as the three other companions sat restlessly in the open area of Han and Leia's living quarters. "Oh, indeed," the miniature translating droid said. "That's a fine idea." Em Teedee's tinny voice caused the other young Jedi Knights to sit up straighter and look at Lowie. "Why, it doesn't even sound very dangerous."

"What doesn't?" Jaina asked.

"Master Lowbacca suggests that perhaps he and you, Mistress Jaina, along with his uncle Chewbacca—if we can convince him—might accompany Master Peckhum up to his mirror station to see if we can effect temporary repairs."

THE LOST ONES 323

"That's a kind offer," Peckhum said, "but I don't see how much you could do without a new central multitasking unit."

Jacen snorted. "I can't remember the last time Jaina *wasn't* able to whip up some kind of solution. She could probably fix the whole place using nothing but her imagination."

"Thanks for the vote of confidence," Jaina growled at her brother. Then, knowing what Zekk would have done, she sighed in resignation and smiled at Peckhum. "He's right, you know. I'm sure we can repair enough subsystems to keep you going until we find Zekk. So what are we waiting for?"

"But why should you want to do that?" Peckhum asked.

"You need the help, don't you?" Jaina asked, momentarily confused. She didn't want to admit that Zekk was the real reason she was doing this. "Besides," she rushed on, "we've been having trouble mapping debris paths in certain areas. Maybe we'll get a better perspective from orbit. Meanwhile, Jacen, Tenel Ka, Anakin, and Threepio can keep searching for Zekk down here in the places you suggest."

"All right," Peckhum said. "You've got *me* convinced, but will your parents agree to it?"

Lowie growled a comment. "Master Lowbacca is confident that he can use his powers of persuasion to convince his uncle Chewbacca to accompany us into orbit," Em Teedee said.

Jaina's eyes lit with confident enthusiasm. "If you can do that, Lowie, just leave my parents to me."

Jacen half-closed his eyes, reached out with the Force, and listened for any sign of Zekk in the deserted building. But he heard only the hollow echo of their footsteps as he and Tenel Ka walked through the gloomy corridor.

He clicked on his comlink. "Hey Anakin—it's Jacen."

"Go ahead," his younger brother answered, transmitting from another building.

"Heading into section seven on the map. Nothing to report so far."

"Okay," Anakin said. In the background, Jacen heard Threepio say in a dismayed voice, "I certainly hope we can locate Master Zekk soon. I'm sure I would much rather be at home than inspecting such . . . unsavory places!"

"I hope we find him soon, too," Jacen said, then clicked off and followed Tenel Ka down the empty hall on the seventy-ninth level of the crumbling building.

The floor was littered with old cartons, canisters, bits of plasteel, and other items too broken-down to be scavenged. Some dry leaves were scattered about as well—though how leaves had come to be in this building, nearly a kilometer below the upper greenhouse levels, Jacen had no idea.

A thin, icy breeze whistled through a crack in the wall, skittering the dead leaves across the floor. The breeze did nothing to dispel the odors of mildew and decay that hung around the old structure, but it did send a chill of apprehension up Jacen's spine. He let his eyes fall half closed again in concentration as he walked slowly along.

Suddenly, something light and warm touched his arm. Jacen's eyes flew open. Tenel Ka's hand rested on the sleeve of his jumpsuit. "I thought you might stumble," she said, pointing at a small pile of rubble ahead of them, where part of the ceiling had given way. In these old buildings, nothing was repaired unless someone planned to use the space. Floors and ceilings were no exception. If she hadn't stopped him, Jacen would have fallen on his face.

"Thanks," he said with a lopsided grin. "Nice to know you really care."

Tenel Ka blinked once. She stood still beside him, not rising to the bait—or perhaps not noticing it. "It is simpler to prevent an accident than to carry an injured companion."

That wasn't the response Jacen had been hoping for. "Well, hey, I'm glad you didn't have to strain any muscles," he said, kicking at the rocky debris with the toe of one boot and sending a cloud of dust into the air.

"It is not a question of strain." Tenel Ka coughed, but her voice remained detached and gruff. "I could lift you easily, should the need arise." She stepped around the rubble. "But I saw no need."

Jacen followed her, wondering why he always managed to make an idiot of himself in front of the calmly competent Tenel Ka. He grimaced. At least if he had twisted an ankle, he might have had the compensating pleasure of Tenel Ka's arm around him to help him out. . . .

Jacen shoved the surprising mental image aside, realizing that Tenel Ka would probably be aghast if she knew the turn his thoughts had taken. Besides, the only thing he should be thinking about right now was finding Zekk.

Using a map on their datapad, they tried to be methodical in their search, concentrating on buildings where old Peckhum said Zekk most often did his scavenging. Walking from one end of the building to another, each of them would reach out with Jedi senses, trying to find their friend, looking for any sign that he had been there.

Once they were convinced Zekk was not close, Jacen and Tenel Ka would take the stairs, a turbolift, or a chute-slide a few floors down, and begin a search of the next level. If they again found no trace of Zekk, they would move to the next likely location, using the aerial catwalks that bridged the gaps between buildings. Many of these walkways had not been repaired for hundreds of years, and they creaked as the two young Jedi crossed them.

Anakin and Threepio were doing the same in other buildings. Jacen's younger brother was absolutely delighted to have a break from the golden droid's daily tutoring.

As the day wore on, Jacen grew tired. The longer they spent in the murky lower reaches, the more uncomfortable he grew. A sense of urgency stabbed like a needle at the back of his mind. Zekk had been missing for days, and they had to find him—soon. Before long, it would be too late for the dark-haired boy. He wasn't really sure *why*, but he knew that it was true.

They searched dozens of buildings and crossed as many walkways, but found no clues. The deeper they descended, though, the more signs of life they found. Low life.

Creatures scuttled past them to hide in every shadowy corner. When corridors were too narrow for them to walk side by side, the two young Jedi took turns leading. Jacen watched Tenel Ka in the light of her glowrod as she headed down another cramped stairwell into the inky darkness. Her reddish-gold braids bounced slightly as she made her quiet descent.

At one point Tenel Ka faltered, then regained her footing and continued her smooth pace. "Broken stair," she said, turning to point out the rough area. "Be careful."

Just then a dark fluttering shape rose up behind Tenel Ka with a keening shriek. Instinctively, she whirled and lashed out at the thing, dropping her glowrod in the process—but the more Tenel Ka batted at the creature, the more frantically it shrieked and flapped about her head.

As soon as Jacen understood what was happening, he reacted. "Hold still!" he said, moving toward the squealing creature, which had managed to tangle itself in Tenel Ka's long braids. "It's probably scared of the light."

Tenel Ka instantly held still, though he knew it must have gone against her instincts. Jacen's thoughts reached out toward the struggling creature, sending soothing messages to it. Gradually, the winged rodent grew calmer and allowed Jacen to touch it. Careful not to make any startling movements, he gently disentangled its claws from

Tenel Ka's hair. Then, still crooning reassurances to the agitated beast, he set it behind himself in the stairwell and backed away.

He picked up the fallen glowrod and returned it to Tenel Ka. "Hey, are you all right?" She nodded curtly, and Jacen suspected that she was embarrassed at having been unable to handle a small flying rodent without his assistance.

As they resumed their search, he tried to get her mind off the incident. "So, do you know why the bantha crossed the Dune Sea?"

"No," she said.

"To get to the other side!" He laughed out loud.

"Ah," Tenel Ka said, without even stopping to look at him. "Aha."

He had expected her to be more subdued after the encounter with the winged rodent, but she continued at her usual pace. Jacen began to wonder if anything could penetrate her cool confidence. Though part of him admired her fortitude, another part wished that she had been more impressed by the way he'd gallantly come to her rescue.

At the next walkway, it was Jacen's turn to go first. The rickety bridgework was littered with the usual debris of rocks and plasteel. It creaked when he stepped out onto it, high above the ground.

"Be careful," Tenel Ka said from behind him—completely unnecessarily, as far as he was concerned.

"I think we're getting close to that old crashed shuttle," he said, choosing to ignore her remark. "I'm pretty sure it's just on the other—"

The walkway shuddered beneath him, and his heart gave a lurch as metal support struts sheared away with a shrieking noise. He grabbed the rusty rail.

"Hold still!" Tenel Ka called, but it was too late.

With a sound of popping bolts and twisting plasteel, the walkway sagged downward, split in the middle. As if in slow motion, Jacen watched large chunks fall away as the bridge floor beneath his feet tilted at a crazy angle.

A whizzing sounded in his ears, followed by a soft *clank*. He felt himself slide toward the deadly gap and he grasped the railing, but the corroded metal broke away in his hand. He yelled for help, reaching back for anything to hold on to—and felt a strong arm wrap around his waist, then found himself being swept forward. Almost before he realized what had happened, Tenel Ka had swung both of them across the chasm on her fibercord rope and deposited them onto a sturdy metal stairway on the opposite side.

With a creaking groan of protest, the remainder of the bridge gave way behind them and fell in ominous, eerie silence into the deep blackness below.

It wasn't until Tenel Ka released him that Jacen realized they had been clinging together for dear life. After what they had just been through, the metal stairway where Tenel Ka had anchored her rope seemed none too safe to Jacen. Nevertheless, the two young Jedi Knights stood in silence for a moment longer, staring down into the bottomless gap between the buildings.

"I guess we make a good team—always rescuing each other," Jacen said at last: "Thanks." Without waiting for an answer, he turned and climbed down a few steps to a building entrance. Once inside, he sank to the floor in relief, reveling in its comparative solidity.

Tenel Ka lowered herself shakily beside him. In the dim light, her face looked troubled and serious. "I was afraid I might lose a friend."

You almost did, thought Jacen ruefully. But instead he said, "Hey, I'm not *that* easy to get rid of."

Although she did not smile, Tenel Ka's mood lightened. "This is a fact."

They came upon the crashed shuttle less than ten minutes after they resumed their search. When they saw it, they both spoke at once.

"Zekk's been here," Jacen said.

"Something is wrong," Tenel Ka said. Hearing her, Jacen realized that something was indeed wrong. Tenel Ka noticed his hesitation, and stepped forward. "It is my turn to go first. You may wait here, if you prefer."

"Not on your life," he shot back. "After all, I've got to stay close to you—just in case you need me to rescue you again."

"Ah," she said, raising a skeptical eyebrow. "Aha." She entered the shuttle, and Jacen heard her say, "It is all right. No one here."

Following her inside, Jacen saw that while the shuttle was unoccupied, someone had been there recently, picking out the remaining salvageable items. Tangles of wire and cable snaked across the dusty deck plates. Stripped bolts and broken fasteners lay strewn about. Several access panels gaped open, showing empty spaces that had once housed the shuttle's vital equipment.

"Looks like Zekk may have been scavenging here after all," Jacen said. "That's a good sign."

"Perhaps," Tenel Ka said, lifting a finger to trace the frighteningly familiar symbol that was etched with crude strokes into one of the access panels. "Or perhaps not."

Jacen looked at the fresh scratches that formed a triangle surrounding a cross—the threatening symbol of the Lost Ones gang. Jacen swallowed hard.

"Well," he said, "I guess we know where to look next."

16

STILL DEEPLY WORRIED about Zekk, old Peckhum piloted his battered supply ship, the *Lightning Rod,* out of its sheltered hangar. The New Republic would have provided him transportation if he'd requested it, but Peckhum liked to take his own ship, though even on its best days it functioned less reliably than the *Millennium Falcon.* And it had never been made to carry so many passengers.

Lowie crammed himself beside Jaina into the back compartment, his ginger-furred legs stiff and awkward as he maneuvered his lanky Wookiee body into a seat built for someone little more than half his size. Lowie wished he had the T-23 skyhopper his uncle Chewbacca had given him the day he started at the Jedi academy, but the small craft was still on Yavin 4.

Peckhum had cleared tools and cartons of junk from the *Lightning Rod*'s cockpit—he usually flew the ship alone—so that Chewbacca could ride in the copilot's seat. Chewbacca brought his own tool kit of battered hydrospanners and diagnostics, gadgets he used while working with Han Solo to keep the *Falcon* up and running . . . if just barely.

When the *Lightning Rod* received clearance from Coruscant Space Traffic Control, Peckhum angled upward through the misty clouds at high acceleration until the glowing atmosphere faded into the night of space. Lowie watched, bending his shoulders to stare out the front viewport as Peckhum maneuvered the ship into a high and stable orbit. The huge solar mirrors remained in position like a lake of silver, spreading a broad blanket of sunlight across the northern and southern regions of the metropolis-covered world.

Although the mirror station was temporarily empty because of the emergency switchover of caretakers, the critical solar mirrors could not be left untended. Peckhum's name was next on the roster, and he had to report for duty, whether or not Zekk had run away from home.

Peckhum brought the *Lightning Rod* to dock against the corroded old station, which looked like a tiny speck dangling beneath the kilometers-wide reflector. Chewbacca and Lowie blatted to each other in Wookiee language, expressing their admiration for the huge orbital mirror.

The thin silvery fabric was like an ocean of reflection, only a fraction of a millimeter thick. It would have been torn to shreds had it approached Coruscant's atmosphere, but in the stillness of space the mirror was thick enough. Space engineers had connected it to the dangling guidance station by dozens of fiber cables, gimbaled to attitude-control rockets that could direct the path of reflected sunlight onto the colder latitudes.

With the *Lightning Rod* docked, Peckhum opened the access hatch, which still bore markings from the Old Republic, and they all scrambled through into the austere station where they would spend the next few days.

"Well . . . isn't this cozy," Jaina said.

"According to my dictionary programming, I should think *cramped* is a better word," Em Teedee observed. "I *am* fluent in over six forms of communication, you know."

The metal ceiling was low and dark, strung with insulation-wrapped coolant tubes and wires running to control panels. A single chair sat in the middle of an observation bubble, surrounded by windows that looked down upon the glittering planet below. Old-style computer systems blinked with reluctant readiness, waiting for Peckhum to awaken standby routines and begin the tedious monitoring of the solar path.

Drawn by the spectacular view of space and the planet, Lowbacca went toward the observation dome. He grasped a cold metal pipe that thrust out from the curved wall and bent down to look at the huge ball of Coruscant. High clouds masked the daylight side of the planet, while the darkened hemisphere gleamed with millions upon millions of city lights that sparkled like colorful jewels in the night.

Lowie had seen planets from space before, but somehow it had never struck him how intimate the setting was. Here, high above the world, he felt a part of the universe and apart from it, a piece of the cosmos and an observer at the same time. It was strange to have such a perspective, and it made the galaxy seem both small and immensely large at the same time.

"Don't just stare, Lowie," Jaina urged. "We've got work to do. Our first priority should be to get those communication systems up and running."

Chewbacca roared his agreement, clapping a strong hand on his nephew's hairy shoulder. Peckhum seemed to be working hard to keep his attention on the routine aboard the station, rather than letting his thoughts wander to Zekk. "I really appreciate what you're all doing," he said.

"Happy to help," Jaina offered as she knelt down to poke around in some control panels. "Lowie, you're good with computers. Give me a hand here."

"Oh, absolutely," Em Teedee said. "Master Lowbacca is exceedingly talented when it comes to electronic systems." Lowie growled a response, and the miniature translating droid answered, "Of *course* they already know that. I was simply reminding them."

"Could you please work on the comm systems first? When I try to transmit, all I can really manage is static," Peckhum said, hovering behind them as he pointed out problems.

Jaina's forehead furrowed with concentration. "Sounds like the power transmission is still working, but the voice synthesis encoders aren't doing their jobs."

With everyone standing around, the area was far too cramped to let Chewbacca push his way in, so the older Wookiee hung back and waited. Lowie suspected his uncle was amused to watch the two young protégés working so hard. Perhaps it reminded him of the way he and Han had worked together, fixing things again and again.

"Well," Jaina said, scratching her cheek and leaving a smear of grime from the corroded control panels, "I expect that by the end of today we'll have these comm systems up and running." She smiled brightly at Peckhum, and Lowie rumbled his agreement. "Just a stopgap measure, you understand, but they'll work."

Peckhum shrugged. "Better than what I've got now. I still wish we had that central multitasking unit," he said dejectedly. "Almost as much as I wish we knew what happened to Zekk."

"I'm sure he's all right," Jaina said, but Lowie knew that she was sure of no such thing.

As Jaina tinkered, Chewbacca went to a different part of the station and roared a suggestion. Lowie readily agreed. Since it was getting toward time for midday meal, it seemed a very good idea to get the mirror station's food-processing units up and running. Lowie's appetite was already large, and his mouth watered as he thought of the excellent dishes they could create, even from the meager ration supplies on board.

Em Teedee tsked. "Really, Lowbacca! There you go again—always thinking with your stomach."

Chewbacca roared an annoyed challenge, and Em Teedee's voice became thinner, less emphatic. "You Wookiees," the miniaturized translating droid said in quiet exasperation, "you're all alike."

17

JACEN HAD GOTTEN distracted so many times during their scavenger hunt for the hawk-bat egg with Zekk that he would never have been able to retrace his steps through the labyrinth of Coruscant's lower levels. Tenel Ka, however, led the way with an unerring sense of direction . . . which didn't surprise Jacen a bit.

The buildings drew closer together, became more dilapidated, more ominous. The walls were dark and smeared with sickly discolored blotches that looked like centuries-old bloodstains. Jacen saw the ever-present cross-in-triangle gang symbol chiseled into the duracrete bricks or splashed on with bright, permanent pigments.

"Ah. Aha. We have found the territory claimed by the gang of the Lost Ones," Tenel Ka said, her senses sharpened like a hunter's blade.

Jacen swallowed. "Let's hope we find Zekk soon. I'd hate to overstay our welcome if that gang is in a bad mood again."

"I suspect they are always in a bad mood," she observed. "They may still be angry at us for escaping them before."

"Well, maybe they've got Zekk. We have to rescue him. That Norys guy seems like a bad customer."

Something skittered along the wall behind them, an ugly spider-roach dashing for cover in a clump of slimy moss. At any other time Jacen would have rushed to study the creature, but at the moment he just wanted to be back home and safe in his rooms.

Tenel Ka looked tall and brave as she marched down the enclosed corridor. Jacen wished fleetingly that he had his own light saber, like the one he had used at the Shadow Academy. He knew the Jedi weapons were dangerous and not for play, but right now he didn't want to *play* with one—he wanted it for genuine protection.

Jacen swallowed nervously and moved closer to the warrior girl, keeping his eyes on her dangling red-gold braids. Maybe humor would turn his thoughts from the sinister gang. "Hey, Tenel Ka—do you know the difference between an AT-AT and a stormtrooper on foot?"

Tenel Ka turned and gave him an odd look. "Of course I do."

He sighed. "It's a *joke*. What's the difference between an AT-AT and a stormtrooper on foot?"

"I am supposed to say 'I don't know'—this is correct?"

"Yeah, exactly," Jacen said.

"I don't know."

"One's an Imperial walker, and the other's a walking Imperial!"

Tenel Ka gave a sage nod. "Yes. Very humorous. Now let us continue our search." She narrowed her cool gray eyes as they approached a corner. "Zekk is your friend. You know him best. Reach out with your Jedi powers again to see if you can sense him. These corridors have many twists and turns."

Jacen nodded. He didn't think his powers were strong enough to locate any person specifically—he wasn't sure if even Uncle Luke could do that—but all he needed was a trickle of thought, an impression, a hunch. He and Tenel Ka were wandering blindly so far, anyway, and the slightest inkling would increase their odds over pure luck.

As he concentrated and closed his eyes Jacen thought he felt a tingle, something that conjured up an impression of the dark-haired boy in his mind. He pointed the way before he could have second thoughts. Uncle Luke had always taught them to follow their Jedi instincts.

He hurried to keep up with Tenel Ka as they moved down one hall, then another. The old skyscraper seemed completely empty, oppressive in its silence despite the inhabited levels far above, but Jacen felt invisible eyes watching him from secret hiding places. He trusted his Jedi senses enough to guess that this was not just his imagination.

"We are getting closer, I think," Tenel Ka said.

They heard voices up ahead, and Jacen recognized the timbre of a clear, strong voice—a young man's voice—though he could hear none of the words. "That sounds like Zekk!" he whispered. "We've found him."

Filled with elation, suddenly dismissing all of his ominous thoughts, he rushed forward while Tenel Ka kept pace, advising caution. "Careful," she said just as Jacen turned another corner and ran into an echoing room filled with battered furniture, half-collapsed ceiling beams, and glowpanels wired to the walls as if someone had rigged them wherever it seemed most convenient to connect electrical power. Other doors leading from the large room were closed, some blocked by crates, others jammed on their hinges.

In the middle of the room Jacen saw a young man, emerald eyes glittering in the uncertain light of the haphazard glowpanels. It was Zekk. His hair, a shade lighter than black, was fastened at the nape of his neck with a leather thong instead of hanging free down to his shoulders. Jacen had never seen Zekk's hair like that. His friend's clothes were also different: clean, dark, padded, as if they were a uniform—and much more stylish than the suit he had worn to the diplomatic banquet for the ambassador from Karnak Alpha.

Sitting on chairs or sprawled on ragged cushions sat a dozen tough, hard-bitten kids, all in their middle to late teens. Most were boys, but the few girls looked wild and rugged enough to take Jacen apart piece by piece, like an obsolete droid.

The Lost Ones.

"Hey, Zekk!" Jacen cried. "Where have you been? We've all been worried!"

Startled from his speech, the dark-haired young man drew himself up, frowning at Jacen and Tenel Ka. His green eyes flashed with momentary surprise and delight, but he quickly masked the expression with a scowl. Zekk appeared to have aged a dozen years in the few days since his disappearance.

"Jacen, now isn't the time," he said in a rough voice.

A brawny boy with close-set eyes and thick eyebrows stood up, glaring. "I don't recall inviting you two." Jacen recognized the bully Norys.

Zekk gestured behind him to calm the burly gang leader. "Let me handle this." Anger showed clearly in Zekk's face as he shook his head at Jacen. "Why couldn't you have left me alone for just a little longer?"

Jacen scratched his tousled hair, completely baffled. When he stepped forward in confusion, Zekk flinched. "Go away," he whispered, "you'll ruin everything!"

The other Lost Ones stood up from their places like a pack of nek battle dogs zeroing in on a target. Jacen swallowed. Beside him, Tenel Ka placed a protective hand on his shoulder, in case they would be required to fight.

"Zekk, it's *us*," Jacen pleaded. "We aren't going to ruin anything—we're your friends."

Just then, one of the corroded doors at the far side of the chamber scraped open. "They are not your friends, young Lord Zekk," said a woman's voice, rich and low. "You know better than that now. They may *claim* to be your friends, but you've seen evidence of just how much they truly value you."

Jacen and Tenel Ka both whirled to see the ominous form of the black-cloaked Nightsister, with her static-charged ebony hair and blazing violet eyes. The upthrust spines on the shoulders of her cloak looked like spears. Two others dressed in similar fashion stood on either side of her: a young dark-haired man and a petite powerhouse of a woman, both of whom looked as rigid as the towering Nightsister herself.

"Tamith Kai . . . ," Jacen acknowledged. "Charming as usual, I see."

"And Garowyn. And Vilas," Tenel Ka said with an astonishing and unexpected expression—a feral smile—on her normally serious face. "So, how is your knee?" she asked Tamith Kai. Her grip on Jacen's shoulder felt tight enough to crack a bone.

The tall woman's face roiled with a thunderstorm of anger. Her wine-dark lips curled down, and she barely controlled her rage at being reminded of how Tenel Ka had humiliated her during the young Jedi Knights' escape from the Shadow Academy. "Jedi brats," she snarled, "you should learn when to leave well enough alone."

"And *you* should have figured out not to mess with us after the first time," Jacen responded in a challenging tone. "Zekk, what are you doing with these clowns? What sort of nonsense have they been telling you?"

Zekk seemed to waver for a moment, but his voice was strong. "They're offering us—all of us—an opportunity. A chance we never had before."

"Like what?" Jacen said, genuinely mystified. "What could these losers possibly offer you?"

"They're taking us back to the Shadow Academy to train us!" the burly gang leader, Norys, said. "Now we'll have our own shot at being powerful."

"But not everybody has Jedi potential," Jacen said reasonably, trying to keep Zekk talking until he or Tenel Ka could figure out what to do.

"*I* do. You would have known that if you'd bothered to test me," Zekk said defiantly. "And anybody who joins us but doesn't have the talent will be recruited into the Imperial military forces, given responsibilities and a chance for advancement in the Second Imperium."

"Oh, Zekk," Jacen said, shaking his head, "those are all lies designed to lure you into dropping your guard—"

"They are not lies!" Tamith Kai interrupted, her melodious voice holding the potential for deadliness. "We will keep our promises. You will all be given equal opportunities, without regard to your social status in the Rebel worlds. The Second Imperium won't judge who you are—only what you do for us."

"Zekk," Jacen cried, "how can you trust them? These are the people who kidnapped me and Jaina."

"Yes," Tamith Kai continued, "and we have learned our lesson. Highborn noble pups such as you are no more worthy of being Imperial Dark Jedi than any other student." Her violet eyes glared daggers at Tenel Ka.

"Zekk," Jacen whispered quickly, "this is your chance. Trust me on this: You're in great danger. You could escape now. Get away!"

But his formerly happy-go-lucky friend gave him a look that was somewhere between pity and a plea for understanding. Jacen thought he saw a glimpse of the deep sadness that touched the young man's heart.

Zekk said, "You don't understand, Jacen. You can't because you've always *had* too much. You've never wanted for anything. These people"—he gestured toward the evil Nightsister and her companions—"they're offering me something I never had in my old life. With them I have a chance to *be* someone."

"Not *much* of a chance, if they're the ones offering it," Jacen muttered.

Tenel Ka tensed, holding her hands at her utility belt, ready to draw a weapon.

One by one, each of the gang members stood and glared at the two young Jedi. The burly Norys and the other Lost Ones seemed to have been hypnotized, and Jacen wondered if Tamith Kai or the others were using some sort of Force trick to make them more susceptible to insidious suggestions.

Tenel Ka whispered, "Jacen, we must leave while we can still bring help."

Jacen tensed, ready to turn and run. He clicked on the comlink, hoping to signal Anakin and Threepio, but before he and Tenel Ka could sprint to the door, Vilas pulled out a blaster.

"We can't risk any more of your meddling," Garowyn said. "There's too much at stake."

Jacen and Tenel Ka managed to take a few running steps before stun bolts slammed into them from behind. They plunged headfirst into helpless unconsciousness.

18

BRAKISS SEALED THE locking mechanism on the door to his private office, changing the access code to make absolutely certain no one could disturb him. He wouldn't allow even Tamith Kai to eavesdrop on his special communications with the great Imperial Leader.

Brakiss always found inspiration on the walls of his Shadow Academy office, where the exploding stars, broken planets, and cascading glaciers reminded him of the fury locked within the universe. By using the dark side as his focus, Brakiss tapped into that incredible energy and used it for his own benefit, to help pave the way for the return of the Empire.

He set the glowpanels to low as he waited for the contact, checking his chronometer. Speaking with his ominously powerful leader filled Brakiss with both terror and awe, and he was forced to use a Jedi calming technique, though patience was very difficult.

The Great Leader of the Second Imperium had enormous burdens and responsibilities. He was frequently late for his scheduled communications—not that Brakiss would ever dare mention it. The Leader set his own schedule; Brakiss was merely the dutiful slave who knew his place in the grand scheme.

Just as the Rebels depended on the overestimated protection of their vaunted Jedi Knights, so the new Leader would have his own secret weapon: an army of Dark Jedi who could use the dark side of the Force to carve a broad place in history for the Second Imperium.

But Dark Jedi were notoriously dangerous and unstable, prone to delusions of grandeur. Realizing this risk, the Great Leader had taken precautions to protect *himself* from the Shadow Academy. The huge ring-shaped station was riddled with deadly explosives, detonators threaded through the life-support systems, the hull, and thousands of other places that Brakiss neither knew nor wanted to consider. The moment his Dark Jedi gave hints that they might get out of control, the Great Leader would detonate those explosives and end the experiment without remorse.

Brakiss had to show success after success to keep his powerful master happy—and the Shadow Academy had recently had several spectacular accomplishments indeed.

With a humming sound, the holographic generators in his sealed office activated, and Brakiss snapped to attention. The air shimmered in front of him as a massive image crystallized into focus, transmitted from some far-distant hiding place in the Core Systems. Static rippled along the edges of the gigantic cowled head that loomed over Brakiss, scowling down at him.

Brakiss instinctively averted his eyes, bowing his head in reverence. After performing the appropriate gestures of obeisance, he looked up into the face of the Great Leader of the Second Imperium—*the hooded, wrinkled form of Emperor Palpatine himself!*

Though the holographic image was fuzzy and fragmented from being transmitted across so many systems on the Holonet, through asteroid belts and solar flares and ion storms, the features of the sallow-faced Emperor were unmistakable. Brakiss looked adoringly at the harsh paternal figure. Here was the man who would make all star systems quake with terror until they learned to live again with respect and glory, in the Imperial way.

The Emperor's skin was ravaged with wrinkles brought on by too deep an immersion in the potent powers of evil. His yellow reptilian eyes blazed from hollowed sockets, and wattles on his neck hung down like the throat sac of a scrawny lizard.

Brakiss knew that the rest of the galaxy thought the Emperor had died many years ago, first in the explosion of the second Death Star, and then six years later in the destruction of the last of Palpatine's clones. But the Emperor's death *must* have been some kind of illusion, because Brakiss could see the transmission with his own eyes. He could not guess how the Emperor had survived, what sort of trick the great man had played on everyone—but with the Force, many things were possible.

Master Skywalker had taught him that.

When he finally spoke, the Emperor's voice was harsh and raspy. "So, Insignificant One, what is your report for today? More successes, I hope. I am tired of failures, Brakiss. I grow impatient to bring about my reign and the Second Imperium."

Brakiss bowed again. "Yes, my master. I have good news to report. We are sending along the hyperdrive cores and turbolaser batteries stolen from the Rebel supply ship, as you ordered. I think your glorious military machine will make efficient use of them."

"Yesss," Palpatine hissed.

Brakiss continued. "Here at the Shadow Academy your new force of Dark Jedi grows more powerful each day. I am particularly pleased that we have uncovered new candidates from the underworld of Imperial Center—exactly as you suspected, my master. No one will notice their disappearance, and we are free to turn them."

"Yesss!" the Emperor said. "I told you it would be simpler to turn candidates whose lives held little hope. It is especially ironic to snatch them from under the very noses of the Rebel usurpers in the government."

Brakiss nodded. "Yes, indeed, my master. We merely offer the new candidates something they need—and they are desperate to take it from us."

"Ah," the image of the Emperor said. He seemed almost—*almost*—proud.

Brakiss drew a deep breath before continuing. "Naturally, many of these new candidates have no Jedi potential, but still they remain eager for opportunities. Therefore, we have begun training one group as elite stormtroopers. They know the underworld of Coruscant very well, and could prove to be effective spies or saboteurs, should we choose to employ them in such a fashion."

The projection of the Emperor nodded inside his cowl. "Agreed, Brakiss. Very good." A ripple of static flickered across the transmitted image, and the Emperor's voice wavered. "You shall survive another day."

"Yes, my master," Brakiss said.

The expression on the Emperor's ravaged face grew stern. "Don't disappoint me, Brakiss," he said. "I should be most displeased if I was forced to blow up your Shadow Academy."

Brakiss bowed low, and his silvery robes pooled around him. "I would be displeased as well," he said.

The holographic image of the Emperor shimmered, then broke into sparkles of static as the transmission cut off.

Brakiss felt himself trembling all over, as he did each time he spoke to the awesome Palpatine. Exhausted, he sat down again at his desk and began to review his next set of plans, obsessively careful not to allow any mistakes.

19

YOUNG ANAKIN SOLO stood next to the comm unit in the living area of his family's quarters, exhausted from his long and fruitless search, and worried about his brother Jacen. Staring at the darkened screen, he willed a message to come in from Jacen, but he knew that none would come—he could *feel* it.

He and Threepio had returned to their quarters an hour earlier after covering their assigned search locations, but they had heard no word from Jacen. And Anakin knew he couldn't delay any longer.

He turned and walked over to the wall, where the golden protocol droid sat enjoying the refreshment of a brief shutdown cycle. Ice-blue eyes looked into the droid's yellow optical sensors. Anakin gave the droid a tap. "Wake up, Threepio. We've waited long enough. Time to get help."

The optical sensors winked to life, and See-Threepio gave a start of surprise. "Dear me, I couldn't possibly have overslept, could I? I thought we agreed to rest two more cycles before going out to search again. And you have a lesson plan to—"

"I can sense that something is wrong," Anakin interrupted. "Jacen and Tenel Ka haven't come back."

"Well, if you ask me—"

"I didn't," Anakin cut in. "Try to signal them again with your mobile comlink connection."

"I'm sure they're quite all right, but I'll try." Threepio tilted his head sideways and stared off into space for a few seconds.

"Any response?" Anakin asked.

"No, Master Anakin," Threepio replied with greater concern in his voice. "None at all."

Just then Leia Organa Solo entered the room, smiling brightly at Anakin—then frowning. "Anakin, what's wrong?"

Anakin considered how much to tell his mother—after all, they had asked for her help earlier, but she had not believed Zekk's disappearance was anything serious. Now, though, maybe Leia would change her mind when she learned that Jacen and Tenel Ka had vanished as well. The young boy spilled the story rapidly, with Threepio adding sound effects and embellishing with unnecessary comments.

"Jacen would have answered our call if he could," Anakin said.

"Most certainly," See-Threepio added with enthusiasm. "Master Jacen may be somewhat disorganized, but he is *always* conscientious."

Her alarm growing visibly, Leia said, "He would answer—unless he's in trouble." She reached some sort of decision and snapped into action, demonstrating one of the qualities that made her a good Chief of State. "We've got to go find them. Tenel Ka wouldn't let Jacen do anything dangerous. But she probably doesn't think *anything* is dangerous."

Leia ran to a wall panel. "I'll summon a group of guards to go with us. Threepio, can you trace the location of Jacen's comlink?"

"Well, it's certainly not as precise a tracking system as I'd like, but I suppose that by sending a continuous signal and monitoring the feedback from the mobile comlink I could probably—"

"So how close can you get us?" Leia interrupted impatiently.

"I should be able to pinpoint the signal to within a radius of ten meters."

"Close enough," Leia said.

Anakin gave a sigh of relief. "Let's just hope both Jacen and Tenel Ka are still somewhere near the comlink."

"We'll worry about that when we get there," Leia said, grabbing a medkit and dashing toward the door. Guards rushed into position, still not clear on what the emergency was. "Let's go, Anakin. You're part of this rescue, too. Which way, Threepio?" Leia called.

The protocol droid followed as fast as his mechanical legs could move. "To your left, Mistress Leia. We'll need to find a turbolift and take it down forty-two levels."

Anakin tried to picture in his head where they were going, but with little success. "Maybe you'd better lead, Threepio."

Leia, the guards, and Anakin followed See-Threepio as he picked his way across another rickety walkway between two gigantic buildings. The protocol droid seemed to be enjoying his new importance immensely.

The buildings stretched out of sight above and below them. Once, at a spot where the side rail was missing, Anakin lost his footing and nearly fell off the bridge, but Leia instinctively grabbed him. She looked at her son with shock, then hugged him quickly. "Be careful," she urged. "We've *all* got to be careful."

Anakin shuddered. This area had not looked so dangerous on the map. As they homed in on the comlink signal, working through abandoned levels and empty, ominous halls, he noticed a design that appeared with increasing frequency on the grimy walls: an equilateral triangle surrounding a cross.

"I wonder what that symbol means," he said, pointing.

"I am fluent in over six million forms of communication," Threepio said. "Unfortunately, that design is not in any of my databanks. I'm afraid I cannot offer any enlightenment, Master Anakin."

Leia looked at the guards. "Do any of you recognize the symbol?"

One of them cleared his throat. "I believe it's a gang marking, Madam President. Several . . . unpleasant groups make a habit of living down in the untended lower levels of the city. They are very difficult to catch."

"I heard Zekk talking with Jacen and Jaina about a gang called the Lost Ones," Anakin supplied. "I think the gang wanted Zekk to become a member."

Leia's mouth formed a grim line, and she nodded, filing away the information for future reference. Right now, she just wanted to find Jacen and Tenel Ka.

See-Threepio paused to study his readings. "Oh, curse my inadequate sensors—I'm certain my counterpart Artoo-Detoo could have been much more accurate—but I believe that we are now within two hundred meters of their location."

As the group walked deeper into the dilapidated level, the hall became darker and darker. The guards held their weapons ready, glancing at each other uneasily. Leia held her chin up and bravely pushed ahead with greater speed. Threepio increased the brightness of his optical sensors, shedding a soft yellow light directly ahead of them. Anakin kept his glowrod out and ready; it made him feel safer somehow, as if it were an imitation lightsaber.

Threepio made a sharp right turn into a low, narrow passageway, ducking under a half-fallen girder. Even Anakin had to stoop to get under it. "Are you *sure* this is the right direction, Threepio?"

"Oh yes, absolutely certain," Threepio replied. "Remember, we are following a direct path, homing in on the signal. Young Master Jacen may have taken a more roundabout way. We are within thirty meters now."

They finally emerged into a large, eerily lit room with flickering glowpanels mounted haphazardly on the walls. Anakin looked around at the set of rickety stairs leading nowhere, the food wrappers, cushions, and broken-down furniture, and the odd assortment of sealed doors on the other side of the room. "This must be the meeting place of the Lost Ones."

"Oh dear," Threepio said. "Didn't Master Zekk say those gang members were rather unpleasant sorts?"

The room was deathly silent, and the flickering lights made Anakin uneasy. The guards hesitated at the low doorway, pushing their weapon barrels inside. Even though the room was empty, Anakin sensed a lingering feeling of darkness as he entered and began to look around. He nearly jumped out of his skin when See-Threepio cried out, looking down at the floor in horror.

"It's all my fault!" Threepio wailed again. "Oh, *curse* the slowness of my processor. We should have come looking for them much sooner."

In a heartbeat Anakin had scrambled over the makeshift furnishings to where Threepio stood berating himself. Leia and the guards rushed over to join him.

Jacen and Tenel Ka lay crumpled on the floor, side by side, unconscious . . . or perhaps dead.

Quickly unstrapping the medkit, Leia pulled out a mini-diagnosticator and examined the two young Jedi Knights. "It's all right," she said. "They're alive—just knocked out." She ran her cool palm over Jacen's forehead, brushing aside his tousled hair.

Anakin and Leia slowly nursed the two back to consciousness. Jacen came around first, and Anakin could tell from the look in his brother's eyes that the news was grim.

"Are you all right?" Anakin asked. He shifted gears as he began to put the pieces of a puzzle together in his mind.

Jacen swallowed hard. "Tenel Ka? . . ." he asked, his voice shaky.

". . . is just fine," Leia said reassuringly. "Looks like you two got stunned. What happened?"

Jacen shivered, as though the room had suddenly become colder. "Tamith Kai was here—the Nightsister from the Shadow Academy—along with two of her friends." His brandy-brown eyes squeezed shut, as if he had just remembered something too painful to bear. He groaned. "And they've got Zekk! I think . . . I think he's gone over to the dark side."

Anakin's breath could not have come out in a greater rush if a bantha had just kicked him in the stomach.

"They're going to train him to be a Jedi," Jacen continued. "A Dark Jedi."

Tenel Ka grunted and sat up. "This is a fact."

"There were other kids here, too," Jacen said. "The Lost Ones. I think the Nightsisters took them all—to the Shadow Academy."

Leia shook her head, her dark eyes flashing. "I think it's about time we did something decisive about that Second Imperium," she said. "That's twice now they've hurt my children."

"Yes, indeed, Mistress Leia! That's all well and good, but we simply must get back home where it's safe," Threepio said in alarm. "Mistress Tenel Ka, are you capable of walking?"

Her granite-gray eyes narrowed, as if she suspected a veiled insult. "I could carry *you*, if I had to."

Jacen chuckled, then groaned as he held his aching head. "Yeah, I think she's just fine."

20

UP ON THE mirror station, Jaina worked with Lowie and Chewbacca to patch up as many of the worn-out subsystems as they could manage. After scraping together the few spare components they could find, they added their own ingenuity to come up with alternative solutions. Although it was impossible for them to program the food synthesizers to create anything remotely resembling gourmet fare, Lowie and Chewbacca did manage to produce a passable midday meal.

Jaina completed the task of reconnecting the communications systems, making it possible to send brief messages, though the transmissions were still plagued with bursts of static. Chewbacca set to work inspecting the life-support systems, the environmental controls, and the station heaters.

Peckhum watched, performing the few duties expected of him on his monitoring shift. He bubbled over with gratitude, emphasizing again and again how much he appreciated all the effort Jaina, Lowie, and Chewbacca were putting in on his behalf. "If I had waited for the New Republic to get around to fixing these things, Zekk would have been an old man by the time—" Peckhum broke off with a sad shake of his head.

With the major and obvious repairs completed, the young Jedi Knights had little to do while Chewbacca continued poking around. Lowbacca devoted his energies to finishing the orbital-debris plotting that he and Jaina had volunteered to do. Jaina had helped Lowie with the task, but tracking thousands of pieces of debris was just too daunting for her at the moment. Lowie, on the other hand, had extreme patience for a Wookiee, especially around computers. He diligently plotted one blip after another, noting the more dangerous space lanes in the heavily traveled orbits around the capital world.

Jaina glanced at Lowie's three-dimensional map, but soon turned back to the puzzling images on her own datapad. She reviewed file copies of the newsnet videoclips that showed the mysterious Imperial attack on the supply cruiser *Adamant*. On the day after the attack, she, Jacen, and Lowie had easily identified the modified assault shuttle, with its Corusca-gem teeth, recognizing the craft that had been used to kidnap them from Lando Calrissian's Gem-Diver Station.

Admiral Ackbar had verified their descriptions. The theft of military equipment was undoubtedly part of the evil work of the Shadow Academy. From Ackbar's description, Jaina knew that the Imperial in command of the attack had been none other than Qorl, the TIE pilot she and Jacen had tried to befriend near his crashed ship on Yavin 4.

She sighed and shook her head, watching the footage yet again. Jaina had hoped Qorl would see the error of his ways—and though the TIE pilot had trembled on the verge of surrender, the Imperial brainwashing had won out in the end. And now Qorl continued to cause trouble for the New Republic.

She replayed the videoclip of the *Adamant*'s capture a third time. The film, taken by New Republic forces as they'd rushed from Coruscant to defend the supply cruiser, had low resolution. But something about the clip bothered her in an indefinable way, as it had since the first time she'd seen it.

Jaina chewed on her lower lip. "Something just isn't right." She watched the shark-mouthed assault ship appear out of nowhere, while shots from the flanking Imperial ships took out the *Adamant*'s communication arrays and weapon systems. She turned her attention back to the replay—and suddenly sat up with a jolt. She had been watching Qorl's ship—but it was the *other* Imperial fighters that didn't fit.

"That's it!" she cried. "It can't be."

Chewbacca growled a question as he stood up from his cramped position in the control modules for the life-support systems. Jaina focused her attention on the images of the smaller ships, pointing. "I know my Imperial fighters," she said. "Dad taught me to identify every ship ever recorded . . . well, almost every one." She leaned closer to the image. "Those are short-range fighters." She jammed her finger at the image on the screen. *"Short-range* fighters! They had to come from somewhere nearby. Their base is close—hidden somewhere in this system!"

Chewbacca growled a surprised comment. Lowie, wedged into a chair built for humans with his knobby knees thrust high and his arms reaching almost to the ground, cradled his datapad in his lap, studying coordinates of the known items of space debris. He roared his own question, and waved the datapad in the air.

"Attention! Excuse me!" Em Teedee shrilled. "Master Lowbacca believes he has also found something of utmost importance, an inconsistency in the positions of orbital debris. I can't see it myself *since he hasn't shown me the datapad*"—the miniature droid huffed—"but I trust it's something highly unusual for him to become so excited. You really must calm down, Master Lowbacca, and explain yourself."

Jaina rushed with Chewbacca to look at the thousands of dots plotted in the three-dimensional map of space around the planet Coruscant.

"That can't be right, either," Jaina said immediately. She was still puzzled by her own results, and now Lowie had made the mystery even deeper. "It's pretty much the opposite of what we expected."

Lowie barked his confirmation. Jaina sighed, biting her lower lip again. The entire reason for their mapping project had been to discover uncatalogued debris that posed a danger to navigation. Instead of revealing the uncharted hazard that had destroyed the *Moon Dash*, though, Lowie's map of space wreckage showed absolutely *nothing* in the marked zone. In fact, it was more like a forbidden area in space, an island empty of all known debris, as if somehow it had already been swept clear. But they knew the *Moon Dash* had struck something large enough to destroy it. . . .

With a burst of static from the communications system, words filtered across the small, confined space. "Hello! Hello, Mirror Station? Can anyone hear me? Jaina, are you there?"

Peckhum perked up. "Well, now we're sure the communications system works."

"That sounded like Jacen!" Jaina rushed to the comm unit and flicked a switch, but was greeted by a flash of sparks from a burnt-out fuse. The sudden heat stung her fingertips. Scrambling, she yanked off the panel face and stared at the singed wires. She probed with the Force, following the path of the short circuit, and rapidly managed to hot-wire the damaged system well enough that she could answer her brother.

The speakers crackled back to life. "—are you there? Jaina, answer me! This is important. We've found Zekk." A burst of static disrupted his next words. ". . . bad news . . ."

"Zekk!" Peckhum hurried forward, leaning over Jaina's shoulder. "Hello?" he shouted into the speaker. "Where is he? Is he all right?"

Jaina tossed her shoulder-length brown hair out of her eyes. "Wait. I haven't got the transmitter back on-line yet." She plucked out a melted cyberfuse and popped in a replacement yanked from her datapad. "That should do it," she said. "Okay, Jacen—we read you. Are we coming through?"

His voice came over the speakers, sizzling and broken. ". . . some disruption, but . . . understand you."

"What about Zekk?" she asked with an indrawn breath. "He's not? . . . ."

"Dead?" Jacen finished for her. The transmission was clearer now, and his voice sounded stronger. "No. We found him—and then Tamith Kai and a couple of others from the Shadow Academy knocked us out."

"Tamith Kai!" Jaina gave a startled cry. Lowbacca roared, and even Em Teedee emitted a squeak of dismay. "But what would she be doing on—"

"They've recruited Zekk and a handful of the Lost Ones gang," Jacen said. "I don't know where they took him, but Zekk seemed to be with them *willingly*. Tamith Kai said she was going to train him to be a Dark Jedi! They're going to the Shadow Academy."

Lowie growled a curious question, but Jaina asked it without waiting for Em Teedee's translation. "But how *could* they train Zekk? He's not a Jedi—"

"Apparently he has the potential," Jacen said. "Remember, Uncle Luke found lots of candidates who never knew they could use the Force. Zekk had a knack for finding things to salvage, even in places where other people have scavenged already. We just never noticed, never put the pieces together."

Jaina hung her head, thinking of all the time they had spent with Zekk, all the fun they had had together, without her ever having recognized his true potential. "So where is he now?"

Jacen's voice became sad. "I don't know," he admitted. "They stunned me and Tenel Ka, then disappeared. Mom and Anakin came to find us, but that was hours ago. They've probably managed to get off planet by now. I have no idea where they might have gone."

Jaina covered her face with her hands. "Not you, Zekk. Not you!" Then she raised her tear-damp face and looked directly into Lowbacca's bright golden eyes. "The Shadow Academy!" she whispered. "Remember, the cloaking device makes the whole station invisible, like a hole in space—just like on your orbital map!"

He snarled in agreement. "Oh, my!" Em Teedee said, too flustered to provide a translation.

Jaina turned back to the comm system. "We know exactly where they are, Jacen." She glanced at Lowie's datapad and the projected map, zeroing in on the empty spot in space.

Jaina shouted into the voice pickup. "Tell Mom to contact Admiral Ackbar. We've got to mobilize the New Republic fleet. Lowie's going to send you some coordinates. We need to strike fast, before the Imperials realize we've caught them in the act."

"Great," Jacen said. "What are you going to do?"

Jaina smiled. "We're going to shine a little light on the subject."

Old Peckhum sat strapped into the command chair in the monitoring station as it dangled beneath the giant solar reflectors, working the outdated attitude adjustment controls. Jaina crouched over the chair, whispering excitedly into his ear. "Turn the mirrors," she said. "Turn, turn, turn!"

"I'm already beyond the maximums," Peckhum said in despair. His jaw was clenched, his neck muscles taut, and beads of sweat glistened on his brow. "These are delicate sheets of reflective material. We'll tear the solar mirrors if we whip 'em around too fast."

Jaina looked out the observation viewports, spotting the New Republic fleet launching from orbit and streaking toward their invisible target. Their weapons powered up as they homed in on the mysteriously empty zone. Before they arrived, Jaina and the others had to expose the Shadow Academy.

Lowie groaned a question, which Em Teedee translated. "Master Lowbacca wishes to inquire if the focusing apparatus has condensed the beam of reflected sunlight to its full-power configuration."

"That's for sure," Peckhum said. "Once we get this thing turned, we'll really make them hot under the collar."

Hanging in orbit over Coruscant, the big mirrors finally swung into position, focusing their bright beam of condensed sunlight into the empty void. The mirror beam cut a swath through space like a searchlight.

The light should have kept flying across the solar system, but when it struck the empty coordinates, space itself seemed to shimmer like golden smoke. The high-intensity flood of sunlight continued to bombard the cloaked area, finally overwhelming the invisibility shields around the Shadow Academy.

"There!" Jaina cried triumphantly.

The Imperial station rippled into view and then snapped into perfect focus, a large circular ring bristling with spiked gun emplacements and observation towers.

Lowie and Chewbacca roared in unison, and Jaina shook her head. "They were hiding right on our doorstep all along. That's why they could use short-range fighters to attack the *Adamant*. That's how Tamith Kai and her companions could slip down to the city and steal Zekk away."

"Zekk must be aboard the station then," Peckhum whispered. "That's where they've taken him."

"And the Lost Ones," Jaina added.

Chewbacca snarled, then pointed as the exposed Shadow Academy began to move. Thrusters along the equator of its donut shape burned blue-white on one side, nudging it away from the bright beam of concentrated sunlight.

"Turn the mirrors," Jaina said. "We can't let them get away before the ships arrive."

"Oh dear," Em Teedee said. "I do hope our fighters manage to apprehend that Shadow Academy. I'm still exceedingly vexed with them for reprogramming me when we were all taken prisoner there."

Peckhum punched new coordinates into the mirror directional systems, but the sudden acceleration and the change in direction proved too much for the already-stressed silvery sheeting. The long webs of cables that held the great mirror in position tore free, and a wide gash began to open up, spilling a seam of stars and black night through the glittering reflector.

"We can't hold it," Peckhum shouted. "It's too much!" He shook his head. "We could never target a moving object anyway." Then he looked up and moaned. "My mirrors!"

The Shadow Academy continued to accelerate, and Jaina watched the approach of Admiral Ackbar's vengeful fleet, silently urging them to greater speed. But she could see they would not arrive in time.

"The Shadow Academy must already have been preparing to leave," she said. "Of course. They've got Zekk and some other recruits. They've stolen a shipment of hyperdrive cores and turbolaser batteries. They were only increasing their danger by staying here."

Though its ringed shape made it appear unwieldy, the Shadow Academy picked up speed as it headed toward its appropriate hyperspace jump point.

The first of the New Republic ships soared ahead, firing laser bursts at the Shadow Academy. Several shots struck home, leaving dark blaster scoring on the outer hull; the intensity of the solar mirror must have burned out some shields.

Jaina reached out with her mind, searching for Zekk, still marveling at the thought that the handsome, dark-haired street boy might have the potential to be a Jedi Knight. Or a Dark Jedi. She muttered to herself, feeling guilty, "He was our friend, and we never even imagined he might become a Jedi, too. Now it's too late."

As the New Republic ships arrowed toward their target, firing numerous laser bursts, the Shadow Academy suddenly shot forward with a bright flash of light. Its acceleration stretched space and bent starlines, then it vanished to its unknown hiding place deep in Imperial territory.

The Shadow Academy was gone. Again.

Jaina swallowed a lump in her throat. And this time the Imperials had taken a friend with them.

21

AT THE OBSERVATION windows of the mirror station, Jaina stood next to Lowie, her hands outstretched, as if she were trying to pull back the vanished Shadow Academy—and Zekk with it. But, with the exception of a few New Republic ships, the area where the Imperial space station had disappeared remained stubbornly empty.

She let her arms fall back to her sides. Her eyes squeezed shut against the un-Jainalike tears that had suddenly welled up, and her mind sent out a silent cry. *Don't go, Zekk! Come back.*

In stunned silence, Peckhum leaned against the station wall next to her. His mirrors were damaged, and Zekk had joined the fragments of the Empire. "He's gone," the old man whispered.

When Lowie placed a sympathetic hand on her shoulder, Jaina felt strength and optimism flow back into her, as soothing as cool water to her burning sorrow. Drawing a deep breath, she searched the observation window again for any sign of hope.

A new movement caught her eye. "There!" she said, turning to grab Lowie's hairy arm. "Did you see that?"

Peckhum squinted, and the young Wookiee gave an interrogative growl.

"What do you mean, 'See what?'" Jaina said. "Look—something else is out there, right where the Shadow Academy was."

Lowie's rumbled reply sounded hesitant, but Em Teedee piped up to translate. "Master Lowbacca is loath even to suggest the possibility, but might that not simply be a New Republic ship, or one of the pieces of debris you've been tracking?"

"Absolutely not," Jaina said stubbornly. "Besides, any debris with a path that intersected the Shadow Academy would have been destroyed already—just like that shuttle, the *Moon Dash*."

Peckhum hunched over the comm system. "Strange. That object seems to be transmitting a pickup signal—if I read this correctly, that is."

Lowie's triumphant roar brought Chewbacca from the main stabilizer unit, where he had been attempting manual repairs to the mirror adjustment systems—to no avail.

"Not very big," Jaina said, studying the mirror station's crude scanners. "Small enough to be an escape pod, don't you think?"

Lowie looked up at his uncle, who rumbled a negative.

"Looks more like a message canister to me," Peckhum said. "Speaking of which, the transmitters are working now, so why don't we send a message to the New Republic fleet? They'll pick it up, whatever it is."

"Well, then," Jaina said, "what are we waiting for? Let's raise Admiral Ackbar."

Lowie transmitted the message while Jaina stared at the screen, still hoping.

"Years ago, Uncle Luke told me about one of his first students, a young man named Kyp Durron, who managed to stow away in a message pod." Jaina sent her mind out toward the object, trying to gather tiny bits of information with the Force. But she felt nothing, sensed no presence of her dark-haired friend. She heard Lowie croon a sad note beside her, but even without his confirmation, she knew that they wouldn't find Zekk inside the message pod.

At least not alive.

Jaina bit her lip and tried to look over Peckhum's shoulder as he piloted his old ship, the *Lightning Rod,* back toward Coruscant. Her view was all but obscured by the hairy form of Chewbacca, who took up the copilot's seat and much of the area around it. Thinking about the retrieved message pod from the Shadow Academy—still sealed against the vacuum of space and possibly containing a message from Zekk—filled her with a sense of urgency.

She wished she could tell Chewie and Peckhum to hurry up, that they had to get back immediately so they could be on hand when the message pod was opened. But that would have been foolish, not to mention rude. The two of them seemed to understand her anxiety and had already pushed the *Lightning Rod* to the highest speed its safety limits would allow. In the compartment behind them, the engines made disconcerting clunking sounds. Jaina bit her lower lip.

Lowie sat in thoughtful silence beside her. Only the deep indentations left by his hairy fingers in the foam padding of the arm cushions told Jaina that the young Wookiee felt a tension similar to hers.

As they reentered the atmosphere, Jaina forced her eyes shut and practiced one of Uncle Luke's Jedi relaxation techniques. But it didn't seem to work.

Finally, a gentle thump and the diminishing whine of the *Lightning Rod*'s engines told her they had arrived at one of the landing pads in Imperial City.

Jaina jumped down onto the landing pad without waiting for the exit ramp to extend fully; she couldn't even remember having unfastened her crash webbing or opening the exit hatch. She immediately caught sight of her parents, brothers, and Tenel Ka, who were standing near another New Republic ship that had obviously just landed. The message pod from the Shadow Academy was already being unloaded. Jaina ran toward her family.

"Any sign of explosives or weapons?" Leia was asking Admiral Ackbar as he stood watching his troops perform their duties.

"Absolutely none. We scanned it," he said. "It's clean. No booby traps."

"What about biologicals?" Han asked. The admiral shook his fishlike head.

"Can't be anything dangerous in there," Jaina said, skidding to a stop beside her parents. "It's from Zekk—I can *feel* it."

Admiral Ackbar looked skeptical, but three young voices spoke up at once.

"Hey, she's right."

"I feel it too."

"This is a fact."

"Even so," the Calamarian admiral said, "in the interest of safety, perhaps we should—"

Unable to bear the suspense any longer, Jaina pushed past the two guards who stood between her and the capsule, and activated the message retrieval mechanism. With a small *whoosh* of depressurization, the double panels slid aside to reveal the contents—a device of some sort, a complicated jumble of knobby plasteel parts and cabling.

"What is that?" Leia asked in surprise.

"Stand back!" Ackbar shouted. The guards tensed, as if expecting an explosion.

Han glanced into the capsule and then looked over at Chewbacca and Peckhum, who had come to join them. "What do you think, Chewie?"

Chewbacca scratched his head and gave a couple of short, surprised-sounding barks.

"Yeah, looks like that to me, too," Han agreed.

"So what is it?" Jacen asked, exasperated at being unable to follow the interchange.

"A central multitasking unit, of course," Jaina whispered in amazement and delight. "From Zekk."

Jaina heard a satisfied grunt from behind her. Old Peckhum muttered, "Kid's never broken a promise to me yet."

Then, as if conjured by Peckhum's words, a holoprojector hummed to life. A tiny image of Zekk resolved itself in the air just above the message pod. Jaina bit down hard on her lip again as the tiny glowing form began to speak. "I'm doing this against the better judgment of my teachers here," Zekk said, "so I'll make this message brief.

"Peckhum, my friend, here's the central multitasking unit I promised you. You always expected only the best from me, and I always gave it. This must be hard for you, but I want you to know that no one has kidnapped me or brainwashed me.

"To Jacen and"—the tiny holographic image hesitated—"and Jaina, it turns out I do have Jedi potential after all. I'm going to make more out of myself than anyone imagined I could be. We were good friends, and I'd never want to hurt you. Sorry I messed up your mother's diplomatic banquet—but that's one reason I'm doing this. I have the chance to become something better—a chance that I was never given by anyone in the New Republic."

Jaina groaned and shut her eyes, but the image continued to speak.

"I know this is something you wouldn't approve of, but I'm doing it for *myself*. If I ever come back, I'll be someone you can all be proud of.

"Don't worry, Peckhum, I'll never let you down. You've been my truest friend, and if there's any way I *can* come back to you, I will."

When Jaina opened her eyes again the tiny image had faded into sparkles, but she wouldn't have been able to see it anyway through her tears.

22

THE HANGAR BAY at the base of the Great Temple on Yavin 4 was quiet and cool, welcoming the travelers back to the Jedi academy. The ship sighed as it settled down on the smooth floor. Luke Skywalker emerged from the hatch and stood in the shadows as his students climbed out after him.

In the days when the Great Temple had been a secret Rebel base on the jungle moon, the hangar bay had been a place of frantic activity, filled with X-wing fighters, noisy equipment, droids, fighter pilots, and miscellaneous weaponry. In recent years, however, this had been a peaceful place of Jedi contemplation.

Luke turned to watch the young Jedi Knights following him out of the *Shadow Chaser,* the sleek Imperial ship he and Tenel Ka had captured from the Shadow Academy while rescuing Jacen, Jaina, and Lowbacca. Luke's thoughts were as troubled as the faces of his young students descending the exit ramp.

With the help of the Shadow Academy, a group of renegades calling themselves the Second Imperium was mounting a serious threat against the shaky peace that had been built over the past two decades by the New Republic. They could all sense it, and the battle was brewing, a great battle that would decide the fate of the galaxy.

The Shadow Academy had become more bold in searching for recruits with Jedi potential. In addition, it seemed to be welcoming trainees with no Jedi skills whatsoever—but why? And then there was the theft of hyperdrive cores and turbolaser batteries from the *Adamant*—components that could be used to build a powerful military fleet. Something big was going to happen—and soon. . . .

Luke had picked the kids up from Coruscant, which had given him an opportunity to see his sister Leia and learn more about the newest Imperial threat to the New Republic. Since then, none of the young Jedi Knights had spoken much, each lost in private thoughts. Now they had arrived back on the jungle moon, where the other students were still training, bringing back the powerful force of Jedi Knights to help strengthen the New Republic. The new government was going to need its Force-trained defenders soon.

Bright sunlight streamed through the broad door of the hangar, bathing the entire bay in light and shadow. Clean shadows. Luke looked up at the sunlight glinting off the burnished quantum armor on the *Shadow Chaser*.

"The *Shadow Chaser* is still a beautiful ship." Jaina's voice cut into Luke Skywalker's thoughts. "Look at those lines, the curves."

"And at least it's one powerful ship the Shadow Academy doesn't have anymore," Jacen added, coming to stand beside them.

Luke nodded. "But it also shows us what our enemies are capable of building. Think of what they can do with that large shipment of hyperdrive cores and turbolaser batteries they just stole."

Lowie grunted agreement. "This is a fact," Tenel Ka said.

Luke turned and strode through the open hangar bay doors, and the young Jedi Knights followed him out into the humid sunlight. Droplets of morning dew still sparkled on the Massassi trees and climbing ferns. The jungle air was filled with the scent of sweet growing things and the croaking, rustling, and twittering sounds of exuberant life.

Jacen's forehead was creased, as if by the weight of his thoughts. He turned and glanced back into the dimness of the hangar bay, catching sight of the *Shadow Chaser*. He sighed, then finally said what was on his mind. "I still can't believe that Zekk willingly chose to go to the dark side," he said. "Uncle Luke, what are we going to do about him? What did we do wrong? He was our friend, and now he's joined the enemy."

Jaina spoke through gritted teeth. "It's our fault for not showing him that he was just as important as anyone else. We didn't even realize he had Jedi potential. *It's our fault,*" she repeated.

Lowie started to snarl a reply, then quickly reached toward his belt and turned off Em Teedee before the little droid could offer a translation.

"It's not so simple to tell who has Jedi potential and who doesn't," Luke said, sensing Jaina's despair and self-reproach. "Especially if they don't know it themselves. Even Darth Vader had no idea that your mother Leia had Jedi potential, though he spent quite a lot of time near her. You can't blame yourself, Jaina."

Tenel Ka spoke up, a distant look in her cool gray eyes. "Zekk made his own choice for his own reasons," she said. "We all do."

"But how could he betray us like that?" Jacen asked.

Jaina winced at the word. "He can't betray us!" Her voice was hot with the strength of her emotions. "He won't—he promised. And he'll be back. I know it."

"The pull of the dark side is strong," Luke answered. "It's possible to turn away from it, but the price is always high. It cost your grandfather his life. . . .

"But there's always hope—for Zekk, even for Brakiss. We have no way of knowing. One thing I do know, though." Luke turned his face toward the sunlight and enjoyed the feeling of the free breeze ruffling his hair. "The forces of darkness are gearing up for a full-scale war."

"Do we have to just wait for them to make the next move?" Jacen asked. "Can't we try to prepare ourselves for the coming fight?"

Luke looked with pride at each of the young Jedi Knights. "Yes, we can. A great battle is coming," he said, his voice tinged with both sadness and hope. "The Jedi Knights—all of us—have no choice but to prepare for it."

LIGHTSABERS

To Jonathan MacGregor Cowan,
whose love, intelligence, imagination, sense of humor,
and sense of wonder constantly inspire us—and
challenge us.

Acknowledgments

We would like to thank Lillie E. Mitchell for her spectacular typing and her love of the books, Dave Wolverton for his input on the Hapes Cluster, Lucy Wilson and Sue Rostoni at Lucasfilm for their constructive comments and their vision, Ginjer Buchanan and Lou Aronica at Berkley/Boulevard for their wholehearted support and encouragement, and Skip and Cheryl Shayotovich for being some of our most faithful cheerleaders.

1

DAYBREAK AT LAST spilled across the treetops on Yavin 4, where Luke Skywalker, Jedi Master, listened to the stirring, rustling sounds of the awakening jungle. The looming stone blocks of the ancient temple had absorbed the deep night's chill, and now glistened with dew.

As the morning brightened, he wished his spirits could lift as easily.

Cool and stiff, Luke had been atop the Great Temple for a long time already, sitting patiently in the primeval darkness and thinking. He had used Jedi relaxation techniques to dispense with sleep; in fact, he had not rested thoroughly for some time, so great was his concern over the growing Imperial threat to the New Republic.

Jungle birds cried out and took wing, searching for a breakfast of flying insects. The enormous gas giant Yavin hung overhead, luminous with reflected light, but Luke stared beyond it with his imagination, envisioning all of the galaxy's dark and secret corners where the Second Imperium might lie hidden. . . .

Finally Luke stood and stretched. It was time for his morning exercises. Perhaps the exertion would help him think more clearly, get his heart beating harder, tune his reflexes.

At the top of the pyramid, he went to the sheer edge of the enormous, vine-covered blocks that formed the sides of the towering temple. It was a long drop to the next level, where the ziggurat widened toward its base. Each squared-off set of blocks displayed decorative etchings and crenellations, carved into the stone thousands of years earlier during the building of the ancient structure, weathered by scorching attack and passing time. The dense jungle encroached at the rear of the temple pyramid, embellishing the massive stones with thick vines and overspreading Massassi tree branches.

Luke paused for a moment at the edge, took a deep breath, and closed his eyes to center his concentration. Then he leaped out into space.

He felt himself falling and rotated in midair, executing a backward somersault that brought him into position, feet down, just in time to see the cracked old stones rushing up at him. Using the Force to slow himself just enough for a hard landing, he rebounded and pushed off toward the nearest vine. Allowing himself a brief laugh of exhilaration, Luke snagged the rough jungle creeper and swung up onto the lichen-flaked branch of a Massassi tree. He landed smoothly and ran along the branch without pausing. Next he jumped across a gap in the jungle canopy and grabbed a small branch overhead, hauling himself higher, climbing, running.

Each day Luke challenged himself, finding more difficult routines in order to continue honing his skills. Even during times of peace, a Jedi Knight could never allow himself to relax and grow weak.

But these were not quiet times, and Luke Skywalker had plenty of challenges to face.

Years ago, a student named Brakiss had been planted in Luke's academy as an Imperial spy to learn the ways of the Jedi and twist them to evil uses. Luke had seen through the disguise, however, and had tried unsuccessfully to turn Brakiss to the light side. After the dark trainee had fled, Luke had not heard from Brakiss again—until recently, when Jacen, Jaina, and the young Wookiee Lowbacca had been kidnapped. Brakiss had teamed up with one of the evil new Nightsisters—Tamith Kai—to form a Shadow Academy for training Dark Jedi in the service of the Empire.

Panting from his workout, Luke continued to climb through the trees, startling a nest of ravenous stintarils. The rodents turned on him, flashing bright teeth, but when he nudged their attack instincts in a new direction, they forgot their intended target and scattered through the leafy branches.

He swung himself up and finally reached the jungle canopy. Sunshine burst upon him as he pushed his head above the leafy treetops. Humid air filled his burning lungs, and he blinked again in the morning light. The lush world around him seemed very bright after the filtered dimness of the thick underlevels. Looking back toward the stepped pyramid of the Great Temple that housed his Jedi students, Luke considered both the new group of fighters he had brought here to help protect the New Republic and the trainees at the Shadow Academy. . . .

In the past few months, the Shadow Academy had begun recruiting candidates among the disadvantaged young men and women of Coruscant, taking these "lost ones" to serve the Second Imperium. One of these had been the teenager named Zekk, a dark-haired, green-eyed scamp who had been a good friend to the twins, especially Jaina. In addition, the TIE pilot Qorl—who had spent over two decades hiding on Yavin 4 after the first Death Star was destroyed—had led a raid to steal hyperdrive cores and turbolaser batteries from an incoming New Republic supply ship.

All this and more had led Luke Skywalker to the conclusion that the Shadow Academy was gearing up for a major battle against the New Republic. Since the death of Emperor Palpatine, there had been many warlords and leaders who had attempted to rekindle the Imperial way—but Luke sensed through the Force that this new leader was something more evil than just another pretender. . . .

Bright sunlight fell across Luke, warming his hands. Brilliantly colored insects flitted about, buzzing in the new day. He shifted against the rough branches and drew a deep breath of the fresh air, catching mingled scents from the lush jungle all around him.

The Shadow Academy was still out there, still training Dark Jedi. Luke hated to rush his training of those who studied the ways of the light side—but circumstances forced him to attempt to bring out powerful defenders faster than the Shadow Academy could create new enemies. A fight was brewing, and they had to be prepared.

Luke grabbed a loose vine and let himself drop, drop, *drop* until, landing with a jarring thump against a wide Massassi tree branch, he set off, running at top speed back to the academy.

The workout had awakened him fully, and now he was ready for action.

It was time for another gathering of students at the Jedi academy—and Jacen Solo knew that meant his uncle, Luke Skywalker, had something important to say.

Life at the academy was not a constant series of lectures and classes, as he had experienced during tutoring sessions back on Coruscant. The Jedi academy was designed primarily for independent study in a place where Force-sensitive individuals could delve into their minds, test their abilities, and work at their own pace.

Each potential Jedi Knight had a range of skills. Jacen himself had a knack for understanding animals, calling them to him, and knowing their thoughts and feelings. His sister Jaina, on the other hand, had a genius for mechanical things and electronic circuits, and possessed engineering intuition.

Lowbacca, their Wookiee friend, had an eerie rapport with computers, which allowed him to decipher and program complex electronic circuits. Their athletic friend Tenel Ka was physically strong and self-trained, but she usually avoided relying on the Force as the easiest solution to a problem. Tenel Ka depended on her own wits and strength first.

In his quarters Jacen's exotic pets rustled in their cages along the stone wall. He hurried to feed them and then ran his fingers through his unruly brown curls to remove any stray bits of moss or fodder he might have picked up from the cages. He poked his head into his twin sister Jaina's chambers as she, too, prepared for the big meeting. She quickly combed her straight brown hair and scrubbed her face clean so that her skin looked pink and fresh.

"Any idea what Uncle Luke's going to talk about?" she asked, drying drips of water from her chin and nose.

"I was hoping you'd know," Jacen said.

One of the other young Jedi trainees, Raynar, emerged from his room dressed in garishly colored robes with an eye-popping display of intense primary blues, yellows, and reds. He seemed terribly flustered as he brushed his hands down the fabric of his robe, let out a sigh of dismay, and ducked back into his rooms.

"Bet the meeting has something to do with that trip Uncle Luke just took to Coruscant," Jaina said. Jacen remembered that their uncle had recently flown off in the *Shadow Chaser*—a sleek ship they had appropriated from the Shadow Academy in order to make good their escape—to discuss the threat of the Second Imperium with Chief of State Leia Organa Solo, Luke's sister and the twins' mother.

"Only one way to find out," Jacen said. "Most of the other students should be in the grand audience chamber already."

"Well then, what are we waiting for?" Jaina said, and took off with her brother at a brisk clip down the corridor.

Behind them, Raynar emerged from his quarters again, looking much more satisfied now that he had managed to find a robe that was, if anything, even more dazzlingly bright than the first one—enough to cause tension headaches in anyone who looked too long. Raynar cinched the robe around his waist with a green and orange patterned sash, then bustled after Jacen and Jaina.

When they stepped out of the turbolift into the grand audience chamber, the twins looked at the restless crowd of human and alien students, some with two arms and two legs, others with many times that. Some had fur, others had feathers, scales, or slick damp skin . . . but all had a talent for the Force, the potential—if they trained and studied diligently—to eventually become members of a new order of Jedi Knights that was growing stronger with each passing year.

Over the background chatter they heard a resounding Wookiee bellow, and Jacen pointed. "There's Lowie! He's with Tenel Ka already."

They hurried down the central aisle, passing other students and slipping between rows of stone benches to reach their two friends. Jaina held back and waited while her brother took a seat next to Tenel Ka, as he always did.

Jacen wondered if his twin sister had noticed how much he liked being with Tenel Ka, how he always chose a place beside the young warrior girl. Then he realized that Jaina would never miss anything of that sort—but he didn't really care.

Tenel Ka didn't seem to object to Jacen spending his time next to her. The two of them were an odd mix. Jacen always wore an impish grin and enjoyed joking around. Ever since they had met, one of his main goals had been to make Tenel Ka laugh by telling her silly jokes. But despite his best efforts, the strong girl with reddish-gold hair remained serious, almost grim, though he knew she was intelligent, quick to act, and profoundly loyal.

"Greetings, Jacen," Tenel Ka said.

"How are you doing, Tenel Ka? Hey, I've got another joke for you."

Lowbacca groaned, and Jacen shot him a wounded look.

"There is no time," Tenel Ka said, pointing toward the speaker's platform. "Master Skywalker is about to address us."

Indeed, Luke had come out onto the stage and stood in his Jedi robe. His face deeply serious, he folded his hands in front of him, and the audience quickly grew quiet.

"A time of great darkness is upon us," Master Skywalker said. The silence grew even deeper. Jacen sat straight and looked around in alarm.

"Not only does the Empire continue its struggles to reclaim the galaxy, but this time it is using the Force in an unprecedented manner. With its Shadow Academy, the leaders of the Second Imperium are creating their own army of dark side Force-wielders. And *we,* my friends, are the only ones who can stand against it." He paused as that news sank in. Jacen swallowed hard.

"Though the Emperor has been dead for nineteen years, still the New Republic struggles to bring the worlds of the galaxy into an alliance. Palpatine did not take so long to squeeze his iron fist around star systems—but the New Republic is a different kind of government. We aren't willing to use the Emperor's tactics. The Chief of State will not send armed fleets to crush planets into submission or execute dissidents. Unfortunately, though, because we use peaceful democratic means, we are more vulnerable to a threat like the Empire."

Jacen felt warm inside at the mention of his mother and what she was doing with the New Republic.

"In days long past," Luke said, walking from side to side on the stage so that he seemed to be talking to each one of them in turn, "a Jedi Master spent years looking for a single student to teach and guide along the path of the Jedi." Luke's voice became graver. "Now, though, our need is too great for such caution. The Empire nearly succeeded in obliterating the Jedi Knights of old, and we don't have the luxury of such patience. Instead, I'm going to have to ask you to learn a little faster, to grow strong a little sooner. I must accelerate your training, *because the New Republic needs more Jedi Knights.*"

From one of the front rows, where he always sat, Raynar spoke up. Jacen had to blink to clear the spots of bright color from his vision when the sandy-haired boy raised his hand. "We're ready, Master Skywalker! We're all willing to fight for you."

Luke looked intently at the boy who had interrupted him. "I'm not asking you to fight for *me,* Raynar," Luke said in a calm voice. "I need your help to fight *for* the New Republic, and *against* the evil ways we thought were behind us. Not for any one person."

The students stirred. Their minds churned with a determination they didn't know how to direct.

Master Skywalker continued to pace. "Each of you must work individually to stretch your abilities. I'll help as I can. I want to meet with you in small groups to plan strategy, discuss ways to help each other. We must be strong, because I believe with all my heart that we face dark times ahead."

Down in the echoing hangar bay beneath the temple, Jacen crouched in a cool corner, extending his mind into a crack between blocks where he sensed a rare red and green stinger lizard. He sent a tendril of thought to it, imaginary enticements of food—dismissing reptilian concerns of danger. Jacen very much wanted to add the lizard to his collection of unusual pets.

Lowbacca and Jaina tinkered with Lowie's T-23 skyhopper, the flying craft that his uncle Chewbacca had given him when he'd brought the young Wookiee to the Jedi academy. Jacen knew his sister was a bit jealous of Lowie for having his own flying machine. In fact, that had been one of the reasons Jaina had so badly wanted to repair the crashed TIE fighter they'd found out in the jungle.

Tenel Ka stood outside the upraised horizontal door of the hangar bay. She held a forked wooden spear that she used for target practice, throwing it with exceptional skill toward a tiny mark on the landing pad. The teenaged warrior could strike her target with either hand. She stared at her goal with cool, granite-gray eyes, focused her concentration, and then let the sharpened stick fly.

Tenel Ka could have nudged the spear with the Force, guiding it where she wished it to go—but Jacen knew from long experience that she would probably tackle him to the ground if he dared suggest such a thing. Tenel Ka had gained her physical skill through faithful practice and was reluctant to use the Force in a way that she considered to be cheating. She was very proud of her skills.

In the rear of the hangar bay, the turbolift hummed. Master Luke Skywalker emerged and looked around. Jacen gave up his designs on the stinger lizard and stood. His knees cracked, and his ankles were sore, which made him realize how long he had crouched motionless. "Hi, Uncle Luke," he said.

Tenel Ka threw her spear one last time, then retrieved it and turned to meet Luke. She and the Jedi Master had shared a special bond from the time the two of them had spent together searching for the kidnapped twins and Lowie and rescuing them from the Shadow Academy . . . though Jacen sensed that Tenel Ka and Uncle Luke shared other secrets as well.

"Greetings, Master Skywalker," Tenel Ka said.

The tinny voice of Em Teedee, the miniaturized translator droid hanging from a clip on Lowbacca's belt, chimed out, "Master Lowbacca, we have a guest. If you're quite finished fussing with those controls, I believe Master Skywalker wishes to converse with you."

Lowie grunted and raised his shaggy head, scratching the remarkable black streak of fur that rose over one eyebrow and curved down his back.

Jaina scrambled up beside him. "What is it? Oh, hi, Uncle Luke."

"I'm glad you're all here," Luke said. "I wanted to discuss your training. You four have been in closer contact with the Second Imperium than my other students, so you know the danger better than they do. You also all have extraordinarily strong Jedi potential, and I think perhaps you're ready for a greater challenge than the others."

"Like what?" Jacen asked eagerly.

"Like taking the next step toward becoming full Jedi Knights," Luke said.

Jacen's mind spun, trying to figure out what his uncle meant, but Jaina exclaimed, "You want us to build our own lightsabers, don't you?"

"Yes," Luke nodded. "I normally wouldn't suggest this so early, especially for such young students. But I think we're in for a battle so difficult that I want you to be prepared to use every weapon at your disposal."

Jacen felt a surge of delight, followed by sudden uneasiness. Not long ago he had desperately wanted his own lightsaber, but he had been forced to train with one at the Shadow Academy . . . and he and his sister had come close to killing each other in a deceptive test. "But, Uncle Luke, I thought you said it was too dangerous for us."

Luke nodded soberly. "It *is* dangerous. As I recall, I once caught you playing with my weapon because you wanted one so much—but I think you've learned an important lesson since then about taking lightsabers seriously."

Jacen agreed. "Yeah, I don't think I'll ever again think of a lightsaber as a toy."

Luke smiled back at him. "Good. That's an important start," he said. "These weapons are not playthings. A lightsaber is a dangerous and destructive instrument, a powerful blade that can strike down an opponent—or a friend, if you're not careful."

"We'll be careful, Uncle Luke," Jaina assured him with an earnest nod.

Luke still seemed skeptical. "This isn't a reward. It's an obligation, a difficult new set of lessons for you. Perhaps the work involved in building your own lightsaber will teach you to respect it as a tool, as you learn how the Jedi created their own personal weapons, each with its special characteristics."

"Always wanted to know how a lightsaber worked. Can I take yours apart, Uncle Luke?" Jaina asked, her brandy-brown eyes pleading.

Now Luke let a smile cross his face. "I don't think so, Jaina—but you'll learn about them soon enough." He looked at the four young Jedi Knights. "I want you to begin without delay."

2

JAINA PAID ATTENTION to her uncle Luke's words with only half a mind, the rest of her concentration focusing on the problem of where to get the precious components for building her very own lightsaber.

She and her brother, along with Lowie and Tenel Ka, were in one of the upper solariums in the Great Temple, a room made of polished marble slabs inset with semiprecious stones. Bright light streamed through tall, narrow windows that had been chiseled into the stone blocks by ancient Massassi tribesmen.

Luke Skywalker sat nearby on a deep window ledge, uncharacteristically relaxed and boyish. He enjoyed being with a small group of trainees, especially his niece and nephew and their friends, talking about things that interested him.

"You may have heard about Jedi Masters during the Clone Wars who were able to fashion lightsabers in only a day or two, using whatever raw materials were at hand," Luke said. "But don't get the idea that your weapon is a quick little project to be slapped together. Ideally, a Jedi took many months to construct a single perfect weapon that he or she would keep and use for a lifetime. Once you build it, the lightsaber will become your constant companion, your tool, and a ready means of defense."

He stood up from his seat on the window ledge. "The components are fairly simple. Every lightsaber has a standard power source, the same type used in small blasters, even in glowpanels. They last a long time, though, because Jedi should rarely use their lightsabers."

"Got some of those power sources in my room," Jaina said. "Spare parts, you know."

"One of the other crucial pieces," Luke continued, "is a focusing crystal. The most powerful and sought-after gems are rare kaiburr crystals. However, though lightsabers are powerful weapons, their design is so flexible that practically any kind of crystal can be used. And, since I don't happen to have a stash of kaiburr crystals"—he smiled—"you'll have to make do with something else, of your own choosing."

Luke held out the handle of his own lightsaber, sliding his palm over the smooth grip, then igniting it with a startling snap-hiss. The brilliant yellow-green blade drowned out even the bright sunlight in the room.

"This is not my first lightsaber." Luke drew it back and forth through the empty air so that its hum changed frequency. "Note the color of its blade. I lost my first lightsaber years ago . . . my father's lightsaber." He swallowed and seemed to struggle against a dark memory from his past. Jaina knew the story of how Luke had lost his other lightsaber during a duel with Darth Vader on Cloud City. In that terrible fight Luke Skywalker had lost not only his lightsaber, but his hand as well.

"My first weapon had a pale blue beam. The colors vary, according to the frequencies of the crystals used. Darth Vader's lightsaber"—he drew a deep breath—*"my father's* lightsaber was a deep scarlet."

Jaina nodded solemnly. She remembered fighting Vader's holographic image on the Shadow Academy—though it had actually been her own brother Jacen in disguise. Her lightsaber experiences had not been pleasant on the Imperial station . . . and now her feelings about the energy blades were even more confused. Her friend Zekk had also been taken by Brakiss and the Second Imperium. Jaina knew she would have to fight to get him back.

Luke continued, "One of my students, Cilghal, a Calamarian like Admiral Ackbar, made her lightsaber with smooth curves and protrusions, as if the handle had been grown from metallic coral. Inside, she used a rare ultima-pearl, one of the treasures found in the seabeds of her watery planet.

"My first true failure as a teacher was another student named Gantoris. He built his lightsaber in only a few intense days, following instructions given to him by the evil spirit of Exar Kun. Gantoris thought he was ready, and my mistake was not seeing what he was up to.

"You, my young Jedi Knights, must be different. I can't wait any longer to train you. You must learn how to build your lightsabers—and how to use them—in the right way. The galaxy has changed, and you must meet the challenge. A true Jedi is forced to adapt or be destroyed."

Tenel Ka spoke up. "Where will we find these crystals to build our weapons, Master Skywalker?" she asked. "Are they lying on the ground?"

Luke smiled. "Perhaps. Or it's possible they could be scavenged from old equipment left here from when this place was a Rebel base. Or maybe you already have resources you haven't yet realized." He shot a quick look at Jacen, but Jaina couldn't decipher what the glance meant.

"I'd like you to start on your lightsabers immediately." Luke switched off his throbbing weapon and looked down at its handle. "But I hope you'll need to use your weapons only rarely . . . if ever."

A few days later, Jaina sat hunched over her worktable inside her quarters. She had strung up extra glowpanels to allow her sufficient illumination to work through the night. Dozens of tools and pieces of equipment lay on the tabletop, arranged in a careful order so that she knew where every component, every wire and circuit might be found.

After Jaina had given each of her friends an appropriate power source to build their own lightsabers, the young Jedi Knights had split up to search for the precious crystals and other components that would make their new weapons function. Jaina, though, wanted to make the lightsaber particularly *hers*, a symbolic extension of her unique personality. She would make it from scratch in a way that the others would never attempt. She smiled at her own ingenuity.

Dark smoke rose from the portable furnace she had brought in, and she blinked to clear the chemical fumes from her eyes as she bent over it. Carefully, she added the next batch of powdered elements in the precise mixture her datapad suggested. She drew on her Force powers, amplifying her vision to observe the chemicals interacting, to watch them bond into a tight, organized lattice.

The precisely pure crystals began to grow. . . .

She adjusted the temperature, watching intently, though the process of crystalline growth took hours. She focused her mind on shaping the facets as they emerged from the molten mixture in the furnace, making the planes tilt at appropriate angles. The growing crystals gobbled up and stored the extra energy pumped into the mixture by the furnace.

Finally, by morning, her eyes bloodshot and gritty from lack of sleep, Jaina shut down the system. She let the furnace cool until she could reach in and take out her beautiful, sparkling crystals.

They were a rich purplish blue, shimmering with inner energy. They had formed perfectly, as she had expected, guided by her own mental skills. She held them in her palm and smiled. Now for the next step.

* * *

The tip of Jacen's tongue stuck out between his lips as he focused with unaccustomed concentration on the mechanical task at hand. It had already taken him a week to get this far.

He wanted to rush through the project, jam the components into place, connect the power, and turn on his lightsaber—his *own* lightsaber—but he took Uncle Luke's words seriously. This was a weapon he would use for the rest of his life, the weapon of a Jedi. A few weeks didn't seem so long to invest in creating it.

Much as it went against his nature to do so, Jacen forced himself to be meticulous and patient, knowing that he had to make sure everything fit together *just so* in the precise configuration required.

He had the power source Jaina had given him, and it was easy to find pieces of metal in the right shape and size to form the casing. He used Jaina's tools to cut the pieces into interlocking configurations and file down the rough edges. After a few days of doing that, he installed the power source, connecting all the leads. Then he added the control buttons.

Jaina could have whipped the casing together in just a few minutes, but it took him days to gather all the parts. Now, even though his scavenger hunt was over, it still seemed to take forever to assemble the thing.

Jacen would rather have been outside hunting for more specimens to add to his menagerie—or better yet, playing with the ones that cheerfully bounced about in their cages, often housed mere centimeters from other creatures that would gladly have had them for breakfast.

He heard the crystal snake rustling in its repaired cage, and then one of the reptile birds began to chirrup—but Jacen steeled himself, focusing on the project at hand. The lightsaber was almost finished, almost finished! He would be the first to complete his, and Master Luke would be very proud.

With the handle mostly assembled, he wrapped special grip-textured bindings around it so that he could hold and wield the blade with the gentle ease of a Jedi swordsman. Now Jacen was ready to install the powerful crystal.

He went to the personal locker box where he kept his valuable possessions and withdrew a small, glittering object—a Corusca gem. He had snared the gem during a mining demonstration at Lando Calrissian's GemDiver Station, and had later used it to cut himself free from his locked quarters in the Shadow Academy. He had offered the jewel to his mother as a special gift—but she had persuaded Jacen to keep the gem, to find a special use for it.

And what could be more special than using it in his own lightsaber?

Lowbacca prowled through the clutter in the former Rebel control room, left over from when the Great Temple had been used as a base in the struggle against the Empire. The soldiers had left most of their old equipment here when they fled the small jungle moon. In the years since, most of the machinery and computers had been gutted for other purposes, since Luke Skywalker's Jedi academy did not rely heavily on gadgets and technology. Although Jaina had already scavenged these rooms, Lowie knew that a great deal of equipment still remained to be picked through.

Poking his snout into shadowy corners, the Wookiee snuffled and rumbled thoughtfully to himself. He lifted metal coverings to look around, rummaging through wires and circuit boards, taking apart flatscreen displays.

"Master Lowbacca, I simply cannot imagine what you think you're accomplishing," Em Teedee said from the clip at his waist. "You've been prodding around here for hours, and you've found nothing."

Lowie let out a short growl.

"Well, really! No, I *don't* believe you can sniff them out with your nose. What an absurd notion! How could anyone possibly sniff out a crystal?" Em Teedee's temper seemed to be getting short and Lowie wondered if perhaps the little translating droid's batteries were running low.

"Anyway, I doubt you'll ever locate any kind of crystal in here. I'm sure the entire control room was thoroughly ransacked years ago."

Lowie barked a comment as he continued his search.

"Quite the contrary," Em Teedee said. "I am not a pessimist—I'm simply being realistic. I don't know why Master Skywalker should expect everyone to simply *find* appropriate crystals here or there. What if one of you created an inferior lightsaber? What good would that do? I daresay it's a possibility. I really think you should give up the search."

With a sudden bellow of triumph, Lowie reached into the cluttered interior of a small, high-resolution projection system and withdrew two glittering components: a flat focusing lens and a spherical enhancement jewel. The items had been used in the high-res display, and Lowie knew instinctively that they could be applied to the same general purpose inside his new lightsaber.

With great delight, he held them in his long hairy fingers in front of

Em Teedee's optical sensors. He growled with pleasure, and a hint of smugness.

Em Teedee replied with some degree of petulance, "Well, of course I could be wrong."

3

DAYBREAK FOUND TENEL Ka atop the Great Temple limbering up in preparation for her new exercise routine. After tying back her wavy red-gold hair with a few simple braids, she stretched each muscle slowly, deliberately, efficiently. Her lizard-skin bodysuit was even more abbreviated than her usual reptilian armor, so as not to restrict her movement. The sparkling blue scales rippled with every flexing of her muscles.

Standing barefoot on the ancient weathered stone of the temple, Tenel Ka reached toward the sky, stretching first with one arm, then the other. She felt her body begin to loosen up, as the jungle around her blossomed with the scents and sounds of the dawning day. A light breeze stirred the leaves, and Tenel Ka took in deep breaths, letting her mind focus on what she needed to do. She would make her new routine as rigorous as the calisthenics Master Skywalker himself performed each morning.

She had been surprised by her reaction to the Jedi teacher's instruction for them to build their own lightsabers. Despite her fierce pride at knowing she would soon begin earnest training for real battles, Tenel Ka had resented the implication that she would somehow be judged on the basis of the *weapon* with which she would fight.

Earlier, she had scaled the Great Temple using nothing more than her grappling hook, her fibercord, and her own muscles. Wasn't the warrior who wielded the weapon much more important than the weapon itself? she asked herself. Even holding a simple stick instead of a dazzling lightsaber, Tenel Ka was capable of defeating an enemy.

When she felt truly limbered up, Tenel Ka hefted the meter-long wooden staff she had carried to the top of the temple. For half an hour she practiced throwing the stick into the air and catching it, alternating between her left hand and her right, first with eyes open, then closed. Next, she practiced twirling the wooden rod over her head and jumping over it as she swung it beneath her feet.

Perspiration glistened on Tenel Ka's neck and forehead, and was trickling down her spine by the time she moved on to the next challenge. Finally, once Tenel Ka was satisfied that her reflexes were as finely tuned as she could wish, she grasped one end of the staff with both hands as if it were a lightsaber and began sword drills.

After an hour of that, Tenel Ka was ready for more exacting physical activity. Taking a deep breath, she sprinted down the steep outer stairs of the pyramid to ground level and began her ten-kilometer run for the day.

The breeze felt cool against her face as she ran. Glancing down at herself, she assessed her lean muscular arms and long sturdy legs, reveling in the unrestricted motion and complete control. She sped up, pleased to note that her muscles were more than equal to the demands she made on them.

Yes, she decided, the *warrior* was what mattered, not the weapon.

After her fifth day of intensive drilling to hone her skills as sharp as any weapon, Tenel Ka felt ready to begin fashioning the handle of her personal lightsaber. Still glowing with perspiration from her morning workout, she decided to swim in the warm jungle river while she considered her next task.

She thought of the many materials available for her lightsaber handle, as she stripped off her exercise suit and dove with easy confidence into the swift current. Tenel Ka was a strong swimmer, trained on both Hapes and Dathomir, at the insistence of both grandmothers. It was one of the few times she could remember that her parents' mothers had ever agreed on anything.

Augwynne Djo, mother of Teneniel Djo, Tenel Ka's mother, had taught her to swim, saying that the strongest hunters and warriors were those who could not be stopped by a mere lake or river. Ta'a Chume, on the other hand, matriarch of the Royal House of Hapes and mother of Tenel Ka's father, Prince Isolder, had taught swimming as a defense against assassins or kidnappers. In fact, her grandmother had once escaped an attempt on her life by jumping from a wavespeeder into a lake and swimming for shore underwater, so that the would-be assassins assumed she had drowned.

Tenel Ka surfaced from the river, drew a deep lungful of air, and struck out upstream against the current. It was difficult swimming, but she used the added strength she had gained in her recent lightsaber training . . . which brought her back to the task at hand.

She supposed she could fashion her lightsaber handle from a piece of metal pipe, or even carve one from hardwood, since a lightsaber gave off little heat. But somehow those did not seem right for her.

Tenel Ka propelled herself forward with long smooth strokes, keeping a steady rhythm. Left. Right. Left. Right.

Stone would be too difficult to shape, and too heavy for her purposes. Tenel Ka needed something that would suit the *image* of a warrior from Dathomir. She pictured Augwynne Djo's proud form clad in reptile skin, a ceremonial helm on her head, riding a domesticated rancor. The taming of these ferocious beasts was an appropriate symbol of the courage of her rugged people, since the huge beasts were powerful and their sharp claws deadly.

Tenel Ka allowed herself to sink below the surface of the river and changed to a new stroke, recalling that she had kept two teeth from her grandmother's favorite rancor when it had died a few years ago. They were not the rancor's largest teeth by far, but each *was* the perfect size and shape to be a lightsaber handle. . . .

A week later, Tenel Ka studied her handiwork with justifiable pride and etched another deep groove into the pattern she had carved on her rancor tooth.

Lowie, sitting ahead of her in the tiny cockpit of the T-23 skyhopper, turned and roared a question at her. She waited for a moment for Em Teedee's translation. "Master Lowbacca wishes to inquire whether you have any preference as to the volcano in which you hope to search for crystals."

Tenel Ka glanced out at the rich green jungle canopy rushing beneath them. "You may choose," she said.

Lowbacca gave a short bark. "It makes little difference to Master Lowbacca," Em Teedee told her. "He has already assembled the components he intends to use for his lightsaber. The primary construction on his instrument is complete, and he has only to tune it now."

Tenel Ka blinked in surprise, not only at the length of Em Teedee's translation after Lowbacca's short reply, but also at the thought that Lowbacca—and perhaps Jacen or Jaina—was so far ahead of her. Well then, she would have to make her search quickly and assemble her lightsaber without delay.

"The closest volcano," she said, reaching forward and pointing. "There." Then, gruffly, because she felt foolish for having asked Lowbacca to take her out on this errand, she said, "I apologize. I would not have troubled you with my request had I known your lightsaber was almost complete."

The Wookiee growled and dismissed this with a motion of one

ginger-furred hand. "Master Lowbacca wishes to assure you that you have not inconvenienced him in the slightest," Em Teedee supplied. "It has been many days since he enjoyed solitude and meditation out in the jungle, and he delights in the opportunity to assist you in this manner."

The Wookiee snorted and gave the little translator droid a flick with one finger. "Oh—that is to say," Em Teedee amended, "it was Master Lowbacca's intention to take a break anyway, and he's pleased he could help."

The young Wookiee sniffed loudly, but accepted this translation. He brought the T-23 skyhopper down on a patch of hard-packed volcanic sand between the jungle's edge and the base of a small volcano. After Lowbacca woofed a few words, Em Teedee said, "When you have completed your search, successful or not, simply return here to the T-23. Master Lowbacca and I will watch for you from the treetops."

Tenel Ka nodded curtly. "Understood. Thank you." Without further ado, she turned and hurried up the slope toward the volcano.

Though none of the volcanoes near the Jedi academy had erupted in quite some time, tendrils of white steam still curled from this one's peak. Skirting the sharp black rocks on the perimeter, Tenel Ka soon found a gaping lava tube leading in toward the core of the volcano, as she had hoped.

A pungent sulfurous odor filled the warm tunnel. Tenel Ka pulled the finger-sized glowrod from a pouch at her belt and ignited it to light her way. Black crystalline sand crunched under her feet and glittered like thousands of fiery sparks, throwing back the light of her glowrod. As she trudged farther in, the sandy floor became hard rock, glassy like obsidian. Ahead of her the rocky corridor radiated an eerie red light, and the heat grew stifling.

Occasionally she heard a rumbling, rushing roar, as if the volcano itself were breathing deeply in its sleep. The stony walls around her took on a cracked, broken look. Some of the larger fissures ran from floor to ceiling and leaked puffs of acrid white steam. But she saw no embedded crystals.

The lava tube wound on and on. Losing patience, Tenel Ka had just about decided to turn back when she rounded one last corner and encountered a wave of searing heat. She had found what she was looking for.

"Ah," she said. "Aha."

She wouldn't be able to bear the heat for long, but she had to risk it. On the floor of the tunnel lay a huge slab of glossy black rock that had broken free from a crack on the tunnel wall. Ripples of scorching air danced before her in the dimness. Rivulets of perspiration ran down her forehead and into her eyes, blurring her vision. Even so, she could not mistake the chunks of spiky crystals that grew on the broken slab, glittering and hazy.

The rock surrounding her was too hot to touch, so Tenel Ka worked quickly. Holding her glowrod in her teeth, she pulled a small scrap of lizard hide from a pouch at her belt, wrapped it around a clump of the crystals, used her grappling hook to chip away at a few of the crystals, then pried them loose.

Tenel Ka tucked the crystals, still wrapped in their protective lizard hide, into her belt pouch, then headed back up the tunnel at a trot. Holding the glowrod high above her head, she raised her voice in a loud ululating cry of triumph that echoed down the length of the lava tube.

Back in her quarters, Tenel Ka sat at a low wooden table with the components of her future lightsaber spread in front of her. Everything she needed for assembling her weapon was here: switches, crystals, the covering plate, a power source, a focusing lens, and the rancor-tooth hilt.

She ran a light fingertip over the intricate battle etchings she had carved on the ivory lightsaber handle. The markings had turned out even better than she had hoped.

After returning from her crystal hunt, she had applied to the rancor tooth a paste made of dampened black sand from the floor of the lava tube. When she polished the tooth to a soft luster, pigment from the dark sand had stained every crevice of her carving to bring each etched line into sharp relief. The decorated rancor tooth was a beautiful piece, worthy of a warrior.

A yawn of contented weariness escaped her lips as Tenel Ka began to piece the components together according to Master Skywalker's directions. She frowned when she realized that the hollow inside the rancor's tooth was not quite large enough to contain the arrangement of crystals she had hoped for. She frowned again when she noticed on close inspection that each of her hazy crystals contained a tiny flaw. She suppressed another yawn and shook her head in resignation. Well, she didn't have much choice. There hadn't been time to examine the crystals more carefully in the searing lava tube, and now it was too late to search for more.

Tenel Ka thought back over the past two weeks, the drills and exercises she had put herself through. Her reflexes were lightning-fast, her skills and senses sharp as a laser. She shrugged, trying to loosen the knot of weary tension that had crept into her shoulders. She would have to make do. After all, in the long run it was the warrior and not the weapon that determined victory.

She nodded to herself as she picked up the lightsaber handle and began placing the components inside.

4

THE JUNGLE CLEARING was alive with thousands—no, millions!—of living creatures and interesting plants, strangely colorful mushrooms and droning insects, all of which offered great distractions to Jacen. He had to work very hard to keep his mind from wandering. At the moment it was far more important to pay attention to Luke Skywalker as he set up the first lightsaber dueling exercise for the young Jedi Knights.

During the construction of their weapons, the trainees had sparred with dueling droids and with each other, using sticks the same length as a lightsaber blade. After completing their lightsabers, they had spent a week practicing with their real weapons against stationary targets, accustoming themselves to the feel of the energy blades.

Now, though, Master Skywalker had deemed them ready to move on to the next step.

The clearing was a burned-out spot where lightning had sparked a brief but intense forest fire. The jungle dampness and lush foliage had quickly smothered the blaze, but a huge Massassi tree—its trunk charred and weakened by the searing flames—had toppled over, taking with it several smaller trees and bushes. The rest of the clearing was a matted maze of pale green undergrowth—weeds and grasses and flowers attempting to reclaim the burned and crumbly soil.

Because today's exercises would be both mental and physical, Uncle Luke wore a comfortable flight suit, as did Jacen and Jaina. Tenel Ka's ever-present reptilian armor left her arms and legs bare, giving her complete freedom of movement. Her long reddish-gold hair had been plaited into intricate braids, with special ornamentation on each one. Lowbacca wore no garment other than his belt, woven of strands he had harvested from a deadly syren plant in the deep forests on Kashyyyk. Em Teedee hung in his accustomed place at the Wookiee's waist.

All of the young Jedi Knights carried something new and special this time, though—their own lightsabers, completed after weeks of delicate construction.

While Jacen stood with his friends, flicking occasional glances in the direction of rustling leaves that hinted at the presence of strange creatures, Luke Skywalker took a seat on the massive fallen trunk. At last he unslung the mysterious pack he had lugged all the way from the Great Temple.

"What's in there, Uncle Luke?" Jacen asked, unable to restrain his curiosity. Since he couldn't investigate the interesting insects and plants, he needed to focus his mind on something else.

Luke gave a secretive smile and withdrew a scarlet sphere the size of a large ball, perfectly smooth except for tiny covered openings that might have been repulsorjets or small targeting lasers. Luke set the ball on the slanted, burned trunk; miraculously, it did not roll down the slope, but remained exactly where he had placed it. He withdrew another of the scarlet spheres, and another, and another.

"Remotes!" Jaina cried, guessing what they were. "Those *are* remotes, aren't they, Uncle Luke? What are they for?"

"Target practice," he said. All four remotes sat balanced on the burned Massassi trunk, refusing to roll, as if they could ignore gravity.

Lowbacca grunted with surprise, and Tenel Ka straightened. "We are going to shoot at them?"

"No," Luke said. "They're going to shoot at *you.*"

"And we deflect the shots with our lightsabers?" Jacen asked.

"Yes," Luke said, "but it's not as easy as you might think."

"I never said I thought it would be *easy,*" Jacen muttered.

Tenel Ka nodded. "A lesson to sharpen our reflexes and concentration. We must react quickly to intercept each burst from the remotes."

"Ah, but it gets harder," Luke said. He reached into the sack again, removed a flexible helmet with a transparisteel visor tinted a deep red, and handed it to Tenel Ka. "You'll each wear these." He withdrew another pair of helmets for the twins, but the last one consisted of only a red visor fastened with crude tie-straps. "Sorry, Lowbacca, but I couldn't find a helmet big enough for your head. This will have to do."

Jacen slipped the helmet over his perpetually tousled brown hair and suddenly saw the jungle through a scarlet filter. The thick forest held a more primeval quality now, as if backlit with smoldering fires. The details were duller, darker, and Jacen wondered what the helmet and visor were supposed to do—protect them against stray shots from the remotes? He looked over at where the bright red remotes had rested on the burned tree trunk . . . or rather where they should have been.

Jacen blinked. "Hey, they're gone!"

"Not gone," Luke said. "Just invisible. When you look at the remotes through the red filters, you can't see them anymore." Luke smiled. "That's the point. When Obi-Wan Kenobi taught me, he made me fight using a helmet with the blast shield down. I couldn't see a thing. You'll at least be able to see your surroundings . . . but not the remotes."

Jacen wanted to ask how he was supposed to fight what he couldn't see, but he knew what Uncle Luke would say.

"I didn't want you totally blind," Luke continued, "because all four of you will be training here in the clearing with different remotes. This way you'll be able to see *each other*. I don't want anyone getting too enthusiastic and causing injuries instead of just deflecting laser bolts."

This brought a small chuckle from Jacen and Jaina, but Master Skywalker looked at all of the trainees sternly. "I wasn't kidding," he said. "A lightsaber can cut through practically any substance known— and that includes people. Remember this warning: lightsabers are not toys. They are dangerous weapons. Treat them with the utmost care and respect. I hope that the time you each spent building your lightsaber has taught you more about its power and its risks."

Luke picked up a set of controls. "Now let's see how well you work with the Force and your own energy blades."

He flipped a switch, and Jacen heard a hissing, whirring sound. But he saw nothing until he pushed up the scarlet visor. The four remotes drifted into the air, spinning around and scanning the vicinity.

"These lasers are low power," Luke said, "but don't think they won't sting if you get hit by one."

Jacen muttered to his sister, "At least he's not throwing rocks or knives at us, like at the Shadow Academy."

"Visors down," Luke said. "Take your positions."

The companions spread out in the clearing, tramping down the weedy underbrush.

"Ignite your lightsabers," Luke said, then sat back. He seemed to be enjoying himself.

As one, the four Jedi trainees held out the handles of their new weapons and depressed the power studs. Brilliant beams sprang out in the red dimness, bright slashes the length of a sword blade burning through the thick crimson in front of Jacen's eyes. The tinted masks drained all other color from their lightsabers, transforming them into glowing red rods. It reminded Jacen of Darth Vader's weapon.

"The remotes are circling now," Luke said. "In the next thirty seconds they'll begin to fire at random. Reach out with the Force. *Feel* them. Sense the impending attack—then use your lightsaber blade to deflect it. A lot of your training has been leading up to this. Let's see how well you do."

Jacen tensed, holding his lightsaber ready. Much as he hated to admit it, he drew upon some of the skills Brakiss had taught him at the Shadow Academy. He felt the energy blade humming in his hand, pulsing with power. The sharpness of ozone reached his nostrils. He heard his friends moving about, preparing for an attack that could come from any direction.

The buzzing lightsabers muted all other sounds, just as the red filter drowned all other colors. Suddenly Jacen heard a snapping shot, though he saw nothing. A loud Wookiee yowl preceded the vibrating hum of a lightsaber blade sweeping sideways and hitting nothing. Lowie roared again.

"Dear me, Master Lowbacca, that wasn't even close," Em Teedee exclaimed. "I do hope you'll improve significantly with practice."

Lowie snarled, sounding hurt, and Em Teedee responded in a somewhat cowed fashion, "Well, all right. I understand it's more difficult since you can't *see* anything. . . . Even so, I should think it inadvisable to allow it to strike you again."

Jacen's interest in the conversation vanished when a sizzling bolt shot out from behind and struck him squarely on the backside. He yelped with pain. The tiny wound burned as badly as if a stinger lizard had zapped him. He whirled, slashing with the lightsaber, but by then it was too late.

From across the clearing another bolt shot out, followed by a crash of underbrush. Through the visor he saw Tenel Ka leap to one side. A branch snapped in two as the invisible laser struck it where Tenel Ka had stood only seconds before. The warrior girl crouched, holding her lightsaber up, her head cocked in concentration.

Jacen reached out with his mind, trying to sense through the Force where his remote would shoot next. He heard two more laser blasts and then a *spang* as Jaina successfully deflected one of the bolts. Jacen focused on the pain at the spot where he had been struck by the laser, using it to intensify his determination. He didn't want to be stung again.

Another laser beam shot out. He swiped the lightsaber at it, barely missing—though his motion was enough to shift him out of its path so that the beam sizzled past. He felt the warmth of its passage, but could not see it.

"That was close," he said, then instinctively swung to strike again as the remote fired once more.

Jaina parried a flurry of bolts as her remote attacked mercilessly, firing five times in rapid succession. One of her bolts ricocheted off the glowing edge of her lightsaber directly toward Jacen. He responded without conscious thought, using the Force and flowing with it, somehow knowing what to do as he shifted his own blade sideways just enough to catch the diverted bolt. The deflected blast bounced up into the trees, where it fried a fistful of leaves.

In a single follow-through motion, Jacen spun, reaching up with the lightsaber blade to ward off a second bolt fired from the other remote hovering in front of them.

Lowbacca bellowed with triumph as he, too, got the hang of defending himself.

Except for her heavy breathing, Tenel Ka was quiet, thoughtful. Through the red filter Jacen watched as she parried one of the lasers and leaped upward with all her might, using her lightsaber like a cleaver. A shower of sparks erupted and a smoking hole appeared in midair. Jacen heard a *thunk* as pieces of Tenel Ka's remote fell useless to the jungle floor.

"All right. That's enough for now," Luke Skywalker said.

Tenel Ka switched off her weapon and stood with her hands on her hips, her elbows spread. Jacen flipped up his red visor to discover his own remote hovering barely at arm's length in front of his face. He stepped back, startled.

Tenel Ka's remote lay on the ground sliced in two, its circuits flickering and sparking. Jaina and Lowie also shut off their weapons and stood panting and grinning. Jacen rubbed the burning pain in his backside and grimaced sheepishly, hoping none of the others would notice.

"Excellent, all of you—except now it looks as if I'll need a new remote," Luke said, smiling wryly at Tenel Ka. "You did very well with the Force."

"Not only with the Force," she said, thrusting her chin upward and squaring her shoulders. "I also used my ears to track the remote. When I concentrated, I could hear it even above the sound of the lightsabers."

Luke chuckled. "Good. A Jedi *should* use all available skills and resources."

Jaina gripped the lightsaber in both hands and positioned the brilliant, electric-violet blade in front of her. She looked past the searing line of controlled fire at Lowbacca, her opponent, who stood opposite her, a lightsaber in his hairy grasp. He growled his readiness.

Jaina looked into the young Wookiee's golden eyes, saw the dark streak of black fur swirling up from his eyebrow and around his head. She swallowed and tensed. Though lanky, Lowbacca was much taller than she, and Jaina knew he was about three times as strong. But in his furry expression she saw an uncertainty, a genuine discomfort that mirrored her own.

"Do I really *have* to fight Lowie, Uncle—uh, Master Skywalker?" Jaina asked.

Luke Skywalker stood. "You're not fighting him, Jaina. You're *fencing* with him. Test your opponent. Gauge each other's skills. Learn to judge reactions. Explore strategies. But be careful."

Jaina thought of her training at the Shadow Academy and how she and Jacen had dueled with lightsabers, not realizing that they had fought each other in holographic disguise.

"Remember," Luke cautioned, "a Jedi fights only as a last resort. If you are forced to draw your lightsaber, you have already forfeited much of your advantage. A Jedi trusts the Force and at first seeks other ways to resolve problems: patience, logic, tolerance, attentive listening, negotiation, persuasion, calming techniques.

"But there are times when a Jedi *must* fight. Knowing that the Shadow Academy is out there, I fear those times will come all too often for us. And so you must learn how to wield your lightsabers."

He stepped back and motioned to Jacen and Tenel Ka, who waited on the edge of the clearing, sitting next to each other on the burned tree trunk. "You two will be next. Jaina, don't worry about Lowie being so much bigger and stronger than you are. Dueling with a lightsaber is primarily skill, and I think you're equally matched in that. Your one true disadvantage is that his reach is much longer than yours. Unfortunately," Luke said with a sigh, "circumstances don't always pit us against equal opponents. As for you, Lowie, be careful not to underestimate Jaina."

He dropped back to watch. "Now, show me what you can do."

"Well?" Jaina stepped forward, keeping her gaze locked with Lowie's. "What are we waiting for?"

The Wookiee shifted his lightsaber, bringing its molten-bronze blade into position. Jaina moved hers up to meet it, crossing her blade against his. She felt the pressure, the sizzling of sparks, and the discharge as the powerful beams drove against each other. She saw the muscles bulging in Lowie's long arms as he strained against her—but Jaina held her own.

"All right, let's try something else." Jaina withdrew her lightsaber, then swung it at her Wookiee friend slowly, cautiously—and Lowbacca met it with another crackle of released energy.

Swinging to strike again, she said, "This isn't so bad."

Lowie defended himself. He seemed reluctant to do battle.

Knowing that Lowie had endured horrifying struggles at the Shadow Academy—and remembering again that she had been forced to fight her own brother—Jaina realized that Brakiss and the violet-eyed Tamith Kai would stop at nothing to bring down the New Republic. She and Lowie would both be needed to defend against the Dark Jedi. She decided now that the best way to rid Lowie of his reservations would be to go on the offensive.

And this time she did not feel strangled by darkness. Today Jaina fought with full willingness, learning to be a defender of the light side, a champion of the Force. Uncle Luke had been correct in his speech in front of the Jedi trainees. She knew in her heart that the Shadow Academy had only begun to cause trouble, and she would have to fight to get her friend Zekk freed.

But first she had to learn how.

Lowbacca responded with greater strength, a better show of his abilities, as he parried her blows and struck back with his own. She had to move quickly to cross blades with him again. They clashed and struck. Sparks flew.

Lowie spun and chopped down, but she met his lightsaber with hers, smiling, intently focused. She heard Jacen cheering from the side.

"Excellent, Master Lowbacca!" Em Teedee said. "Now do be careful—you wouldn't want a flying spark to damage me."

Jaina felt the Force flowing through her; Lowbacca wore an expression of exhilaration on his furry face. He opened his mouth, showing fangs and letting out a bellow of challenge—not mean or angry, simply an outpouring of excitement.

Lowie grasped the handle of his large lightsaber with both hands and swept sideways, attempting to catch Jaina by surprise—but she turned the tables on him. Summoning a burst of energy, she astonished the Wookiee by leaping high into the air up to the level of Lowie's head. His lightsaber swept harmlessly beneath her, and she landed lightly on the weed-covered ground behind him, laughing and panting.

"Oh my! That was *most* unexpected," Em Teedee said. "Splendid work, Mistress Jaina."

"Hey, that was great, Jaina!" her twin brother called.

Lowie raised his lightsaber in salute. Jaina grinned, her eyes gleaming.

"Most impressive," Luke said, turning to Jacen and Tenel Ka. "Next, let's see how well our spectators can do."

5

TENEL KA HESITATED, rubbing her fingers along the ivory surface of the rancor-tooth lightsaber handle. She held the deactivated weapon in front of her, drawing deep breaths. Intent on her body, her surroundings, she tightened her muscles and brought them to full readiness. Jungle sounds filled the clearing: the whisper of breezes ruffling leaves, the song of insects, the flutter of birds in the canopy.

She centered her thoughts, making sure her reflexes were primed and ready for action. Tenel Ka relied on her body and pressed it to its limits, but she always knew how far she could take it. So far, her muscles had never let her down.

Slowly, she opened her cool, granite-gray eyes and looked at the young man who stood in front of her, ready for the next duel.

He grinned at her. "Good against remotes is one thing, Tenel Ka," Jacen said, "but good against a real opponent? That's something else."

"This is a fact."

Depressing a button, Jacen switched on his lightsaber. The emerald-green blade sprang forth, snapping and glittering with power. "Hey, I'll try not to be too hard on you."

Tenel Ka's fingers found the recessed power button on the rancor-tooth handle. A shimmering gray-white blade extended like crackling electric fog shot through with golden sparks. The lightsaber's color reminded her of the hazy crystals she had taken from the lava tube.

"And I will try not to be too hard on you, my friend Jacen," she said. Tenel Ka tested the weapon by turning her wrist, flicking the blade from side to side. The beam sparked and sizzled as it encountered moisture in the air.

"Be careful," Master Skywalker said from his vantage point on the burned tree trunk. "Don't get cocky. You both have a great deal to learn."

"Don't worry, Uncle Luke," Jacen said. "I know it was a bad time for me, but I *did* have some training at the Shadow Academy." He grinned. "Fighting Tenel Ka will be more of a challenge than battling holographic monsters, though."

Jaina cleared her throat and spoke from where she sat, sweating and worn out after her session with Lowbacca. "And better than fighting your own sister in disguise?"

"That too," Jacen said.

Tenel Ka flicked her lightsaber back and forth again, taking a step closer to Jacen. She squared her shoulders, knowing that she stood taller than her good-humored friend. The lightsaber thrummed with power in her hand. "Are we going to talk all day, Jacen?" she said. "Or will you leave time for me to defeat you before the morning is over?"

Jacen laughed. "Hey, we're not supposed to be enemies, Tenel Ka. It's just a practice session."

She nodded. "This is a fact. Even so, we *are* opponents."

She swung her lightsaber slowly enough that he wouldn't perceive it as a real attack, but instinctively Jacen brought up his own weapon. Their blades intersected with sizzling force.

Jacen blinked in surprise, then drew back and struck against her nebulous gold-shot blade, testing. "All right then—let's go, Tenel Ka!"

She deftly sidestepped the thrust and returned with a parry of her own as he stumbled to regain his balance. Had he been a real enemy, she could have finished him then, but she pulled her blade aside for a split second, just to demonstrate that Jacen had let his guard drop—a lesson a Jedi Knight would need to learn to avoid defeat.

Unexpectedly, Jacen whirled and came up with a backhanded strike that forced her to retaliate. "I figure we should do something about that lack of confidence you've got, Tenel Ka," Jacen said, still grinning.

"I have no such lack," she said, and found that perspiration had broken out on her forehead. She swung, and Jacen caught her blow on his blade, laughing. She noted the degree of strength he used, the speed with which he maneuvered his weapon. They clashed again. Her cheerful friend, usually so scattered and disorganized, was giving her a surprisingly difficult workout.

"Hey, Tenel Ka," Jacen said as he struck twice more, as if he always held conversations while fighting with a lightsaber, "you know why a wampa snow monster has such long arms?" He paused for just a beat. "Because his hands are so far away from his body!"

Lowbacca groaned with miserable laughter, prompting the little droid at his waist to speak up in a tinny voice. "I fail to perceive the amusement value in Jacen's explanation of a zoological anomaly," Em Teedee said.

"Your jokes cannot distract me, Jacen," Tenel Ka said, swinging her lightsaber once more. Did he really think he could break her concentration so easily? "I do not find them humorous."

Jacen sighed as he met her blade with his own. "I know. I've been trying to get you to laugh ever since I've known you."

Tenel Ka watched her opponent closely, trying to judge from the tension in his muscles how soon he intended to make a surprise move, in which direction he would react, when the motion of his blade was a genuine attack and when it was merely a feint.

"Good," Master Skywalker said from where he watched. "Feel the Force. The lightsaber is not just a weapon. It is an extension of yourself."

Jacen pressed Tenel Ka hard, and she skipped backward a couple of paces. It was obvious he was trying to drive her toward an outcropping of broken boulders at the edge of the clearing. Jacen must have thought she had forgotten about them, but Tenel Ka filed away every detail of her surroundings in her mind.

Just as she reached the rocks, Jacen gave away his plans even more clearly with a broad grin. He pushed forward abruptly, no doubt expecting her to trip. But Tenel Ka leaped lightly backward over the boulders and landed on the other side, her legs planted firmly in a fighting stance. Suddenly foiled, Jacen stumbled and fell toward her, almost hitting the rocks himself. He came up sputtering in disbelief.

"Hey," he said, then smiled. "Good one!"

Tenel Ka stood waiting for him, her braided hair dangling about her head, drenched with sweat. Allowing herself a brief moment of self-indulgence, she switched the lightsaber to her left hand to prove she could fight just as well with either arm. She had practiced equally with her left and right hands, knowing it might prove a useful skill sometime.

"Show-off," Jacen said. After a heartbeat of hesitation, he switched his own blade to his left hand and charged at her, swinging hard with the emerald-green lightsaber. She raised her own misty-white and gold blade, struck at him, then struck again. Sparks flew as the blades met.

When Jacen laughed with exhilaration, she allowed herself a satisfied grin as well. "You are a good opponent, Jacen Solo," she said.

"You bet I am," he answered.

Tenel Ka knew that her skill was based on her prowess, her physical ability. Though she had constructed a fine lightsaber, she would become a great warrior because of her *fighting abilities,* not because of the strength of any weapon, no matter how powerful.

Jacen's lightsaber pressed against hers, and she took a step back. They stood deadlocked, slamming energy blade against impenetrable energy blade. Fiery electricity crackled, and the air thickened with the sharp scent of ozone. Tenel Ka pushed with all her strength, but Jacen countered with equal force.

Her palm was sweaty, but her hand maintained its grip on the rancor-tooth handle. Inside, the components of her lightsaber vibrated, as if struggling to maintain the full energy of the blade while Tenel Ka pressed so furiously against an equally powerful weapon. She pushed harder. The handle rattled.

Jacen grinned at her. "Hope you don't expect me to surrender too easily."

"Perhaps you should," she panted, and pressed harder, ignoring the strange, unsettling sensations from her weapon. She gritted her teeth. Her arm strained. The lightsabers whined and buzzed. Jacen shoved back with all his might. His eyes glittered with the effort.

Over by the edge of the clearing, Master Skywalker stood watching the tense battle, as did Lowbacca and Jaina.

Tenel Ka narrowed her gray eyes, not easing up for an instant, wondering how best she could defeat Jacen and end this match.

Suddenly, something changed inside her lightsaber. She heard a sharp crack and then a loud hissing sizzle.

Jacen pressed harder with his emerald-green blade. For the briefest instant, the golden sparks that shot through her white pulsating energy beam flickered wildly. Her blade blurred with static, grew less focused.

Intent on the battle, Jacen gave a final, extra push with all his strength.

It happened all at once.

The power source in Tenel Ka's lightsaber gave a shriek of electrical overload—and the blade winked out like a snuffed candle. Sparks and smoke poured from the end of the handle where an energy blade should have glowed.

Suddenly, encountering no resistance as Jacen thrust with his last reserves of strength, the emerald-green lightsaber sliced through the opening where Tenel Ka's own blade had been just a moment before—plunging down to the only thing that stood in its way.

Tenel Ka felt a line of blazing agony sweep across her arm just above the elbow. It *burned* . . . and yet below the burn she felt only a sickening, horrible coldness—a bone-deep chill like none she had ever felt before.

Somehow her lightsaber thumped on the ground with a soft *thud*. Impossibly, she saw her hand clenching the carved rancor's tooth. Sparks the size of lightning bolts flashed around the handle as her weapon exploded in a burst of blinding light.

Bright. So very bright . . .

Tenel Ka felt a dizzying haze swirling up to engulf her. Everything was so confusing. Jacen screamed something she couldn't understand. Tenel Ka hoped intensely that she had not hurt him.

Jaina, Lowbacca, and Master Skywalker all ran toward her, shouting, but Tenel Ka couldn't find the energy to stay upright any longer. Just as Jacen reached a hand out toward her, she felt herself falling to the ground.

Then the pain and shock were completely swallowed up in blackness.

6

ON THE FRINGES of the unmapped heart of the galaxy, the Shadow Academy found a new hiding place near the flaming shells of two stars that had been dying for the last five thousand years.

Without its cloaking device, the dark Imperial training center hung like a circlet of thorns, washed in the blaze of solar radiation. The whispering trails of thrown-off star gas would camouflage the station from prying Rebel eyes.

Zekk stood before the broad windowports of the tallest observation tower, staring into the dazzling maelstrom of starfire. The darkened transparisteel of the viewport filtered out the deadly radiation—but even dimmed to a fraction of its true power, the fury of the universe left Zekk breathless.

Beside him stood Brakiss, Master of the Shadow Academy, a tall and statue-handsome Jedi. As an Imperial spy, Brakiss had once studied at the New Republic's Jedi academy; when Master Skywalker had tried to turn him away from the dark side of the Force, however, Brakiss had fled back to the Empire. There he gathered a group of Dark Jedi trainees and conditioned them to serve the great leader of the Second Imperium, the resurrected Emperor Palpatine himself.

Brakiss lifted his serene face, drinking in the view of the double suns. "This reality makes the image in my office seem like a pale glimmer by comparison, doesn't it, Zekk?"

Zekk nodded, but found himself without words.

"More than five millennia ago the Denarii Nova exploded, ripping through these stars and reducing them to cinders," Brakiss said. "The powerful Sith sorcerer Naga Sadow caused this cataclysmic event to gain his freedom from pursuing Republic warships. With the extravagant power of the dark side, Naga Sadow tore these two stars apart and used giant flares like two slapping hands to crush the fleet behind him."

Zekk nodded again and finally found words. "Another example of the power of the dark side."

Brakiss smiled proudly at him. "It is a power your friends Jacen and Jaina would never have shown you—much less taught you."

"No," Zekk agreed. "They never would have." For years, he had been friends with the twin children of Han Solo and Leia Organa Solo. Zekk was just a street kid, though—a nobody, who lived by his wits scavenging items in the dangerous underlevels of the city-covered world of Coruscant. His hopes for a better life had been little more than dreams until the Nightsister Tamith Kai snatched him and brought him to the Shadow Academy as part of a new recruitment drive.

In an earlier attempt to gain talented candidates, Brakiss had made an error by kidnapping the high-profile trainees Jacen, Jaina, and Lowbacca. When that failed, he had decided the Shadow Academy might do better with a different sort of person: downtrodden young ones who wouldn't be missed, yet had just as much potential to acquire Jedi powers—and more to gain by swearing allegiance to the Second Imperium.

Zekk had resisted the transformation at first, fighting to stay loyal to his friends. But gradually Brakiss lured him, showing Zekk how to use the Force for one small thing, then another. Zekk discovered that he was strong in the Force, and he learned quickly.

The experience altered his feelings toward the twins from friendship to resentment. Jaina and Jacen had never thought to include him in Jedi testing, though he felt he had as much innate talent as any of their highborn friends. Zekk's main regret in leaving his old life was that he missed his companion, old Peckhum. But now he had much more of a future. Zekk was beginning to understand Jedi powers, and he had already done things he'd never dreamed of.

Gazing at the stormy suns, Brakiss raised his arms to each side, spreading his fingers. His silvery robe flowed around him as if knit from silken spiderwebs. He stared into the swirling flares of the Denarii Nova. "Observe, Zekk—and learn."

Closing his eyes, the Master of the Shadow Academy began to move his hands. Zekk watched through the observation port, his green eyes widening.

The ocean of rarefied incandescent gases between the dying stars started to swirl like arms of fire . . . writhing, changing shape, dancing in time with the hand motions Brakiss made. The dark teacher was manipulating the starfire itself!

He whispered to Zekk without opening his eyes, without observing the effect of his work. "The Force is in all things," Brakiss said, "from the smallest pebble to the largest star. This is just a glimmer of how Naga Sadow reached out to the stars and delivered a mortal wound five thousand years ago."

"Could you make the sun explode?" Zekk asked in awe.

Brakiss opened his eyes and looked at his young student. His smooth, perfect forehead creased. "I don't know," he said. "And I don't believe I ever want to try."

Zekk remembered the way Brakiss had first enticed him to experiment with his innate Jedi powers, by giving him a flarestick and showing how simple it was to draw shapes in the flames with the Force. Here in the Denarii Nova, Brakiss had done the same thing—only on a scale the size of a star system.

"Could I try it?" Zekk said eagerly, leaning forward. He touched his fingertips to the light-filtering viewport, looking out at the double star and its brilliant corona, which rippled like a barely contained inferno.

Brakiss smiled again. "You're ambitious as always, young Zekk." He placed a firm hand on his prize student's shoulder. "But do not be impatient. There is more you must learn, much more. You've been such a voracious learner, surpassing my greatest expectations about how capable you are of using the power you were born with. You easily accomplish the exercises I set for you—but there comes a time when every Jedi trainee must be tested to the limit." Brakiss raised his eyebrows. "Tamith Kai continues to flaunt her greatest student, Vilas, who has been training here for more than a year. But you are learning so much faster. I believe you have reached that stage, Zekk."

He reached into his silvery robes and grasped something there, but hesitated, meeting the dark-haired boy's steady gaze. "I know you are ready for this. Do not disappoint me."

"What is it, Master Brakiss?" Zekk asked.

From the folds of his robe Brakiss removed a dark, ornate cylinder. "The time has come for you to have your own lightsaber."

Zekk took the ancient Jedi weapon and stared at it in wonder. Even deactivated, it felt powerful in his hand. He squeezed the grip and swung the handle back and forth, imagining a crackling energy blade. It felt good. Very good.

"Normally," Brakiss said, "I would have suggested that you build your own weapon. But it takes time and intense concentration to assemble the components, understand the workings. And we have not the time. Through the dark side, many things are easier, more efficient. Take this lightsaber as my gift to you; wield it well in the service of the Second Imperium."

"May I turn on the power?" Zekk whispered, still in awe.

"Of course."

Brakiss stood back as Zekk activated the lightsaber. A scarlet beam lanced outward, glowing like lava. "This is a masterful weapon," Brakiss said. "It has already been attuned for use by the dark side."

Zekk swiveled his wrist left and right, listening to the hum of the powerful cutting edge.

"In fact, this lightsaber is very similar to the one Darth Vader used," Brakiss pointed out.

Zekk struck out against the air. "When can I train with it?" he said. "How will I learn?"

Brakiss led the young man out of the observation tower. "We have simulation rooms," he said. "A while ago, I spent some time training your friends Jacen and Jaina. Very disappointing. They did learn how to use lightsabers, but they resisted me each step of the way.

"I expect you, on the other hand, to excel in every routine. *You*, Zekk, will quickly surpass anything your friends accomplished. And I know Master Skywalker and his fears—he is too nervous to train his precious younger students with their own lightsabers. He considers the energy blades too dangerous." Brakiss laughed. "His fears are misplaced. The most truly dangerous thing is a Dark Jedi *wielding* such a weapon."

As Zekk accompanied his teacher down the corridor, he switched off the lightsaber and held its sturdy handle in his grip. He looked down at the legendary Jedi weapon and ran his finger over its case.

The lightsaber felt warm, ready . . . begging to be used. The afterimage of the scarlet blade still blazed across his vision.

Zekk tried to blink it away, but the bright line remained. At last he said, "Yes, I can see how such a weapon could be very dangerous indeed."

7

JACEN COULDN'T HELP brooding as he wandered aimlessly through the halls of the Jedi academy, keeping to the shadowy corridors that were least used by other students. Jaina walked beside him in stunned silence, as she had for the past two hours. She seemed to need her brother's company as much as he needed hers, though neither of them knew quite what to say.

Jacen still couldn't understand why Uncle Luke hadn't allowed anyone else to stay with the unconscious Tenel Ka while the medical droid tended her. Neither had he allowed anyone to be present when he went to the Comm Center to contact Tenel Ka's family and inform them of the accident.

Uncle Luke himself had scooped up Tenel Ka's limp form and rushed her back to the Great Temple. As the twins hurried behind, Jacen had sensed the Jedi Master drawing on the Force to help the injured young woman maintain her strength, as well as to move faster and to keep from jarring her. At the same time, he had sent a continuous stream of soothing thoughts toward Tenel Ka's unconscious mind, thoughts of peace and healing.

Jacen had known he should try to do the same, to help his friend in any way he could, but his thoughts were in such a turmoil that he was afraid his attempts would only make things worse. Perhaps that was why Master Skywalker hadn't let any of them stay with the warrior girl once they returned to the Great Temple. He had assured the friends that he would call instantly if Tenel Ka asked for them.

Since then, the twins had roamed up and down stairways and dim passages, both of them alone with their private thoughts. When Lowie joined them without a word, neither asked where he had been. After all, he often went out to the tall trees alone, to sit and think about his home on Kashyyyk, his parents, his younger sister. . . . Now he was ready to be with friends again. But Jacen was not surprised to note, when he glanced down at Em Teedee, that the little droid had been shut off.

They were all disturbed by what had happened—no one more so than Jacen. He replayed the scene over and over in his mind as they walked: the sizzling, popping sound of the lightsabers as they clashed, the look of challenge in Tenel Ka's eyes, the glowing green of his own energy blade passing *through* hers. . . . He squeezed his eyes shut in an effort to block the rest from his mind, but that was a mistake. The scene was too vivid in his memory. His eyes flew open again.

"I can't wait any longer," he choked. "I have to see Tenel Ka to make sure she's all right—and to apologize to her."

"We'll go with you," Jaina said. Lowie purred his agreement.

When the three Jedi trainees reached the room where their friend had been treated, they saw Luke Skywalker emerging, Artoo-Detoo at his side.

"How's Tenel Ka?" Jacen asked immediately. "Is she awake? Can we see her?"

Luke Skywalker hesitated, and Jacen could see the concern written on his face. "She's still recovering from the . . . shock," he said. "She *is* awake now, but she's not quite ready to see you yet."

"But a time like this is when she needs her friends most," Jaina said.

Artoo-Detoo swiveled the top of his domed head back and forth once and buzzed an emphatic negative.

"But I have to see her," Jacen objected. "I need to do *something* for her—tell her jokes, hold her hand. . . . Blaster bolts! She only *has* one hand now, and I'm the one who's responsible."

Artoo gave a low mournful whistle, and Luke looked at his nephew in sympathy. "I know this is hard for you," he said, "but it's even harder for Tenel Ka. I remember the thoughts that went through my head when I lost my own hand on Cloud City, fighting with Darth Vader. I had just learned that he was my father. It felt as if I had lost a part of myself, a part of who I was . . . and then I lost my hand, too."

"But hands can be fixed," Jaina pointed out. "They can be reattached and healed in bacta tanks."

Luke shook his head. "My hand was gone. There was nothing to reattach."

"But your synthetic hand works just as well as your old one did," Jacen said.

"Perhaps," Luke said, flexing his lifelike prosthetic and running the artificial thumb along his fingertips, "but it was a difficult decision to make. I remember thinking that maybe I had just taken another step toward becoming more like my father, like Darth Vader—partly alive, but partly a machine. Tenel Ka will have to face the same decision herself. When her lightsaber exploded, it destroyed any chance we had of reattaching that arm."

"Uncle Luke, I need to see her," Jacen pleaded. "I *have* to apologize."

Luke squeezed his shoulder. "I promise to call you the moment she's ready to talk. Try to get some rest now."

Jacen slept fitfully, tossing and turning as images of a wounded Tenel Ka haunted his dreams.

"We are opponents," he heard her say.

"No. I'm your friend," Jacen tried to answer, but his voice was trapped in his throat; he could make no sound. He felt again the sickening jolt as her lightsaber dissolved beneath his and the sizzling green energy blade sliced through her arm.

The smell of singed flesh clawed at his nostrils. The sound of her exploding rancor-tooth weapon crashed against his eardrums, and his vision filled with the image of Tenel Ka's cool gray eyes, clouded with accusation.

"We are opponents. . . ."

Jacen felt something push at his mind, and he woke drenched in sweat, his single light blanket damp and tangled around his legs. He wasn't quite certain what had awakened him, but he knew it was somehow urgent. *It's Tenel Ka. She needs us.* The thought came unbidden to his mind. Through his open window, from the direction of the jungle he heard the faint ululating howl of a Wookiee.

Jumping from his sleeping pallet, he hurriedly fastened the front of the rumpled orange flight suit he had never quite bothered to take off when he'd lain on his bed. The distant howl came again, and Jacen could sense that Lowie, meditating at the top of a high Massassi tree, must be trying to tell him something. Without bothering to put on a pair of boots, he bolted out of his room and called at his sister's doorway.

"Jaina, wake up. Something's wrong." He raced on down the hallway, not waiting for her reply. But something—perhaps Lowie's call—had already wakened his sister, because he hadn't even turned the corner before he heard Jaina running down the hall after him. He didn't slow, though. Bare feet slapping against the cold flagstones, he rushed out the nearest exit and down one of the Great Temple's external stairways, taking the torchlit steps three at a time. He felt the nudge against his mind again and headed in the direction it had come from: the landing pad.

As he rounded the corner of the temple, with Jaina hard on his heels, he was surprised to see Lowie coming toward them from the jungle, where eerie night mists blanketed the ground with translucent white. On the landing field, though, Jacen saw something that surprised him even more.

A small, sleek shuttle, about half the size of the *Millennium Falcon*, lifted off the grassy stubble of the landing pad, blasting away wisps of ground fog. And there, bathed in the blue glow from the landing lights, his hair whipping wildly in the breeze, stood Luke Skywalker.

The Jedi Master was facing the shuttle, one arm raised as if in farewell, as the three young Jedi Knights raced up to him. Jacen and Jaina spoke at the same moment.

"Who was that?"

"What's going on?"

The tall, gangly Wookiee added a questioning bark of his own.

Luke Skywalker lowered his eyes to look at his Jedi students.

"It was Tenel Ka, wasn't it?" Jacen persisted, without really needing to hear the answer. In the dimness, his gaze locked with his uncle's, and the Jedi Master nodded.

"Her family insisted on coming immediately to pick her up. She should be in good hands now—don't worry."

Jacen felt as if a bantha had just stepped on his chest. He struggled for enough breath to speak. He felt betrayed. "She's gone! You said you'd call us when Tenel Ka was ready to see us."

Luke Skywalker cleared his throat. "She wasn't ready."

Lowie gave a despairing groan.

"But we didn't even get a chance to say good-bye," Jaina said.

Her uncle sighed. "I know. But she's with family now. They'll take care of her."

Jacen saw his sister shake her head in confusion. "But how can that be true?" Her question made no sense to him, and he looked at her, waiting for her to explain. "What I mean is," she went on, "why would Tenel Ka's family from Dathomir come for her in *that* shuttle?"

Jacen shrugged, feeling as if she expected him to understand. He didn't. "What's so strange about it?" he asked finally.

"That was an *Express*-class ambassadorial shuttle," she said. "And it had the markings of the Royal House of Hapes."

Three pairs of questioning eyes turned toward Luke Skywalker.

8

THE PASSENGERS' QUARTERS aboard the Hapan royal shuttle *Thunder Wraith* were spacious and equipped with every convenience a space traveler could desire. The elegant appointments of the cabin fell just short of ostentation; the chief adornment on each wall consisted of an ornate gilt frame surrounding a massive viewscreen.

Tenel Ka took no notice of the spectacular view, however. She had seen hyperspace before. She had no desire to see anything. Or anyone.

Or to *feel* anything. Numb. That was what she felt. Mind, emotions . . . even her arm. All numb.

The thought crossed her mind briefly that perhaps she ought to eat something. She'd had no food since before . . . since *before*.

No, she decided. No food. She could not work up enthusiasm for eating, or anything else, for that matter.

Her reddish-gold braids hung in tangled disarray around her face. Though the medical droid had done a serviceable job of washing her body and disinfecting the wound before cauterizing it, the droid had no programming on what to do with hair. It had kindly offered to shave Tenel Ka's head for her, but she had declined. One of the twins might have been willing to help her comb through the mess and rebraid it. But she'd been too proud to let her friends see her in her current condition, afraid of the disgust she might see on their faces—or worse yet, pity.

At least that was one good thing about having been spirited away from Yavin 4 in the middle of the night, Tenel Ka thought: she didn't have to see anyone, and so would be spared both sympathy and derision.

As if to dispel Tenel Ka's only comforting thought, Ambassador Yfra chose that moment to appear. Her grandmother's aging henchwoman, for all her kindly smiles and refined features, was still cut from the same cloth as the former queen—power-hungry and more than willing to do whatever it took to add to her personal power. Not long ago, Yfra had tried to visit Yavin 4, but when her friends were kidnapped by the Shadow Academy, Tenel Ka had gone with Master Skywalker to rescue them. Tenel Ka had not been disappointed to miss the ambassador, who had canceled the visit. She had never trusted the woman and disliked her instinctively.

"Are you feeling any better, my dear?" the ambassador said with nauseating insincerity. "Would you like to talk?"

"No," Tenel Ka said stubbornly. "Thank you." Then curiosity began to tickle her numbed brain, and she asked, "Why were you the one chosen to bring me home?"

"Actually," Yfra said, not meeting Tenel Ka's eyes, "I wasn't so much *chosen* as I was . . . convenient. I was in a nearby star system on business, you see, when your grandmother received word of your . . . unfortunate accident.

"Now, my dear," she continued, "we'll be coming out of hyperspace in a few hours, so if there's anything I can do in the meantime—"

"Yes, there is," Tenel Ka interrupted in her usual forthright manner. "I wish to be left alone."

If the ambassador was put off by the abrupt answer, she covered it well. "Why, of course you do, my dear," she said with gracious insincerity. "You've been through *such* an ordeal." She looked meaningfully at Tenel Ka's arm and artfully pretended to suppress a shudder of revulsion. "You must feel simply terrible."

With that, Yfra withdrew, managing to leave Tenel Ka feeling even worse than she had before—which might actually have been what the ambassador wanted. The ruthless henchwoman was a skilled manipulator.

Tenel Ka looked at her left arm—what remained of it, after her faulty lightsaber had exploded. There had been no chance of salvaging the limb and allowing it to heal in a bacta tank. She was no longer complete.

How could she be a true warrior now? She could not even claim her wound as the honorable result of battle. Her injury had, in fact, been caused by her own pride. And haste. And stupidity. If only she had taken more care in choosing her lightsaber components. If only she had been more meticulous in assembling the weapon. . . .

Certain that her success or failure in battle would depend on her physical skills, she had not bothered to use her best talents when constructing her weapon. Even during her Jedi training, Tenel Ka had always proudly tried to rely solely on her natural abilities, refusing to use the Force unless there was no other way to accomplish her goals.

But now what had become of her fighting prowess? How could she ever again climb a building using nothing but her fibercord, her grappling hook, and her own wits? How would she climb a tree? Or hunt? Or swim? Why, she couldn't even braid her own hair! And who would respect a Jedi with only one arm?

Lost in such grim thoughts, Tenel Ka drifted into sleep. The next thing she heard was a tapping on the door to her stateroom.

"My dear, are you resting?" Ambassador Yfra called in her cultured voice. "Time to come out now. We're almost home. We're near Hapes."

Tenel Ka shook herself awake, stood, and looked at the viewscreens around her. The *Thunder Wraith* was no longer traveling in hyperspace. The stars and planets of the Hapes Cluster lay all about her, like handfuls of rainbow gems from Gallinore scattered on rich black velvet.

"Did you hear me, my dear?" the ambassador's voice came through the door again. "You're home."

"Home," Tenel Ka repeated. The dread she had been feeling congealed into a ball of ice in the pit of her stomach, as she considered that this place might indeed be her home from now on.

Immense warships, Hapan Battle Dragons, appeared as if out of nowhere to escort the tiny shuttle to its landing area. When the *Thunder Wraith* finally landed and Tenel Ka disembarked, she looked around with the first trace of eagerness she had felt since the lightsaber accident, searching for her parents. She was surprised, however, to find that her grandmother, Ta'a Chume, was the only relative present.

The former queen, accompanied by a large honor guard in full ceremonial garb, stepped forward to greet her granddaughter. Tenel Ka endured an embrace and a showy display of affection—although her grandmother *never* hugged her in private—and asked, "Why did my parents not come?"

"They were called away," Ta'a Chume answered smoothly, "on an urgent and top-secret diplomatic . . . matter. Only I and my most trusted confidant know their whereabouts." She motioned to one of her retainers, who strode forward to drape a royal robe across Tenel Ka's shoulders. Its thick, soft folds hid Tenel Ka's arms, and she did not have the energy to object. "But," her grandmother continued, "I assure you that your parents will return as quickly as they are able."

Four pairs of scantily clad male servants appeared, bringing cushioned seats for the princess and her grandmother. Tenel Ka sat, and only then noticed that at least two dozen more handsome servants had filed onto the landing pad. She closed her eyes and sighed. She might have known. It seemed that in her parents' absence, Ta'a Chume had decided to receive Tenel Ka with as much spectacle and fanfare as possible—perhaps to prove to her aspiring-Jedi granddaughter how wonderful it was to be a member of the royal family.

Tenel Ka was not thrilled.

Three brawny young men, dressed only in loincloths, moved to the center of the landing pad and began a rhythmic display of their gymnastic abilities. Other servants along the sidelines produced stringed instruments and flutes and began a musical accompaniment. During their performance, the former queen leaned toward her granddaughter and murmured, "You are so fortunate."

Tenel Ka blinked in surprise.

Her grandmother made an all-encompassing gesture. "Everything you see—Hapes and its sixty-three worlds—is yours to command." Her voice took on a persuasive tone. "Not many who fail to become Jedi Knights have such a pleasant alternative. After all, unlike the weapons of battle, wielding political power does not require the use of both arms."

Tenel Ka grimaced, not only at her grandmother's unfair assertion that she had failed in her Jedi training, but also because one of the acrobats had performed a double handspring—an act she had done countless times herself, and one she'd always assumed she'd go right on doing. She had even included flips, cartwheels, and handsprings in her daily exercises at the Jedi academy. The Jedi academy . . . she missed it already.

When the gymnasts finished, a young man stepped forward and began to juggle with phenomenal agility. Tenel Ka grew more uncomfortable as she watched him pass fire crystals, hoops, and blazing torches from hand to hand, tossing them high into the air with ever-increasing speed.

Another thing I will never be able to do, Tenel Ka thought, pressing her lips into a grim line.

She tried to concentrate on the juggler's face instead. The young man was indeed beautiful, but right then Tenel Ka would have traded every servant and guard on the landing platform for just a glimpse of a face that was friendly: Jacen, Jaina, Lowbacca, even Master Skywalker. . . .

"You know," her grandmother said, leaning toward her again, as if a thought had just occurred to her, "perhaps your injury was the

Force's way of showing you that you were never meant to be a Jedi Knight—that your destiny has always been to rule Hapes."

Tenel Ka's breath left her in a rush, as if a rancor had stepped on her stomach. She wondered if perhaps, for once, her grandmother might not be right.

9

THE ACOUSTICS IN the grand audience chamber on Yavin 4 could carry even a whispered word from the stage to every seat in the hall. But today no lecturer stood at the far end of the long chamber, and Jaina's steps were so slow and hesitant that her booted feet made no sound. With the exception of Jacen and Lowie, who sat on stone benches near the front, the audience chamber remained completely empty.

No, not quite empty. Images of a confident young warrior from Dathomir filled Jaina's vision: Tenel Ka raising her cup in a pledge of friendship, Tenel Ka braiding her long hair in preparation for Jedi training exercises, Tenel Ka scaling the outer walls of the Great Temple, pulling herself up easily hand-over-hand. Jaina could sense through their connection in the Force that similar thoughts troubled her twin brother.

Just moments after Jaina took a seat near Jacen, the Jedi historian and instructor Tionne appeared through a side door and came to stand near the three trainees. Jaina felt her brother's mood brighten at the sight of the silvery-haired Jedi woman. Tionne had taught them to look for multiple solutions to any problem, to find choices, fresh perspectives, new alternatives. As always, Jaina was struck by the wisdom in the mother-of-pearl eyes, wisdom gained from years of studying the tales and lore of ancient Jedi.

Tionne's voice was soft and melodious. "Master Skywalker has asked me to . . . help you to move forward in your lightsaber training."

Jaina shifted uncomfortably, not wanting to think about the deadly weapon she wore clipped to a utility loop on her orange jumpsuit.

Tionne motioned to the three seated trainees. "Please. Come up on the platform where we have more room to work."

Jacen and Lowie mounted the steps, but Jaina hung back, not sure if she could express her reluctance. But when Tionne beckoned again, smiling at her with kind patience, Jaina found herself moving to join the others.

With each step, her lightsaber bumped against her leg, a grim reminder of its deadly presence. Her heart began to pound with dread, and a cold sweat broke out on her neck and forehead. Continuing with her lightsaber training, she could see now, was going to be even more difficult than she had expected, and Jaina could tell from the set of Jacen's jaw that her brother was also struggling to control his own anxiety. He must have sensed her difficulty too, because he turned to her with a shaky smile. "Want to hear a joke?"

She forced a laugh. "Why not?"

This took her brother by surprise, and he paused a moment to think. "Okay, why is a droid mechanic never lonely?"

Jaina shrugged, knowing better than to attempt an answer.

"Because he's always making new friends!"

Jaina giggled in spite of herself, grateful for the release in tension. Lowie let loose a bark of laughter as well. A dimple appeared in Tionne's cheek, and the approving glow in her alien eyes showed that she understood how hard this must be for all of them.

Then, spacing the trainees two meters apart, each facing the same direction, Tionne took them through a series of exercises, using only the hilts of their lightsabers. Clearing her mind of all else, Jaina echoed the instructor's strong, fluid movements as if she were performing a dance.

Apparently satisfied with their progress, Tionne ended the exercise and came to stand in front of Lowie. Gesturing for Jaina to take a position beside her, facing Jacen, Tionne pressed a stud on the handle of her weapon and a shimmering silver beam sprang from it, coruscating with energy.

"Please ignite your lightsabers," she said.

Though a frown of doubt crossed Jacen's face, he soon held a glowing emerald blade. With a snap-hiss, Lowie's blade appeared too, blazing a deep gold, like molten bronze. He held it at his side.

"Oh, *do* be careful, Master Lowbacca," Em Teedee said from the Wookiee's waist. "You know how delicate my circuitry is."

Biting her lower lip, Jaina closed her eyes and touched a button on her lightsaber. Her weapon whooshed to life; the flare of its electric-violet beam and the light of the three other energy blades penetrated even through her shut eyelids, bringing with them a flood of vivid memories.

Violet. The color of the evil Nightsister Tamith Kai's eyes.

Silver. Brakiss's flowing robes. The Shadow Academy. Jacen and Jaina dueling with each other in holographic disguise. A mistake by either of them could have meant death.

Bronze. Almost the reddish gold of Tenel Ka's hair. Tenel Ka's severed arm, still holding the handle of the failed lightsaber as it exploded. The shock on Tenel Ka's face as an emerald blade sliced through her arm.

Emerald green. The color of Zekk's eyes, surrounded by a dark corona. Zekk, who was even now being trained on the Shadow Academy, learning to serve the Second Imperium and using the dark side of the Force. And if the Second Imperium attacked the New Republic as planned—the New Republic that Jaina and Jacen and Luke Skywalker's other Jedi Knights had sworn to protect—she would be forced to fight. How could she not defend the New Republic, when her mother was its leader?

Would she have to face Zekk with a lightsaber to protect her own mother?

With a cry, Jaina switched off her weapon and dropped it to the flagstones, backing away from it as if it had turned into a krayt dragon. An instant later all lightsabers were extinguished, and Jaina shuddered with relief.

Tionne's pearly eyes were grave as she looked at her three young charges. Picking up Jaina's discarded lightsaber, she seated herself on the cool stone of the raised platform and said, "Please, make yourselves comfortable. I need to tell you a story."

Jaina, Jacen, and Lowie settled in a tight half-circle around her, crowding close, needing the contact. Tionne sat straighter and held her delicate hands before her, moving them as she wove her tale like an invisible tapestry before their eyes.

"Thousands of years ago, in a time of great evil and great good," Tionne began in her rich musical voice, "there lived a woman named Nomi Sunrider with her husband Andur, who was training to be a Jedi Knight.

"When Nomi and her husband traveled to take a gift of precious Adegan crystals to Andur's new Jedi Master, they were stopped by a group of greedy bandits, who killed Nomi's husband and tried to steal the crystals. But when Nomi saw her husband lying dead, she snatched up his lightsaber and took a deadly revenge on his murderers. Afterward, seeing what she had done, Nomi was so filled with revulsion that she vowed never to touch a lightsaber again.

"To fulfill the dying wish of her husband, Nomi carried the crystals to his Jedi Master, Thon. There she stayed with her baby daughter Vima and began her own training to become a Jedi. She learned and grew in wisdom and the Force, but still she refused to touch a lightsaber, although it was the weapon of the Jedi.

"Eventually, however, there came a day when she discovered that her power with the Force alone could not protect the ones she loved. To save her beloved Jedi Master and to guard her daughter, Nomi once again took up a lightsaber and fought for what she knew was right.

"But by this time Nomi understood the purpose and meaning of the lightsaber—and from that day forward she fought with all the power of the light side of the Force. She was never eager to use her lightsaber, but she knew it was occasionally necessary. By learning to accept this, she became a great Jedi Master and a great warrior."

As the story ended, Jaina drew a deep refreshing breath, coming out of the near trance she entered whenever listening to Tionne's tales. Jaina sensed that much of the horror she had felt earlier had already drained away, though her muscles were as sore and weary as if she herself had fought all of Nomi Sunrider's lightsaber battles.

Jaina felt something heavy and solid slide into her hand. She glanced down to see the handle of her lightsaber. Tionne had slipped it to her.

"No need to turn it on for now," the Jedi instructor said gently, looking directly into Jaina's brown eyes. "I think we've come far enough for today."

10

DOCTORS WERE BORN meddlers, Tenel Ka decided with annoyance.

The fifth court physician in as many hours continued explaining in a calm, patronizing voice that, although Tenel Ka was perfectly correct in not desiring a crude droid arm, she could have *no* objection to a lifelike biomechanical prosthetic replacement. (Apparently they thought they knew her better than she knew herself.) Tenel Ka finally raised the stump of her arm in exasperated surrender and let the doctor have her way. The physician looked satisfied and not at all surprised that Tenel Ka had agreed. After all, it had been the only reasonable choice.

The doctor beckoned to one of her nurses, and the man came forward to begin taking measurements of the stump of Tenel Ka's left arm. Next, an engineer placed electrodes against her scarred skin and sent intermittent jolts of electricity into the flesh—to measure the nerve conduction, she explained.

Meanwhile, the nurse placed Tenel Ka's right arm in a holographic imaging chamber. Each time the engineer administered a jolt to Tenel Ka's stump, the nurse patted her shoulder comfortingly and asked her to hold still. The man took great pride in telling her how the holographic image would be reversed to make a pattern that could be used as the mold for her new biosynthetic left arm.

Like children let loose at a sweets bazaar, physicians buzzed around the room snapping orders, conferring with each other, and making preparations. Allowing the poking and prodding and the chaos of voices to fade into the background, Tenel Ka sank into her own thoughts.

As the daughter of two strong ruling families, one from Hapes and one from Dathomir, Tenel Ka had long known who and what she was. Her philosophy of life had been as clear in her mind as her views on lineage, loyalty, friendships, and even her own physical abilities and limitations.

If one of those components changed, did everything else change as well?

From childhood, Tenel Ka's parents had taught her to make her own decisions based in equal part on reason, fact, and personal belief. Therefore, she had never been one to sit passively while others made choices for her. Yet, since the loss of her arm, hadn't she done just that?

She had hardly given it a thought when Ambassador Yfra appeared in the middle of the night to whisk her away from Yavin 4 in secret. In these last few days on Hapes, Tenel Ka had allowed her grandmother to control her movements and communications, tell her when to sleep, bring all her meals, and select appropriate clothing for her. And now Tenel Ka, who had always relied on her own mind and body, was allowing herself to be fitted for a biomechanical arm.

Had she truly changed so much?

The Force was a part of her, flowing through her just as the blood of her parents flowed through her veins. But this artificial arm was no part of her. If she accepted it, then she was allowing the loss of her limb to change her in ways that reached deeper than the eye could see. She didn't object to changing—but this change was not for the better. If she allowed herself to be transformed, it should be in the direction of becoming stronger or wiser.

Tenel Ka's reverie was cut short by the sound of whirring servomotors. The doctor and an engineer stood before her holding a grotesque metallic arm. A droid arm. It reminded Tenel Ka of the unwieldly contraption she had heard the former TIE pilot Qorl now wore since going back to serve the Second Imperium. Tenel Ka shook her head in wordless denial.

"Now this is only temporary, of course," the doctor said with the same infuriating condescension she had used before. "Just accustom yourself to it while we're synthesizing the biomechanical arm."

Tenel Ka decided then and there that she had not, in fact, changed that much. If she needed to use the Force from now on to assist her in small ways, then so be it. But she refused to become dependent on a machine that masqueraded as part of herself.

"No," she managed to croak when the doctor moved to attach the mechanical arm to her severed limb. The engineer backed away uneasily, but the doctor continued as if Tenel Ka had not spoken.

"This is all part of the process of making you whole again," the doctor said in her maddening voice, "and that is exactly what you want."

"No," Tenel Ka repeated, setting her jaw stubbornly. Anger seethed inside her at the doctor's confident presumption that she knew what was best.

The doctor shook her head and bent down, as if chiding a young child. "Now, you agreed to be fitted for this new arm and—"

"I've changed my mind," Tenel Ka gritted, clamping down on her temper to hold it in check.

The doctor's lips were still smiling, but grim determination shone in her eyes, indicating she would never take no for an answer—not from any patient of *hers*. The woman kept up a steady stream of talk and motioned for the engineer to help her position the droid prosthetic against the stump of Tenel Ka's arm, as if the doctor thought that by forging ahead she could overwhelm her patient's determination with her own.

"Now, there's no disgrace in having a biomechanical arm, you know. Even your great Jedi Master Skywalker has a prosthetic hand."

Tenel Ka acknowledged inwardly that there had been no weakness in Master Skywalker's choice. It made him no more or less than what he was. He had wrestled with his own decisions and made his own choices, just as she must make hers. The Jedi Master would not ask her to do otherwise—as the people who surrounded her here on Hapes seemed intent on doing.

"Your new arm will look quite natural," the doctor went on in her exasperating, soothing voice, "and your grandmother has spared no expense."

When the cold metal of the mechanical limb touched Tenel Ka's arm, she lost the last vestiges of control over her anger.

"No!" Tenel Ka cried, unconsciously using the Force to give the engineer and the doctor a backward shove. The droid arm was already clamped in place against her skin, however, like a protruding cancerous growth.

"*I said NO!*" Tenel Ka quite consciously used the Force to yank the contraption free and fling it with blinding speed against the nearest wall. It hit the stones with a clang and a crunch and fell in pieces to the cold tile floor.

Gasps went up from all around the room, and a dozen pairs of eyes regarded her with shock and apprehension.

Having vented her fury, Tenel Ka's voice was now quite calm. "And I meant no."

11

THE BUZZING VIBRATION of the T-23 skyhopper both soothed and unsettled Jacen for some reason he could not define.

Up in the cockpit with Lowie, Em Teedee amplified his speaker volume to be heard above the whine of the engines. "Really, Master Lowbacca, I don't see what the point of all this flying about could be, without even so much as a destination in mind."

At Lowie's soft growl, the little droid replied, "Therapeutic? For what? And in any case, I should think that performing some sort of physical exercise would be far more beneficial than flying aimlessly over the treetops."

Jaina sat pensively beside Jacen in the skyhopper's cramped passenger seat, toying with her lightsaber. "We actually tried that, Em Teedee, but lately it seems like any exercise we do only reminds us of the things we were trying to get our minds off of in the first place."

Jacen was surprised to hear Jaina answering the pesky little droid just as Lowie had addressed it a moment earlier—without annoyance, and as a friend. In fact, a full day had passed since any of them had had the heart to switch Em Teedee off. It was as if they hoped the little translator's chatter might fill the void that none of them wished to think about.

But something *was* missing, Jacen thought. Different. Under normal circumstances he probably would have been crowded into the tiny cargo well behind the passenger seat . . . and he would have happily endured that discomfort, if it meant that Tenel Ka could have been with them, sitting where he now sat.

"Oh, dear me!" Em Teedee said in a much subdued voice. "How terribly insensitive my processor can be. You've all been thinking of Mistress Tenel Ka, haven't you? I *am* dreadfully sorry."

Jacen saw Lowie reach down to give the little droid what looked like a comforting pat. Now that Em Teedee had brought up the subject the friends had been avoiding, Jacen felt Tenel Ka's absence all the more keenly.

"It's okay, Em Teedee," Jaina said. "We all miss her."

Jacen sighed. "I wish I could just talk to her."

Jacen, Lowie, and Em Teedee voiced agreement. Then, as though they had discussed it and come to a unanimous decision, Lowie turned the T-23 about and headed back to the Jedi academy.

Master Luke Skywalker looked down at his small barrel-shaped astromech droid as they entered the hangar bay at the base of the Great Temple. "I'm fine, Artoo," he said, answering the droid's questioning whistle. "I just have an important decision to make."

Luke frowned and thought back on the direct communication he had just sent to the Fountain Palace on Hapes. He had been unable to get hold of Prince Isolder and Teneniel Djo, Tenel Ka's parents. Instead, Ta'a Chume, the matriarch of the Royal House, had come on-screen and told him in no uncertain terms that Tenel Ka's parents were traveling outside the Hapes Cluster and could not be reached, and that the princess herself had already endured enough trauma because of her Jedi training. Under no circumstances would the young woman be allowed to speak with Master Skywalker. With that, the former queen had abruptly terminated the connection, leaving Luke with an entirely new set of concerns.

Tenel Ka's grandmother had never approved of the direction the girl had chosen for her own life. The harsh old woman had always wanted to mold her granddaughter into a scheming politician of whom she could be proud—someone just like herself.

What if, Luke wondered, instead of supporting and comforting Tenel Ka during this time of turbulence, her grandmother chose to use Tenel Ka's weakness to her own advantage? Without Isolder and Teneniel Djo to support their daughter emotionally, Tenel Ka might be too despondent or confused to make her own choices. It was possible she would blindly accept any decision the matriarch might make on her behalf.

Luke shook his head. Political considerations aside, Tenel Ka would not find the comfort she needed from her grandmother. He thought of the close bond the four young Jedi Knights had developed from working and training together at the academy. Tenel Ka needed that kind of closeness right now. She needed the unselfish caring that Jacen, Jaina, and Lowie could provide.

Luke had no wish to influence Tenel Ka's decision about whether or not to return to Yavin 4; that would have to be her choice, and hers alone. And certainly any competent medical droid could be trusted to tend Tenel Ka's physical wound. But she needed the warmth and support of friends in order to heal her emotional wounds and come to her own decision.

Luke smiled as he saw Lowbacca maneuver the T-23 skyhopper onto its pad in the hangar bay. Those Jedi trainees needed to have their emotional wounds healed as well. He straightened and walked toward the T-23. "I think we'd better do a preflight check on the *Shadow Chaser,* Artoo. Let's get ready to fly."

Artoo warbled and beeped, asking a question.

"Yes," Luke Skywalker said. "I've made my decision."

From the moment her uncle announced he would take them to see Tenel Ka after all, adrenaline began to rush through Jaina's veins. She made a mad dash for her chambers, snatched a fresh jumpsuit, a Jedi robe, and a few other odds and ends, then stuffed them along with her lightsaber into a small flight duffel. By the time she raced back out of her quarters, down the echoing stone stairs and hallways, and out onto the landing pad, where their ship waited, she no longer had any idea what she had packed.

Jacen arrived ahead of her, running up the ramp of the sleek *Shadow Chaser,* a disordered pile of clean clothes tucked under one arm, his lightsaber under the other. Jaina didn't slow as she followed him up the ramp, marveling as she always did at the powerful ship and its glossy quantum armor. The ship had once been the finest craft created by the Second Imperium. After Master Luke Skywalker and Tenel Ka had used it to rescue the twins and Lowie from the Shadow Academy, the New Republic had given the *Shadow Chaser* to the Jedi Master for his own use.

Once Lowie had scrambled aboard with Em Teedee, his lightsaber clipped to the webbed belt at his waist, Luke instructed Artoo-Detoo to raise the boarding ramp, and the *Shadow Chaser* lifted off.

Jaina felt a thrill as the *Shadow Chaser*'s repulsorlifts boosted them off the landing field; sublight engines kicked in, launching them away from the jungle moon. The last few minutes of rushed preparation were a blur in her mind, and she looked around for something else to speed them on their way.

Lowie rumbled a question from the navigation console, and Em Teedee answered, "No, I'm certain Master Luke doesn't need our assistance in plotting the most efficient route."

Her uncle smiled down at the Wookiee. "We'll be going to lightspeed in just a few minutes. Why don't you all try to relax, get some rest."

Jaina took a deep breath and watched the stars through the viewports—like glittering gems sinking in a depthless black sea—until each pinprick of light elongated into a starline and the *Shadow Chaser* made a smooth jump into hyperspace.

The three Jedi trainees found they were too excited to rest, though. They spent the remainder of the journey trying to distract themselves aboard the tiny ship. Jaina and Lowie were just about to remove an access panel to the rear thruster stabilizers to study how they worked when Luke announced their final approach to Tenel Ka's home planet.

The three friends rushed to the cockpit. As they took their seats behind the Jedi Master, Lowie squinted and scanned the star system around them. When she saw his ginger-furred face register surprise, Jaina looked around, seeing no nearby planet that could have been Dathomir.

"That's odd," she said at last. "From the descriptions I've heard and the star charts I've studied, I could swear we were in the Hapes Cluster."

Her uncle swiveled in the pilot seat and met each pair of eyes in turn.

"We *are* in the Hapes system," Luke said gravely. "It's time I explained to you that Tenel Ka is more than just a simple warrior from a backward planet."

12

BROAD-SHOULDERED NORYS, former leader of the Lost Ones gang and new stormtrooper trainee, spread his white armor on the bunk in front of him. He studied the pieces carefully, then began to assemble the glossy outfit, donning the components one at a time—and enjoying every minute of it.

The boots went on first, stiff and sturdy. Then the greaves, the shin armor, the leg plates, body armor, arm plates, and finally the flexible but tough gloves. He felt as if he had been transplanted into the body of an assassin droid, a fighting machine encased in an impenetrable shell.

Norys allowed himself a satisfied smile. This was much more impressive than anything his gang members had ever scrounged deep in the decaying alleys of Coruscant's underworld. He had been the toughest, meanest, angriest young brute of all the gang members. But being a stormtrooper was better . . . so much better.

All of his former companions were also soldier recruits undergoing training. Norys fully expected to be the best among the new troops, just as he had been toughest among the Lost Ones.

On the downside, he was no longer his own boss, free to do as he wished. He had to follow the orders of the Second Imperium. But with armor such as this and the military might of those who followed their Emperor, it was all worth it. Besides, if Norys proved himself valuable enough, his rank would increase, and he'd be placed in command of more soldiers, maybe even fly a TIE fighter. Without a doubt, he would have more power and cause much more damage than he'd ever imagined when he was just a gang leader.

Things were looking up.

The last piece of his stormtrooper outfit was the hard white helmet with black eye goggles and mouth speakers. He slipped the helmet over his head and locked it into place at the neck joint. At last he stood totally encased, completely protected—no longer a disreputable bully with a grimy outfit and stolen scraps as his only possessions.

Now he was someone to be reckoned with: a *stormtrooper*.

Norys marched down the corridor, taking care to clomp loudly on the deck plates with his armored boots. They made such a satisfying sound.

He had memorized the layout of the Shadow Academy station and knew exactly how to get to the private training room where old Qorl, the former TIE pilot, had ordered him to report. Standing outside the sealed door, he keyed in the access code—he'd felt a private thrill when Qorl had given him the secret numbers—and waited for the computer to process his entry request.

With a hiss like an angry serpent, the door slid aside. Norys marched boldly into the shielded room, and the door sealed itself behind him.

Qorl stood inside the training chamber holding a wicked-looking spear in his black-wrapped left hand. His droid replacement arm gripped the gleaming shaft with enough force to dent the metal. The serrated head of the spear had a long central prong with two side spikes curving up like a dragon's barbed tail.

"You're late," Qorl said. He cocked his droid arm back—and hurled the deadly weapon at Norys with all the strength in his robotic servomotors!

Norys stood astonished as the deadly spearpoint hurtled toward his chest plate. He just had time to cry "Hey!" in a panicked voice amplified by his helmet speakers before the barbed tip impacted squarely with enough force to smash him backward.

Norys slammed into the wall, his helmet ringing against the hard metal bulkhead. His vision sparkled with impending unconsciousness. He expected to see a spear sprouting from his heart and waited for his nerves to send shouts of mortal pain. He wanted to scream that Qorl, his supposed teacher, had betrayed him, murdered him—

But a split second later his thoughts cleared enough to hear the clatter as the spear shaft fell harmlessly to the floor. He looked down at his chest in amazement and saw only a nick in the white armor where the spear had struck.

"What did you do that for?" Norys shouted.

Qorl answered in a gruff but calm voice. "To teach you respect for your stormtrooper armor, Norys," he said, "but also to warn you not to become overconfident. Yes, that armor is powerful enough to stop many weapons, such as this crude spear." The TIE pilot nodded toward the jagged weapon on the floor plates.

Norys bent down to grab the spear, narrowing his eyes in rage as he looked at his teacher. The old pilot had made a fool out of him. He felt a dangerous anger boiling through his veins. He had a good mind to take the triple-pronged spear and attack the pompous old man with it.

"But don't think your armor is invincible." Qorl reached inside his uniform, pulled out a deadly blaster pistol, and pointed it directly at Norys. "For instance, this blaster could slice through that armor as if you were wearing nothing at all."

Norys stiffened, looking into the ominous snub barrel of the pistol. His mind raced. What had he gotten himself into? Why was Qorl so upset with him? He wondered whether he could swing the spear, knock the blaster away, and strike down the TIE pilot. That would serve the old man right. . . .

Qorl turned the blaster pistol around and extended it toward Norys, butt end first. "Here. This will be your personal weapon," he said.

Norys dropped the spear to the floor and tentatively took the blaster. The pistol felt very good in his gloved grip. Qorl nodded at him. "For target practice," he said, then went over to the controls by the door.

The gray light-absorbing walls of the windowless room shimmered.

Suddenly Norys found himself standing in a dank, dim cave with fanged stalactites dripping from the walls and ceiling. Long spikes of stalagmites rose like blunt knives from the floor. Unseen water trickled somewhere, and a pallid light seemed to ooze from the pale rock itself. Despite the room's visible transformation, Norys could detect no change in the smell of the air through his helmet filters.

"The walls of this chamber will absorb blaster bolts," Qorl said. "Your weapon has already been set to full power. There won't be much recoil, but you must become accustomed to how it feels to aim and shoot and hit a target. Pay attention now. Watch for them as they attack."

"Watch for what?" Norys said, looking around from right to left. "What's going to attack me?"

The cave seemed more sinister now. The eye goggles distorted his vision, and he tried to compensate. Strange creature noises burbled and hummed from every direction. He couldn't tell if they were insects or rodents, but they sounded vicious to him, as if everything within this chamber might be a predator.

Norys had hunted in the lower alleys of Coruscant, tracking giant granite slugs, multifanged spider-roaches, mutated feral rats—and his intuition told him this was simply a testing chamber on the Shadow Academy. He didn't think there could be any real danger. Not really.

However, this cave certainly seemed real enough. . . .

With a squalling cry, a leathery-winged creature dropped out of its hiding place in the ceiling and swooped toward him. Its eyes were huge and slitted, and Norys could see pointy ears or antennae on top of its head and razor claws at the ends of its flapping wings as it swept down.

A mynock. They weren't supposed to be terrible predators—but from the wicked fangs and claws as it swooped toward him, Norys decided this was one mynock with a bad attitude.

He pointed the blaster and squeezed off an energy bolt, but the beam went wide, striking a stalactite and startling up four more of the angry flying creatures. The new batch of mynocks also attacked, annoyed at him for disturbing their dark slumber.

Norys squeezed the firing button again and again, adjusting his aim as he watched the bright bolts streak through the dimness. The brilliant spears of light dazzled his eyes, and he could barely see through his filtered goggles.

The devilish mynocks swooped and avoided the deadly beams.

This wasn't fair! It was supposed to be target practice. He should have been able to point at a bantha's-eye or hide behind a window while shooting at an unsuspecting target in the streets below, as he had often done on Coruscant.

The blaster missed again and again as mynocks swirled around him, flapping their wings and assailing his ears with skull-splitting screeches. Norys wondered if Qorl had intentionally adjusted the blaster's aimpoint to throw the beam off.

He suddenly realized that he had been aiming wrong. It was his own fault. Reacting wildly to his sudden fear, he had overcompensated.

As the first mynock came toward him again, claws outstretched and long fangs ready to tear him to shreds, he took a second to aim and squeezed off a long bolt that sizzled through the creature's body. The mynock gurgled and fell to the floor, where it was impaled by one of the stalagmites.

"Yes!" Norys shouted in triumph—but three new mynocks swirled around him, attracted by his shout. He fired again and missed. The creatures came at him from the front, side, and behind. Norys turned, remembering to *think,* point, aim, and shoot. He eliminated another creature.

Two more emerged from the ceiling, but Norys swiveled at the waist and forced himself to concentrate. One of the two struck from behind, though its claws skittered off Norys's white stormtrooper armor. He ignored it as he set the second mynock firmly in his sights and shot it.

"Gotcha!" He turned and carefully targeted the remaining creatures, one after another. Gradually, his shooting improved. He learned how to aim. He had learned how to be deadly.

Finally, his blaster pack winking from low charge, Norys stood still and waited—but no more of the creatures emerged from the illusionary cave. He squinted through his goggles, alert for a new attack.

The walls of the cave shimmered and vanished, leaving only the flat metal shell of the training chamber. He allowed himself to relax.

"Good," Qorl said.

Norys turned to see the old TIE pilot standing next to the controls. In the excitement of the exercise, he had forgotten entirely about the military instructor.

"That was fun," Norys said. "I'm getting good at it." He looked down at the blaster, wondering when he'd be able to use it next, when he'd be allowed to practice against a real target.

"You did well enough, Norys," Qorl said again, "but you must remember—*mynocks don't shoot back.*"

Qorl pushed another button on the controls, and the door to the training chamber opened. "Come, we must go to the assembly rooms. Everyone will be there." The old TIE pilot waited for Norys to march ahead of him. "Our Great Leader is planning to address the Shadow Academy."

Zekk sat smothered in his private shell of self-confidence as dozens of Dark Jedi students gathered in the confined room where Master Brakiss and Tamith Kai lectured them in the ways of the dark side.

Zekk wore his padded suit of dark leather armor and sat straight and proud, shoulders squared. His lightsaber hung comfortably at his side. After weeks of training, he had grown fully comfortable with it. It was like a part of him, an extension of his body. That, more than anything else, convinced him he was destined to be a Jedi Knight. He was a loner, but he was also the most powerful of Brakiss's students. The other trainees flashed him occasional glances. Zekk had rapidly surpassed all of them, even those who had been at the Shadow Academy for months and months.

But then, Zekk had the greatest motivation. He wanted to be strong. He wanted everything the Force could give him.

Among those gathered in the assembly hall he noticed Vilas, the Nightsister Tamith Kai's dark-haired and brooding trainee. Vilas, who was from Dathomir, was arrogant and smug, always looking down at him, never letting him forget that it was *he* who had stunned Zekk when he'd resisted capture on Coruscant. Zekk wasn't about to forget. He felt a rivalry with this swarthy young man who talked too often about how he had ridden rancors and summoned storms on Dathomir—as if Zekk was supposed to be impressed.

The ominous Tamith Kai stood next to her protégé Vilas. She and the new Nightsisters had begun training Vilas during the Shadow Academy's construction. They therefore considered him the first of the new Dark Jedi, stronger than the others. For now.

Zekk crossed his arms over his leather-armored chest, knowing that they were wrong. And one day, Zekk told himself, he would prove it.

Burly Norys and the Lost Ones—new stormtrooper recruits taken under the wing of military commander Qorl—stood at attention. The other senior-ranking stormtroopers seemed at ease, while the Lost Ones appeared restless and uncomfortable in their new body armor.

But everyone listened intently to the Great Leader's speech.

In the center of the chamber the overwhelming and awesome image of the Emperor Palpatine filled the open space in the confined room. The glowing hologram towered taller than any person present, a paternal figure and stern watchman.

Crackling from transmission static, the image of the cowled Emperor addressed them from his hideout somewhere in the Core Systems. Yellow reptilian eyes under hooded brows watched the gathered students. The eye of Palpatine was always on them.

"Our plans for the Second Imperium are close to completion," the Emperor said. "All beings are doing their part to return a New Order to our galaxy. Each of you will help my Second Imperium become powerful. Each of you is an important part of a great machine that will crush the Rebellion and put an end to their so-called New Republic."

The holographic image pivoted, giving the impression that Palpatine's gaze was sweeping across each and every person there.

"Our space fleet grows day by day, thanks to the hyperdrive cores and turbolaser batteries stolen in a recent brilliant military ambush. That equipment is helping us create our own battle fleet. Our ships will at first be smaller than the behemoths the New Republic can bring against us—but we shall fight, and we shall win. Our army of Dark Jedi is nearly complete."

The Emperor seemed to grow larger, his image swelling to loom above them. The rippling hood around Palpatine's shriveled face seemed to blow in an unseen wind. His eyes widened, blazing with the light of twin white suns.

The Emperor's voice boomed out, raised to such a volume that Zekk flinched. "Hear me, my Jedi Knights and stormtroopers. The Force does not favor weaklings. *We* have the strength. The Force is with *us*—to victory!"

Then the transmission ended, and the Emperor's cowled silhouette dissolved into sparkles and static.

The entire assembly set up a deafening cheer, in which Zekk joined wholeheartedly.

13

FLANKED BY A pair of Hapan Stinger security escort vehicles, the *Shadow Chaser* touched down lightly on the main landing pad of the Fountain Palace. In the cockpit, Luke Skywalker gave a small sigh of relief. Letting his eyes fall closed for a moment, he reached deep within himself, found the calm core of Force at his center, and then focused outward.

Artoo-Detoo gave a short warble, and Luke opened his eyes to find all three young Jedi Knights already unbuckled from their crash webbing and scrambling toward the exit hatch, barely able to restrain their impatience. Jacen bounced nervously from one foot to another, while Lowie raked fingers through his ginger fur in an effort to smooth it down. Jaina shrugged and looked at him. "Well, what are we waiting for, Uncle Luke?"

Chuckling, Luke released the flight interlocks, and the three Jedi trainees tumbled down the ramp as soon as it began to extend. Ta'a Chume, in the customary half-veil she wore for public appearances, was already waiting on the landing pad with a retinue of guards and attendants. Luke was pleased to see the twins and Lowie greet the old matriarch with courtesy and respect.

The former queen looked coldly at Luke as he began his greeting. "I'm sorry, but your journey here has been a complete waste, Jedi Master. You see, my granddaughter will not be able to speak with—"

Just then Jaina gave a delighted cry, and Jacen yelled, "Hey, Tenel Ka, are we ever glad to see you!" Lowie bellowed a loud Wookiee greeting. The three young visitors rushed across the landing platform to embrace their friend, who had emerged from the sparkling palace. Snatches of the excited conversation drifted to where Luke stood.

"Master Lowbacca wishes to compliment you on how, er, well-rested you look."

"Thought we'd never see you again."

"I am glad you came."

"Want to hear a joke?"

Luke's attention was drawn back to Ta'a Chume when she spoke to her nearest attendant. "I didn't call the princess. How could she possibly—"

"I called to her," Luke said simply.

Ta'a Chume shook her head. "Impossible. We would have picked up any transmission from your ship."

Luke allowed himself the barest smile at her mystification. "I didn't use a transmitter," he said. "I called her through the Force. You may wish it weren't true, but Tenel Ka is already more Jedi than you know."

The matriarch raised her brows, but her eyes were unreadable. "We shall see, Jedi Master. The princess may yet get over that foolish notion."

"Does it matter to you what your granddaughter wants for herself?" Luke asked bluntly. "I know it matters to her parents. When I let her leave my protection on Yavin 4 to return to Hapes, I thought her parents would be here for her. But maybe I shouldn't have sent her away so quickly. Where are Teneniel Djo and your son Isolder?"

Luke saw indecision cloud the matriarch's eyes, and he sensed that she was trying to decide whether she would be better served by the truth or a lie. At last she said, "Although I no longer rule the Hapes Cluster, I still have my sources of information. I learned that an attempt would be made on the lives of the royal family, so I urged my son and his wife to pay a visit of state to another system—to negotiate a liberalization of our trade agreements. The negotiations called for a royal touch, and so my son and his wife were easily persuaded. No one but myself and my most trusted advisor knew when they left or where they went.

"Tenel Ka's accident was an unexpected complication that, unfortunately, may put her in danger, drawing assassins to her, like piranha beetles swarming toward the scent of blood. The princess will be safer here with me than at your primitive temple. She is no longer any of your business, Jedi."

Luke shook his head, unwilling to back down. "Whether or not she remains my business will be for Tenel Ka to decide, when *she* is ready."

Jacen looked around his assigned room and shook his head in amazement. It had been scarcely two hours since he had learned that Tenel Ka was a genuine princess, heir to the entire Hapes Cluster. He hadn't even adjusted to that idea yet. And now this.

His room was more luxurious than any in the Imperial Palace on Coruscant. Rich, exotic scents filled the air, along with the sounds of trickling water, faint music, and chirping avians. Decorative fountains spattered in every room, every corridor, every courtyard, striking musical water chimes.

This was where Tenel Ka had grown up? He still couldn't believe it. Why hadn't she told any of her friends? Uncle Luke had known, of course, but what possible reason could Tenel Ka have had for hiding the truth from her friends for so long? Jacen didn't understand that any more than he understood her refusal to speak to him after he had injured her with his lightsaber.

He cringed again at the thought of the harm he had caused his friend. Jacen had no idea how Uncle Luke had ever talked Tenel Ka's sharp-tongued grandmother into allowing the twins and Lowie to stay on Hapes for an entire month. He only knew that at the appointed time Luke would return to pick up three or—he hoped—four young Jedi Knights.

A whole month. He'd have to talk to Tenel Ka about the accident soon, to clear the air. But what would he say? She wasn't the same person he had known on the jungle moon. Not now. But then, she had never been the person he thought she was, had she? A real Hapan princess! What *could* he say to her?

"May I enter?" The voice startled him out of his reverie, and Jacen turned to find Tenel Ka standing at the door to his chambers.

"Sure . . . I mean, um, of course," he said, blinking in surprise. "I was just thinking about you."

Tenel Ka nodded as if she had known this and swept into the room. Dressed in a long wine-colored gown topped by a rich cape in velvety silver-gray, hair flowing freely down her back in loose, golden-red ripples, Tenel Ka looked like a stranger to Jacen. He found himself tongue-tied.

She stared at him for a long moment, as if he too were a creature from some unknown world, but when she spoke it was the same Tenel Ka. "The room—it is acceptable?"

A thousand questions, apologies, and bits of news clamored in Jacen's mind, waiting to be spoken. But all he could manage to say was "Hey, it's a great room. This is an amazing place. All those fountains."

Tenel Ka nodded again. "This is a fact."

Jacen tingled with an odd pleasure at Tenel Ka's old familiar phrase. Looking into her cool gray eyes, Jacen struggled to collect himself and harness his racing thoughts. At last he managed to blurt out, "I'm really sorry I hurt you, Tenel Ka. It was all my fault."

"I was to blame."

"No," Jacen hurried to say, "I was being stupid. I was so busy trying to impress you with my dueling skills that I didn't even notice when your lightsaber blade started to fratz out!"

"This is not a fact," Tenel Ka said, frowning. "My own pride caused the accident. I believed my fighting prowess could compensate for any deficiency of my weapon. I foolishly believed that the quality of the energy blade was insignificant compared with the quality of the warrior. This was also not a fact."

Jacen shook his head. "Even so, it should never have happened. I should have—"

"The responsibility is *mine,*" Tenel Ka broke in, stamping one foot adamantly, her face flushed with emotion. As if she suddenly felt too hot, she unclasped her cloak and tossed it over the back of a cushioned bench, leaving both of her arms bare.

With a stubborn lift of his chin, Jacen looked at the stump of her left arm. It made him feel sick, and he wanted to turn away. This was the first time he had really seen her injury. "I . . . I won't let you take all the blame. If I'd been letting the Force direct my movements, I would have sensed something was wrong." He pointed to where her arm ended so abruptly. "And *that* would never have happened."

Tenel Ka's eyes flashed with smoky gray fire and, using her right arm to hike up her gown to a comfortable thigh level, she plopped onto the cushioned bench. "And had *I* been using the Force," she argued, "I would already have known my lightsaber blade was inadequate."

"Well, I . . ." Jacen stopped, unable to dredge up a counterargument to convince his infuriatingly proud friend. "I . . ." He cast about furiously for something else to say and finally finished, "Um, want to hear a joke?"

His mouth dropped open in amazement as Tenel Ka burst into peals of laughter. He could tell that this was neither polite amusement nor hysteria, but the laughter of enjoyment that sprang from the heart. It was a wonderful sound—one he had wanted to hear since the first day they met.

"But . . ." Jacen shook his head in confusion. "I didn't even tell my joke."

"Ah," Tenel Ka gasped, and tears of merriment began to stream from her eyes. "Aha. I am so glad you're here."

Jacen shrugged as fresh waves of mirth assailed her. "I'm not objecting, mind you. I just don't get it. What's so funny?"

"We have often been in competition, you and I," she said. "I have missed that. Shall we now compete for the greater share of blame?"

Jacen gave her a lopsided grin. "Nah. I guess all I really need is for you to accept my apology."

Tenel Ka began to object but stopped herself. Her laughter faded and her expression turned sober. As if it took a great deal of effort, she said, "Apology accepted. I . . . forgive you, if that is what you desire." Her last words came out in a whisper: "Jacen, my friend."

Relief rushed through Jacen like a morning breeze clearing remnants of lingering fog. He had been holding his breath, and he nearly choked with emotion at her reply. There were no words to express the flood of feelings that welled up in him, so he sat beside Tenel Ka and put both arms around her.

Tenel Ka returned his hug, as best she could, with both arms. Shaking, she pressed a face wet with tears against his shoulder, and Jacen did not think that they were tears of laughter anymore.

When Tenel Ka and Jacen had both composed themselves, they went in search of Jaina and Lowbacca. Then Tenel Ka took the companions on a whirlwind tour of the Fountain Palace, ending at her own chambers. Because chattering went against her nature, the descriptions she provided were brief and succinct.

When they were alone in her rooms, Tenel Ka showed them her favorite—and most private—place in the Fountain Palace, a completely enclosed terrace garden at the center of her suite of rooms. The three-story-high ceiling was domed, and could be adjusted to simulate any kind of weather and any time of day or night.

The garden room was fifty meters across, its curved walls decorated with scenes from Dathomir. Terraced planters held bushes and trees, cunningly arranged to look as if they were part of the painted primitive landscapes.

At the middle of the garden, smooth stone benches surrounded a tiny artificial lake. Centered in the crystal-clear water, like a miniature volcano emerging from a primordial sea, stood a peaked island with a real waterfall flowing down one side.

"I come here when my heart is heavy, or whenever I miss my mother's homeworld."

"Beautiful," Jaina whispered.

Warmed by her friend's approval, Tenel Ka took a seat on one of the stone benches and gestured for the others to join her. "We may speak freely here," she said, "and I will answer your questions."

And so the friends talked, more frankly than they had ever dared before, until Tenel Ka's grandmother arrived to summon them to evening meal.

"The banquet hall is ready," Ta'a Chume announced.

Tenel Ka's jaw took on a stubborn set. For the first time since her return to Hapes, she felt *alive*. How could her grandmother interrupt now? "We would prefer to eat in privacy," Tenel Ka said, knowing that she was displaying an appalling lack of courtly manners. But she didn't care.

The matriarch gave her granddaughter a smug smile. "I've already taken care of that," she said. "I sent away all my attendants and advisors for the evening."

This was an old game that she and her grandmother played—who could outmaneuver whom—and Tenel Ka took up the challenge. "Then it should be no problem if we choose to eat here."

"Oh, but the serving droids have already gone into the banquet hall," the former queen objected. "The meal will be served directly on the hour."

Tenel Ka saw Jaina glance at her chronometer. "But that's only five minutes from now," Jaina said, her eyes registering surprise. "I'll need some time to wash up first."

Lowie grunted his agreement, and Jacen said, "Hey, me too. I think we'd all be a lot more comfortable if we weren't so formal on our first night here." His grin, aimed at Ta'a Chume, was charming and infectious. "And we're all pretty tired from our travels."

Flashing Tenel Ka a look that said she would not give in so easily next time, the matriarch nodded. "Very well, then. I will have the serving droids sent in."

Ta'a Chume withdrew from Tenel Ka's private sanctuary, and they all relaxed, glad of the reprieve. Tenel Ka looked gratefully around at her friends and then said, "Let me show you to the refresher units before our meal arrives." She had just stood up to lead them to the door when suddenly the polished stone shook beneath her feet. An ear-splitting roar rent the air, along with a heavy blast, throwing Tenel Ka to her knees.

Lowbacca yelped with alarm, and Em Teedee replied, "Dear me, yes! Master Lowbacca wishes to inquire as to the origins of all this noise and commotion."

"Yeah," Jacen said, "you didn't warn us you had groundquakes."

Tenel Ka looked back to see the Wookiee scrambling to his feet and helping the twins back up as well. "That was no groundquake," she said, grimly launching herself toward the door. "Come with me."

Tenel Ka's heart raced, though not with exertion, as the four of them pelted down the corridor toward the private dining hall. Thick smoke billowed from the far end of the vaulted passageway. She felt her stomach clench.

Her dread lessened when a pair of guards emerged from the roiling, sooty clouds, supporting her grandmother. Emergency squads rushed to extinguish the fires still blazing inside the dining hall. Ta'a Chume coughed a few times and waved imperiously for the guards to allow her to walk on her own.

"No one hurt," she croaked.

"It was a bomb?" Tenel Ka asked.

Her grandmother motioned them all back the way they had come. "Yes. In the dining hall," she said. "Must leave immediately."

"*We* were all supposed to be in the dining hall!" Jaina blanched. "So that bomb—"

The matriarch nodded. "—was meant for the princess and me."

14

THE ROYAL YACHT, a Hapan Water Dragon, skimmed across the ocean waves at top speed, its repulsorjets kicking up spray. Bright sunlight shone through its transparisteel windowports, and the fresh smell of saltwater and rafts of seaweed filled the air.

Leaning against a windowport, eyes half shut, Tenel Ka watched the water dance and sparkle. She had always thought of Reef Fortress Island as her summer home, a place to enjoy the warm sun, the surf, and the ocean breezes. But in truth, it was a stronghold, a safe haven in time of danger.

"I feel ill," Jaina said. "Mentally and physically."

Tenel Ka, having been lulled by the yacht's rocking movement as it sped across the water, now straightened and blinked in surprise. "What is wrong, Jaina?"

"Do you realize that a few minutes one way or another, and we might all have been blown to bits by that bomb?" Jaina asked incredulously. "Or maybe I'm just a little seasick from these waves."

Tenel Ka looked at each of her friends in turn. Jaina did not look well. Her straight brown hair, dull with perspiration, clung in damp clumps to her pallid face and neck. Lowie, sitting beside Ta'a Chume as she steered the yacht with nonchalant confidence, seemed too interested in the navigational computer to be affected by the waves. Jacen, on the other hand, looked boyishly enthralled by the experience.

Tenel Ka said to Jaina, "You will recover."

Tenel Ka's grandmother spoke from her position at the helm. Although royal guards accompanied them, the former queen preferred to pilot the craft herself. "We're almost to the fortress now. You'll be safe there."

Tenel Ka's eyes narrowed shrewdly as she noted her grandmother's words. "Should you not have said *we* will be safe?"

"You and your friends will be safe, yes," her grandmother said evasively.

"Where will you be?" Tenel Ka asked.

"Much of the time I'll be with you, but I'm not sure I can trust the investigation of this bombing to anyone else. Until I get to the bottom of the plot against us, I may have to travel back and forth between Reef Fortress and the Fountain Palace."

Jaina looked startled. "And leave us on the island alone?"

"You will have a full complement of guards," Ta'a Chume said soothingly. "And Ambassador Yfra will stay with you whenever I'm away."

Lowbacca snuffled a question from the navigation station. "Master Lowbacca wishes to inquire whether that island up ahead is our final destination," Em Teedee elaborated.

Jacen and Jaina went to the front windowport to look out at the smear of darkness rising from the sun-dappled water.

"Yes," Tenel Ka's grandmother replied, "that is Reef Fortress."

Tenel Ka didn't move forward to look out at the island. She'd been there so many times, she already knew what she would see. It never changed. She closed her eyes, picturing the rocky spires jutting up from the foamy waters of the ocean. She envisioned the water-level entrance to the cave grotto, the steep stone walls of the fortress itself, the crystal-clear cove where she had once loved to swim, the dizzying heights from the parapets along the impenetrable walls where she could walk or run with the wind in her hair, the gently steaming thermal springs in the cellar that provided fresh water for bathing, cooking, and drinking.

Tenel Ka suddenly realized that she had felt homesick after all for this place that held so many of her happiest memories from her childhood, memories of carefree time spent with her parents. The corners of her mouth turned up slightly. Opening her eyes, she moved to stand beside Jacen. "I can't wait to show you my home."

Although the matriarch offered to select quarters for their guests, Tenel Ka insisted on personally choosing an appropriate room for each of the young Jedi Knights.

Lowbacca's chamber was massive, built at a corner where two of the fortress's protective walls met. The room's appointments were basic, its only decorations an ornamental spear on one of the inner walls and a threadbare tapestry on the other. But through the windows on the two outer walls, the room had a spectacular view of the sheer drop from the stone fortress down to the reef rocks and ocean below. Lowbacca stood by the window casement, staring through the force-field screening with such rapt wonderment on his face that Tenel Ka knew she had chosen well for him.

"Do be careful, Master Lowbacca," Em Teedee squeaked in alarm. "If I were to fall down there, I'm sure the damage to my circuits would be irreparable."

For Jaina, Tenel Ka chose what she had always known as the "gadget room." It had belonged to Tenel Ka's great-grandfather, whose hobby had been inventing and tinkering with machines. Fully half of the chamber was filled with workbenches, adjustable-intensity glowpanels, power droids, electrical implements, and odd-looking equipment in various stages of assembly or disassembly. Jaina stayed behind to investigate the fascinating workshop while Tenel Ka showed Jacen the special room she had picked for him.

When they reached the arched doorway, Tenel Ka found herself assailed by an inexplicable bout of nervousness. What if she had judged wrong for her friend? What if Jacen found this room gloomy or dreary, instead of peaceful and soothing? Oh well, she finally decided, she might as well try for the whole effect.

"I would request," she said uncertainly, "that you close your eyes."

"Sure," Jacen said. "Need to clean it up a bit?" He squeezed his brandy-brown eyes shut.

Tenel Ka opened the door with her right hand and reached out to take his arm with her other—only to remember that she had no left hand. Even though Jacen could not have seen, she felt a flush of embarrassment creep into her cheeks as she grasped his arm with her good hand and led him into the room.

"Uh, if it'll make you more comfortable," Jacen quipped, "I can keep my eyes shut the whole time we're at the fortress."

"That will not be necessary." Tenel Ka shut the door behind her and adjusted the lighting. The room was still dim, but that was unavoidable. "You may look now."

She heard his quick intake of breath, and then a whispered exclamation. "Blaster bolts!"

"It is . . . to your liking?" Tenel Ka moved closer to observe Jacen's expression. In the glow of the violet lighting, his smile flashed a fluorescent white. She noted with great satisfaction the delight that lit his face as he used all of his senses to experience this special room.

Tenel Ka's own sense of wonder was renewed as she looked around with Jacen, as if for the first time. A four-meter-high curved aquarium lined the walls of the circular room, unbroken except for the arched doorway through which they had entered. The air tasted salty and tingled pleasantly in her nostrils. Almost hypnotic in its effect, the bubbling and whishing of recirculating water surrounded them. Colorful creatures of all shapes and sizes propelled themselves through the seawater, lit only by specially regulated glowpanels. Moist tropical warmth wrapped them like a blanket, and Tenel Ka stifled a contented yawn.

Jacen followed suit and then chuckled. "I don't think I'll have any problem sleeping in here," he said. "This is just perfect."

She felt him reach out, grope around for her hand, and then give it a squeeze. Tenel Ka sighed. This room was indeed filled with peace.

After they had had an opportunity to refresh themselves, Tenel Ka took her friends to one of her favorite places on the rocky shore of the island, a tiny cove with calm water in an amazing shade of living green. The four of them waded in the sparkling warm waters, joking and splashing, able to forget for a moment the dangers that had brought them to this place.

Jacen and Jaina wore only the undergarments from their flightsuits, which served admirably as swimming gear as well. Tenel Ka herself had changed into a brief lizard-hide exercise suit and felt more like herself than she had at any time since returning to Hapes.

"If you won't be requiring my services, Master Lowbacca," Em Teedee said, "might I stay on shore and shut down for a rest cycle? I have no idea what saltwater might do to my delicate circuitry."

Tenel Ka watched Lowbacca grumble a reply and splash out of the shallows to place Em Teedee high up on a dry rock. After the Wookiee returned, the four friends waded out toward deeper water, enjoying one another's companionship, along with the feeling of the silky water around them.

When Jacen, Jaina, and Lowie turned onto their backs to float lazily on the surface while they conversed, Tenel Ka absently flipped over and floated as well. In that instant she remembered yet again that one of her arms was missing—but she also realized that, with only a slight adjustment of her posture and weight, she was able to float quite easily. By experimenting, she discovered she could propel herself at surprising speed, using nothing more than her strong legs.

Jacen, who had noticed her tentative attempts, swam over and favored her with what she could only interpret as a challenging grin. Starting to tread water, he raised his eyebrows at her. She met his gaze and began treading water as well—at first with little coordination, then finding her rhythm. When Jacen narrowed his liquid-brown eyes and moved to a sidestroke, Tenel Ka did the same.

Tenel Ka met one challenge after another with varying degrees of success. She found that she was able to do much more than she could ever have imagined. And even when her performance was less than stellar—as when she tried to perform an underwater somersault—she *enjoyed* herself.

When she resurfaced sputtering and coughing after one such attempt, she noticed a measuring look in Jacen's eyes, daring her to push herself to her limits. "Race you to the shore," he said.

Tenel Ka gave him a solemn warning look. "Only if you truly intend to beat me," she said.

Jacen's face was equally grave as he said, "I'll give it everything I've got."

She nodded. "Then—go!"

Tenel Ka drew on all of her strength, endurance, coordination, and ingenuity as she threw her body into the mad race for shore. Her entire consciousness was focused on one goal, and she drove forward with every bit of determination she possessed.

Before she even understood what had happened, she was standing on the shore being greeted by loud cheers from Jaina and a very bedraggled-looking, wet Lowbacca, who were already standing on the rocky beach.

Disoriented, Tenel Ka turned, looking for Jacen, and found him just emerging from the water behind her. From the surprised expression on his face, she knew their competition had been real: he had not "allowed" her to win.

Jaina ran forward to hug them both just as Lowbacca, with a loud Wookiee yell, shook himself dry, sending sprays of salty water in every direction. Jacen yelped, and Jaina gave a small shriek of surprise.

Tenel Ka was glad of the diversion, however, because some of the salty droplets glistening on her face were not seawater.

15

TWO DAYS LATER, the royal matriarch Ta'a Chume looked sternly at her granddaughter as Tenel Ka defiantly tossed aside the embroidered robe of state, as well as the glittering and gaudy tiara.

The former queen was not pleased. "You must dress in a manner befitting your station, child," she said in an indignant tone. "And you might show a bit more respect for your heritage. Take your tiara. It is an heirloom, known throughout the cluster." She held up the delicate crown studded with beautiful, iridescent jewels. "These are rainbow gems of Gallinore, worth enough to buy five solar systems."

"Then buy five solar systems," Tenel Ka said. "I have no use for such wealth."

"You can't avoid your duties by being impertinent. This is not a carefree vacation. There is still work to do. We have an important diplomatic meeting to conduct, and you must prepare yourself."

"I have no interest in your important meeting, Grandmother."

Jacen, Jaina, and Lowbacca stood uncomfortably, not sure what to say as Tenel Ka argued with the matriarch.

"So long as you remain part of the Royal House of Hapes, Tenel Ka, you will continue to receive diplomatic instruction and learn how to become a useful member of our bloodline," her grandmother snapped.

Tenel Ka glared back, her one hand clenched into a fist. "What makes you think I wish to stay here as part of the Royal House? I am still in training as a Jedi Knight."

The matriarch laughed. "Spare me your fantasies, child, and face reality. The Mairan ambassador is on his way to us underwater right now, and we must go meet him at the shore. Put on your robe. I promised him that *you* would be the one to greet him."

"You didn't ask me," Tenel Ka said.

"There was no reason to," the matriarch answered. "You couldn't possibly have other plans, so I just told you."

"I have no need for diplomatic training. I am a fighter, not a politician," Tenel Ka said, indicating with a sweeping gesture the reptile-skin armor she had changed into to emphasize that her preferred heritage was from Dathomir.

"Hey, um, Tenel Ka?" Jacen said uncertainly, clearing his throat. "Uh, I mean, you've got to make up your own mind and everything . . . but remember what Master Skywalker says? Jedi ought to be open to all learning, to draw strength from knowledge—wherever they might find it? Seems to me that even though you're a good fighter, you might someday find a use for the skills your grandmother wants to teach you."

"I disagree with her politics," Tenel Ka said.

Jacen shrugged. "Nobody said you had to do everything the *way* she wants you to."

The matriarch scowled at the insolent young Jedi boy, and that made up Tenel Ka's mind. "Very well. I will do it," she said, "but I will do it my way. This is a fact."

"Oh, excellent!" Em Teedee said from Lowbacca's waist. "Might I take this opportunity to remind you, Mistress Tenel Ka, that a goodly portion of my programming was adapted from protocol droid subroutines? If I can be of any assistance in your political efforts, I gladly offer my services."

The old matriarch looked horrified.

Tenel Ka smiled inwardly. "Thank you, Em Teedee. I accept your offer. Lowbacca, I would like you at my side when I meet the Mairan ambassador."

Tenel Ka picked up the robe and with her one hand attempted to fling it about her shoulders, but the left side slid off, leaving the stump of her arm bare. When the matriarch moved to help her, Tenel Ka pulled away and quickly reached over to tug the garment into place.

"It is good to be an independent thinker, my granddaughter," the matriarch said. "Just have a care you don't do it to excess."

Royal guards had set out a plush chair on the outer edge of the reef, where curling whitecaps chewed against the rock. The damp air smelled of salt and freshness. The old matriarch stood back, observing.

Tenel Ka, in her rippling robe, marched to the chair without waiting for her grandmother to issue instructions. Adjusting the rainbow-gem tiara on her thick red-gold hair, she looked directly into the brisk wind that blew off the choppy waters.

Lowbacca, the breeze ruffling his ginger fur, stood beside Tenel Ka as she seated herself and looked out across the black rocks and the endless sea. She blinked against the bright sunlight and watched the waves for any motion.

The Mairans, a race of intelligent, tentacled, undersea dwellers, came from the ocean world of Maires, one of the planets in the Hapes Cluster. Their ambassadors had set up a consulate on the ocean floor of the Hapes central world. It seemed that, even from their undersea consulate, the Mairan ambassadors had managed to raise a political dispute with their traditional rivals from the planet Vergill.

The Mairans could leave the sea for short periods, but only if the tentacled creatures were periodically showered with a fine spray from bubbling tanks of filtered water they carried on their backs. By keeping their rubbery skin moist, the Mairans were able to spend hours on dry land, and the ambassadors had insisted on coming personally to the island fortress. They would allow the matter to be resolved by no one but the matriarch herself—or a member of the Royal House who was her designee.

The matriarch had designated Tenel Ka.

The princess sat waiting, watching the waves. She had not brought her chronometer along and wondered if the ambassador was late . . . or if she was just impatient for this ordeal to be over with.

Lowbacca stood watch at her side, tall and shaggy; Em Teedee gleamed silver in the sunlight. Jacen and Jaina, who hadn't been briefed, hung back.

"Uh, what are we doing here, exactly?" Jacen asked.

Tenel Ka turned to answer him, but Em Teedee chimed in first. "If I might be permitted to explain, Mistress Tenel Ka? I believe I can provide an appropriate summary." The little droid made a sound as if it were clearing its voice speaker. "Now, then. The Mairan underwater consulate—a domed structure built on their own planet and transported here to the Hapes homeworld—is perilously close to a subsurface mining project opened by the Vergills just after the Mairan consulate was established.

"Although the Vergill mining business is terribly productive, the Mairans have filed a formal complaint because of the noise and the silt stirred up by the drilling and excavation operations. They contend that, since the Mairans were there first, the Vergills should be required to clean up the muddied waters, cease their disruptive mining, and relocate to a place at least fifty kilometers from their consulate."

Tenel Ka nodded. "Yes, these are some of the facts. But not all."

Before she could elaborate, Tenel Ka saw a hulking shape rise out of the water and shamble in her direction, sloshing through the surf.

Forty or so black tentacles—which Tenel Ka knew the Mairans let drift free underwater, to grasp any fish that might flit within reach—dangled from its slumped shoulders, and it weaved from side to side on two legs as it walked. The spherical discolored lumps on its sloping head must have been eye membranes. The entire creature looked dark and oily.

Tenel Ka's initial reaction upon seeing the alien ambassador was one of fear—a giant primeval monster nearly one and a half times her own height rising out of the surf and lumbering toward her—but she pushed the reaction away. Fear could only weaken her judgment right now.

Waves rippled around the Mairan's legs, which were like tree trunks clinging to the beach. Stopping in the low surf, the ambassador held a heavy convoluted shell, into which a pattern of holes had been drilled.

The Mairan ambassador spoke from a vibrating membrane beneath its tentacles in a resonant and burbling voice that was very difficult to understand. *"I am capable of speaking Basic if this is how we must proceed."*

Tenel Ka shook her head. "That will not be necessary. Use your native language." She cast a glance sideways at the silvery ovoid of Em Teedee at Lowie's side. "I have brought my own translating droid."

"Oh, my," said Em Teedee, who just an hour earlier had downloaded the Mairan language from the fortress databanks. "This is quite exciting!"

The tentacled hulk bowed once, then straightened. Placing the drilled side of the shell against its blowhole, it played a skirling, complicated series of flutelike notes.

"Ah, yes," Em Teedee said. "This musical language was indeed properly loaded into my memory banks. Thank the Maker! The Mairan ambassador formally greets you, Princess Tenel Ka."

The tentacled creature blew another series of notes. Em Teedee translated. "And he commends you on your capture of such a magnificent and well-trained pet, with its coat of silky brown seaweed—oh, dear!" the droid chirped. "I do believe he's referring to Master Lowbacca!"

Lowbacca growled and flashed his fangs. Tenel Ka stood, indignant, letting the robe fall away to reveal her reptile-hide armor and her arm stump. Behind them on the rocks, the matriarch frowned in disapproval at her granddaughter's performance.

"Wookiees are an intelligent species. They are *no one's* pets," Tenel Ka said. "This is my friend."

The Mairan appeared flustered, flailed his tentacles in agitation, and played another series of notes. "The ambassador offers his apologies for having misunderstood, Princess Tenel Ka. He grieves for your loss of one . . . tentacle—I believe he means your arm—and hopes that you exacted tenfold retribution on the fool responsible for your loss."

"How I have dealt with the loss of my 'tentacle' is not his concern." Tenel Ka's voice was crisp and hard. "If he has a diplomatic matter to raise, he had better do so immediately. If he tries my patience, I will leave. I have other things to do."

The Mairan ambassador hesitated, its tentacles stirring uncertainly, then raised the shell flute again, drawing forth a long and tangled melody.

"The Mairan ambassador apologizes again and says that he understands the matriarch gave you this decision to make as part of your diplomatic training. Since it is to be your first ruling of major import, you will most assuredly want to give it the utmost time and consideration to choose the best course of action."

Tenel Ka did not back down. Her voice remained stern. "The ambassador is sorely misinformed. I have made *many* important decisions in my life. Although this may be the first one that affects *him* and his kind, he may rest assured that I am no stranger to making tough choices."

Some of those other choices flashed through her mind—particularly her decision to join Master Skywalker's Jedi academy, and her insistence on embracing the Dathomir side of her heritage as well as that of the Hapan Royal House.

"Please present your case without further digression," she said. Her one hand gripped the chair, but she remained standing to minimize the height differential between herself and the towering tentacled ambassador.

"Very well, Princess Tenel Ka Chume Ta' Djo. The Mairan ambassadorial delegation begs the intervention of the Royal House in a matter that has distressed us greatly." Em Teedee had a difficult time keeping up as he translated the fluting notes of the tentacled ambassador's speech.

"Our peaceful undersea settlement is our home on this world, set up by our first delegation no more than six months ago. We have been delighted with the beautiful and tranquil setting of our consulate under the sea. If only you air-breathers could come to see it, I'm certain you would agree that—"

"I'm not a tourist," Tenel Ka said. "What is your grievance?" She already knew, but she wanted him to spell it out.

"Only a month after we established our consulate," the ambassador whistled, "a mining crew of oafish, inconsiderate Vergills set up a floating platform and began drilling less than a kilometer from our settlement structures. The currents are now perpetually stirred up and dirty. The noise vibrates through the water, disturbing our concentration and frightening away fish. They have ruined our home."

The Mairan raised its tentacles beseechingly. "We had established our dwelling there first, most knowledgeable Princess. We beg you to order the despised Vergills to move their pollution away from our home. After all, they have the entire ocean. They need not disturb our peace."

"I understand," Tenel Ka said.

The tentacled ambassador bowed deeply in respect, but then Tenel Ka continued sharply, "I also understand that the Vergills conducted a mining survey of the oceans by satellite, well before you established your consulate city. When I consulted the access records, I learned that you Mairans received a copy of this mining report several months *before* you chose a location for your domed consulate. Finally, I have discovered that you identified the richest vein of ditanium picked up on the survey and chose to place your structure *exactly there,* knowing full well that the Vergills would eventually commence mining operations in the vicinity.

"Yes, Ambassador, the entire ocean *is* available," she said as the wind whipped her hair about like red-gold flames, "but it is you who chose to bring about this dispute. You erected your consulate *after* you knew for certain that the Vergills would desire to mine that very same spot."

She waited, but the Mairan said nothing. She continued. "The Vergills have also petitioned for our intervention. And so you may either change the location of your consulate—which is quite easily done, as I understand from the modular construction of your domes—or you may simply choose to tolerate the noise and disturbance."

After a moment of stung silence, the Mairan ambassador fluted stridently, waving his tentacles. "Don't even bother translating that," Tenel Ka said sharply to Em Teedee, then turned to face the hulking black creature. "You came to me asking for a decision, and I have made it. In the future perhaps you will attempt to work out your own problems instead of wasting our time with your petty squabbles. I have spoken."

She sat back down and shrugged into her robe again. After another moment the Mairan ambassador shuffled backward into the surf and disappeared beneath the waves.

"All right, Tenel Ka!" Jacen cried, running toward her. Lowbacca chuffed with laughter.

Tenel Ka felt her head spinning, exhilarated at what she had done. It surprised her that the speech had come easily after all. She adjusted the rainbow-gem tiara on her head.

She was actually startled, though, when she looked behind her to see her grandmother, the iron-hard and impossible-to-please matriarch, *smiling.*

"Perhaps your methods are a bit rough yet, child," her grandmother said, "but your judgment was sound."

16

REST AND SAFEKEEPING were all well and good, Jacen thought—but after several days staying at the Reef Fortress with no place to go but to the tiny cove to swim, he began to get restless. Terribly restless.

Tenel Ka, too, was a person of action—Jacen knew that better than anybody. She wanted to be out and around, having adventures, not coddled and sheltered like a pet. The injured warrior girl certainly didn't want to sit like an old woman, merely watching waves pound against the rocks.

Ta'a Chume had returned to the Fountain Palace to supervise the investigation of the bomb blast, leaving Tenel Ka and the young Jedi Knights under the questionable care of thin-lipped Ambassador Yfra. The ambassador was a hard woman, as if all the muscles in her body were made of durasteel rather than flesh . . . but then, everyone within the Hapan government lived a harsh life, trusting no one, always struggling for personal gain. Jacen supposed Ambassador Yfra was no worse than anyone else in this society. On the other hand, he could see why Tenel Ka preferred the honest ruggedness of her mother's world of Dathomir to the hypocritical and often poisonous dealings of Hapan politicians.

He found Tenel Ka outside the towering Reef Fortress standing on an outcropping of black rock. She was throwing stones with her good arm into the swirling pools of water that hissed around the outer reef. Deep in concentration, she took careful aim and was clearly pleased whenever she struck her imagined target. Reluctant to disrupt her reverie, Jacen stood behind her, content just to watch.

Jaina and Lowie, who had followed Jacen out of the fortress, also looked on as Tenel Ka threw stones. All of them seemed to feel the same restlessness—stuck on a minuscule island with no place to go.

After a few minutes, the balcony doors above them opened, and a flash of sunlight from polished transparisteel dazzled Jacen. Ambassador Yfra stepped out onto the high balcony, whip-thin, looking like a bird of prey as she scanned the rocks to find them. She waved, catching their attention. "Children, come here please."

Lowbacca sniffed the salty air and groaned a comment. Em Teedee made an electronic sound of disagreement. "I'm sure I don't know what you mean, Master Lowbacca! Whatever makes you think the air has changed for the worse? It still smells every bit as salty and refreshing to *me* as it has for the past hour."

Tenel Ka glanced behind her when Em Teedee spoke and looked momentarily startled to find the others watching her. She clambered off the rock outcropping and joined her three friends. "Let us see what the ambassador wants," she said in a gruff voice, leading the way.

"Maybe it'll be something fun," Jacen suggested.

Tenel Ka looked at him with her granite-gray gaze, raising her eyebrows. "Somehow the ideas of Ambassador Yfra and 'fun' do not go together in my mind."

Jacen snickered at that, wondering if Tenel Ka had purposely made a joke. By all outward appearances she had merely stated a fact.

Inside the fortress, the ambassador met them in the warmly lit balcony room with a surprise for them all. "My dears, I think it's time for you to have a little enjoyment!" she said, smiling with her face, but not with her mind. Jacen could sense it. Although she went through all the correct motions of being friendly and understanding, Jacen could tell that Yfra had no great love for children—or for anyone else who took up so much of her time and interfered with governmental business.

Tenel Ka placed her hand on her hip. "What would you suggest, Ambassador?"

"You children seem so bored," Yfra said. "I can understand that. Sometimes having no cares or worries *is* bothersome." She gave the briefest disapproving frown, then covered it with another false smile. "I've taken the liberty of reprogramming one of our wavespeeders so that you can get away for a while, cruise the ocean, and have a good time out in the sun."

"Are you planning to come along, Ambassador?" Jaina asked.

Yfra made a sour frown, then covered her expression with a cough. "I'm afraid not, young lady. I've terribly important work to attend to. My, you can't imagine the responsibilities I deal with. The Hapes Cluster has sixty-three worlds, with hundreds upon hundreds of different governments and thousands of cultures. Ta'a Chume is a very powerful woman, and we all have so much to do in the absence of

Tenel Ka's parents." Yfra clasped her clawlike hands together. "You children ought to enjoy your younger years, while people like me take care of the difficult work."

She shooed them away. "Run along now. Down in the docking bay you'll find the speeder I programmed. It's completely safe, I assure you. I've input a simple loop course that will take you out beyond the reef into the open ocean and then back here by nightfall. I've even seen to it that you have a basket of food, so you can enjoy a meal together while you're out." She drew a deep breath and smiled her insincere smile. "I'm sure you'll have a wonderful time."

Jacen studied the ambassador, trying to determine whether or not to be suspicious. He certainly understood how time-consuming the demands of government could be, since his mother was a Chief of State herself. He also thought of how restless the four companions had been for the past day.

"Blaster bolts! Let's go out and have a good time," he said. "It'll be great to be away from the watching eyes of parents and escorts and ambassadors. I promise you we're going to have fun."

Tenel Ka nodded seriously. "This is a fact." Then she gave him one of the most remarkable gifts Jacen had ever received.

She smiled at him.

The wavespeeder roared across the sea, bouncing and thumping as it crossed the troughs and crests like a wheeled vehicle traveling at high speed across a heavily rutted road. Though the autopilot followed a predetermined course, Jaina and Lowie each took turns at the wheel guiding the rudder, seeing just how far the autopilot would let them deviate from its course. Lowbacca let out a happy-sounding bleat.

Em Teedee said, "Master Lowbacca observes that this vehicle bears some similarity to his own T-23 skyhopper."

Jaina looked at the ginger-furred Wookiee. "Reminds me more of the controls of the *Millennium Falcon*. You and I wouldn't have any problem piloting this thing, Lowie," she said. Lowbacca rumbled in agreement.

The wavespeeder took them away from the rough foamy waters around the reef, on which the isolated fortress towered like a citadel overlooking the blue-green ocean of Hapes.

Jacen sat back and talked with Tenel Ka as they let themselves be lulled by the reflected sunlight and the hypnotic undulation of the waves. "Hey, Tenel Ka," he said tentatively. "I've got a great joke—listen. Which side of an Ewok has the most fur?"

Tenel Ka looked at him seriously. "I have never considered the question."

"The *outside!* Get it?"

"Jacen, why do you so often tell me jokes?" she asked. "I do not believe I ever laugh at them."

Jacen shrugged. "Hey, I was just trying to cheer you up."

Tenel Ka threw him an odd glance. "You think I need cheering up?"

When he answered her, Jacen noticed that he had a difficult time keeping his eyes away from the healed pinkish stump of her arm. "Well, you just seemed kind of quiet and serious."

Tenel Ka raised her eyebrows. "Am I not always quiet and serious?"

Jacen forced a laugh. "Yeah, I guess you're right."

Tenel Ka continued, "We have discussed this, Jacen. Please do not assume that I need cheering up, that I am helpless, or that I have somehow turned into a whimpering weakling. I am still a Jedi trainee, and I believe I will still become a Jedi Knight . . . as soon as I figure out how."

Jacen reached over tentatively to rest his fingers on her arm and slid them down until she caught his hand in her strong grip.

"If there's any way I can help you, let me know," he said.

She gave his hand a brief squeeze. "I will."

The wavespeeder cruised around a set of sharp rock points that thrust up from the water. The Dragon's Teeth, Tenel Ka called them. The jagged pinnacles hunched together, and the surging waters spurted between them with a slamming sound, regularly erupting in a geyser of white foam.

The engines roared as the craft turned to skirt the turbulence near the Dragon's Teeth, then picked up speed again, shooting out toward the open waves. Jaina and Lowie studied the course, each making calculations and trying to guess how far the craft might take them before they circled back.

"It's about time for lunch," Jacen said, rummaging through the food baskets and handing out meal packets.

When Lowie roared in agreement, Em Teedee said, "Well, of course, Master Lowbacca—aren't you *always* hungry?" The young Wookiee chuffed with laughter, but did not disagree.

The wind from their passage whipped spray in their faces, and the salty-fresh air made Jacen ravenous. He and his friends ate the self-warming meal packs and filled their cups from a thermal beverage container.

Jaina stared through the wavespeeder's transparisteel windscreen while she munched. She glanced at the course again. "I wonder how far this is going to take us."

Up ahead Jacen noted that the water seemed to have a different color and consistency . . . to be more greenish and rough-looking.

Lowie sniffed, sniffed more deeply, then growled a query. Em Teedee answered, "I couldn't tell you, Master Lowbacca—my scent analyzers can't seem to match this with the appropriate data to provide a clear answer. Salt, of course, iodine . . . and some sort of decomposing biological matter, perhaps?"

Jacen caught it too: a sick, sour stench that clogged the air and weighed it down. "Smells like dead fish."

Tenel Ka narrowed her eyes in concentration. "And rotting seaweed. Something very old is there. Something . . . not healthy."

Jaina scanned their course again. "Well, the wavespeeder's taking us right toward it."

Before anyone else could speak, they cruised into the strange, gelatinous area. The water was covered with leafy, floating seaweed as dense as jungle undergrowth. Thick, rubbery tentacles with long wet thorns glistened in the water. Huge, scarlet flowers as big as Jacen's head opened up in the thickest portions of the morass.

Jacen leaned over the edge of the wavespeeder to get a better look. The center of each fleshy-lipped flower held a cluster of moist blue fruits that made the entire blossom look like a wide-open eye. This impression was heightened when the wavespeeder's passing triggered some sort of reflex and the petals of the floating plants blinked closed like eyelids squeezing shut.

"Weird," his sister said next to him.

"Interesting," he replied.

Ahead, the tangled mass of spiny seaweed extended as far as they could see. The wavespeeder continued automatically across the undulating surface of the water, and the foul smell grew stronger. The thick stems and fronds of weed twitched, as if moving by themselves, although Jacen decided it must be caused by swirling currents in the water underneath.

Some of the large eye-flowers rose on their stalks and turned in their direction, as if studying them. Jacen shivered and glanced at Jaina. "Uh, then again . . . maybe 'weird' *is* a better word for it," he agreed.

Lowie looked around, moaning uneasily. Jaina met the Wookiee's gaze and bit her lower lip. "Yeah, I've got a bad feeling about where this boat is taking us. I don't know if I want to go any deeper into this seaweed desert."

"But we're stuck with the autopilot, aren't we?" Jacen said. "If you shut it off, how'll we get back?"

The young Wookiee barked an answer at the same time as Jaina replied, "Been keeping an eye on the course. Lowie and I could probably find our way back home. Ought to be pretty easy."

Tenel Ka stood up, scanning the seaweed, as if trying to remember something. "Jaina is right," she said. "We should return now. To remain here would be unwise."

Jaina and Lowie took over the controls, throttling back while they disengaged the autopilot. As they eased the craft around to head back out of the seaweed, the engine sputtered to a stop.

Since he loved to investigate strange plants and animals, Jacen took the opportunity to lean over the side of the speeder again. He reached down to touch the rubbery, interesting-looking seaweed.

Suddenly, every red eye-flower swiveled to stare at him.

"Whoa!" Jacen said. He waved his hand experimentally, and the flowers turned, attracted by the motion.

Intrigued, he reached for the closest blossom—and a slick tentacle of seaweed whipped up to wrap around his wrist, capturing him in its barbed embrace.

"Hey!" he shouted. Thorns stung his arm. The seaweed began to pull. "Help!"

He grabbed the railing of the wavespeeder with his free hand to keep from being yanked into the mass of ravenous seaweed. The tentacles thrashed wildly now . . . *hungrily*. Other fronds reached up to slap the side of the boat, twining themselves about the rail.

Lowbacca leaped from the nearby pilot station and grabbed his friend's legs just as the tentacle, redoubling its efforts, gave a sharp jerk and pulled Jacen over the railing. He dangled over the water, struggling to free his arm from the seaweed.

Tenel Ka suddenly appeared beside them. Wrapping her legs around the deck rail, one of her throwing knives gripped tightly in her hand, she bent to slash at the tentacle that grasped Jacen's arm. The seaweed cut free with a snap, and in the recoil Lowbacca managed to yank Jacen back onto the deck.

"Blaster bolts!" Jacen cried, wiping blood from the oozing wounds on his hand. "That was close."

But it was just the beginning. With dread, he looked at the water all around them. The seaweed roiled angrily in every direction, as far as the eye could see. Large fronds thrashed into the air, grabbing the deck rails, as if intending to heave the wavespeeder down. The monster had tasted Jacen's blood, and now it had decided that Jedi Knights were exactly what it wanted for lunch.

Another writhing tentacle rose above the boat's side, searching for a target to skewer with its thorns. Tenel Ka leaped in front of the deadly frond, wielding her throwing dagger. She stabbed into the thick stem of seaweed, and a syrupy green ooze gushed out.

The seaweed recoiled, then lashed back, slapping Tenel Ka across the side of the head. A trickle of blood traced a scarlet line down her cheek. Rather than cry out in pain, Tenel Ka chose to respond with her knife, slashing through the coiled weed—and another fat tentacle thumped to the deck.

Jacen shook his injured arm to restore the feeling then grasped the lightsaber clipped at his side. He had not used it in some time, but there was no room for hesitation now—not if he ever intended to be a Jedi Knight . . . not if any of them wanted to get out of this mess alive. He flicked on the emerald-green blade. "I'm not letting some *weed* get the best of me!" he said.

The humming weapon sliced off one of the large tentacles twined around the rail. "Take that," Jacen said. Gray fumes burned his eyes as the chunk of severed seaweed fell away.

Out in the water the tentacles thrashed. Now they seemed to be in pain. The scarlet eye-flowers blinked and gyrated furiously. The smell of seared vegetables and saltwater filled the air.

"I'm getting us out of here," Jaina called from the controls, restarting the engines. But grasping tentacles held them in place, and the wavespeeder could not break loose.

Roaring, Lowbacca ignited his own blazing lightsaber and held it with both hands, a glowing bludgeon of molten-bronze light.

Larger stems rose now from the deeper water, each with a pair of serrated shells on the end, like vicious pincers ready to tear apart prey. The tentacles writhed and clacked their sharp edges together, looking for something to bite into.

Jaina pushed hard on the controls. The wavespeeder's engines whined as it strained against the grasping tentacles.

Lowie raced to the rail. Bellowing a warning, he swept down with his lightsaber blade again and again, slicing through the seaweed that still held their craft.

"Oh, do be careful, Master Lowbacca—here comes another one!"

Grunting a reply, Lowie slashed at the tentacle, and the little translating droid said, "Excellently done, Master Lowbacca! And it's *quite* a comfort to hear you would rather I didn't wind up as an appetizer for a mass of salivating seaweed."

Tenel Ka turned to fend off an attack from one of the sharp-shelled tentacles. She slashed with her knife, but one of the clamshell pincers clenched the point of her dagger with a loud click. The razor-edged shells clacked again, pushing to reach closer to her face.

Then Jacen was there, chopping the tentacle away with his brilliant green energy blade. He flashed Tenel Ka a roguish grin. "Just wanted to keep the score even!"

"My thanks, Jacen," she said.

Lowie hacked with his blade, severing the last of the seaweed tentacles holding the boat. The wavespeeder broke loose and lurched away while thorny fronds writhed and lashed out, struggling to recapture their prize.

As quickly as she could, Jaina pushed the wavespeeder to its highest velocity, roaring over the twisted weed. The malevolent eye-flowers stared at them. Other thrashing tentacles rose up, but the seaweed seemed unable to respond fast enough.

Jacen gripped his emerald-bladed lightsaber, ready. This thing was more than a plant. It was . . . something sentient, something that could *respond*. He used the Force, hoping to calm it, make it leave them alone. "I can't find its brain," he said. "It seems to be all reflexes. All I can sense is that it's hungry, *hungry*."

"Yeah, well it's going to stay hungry a while longer," Jaina said.

"Yes, indeed! I agree wholeheartedly," Em Teedee answered.

Moments later they were out into open water again. Jaina and Lowie plotted their new course, made the appropriate calculations, and manually set the wavespeeder's direction to take them back to the Reef Fortress.

Glancing over at Tenel Ka to make sure she wasn't hurt, Jacen was surprised to see her wearing a calm and satisfied expression as she slid her throwing dagger back into its sheath at her waist. She seemed more alive and confident now than he had seen her at any time since their fateful lightsaber duel on Yavin 4.

"We are fine warriors," Tenel Ka said. "There is nothing like a physical challenge to make the day more relaxing."

Lowbacca gave a low grunt. Em Teedee bleeped, but refrained from articulating a comment. Jaina looked at Tenel Ka in surprise, but Jacen laughed. "Yeah, we *are* quite a team, aren't we? Real young Jedi Knights."

Tenel Ka helped Jacen bind up the minor wounds on his arm, and he applied some salve from the wavespeeder's emergency medkit to the stinging cut on her cheek. "I do not believe Ambassador Yfra had this in mind when she sent us out for a day of recreation," she said, "but I found it enjoyable nevertheless."

Lowbacca growled and pointed toward the navigation console. "Oh, dear! Master Lowbacca suggests that it might, perhaps, be premature to feel safe and comfortable quite yet," Em Teedee translated. "You see, he hypothesizes that this wavespeeder was purposely sabotaged."

"What do you mean?" Jacen asked. "Those numbers don't mean anything to me."

"I think he means *this*." Jaina nodded down at the console, indicating the preprogrammed course coordinates. "The autopilot was set to take us into the middle of that killer seaweed—with no return course!"

17

THE GURGLING, SHUSHING sound of gentle waves lapping against stone docks and anchored boats filled the cave grotto. With each breath, Tenel Ka drew comfort from the salty smells and the cool, solid rock around her. Sitting with bare, crossed legs, using a Jedi calming technique to help herself think clearly, she let her gaze drift across each of her friends.

Jaina, head under the control panel and feet high in the air, checked the wiring of the wavespeeder's directional controls. Lowbacca tinkered with the navigational computer from above, handing Jaina tools as she asked for them. Tenel Ka felt a pang of loss as she watched her two friends working with such confidence and agility, completely unconscious of how easy it was for them to use either one hand or the other.

Jacen lay stomach down on a ledge beside Tenel Ka, his right hand reaching deep into the water while the fingers of his left teased the surface, trying to lure a glowing amphibious creature close enough to grasp it.

"Hand me that hydrospanner, would you, Lowie?" Jaina said in a muffled voice. "I need to take this access plate off." Without looking up from his work, the Wookiee plucked the tool from the case behind him with one nimble-fingered hand and passed it to Jaina.

It is so simple with two arms, Tenel Ka thought. As quickly as the jealousy rose within her, she squelched it, chiding herself for being irrational. Even if she still had both hands, she might not have been able to do the things Lowbacca could do with his long, limber arms. He used everything he had, body and mind, to the best of his ability. Just as Jacen and Jaina did.

Just as Tenel Ka always had.

Was she still that same determined person, using her skills and abilities to their fullest, she wondered, or was that person gone now that she had lost her left arm?

She scowled at the thought. If the missing limb was the only thing that bothered her, then surely she could have accepted the biosynthetic replacement her grandmother offered. . . . So perhaps the injury itself was not her primary problem, after all.

Tenel Ka noticed then that Jacen had propped himself up on his elbows and had turned to look at her, his eyes serious. "Hey, you fought really well out there yesterday, against that killer seaweed."

"You mean for a girl with only one arm?" Tenel Ka said bitterly.

"I . . . no, I—" Jacen's cheeks turned crimson and he looked away. His voice was low when he spoke again. "Sorry. All I remembered was you fighting that plant. I didn't even think about your missing arm—it didn't slow you down a bit."

Tenel Ka flinched as if he had slapped her. He was right, she realized: she had not fought like some weak, pitiable invalid. Instinctively, she had battled with everything in her repertoire, drawing on all of her resources. She had truly been *herself,* using every weapon at her disposal.

"Do not be sorry, Jacen," she said. "Your words were meant kindly. It is I who must apologize." She thought again of the battle, musing over what she had accomplished. "I might have fought better, though, if I—"

"—if you had had your other arm?" Jacen finished for her. "Hey, *I* might have fought better if I'd had a blaster cannon, but I didn't. I just did my best."

"No." Tenel Ka looked at him in surprise. "I meant to say, I might have fought better had I used a lightsaber."

With a hesitant smile, Jacen looked up at her again. "Yeah . . . you're pretty good with a lightsaber. Of course, you're pretty good at a lot of things."

This was a fact, she thought in wonderment. She was indeed good with a lightsaber. *Still.* And she was also still a good swimmer, fighter, runner. But she had stopped believing in herself, stopped using every portion of her body and mind to their fullest ability. These things were an integral part of the person Tenel Ka had always prided herself in being—and *that* was what she had been missing since the accident.

"Thank you, my friend," she said. "I had begun to forget who I was."

He dazzled her with one of his famous lopsided grins. "Hey, if it was as dangerous to be *me* as it is to be *you,* I might try to forget who I was, too."

"There, that ought to do it." Jaina's voice was loud and clear as she climbed out of the wavespeeder. Lowbacca growled and gesticulated.

"Yep," Jaina agreed. "Sabotage, no doubt about it." With her usual directness, Jaina looked at Tenel Ka and asked, "Any possibility your grandmother could be behind this?"

Jacen gulped. The thought had not occurred to him. "Your grandmother? She wouldn't try—!"

Tenel Ka considered the question seriously. "No," she said at last. "Had that been my grandmother's intention, she would have . . . disposed of me long before you arrived." Lowbacca gave an interrogative growl, and Tenel Ka continued. "Do not misunderstand me. I believe her capable of murder—but I also *sense* that her intention is to keep me from danger, to protect me, whether I become a queen or a Jedi."

Lowbacca growled a reply, and Em Teedee said, "Master Lowbacca points out—and quite rightly, I might add—that with Ta'a Chume traveling back and forth between here and the Fountain Palace, as she did today, she can hardly be counted on to provide protection."

"Well, she did leave some guards on duty," Jaina said.

"And Ambassador Yfra," Jacen added, rolling his eyes. "Oh boy."

Jaina bit her lower lip. "Yfra's the one who suggested we go out in the wavespeeder, you know."

Lowbacca barked a comment. "Not to mention the fact that she claims to have programmed the wavespeeder herself," Em Teedee supplied. "Oh, my!"

Tenel Ka, who had never trusted Ambassador Yfra, made no comment as her friends voiced their suspicions. In the distance she could hear the sound of the large Hapan Water Dragon approaching. "Perhaps it would be safest for the moment to trust no one," she suggested.

Jaina and Lowbacca agreed.

"And maybe we'd better stay as far away from Ambassador Yfra as possible," Jacen added.

Just then, the royal yacht floated into the grotto on a wafer-thin cushion of air. Tenel Ka's grandmother stood at the helm. Ta'a Chume brought the Hapan Water Dragon to a complete stop near one of the stone piers and climbed out onto the dock while her guards secured the craft.

Stepping forward to greet her grandmother, Tenel Ka tried to sense any harmful intentions the matriarch might have. The only emotions she picked up, however, were weariness, frustration, and a sense of grim determination.

"We had one of the bomb conspirators in our grasp today," her grandmother said in a tired voice, "but before I managed to question her, she was poisoned." Ta'a Chume shook her head. "She was under guard the entire time. I don't see how an assassin was able to get to her so quickly."

"You appear to require rest, Grandmother," Tenel Ka said, trying not to seem unduly concerned at the former queen's haggard appearance. "Perhaps you should not conduct this investigation yourself."

Ta'a Chume's eyes narrowed shrewdly. "For decades I ruled the entire Hapes Cluster by myself." The woman sighed and seemed to relent. "But perhaps you are right. I will send Ambassador Yfra back to the mainland to continue the search."

Tenel Ka bit her tongue to keep from voicing her suspicions that Yfra might sabotage the investigation rather than help it. But at least such an assignment would get the possibly murderous ambassador away from the Reef Fortress. Far away.

18

BY NOW ZEKK considered his lightsaber an old friend.

Though he had not taken the time or care to build his own weapon, he practically lived with the scarlet beam. He knew how to make it dance against imaginary enemies. He had fought and defeated every simulated monster the computers could portray in the training room. He had slain mynocks, Abyssins, krayt dragons, wampa ice monsters, piranha beetles, and hordes of angry Tusken Raiders.

In one battle he had even felled a ferocious rancor with his lightsaber. After that difficult victory, Zekk wished he could have watched the reaction of his rival Vilas, who seemed so enamored of the hideous beasts.

Now Zekk strode beside Brakiss as the Master of the Shadow Academy led him down corridors toward the station's central hub. Busy with his training, Zekk had never thought to venture here before. No longer an underconfident and overwhelmed trainee, Zekk walked in his full leather armor with ease, lightsaber at his side, as if he were almost Brakiss's equal.

The Shadow Academy Master seemed quiet and withdrawn, though. The perfectly chiseled features of his handsome face were set in an unreadable mask, his forehead showing just a trace of a frown.

Zekk cleared his throat, finally curious enough to speak. "Master Brakiss, I sense . . . uneasiness in you. You haven't told me about this next exercise. Is there something I should know?"

Brakiss paused and fixed the young man with a calm, piercing gaze. "You are about to face your most difficult trial, Zekk. Everything depends on this. You must demonstrate how talented you truly are."

Zekk lifted his chin and drew a deep breath, flaring his nostrils. His hand moved instinctively to his lightsaber. "I'm ready for anything."

They reached a thick metal door, and Brakiss punched in a code that opened pneumatic locks. The heavy hatch opened slowly, revealing a small airlock chamber and a second sealed metal door blocking the other side.

Brakiss said, "Trust in your abilities, Zekk. Feel the Force."

Zekk nodded solemnly. "As always, Master Brakiss. I will pass your test. But why is this so important? Why should you be so concerned?"

Brakiss gestured the young man inside the chamber. Zekk entered and stood waiting, but Brakiss remained outside. "Because it will be a fight to the death," he said, then slammed the door, locking Zekk inside.

Within the echoing airlock chamber, Zekk waited. Master Brakiss's words reverberated in his mind. The doors remained sealed, and he forced himself to breathe calmly, though he felt claustrophobic and trapped. Drawing his trusted lightsaber, he gripped it until his knuckles turned white, but he did not yet turn on the blade.

The seconds pounded by, and still the other door didn't open. Fear swelled within him, but he pushed it aside. A Jedi had no place for fear, no reason to fear. The Force was in all things, and the dark side was his ally.

Still, although Zekk had defeated ferocious creatures in the simulation chamber, those opponents had been mere phantoms. He knew that many more dangerous things might happen in a real battle with a real opponent.

He looked at the inner door, wondering if he should hack it open with his lightsaber and force his way free. He needed to see what lurked on the other side. Was this perhaps part of the test? How long should he wait?

Patience, he told himself. He began to count to a hundred—but before he reached ten, the automatic locks on the inner door gave a thump that vibrated through the metal wall. The door swung open by itself.

Zekk felt a disorienting lurch as he stepped out into well-lighted *nothingness.* . . . The floors and ceilings and walls spun about in a blur until he finally realized that he had tumbled into a chamber where the artificial gravity had been turned off—the zero-gravity arena at the hub of the Shadow Academy! He floated free in the open air of the spherical chamber, with no sense of down or up, with nothing to stop his motion.

Zekk's stomach gave a lurch, but he drew a deep breath and concentrated on not throwing up. He focused on the images around him, trying to snatch answers from the briefest glimpses. Grasping the hilt of his lightsaber, he slowed his weightless tumbling and balanced himself. Only then did he notice the seats and standing areas that studded the walls of the chamber, the dozens of noisy onlookers, the balconies pasted on at haphazard angles to accommodate spectators in zero gravity.

Stormtroopers stood in ranks, gripping the balcony rails. The other students at the Shadow Academy sat all around, ready to watch the spectacle. He stiffened, wondering just how difficult this test was going to be. What had Brakiss meant? What was Zekk supposed to do now?

Boulders like miniature asteroids floated in the center of the open arena, along with metal boxes, small cargo containers, and artificial geometrical constructions. Long durasteel pipes drifted free. Zekk could make no sense of the random mix of large and small objects.

Suddenly he understood: they were obstacles.

On the curved wall at the far side of the arena, Zekk saw the clear blister of an observation dome. With his sharp eyesight he spotted figures inside, figures he recognized: the silver-robed figure of Brakiss; the intimidating Nightsister Tamith Kai, with her voluminous ebony hair and her black-spined cape; and the black-armored figure of Qorl the TIE pilot.

Master Brakiss leaned forward and spoke into a voice amplifier. His words boomed through the amphitheater, and all background noise faded.

"You are all here to witness the selection of a leader for our new Dark Jedi trainees—a leader who shall be the first general of our Shadow Academy forces when the Second Imperium makes its grand foray to reclaim the galaxy. Here, before you, we will witness the great battle."

On the other side of the chamber, where the view was partially blocked by drifting obstacles, another airlock opened, and a dark figure emerged. Because of the floating debris, Zekk couldn't see who it was.

Brakiss continued, "This will be a duel to the death between Zekk"—he paused, but none of the students cheered; they knew better, for they would have to follow whoever the victor of this contest might be—"and Vilas!"

Zekk turned, keeping his lightsaber handle in front of him as he faced the thick-browed young man from Dathomir, Tamith Kai's most powerful trainee. Vilas held his ignited lightsaber ready for the duel.

Vilas pushed off from the far wall and flew toward the obstacles at the center. Zekk switched on his weapon and did the same, moving to meet his opponent in the open space. Zekk's heart pounded, and he realized that despite his anxiety, this was a battle he had longed for. How many times since he'd come to the Shadow Academy had Vilas been his rival? After today there would be no question as to who the greater student was.

Vilas shouted in his mocking, oily voice, "If you surrender now, young trash collector, I may only cripple you." He laughed. Zekk felt himself flush. Norys or one of the other Lost Ones must have told Vilas their derogatory nickname for him. *Trash collector.*

Zekk reached the floating debris and found a pitted oblong stone, an iron-hard meteorite. He grasped it. "If you think victory is going to be *that* easy, Vilas, I'll defeat you before you can blink!"

Zekk hurled the stone with all his strength. In zero gravity the meteorite shot toward the other Dark Jedi—but the equal and opposite reaction after he threw the stone surprised Zekk, and he found himself tumbling backward from the momentum. He slammed head-first into one of the floating metal cargo containers. A flash of bright pain burst inside his skull. His ears rang. He cleared his vision just in time to see Vilas easily nudge himself out of the path of the flying rock.

Vilas laughed. "Is that the best you can do, trash collector?"

Zekk realized he had been foolish. He concentrated, using the abilities he had recently acquired. Since Vilas was no longer looking at the stone, Zekk used the Force to yank it back toward his enemy. The rock didn't have enough distance to build up much speed, but it struck a sharp blow to Vilas's shoulder. The other young man cried out, rebounding from the impact.

Zekk found himself floating out of control, unable to move where he wanted. He couldn't swim through the air, and he felt entirely disoriented. The walls spun around him. Finally, his feet pressed against the side of a drifting cargo container, and he propelled himself toward Vilas again. His lightsaber drew a fiery streak through the air as he plunged forward.

Vilas was ready for him, though, his glowing energy blade held up as he spun forward. The two opponents approached like colliding cannon balls.

Zekk swung, and Vilas met his lightsaber with his own. The blades clashed and sparked. Bolts of electricity splashed off in random directions. Then Zekk shot past while Vilas scrambled in the empty air, trying to pursue.

Zekk tried to locate one of the floating obstacles for something else to bounce off of—but suddenly Jedi instinct warned him to twist out of the way. In that instant, Vilas came flying by, his lightsaber slashing and humming through the air. Zekk contorted as if leaping backward over a low fence—but not quite fast enough. His enemy's fiery weapon skimmed too close, nicking Zekk's prized leather armor and leaving a smoking gash.

When Vilas turned with a hoot of victory, Zekk felt anger boil up from the depths of his mind, allowing him to draw more strongly on the dark side of the Force. Reaching out into the floating debris, he grabbed a pyramidal greenhouse module and smashed the massive object into Vilas with enough force to shatter its transparisteel panes.

As Vilas reeled, he chopped with his lightsaber to cleave the greenhouse module in half. The two smoldering portions tumbled in opposite directions.

His face contorted with rage, Vilas kicked off of one of the floating segments and hurtled toward Zekk, who waited with his lightsaber held low. Vilas made ready to swipe his blade across the space where Zekk was. Zekk knew that if their blades clashed again, the momentum would send them both tumbling out of control. Just as Vilas drew back his lightsaber for a mighty blow, Zekk used the Force to give himself a sharp shove—*away*.

Vilas swept out with full force—and the energy blade buzzed through empty air. Because nothing had stopped the stroke of his sword, Vilas spun about like a slow tornado, tumbling and disoriented.

Zekk saw his opportunity to buy time. He shot up behind one of the larger meteoroids hanging in the center of the weightless arena and plastered himself to the rock surface, pressing his back against the rough stone.

He could hide here for a moment, and then come back fighting.

Inside the arena's observation blister, Qorl remained standing while Brakiss and Tamith Kai both sat in padded chairs, watching their respective champions and hoping for a personal victory. Qorl tried to hide his uneasiness, but could not divert his attention from the two talented young opponents fighting viciously out in the zero-gravity chamber.

Tamith Kai's eyes blazed with violet fire as she fixed upon the battle. She spoke out of the corner of her wine-dark mouth, mocking Brakiss. "Your boy has no chance," she said. "Vilas is much more ruthless. I have trained him. Vonnda Ra has trained him. Even Garowyn has trained him. That young man is the culmination of our efforts on Dathomir. Why bother with this wasteful contest? Just give Vilas command of the new Dark Jedi."

Brakiss sat, exuding outward calm, though Qorl could tell from the subtle reflexive expressions on his face each time the battle reached a new peak that this duel had filled the Shadow Academy Master with tension.

"Ah, Tamith Kai," he said, "you forget that *I* trained young Zekk. That counts for more than all the schooling of all your Nightsisters put together."

Tamaith Kai tore her gaze away from the contest and glared at him. She gave a derisive snort.

"I think," Qorl said, "that Tamith Kai has a point. This type of contest is an utter waste—no matter what the outcome, we still lose our second-best trainee, someone far superior to any of the others we keep."

"This is a different kind of contest," Brakiss said, as if explaining to one of his students. "Those other trainees know their places and will follow orders without second thoughts. These two, though . . . each thinks he is best. But only one can command. Only one can be the greatest warrior. If we allowed the loser to live, he would always resent the rule of the other—perhaps even try to undermine his authority. No, it is better that we see who is the stronger."

Tamith Kai agreed. "Yes. It is good for the other Jedi trainees to see one of their number die. Only then will they understand the depth of our convictions . . . and realize that the Second Imperium may demand the supreme sacrifice of them, as well." Brakiss nodded.

Qorl made no answer. He did not wish to argue with his two superiors. Obviously, both Brakiss and Tamith Kai believed in the process; who was he to question it? And even if one of the two contestants out there were to forfeit the battle in hopes of saving his life, it would be a terrible blow to morale. *Surrender is betrayal,* after all. Qorl leaned forward to watch the struggle.

But he still thought it a wasteful exercise.

Zekk tried to catch his breath. He couldn't hide for long, of course—not in front of so many cheering spectators, who were growing more and more enthralled as the battle grew more vicious. His hands were slippery with sweat, and he knew he couldn't afford to lose his weapon at the wrong moment during this battle. He would have to be alert and aggressive. Just to be certain, he locked his lightsaber in the ON position and cast about in his mind for a plan that might let him take out Vilas once and for all.

Then, behind him through the rock, he heard a crackling sound and instinctively threw himself away just as Vilas's blazing blade sliced completely through the meteoroid, leaving each chunk of tumbling rock with a flat edge that was so smooth it looked like a molten mirror.

If he hadn't moved at the last instant, the lightsaber would have bisected Zekk just as it had the meteoroid!

He turned in the air to see Vilas hurtling toward him, slashing again. Zekk raised his blade to meet the other lightsaber, and their edges crossed in a shower of sparks. They pushed against each other, but found nothing for traction in weightlessness. They drifted aimlessly, blades locked, jaws clenched, glaring defiantly into each other's eyes.

When Vilas's eyes were drawn for a moment to a point just behind Zekk's shoulder, Zekk barely had time to wonder what his opponent was doing before a drifting metal rod crashed into the small of his back, sending an avalanche of pain along his spine. He gasped, then released his held breath in a rush. His lightsaber, still blazing, tumbled out of his hand.

The crowd roared as Zekk flailed in the air, trying to move away from his opponent. With an evil grin, Vilas charged toward him. Zekk could not reach his lightsaber in time: it spun like a fiery glowrod toward one of the balconies, where spectators scrambled to get out of the way.

With no weapon at hand, Zekk reached beside him to grasp the still-drifting metal rod. He grabbed the pole and swung it through the air with such speed that it made a sighing sound. But, in zero gravity, he was on the other end of the pivot point, and he began to spin around like a baton.

Vilas slashed at the oncoming metal pipe, slicing off half a meter of it. Zekk continued to spin, and Vilas swung again. The blow went wide. Zekk jabbed with the superheated end of the severed pipe, and the hot tip burned through Vilas's armor, searing his ribs.

Vilas yowled in pain and grabbed the pipe himself, flinging it sideways and using the momentum to toss Zekk free. Zekk sailed across space, rebounded off one of the floating meteoroids, and reached out with his mind to call his lightsaber back to him. The weapon stopped its spiraling plunge toward the wall, reversed itself, and zipped into his grasp.

When Zekk turned and looked for Vilas again, though, he found that his opponent had vanished. The brooding young man from Dathomir was hiding, just as Zekk had. Zekk narrowed his eyes and opened his mind to the Force, listening, trying to sense Vilas among the obstacles.

The noise of the crowd gave him no hints . . . but somehow he was able to hear a faint *tink-tink-tink,* coming from behind two joined cargo containers. Zekk struck out for that point. He didn't know what Vilas was doing, but he wouldn't give the other young man time to complete his plan.

Zekk used the Force to direct himself toward the noise, but when he grabbed the edge of the cargo container and pulled himself around it, his lightsaber at the ready, he found only a small chunk of rock invisibly tapping itself against the metal wall. Vilas had managed to distract him, creating a diversion with the Force, while he hid elsewhere and prepared to strike—

With a sudden powerful premonition, Zekk whirled. Vilas *had* to be coming for him. Using his instinct, his sense with the Force, Zekk acted without thinking.

Before he could see, before he could consider what he was about to do, he pulled back to strike with his lightsaber, putting everything he had behind one powerful stroke.

In that instant, through the blaze of light smearing across his eyes, he saw Vilas launch himself out of the cargo container, wearing a predatory grin. He had hidden in ambush, hoping to kill the unsuspecting Zekk.

But Zekk had outsmarted him.

Zekk's slashing blade encountered resistance as Vilas flew across his path. Then, with a flash of smoke and a terrible stench, the bright energy blade cleaved through flesh and bone, cauterizing as it went. Vilas made a choking, gurgling sound and continued his tumbling flight through the air—but now his body moved in two separate, smoking pieces.

Vilas's death rattle was swallowed up in the triumphant roar of the crowd.

Zekk stared down at his pulsating scarlet lightsaber, too horrified at what he had done even to look at the body of Vilas. The spectators still cheered. This had been no simulation, he realized. *This was real.*

Zekk knew he had taken one giant step farther down the road to the dark side. He raised his head, speechless, as the voice of Brakiss echoed through the zero-gravity chamber, drowning out the praise of the onlookers.

"Excellent, Zekk! I knew you could do it."

Tamith Kai's somewhat petulant voice came next. "My congratulations, young Lord Zekk."

Then, to his absolute amazement, overwhelming even his shock at the violence he had committed, the air in the center of the arena shimmered until an ominous image engulfed the drifting obstacles. The huge hooded head of the Emperor himself offered its grim congratulations directly to Zekk.

"You have won this battle, Zekk," the Emperor said in a voice so filled with cold power it could freeze blood. Zekk drew in a quick gasp. All of the other trainees watched, absorbing their Great Leader's words.

"You are my Darkest Knight, Zekk. I have chosen you to personally lead my Jedi into battle against Skywalker's Jedi academy."

19

THE MUFFLED THUMP of an explosion in the middle of the night was already fading by the time Tenel Ka reacted and sat up, suddenly wide awake.

She strained her ears, but heard nothing more. She had slept fitfully a few times since coming to the thick-walled Reef Fortress—but she had never woken up without cause. Had she really heard the sound of a blast? She couldn't be sure. Perhaps it had merely been a part of her uneasy dream. . . .

Around her, the room was dark and shadowy, lit only by the metallic silver glow of moonlight spilling in from the window. The deep darkness was quiet. Too quiet. With a fluid motion Tenel Ka slid off her bed, stood, paused to listen, then crept forward to the fortress window.

Her skin prickled, but not from cold. She recognized the reaction of her Jedi senses transmitting messages of danger—an indefinable uneasiness that was rapidly growing closer to full-fledged alarm. Something was definitely not right.

Tenel Ka looked out the stone-framed window down to the glossy midnight ocean that stretched into inky blackness. The breakers, capped with moonlight, crashed against the dark reefs. She heard the rushing, hissing ocean—and realized that the sound should not have been so clear.

Where was the background hum of the night perimeter shields?

Leaning forward, Tenel Ka narrowed her eyes to study the air. A telltale shimmer should have been visible to demonstrate that a protective field surrounded the fortress—but she saw nothing. Then her attention turned to a glimmer of light and a smudge of smoke rising into the air near the generator station.

The shield generator had been destroyed! That meant Reef Fortress now stood unprotected.

Tenel Ka drew back, intending to whirl around and sound the

alarm—when a faint motion far below caught her eye. Her heart pounding, all Jedi senses alert, she glanced down to where the steep stone walls blended into the uneven lumps of the reef. A strange camouflaged ship, long and angular, floated just above the waves on repulsorfields.

"Ah. Aha," she said. "Assault craft of some sort." Then she sucked in a sharp breath as she saw figures moving—more than a dozen.

Black, many-legged creatures like large insects swarmed up the base of the fortress—*and scaled the sheer walls effortlessly.* Tenel Ka instantly recognized the tactics, the black body armor, the skittering, segmented movements. Her stomach tied itself into an icy knot, and adrenaline shot through her veins. The Bartokks, deadly humanoid insects, were legendary for their relentless and resourceful assassin squads.

Tenel Ka raced over to the comm unit mounted on a stone wall near her door and slapped the alarm button to sound a general call to arms—but nothing happened. She pushed the alarm firmly once again with her hand, and found that the entire warning system was dead.

"Lights," she called, but her room remained dark. All power, including backup generators, had been cut off to Reef Fortress.

They were in deep trouble.

Bending over and using the stump of her arm to hold the buckle in place, she took a moment to fasten her utility belt over the supple reptilian armor in which she slept. Tenel Ka pulled her hair back with a thong, letting the long red-gold braids drape like a crown around her head. It was time for action. She would have to rouse everyone.

Tenel Ka rushed down the corridor and pounded on the door to Jacen's room. Lowbacca bellowed from his own chamber and flung the door open. Jaina hurried out of the gadget room.

"What's going on?" Jacen asked, dragging unsteady fingers through his sleep-tousled hair.

"Something . . . dangerous," Jaina said, already sensing the situation. "A serious threat."

Lowbacca roared, his wildly disheveled fur standing out in every direction as he attempted to strap on the glossy white belt made of syren-plant fiber. "Emergency?" Em Teedee said. "Perhaps we are all simply overreacting."

"No. We are not," Tenel Ka answered. "The power to the fortress has been cut off, and our defensive force field no longer functions. The generating station has been destroyed. We are currently under attack by a Bartokk assassin squad."

Jacen shuddered. "Hey, I've heard of them. Insects, right? And they all work together as a hive, to assassinate their assigned target."

Tenel Ka nodded. "They are fearsome mercenaries, fighting as one organism. Once given a target, they continue to fight until the very last member of their hive has been killed—or until their victim lies dead."

"I'm sure that's terribly efficient," Em Teedee observed, "but they certainly don't sound very friendly."

Jaina frowned, looking determined. "Well then, what are we waiting for?" She retrieved her lightsaber from her quarters while Jacen ran back into the aquarium room to fetch his weapon, too.

Lowbacca, his lightsaber already at his waist, roared in challenge. "Now, Master Lowbacca, getting delusions of grandeur can be hazardous to your health," Em Teedee said. Lowie just snarled, the black streak across the top of his head bristling with anger.

Tenel Ka stepped into the Wookiee's room, marched to the far wall, and yanked free the jagged ceremonial spear mounted there as ornamentation. Holding the spear one-handed, she said, "We must fight them."

Suddenly they heard a crash and a shout, then brief weapons fire from the far end of the corridor that led to the isolated tower containing the matriarch's quarters.

"My grandmother!" Tenel Ka said. "She must be their primary target."

Still holding the spear, she raced down the cold flagstones of the dim hall. All glowpanels had gone out, and only the moonlight streaming through the corridor windows lit her way—but Tenel Ka had known these twists and turns since childhood.

Growling, Lowbacca sprinted after her while the twins ran at top speed to keep up. Jacen and Jaina ignited their lightsabers, and the brilliant energy glow splashed ahead, shedding enough light for them to see. Tenel Ka heard more shouts, a loud scuffle, and her grandmother's voice calling for help.

"We must hurry," Tenel Ka said, putting on an extra burst of speed. Someone had to have contracted the assassin squad to remove the former queen, she reasoned. Was it Ambassador Yfra? Once Ta'a Chume was dead—and with Tenel Ka's parents gone—the ambassador probably would not consider a one-armed girl in lizard hide much of a threat to her power. She could easily take over the rulership of the Hapes Cluster.

While the idea enraged her, Tenel Ka could not afford to think about it at the moment.

Just ahead, a couple of black, clattering insects emerged from side corridors. The Bartokks, as tall as Tenel Ka, stood on two powerful legs and had a central pair of arms at their waists for grasping and manipulating objects, while their upper set of arms ended in long, hooked claws like scythes used to harvest grain. The serrated edges of the scythe claws swept from side to side, with razor edges that could clip an enemy to pieces.

The Bartokks chittered upon seeing these new and unexpected opponents, but Tenel Ka raced ahead with full momentum. Using all the muscles in her single arm, she jabbed with her spear, plunging it through the body core of the left assassin. Its upper four arms flailed in reflex, trying to bat the weapon out of Tenel Ka's grip—but she twisted the long blade, ripping it sideways. The insect's hard exoskeleton cracked and split open, spilling thick greenish-blue goop onto the stone floor. She yanked the spear free as the Bartokk clattered to the flagstones, its legs still flailing.

Beside her, Lowbacca met the second assassin with a sideways sweep of his lightsaber that sliced the Bartokk into smoking halves that fell twitching to the floor.

The twins rushed up. "Good one," Jacen said, panting. "That's two down."

Tenel Ka spoke over her shoulder as she continued running. "We cannot be certain those two are dead," she said. "And do not forget, the Bartokks have a hive mind. Now all of the assassins—there are usually fifteen in the hive—know we're coming to help my grandmother."

As they skidded around the corner near the armored door to the matriarch's chambers, five more of the insects moved to block their way. Ta'a Chume's two personal guards fought fiercely at the threshold to her chambers, but the remaining Bartokks had nearly succeeded in breaking in.

As the young Jedi Knights ran forward, Bartokk assassins captured both loyal guards outside the matriarch's door and dragged them away. The guards struggled, cried out, then ceased all movement.

Although this capture was intended to free the opening for a fresh assault on the matriarch's chambers, it also created a diversion for Tenel Ka and her friends to plow forward. With their lightsabers ignited, Jacen and Jaina slashed in, chopping the two frontmost Bartokks into quivering bug pieces. Lowbacca barreled into a third assassin, knocking it against the stone wall with such force that its black carapace split open.

"Inside," Tenel Ka shouted. She could hear the matriarch calling for more guards, but there were none. Instead, four young Jedi Knights charged into her chamber.

"Lowie, help me get this closed," Jaina cried. The lanky Wookiee shoved his shoulder against the armored door as he and Jaina swung it shut against the powerful press of Bartokk arms and snapping claws. Startled, most of the insects jerked back, but then began to push and claw at the entrance again almost immediately. In that instant of surprise, however, the door groaned shut.

"Lock it," Jaina gasped, and Tenel Ka snapped a bolt into place.

Outside, Bartokk assassins pounded, scraping with their razor-edged claws against the doorjamb. The metal door rattled in its frame, and Tenel Ka knew their defenses couldn't last long against the onslaught.

But that was the least of her worries at the moment.

Three Bartokk assassins had been trapped *inside* the chamber with them, and now the ruthless black-shelled insects moved forward, focusing on their main target.

The old matriarch had barricaded herself in a corner and was doing her best to knock the creatures away with a broken piece of furniture. The young Jedi Knights rushed to defend the former queen, but one of the assassins lashed out with its razor claws at them.

Tenel Ka charged forward as the insect killer moved to meet her. She plunged her ornamental spear into it until the tip of her weapon bored all the way through the glossy shell and wedged into a crack between the wall blocks. She left the Bartokk pinned to the wall like a bug in a child's collection. Even so, the creature still writhed and snapped, thrashing to get at them.

Jacen ran forward and with a hissing sweep of his lightsaber, sliced off the multi-eyed head of another assassin as it leapt toward the matriarch.

With a roar, Lowbacca left his post at the rattling door and grasped the remaining Bartokk, lifting it bodily off the floor. Its many sharp arms thrashed as Lowie pushed forward to the high open window and heaved the creature over the ledge. The assassin tumbled nearly thirty meters to splatter on the jagged reef far below.

"Hey!" Jacen said, as the Bartokk he had beheaded, instead of collapsing into twitching death, continued to fight its way toward the alarmed matriarch. "Aren't you supposed to die?"

He slashed again with the lightsaber, this time cutting the legs out from under the headless Bartokk. The insect torso crashed to the floor, but with its remaining limbs it still hauled itself toward Tenel Ka's grandmother. The severed head lay on the flagstones near the wall, staring at its target through faceted eyes, somehow continuing to direct the body.

"These hive-mind assassins," Tenel Ka explained, "their brains are distributed through major nerve networks inside their bodies. Simply cutting off a head won't stop them. The pieces will still attempt to continue their mission."

With another blow from his lightsaber, Jacen chopped the remaining torso in half. "This is getting ridiculous," he said.

Lowbacca marched over to where the severed insect head lay near the wall. Then with great pleasure he stomped down, squashing it as one might step on an annoying beetle.

The wiry old matriarch tossed aside the broken piece of furniture she had been using as a weapon. "I thank you for your efforts to save me, my granddaughter," she said, "but it would seem that this plot is rather extensive. Our entire fortress is overrun, and I see no means of escape."

Across the floor the ichor-dripping pieces of the chopped-up assassin continued to squirm toward the former queen, blindly groping, yet still deadly. The skewered Bartokk hanging from the wall thrashed and flailed, trying to break free from Tenel Ka's spear.

Outside, in the corridors, the rest of the assassin hive hammered without pause against the armored plates of the door. From where Tenel Ka stood, she could see the rivets popping out and blocks crumbling to powder at the edges of the sealed door. The metal began to bend inward. . . .

It certainly wouldn't last much longer.

20

JAINA LOOKED AROUND the dim room where they had barricaded themselves, desperate to find some means of escape. With the hammering of assassins outside the door growing louder and louder, she found it hard to think. Pale moonlight streamed through the window from a deceptively calm sky, bleaching all colors in the room to black and white and gray.

"We have to get out of here somehow," Jaina said.

Tenel Ka nodded grimly. "This is a fact."

Jacen turned to the matriarch. "Hey, if you know of any secret passages that lead out of here, now might be the time to tell us."

"There are none," Ta'a Chume said. "This tower room was designed as a protected chamber, with no secret ways for an assassin to gain entrance. Reef Fortress itself was built to be impregnable."

Jaina snorted. "Maybe you'd better fire your architect."

Tenel Ka felt at her utility belt and removed her grappling hook and the strong fibercord. "I see no better way. We must escape by the same route those creatures used to break into the fortress. Not only must we flee the fortress, we must flee the reef island itself."

"Where can we go, Tenel Ka?" Jacen said. "We're stranded."

"I get it!" Jaina cried, seeing what her friend intended. "We take one of the fast wavespeeders and zoom out across the ocean. It's our best chance."

The stern matriarch went to the window and gazed at the sheer drop. "You mean *climb* down?"

"Yes, Grandmother," Tenel Ka said, setting the grappling hook firmly against the stone of the windowsill. "Unless you'd prefer using your diplomatic skills to negotiate a settlement with the Bartokks."

The matriarch's sharp eyes flashed with determination. "I've never allowed anyone but myself to control my fate—so I suppose falling to my death while escaping would be preferable to waiting around to be killed by giant insects in my own bedchamber. It's agreed, then. We'll try the climb, as you suggest."

Tenel Ka shook her head. "No, we shall *do* the climb. There is no try."

Jaina tugged on the cord. The grappling hook did not budge. "All right, let's get out of here."

Lowbacca blatted a comment and Em Teedee said, "Oh, dear—*must* I?" At the Wookiee's growled response, the little droid heaved an electronic sigh. "Master Lowbacca believes he would be the most sensible choice to go first—and unfortunately I'm forced to admit that he is correct. Firstly, because he is an experienced climber, and secondly because he is strong and will be able to hold the rope steady for the rest of you once he reaches the bottom."

"Can't argue with your logic," Jaina agreed. "Go ahead."

While Em Teedee twittered about the impending danger, Lowie swung himself over the sill and supported his full weight on the glistening fibercord. Then, using his long arms, he lowered himself hand-over-hand down the vertical stone wall. Em Teedee's pitiful moans grew more and more faint until finally Lowie touched down on the rocks below, stood away from the wall, and gave the rope a yank.

"Good," Tenel Ka said.

Persistence finally paid off for the Bartokks, who had continued their relentless battering at the armored door. One of the hinges groaned and popped out of the wall. With a loud creak, a corner of the door bent inward. Chittering insect assassins thrust their sharp scythe claws through the gap.

"No more time," Tenel Ka said to the twins. "You two go now. The rope will hold both of you."

"We'd better be careful," Jacen said. The door rattled in its frame and the metal screeched, caving in further.

"Guess we can't afford that luxury," Jaina said in a terse voice. "What are we waiting for?" She slipped over the sill, grabbing the fibercord, and began rappelling down the slick dark stones.

Jacen came after her. The rope was thin, and the descent treacherous, but they used their Jedi skills to keep their balance and make themselves lighter. At the bottom Lowbacca stood with his feet planted far apart on the rocky reef, holding the rope.

"Excellent climbing, Master Jacen, Mistress Jaina," Em Teedee encouraged. "You're almost here—you can make it!"

Even before they reached bottom, Jaina looked up to see Tenel Ka and her grandmother easing over the sill. The matriarch, unable to grasp the slender cord tightly enough in her old hands, steadied herself with an arm around Tenel Ka's waist. The young warrior girl had looped the rope once around her arm to allow herself more friction to control their descent.

With a firm hold on the fibercord, she slowly leaned backward, letting the strand slip through her fingers as her feet pressed against the outer wall of the fortress. The dangerous climb may have been more difficult and awkward with her handicap, but Tenel Ka did not seem the least bit hesitant. Despite her usual reluctance to use the Force, she took advantage of it this time without reservation.

"Come on, Tenel Ka!" Jacen called.

Before the girl and her grandmother had gotten more than halfway down the rope, though, a loud crash sounded from above. Suddenly swarms of multilegged figures surged to the open window, squealing their triumph.

Jaina heard Tenel Ka shout, "Hold on!" as she doubled her speed, sliding down the cord so quickly that Jaina was sure she would get a rope burn on her hand and arm.

The Bartokks grabbed the fibercord and sawed at it with their serrated scythe arms.

Tenel Ka slipped down faster, faster.

Suddenly the strand parted. The insectoid assassins above gave a triumphant chitter.

Lowbacca roared and with lightning-fast reflexes dropped the end of the severed rope, held out his arms, and caught the old matriarch as she plunged. Using the Force to control her own fall, Tenel Ka landed heavily on her feet, but without injury.

"Good one, Tenel Ka," Jacen cried. "We made it!"

"Not quite yet," Jaina said, pointing upward. The remaining black Bartokk assassins started to boil through the upper window, crawling headfirst down the vertical stone block.

"We must hurry," Tenel Ka said, pointing toward the grotto. "To the wavespeeders."

At the far edge of the reef, Jaina saw the sharp-edged assault boat from the Bartokk hive near the smoldering wreck of the shield-generator station. For a moment she contemplated taking that craft instead—but when she noticed the knobby, alien controls designed for simultaneous use by four claws, she couldn't be sure she or Lowie could pilot such a ship. Their best chance would be to grab one of the smaller wavespeeders.

Ducking under the moss-edged rock of the entrance, they ran into the sea cave. A wavespeeder, tied to the dock closest the entrance, bobbed gently on the water of the grotto.

"Everybody in," Jaina said. "Lowie and I can handle this. Let's just hope its top speed is better than what that assassin craft can manage."

"And that Ambassador Yfra hasn't sabotaged it!" Jacen muttered.

Lowbacca bellowed his agreement. Still dazed after her fall, the grim matriarch shook herself and climbed aboard as Jacen and Jaina hopped over the rail, followed by Tenel Ka.

With a roar, the repulsorlift engines raised the wavespeeder up off the calm waters inside the sheltered cave. Before Tenel Ka had managed to seat herself, Jaina pulled the boat away from the dock, whipped it around, and accelerated through the cave entrance, churning the water into froth beneath them. The wavespeeder shot away from the darkened, overrun Reef Fortress.

Lowbacca, sitting in the navigator's chair, turned his shaggy head to gaze back at the tall citadel with his dark-adapted Wookiee eyes. He growled, stretching out a hairy arm. Jaina risked a glance and saw the insectoid murderers swarming down the tower wall toward their assault craft.

"Better get our head start while we can," Jaina said grimly. She pushed hard against the accelerators, although they were already traveling at maximum speed. The small boat sped out to where the sea grew choppier.

Moments later an ear-splitting mechanical roar erupted behind them. Jacen shouted, and Jaina glanced back to see the Bartokk assault craft pull away from the reef, infested with black insect assassins.

The assault craft's engine thundered like a Star Destroyer in pursuit. "They must have come in using stealth silencers on their engines," Jaina said. "They're at full power now, though—no need to keep quiet." She watched the tactical panel in front of her and swallowed a lump in her throat.

Lowie growled. "Master Lowbacca estimates that they will overtake us within minutes," Em Teedee wailed. "What *are* we to do?"

The ocean was lit only by the twin moons high overhead in the midnight sky. Jaina saw froth ahead as the water surged around a rocky obstacle jutting from the sea—the Dragon's Teeth. "We'll go there," she said, "and try to cause some trouble as they dodge around the rocks. We're smaller, more maneuverable."

"I doubt they'll give up because of a navigation hazard," Jacen said.

"No," Jaina replied, "but we can hope they crash."

The pointed rocks thrust out of the water like jagged spires. Waves crashed against their faces, running like saliva drooling from a krayt dragon's mouth, and rippled around the submerged reefs at the base of the Teeth. The Bartokk assault craft screamed after them.

"Watch the waves—and count," Tenel Ka said, pointing as a plume of white water jetted up between the two sharp rocks. Five seconds later another plume spurted up just as high. "Timing could be our advantage."

Jaina nodded. "I see what you mean. Lowie, I'll need your help on the controls." They slowed just enough to let the assault craft approach them as they headed toward the narrow gap between the treacherous rock spires.

"It's going to be close, Jaina," Jacen said.

"Don't I know it," she agreed. "Okay, punch it, Lowie."

The Wookiee hit the accelerators full force just as the Bartokk assault craft nearly rammed them from behind. The insect assassins waved their clacking arms. One fired a deck-mounted cannon, and the blaster bolt struck the waves, creating a geyser of steam just beside their wavespeeder.

"Whoa," Jaina said as Lowie yowled. "Didn't expect that."

Unconsciously ducking her head as they streaked between the black rocks, she canted the wavespeeder to fit through the narrow gap. The hiss of their passage boomed and echoed, and a fine cold spray splashed them all.

The assault craft charged in behind them. Jaina didn't think the assassins could possibly fit through the narrow opening, but the ship slid into the gap with only a few centimeters of play on either side.

The ocean roiled just as the assault craft spat from the narrow cleft between the rocks. A jet of water rocketed through the gap, shooting out a high-powered plume that catapulted the Bartokk assault craft into the air and spun it end-over-end.

Three assassins toppled overboard and vanished into the churning seas before the assault craft righted itself and crashed back onto the water. The Bartokk pilot wrestled with the controls as Jaina streaked onward at top speed, stretching the gap between them.

Before long, though, the assault craft was hot on their tail again.

Sitting in back, Ta'a Chume recovered enough to reach inside her plush robes and withdraw a tiny holdout blaster. "For what it's worth," the matriarch said, "I'll use this—but it's designed for only two shots."

"What good is a blaster that only has two shots?" Jacen asked.

"The first shot is for an attacker," Tenel Ka's grandmother answered. "The second shot . . . well, sometimes it is preferable not to be taken alive."

Jaina gulped and continued to guide the wavespeeder away from the reef. Waves crashed against the front of their craft, but she couldn't gain any more height from their repulsorlifts. Fortunately, the Bartokk assault craft had sustained some damage in its passage through the Dragon's Teeth, and now the pilot of the impaired vessel had no choice but to hang back.

Pushing the wavespeeder to its redlines, Jaina maintained their lead—but just barely. Another hour went by as they sped over the dark wavetops under the pale light of the moons. The assault craft edged closer and closer.

"Is there any way to get back to civilization, get some help?" Jacen asked.

"Our fortress is extremely isolated—theoretically for our protection—and this wavespeeder travels much too slowly," the old matriarch said. "It would take us many hours to get back. I fear the Bartokks will have taken care of us before then."

"Not if I can help it," Jaina said, gritting her teeth as she diverted them toward a pale patch of water ahead, a wasteland covered with a rough, flattened texture and exuding a spoiled fishy smell. She realized full well where they were going. The coordinates had been familiar, and now she hoped to use her knowledge to their advantage.

Lowbacca, guessing her intention, let out a questioning whine.

"I know what I'm doing, Lowie," Jaina said.

Jacen must have smelled the same thing. He leaned toward his sister in alarm. "You're not actually going into that seaweed field, are you?"

Jaina shrugged. "They'd be crazy to follow us, wouldn't they?"

"The Bartokk assassin hive will follow us to the ends of the planet," Tenel Ka said. "They have no concern for their own danger."

"Good," Jaina said, "then maybe they'll get sloppy."

Suddenly the sound of the engines grew muted as they streaked over the writhing forest of carnivorous seaweed. Just below the hull of their wavespeeder, the weed thrashed in agitation. Clusters of red eye-flowers rose up, keeping a vigilant watch for new prey even in deepest night. The seaweed flickered and snapped, as if it remembered its near miss with the group of young Jedi only days before.

"I sure hope this thing is still hungry," Jacen said. "How about we give it some plant food?"

"As long as it's not us," Jaina responded.

The Bartokk assassins paid no heed to how the sea had changed, intent only on closing the gap between them and their prey.

The matriarch stood at the rear of the wavespeeder, holding her small blaster. "Two shots," she said, pointing her weapon at the approaching boat.

"Target their repulsorpods," Jaina shouted. "That's the only weak spot on a big assault craft like that."

The wavespeeder jostled, but the matriarch took careful aim and fired a high-powered blaster bolt. The streak of energy skimmed the bottom of the pursuing assault craft, leaving the repulsorpod undamaged. The shot reflected off the Bartokks' metal hull and sizzled into the churning seaweed creature.

"No damage," the matriarch said. "One chance left."

"Your shot was not wasted," Tenel Ka said. "Observe the plant."

The seaweed now seemed fully awake and *angry*. Its spined tentacles thrashed in the air and slapped at the craft roaring over its fronds.

The Bartokk assassins approached the wavespeeder, apparently unconcerned that one of their intended victims had just used a blaster. The Bartokk craft fired a return shot with one of its laser cannons, but Jaina, sensing the impending bolt through the Force, rocked the wavespeeder to the left. The blast struck the seaweed again, eliciting a hissing, low-frequency roar from the plant monster.

Ta'a Chume stood again, raised her tiny blaster, and aimed a second and last time.

"May the Force be with you," Tenel Ka murmured.

The matriarch took her final shot. This time the energy bolt struck one of the Bartokk repulsorpods squarely. Though the tiny weapon was not powerful enough to cause great damage, it was enough to throw the pursuing assault craft into a spin.

The stern of the assassins' boat rose up and, as the Bartokk insects scrambled for control, the bow plunged, grazing the ravenous seaweed. Before the pilot could regain stability, a dozen spiked tentacles whipped up to wrap themselves around the rails, snatching at the hull, the repulsorpods, the laser-cannon emplacements. The insect assassins chittered, more in anger than fear, because the hive mind couldn't comprehend its impending death.

Within moments, however, Bartokk assassin legs were flailing as spiked weed tentacles plucked the insects from their stations at the side of the boat and dragged them thrashing beneath the foaming waves. Soon the seaweed had engulfed the entire sharp-edged craft, dragging it under the roiling water.

Pincer-ended tentacles clamped down on hard chitinous shells, and Jaina heard muffled crunching sounds as the seaweed monster snapped exoskeletons apart to reach the tender parts inside. She stared at the water in horrified fascination.

"I think maybe this is our cue to leave," Jacen pointed out, giving his sister a nudge. Lowie roared his agreement.

Bloodred eye-flowers blinked hungrily up at them.

"Okay, what are we waiting for?"

Lowie revved the engines and then accelerated as Jaina guided the wavespeeder back out of the deadly tangle of seaweed.

Ta'a Chume made her way to the front of the wavespeeder. "I can pilot us to safety from here," she said. Jaina gladly relinquished the controls as the former queen headed the craft toward the mainland.

"An excellent shot, Grandmother," Tenel Ka said.

The matriarch nodded and looked with renewed admiration at her granddaughter. "So much for diplomacy."

Some five hours later, the entire bedraggled crew finally hauled themselves into the Fountain Palace.

Ta'a Chume was outraged to find that Ambassador Yfra had already assumed control. Declaring martial law, the ambassador had announced that there would be several hours of mourning over the untimely death of the dear, departed matriarch.

Tenel Ka marched beside her grandmother into the central throne room amidst gasps of horror, delight, and surprise from the guards. The most appalled expression, however, showed on the hardened face of Ambassador Yfra herself.

"Ta'a Chume!" she cried, standing up and trying unsuccessfully to hide the brief storm of anger that clouded her eyes. "You're—you're alive. But how—?"

"Your plot failed, Yfra. Guards, arrest this traitor!"

"On what charge?" Ambassador Yfra said in a reasonable tone, her confidence not yet shaken.

"Plotting to kill the entire royal household. I am only happy that Tenel Ka's parents were absent, for I'm sure they would have been at risk as well."

"Why, Ta'a Chume—I've never shown anything but loyalty to you." Yfra's voice was full of sweetness and offended innocence, though Tenel Ka could sense that she was lying. "How can you make such an accusation?"

"Because you took control. How could you possibly have known we were in danger if you hadn't set up the plot yourself?"

"Well, I—" Yfra blinked. "I simply responded to the distress call sent out from Reef Fortress, of course."

"Ah." The matriarch pointed her long knobby finger and a smile curved her thin wrinkled lips. "Aha! But no distress signal was sent. Your Bartokk assassins blew up our power-generating station. We escaped. This is the first word that has gotten out—but *you* knew." The matriarch nodded confidently. "Yes, you knew."

Before Yfra could sputter another excuse, the guards came forward and took her into custody.

"Oh, she'll be given a fair trial," the matriarch said, "but I think we have more than enough proof—don't you, Tenel Ka?" She raised her eyebrows.

"This is a fact," the young warrior woman replied. "And I believe I have more than enough proof for something else, as well." She stood straight, looking proudly into her grandmother's eyes.

"This adventure has shown me that I am fully recovered from my injuries. I wish to return to Yavin 4."

21

TENEL KA SAT up and looked around with brief disorientation before she remembered where she was. Letting her gray gaze skim across the ancient stone walls, arched doorway, and modest sleeping pallet, she experienced a sense of warmth and safety—and excitement.

It felt right to be back on Yavin 4, in her own student quarters in the Great Temple. She sat back on her pallet and began practicing her new skill—braiding her hair with one hand and her teeth.

Over the past weeks, the wrongness in her life had slowly dissolved, beginning with her parents' safe return to Hapes. Having foiled an attempt on their own lives by Ambassador Yfra's henchwomen, Teneniel Djo and Isolder had hurried back to find their daughter and her grandmother unharmed. They immediately sought out and purged the remaining conspirators from the royal court, while Ambassador Yfra awaited trial.

To Tenel Ka's great surprise, neither of her parents had tried to talk her into wearing a synthetic arm or discontinuing her studies at the Jedi academy. In fact, when she had expressed her desire to continue her training, her mother and father had readily agreed, asking only that she stay to visit with them for a few weeks before returning to Yavin 4.

"I believe you may become a stronger warrior than ever you imagined," Teneniel Djo said. "You have powerful legs, fast reflexes, and you still have your better fighting arm. From what your grandmother tells us, your wits have not been dulled, either."

"And I think you may teach many a future opponent that one cannot judge a warrior's worth by her outward appearance," her father added, hugging her. "Never be ashamed of what you are—or *who* you are."

When Luke Skywalker had returned in the *Shadow Chaser* to take Tenel Ka and the other young Jedi Knights back to Yavin 4, there had been no mistaking her parents' pride. Her mother's final whispered words still echoed through her mind: "May the Force be with you."

Now, after a good night's rest in familiar quarters, Tenel Ka felt ready to take her next step to recovery. She stood and stretched, delighting in the well-controlled response of her muscles.

She spent the next few minutes ransacking her belongings until she had collected the objects she needed. She found her remaining rancor-tooth trophy wrapped in its supple leather covering. She tucked it under the stump of her severed arm—not a completely useless limb after all, she noted with some satisfaction—while she searched for another item. When at last she located the jewel-encrusted tiara from Hapes, which her grandmother had insisted she take, she placed the two articles side by side on a tiny worktable in the corner and studied them.

Both objects were symbols of who she was, of her upbringing. The rancor's tooth came from Dathomir, a planet that was wild, untamed, fierce, and proud. The tiara symbolized her Hapan inheritance: regal bearing, refinement, power, wealth, and political shrewdness.

Tenel Ka had long believed that honoring one part of her heritage implied that she must *dis*honor the other. Just as she had believed that trusting in the Force implied a lack of trust in herself. Wincing at the thought, she was compelled to acknowledge that she had actually gained wisdom from the loss of her arm. She knew now that she had to use every ability she possessed—including her talent with the Force—to become the best possible Jedi.

But what of her heritage? she thought, picking up the rancor's tooth and turning it over in her palm. Hapes and Dathomir. Could she combine the best of both? She was, after all, only one person.

Coming to a decision, she grasped the rancor tooth tightly, lifted it over her head, and brought it smashing down on the glittering, jewel-studded tiara. The delicate crown broke into pieces.

Tenel Ka hammered again and again until bits of precious metal and gems lay strewn across the tiny table.

Yes, she decided. She was a product of two worlds, and she would learn to blend the best of her mother's *and* her father's. She laid down the rancor's tooth and reached for the other items she had assembled.

Then, selecting the finest jewels from her Hapan tiara, she began to build her new lightsaber.

Brilliant morning sunlight played across the top of the Great Temple and filtered through Tenel Ka's partially braided hair to form a red-gold nimbus around her. Jacen stood about a meter away, facing her, a gentle breeze ruffling his unruly brown curls. His face was filled with apprehension.

"You sure you want to do this?" he asked.

"Yes," she said simply, though she felt an uncertain fluttering in the pit of her stomach.

"Well, I'm not sure *I* can go through with it," he said in a low voice.

"You? But why—"

"Blaster bolts! The last time we did this, I ended up . . ." Jacen's voice trailed off and he looked significantly at what remained of her arm.

"Ah," Tenel Ka said. "Aha."

"So I'm asking you if you're sure," Jacen said, "because I'm not."

Gray eyes searched brandy-brown while Tenel Ka considered this. Her throat was tight with unaccustomed emotion when she finally spoke. "Jacen, my friend, I know of no better way to show that I trust you . . . that I do not blame you for what happened."

Jacen's face was solemn as he nodded his acceptance. "Thank you." He let his eyes fall half shut and took a deep breath.

Tenel Ka did the same, feeling the Force flow into her, through her. Her muscles tautened—not with fear, but with a delicious anticipatory tension. Reaching for the rancor's tooth clipped to her belt, Tenel Ka held it steady in front of her and pressed the power stud.

A blade of sizzling energy sprang from the ivory hilt, glowing a rich turquoise, produced by the rainbow gems she had installed from her tiara. A heartbeat later, Jacen's emerald lightsaber hummed to life.

As if in slow motion, the two friends raised their blades until they hovered at eye level, just centimeters apart. With a crackle of discharged energy, their lightsabers touched once. Then again.

Hesitantly at first, Tenel Ka thrust with her turquoise blade, and Jacen parried with a barely perceptible nod.

The Force flowed between them, around them, and soon they were moving in ancient patterns and rhythms, as in a well-rehearsed exercise routine, an intricate dance. Somehow both of them knew that neither would come to any harm.

Their eyes locked, while the silent music that accompanied their movements built to a crescendo, then began to fade. But their confidence in each other did not wane as their movements slowed.

They stood still at last, lightsabers barely touching, a look of amazement on both of their faces. Jacen opened his mouth as if to speak, but no sound came out.

A moment later, an ear-shattering roar split the air as Lowbacca and Jaina ran across the rooftop to greet them.

Jaina laughed. "I agree with Lowie: it's good to see you holding a lightsaber again, Tenel Ka. For a while I was worried that you thought you were too different from us, that you couldn't be our friend anymore."

"Perhaps for a while I did," Tenel Ka said. "But I have learned that differences can be positive, that they can be blended together to form a stronger whole."

"We *are* pretty different," Jacen pointed out.

Jaina switched on her amethyst energy blade with a snap-hiss. "But we're all going to be Jedi Knights."

Lowbacca ignited his lightsaber as well. Its shaft glowed a molten bronze.

"Stronger together," Tenel Ka said, raising her turquoise lightsaber high over her head.

Lowbacca lifted his lightsaber to touch hers.

"Yes, stronger together," Jacen and Jaina said in unison, crossing their glowing blades with the other two.

The four lightsabers blazed into the morning light.

DARKEST KNIGHT

To Skip Shayotovich,
whose enthusiasm knows no bounds

Acknowledgments

The usual round of thanks to Lillie E. Mitchell and her fast fingers for transcribing our dictation; Lucy Autrey Wilson, Sue Rostoni, and Allan Kausch at Lucasfilm for their helpful suggestions; Ginjer Buchanan at Berkley/Boulevard for her wholehearted support and encouragement; and Jonathan MacGregor Cowan for being our test reader and brainstormer.

1

THE MASSASSI TREES that towered over Yavin 4's jungles were smaller than the enormous wroshyr trees on the Wookiee homeworld, but Lowbacca considered them to be the next best thing. Especially when he needed to be alone, in a place where he could sort out his thoughts.

As twilight descended on the jungle moon with a blanket of colors deepening in hue, Lowie ascended one of the thickest, tallest trees in the vicinity of the Great Temple, the site of Luke Skywalker's Jedi academy. With his retractable Wookiee claws and muscular arms, he grabbed on to branches and hauled his lanky body up one level after another, increasing the distance between himself and the ground. It seemed that if he kept climbing, he might almost be able to reach the stars . . . and be closer to home.

Stopping to rest momentarily, Lowie reached out to grasp a hairy green vine, tugged to make sure it would hold his weight, then used it to climb even higher. He had to reach the top. The top was the best place.

The best place to think.

It had been a long time since he had been back to the Wookiee world of Kashyyyk. He hadn't seen his immediate family since departing for Yavin 4 to begin training as a Jedi Knight. Although Lowie loved tinkering with computers—as did his sister and his parents—he wanted more than anything to make use of his special, undefinable talent, a potential for using the Force that few Wookiees in his family line had ever exhibited.

When Lowie first arrived at the Jedi academy, uncertain and alone, his uncle Chewbacca had given him a T-23 skyhopper as a gift, so he could cruise far out into the jungle. Sometimes he brought his friends Jacen and Jaina and Tenel Ka. At other times, though, he just needed to be by himself, far from everyone. And this was one of those times.

He missed his family very much, especially his younger sister Sirrakuk. A very dangerous time in her life was fast approaching. . . .

With a great heave, Lowie used one long arm to draw his body up to a leafy nest of branches, where he disturbed a shrieking horde of the voracious tree rodents called stintarils. Stintarils normally ate anything in sight, anything that moved—but when Lowie treated them to his best Wookiee roar, the chittering rodents scampered away through the trees, kicking up clouds of broken twigs and leaves.

At last, surrounded by the dimming colors of dusk, Lowie parted the final blanket of leaves overhead. He braced his broad, flat feet on a sturdy branch, pushed his head above the treetops, and stood there, drinking in the distance. He looked across the sprawling jungle that spread all around him like an ocean of greenery, occasionally broken by the protruding ruins of temples. He smelled the damp scents of approaching evening: night-blooming flowers from vines that curled through the leaves, the rich moistness of the Massassi trees themselves, a fine mist rising above the canopy as if the forest itself were exhaling in its sleep.

The looming coppery gas-giant of Yavin shimmered low in the sky like a dying ember, a huge sphere of swirling gases. Not far from the orangish planet, though invisible to Lowie's eye, orbited GemDiver Station, Lando Calrissian's mining operation that retrieved valuable Corusca gems from the gas-giant's core.

Lowie looked away from the planet setting on the horizon, though, as deeper night seeped into the sky. Specks of starlight dusted the midnight blue canopy.

Finding a comfortable spot to lean against the outspread crown of the Massassi tree, he remained still, breathing deeply, drawing comfort from the sight of the endless trees . . . and thinking of Kashyyyk.

He should be calm, but he was very worried about his sister. He could do nothing to help her, and she had to make her own choices—and face the consequences of those choices. Even so, Lowie understood the dangers she intended to face deep in the underlevels of the rain forest on the Wookiee planet.

He ran his long, strong fingers over the pearly strands of his fiber belt, woven from threads harvested from the deadly jaws of the carnivorous syren plant. It had been quite an ordeal for him to obtain those strands, but he had succeeded. Alone.

Lowie sat still as the air cooled and the noises of the jungle grew louder. Evening insects and predators stirred and went about their business.

At his side the miniaturized translating droid, Em Teedee, remained silent—switched off, so that Lowie could ponder his concerns without being interrupted by synthesized chatter. He sat back, and time passed. He would be late for evening meal back at the Jedi academy, but he didn't mind.

He had more important things to worry about.

By the time Jaina Solo finished her meal inside the Great Temple, most of the other Jedi trainees had left the eating area. Preoccupied, she slurped the last morsels of roasted crab nuts and salted boffa fruit, dabbing up the juice with a chunk of fresh bread.

Beside her at the table, her twin brother Jacen had only half finished his meal; a droplet of greenish syrup ran unnoticed down his chin. Jacen spoke excitedly, his brandy-brown eyes blinking as he ran a hand through his tousled brown hair.

"And I did manage to catch that stinger lizard down in the hangar bay. It's taken me weeks to coax him out of hiding. He's all by himself now in that new cage you built for me, but I'm not sure what he eats." He paused briefly to stuff some food into his mouth.

Jaina nodded, only half listening. She was concerned that Lowbacca hadn't shown up to eat. Their Wookiee friend had been reserved lately, keeping to himself, speaking little even to his closest friends.

"Not to mention that several of the cocoons for my beetle moths are about to hatch!" Jacen continued. "I think I'm going to let most of them go, but I want to keep two as specimens, to see if they'll lay eggs in captivity. And you should see the fascinating blue fungus I found in a crack between some stones down by the river."

He gulped more juice, then suddenly held up a finger as he remembered something. "Oh yes, I've been meaning to ask—could you check the cage for my crystal snake? I think he's up to some mischief, maybe even trying to break out again—and you *know* what trouble that would cause."

Jaina couldn't help indulging in a quick giggle, remembering the pandemonium the nearly invisible snake had caused the last time it had gotten loose: the serpent had bitten the uppity student Raynar, sending the boy instantly to sleep. Not all of Jacen's pets caused trouble, though. Another crystal snake had helped to divert the lost TIE pilot Qorl from his attack on the Jedi academy, shortly after the twins had found Qorl living in self-imposed exile deep in the jungles of Yavin 4.

Jaina had hoped the old TIE pilot might have a soft spot for them after their efforts to help him, but Qorl had chosen not to become their ally. Instead, the Imperial brainwashing he had undergone resurfaced and became even more deeply entrenched. The pilot had returned to the remnants of the Empire, where he had fallen in with the Shadow Academy.

Jaina nodded to her brother, shaking herself from her reverie. "Okay, I'll take a look at the crystal snake cage."

She whirled as she heard the tinny mechanical voice of Em Teedee saying, "Master Lowbacca, I must urge you to ingest a wider variety of nourishment than that. According to your species' nutritional requirements, those foods are insufficient for a growing Wookiee to maintain a healthy level of energy . . . though I must admit you *have* been sulking lately instead of engaging in physical activities. Your diet should consist primarily of large quantities of fresh meat, which is substantially higher in protein than those fresh fruits and vegetables you're presently consuming."

Lowbacca answered with only a half-hearted growl as he carried his food into the eating area. Without even looking for his friends among the other Jedi trainees, he sat by himself at a small table against the stone wall.

"Lowie!" Jaina got up and hurried over to the ginger-furred Wookiee. "We were worried about you. You didn't come join us for the meal."

Lowie grunted something too brief for Em Teedee to translate.

Jaina pulled up a wooden chair across from their Wookiee friend and straddled it. Tucking a long strand of straight brown hair behind her right ear, she looked with concern at Lowie's shaggy head. The Wookiee turned his golden eyes down and studied the fruits and greens on his platter.

"Lowie, will you please tell us what's wrong?" Jaina said. "You can talk to us. We're *friends,* remember? Friends help each other."

Em Teedee spoke before Lowbacca could respond. "He won't answer you, Mistress Jaina. Even *I* can't get a response out of him. I'm afraid I'll never understand Wookiee behavior. Do all biological creatures have these unpredictable moods?"

Jacen sat down beside his sister. "Hey, maybe Lowie just wants to be left alone."

The young Wookiee groaned and nodded dejectedly. Jaina sighed, gradually realizing that perhaps the best thing she could do for her friend would be to respect Lowie's wishes and let him solve his problems on his own. He knew he could talk to Jaina or Jacen anytime he wanted—but right now he didn't want to.

"All right," Jaina said, maintaining her deeply troubled expression, "but remember we're here for you, whenever you need us."

Lowie nodded, then stretched out one hairy arm to clasp Jaina's hand in his. The Wookiee's large grip engulfed her entire hand. During the brief touch, she reached out with the Force, hoping to find a clue to Lowie's strange behavior, but all she sensed was warmth and friendship.

Jaina stood up and gestured to her brother. "Come on, Jacen. Let's have a look at that crystal snake cage."

Lightsabers flared into the night, reflecting off the ancient stone walls of the Great Temple. Tenel Ka gripped the carved rancor-tooth handle of her new weapon as its brilliant turquoise beam pulsed through the activating crystal, a precious rainbow gem of Gallinore she had taken from her own royal tiara.

The warrior girl stood in the flagstoned courtyard at the side of the ziggurat temple, a newly refurbished training area the students had reclaimed from the ever-encroaching jungle. The hardworking Jedi candidates had cleaned and polished the carefully set stones for exercises just such as this.

Tenel Ka gazed across at the alien mother-of-pearl eyes, elven features, and long quicksilver hair of her opponent—Tionne, the Jedi trainer and historian who often assisted Master Skywalker. The Jedi woman used her lightsaber with precision, matching Tenel Ka's moves stroke for stroke.

During an earlier training accident, Tenel Ka's poorly constructed lightsaber had exploded, and her friend Jacen's lightsaber blade had severed her left arm. Now Tenel Ka lived and fought with only one hand. But she wielded her glowing energy blade with strength and confidence.

Although skilled biotechnicians had offered her the best prosthetic arm replacement in the Hapes Cluster, Tenel Ka had turned them down. She prided herself in *being* herself—relying on her own abilities, her own strength and prowess. She did not want the artificial assistance of a biomechanical limb. Instead, she chose to alter her means of achieving her goal. She was determined to be as strong and as capable as ever before.

And when Tenel Ka determined to do something, she usually accomplished it.

Bright lights on the cleared landing grid in front of the temple illuminated the jungle, attracting thousands of nocturnal insects and the flying predators that fed on them. In the flagstoned courtyard, though, only the flares and flashes of intersecting lightsaber blades disturbed the night, bathing the area in a dazzling multicolored glow.

Tionne countered the warrior girl's stroke. "Very good, Tenel Ka," the teacher said. "You are learning to focus on precision rather than brute strength, to anticipate my moves and your own reactions using the Force."

Tenel Ka nodded, and her heavy red-gold braids danced around her head. The beads she had woven into the braids jingled and clacked together. She fought harder, sensing the control and skill of this older Jedi, who had been training for more than ten years now.

Several other students had come out to watch the exercises. All of Master Skywalker's Jedi candidates had intensified their training efforts, now that the New Republic was sure of the growing threat posed by the Shadow Academy and the Second Imperium. For more than a thousand generations, Jedi Knights had been the forces of light throughout the galaxy, and Luke Skywalker intended to continue the tradition.

Tionne swung her weapon with a calm, smooth gesture so unexpected that Tenel Ka barely reacted in time. She had sensed no intention of a counterattack from the silver-haired scholar, and so Tionne had surprised her. Their blades locked and sizzled—and then Tionne pulled her lightsaber back.

"Halt," she said, and switched off her weapon, leaving the warrior girl to stand with her own lightsaber blazing in her hand.

Tionne gestured up into the night sky of Yavin 4. The other students around the flagstoned courtyard stood up to watch. Just then, the twins Jacen and Jaina emerged from a low stone arch in the side of the Great Temple, hoping to observe Tenel Ka at her exercises. Instead, they all saw a glowing light streaking toward them like a tiny meteor.

"Hey, it's a ship!" Jacen said.

"Not just any ship," Jaina added. "I'd recognize it anywhere!"

Jacen blinked. "Hey, Dad never told us he was coming!"

Within a few moments the ship swooped down with a roar of its sublight engines and powered-up repulsorlifts. The flat, pronged disk of the *Millennium Falcon* settled with a loud hiss onto the landing pad.

Talking excitedly with each other, Jacen and Jaina rushed from the courtyard out onto the close-cropped weeds of the landing field to greet their father. The modified light freighter's boarding ramp extended, and Han Solo strode down it. A lopsided grin appeared as his children greeted him with wild enthusiasm.

When Chewbacca bounded down the ramp, Tenel Ka heard a bellow of greeting from behind her. She turned to see Lowbacca on one of the pyramid's stone ledges above the training area. He swung himself over the ledge and scrambled down the sloping temple blocks to reach the ground. Chewbacca roared a response to his nephew.

Lowbacca had been very troubled recently, and Tenel Ka could sense many deep thoughts working through his brain. She had decided to honor her Wookiee friend by letting him fight his own battles . . . unless he asked for help. But when she saw the expressions on Chewbacca's and Lowie's faces, Tenel Ka grasped a strange and interesting fact.

Although the twins had been surprised by the unexpected appearance of the *Millennium Falcon,* Lowbacca had known full well that the ship was coming.

2

JAINA REALIZED SHE was grinning like an idiot as she hugged her father. "What are you doing here? We didn't even know you were coming."

Beside her, Jacen gaped at Han Solo's unfamiliar costume of tattered cloth and furs. His hair had been cut raggedly, and he looked much tougher. "Blaster bolts, Dad! Why are you dressed like that?"

Before Han Solo had a chance to reply, Jaina glanced behind him. Even in the dimness she could see that some of the *Millennium Falcon*'s plating had been replaced with dark anodized hunks of metal, new storage pods had been mounted on the bow, and a second transmitting dish was attached to the rear. Her jaw dropped. "And what did you do to the *Falcon?* It looks so . . . different!"

"One question at a time, kids," Han said, laughing and holding his hands palm out at chest level, as if to ward off an oncoming charge. "There've been a few problems in the Outer Rim recently, so in her official capacity, the New Republic's Chief of State—"

"You mean Mom," Jaina said.

"Right." Han's grin was boyish. "Anyway, she's been after me and Luke to do some scouting for her. Says I need to keep busy or I'll get old too fast. And ever since he started this Jedi academy, your uncle's made it a practice to spend some time away from Yavin 4, just to make sure his skills stay at their peak performance. Still, we figured it might be a good idea to keep a low profile, though, so—"

"You disguised yourself and the *Millennium Falcon,*" Jacen finished for him. Jaina continued to stare at all the lumpy, patchwork modifications to the light freighter.

"And Luke, too." Han Solo nodded behind them to where their uncle, clad in a rumpled brown flight suit, emerged from the base of the temple. "Hey, Han, did you bring the last components for those new shield generators?" Luke called. He brushed a greasy hand down the front of his stained outfit. He looked very much like a down-and-out pilot who had deserted his post.

"You bet, Luke," Han said. "Leia's worried about your Jedi academy with the Second Imperium on the loose, so we've got to install those new shield generators and get them running with enough power to stop an attack."

"I still think my Jedi Knights would do a good enough job defending themselves if it came to that," Luke said, smiling at the trainees standing around the temple. "The Shadow Academy would be foolish to underestimate us."

Han shrugged. "Doesn't matter what you say, Luke—indulge me, or Leia will never sleep a wink."

Laughing, Luke called for Jedi students to unload the heavy components from the *Falcon*'s storage bay. "I'll have some of my students install the systems while you and I are away."

The disguised Jedi Master strode over to the pair of Wookiees, who stood in earnest conversation. He seemed to be bidding Chewbacca farewell. Jaina thought she heard Luke say something about the time being near, but before she could ask about it, her brother spoke up.

"But what about Chewie?" Jacen asked. "Isn't he going to be your copilot this time?"

Their father looked a bit uncomfortable. "I'll manage without him somehow. Back home on Kashyyyk, he and Lowie have kind of a family emergency, you might say."

"Emergency?" Jaina said. "Is anyone hurt?"

"Naw, nothing that simple. You've never met Lowie's sister Sirra, have you?" Han lifted his chin to point in the direction of his Wookiee copilot, who was deep in conversation with Lowbacca. "Anyway, give the two of 'em a chance to talk first. Afterwards I have a feeling Lowie'll tell you all about it. Meanwhile, I've brought messages from your mom and Anakin—and I've got a couple of surprises for you on the *Falcon*."

"Uh-oh," Jaina said. *"More* surprises on the *Falcon?"*

Han chuckled and put an arm around each of the twins' shoulders. "Yeah, presents for you two."

"Hey, that reminds me," Jacen said, "I've got a new joke. Wanna hear it?" Before either of them could talk him out of it, he forged ahead. "What do Jawas have that no other creature in the galaxy has? Give up?" He raised his eyebrows. *"Baby Jawas!"*

Even their father had difficulty feigning amusement. Jaina studied her brother in silence for a moment, then turned to Han, getting back to the subject at hand. "So, what were you saying about those gifts you brought us?"

"Well, I brought a mate for Jacen's stump lizard, along with some of those starflower blossoms they like to eat so much, and a refurbished micromotivator that still needs some tinkering. 'Course, you two'll have to fight over who gets which gift," he added, ruffling the twins' hair as they walked up the boarding ramp together.

Jaina snorted indelicately. "That shouldn't take long."

In her quarters, Tenel Ka sat fascinated by the tiny holographic image of dark-haired Anakin Skywalker holding a cluster of brightly colored twine. She couldn't figure out why the twins' little brother would have sent *her* a message. She had only met the boy once, on Coruscant not long ago.

"I know how independent you are, Tenel Ka, so I hope you don't mind my doing this," Anakin's recorded voice said. "But when Jacen and Jaina told me how hard it is for you to braid your hair since the accident, I took it as a problem to solve. You may have figured out a bunch of this stuff for yourself already"—Anakin's holographic face smiled faintly—"but even if you have, it was still a challenging puzzle, and I enjoyed it."

The Solo twins, who had delivered the holographic message to Tenel Ka after a long visit with their father, sat nearby on the floor of her chambers. Jaina rolled her eyes and chuckled. "That's my little brother."

"This is a fact," Tenel Ka said, shifting her concentration back to the glowing hologram.

The boy's image held the multicolored twine in one hand and threaded the fingers of the other hand through it, neatly separating the colors into individual clumps. Tenel Ka unconsciously lifted her hand to her head and threaded her fingers through some unbraided strands of her red-gold hair.

Moving with deliberate precision, Anakin slid his hands down the brightly colored strands, twining them together with the fingers of one hand as he went. "See, it can be done, if you approach the task from a different perspective." The sequence cycled through again in slow motion while Anakin said, "I tried adding decorations several ways, but it worked best for me if I put the bead or feather in my mouth first. That way I didn't have to let go of the braid to pick it up."

"Ah." Tenel Ka nodded her approval of the logic. "Aha." Experimentally, her fingers began to twine a few strands of hair, following the single-handed technique Anakin had concocted.

The hologram shifted to a different scene, Anakin standing beside a fall of long glossy brown hair, caught up in a dozen Dathomiran warrior braids decorated with feathers and beads. The view pulled back, and Anakin gestured to his handiwork, looking both pleased and a bit embarrassed. "As you can see, Mom let me practice on her." The tiny holographic image of Chief of State Leia Organa Solo turned with a warm smile and then spun in a graceful pirouette to give a better view of the braids.

As the holorecording ended, Tenel Ka nodded seriously, considering the new technique. With practice, she thought she could manage it herself.

A loud questioning growl sounded from the doorway of Tenel Ka's quarters. She looked up to see Lowbacca standing at the arched entrance.

"Enter, friend," Tenel Ka said, indicating a spot on the floor beside her. "Sit with us if you wish."

"Lowie, is everything all right?" Jaina asked with a look of concern.

The lanky ginger-furred Wookiee ambled over and sat between Tenel Ka and Jaina on the floor. For a long time none of the companions spoke. Then Lowbacca reached toward his belt and flicked a small switch on Em Teedee's back. "Ah, thank you, Master Lowbacca," Em Teedee said. "That was indeed a refreshing shutdown cycle, although considerably longer than I had anticipated. Oh, look—we have company."

Lowbacca interrupted the little droid with a rumble and a short bark. "Why, most assuredly, Master Lowbacca. I'd be delighted to provide a translation. That *is* my primary function, you know. I am fluent in over six forms of communication."

Preoccupied, Lowbacca didn't even scold the translating droid. Slowly, haltingly at first, the Wookiee began to speak, and Em Teedee translated. "Master Lowbacca knows that his recent . . . *distress* has been apparent to all of you, causing you no small measure of concern—a concern shared by myself, I might add."

Jaina put a hand on Lowbacca's shoulder. "Well, you did have us worried. We wanted you to be able to talk to us."

"We're your friends," Jacen added.

Tenel Ka merely nodded and waited for Lowbacca to continue.

He squared his shoulders and went on with his explanation. "In recent months a family matter has arisen that has caused Master Lowbacca no end of worry over his sister Sirrakuk's safety.

"As you may recall, young Wookiees occasionally take it upon themselves to perform a feat of great danger and difficulty, either alone or accompanied by friends. This gains them much respect, especially at a time when they are choosing their life path.

"Master Lowbacca decided to prove himself with such an act of bravery, since he knew that it would be difficult for many Wookiees to accept his decision to train at the Jedi academy rather than follow a more traditional calling. He was so proud of his intellectual skills that he chose to rely only on his wits; he descended to the deep forest levels on Kashyyyk without telling a single friend. Alone, he harvested these fibers from the dangerous syren plant. Though Master Lowbacca emerged unharmed with the trophy he had sought, he now admits that his solo expedition was foolhardy and ill-advised. And he fears that Sirrakuk is considerably more impulsive, more impetuous than he."

Here Lowbacca paused to finger the glossy fiber of his webbed belt. Its intricate braiding reminded Tenel Ka of Anakin's message to her, his technique of one-handed braiding.

Jaina gave Lowie a measuring look. "Ah, so now you're afraid that your sister might try to go it alone just because you did?"

Lowbacca looked down at the floor and gave a series of low rumbles and growls. Resting both elbows on his furry knees, he held his head in his hands as he spoke.

"I'm afraid the situation is rather more serious than that, and Lowbacca believes that the responsibility is largely his," Em Teedee said. "You see, since childhood Sirra's best friend was Raabakyysh—or Raaba, as Master Lowbacca's family referred to her—intelligent, strong-willed, beautiful, and adventurous. In fact, Master Lowbacca had always felt that . . . Well, go on," the little droid prompted. "You thought that *what?* You can't simply stop in the middle of a sentence."

Lowie gave a low groan and began to speak again. The dark streak of fur over his eyebrow fluffed up, showing his agitation.

"Approximately one month ago, Raaba prepared to show her own skills in the face of danger, since she wanted to join a difficult and exclusive pilots' school, hoping one day to become the captain of her own ship. Sirra and Raaba had agreed to accompany one another—but the night before they had planned to go, Raaba impulsively decided to go alone.

"In secret, she descended to the lower jungles at night, leaving behind nothing but a brief message to explain to Sirra what she had done and why. According to her note, Raaba had hoped that by duplicating Lowbacca's feat of bravery she might impress him enough that he would someday consider her a worthy mate for a Jedi—when they were old enough. However . . ."

Lowbacca paused and heaved a deep sigh before continuing. "However—oh dear!—I'm afraid Raaba never returned from her ordeal," Em Teedee continued. "When her family searched for her they found only her bloodstained toolpack. Nothing more. Raaba was gone."

"Oh, Lowie." Jaina leaned her head against the Wookiee's shoulder.

Tenel Ka looked at her friend, sensing his pain. "Ah. This is why you feel responsible."

Lowie spoke again, this time in strangled tones. "Since Raaba's . . . loss, Sirra has become increasingly reckless, as if she hardly cares whether she lives or dies. Sirra has refused all offers from other friends to accompany her on her rite of passage, insisting that Raaba was the only one she trusted enough to take along. A while ago, in desperation, Master Lowbacca sent Sirra a message asking if she would accept *him* as a suitable substitute. Chewbacca has just brought word of her answer." Em Teedee paused for a moment. "Oh, thank goodness—she's accepted!"

"Hey, that's great," Jacen said in a relieved voice.

"Oh, indeed," Em Teedee chirped.

Lowbacca didn't respond immediately. He seemed to be intently studying a chip in the flagstoned floor.

"Something's still bothering you, Lowie," Jaina said.

Tenel Ka glanced down at the stump of her severed left arm, then gave Lowie an understanding look. "You fear to face your loss. The loss of Raaba."

"That's it, isn't it?" Jaina said. "It's going to hurt to go back to Kashyyyk, because your friend Raaba won't be there. And you feel responsible that she died trying to copy something you did."

After Lowie's response, Em Teedee said, "Master Lowbacca is also concerned that his grief over the loss of Raabakyysh will render him less capable of supporting his sister at this critical time. He realizes that it may not be feasible, but he was hoping to impose on one of you to accompany him to his home-world."

Tenel Ka answered immediately. "You came when I needed you, after my accident. I can do no less, my friend." She reached out her hand to touch Lowbacca's.

"Hey, I'll come too," Jacen said, placing his hand over both of theirs. "We're stronger together. All of us."

Jaina placed her hand over the others. "I guess we all go then," she said. "Stronger together."

* * *

Lowbacca hung back, standing near the disguised *Millennium Falcon* while the Solo twins said goodbye to their father.

Han Solo gave his kids a lopsided grin. "Yeah, I kinda had a hunch that all of you were gonna volunteer to go with Lowbacca," he said. "As soon as Chewie told me the situation, I cleared it with your mom. Should be a good opportunity for you kids to brush up on Wookiee language comprehension, too."

Just then Luke Skywalker, wearing his tattered jumpsuit, emerged from the hangar bay with Chewbacca. Lowie could smell the grease stains and solvents on the old fabric. "Everything ready?" Master Skywalker asked.

"Ready as it'll ever be," Han Solo replied with another grin. "You and Chewie finished prepping the *Shadow Chaser?*"

Luke turned to Chewbacca, who had come up beside him, and said, "The *Chaser*'s a good ship; don't let anything happen to her." The big Wookiee shrugged and gave a bark of agreement.

Han Solo thumped Chewie on the back. "Take care of yourself. I'm trusting you with my kids, you know. Keep 'em all in one piece, okay? We'll see you in a couple of weeks." With that, Han gave the twins one last hug and went aboard the *Millennium Falcon*.

Before walking up the ramp, Master Skywalker looked around at the young Jedi Knights with calm confidence. "Don't forget that you're stronger together," he said. "May the Force be with you."

When the departing *Falcon* was just a speck in the distance, its bank of sublight engines glowing white, Lowbacca heaved a sigh and growled questioningly at Jaina.

She chuckled. "Right. What are we waiting for?"

3

THE SLEEK *SHADOW CHASER,* with its Imperial design and oily-looking quantum armor, glistened in the early-morning sun as Chewbacca piloted it slowly out of the sheltered hangar bay beneath the Great Temple.

Jacen stood next to his sister and Tenel Ka, watching the vessel move under silent power. Considering Lowie's recent distress, Jacen was glad his uncle Luke had let them take the *Shadow Chaser*—just the kind of fast, stealthy ship needed for an urgent mission. He was proud that Lowie wanted them along, that he and his sister and Tenel Ka could be of some help to their Wookiee friend.

Lowie stood at the far end of the clearing, motioning with his shaggy arms to direct Chewbacca's piloting. When the *Shadow Chaser* came to a halt, its entry ramp extended. Chewbacca stood at the top, gesturing with his cinnamon-furred arms and bellowing.

"Master Chewbacca cordially requests that we all come aboard," Em Teedee translated, speaking in a wobbly voice as he bounced with each running step Lowie took.

Jacen slung his satchel of belongings over one shoulder. He turned to see if he could offer any assistance to Tenel Ka, but when he saw the determined look in the warrior girl's gray eyes, he decided he'd be better off if he didn't ask.

They climbed aboard the *Shadow Chaser* and waved a brief goodbye to the other students and Tionne, who held up a hand in farewell. Even before the ship was completely sealed and ready to take off, Tionne had ushered the trainees back to their studies. With the threat of the Second Imperium loose in the galaxy, the new Jedi Knights had no time to relax.

With a smooth surge of acceleration, so powerful yet gentle it seemed almost to glide against gravity, the *Shadow Chaser* aimed its nose upward and arrowed straight into the mist-shrouded skies of the jungle moon.

* * *

En route to Kashyyyk, Jacen watched Lowie and Chewbacca in the two front seats of the narrow cockpit as the *Shadow Chaser* lurched into hyperspace. When the pair spoke rapidly in the Wookiee language, they sounded like two ferocious beasts challenging each other—but Jacen knew it was just a conversation, though he could make out only a few words. Em Teedee had been instructed not to bother translating, so that Lowie and Chewie could have some uninterrupted words in relative privacy.

While his sister tinkered with her multitool, disassembling a tiny mechanical gadget she had brought from her workshop on Yavin 4, Jacen took the opportunity to amuse Tenel Ka. He decided that, rather than telling jokes this time, he would explain to the gruff girl *why* certain things were funny, why she should be laughing at his punch lines—well, some of them, anyway. Jacen had begun to wonder if perhaps the girl simply didn't understand, and that was why she didn't laugh.

After all, it couldn't be that *every one* of his jokes was bad.

He explained how ridiculous answers to straightforward-sounding questions were supposed to be funny. He showed her how doing unexpected things with food or simple items of clothing might be considered amusing.

Tenel Ka watched him gravely, with full and unwavering attention. But she never cracked a smile.

With a sigh, Jacen told a few of his best jokes, then gave her some of his worst, trying to explain the difference by way of example. Tenel Ka didn't laugh at either.

In desperation, he considered going to the food-prep unit, ordering a pan of chilled Deneelian fizz-pudding, and then comically tripping so that the entire mess splatted in his face—but by this time, Jacen figured that even such a spectacular pratfall would have no effect on the young warrior woman.

Shaking his head in surrender, Jacen decided to leave Tenel Ka alone. He would occupy himself with something less discouraging for the time being. His spirits instantly perked up as he reached out with Jedi senses and detected something interesting in the back of the *Shadow Chaser* . . . the faint glow of a life-form, some creature out of place by the engine compartments. Jacen decided to go snoop. Nobody else was likely to be interested, anyway.

In the shielded rear compartment beyond the sleeping bunks and the food-prep area, Jacen heard the pulsing, pounding thump of engines as the *Shadow Chaser* sped along through hyperspace. He looked at the intricate control panels and access grids, the weapons batteries charged with spin-sealed Tibanna gas, and the shield generators that projected a canopy of protection around the sleek ship. But through all the din and the vibrating power of the engines, Jacen could still detect the faint emanations of some small creature, lost and frightened.

"Don't be scared," Jacen said, speaking with his voice and at the same time thinking the words through the Force. "I'm your friend. I can help you. Let me see you. It's okay."

He lowered his voice to a whisper as he bent down, looking in crannies between the control grids. He followed his senses. "I won't hurt you. I just want to see you. I know you're afraid. You can trust me." He touched his fingers lightly to one of the cool metal access panels, gently brushing the ion shield generators with his mind.

He sensed the creature hiding back there, trembling, guarding something. A little nest?

"It's just me," Jacen said. "Relax. I'll take care of you."

He popped the metal covering off the access panel to the ion shield generator. Inside, in a comfortable little pocket of colorful debris, cowered a furry eight-legged rodent, a mouselike creature with puffy frost-gray fur. It looked up at him with tiny black eyes that glittered in the dim light. It wiggled its damp nose. Judging by the pair of long teeth that protruded from the center of its snout, this rodent was a gnawer, not a flesh eater.

"Come here," Jacen said. "That's not a safe place for you to be." He reached in and calmly drew the rodent out. Its eight legs trembled and tickled against his palm like a plump furry spider, but a friendly and gentle one.

Jacen stroked its back, then bent to peer at the nest again. The rodent had chewed tiny strips of insulation from the power cables, yanked threads and wires and fabrics and plastics from the shield generator to create a soft pocket in which squirmed four smooth cylindrical grubs, the creature's young.

"Oh, what a nice nest you have," Jacen said soothingly. "But I don't think you were supposed to use those components. We need this ion shield generator, you know. It protects the whole ship."

He continued stroking the rodent and retrieved the nest carefully so as not to disturb the young. He held the nest in his hand and placed the mother back on top, snuggled against her little ones. "I'll keep you safe," Jacen said, "but we'll have to tell Jaina and Lowie about this, so they can make repairs."

Preoccupied with calming his new pet, Jacen returned to the forward compartments. He went to his sister who was still tinkering with an incomprehensible mechanical gadget. "Hey, Jaina? I've got some bad news."

She turned, holding up a small hydrospanner. "What?"

Before he could answer, though, the *Shadow Chaser* gave a sudden lurch and rocked as if it had slammed into something invisible. The deck tilted sideways, throwing Jacen to his knees. He struggled to protect his new pet.

The colors of hyperspace swirled like a psychedelic flood in all directions out the windowports. When the *Shadow Chaser* gave another violent lurch, Jacen tumbled backward to the deck; it took all his concentration to guard the precious nest.

"Uh, never mind," he said. "It can wait."

Jaina gripped the armrests of her seat while the ship rocked back and forth. Her tools and the electronic di-scanner remote she had just repaired flew like projectiles to the bulkheads, then smashed onto the deck-plates, ruined.

When the ship momentarily stabilized, her brother crawled to his feet, cradling something in one arm, his hair even more tousled than usual. He checked to make sure Tenel Ka was okay. The warrior girl stood up, planting her booted feet wide apart, seeking balance as the *Shadow Chaser* shuddered and bucked its way through the disturbance.

"What is happening?" Tenel Ka said.

Ahead in the cockpit, Lowie and Chewbacca roared to each other, fighting the controls.

"An ion storm?" Em Teedee chimed in with an electronic wail. "Are you absolutely certain? We're doomed!"

Jaina's lips pressed into a tight, grim line. "It's an ion storm, all right. Just bad luck. Couldn't predict this. We plotted the shortest path to Kashyyyk using the navicomputer. The on-line catalogs only display stable astronomical hazards—star clusters, black holes, and high-energy nebulas—but ion storms come and go. They don't have any set position, but they sure ripple up hyperspace when you pass through 'em."

"Is it serious?" Jacen asked. Droplets of sweat broke out on his brow. "I've got a bad feeling about this."

"Just have to wait and see," Jaina said.

Tenel Ka stood with her hand to her utility belt, ready to fight some tangible foe with a throwing knife, her lightsaber, even her fibercord. But none of those would do any good against an ion storm.

Chewbacca and Lowie grappled with the controls, hairy fingers flying over panels, yanking levers. The *Shadow Chaser* winked out of hyperspace and lurched back into the fringes of the furious ion storm.

"Uh-oh," Jacen said. "I forgot to tell you that we might have some damage to our ion shield generator." He held up the nested bundle of wires and insulation.

Jaina whirled, more worried than ever. "Oh, no! That could—"

As the *Shadow Chaser* plummeted into the space storm, they were immediately surrounded by a spiderweb of high-energy lightning bolts, powerful discharges that arched across the seething knot of hot gas that formed the unexpected interstellar hurricane. The ship thrashed like a mad bantha, throwing its passengers about.

Jacen braced his shoulder against a control bar, and Tenel Ka fell into him. He held the warrior girl upright, pinning both of them against the wall, still cradling his newfound pet in one hand. Jaina, trying to struggle toward the cockpit, fell flat on her face.

The *Shadow Chaser*'s rear engines kicked in, and the sublight drive heaved them away from the rippling ion cloud. In the pilot seat Chewbacca groaned, gripping the controls and wrestling to keep them on a straight course, the shortest path out of danger.

Lowie cried out as fingernails of icy blue electricity skittered across the control panels, burning out subsystem after subsystem.

Behind the back bulkheads, the straining ion shield generators squealed loudly in surrender. Then, with a loud bang, they fell silent.

The rippling colors dwindled outside the cockpit window, and the *Shadow Chaser* careened onward, spiraling out into open space, safe at last from the storm. Still, Jaina shuddered to think of how much damage the stray ion bursts must have caused.

Jacen brushed himself off and forced a lopsided grin. "Now, uh, as I was saying about that damage to the ion shields . . ." He held out the eight-legged rodent, which cowered in her nest, as if she comprehended the trouble she had caused. "I found this critter's nest in the machinery. I took her out, but I needed one of you to fix the damage."

"It would appear that we now have plenty of time to fix it," Tenel Ka said. "We are *capable* of fixing it, are we not?"

From the cockpit Lowie and Chewie consulted in growling voices.

"Oh, excellent!" Em Teedee said. "Master Lowbacca says we have been quite lucky. Our propulsion and life-support systems are largely intact and can be repaired quite easily. My, that *is* wonderful news."

Em Teedee fell silent as the Wookiees continued, and then the little droid piped up. "Excuse me—what did you say, Master Lowbacca? Oh dear! It seems, however, that our navicomputer has been completely disabled. We have lost all coordinates for getting from here to anywhere else. Oh my. We're . . . we're lost in space."

Chewbacca and Lowie both roared in outrage at the translating droid, and Em Teedee quickly fell silent. "Well, I suppose I *should* find it comforting that you both have such confidence in your navigational abilities," Em Teedee muttered after a moment.

The two Wookiees busily consulted with each other and began punching and programming numerical values into the navigational control panel, double-checking each other's calculations. Before long, after everyone had helped with temporary repairs, the *Shadow Chaser* was on its way again.

At first Jaina was surprised that they were back on course—then she realized that she shouldn't have been. After all, Kashyyyk was the only Wookiee planet, and both Lowie and Chewbacca greatly revered the place.

Why should she find it unusual that they had both memorized the coordinates for their homeworld?

4

IN A SECLUDED meeting chamber at the Shadow Academy, Zekk stood proudly, struggling to hide any sign of nervousness. He raised his chin and waited to receive his long-anticipated reward. It had come to this, at last.

The air smelled cold and metallic, exhilarating. Brilliant light stabbed down from the metal ceiling, making him squint his emerald eyes; the irises were ringed with a darker corona, like the shadowy outline around his personality. Zekk tossed back his shaggy dark hair, one shade lighter than black, and looked up, blinking, as Lord Brakiss approached him in the harsh light.

The master of the Shadow Academy was wrapped in rippling silvery robes of a fabric that looked as if it might have been spun by deadly spiders. Against one wall, wearing her spined and glittering black cloak, stood Tamith Kai, the fierce commander of the new Nightsisters. Her violet eyes burned beneath a generous mane of ebony hair.

Beside Tamith Kai waited two other prominent Nightsisters—attractive and petite Garowyn and muscular Vonnda Ra, both from the planet Dathomir. In their black-spined capes and lizard-hide armor, the three Nightsisters reminded Zekk of hungry birds of prey.

Next to them, the grizzled TIE pilot, Qorl, stood at attention, surrounded by a stormtrooper escort of his most promising Imperial trainees. Beneath the white armor, one of the burliest of these was the gangleader Norys, who had led the Lost Ones on Coruscant not long ago. While the other stormtroopers stood rigidly at attention, weapons shouldered, Norys fidgeted and seemed angry and uncomfortable with the ceremony. His senses finely tuned by his own anxiety, Zekk could pick up the harsh muttering words from behind the bully's white helmet. "Trash collector . . . gets all the breaks."

Moving quietly and unobtrusively, Qorl rested his powerful droid replacement hand on the stormtrooper's shoulder armor in a gesture that was firm and clearly meant to quiet the bully. Zekk knew Qorl's droid arm was powerful enough to crack the white armor like an eggshell. Norys fell silent, though he obviously remained upset.

Zekk didn't mind. This was his moment of glory, and he smiled faintly at the thought of how much had changed in only a few months—and how now he had arrived at the peak of his triumph.

For this presentation and initiation, Zekk had worn his new leather uniform; heavy round studs decorated the reinforced pads on his shoulders, creating a kind of armored hide. His hands were encased in thick black gloves that made a warm, satisfying creak as he clenched and unclenched his fists.

Brakiss's porcelain-perfect face smiled with pride. He held out a gift, a flowing black cape lined with deep, vibrant crimson, like fresh dark blood.

"Young Zekk, I present this to you as a symbol of your importance to the Shadow Academy," Brakiss said. "You have proven to be an avid pupil, a true asset to the Second Imperium. Our efforts would be greatly disadvantaged had you not joined us in our struggle. In your duel to the death with Vilas, our other powerful candidate, you proved yourself to be our champion, our new hope—our Darkest Knight."

Zekk blinked back stinging tears of pride and accomplishment as Brakiss draped the heavy fabric over his padded shoulders, then fastened the cape at his throat with a clasp shaped like a ferocious silver scarab.

Zekk watched Tamith Kai, who stood coiled with deadly energy, like a rogue assassin droid. He saw the tall Nightsister flinch at the mention of the slain Vilas, who had been her student, her candidate for the Shadow Academy's champion. But Zekk had defeated the surly, overconfident young man, and now *he* wore the black cape . . . while Vilas was little more than space dust ejected from the garbage port.

Brakiss stepped back and folded his hands in front of him; silvery sleeves flowed down his wrists, swallowing up his manicured hands. "The time has come for you to embark on your first important mission for us, Zekk. You will be given command of troops to prove your skills."

Zekk's heart leaped. He didn't think he could stand any more exhilaration in one day. "What," he stammered, "what do you wish me to do?"

"As a final stage in preparing for our attack on Rebel fortifications, we must launch another raid to obtain vital supplies. You will lead an assault team to the Wookiee world of Kashyyyk. There, in one of their technological tree cities, is the fabrication facility for the most sophisticated computer equipment used by our enemy's ships.

"If your raid is successful in obtaining guidance and tactical systems, we will have an enormous advantage in our overall conflict. We will then be able to throw the Rebel fleet into confusion and use their own computers against them to transmit conflicting signals. We can also use these systems to mimic their secret ship ID patterns, so that Second Imperium fighters can travel freely in enemy territory by identifying themselves as Rebel ships.

"Because of the importance of this mission, you will be assigned a powerful team. I am giving you use of the new holographic disguises we have developed for just such an infiltration effort. Everything depends on you, Zekk. Do you feel up to the task?"

Zekk nodded enthusiastically. "Yes! Yes, I can do that for you."

Tamith Kai strode forward into the pool of bright light that poured down on Zekk. He turned to look at the tall, ominous woman. Her wine-dark lips curved down in a serious expression. As if pronouncing his doom, she said, "There is one other part of the plan. Through an intercepted transmission, we have learned that those troublesome young Jedi brats are even now on their way to Kashyyyk. They sent a message to say goodbye to their mother—luckily Qorl has been monitoring all comm traffic from the vicinity of Yavin 4 back to the capital world." She stared at her clawlike fingernails, as if she found something interesting there.

"We had originally planned to wait a few more weeks before conducting this raid, but now . . . the timing couldn't be more perfect." Her violet eyes flashed with pleasure. "Your second assignment is to make sure that Jacen and Jaina and their difficult friends are . . . removed, so that we can proceed with our galactic conquest without worrying about their meddling."

Zekk swallowed hard when he heard the new orders, but did not reply. Jacen, and especially his sister Jaina, had been good friends for much of his youth. They had parted ways, though, when the twins went off to the Jedi academy, abandoning Zekk to his squalid life in the underworld of Coruscant. He had had no hope for a bright future until the Shadow Academy found him.

"All right," Zekk said in a voice low and hoarse. He tried to speak louder, not willing to let self-doubt show through. He had made his own choices, and now he had to follow through on them despite the difficulties his conscience might encounter. "All right," he repeated. "When do we leave?"

"As soon as possible," Tamith Kai answered.

* * *

In the outer docking bay of the Shadow Academy, Tamith Kai and the other two Nightsisters loaded the ship for its assault mission. The vessel, marked with neutral insignia, was a small cargo freighter stolen from a lost trader who had ventured too close to the Core Systems. Tamith Kai wondered idly if the trader still languished deep in an Imperial prison . . . or if the guards had gotten around to executing him yet, since the Second Imperium could never afford to let the man loose with his knowledge of the Core Systems and the commandeered freighter.

In the observation bubble above the docking bay, Qorl stood by the cloaking shield controls, monitoring preparations for the launch of the mission. The old pilot would not accompany them himself, but he had chosen a handful of the Second Imperium's newly constructed TIE fighters and bombers to be loaded into the freighter's cargo bay.

"We'll see if Brakiss was wrong to place confidence in his young pet," Tamith Kai murmured in her low, rich voice. "I still don't trust him. What is it Norys calls the boy—trash collector? I sense that Zekk hasn't yet given himself entirely over to the dark side."

Vonnda Ra frowned, her squarish face puzzled. "But after all the work he's done—look at his training. How can you question Zekk's abilities?"

"It is his *motives* I question, not his abilities. I had no such doubts about the loyalty of my Vilas."

Garowyn interrupted. "Perhaps, Tamith Kai. But Vilas is dead. Zekk proved to be a better fighter. Perhaps you're simply being a sore loser."

Tamith Kai's eyes flared like twin violet stars about to explode. "I am *not* a sore loser," she snarled.

"Obviously not," Garowyn said, turning away with an ironic smile.

Tamith Kai clenched her fists in rage. "I think Zekk still has feelings for those obnoxious Jedi twins. His friendship is not so easily given up." She calmed herself. Her lips, dark as overripe fruit, twisted into a smile. "That's why I made sure this mission would be more than just a simple raid. Let us watch how Zekk takes care of his other assignment."

Vonnda Ra stored a crate of weapons inside the cargo shuttle and went to fetch the heavy belts that carried their holographic-disguise generators. "I thought the computer guidance and tactical systems were our most important objective."

"For you, perhaps, and for the Second Imperium," Tamith Kai said, nodding distractedly, "but not for me."

Garowyn crossed her wiry arms over her small chest. "You may be my nominal superior, Tamith Kai, but I can set my own priorities as well. I'll assist you in this raid, but the main reason *I'm* going along is to retrieve our . . . stolen property."

"What stolen property?" Vonnda Ra asked, the belts and holographic control packs still dangling from her outstretched arms.

"Our greatest ship, our most ambitious design, with quantum armor and powerful weapons—the *Shadow Chaser*. It is the peak of the Second Imperium's engineering success, my one joy. But Skywalker and that traitorous girl from Dathomir tricked me into an escape pod and stole my own ship out from under me! The Jedi academy has been using it ever since. I had all but given up hope of ever regaining what was rightfully mine, but now I've learned that the Wookiee and the Jedi brats have taken my ship to Kashyyyk. Now is our perfect chance to retrieve what is ours."

"Well, if you do get the *Shadow Chaser*, there will be more room for us when we return in the assault shuttle, then," Vonnda Ra said.

Tamith Kai directed a cool stare at the short, bronze-haired Nightsister. At last she smiled, with just a trace of warmth. "So. I see we each have our own agendas," she said. "Let us hope we all succeed."

5

"WHY, CERTAINLY, MASTER Lowbacca. I'd be happy to be of service in such a manner," Em Teedee said as they approached Kashyyyk. "Calculation of that trajectory is really quite simple."

Lowie accepted the finding from the little droid and input it manually on the *Shadow Chaser*'s control panel. Beside him, his uncle drew in a deep, happy breath when the rich brown-green planet appeared in the viewport, as if anticipating the tastes and smells and sounds of home. Despite the heavy heart with which he was returning, Lowie also felt a rush of excitement and pleasure. He would soon be in the safe, peaceful treetops of Kashyyyk.

"Well done, Masters Lowbacca and Chewbacca!" Em Teedee caroled. Lowie grunted an absentminded acknowledgment, still captivated by the sight of his planet. It looked much the same as it had on the day he left with his uncle and Han Solo in the *Millennium Falcon* to become a Jedi student. How long ago was it now?

Too long. Lowie's yearning to see his family again became almost overwhelming. The two Wookiees worked at the piloting controls with an urgency that came from happy anticipation. As the *Shadow Chaser* approached the thick canopy below, Chewbacca pointed with a certain wistfulness toward the treetop city in which he and Lowie's mother had grown up. With all of Chewie's travels across the galaxy, Lowbacca wondered if his uncle ever felt as homesick as he himself occasionally did on Yavin 4. He knew Chewbacca would somehow find the time to visit his own city and the rest of his family in the next day or so.

Behind him, the twins and Tenel Ka uttered exclamations of admiration at the beauty of Kashyyyk and the size of the trees. "Even though I've been here before, I always forget how big they are," Jaina murmured, pressing her fingers against the windowport.

"Impressive," Tenel Ka agreed. "But where are the cities?"

Chewbacca let the sleek ship dip a bit lower, and Lowie pointed to where clusters of high trees extended their crowns above the lower canopies. Nestled in the masses of thick branches, gleaming towers and platforms were visible, signs of habitation that folded into the natural formation of the trees. "Ah," she said, sounding somewhat surprised. "Aha."

"Neat, huh?" Jacen said, leaning closer to the warrior girl. "They like to make nature and technology work together."

Lowie growled his agreement. "Master Lowbacca points out that technology and nature need not be mutually exclusive," Em Teedee translated. "Blending the two can be more pleasant than separating them."

When he finally caught sight of his home city, Lowie felt a renewed impatience. It was all he could do to keep himself from unbuckling his crash webbing while Chewbacca guided their damaged ship toward the nearest landing platform.

The moment the *Shadow Chaser* touched down, Lowbacca sprang from the copilot's seat and rushed to the exit hatch. Through the cockpit window, he could see his family waiting for him on the platform—his father, Mahraccor; his mother, Kallabow; and his younger sister, Sirrakuk.

Lowie opened the hatch and stood in the sunlight for a split second, taking in every detail, sniffing the air, letting his eyes be bombarded by the rich greens and browns of the treetops. Then he and his family all roared greetings. His parents looked well and happy, if a little tired. His mother's kind blue eyes, surrounded by auburn whorls of fur, shone with pride. The dark streak in his father's fur showed no signs of graying with age.

Only his sister looked different—taller, sleeker and prettier than he had remembered her, but with a heavy sadness about her face. Sirra had trimmed her fur in unusual patterns, had shaved decorative designs around her head and arms. But her fangs were white and sharp, the fur around her nose and mouth well-groomed and long. She was definitely growing up.

His father raised both arms over his head and bellowed another greeting. Lowie roared back and ran toward them.

Jacen looked around the dining table in consternation, wishing for the tenth time that he understood the Wookiee language better. Ensconced between Lowie and Sirra, he looked across the table to where Jaina and Tenel Ka sat on either side of Chewbacca; he wondered if they felt as confused and overwhelmed as he did in the middle of the loud and incomprehensible dinner conversation.

Transparent mesh cages filled with swarms of tiny, luminescent bugs hung from the ceiling branches, providing a fuzzy, warm light. Exotic spices and incense wafted around the room and out the open window notches into the humid night. The air was thick with mouthwatering smells of the welcome meal Lowie's parents had prepared.

The table was a huge slab of wood, a slice from a broad-boled tree: its hypnotic concentric rings indicated how long the tree had lived. All the chairs and furniture in Lowie's home seemed overlarge, built for bodies much taller than the average human. Jacen shifted uncomfortably on the high bench at the table.

Something finally clicked in his head. "Hey, where's Em Teedee?" he asked. "We could really use his translating skills here."

Jaina flushed, her mouth forming a small "oh" of surprise. "I, um, guess that's my fault," she stammered. "I kind of borrowed him and hooked him up to the *Shadow Chaser*'s diagnostics so he could give us a readout of the parts we need to repair the ship." She bit her lower lip. "I suppose it would have been more polite to wait until *after* we had had a chance to chat with Lowie's family a while."

Jacen shrugged and squeezed his eyes shut. He tried to concentrate in the new environment, to pick out individual words. But with five Wookiees barking, bellowing, growling, and roaring, it was difficult to make sense of their speech. He took a slow breath and tried to relax, planning to reach out with the Force to see if he could sense some meaning in the conversation.

Outside, Jacen could hear a warm afternoon rain running gentle fingers through the leaves of the stately wroshyr trees. Inside, the battle of tones continued, strange voices mixing with familiar ones. In the undertones, he felt joy and apprehension, hope and sorrow. He felt . . .

He felt the touch of a furry hand on his arm. Jacen looked up in embarrassment to find Lowie's sister Sirra holding out a platter laden with roasted meats and vegetables. Sirra uttered a polite but curious woof.

"Blaster bolts! I'm sorry, is that plate for me?"

Lowie chuffed a laugh and then swept a hand around the table to indicate that everyone else had already been served. Each of the Wookiees' plates was filled with coarsely chopped fresh meat and mounds of raw vegetables. Jaina had a platter of food similar to his own, while Tenel Ka's held a mixture of vegetables and meats, both cooked and raw. Jacen was amused to note that Tenel Ka's appetite reflected the conflicting preferences of her primitive and refined upbringings. Kallabow and Mahraccor had worked hard to accommodate the dietary preferences of their human guests. Jacen accepted the platter from Sirra and thanked her.

When the Wookiees all fell silent, expectant, and turned to Lowbacca, he held one furry hand over his plate of food as he crooned a few short phrases in a low voice. Jacen recognized the Wookiee ceremonial speech of thankfulness that he had heard from Chewbacca so often.

Lowie stood then, raised his arms high and spread his hands as if forming a protective leafy canopy over his family and friends, and repeated his brief speech. Lowie's mother crooned a sad, low note.

A moment later, both Wookiees and humans attacked their food as if none of them had had a decent meal for weeks.

The next day, Jaina murmured something noncommittal and looked dubiously at the list that Em Teedee had downloaded to her datapad. Jacen and Tenel Ka sat near her in Lowie's spacious room, which had been hollowed out from part of a massive wroshyr tree. Lowie disconnected the lead wires from the diagnostics panel, tucked them back into Em Teedee's casing, and closed it with a snap. While Jaina and Lowie worked together to catalog the *Shadow Chaser*'s ills, Chewbacca had taken the opportunity to go to the other side of the planet to visit the rest of his family, whom he had not seen in some time.

A few leftover spatters of rain from another brief shower dripped outside the open window. Sirra sat with them, her patchy fur standing on end. She didn't want to be alone, apparently, but she didn't participate much in the conversation either.

"Take a look at this, Lowie," Jaina said, holding up the datapad.

The Wookiee studied the list of ruined components with a thoughtful growl. Jacen and Tenel Ka crowded in to get a look as well. Jacen flashed his sister a mischievous grin. "Hard to believe that an itty-bitty ion storm could cause so much damage, huh?"

Jaina sent him a withering look. "If that furry pet of yours hadn't chewed all the circuits—"

"Hey, that's not fair! I'd never even seen her before we left Yavin 4." Jacen removed the fluffy creature from the temporary cage he had made for her and her babies. The little eight-legged rodent seemed very pleased with her soft new nest. "She didn't mean to cause any trouble—did you, Ion?"

He held the fluffy ball close to his face and stroked her with one finger. The tiny creature made a faint cooing sound. Jacen would set the rodent free when they returned to Yavin 4, but for now he would take good care of her.

"The fault was not Jacen's," Tenel Ka said in a mild voice. "And blaming the creature serves no purpose."

Jaina shrugged one shoulder. "Yeah, I know. I'm sorry. Just don't let Chewie catch sight of that pesky little thing when he gets back tonight."

Lowie handed the datapad back to Jaina with a confident bark. "Master Lowbacca believes that we can obtain most of these parts at the local fabrication facility, or create reasonable substitutes," Em Teedee said.

Jaina felt hopeful. "You mean the factory where your parents work?"

"Blaster bolts," Jacen said. "Are you sure? There's a lot of stuff on that list. What do they make at the factory, anyway?"

Lowie gestured with his hands and growled an answer. Jaina could vaguely sense what he was saying. Em Teedee said, "The fabrication facility that employs Master Lowbacca's parents, as well as most of the other inhabitants of this tree city, produces a variety of sophisticated computer equipment for use in a wide range of transportation applications."

Jaina's interest sharpened at the idea of a factory filled with exotic and complex systems.

"Like what?" Jacen asked, placing Ion back in her cage. The little rodent inspected her grubs, rooting around in her fuzzy nest.

After more of Lowie's growling and gesticulating, Em Teedee said, "Among other things, the facility produces guidance control systems for planetary control towers, navigational subsystems and backups, tactical systems, communication encryption generators, multiphasic—"

"Hey, I think we get the idea. Thanks, Em Teedee," Jacen broke in.

Jaina tried to suppress a chuckle. Her ever-curious brother had gotten more explanation than he had bargained for. "Lowie, is there any way we can move the *Shadow Chaser* closer to your home so we can work on it more easily? The hangar bay where we stored it is way on the other side of the city. Not very convenient, if you know what I mean."

Lowie shook his head, but growled a suggestion. "Master Lowbacca proposes—" Em Teedee began.

"Yeah, I think I got it," Jaina said, struggling to understand a few of the Wookiee words. "We can pull out the damaged subsystems one or two at a time, bring them here to Lowie's house, and work on 'em." She beamed. "That's a great idea. So what are we waiting for?"

6

THE MORNING BREEZE ruffled Lowie's ginger-colored fur as he stood with his friends outside on the treetop observation platform. The area was broad and smooth, empty of equipment or visitors—the perfect place for them to stretch their muscles and perform Jedi exercises in the fresh outdoors.

The air was enriched with the scent of spring blossoms, new leaves, and sun-warmed wood. Beside him on the wooden platform, Sirra crouched in pensive silence, watching the Jedi trainees as they worked through their individual exercise routines.

Lowie tried not to make it obvious that he was keeping an eye on Sirra. Too great a show of concern on his part, he figured, would probably only annoy his sister and make her more stubborn. They had left many issues unspoken between them, but he knew they would have to talk soon.

He flicked his golden eyes around the platform and watched as Jacen did push-ups and Jaina practiced gymnastic tumbles. Tenel Ka, limber as ever, stood on one leg, the other pulled up high behind her, pointing toward the sky.

Lowie bent over, placed both hands flat on the warm wood of the platform, kicked his feet into the air, and balanced there. When Jaina turned a cartwheel past him, he risked another look at Sirra. His brash younger sister had spoken very little since his arrival yesterday, though she had instinctively remained close to him. Lowie couldn't help wondering what she was thinking. Did Sirra in any way resent him because he had inherited Jedi potential, while she had not? Did she blame him for Raaba's death? Did she resent the friends he had brought home with him?

He and his sister were so different that Lowie wondered if there had ever been a time when they understood each other completely. Lowie was thoughtful, analytical, introspective, while Sirra was wild, confident, outspoken. He preferred not to draw attention to himself, while she enjoyed surprising people with her appearance—why else would she trim the fur at her ankles, knees, wrists, and elsewhere in such a strange patchwork style?

Sirra and Lowie had always trusted one another, though—but did she *still* trust him?

Tenel Ka whirled through Lowie's field of vision, performing aerial somersaults. He felt himself begin to lose his balance, but quickly regained it and began doing vertical push-ups.

"Hey, Lowie," Jacen yelled from behind him, "can you spare a little concentration from your exercises to teach us a few words in your Wookiee dialect?"

Lowie grunted his assent. "Master Lowbacca says he would not be averse to the possibility of instructing you," Em Teedee translated.

Jaina chuckled. "Gee, that's funny, Em Teedee—it sounded to me like all he said was 'yes.'"

"Well, I suppose that *is* an alternate translation," Em Teedee said, sounding somewhat miffed. "Though it's rather unimaginative."

Lowie gave a bark of laughter and looked over at Sirra to see if she had listened to the interchange. She returned his look for a moment, then deliberately turned and sat with her back to him at the edge of the platform, dangling her legs over the side, above the leafy canopy far below. She stared down toward the unseen depths . . . where Raaba had disappeared.

"Well then," Em Teedee said, sounding hurt now, "once you've taught the others your dialect, Master Lowbacca, I suppose you won't require my services anymore."

"Of course we'll still need you, Em Teedee," Jaina said. "We'll never be able to understand *every* word Lowie says."

Lowie absently grunted his agreement, still looking at Sirra's hunched shoulders. It occurred to him that although he had come home to support her in this difficult time, he had no idea *how* to do it. Clearly, his presence alone was not enough. He wanted to try talking with her, but what if she had problems he couldn't solve? What if *he* was part of the problem, having set a dangerous example that his sister felt obligated to follow, though it might mean her death?

Still balanced on his hands but deep in thought about Sirra, Lowie lost his concentration and his balance again, this time with embarrassing results. He teetered precariously for a moment, trying to regain his equilibrium. Em Teedee let out a squeal of surprise, then Lowie toppled over, landing on his rear end with a loud thump.

Jaina rushed over, adding to the Wookiee's embarrassment. "Are you all right?"

Lowie wished his friends had ignored the entire incident. To Jaina's credit, as soon as she had determined he was unhurt, she made a hasty retreat and became absorbed in her exercises again, studiously pretending not to notice while Lowie picked himself up off the platform's floorboards and dusted off his fur.

Still a bit self-conscious at his clumsiness, Lowie told Em Teedee to shut down for a rest cycle as he ambled over and seated himself by Sirra at the platform's edge, letting his legs swing free beside hers. He waited for a while, hoping his withdrawn sister would say something, since he had no idea where to begin. Watching her out of the corner of his eye, he pondered again what had caused them to turn out so different from each other, how two such opposites could spring from the same set of parents.

Lowie had a strong aptitude for the Force, whereas Sirra showed neither potential nor interest in the Jedi Knights. Lowie's quiet introspective nature had always been a sharp contrast to her confident outspokenness—until recently, that is, when she'd become so quiet. And, while Lowie could sit engrossed for hours in the intricacies of a computer system, Sirra became restless quickly and longed for excitement and adventure. In addition, Lowie had always prided himself in being obedient, finding it simpler to do what was expected of him than to expend effort on meaningless acts of rebellion against authority.

At that thought, Lowie's eyes were drawn to the bands of close-cropped fur on Sirra's body. It was not a style sported by any adults that Lowie knew, and very few youth. He finally decided to ask her about it, hoping to start a conversation somehow. Lowie blurted out the question, asking if the style kept her cooler during warm weather.

Sirra shrugged. That was not why she did it.

A symbol of mourning, then? For Raaba?

Sirra snorted at the suggestion.

Rebellion, then?

Sirra thought for a moment before sighing in confusion, obviously at a loss about how to explain. She thought of it as . . . a way of showing on the outside what did not show on the *inside:* that she was different.

Lowie considered this, rumbling deep in his throat. He had thought it was already clear enough that everyone was different.

Sirra shook her head and sprang to her feet on the platform. Lowie saw at once that she was irritated, that he had misunderstood her, for his sister walked all the way around the edge of the platform before motioning for him to join her. When he did, he practically had to run to keep pace with her.

At last Sirra spoke again, her agitation apparent in her voice. She pointed to her shaved wrists and elbows, explaining in more detail that she did this to show others that she was not like *them*.

Lowie cocked his head quizzically, trying to think of a response, but Sirra resumed her explanation. She said that since she didn't have Force potential as he did, their parents had always just assumed that she would work in the fabrication facility. But Sirra had no wish to work there like everyone else did. She didn't enjoy assembling computers, and was only a mediocre programmer. She raised a fist and barked loudly—she wanted something much more exciting!

Lowie shook his head sternly. Wookiees could excel in engineering, in science, in piloting—anything they wanted to. But such success did not come easily. He nodded toward his friends to indicate how hard they were training at the moment. Lowie and Sirra walked together for a while in silence.

Jacen, Jaina, and Tenel Ka finished their exercises and perched at the edge of the platform, looking down at the beautiful tree canopy. Jacen pointed. "Hey, Lowie—how do you say the name for those trees?"

Lowie barked the answer—wroshyr.

After he and Sirra had skirted the trio, Lowie asked his sister what she wanted to do with her life. Sirra groaned and shrugged uncertainly.

Lowie thought for a moment. Well, what did she *like* to do? he asked.

Sirra heaved a heavy sigh, spreading her hairy arms wide to encompass the forest and the sky. She loved to be out and around, to visit new places and learn new things. She enjoyed feeling free, the way Lowie himself did when he'd travel alone in his skyhopper. And Sirra liked making her own decisions, not being told what she had to do and when.

Lowie growled the names of distant cities of Kashyyyk, suggesting other factories, other jobs. Sirra waved a hand as if to brush the idea away. She wanted to do something important, something unusual. Her voice suddenly sounded resentful of Lowie and his Jedi friends. They had been given a tremendous opportunity, and she wanted one for herself.

The twins and Tenel Ka took turns reaching out with the Force to make temporary furrows in the leafy canopy below, as if a giant invisible bird of prey were skimming over the leaves in search of its quarry. Sirra grumbled in disgust and pointed to the Jedi trainees "racing" their Force furrows through the leaves, crisscrossing and intertwining them.

She would never squander talent like that, she insisted. Knowing that she soon intended to prove her strength and bravery against a syren plant, Sirra expressed her doubts that the young Jedi Knights would last even five minutes down in the forest underlevels. Their Force powers would not keep them safe, she asserted, if this was how they used them.

Lowie fixed his sister with a challenging look, trying to explain difficult concepts. His friends were merely "exercising" their abilities. Learning and practice were never wasted. He insisted that his friends were much stronger than they appeared.

Sirra shrugged away the comment and began pacing the flat, sun-drenched platform again. Exasperated, Lowie demanded to know how she expected him to help her solve her problem.

Surprise registered on Sirra's face. She hadn't *asked* him for a solution.

It was Lowie's turn to be perplexed. If he saw his sister confused or in pain, he asked, shouldn't he assume she wanted help?

Sirra's eyes narrowed. With a quick series of gruff words, she reminded him of when he had fallen down a few minutes earlier and bruised his . . . his *dignity*. Had he wanted anyone to solve his problem for him?

Lowie shook his head. Sirra raised her eyebrows, asking if now he understood.

Lowie saw what his sister was getting at, but that had not been the same thing. He *knew* she needed help.

Sirra sat down again at the platform's edge, looking out across the wroshyr trees. Lowie squatted beside his sister with earnest concern, and her expression softened. She didn't want him to solve her problem, she said, but that didn't mean he wasn't helping.

Lowie realized that it was helping her just to have someone who listened.

He clasped her shoulder, and Sirra sat closer to him. For now, that seemed to be enough.

7

FROM HER UNUSUAL perch, Jaina surveyed the high-tech tree city and realized how much Kashyyyk looked like an organic version of Coruscant.

Here at the canopy level, surrounded by industrial structures and Wookiee living quarters, Jaina saw tall exhaust ports and crystalline windows that reflected the hazy gray-white sky. The crowns of tall trees thrust above the main canopy like skyscraper towers covered with foliage. A huge clump of majestic growth in the distance sat like an island above the leafy waves of the unbroken treetops; from this distance, it reminded her of the pyramidal towers of the Imperial Palace.

Jaina thought with a twinge of homesickness that she missed her mother. The last time she and Jacen had returned to the capital world, though, they had lost their friend Zekk, who had been captured by the Shadow Academy. . . .

Clusters of Wookiee homes dotted the canopy, compact dwellings connected to the computer factory complex by natural roadways that extended like the spokes of a wheel across the treetops. Imported banthas trudged along the wide, wooden roads, brushing against encroaching leaves. They plodded along sturdy worn branches hundreds of meters above the untraveled and treacherous lower levels of the primeval forest.

The bantha Jaina and her friends rode from Lowie's home to the computer fabrication complex was large enough that all five companions could ride on the padded seats strapped to the beast's back. The bantha had a rich, spicy animal scent that tingled in her nostrils. A harness made of bright red ribbons jingled with burnished brass bells.

Her brother Jacen patted the wiry cinnamon-brown fur of the enormous beast of burden. Riding this bantha seemed to be the most enjoyable part of their trip for him so far. The driver, a mousy Sullustan with huge dark eyes that glinted in the sunlight, hunched between the enormous ridged horns that curved around the bantha's head. The docile beast moved along the wooden walkway, paying no heed to the lush vegetation on all sides.

"Banthas were bred for desert travel," Jacen piped up, "but this guy seems to love it here."

Indeed, Jaina thought, the beast seemed fat and healthy, content to carry passengers from the residential districts to the main fabrication facility. They passed other Wookiees walking to work, eating up the distance with long-legged strides.

Beside her on the padded riding structure, Tenel Ka stared ahead, her expression unreadable but alert, ready for anything. Lowie and Sirra sat on the back cushions, chatting comfortably in the Wookiee language.

Jaina looked forward to her tour of the computer factory. She couldn't wait to see the engineering marvels and industrial facilities the Wookiees had installed on their wilderness world. Lowie probably would have been eager as well, if he hadn't been so concerned about his sister.

The bantha stopped and let them off at an outer checkpoint that gave access to the technical complex. Using handholds on the padded seats, the companions climbed down the hairy back of the bantha and jumped to the interlocked wooden deck. Since the bantha transportation systems were designed for use by tall Wookiees, the drop was a meter longer than Jaina expected. She wondered how the diminutive Sullustan driver ever managed to climb his way onto the beast's head.

Lowie paid the driver a few credit chips, and the bantha trudged back down the cleared arboreal highway toward the residential islands in search of new passengers.

Jaina looked at the multiplatformed industrial facility, seeing decks mounted in tiers on the uppermost branches. Lowie growled in excitement and pointed to a level platform high above and behind them. From this angle, Jaina couldn't see anything on its surface, but then a small craft rose with a grating roar of supercharged sublight engines.

"That's an old Y-wing," she said, recognizing the outdated designs of the craft. The Y-wing had a triangular cockpit flanked by two long engine pods that together gave the fighter its characteristic shape like the letter for which it had been named. This starfighter had been refurbished and upgraded, and its engines were loud and powerful. The craft's afterburners kicked in behind the engine pods, and the Y-wing streaked into the skies of Kashyyyk.

Another identical starfighter rose from the platform, hovered for a moment as the pilot adjusted the controls, then streaked off after its companion. A third and a fourth Y-wing also soared away.

"How many of them are there?" Jacen asked.

Jaina watched in admiration. "Probably an entire squadron," she suggested, then suddenly remembered something she had heard. "The New Republic needs all the military strength it can get if we're going to fight the Second Imperium. We don't have time to build all new ships, so I think they're refurbishing the old ones that have been mothballed since the fall of the Emperor."

"What do you mean, refurbishing?" Jacen asked.

"Well, there's nothing actually *wrong* with the old Y-wings," Jaina said with a shrug. "They were great fighters during the Rebellion, but with new technology we can modernize the engines, increase their hyperdrive multipliers. Since we're on Kashyyyk, I'll bet they're getting new navicomputers, guidance and tactical systems, and central processors installed."

Lowie and Sirra nodded their shaggy heads vigorously to show that Jaina was right. She looked into the sky and watched as, one after another, Y-wings shot upward in a spectacular aerial display.

Sirra said something else, and Em Teedee translated. "Mistress Sirra suggests we remain here to watch, since the upgraded ships often test their new systems. She assures us it is quite a breathtaking sight." Lowie bellowed in agreement. Jaina wanted nothing more than to witness the demonstration.

When twelve of the ships had been launched into the air, circling over the treetop industrial facility, they flew in tight formation, one behind the other, a chain of powerful spacecraft. Their engines boomed like distant thunder through the upper atmosphere. The pilots followed their leader, swooping down, cracking the whip in the sky.

The Y-wings formed convoluted figure eights, flying so close to each other that their hulls were almost kissing. But the new guidance systems and engines did not fail them. The refurbished Y-wings performed flawlessly, and Jaina felt a warm satisfaction inside. She held her breath, amazed.

If Qorl and the Second Imperium could see this demonstration, she mused, they might think twice before attempting to tackle the New Republic.

From one of the connecting structures that linked the perimeter platform to the central levels of the fabrication facility, a door dilated open. An excessively tall, spindly droid appeared, its legs like thin support pipes, its long arms coppery. The droid had a squarish head with rounded corners and optical sensors mounted on all sides. It strutted out, moving with spidery grace as it balanced round footpads on the deck.

"Greetings, honored guests," the tall droid said, weaving on its leg hinges as it walked. "I am the Tour Droid, happy to serve you this morning. I have received instructions to give you the complete tour of our facilities—in fact, the expanded VIP tour. I will speak Basic, unless you prefer to converse in Wookiee, Sullustan, Bothan, or another native language."

Jaina shook her head. "Basic will do fine, thanks."

The Tour Droid turned a pirouette on one long rodlike leg, and Jaina guessed that the droid had been constructed so tall in order to comfortably accommodate speaking with Wookiees.

The droid strode ahead with a mantislike gait. "You've already seen our air show for this morning," it said. "Now for the good stuff."

Since Jaina loved learning about the way things functioned, every workstation inside the fabrication facility intrigued her. Interesting smells of lubricants, cryogens, and electrical solder surrounded her. The air was filled with buzzing, humming sounds against a background of white noise from thousands of complicated manufacturing labs.

Jaina looked to the ceiling high above their heads and saw embedded glowpanels that suffused the corridors with a constant white light. At regular intervals, where hallways intersected, they passed trapdoor hatches that provided access to the underside of the factory and emergency evacuation routes down into the lower forest levels.

The Tour Droid led the group into a room full of transparent cylinders that stretched from floor to ceiling, pillars filled with a bubbling fluid and sparkling diamondlike matrices.

"Here you see our crystal-growing tanks," the droid said, raising the volume of its speaker patch to drown out the gurgling noises and whir of air-recirculation fans. "In these carefully modulated tanks we send electrical impulses in specific currents through the nutrient fluid to distribute crystalline molecules in solution. This encourages them to grow into a precise matrix with facet angles and electronic pathways mapped for our galaxy-renowned computer cores. A building is only as strong as its foundation, and these crystalline cores form the critical foundation of our computer architecture."

Jacen rubbed his fingers against a curved tank, tracing the paths of tiny bubbles as they rose toward the ceiling. "This is neat," he said.

"Please don't touch the cylinders," the Tour Droid said. "Faint electrostatic discharges from your body could disturb the crystallization processes inside."

Jacen pulled his hand away and looked sheepishly at his sister. She didn't bother to chide him for it, though, since she had wanted to do the same thing herself.

The next room was exceedingly cold, with puffs of white steam curling around the door frame. The air smelled of scoured metal and frost. Inside, robotic arms moved about, sloshing thin metallic wafers through baths of liquid oxygen, pools of ultracold fluid that halted any contaminants from spreading across the surface. "These wafers are delicate circuit boards," the Tour Droid said, "a perfectly pure substrate on which we pattern complex memory maps."

Jaina drew a long frigid breath, blinking her eyes. Even with their thick Wookiee fur, Lowie and Sirra shivered, though Tenel Ka in her scanty reptilian armor displayed no sign of discomfort. "Fascinating," she said.

The Tour Droid turned and, with long scarecrowish strides, led them through the cold room. The next chamber was large and bustling, filled with hardworking Wookiees, each wearing a mesh bodysuit made of fine wires that held their fur in place. White cloth masks covered the lower halves of their hairy faces.

The workers looked up and chuffed greetings to the visitors. Lowie waved, recognizing his mother at her workstation. Kallabow nodded, blinking her eyes in their whorls of dark fur, then bent back to her tasks, carefully concentrating on the circuits.

"For the past few months our workers have logged extralong shifts and odd hours to meet the heavy quotas necessary to prepare our defense against the Second Imperium," the Tour Droid said. "Here the Wookiees are installing finished chips. The mesh suits you see them wearing are electrostatic screens to prevent even the faintest stray foreign particles from drifting into the air. Any contamination could be disastrous, since these components are so complex."

"I can believe it," Jaina said.

The Wookiee technicians bent over their workstations, using delicate forceps and tweezers to remove minuscule chips patterned and cut from the large glittering wafers they had just seen in the cryogenic lab.

"These basic designs are used for many different systems," the Tour Droid said. "While our specialties are in tactical systems, central guidance computers, and mainframe system controls, some of our chips are used in sophisticated droid models. Most droids are manufactured on robotic industrial worlds, however, such as Mechis III."

"Oh my, did he say *droids?*" Em Teedee chirped. "Do you suppose any of my components might have been manufactured here?"

Lowie rumbled a comment, and Jaina nodded. "Chewbacca helped put you together, Em Teedee. I suspect that lots of your components came from here."

"Oh dear, you don't think he used defective or rejected parts, do you?" Em Teedee asked. Lowie chuffed with laughter, and the little droid scolded him. "My question was entirely serious, Master Lowbacca."

After they walked through the chamber, Em Teedee continued to exhibit his curiosity. "Master Lowbacca, would you mind turning around so that I can see the entire room? If this is my birthplace, I'd like to give it a good look. . . . How fascinating!"

Lowie obliged, turning his waist so that the small translating droid's optical sensors could record every detail. "And I thought this trip was going to be dull," Em Teedee said. "This is ever so much more interesting than those dangerous adventures you insist on having."

For the end of their tour the long-legged droid took them to the highest platform in the entire facility, the transportation control and shipping tower, a computer-filled room with workstations so high off the floor they were at Jaina's eye level where she couldn't easily reach them. Several Wookiees stood around the stations, gazing up through the transparent dome overhead. The dome was reinforced with support girders that crisscrossed in triangular patterns against the hazy sunlight shining down.

"Because we are such a busy commercial facility," the Tour Droid said, "a constant stream of space traffic comes through this complex. Here we verify every incoming transport craft to make certain we receive no unwelcome visitors. We also have security monitoring satellites in orbit, ready to defend Kashyyyk, once they receive orders from the control tower."

The Wookiee traffic controllers worked as a team, communication headsets mounted to their shaggy heads and voice pickups clamped to their throats. They did not divert their attention even for a moment as the visitors entered.

Before the Tour Droid could continue, Chewbacca strode in, accompanied by Lowie and Sirra's father, Mahraccor. Mahraccor waved at his children; his dark streak of fur stood out much like Lowie's. Chewbacca bellowed a greeting and held out a large misshapen object, a blackened device that had once been a polished, precisely angled crystal.

"That's the *Shadow Chaser*'s computer core," Jaina said.

Chewbacca nodded vigorously and spoke low growling words.

"Chewbacca and Mahraccor here say they have been searching for you children," said the Tour Droid.

"Excuse me," Em Teedee chimed in, "but *I* serve as the translator droid here. Master Chewbacca, after returning from a pleasant visit with his family, has removed the *Shadow Chaser*'s damaged navicomputer central processor core. As you can see, he has spoken with Master Mahraccor, and they have successfully located the suitable replacement components to get the ship up and running again. Hooray!"

Chewie pointed to the burned pathways on the *Shadow Chaser*'s removed navicomputer core. Lowie's father also spoke up, and Em Teedee said, "Master Mahraccor asserts that this is an exciting new design, an Imperial configuration he has never seen before. Fortunately, however, he is confident that the facilities here on Kashyyyk can repair it quite nicely."

The Tour Droid bent over on its long, stretched-out body. "You are quite good at translating Wookiee speech, my colleague," it said, "but you lack the finesse for being a true Tour Droid. You seem not to have the ability to make interesting comparisons that customers can understand. For instance, you might have said, 'With our facilities here we can place this damaged core in one of our crystal baths, flush out the impurities and the carbon scoring, and use our own master computers to retrace the circuits and map the electronic pathways. In short, we will provide a bacta tank to heal the computer core.'"

Em Teedee wasn't impressed. "They certainly didn't *need* to hear all of that. Of course, I wouldn't presume to tell you *your* job," he said. "We have more important things to do."

The Tour Droid did not respond to the insult, since he had no doubt been given thorough programming in tactfulness.

"Thank you for the tour," Jaina said. "It was very interesting."

The Tour Droid stood up straighter, and the optical sensors mounted on all sides of its boxy head brightened with pleasure. "That is the finest compliment you could have given me, Mistress Jaina Solo."

8

SURROUNDED BY DIMNESS in his private office, lit only by recorded starlight from distant parts of the galaxy, Brakiss contemplated the plans of the Second Imperium.

Time slipped away from him as he allowed himself to be swallowed up in thoughts. Possibilities for conquest engrossed him, and he ran them over and over in his head, contemplating the complete destruction of the Rebels and his former mentor, Luke Skywalker. Such imaginings soothed him. Resting his elbows on the polished black desk, Brakiss touched his fingertips together and smiled.

Suddenly, a startling signal destroyed his concentration like a thunderbolt. The potent alarm pulsed again, and he used his much-needed Jedi skills to calm himself. "This is Brakiss," he responded.

"Qorl here," a voice replied. An image appeared on the flatscreen communicator built into his desk. The old TIE pilot seemed rattled—and that surprised Brakiss even more than the alarm had. Qorl was one of the steadiest officers in the Second Imperium.

"We have a coded message coming into the Shadow Academy, sir. It carries the highest level of encryption. Every marking indicates that the transmission is of the utmost importance. You must receive the message yourself and respond personally."

Brakiss blinked. "Any indication of the sender's identity?" His thoughts whirled. Tamith Kai and Zekk had already departed on their mission to Kashyyyk, but even they were incapable of sending such a high-level message.

"No indication, sir," Qorl said, "but I would recommend that you respond without delay."

"I'm on my way," Brakiss said, and switched off, propelling himself out of his chair in one fluid motion.

He raced through the curved metallic corridors, taking an automated lift platform to the transmitting and receiving tower, which

DARKEST KNIGHT

contained the machinery that cast a cloaking field around the spike-ringed station.

Several stormtroopers stood alert as Brakiss swept into the transmitting tower. Qorl worked at the receiving stations, scanning computerized readouts and recording the coded signal. Brakiss noted that the man used his biological right hand, letting his bulky robotic limb hang motionless at his side. Qorl blinked at the Shadow Academy leader. "They have begun transmitting again, Lord Brakiss," he said. "They seem to be quite impatient."

"All right, let's input the decryption routine." Standing beside Qorl, Brakiss had to think for a moment to summon the correct string of symbols and numbers, then keyed in his password so that the Shadow Academy computers could translate the high-level coded message.

Qorl handed Brakiss a dangling headset. "The message is for your ears only. Listen on this channel." Qorl helped Brakiss mount the earphones and microphone snugly against his head.

Brakiss listened to the crackle of static as the convoluted message ran through its code-deciphering algorithms and finally resolved itself into coherent words. The voice pounded against his eardrums, harsh, almost reptilian, dripping with evil.

Brakiss's eyes widened, and fear drove a spike through his mind. He cleared his throat twice before he could respond. "Yes, my lord," he finally answered. "Yes, at once." He drew a deep breath to continue, but the sender terminated the signal. Brakiss heard only static.

He stood rigid, using all of his Jedi strengths to keep himself from trembling. Qorl waited beside him, leathery face emotionless, his eyes unblinking. Only a slight furrow across the TIE pilot's forehead showed how concerned he was.

Brakiss spoke quietly, looking at Qorl but knowing that the stormtrooper guards were also listening intently. "The Emperor," he said hoarsely, "the Emperor is coming here!"

An ominous transport shuttle dropped out of hyperspace in the vicinity of the Shadow Academy. The shuttle was an Imperial design, the Emperor's private escort ship, armored with tarnished hull plates. Its configuration was similar to a triangular *Lambda*-class transport, except that this craft bore very special weaponry, sensing devices, and ultrapowerful hyperdrive engines. Even such extreme modifications, though, were of little consequence when compared to the importance of the passenger it carried.

Brakiss stood within the hangar bay, struggling to drive back his anxiety. In all this time he had never met the Emperor face-to-face, despite his unwavering service to the Second Imperium.

The Great Leader of the Second Imperium, Emperor Palpatine, must somehow have escaped death years earlier—though Brakiss had been sure the Emperor had been destroyed . . . several times, in fact. He did not know what secret Palpatine had used, or how he had managed to restore himself to life, but Brakiss didn't care—all that mattered was that the Second Imperium was in the most capable hands imaginable.

The comm buzzed and Qorl's voice made an announcement. "Lord Brakiss, the Emperor's private transport has just come out of hyperspace. I await your orders."

Brakiss leaned closer to the wall speaker. "Very well, drop the Shadow Academy's cloaking field and transmit our greetings to Emperor Palpatine. We are honored by his visit."

"Yes, sir," Qorl said, signing off.

Brakiss could feel no difference, not even through the Force, as the invisibility shield dissolved around the station. He stood with an honor guard of stormtroopers inside the cleared docking bay. The transparent atmosphere containment field flickered.

Brakiss stared out into open space, watching the awesome craft approach. The stormtroopers stood more rigidly, their armor locking into place, boots clicking together.

The Emperor's transport followed Qorl's signal. The three-bladed shuttle glided through the atmosphere containment field, which flickered and sparked as it folded around the hull of the ship. The Imperial transport coasted to the center of the broad deck, then lowered itself to a stable position.

Brakiss swallowed a large lump in his throat. He transmitted to Qorl. "Reactivate the cloaking shield, please—we don't want to expose ourselves any longer than necessary."

"It is done, sir," Qorl said.

The stormtroopers shouldered their weapons and stood in perfect ranks. Brakiss stepped forward to offer greeting, but paused when nothing happened. The Emperor's transport remained silent except for a few hissing and ticking sounds as the ship settled. He saw no movement inside. The hatch remained stubbornly shut. Brakiss waited for any sign.

Finally, a voice boomed from loudspeakers mounted outside the Emperor's shuttle. "Attention, all Shadow Academy personnel! The Emperor has arrived. As a security precaution, we insist that everyone depart the docking bay immediately. The Emperor has a private escort of Imperial guards and wishes no further contact at this time."

The announcement took Brakiss completely by surprise. When he noticed that his mouth was hanging open in foolish astonishment, he closed it so quickly that his teeth clicked together. The Emperor had come to the Shadow Academy—and now Palpatine refused Brakiss's honor escort. The Great Leader wanted to be left *alone?*

Brakiss realized that he had hesitated in following Palpatine's instructions. Aghast and trying to make up for lost time, he turned and clapped his hands smartly. "You heard the orders! Everyone, about-face. Clear the docking bay. The Emperor wishes his privacy."

The stormtroopers turned and, with a booming clatter on the metal deck, marched out of the docking bay and into the curved corridors.

"Sir," one of the stormtroopers said, breaking ranks to stop in front of Brakiss, "I had requested to be part of the Emperor's personal escort squad. I'll stay here to greet him as he disembarks."

Brakiss blinked in shock, noting the stormtrooper's service number. He recognized Qorl's trainee, Norys. Qorl had said the burly young man was ambitious and ill-tempered, but Brakiss was nonetheless stunned at the impertinence.

"You will follow my orders, trooper," Brakiss snapped. "The Second Imperium has no room for those who don't understand discipline." He drew in a cold breath. "If I see any further instance of your failure to obey commands, you will be ejected from the airlock into space. Is that understood?"

As Norys clomped off without acknowledging Brakiss's rebuff, the master of the Shadow Academy turned to look back at the silent Imperial shuttle. He himself was unable to comprehend why the Emperor had come here if he had no intention of interacting with the Shadow Academy, or at least meeting with Brakiss personally.

However, the Emperor was the ultimate master, and Brakiss would not dare question Palpatine's orders.

The last one to leave the docking bay, he turned with a swirl of his silvery robes and stepped outside before transmitting the signal that closed and sealed the doors to the docking bay.

As he stood in the outer corridor, though, Brakiss made a decision of his own. He was master of this station—and was required to know what happened aboard it, wasn't he? He had followed the Emperor's wishes to the letter, but now he needed to see what was going on. Brakiss went to a videomonitor designed for observation of docking and loading procedures.

With the docking bay emptied of stormtroopers and Shadow Academy representatives, the hatches finally opened on the Emperor's shuttle. On the monitor Brakiss was impressed to see four Imperial guards stride out, shrouded in scarlet robes. The intimidating red guards had been the most feared elite corps of Palpatine's forces, and now four of them had accompanied the Emperor here. Smooth red armor covered their heads and shoulders like cowls, reminding him of historical images he had seen of ancient Mandalorian uniforms.

The red Imperial guards moved away from the ship and took up defensive positions, their robes flowing like flames around them. A shudder ran down Brakiss's spine. He tried to feel the intense dark force crackling from the core of the Imperial transport ship. The Emperor, he knew, must be in there somewhere.

Through the voice pickup mounted in the docking bay, Brakiss heard a clanking, slamming sound. Two pairs of squat, powerful worker droids tromped down the wide extended ramp, carrying an enormously heavy isolation chamber. The worker droids, little more than the powerful arms and legs mounted on a stocky body core, hauled their burden without complaint.

The droids were gentle with their cargo, moving smoothly, carefully, despite the immense power in their hydraulic limbs. They carried the huge tank off the Imperial ship and into the docking bay. Side panels on the isolation chamber's black riveted walls blinked with multicolored lights; computer displays showed life monitors and external communications.

The four red guards surrounded the chamber, looking protective and menacing. Then they marched toward the broad doors—two in front of the chamber, two behind—into the main core of the Shadow Academy.

Brakiss hurried to open the doors for them, but somehow the computer-locked seals were automatically broken before he could do so. The doors slammed open, as if controlled by the Emperor's dark side powers.

The red guards strode forward, still surrounding the worker droids. The huge isolation tank hissed and buzzed and bleeped as a thousand electronic systems monitored its supremely important occupant.

Brakiss stopped in front of the foremost pair of Imperial guards. "Greetings. I am Master Brakiss of the Shadow Academy."

The leader of the red guards turned his armored head, and Brakiss felt a cold scrutiny through the black eyeslit. "You will leave us alone. We have important work, and we require privacy. You may guide us to our chambers—and then leave."

Brakiss could barely contain his dismay. "But . . . I am the Master of the Shadow Academy."

The red guard said, "And the Emperor is the master of the galaxy. He wishes privacy for now. We suggest that you do not displease him."

Brakiss backed away, bowing quickly. "I have no wish to displease the Emperor. Forgive my impudence."

After Brakiss indicated the quarters to which the visitors had been assigned—the plushest and most spacious accommodations aboard the station—the red guards and worker droids marched into the chambers, leaving Brakiss alone out in the corridor.

He felt belittled, insignificant, stepped on, as if all of his accomplishments and work meant nothing to the Emperor. It baffled him. What could be the purpose of it? He frowned as thoughts whirled inside his head.

The Emperor had originally died in the destruction of the second Death Star, but six years after his defeat, Palpatine had been resurrected in a series of clones, which had also—presumably—been destroyed.

Now, after observing the isolation tank, the secrecy, the inexplicable behavior of the four Imperial guards, Brakiss felt a new and deeper fear coil through his body. He wondered if something could be wrong, if the Emperor could perhaps be in failing health again. . . .

If that was the case, the Second Imperium was indeed in great trouble.

9

AS A FORMER TIE pilot, Qorl had been trained in the Imperial way, with loyalties and duties and responses drilled into him. No questions, only orders. His mind had been programmed to turn him into a perfect fighting machine for the Empire.

The cornerstone of that training had been *discipline*. And one thing Qorl knew: the young man who stood before him was not disciplined.

He wondered if perhaps Brakiss and Tamith Kai had been too hasty in accepting Norys and his band of young ruffians from Coruscant to be trained as stormtroopers and pilots. True, the battles ahead to recapture lost glory, to reclaim stolen territory, would require every set of capable hands for the Second Imperium. But even if Qorl did manage to turn the rest of the Lost Ones gang into serviceable troopers and pilots, this one was *trouble*.

At the control pad of the simulation chamber, Qorl programmed in a new set of targets while Norys recharged his blaster rifle. He vowed to train this one, and *keep* training him, until he saw some genuine progress in the ambitious fighter.

"I still say I should have been sent on the raid with Tamith Kai," Norys grumbled, waving his weapon as if it made him feel more secure. "I could have taken out a few enemies, evened the score a little bit for our side. Set a few of those big Wookiee trees on fire."

Qorl set the simulated targets in rapid motion: black, orange, and blue for Rebels, and white for stormtroopers. "It's a small raid," Qorl said. "Zekk is directing the troops. There was no need for a second leader."

Norys took aim at a blue target and missed. He liked target practice better when the targets were slow simulations like mynocks. It was fun to kill them. "Then they should have sent me alone, old man. I'm a better leader now than that trash collector will ever be."

Trouble, Qorl thought, *definitely trouble.* "Why do you say that?"

"Because," Norys said, taking aim at an orange target, but only nicking the edge of it, "my followers are so afraid of me they'd never *dare* disobey my orders." He missed once more. "Is the aim-point on this blaster offset again?"

"You aren't concentrating on your target," Qorl said, then addressed the candidate's comment in a neutral tone. "Your example is indeed one method of leadership. But you have much to learn."

Norys bristled and missed another shot. He rounded on the former TIE pilot with a menacing growl. "Like what, old man?"

Qorl didn't flinch or back down. He had faced tougher adversaries than this young bully—though perhaps none with such pure mean-spiritedness. "You could learn to concentrate on your weapon and shut out distractions. You could also learn how to aim and hit your intended target each time, rather than just talking about it," Qorl pointed out. "The way you are shooting today, you would have become a casualty in only a few seconds in a real firefight."

"Really, old man?" Norys's lips pulled back in something between a snarl and a grin. He turned back toward the targets and, moving his blaster rifle in a slow semicircle, flooded the area with blaster bolts, never removing his finger from the firing stud. When he was finished, every target had registered a hit. A complete slaughter. Norys turned back toward Qorl with a satisfied smirk. "How much more target practice do I need, old man?"

"Enough practice so you don't destroy our own troops during a raid," Qorl replied.

Norys shrugged. "We all make a few sacrifices to meet our goals." He glanced back at the targets. "Seems like a fair trade-off to me." He tossed the spent blaster rifle at Qorl, who caught it with his good arm.

Trouble, Qorl thought, *definitely trouble.*

10

STARS BURNED IN the midnight sky like a billion white-hot embers on a slab of black marble. Jacen, Jaina, and Tenel Ka had long since retired to their beds—but Lowie couldn't sleep. Perched comfortably on the wide railing of the upper verandah, with the simmering night sounds of the forest all around him, he kept a watchful eye on his sister's window.

Sirra still insisted she wanted to imitate Lowie's feat with the syren plant, and he could not talk her out of it. Now he feared she would leave him behind at the last moment, go alone on her dangerous quest—as Raaba had done. So far, though, he had seen no sign that his sister was planning anything so foolish.

Because of increased production quotas for the New Republic's military requirements, their parents had both volunteered to work the night shift at the computer fabrication facility. Kallabow and Mahraccor had spent their lives at their jobs, contented if somewhat unchallenged, and seemed baffled that neither of their children wanted to follow in their footsteps.

But Sirra demanded constant challenges, and went out of her way to create some when life didn't provide her with enough of them.

The light in Sirra's room shimmered like a warm fire behind the window's leafy shade. Small glowing mesh cages rested outside her window and on various platforms throughout the Wookiee residential district—containers filled with a sweet-smelling substance that proved an irresistible attractant to a species of tiny glowing gnats called phosfleas. When the cages were placed outside, clusters of the harmless phosphorescent insects swarmed around them to provide a natural, pollution-free light source.

Sitting alone outside under the starlight, Lowie had watched Sirra's shadowy figure moving about in her room, pacing as if agitated, but he had seen no sign of her for some time now. Perhaps his sister was trying to sleep, he thought.

But though vague foreboding crackled like static through his mind, he liked being alone in the restful darkness, high above the ground, where he could think. It felt good to be home on Kashyyyk. He drew in a lungful of the wood-scented air and practiced a Jedi relaxation technique, slowly willing his tense muscles to unknot—

—only to jump a meter into the air as a set of cold claws pricked his back. Lowie stumbled to his feet and spun toward the railing, his defensive Wookiee instincts coming into play.

Sirra, shaking with silent laughter, hauled herself up over the railing onto the verandah and resheathed her claws, complimenting him on his reflexes. At least, she said, he had convinced her that he might be of some help during her quest. Lowie groaned, trying to quell the surge of adrenaline. He asked her if the surprise had been designed strictly to test him.

Sirra's voice grew more serious, and she lowered her head. She had wanted to demonstrate that she could slip off alone, if she wanted, and Lowie wouldn't have been able to stop her. Sirra turned her head up so that the starlight gleamed on the pattern-shaved tufts of her fur. Then she looked at her brother and promised that she wouldn't go without him.

Lowie reseated himself on the railing and gazed up at the stars. He grumbled about the unexpected ways she made her points.

Sirra purred, thanking him for the odd compliment, making herself comfortable beside him.

Lowie grunted, not sure he had intended his remark as praise, but the fact that Sirra was pleased by the comment spoke volumes. She enjoyed being different, just as her friend Raaba had. . . .

As if sensing the direction of his thoughts, Sirra began talking about Raaba, how the sleek, dark Wookiee had loved the stars. Even when they were small, the two young females used to sneak out at night and watch the skies for hours.

Lowie's shoulders slumped. Raaba should not have died. She had taken a foolish risk, going alone.

Sirra growled, pointing out that Lowie had taken exactly the same risk.

Lowie barked in agreement—yes indeed, he had been a fool.

His sister's voice was harsh. If he had it to do again, would he do anything different? Would he take a friend?

Lowie nodded a quick affirmative. Sirra said nothing, but even in the darkness Lowie could see her fur bristling in disbelief. After a long silence he finally sighed, then shook his head.

After another long pause Sirra told her brother how much Raaba admired him, how much she had wanted to be like Lowie.

Lowie looked up at the sky again, at the stars that Raaba had loved. He gave a questioning growl. When he had left for the Jedi academy, Lowie and Raaba had been too young to speak of making a life-bond. He still had his Jedi training ahead of him . . . and Raaba had plans too. With Sirra.

Here Sirra's voice broke. She crooned a low mournful note and then another. After a time, Lowie added his voice to hers, and together beneath the stars, they poured out their grief for a lost friend.

Hours later, Lowie felt more refreshed than he would have thought possible, even had he slept the entire night. It had been better to spend the time growing closer to his sister.

Sirra's husky voice broke into his thoughts, asking about his Jedi friends. Would they grieve for him, if he were gone? Like she and Lowie had done for Raaba?

He nodded emphatically, and she told him he was fortunate to have found them.

Encouraged, he asked her more about the plans she and Raaba had made.

Sirra did not speak for so long he was afraid he had offended her or reopened an old wound. Finally she described how they were going to be pilots, galactic adventurers. They had planned to work on freighters until they earned enough credits to buy their own ship and explore the stars. They could have been rich traders. She chuffed with bitter laughter. Raaba even had some fur-brained notion that they could make their names by charting out new hyperspace routes.

Lowie's fur bristled, and he commented that such a career was a dangerous business.

Sirra's tone was wry, pointing out that danger had never deterred their friend Raaba. Sirra spread her hands, confessing that she didn't want to do that anymore. Not without Raaba. She didn't know what she wanted to do now—but she definitely didn't want to stay on Kashyyyk.

Sirra paused again and stared upward. Lowie followed his sister's gaze, wondering if she imagined Raaba out there among the stars, exploring and having the adventures the two of them had always dreamed of.

Sirra sighed. It was difficult to lose a friend, she said.

Lowie realized how easy it was to take friends—and family—for granted. He found it hard to imagine how lonely his sister must be.

Sirra hesitantly asked him if he would spend the day with her while Chewbacca and Jaina continued to tinker with the *Shadow Chaser*.

Remembering his earlier feeling of foreboding, Lowie gladly agreed.

11

AS MIDMORNING SUNSHINE drove off the last shreds of mist that clung to the wroshyr treetops, four muscular Wookiees marched to the transportation control tower of the computer fabrication complex.

The four looked just like any other Wookiees dressed appropriately for work in the high-tech factory. They were tall and powerful and carried no visible weapons. The newcomers punched in the correct access codes and passed into the high-security tower that rose high above the other tree platforms. Their timing was perfect for the morning shift change.

When they crossed the checkpoint station into the control tower, the four passed an electrostatic air-filtration grid. The images of the four Wookiees flickered in the unseen discharge, just for an instant, before their appearance restored itself.

No one noticed.

The real Wookiees who had been assigned to the next shift lay stunned inside a small supply chamber in an outer storage platform. The Wookiees on duty, weary from hours of monitoring the ships that came and went from the computer facility, were happy to finish their shift and return home. They signed off their stations and handed over the equipment to the new crew, who gruffly acknowledged them in synthesized Wookiee grunts and growls.

The earlier crew departed, leaving the facility's control points, the lockout systems, and Kashyyyk's satellite defense functions in the hands of the newcomers.

One of the new Wookiees sealed the control tower door, pulled out a concealed blaster, then melted the alarm systems and intruder detection devices. Sparks flew. Metal and plasteel dripped, smoldering black. All four Wookiees then touched their waists, switching off the hidden holographic generators belted there. Their images shimmered, dissolving away, to reveal a commando team from the Shadow Academy.

"The holo-disguises worked perfectly," Zekk said, brushing at his leather armor and straightening his crimson-lined cape, happy to be himself again.

The stormtrooper stationed at the door said, "Alarm systems disengaged. No problems here."

The other two infiltrators, the Nightsisters Tamith Kai and Vonnda Ra, stood before the complex computer systems. The Wookiee-level panels forced them to reach up to use the controls. Vonnda Ra craned her neck to examine the readouts and identify systems.

Tamith Kai brooded, mulling over various details. She clasped her long-nailed hands together. "This plan must proceed according to schedule," she said. "If it does, it looks as if success will be ours."

"We'll succeed," Zekk said confidently. "I won't disappoint Master Brakiss."

Vonnda Ra worked at two of the control panels, studying keyboards and diagnostics. Satisfied, the Nightsister slipped an insulated vibroblade from her belt sheath and flicked on the humming knife. She bent down under the panels and slashed sideways to sever the power cords. Bright sparks spat out, followed by curling white electrical smoke.

She backed away, covering her nose against the acrid smell, then stood up straight again, looking satisfied. "Kashyyyk's orbital defense systems have been permanently disabled."

Zekk nodded at the destroyed control panel, his green eyes flashing. "Sure looks permanent to me."

"You're in command of this mission, Zekk," Tamith Kai said, plugging a hand-held translator into the communications console. "Don't you think it's time you transmitted your signal to lure those Jedi brats here, where we can take care of them?" The Nightsister looked insufferably pleased with herself.

Zekk swallowed, his mind whirling. He had known this moment would come, and he had to face it.

"Do I sense hesitation?" Tamith Kai snapped.

"No," he answered, "just working out the proper wording for the message. They must be intrigued and concerned . . . and convinced."

Zekk hovered over the communications console, pondering his words, then punched them into the translator that would convert them to the appropriate Wookiee dialect and send a text message with the highest priority to where Jacen and Jaina were staying with their friends.

If he worded it correctly, he knew the twins would come.

Back in the Wookiee home high in the trees, Jacen did his best to keep up with his friends in the fast-paced computer skill game. But the other players—Lowie, Sirra, and Tenel Ka—far outmatched his reflexes. Jaina, meanwhile, had gone with Chewbacca to work on their damaged ship.

The friends sat at the four sides of a rectangular control grid, each with one hand on the small, flexible motion sensors that guided tiny laserprojected simulations of space fighters. They fought a miniature reenactment of the original Death Star battle.

Lowie and Sirra flew fast X-wing fighters, while Jacen and Tenel Ka were stuck with flanking defensive ships, sluggish old Y-wings. The computer did its best to pursue them all, its simulated TIE fighters firing repeatedly, while enormous turbolaser cannons emplaced in the Death Star trench crisscrossed space with deadly fire-lines.

Jacen was good at target shooting; he and Jaina had often used the *Millennium Falcon*'s quad laser cannons to blast chunks of space debris out of Coruscant orbit. But Lowie and his sister were more intimately familiar with complex computer games, and Tenel Ka had the finely honed reflexes of a warrior from Dathomir.

Jacen's fingers flew across his motion sensor, banking his Y-wing—but a TIE fighter clung close to his rear engine pods. Jacen spun about. "Hey, get off my back," he cried. By sheer luck, the TIE fighter crossed into one of the turbolaser blasts from the trench guns, conveniently saving Jacen.

Anxious to divert attention from his so-so performance in the game, Jacen tried to distract the other players in the most obvious way. Between spins and banks and firing, he told a joke.

"Hey, guys, do you know what sound Whiphids make when they kiss?"

"I have neither seen nor heard Whiphids kiss," Tenel Ka said.

"Master Lowbacca says he's certain he would never wish to," Em Teedee said.

"Come on," Jacen interrupted. "It's a joke. What sound do Whiphids make when they kiss?" He paused a second, cocking an eyebrow. *"Ouch!"*

Tenel Ka looked perplexed, and Lowie groaned, but Sirra endeared herself forever to Jacen by chuffing uproariously at the joke. Then, after only a moment, Sirra sent her holographic fighter ahead of his with redoubled effort.

Little green lances of laser fire shot toward him, but he managed to roll his Y-wing and avoided getting himself blasted. Another Imperial ship clung to his tail, scoring hits and causing increasing damage as it came inexorably closer. Suddenly the pesky TIE fighter erupted in a tiny puff of an explosion with spangles of computer-imaged debris as Tenel Ka brought her Y-wing fighter to the rescue.

"It appeared that you needed some help, Jacen," she said.

"I did—thanks." He and Tenel Ka flew side by side as they followed close behind the streaking X-wings piloted by Lowie and Sirra. Their target approached, a small thermal exhaust port just waiting for them to drop a proton torpedo inside so they could blow up the horrendous superweapon Grand Moff Tarkin had built and—

The comm system chimed with a high-priority signal. Sirra reached out to pause the game, freezing the fightercraft images in position over the grid. Lowie hurried to receive the message, already blinking his golden eyes at the sudden emergency announcement that appeared on his screen.

Jacen and Tenel Ka went to look as Lowie bellowed in alarm. "Master Lowbacca, what is it? Let me see," Em Teedee said. "How can you expect me to translate if you won't let me read the text?"

Lowie punched a button so that Jacen and Tenel Ka could see the message. The comm system translated the words on the screen back into Basic.

"Just a fragment," Jacen said, his blood growing cold. "Something interrupted the transmission."

"It appears serious," Tenel Ka said.

Jacen read, "Emergency . . . injured at computer fabrication facility . . . need your help . . . please come right away. We—" He frowned, feeling his heart start to pound. "But who sent it? Who could it be from?"

"It was sent specifically here, to this house," Tenel Ka said. "Someone must have wished to contact us directly."

"But only Jaina and Chewie know we're here," he said, "and they went off to one of the repair docks to work on the *Shadow Chaser*, not to the computer fabrication facility."

"Perhaps they changed their plans," Tenel Ka said.

Sirra yowled, and Lowie added his own roar. "Oh my," Em Teedee said, "Master Lowbacca and Mistress Sirra's parents are at the facility."

"We cannot ignore this problem," Tenel Ka said. "We must go now and confront it. This is a fact."

"You're right about that," Jacen said.

Lowie punched some buttons on the comm system controls a few times, then pounded the apparatus in frustration. "Master Lowbacca says he is unable to reply to the message," the translating droid said. "Something appears to be wrong with communications at the facility itself. They've been completely cut off from outside transmissions."

Lowie roared for his sister to summon the fastest bantha mount in the area, while he, Jacen, and Tenel Ka fastened lightsabers to their belts, ready for the worst. The four of them rushed out the door of the tree dwelling.

A shaggy bantha lumbered to their platform in response to Sirra's frantic call. The Sullustan crouching on the beast's wide neck appeared deeply weary, ready to go off shift—but when the two young Wookiees bared their teeth and roared that this was an emergency, the mousy alien perked up instantly. Jacen clambered aboard and reached down, offering his hand to help Tenel Ka up; she took the aid without complaint. Sirra and Lowie leaped onto the beast of burden's back, and the bantha plodded off.

"This thing can go faster," Jacen cried. "I saw them stampeding once on Tatooine."

Lowie barked an order and the Sullustan urged the creature to greater speed until its pounding feet vibrated the entire wooden walkway.

High in orbit over Kashyyyk, defensive satellites bristled with weapons, designed to target on invading enemy forces. But the satellites remained silent and motionless as a disguised shuttle, drifting in place, opened its hangar bay doors so that a squadron of TIE fighters could drop out.

Weapons powered up, the Imperial fighters ignited their twin ion engines with a loud roar and streaked toward the thick forest below, flying in tight formation. The general battle plan had already been input into their computers. The Imperials intended to strike swiftly, surgically, causing the greatest damage possible in as little time as necessary. They needed to grab their prize, then vanish into space.

Kashyyyk's defensive satellites picked up the enemy on their sensors and transmitted an urgent report, a call for action, to the control tower in the computer fabrication facility. The sensors continued to track the enemy's flight path, but they received no arming instructions or attack confirmation from the control tower. The planet remained silent. The satellites did not fire.

Although the satellites' weapons were inactive, the sensors continued to file data from the impending attack for future reference . . . if anyone on Kashyyyk survived the Imperial assault.

When the weary bantha finally arrived at the fabrication facility, Lowie, Sirra, Tenel Ka, and Jacen leaped off its back and rushed to the entrance.

The tall, spindly Tour Droid stood waiting. Seeing new visitors, it unplugged itself from a recharge port and assumed its security posture, since no guests were expected at the moment. "Halt!" it said.

"Where's the emergency? We've got to get inside," Jacen shouted.

"We are responding to the distress call," Tenel Ka said.

Lowie and Sirra both roared an explanation, believing that the Tour Droid might respond better to Wookiee than to Basic.

"No emergency has been reported," the Tour Droid said, its arms dangling from its shoulders like metal rods.

"There *must* be," Jacen said. "We received a high-priority transmission telling us to come immediately."

"Accessing," the Tour Droid said as it plugged one of its dowel-shaped fingers into a computer port. It paused a moment as a blur of characters streamed across the screen. "Are you certain you have the right coordinates? Could I offer you some promotional brochures?"

"Ah. Aha." Tenel Ka looked gravely toward Jacen. "Perhaps we have been tricked."

"Blaster bolts!" Jacen said. Hearing a roaring sound from high above, he pointed frantically to the sky. "It looks like there's *about* to be an emergency!"

Lowie tilted his head back and exposed his long fangs, howling in rage.

A wave of Imperial TIE fighters dropped out of the clouds, arrowing straight for the computer fabrication facility. Their weapons began blazing even before they arrived.

12

IT WAS COMFORTING to work with someone who loved machinery as much as she did, Jaina thought. Apparently she and Chewbacca were the only ones around today.

Cool breezes crept in through the open bay doors. The fresh air and the view out over the ocean of leaves made her glad they kept the hangar open. Constructed in a crown of trees rising above the overall canopy level in an outlying area beyond the Wookiee residential district and the computer fabrication facility, this hangar bay was used for major vehicle repairs.

Aside from Jaina's and Chewie's clanking and thunking noises as they tinkered, the cavernous, wooden-walled bay remained relatively quiet and deserted. That was fine with Jaina. She loved nothing more than relaxing with a fine piece of equipment, making the pieces fit together properly, fiddling with the components.

And the *Shadow Chaser* was still state-of-the-art.

When Chewbacca bellowed a request up the boarding ramp, Jaina crawled out from under the cockpit control panel she was working on and hollered back. "Didn't get what you said, Chewie. *Which* tool are you looking for?"

A large hairy head appeared in the entryway and Chewbacca pointed to the tools he needed.

"Just about done here," Jaina said, hoisting the case up to where the Wookiee could reach. "I can finish up with my pocket multitool, so go ahead and take the rest of 'em." Chewie growled his thanks as Jaina crawled back under the console.

She completed her task, reattached the access panel, and trotted down the ramp, where she found Chewbacca cleaning lubricant off the lower armored hull. He rumbled a question.

"Did you ask me if I was hungry?" Jaina asked, struggling with the Wookiee language. She grinned. "Sure. Working on mode-variance inhibitors always gives me an appetite."

With another growl, Chewie spread his arms and shrugged.

"What are we waiting for?" Jaina interpreted with a chuckle. "Couldn't have said it better myself." Hearing a faint roar, like the sound of distant thunder, Jaina chuckled again. "Is that your stomach? You must really be hungry."

Chewbacca suddenly went still and cocked his head, as if listening. He squinted his blue eyes. The sound came again, this time punctuated by sharp thuds like blaster bolts hitting their targets, underscored by a low-pitched buzzing Jaina couldn't quite identify. "That's coming from outside," she said. "What could it possibly—"

Chewbacca held up his hand for silence. The Wookiee woofed and loped toward the hangar bay door, with Jaina hot on his heels. Outside, the treetops spread in a green and brown carpet well below the sheer edge of the hangar bay. Uprising branches held the hangar platform high above the remainder of the forest.

Peering out into the hazy sky, Jaina had no trouble identifying the overlapping sounds: explosions, blaster bolts, and a distinctive engine howl.

"TIE fighters! What would TIE fighters be doing here? And what are they firing at?" She looked at Chewbacca in alarm.

The Wookiee pointed in the direction the sounds had come from and barked an explanation: the computer fabrication facility.

Jaina groaned. "It has to be the Second Imperium! We never thought they'd strike here." Chewbacca roared in anger, and she needed no translation. "I know. We've got to get over there. Let's call for help—where's the closest comm unit?"

The Wookiee bounded to the communications panel next to the open bay door, slapped the switch, and bellowed an alarm. Jaina whirled as a stuttering whine erupted behind them. "Now what?"

The sound came from the *Shadow Chaser* itself. Chewbacca and Jaina exchanged glances and sprinted toward the sleek ship they had been repairing. Through the viewport, inside the cockpit, Jaina could see a petite woman with wavy bronze hair clad in polished lizard hide—a Nightsister.

"How did she get in there?" Jaina cried. "Hey, she's trying to steal the ship!"

The *Shadow Chaser*'s engines filled the hangar bay with a sound like millions of swarming insects. The whine stopped, started, then stopped again with a cough. The engines wouldn't fire. In the cockpit, the face of the Nightsister twisted into a scowl. Her creamy brown skin mottled with rage.

Jaina looked up with equal anger. "We've got to stop her."

Chewbacca dove under the belly of the ship, barking reassurance.

"You're sure it won't start?" Jaina said. "How do you know?"

His head inside the still-open engine access hatch, Chewbacca grunted and nudged a piece of equipment on the floor with his foot. Jaina recognized the primary initiator module that the Wookiee had pulled for repairs.

The *Shadow Chaser* would never start—much less fly—without it.

The annoying whine came from the engines again, and Chewbacca yelped. There was a sharp thunk, and the noise stopped as a shower of sparks sprayed from the engine hatch. The Wookiee ducked back out.

Then Jaina heard the low hum of an extending entry ramp. But before they could rush aboard to apprehend the would-be thief, the Nightsister herself sprang out onto the hangar bay floor and faced them. Jaina thought there was something familiar about the set of the woman's face, the icy beauty and cold anger.

Chewbacca bellowed a challenge, but the petite warrior rounded on the Wookiee, eyes blazing. "I came to reclaim my rightful property. You would be a fool to stand in my way. The *Shadow Chaser* is mine."

"Then you're that Nightsister—Garowyn," Jaina said. "Tenel Ka and Uncle Luke told me about you."

Garowyn shifted her glance to Jaina, her anger turning sour. "Why aren't you at the factory with the rest of your friends, Jedi brat?"

"Factory?" Jaina said in confusion. Why would her friends go there?

"No matter—it is too late to save them," Garowyn snarled, raising her arms overhead as if to hurl something, though her hands were empty. "It will all end here now—with me." She laughed. "You never had a chance."

Chewbacca bared his fangs and coiled his body, ready to lunge.

Suddenly, the meaning of Garowyn's words sank in, and Jaina cried, "We've got to help the others, Chewie! Forget about her." She ducked, hoping to make a run for the hangar bay door and the lift mechanism that would take them down to the main levels of the tree city.

"You're going nowhere!" Garowyn shouted.

One of several large wooden crates of engine components sailed through the air and knocked Chewbacca to his knees. He went down with a *woof* of pain and surprise.

Garowyn stood by the *Shadow Chaser*'s ramp, her hands on her scale-armored hips. With dark fire flickering behind her eyes, she used the Force to snatch other heavy objects from where they rested.

Jaina cried out as a similar crate flew directly at her head. She instinctively deflected it with a shove from the Force. Eerily, it reminded Jaina of the training sessions she had undergone while a prisoner at the Shadow Academy. Fear gripped her as the Nightsister tossed barrels, heavy bolts, mallets, metal sheeting, hydrospanners, and anything else she could fling, quickly and without moving a muscle, at her two captives.

Chewbacca tried to scramble for shelter behind a half-dismantled skyhopper, but Garowyn sent more sharp and hard objects flying after him.

While doing her best to deflect the flying objects from herself and Chewbacca, Jaina huddled behind one of the fallen crates and concentrated. Even in the midst of her own danger, she felt an urgency about reaching Jacen, Tenel Ka, Lowie, and Sirra.

Unfiltered lubricant oozed out of a broken container, making an acrid-smelling puddle on the floor. Jaina was frustrated that she only had time to *react*. She was too busy defending herself to formulate any plan.

Though Chewbacca had no Jedi defenses, he also had no intention of remaining a stationary target. Jaina saw him slip away from the skyhopper's fuselage and lift a crate with his strong, hairy arms. With a powerful heave, he sent the crate smashing into an incoming pail of lubricant tossed by the Nightsister. As iridescent liquid sprayed into the air and splashed to the floor plates all around Jaina and Garowyn, Chewie scooped up his discarded toolkit and, with a mighty bound, leaped onto the hull of the *Shadow Chaser*.

"Tell me what you've done to my ship," Garowyn shrieked, now directing the barrage of objects at Jaina. "How can I fix it?"

The crate Jaina was crouched behind finally splintered under the attack, spilling hundreds of rattling, loose cyberfuses in every direction. Jaina scrambled to find other cover.

Panting, she dodged some of the thrown objects and deflected others with her skills. Perspiration streamed from her forehead and into her eyes, making it difficult to concentrate. "Damaged in an ion storm," she gasped, wiping an arm across her eyes. "You'll never be able to fly it."

"In that case, you're worthless to me," Garowyn sneered. "I'll take care of you immediately." Even as the Nightsister stretched out her hands, her fingers crackling with blue fire, Jaina cast about for a way to distract her.

From out of nowhere an impedance tester sailed toward Garowyn, followed by a hydrospanner and a barrage of rivets and heavy clampbolts. Chewbacca did not need the Force to hurl heavy objects.

Now it was the Nightsister's turn to dodge and deflect. Garowyn directed her attention to the Wookiee, and with a muttered oath sent a bolt of blue fire sizzling up at him. Chewbacca yowled and ducked, tumbling back over the opposite side of the sleek ship.

The distraction was brief, but it was long enough for Jaina. Reaching out with the Force, closing her eyes in concentration, Jaina gave the Nightsister's body a powerful shove.

Caught completely off guard, Garowyn slipped in the lubricant that coated the floor around her. With another forceful shove, Jaina sent her sliding toward the yawning hangar bay entrance.

"Give it up, Garowyn," Jaina said, her voice harsh with exertion. "You'll never get the *Shadow Chaser*."

"You haven't seen the last of me yet," the Nightsister yelled.

Then, to Jaina's amazement, instead of trying to stop the momentum of her slide toward the gaping outer door, Garowyn gave herself an invisible shove in the same direction. Chewbacca scrambled after the woman, but the floor was too slippery for him to overtake her.

As she reached the entrance, Garowyn flung out one arm to grasp a vertical railing that ran along the edge of the doorway. Without slowing, she used her momentum to swing herself out and around in a tight half circle to land on the verandah that ran along the side of the hangar.

Wind whistled around the open door. Inside, the sounds of loose equipment clattered and clanked, and small components rattled out of broken crates. Jaina scrambled across the slippery floor plates, trying to reach the doorway through which Garowyn had escaped. Before she could reach the outside, Jaina heard a puttering, buzzing sound.

"Quick, Chewie," she cried, "she's got a speeder bike."

Jaina stumbled toward the entrance, slipping as she went. She grabbed on to a wall rail to prevent herself from pitching forward in a long drop to the canopy below.

Her heart sank when she saw the fleeing Nightsister on a speeder bike zip across the hangar bay opening, heading toward the computer fabrication facility, which Jaina knew was under attack from Imperial forces.

Moving with amazing speed, Chewbacca launched himself forward. To Jaina's horror, the Wookiee gave a ferocious howl and leaped straight out the door toward Garowyn's buzzing vehicle, with nothing beneath him but thin air—

—and grasped a pipe on the speeder bike with one strong, furry hand.

Still slipping, Jaina held the wall rail and watched Wookiee, Nightsister, and speeder bike spiral down toward the leafy sea. Jaina clung to the rail and reached out with one hand, but she was too far away to help Chewbacca.

As the speeder bike crashed on the treetops, Chewie quickly regained his balance. The Nightsister, still covered with slimy lubricant, dismounted and scrambled for purchase on one of the narrow branches. Chewie swung himself to the thicker branch beneath her and shook the limb on which she stood, growling a challenge.

A harsh laugh escaped Garowyn's lips, and a triumphant look lit her face. Jaina could hear her voice even at this distance. "So you wish to die?" The Nightsister stretched out a hand that crackled with discharges of blue electricity. "You deserve it for what you've done to my ship."

Chewbacca, though defenseless in the face of her discharge of dark power, snarled at her.

In desperation Jaina tried the only trick that sprang to mind. Letting her eyes fall half closed, Jaina sent a rippling furrow through the leaves behind Garowyn. This time the invisible plow made a loud, rustling sound, like a stampede.

The Nightsister whirled to defend against the supposed attack on her from behind. Flinging up an arm to ward off her unseen enemy, Garowyn lost her footing on the narrow branch. She fell backward.

Jaina gasped as she heard Garowyn's head strike a lower tree branch with a solid *thud*. Without another sound, the Nightsister's compact body tumbled like a shooting star, through the sharp and clinging branches into the depths of the jungle far, far below.

13

THE SCREAMING SOUNDS of TIE fighters ripping through the atmosphere sent a chill of primal terror down Jacen's spine. He knew the howl was only exhaust from the powerful engines, but he felt certain the Imperial ship designers must have delighted in the hellish noise.

In the bustling fabrication facility, a cacophony of alarms rang out from platform loudspeakers. Growling, barking announcements hammered through the air. Wookiee workers ran in all directions, activating security systems or evacuating the area.

TIE bombers streaked low over the treetops, dropping proton explosives that set the dense network of branches aflame. Dark gray smoke billowed from burning leaves.

"We must help defend against this threat," Tenel Ka said, looking for some weapon substantial enough to use against the invading fighters. Her face wore an expression of stony determination.

Sirra and Lowie howled in rage at seeing the destruction of the tree dwellings. The spindly Tour Droid spun its boxy head around, despite its numerous optical sensors. "Do not panic. Have no fear," it said in its tinny voice. "This must be a drill. No attack has been scheduled for today."

At Lowie's waist, Em Teedee piped up in a scornful tone. "Why, you silly Tour Droid, switch on your optical sensors! Can't you see this is a crisis situation? Hmmmf!" The miniaturized droid muttered a deprecating comment about the questionable intelligence of public-relations models.

The Tour Droid continued to issue calming messages, though its thoughts were obviously scrambled. "Kashyyyk has numerous satellite defenses. No enemy ships can approach this facility. We have sophisticated defense mechanisms, including powerful perimeter guns. They should begin firing any moment now."

"Perimeter guns?" Tenel Ka said, her cool gray eyes flashing. "Where? Perhaps we can use them against these enemies."

Sirra roared, gesturing with her long hairy arm to show that she knew the way.

"A splendid idea," Em Teedee said. "I do hope we won't be blown to bits before we can implement Mistress Tenel Ka's plan. Oh my!"

"As my sister would say," Jacen said, "what are we waiting for?" He, Tenel Ka, and the two young Wookiees barged past the Tour Droid into the complex.

Sirra led them down an open-air corridor amid the din of explosions and laser blasts. They reached a network of pulley-driven vines, ropelike lifts that yanked them to a higher level. Sirra grabbed one vine, tucked her foot into a loop, and the rope sprang upward, drawing her toward the higher platforms. Lowie did the same. Jacen followed suit, looking down to watch Tenel Ka, who wrapped her arm around the vine and stepped into a loop with no problem whatsoever. Within seconds, they were all whisked to an upper platform at the outer perimeter of the complex.

Because of their quick reaction, the companions reached the defensive guns before most of the Wookiee defenders. Jacen saw unattended ion cannons with spherical power sources and needlelike barrels aimed toward the sky—but his eyes lit upon a pair of old-model quad-laser cannons, exactly like those in the *Millennium Falcon*'s gun wells.

"Hey, we can use those!" Jacen said. He raced over to the nearest emplacement, checking the status panels. "They're powered up and ready to go." Tenel Ka gruffly agreed and stationed herself behind one of the other weapons.

The two Wookiees chattered to each other. Em Teedee called, "Master Jacen! Master Lowbacca and Mistress Sirrakuk have decided to use the computers to determine where the breakdown in the facility's defensive systems occurred. Perhaps they can prevent further Imperial fighters from getting through. Oh, I do hope they're successful."

"They'll do their best," Jacen said, grabbing the quad-laser's targeting controls. He sank down into the voluminous seat in front of the cannon, feeling the energy thrum through the firing sticks in his fingers. Since the widely spread controls had been designed for large Wookiee bodies, he adjusted the targeting circle.

Imperial fighters continued to howl overhead, launching strikes against the Wookiee residential districts, but leaving the central computer facilities relatively untouched . . . though thrown into complete chaos.

A glance to Jacen's left told him that Tenel Ka was in position. Gripping the firing stick with her right hand, she seemed already familiarized with the weapon's control systems. In seconds her eyes began to track the enemy fighters overhead.

Three tall Wookiees charged onto the defensive platform and took up positions at the ion cannons, glancing curiously at the two humans, confused by this unexpected assistance. But they didn't waste time asking for explanations. Instead, they fired powerful blasts from the ion cannons.

One of the crackling yellow-white shots caught a TIE fighter that soared through the edge of the blast. The Imperial control systems flickered out and the TIE fighter spun dead in the air, its engine silenced. Unable to regain control, the pilot crashed into the distant forest canopy with a dull, booming explosion.

Jacen used his targeting circles to lock onto a sluggish, fully loaded TIE bomber that arrowed toward the clustered residential structures. The bomber came in, picking up speed while preparing to drop its deadly explosives.

Jacen grasped the firing controls and gritted his teeth. "Come on . . . come on," he said. Finally, the target lock blinked as the TIE bomber settled directly in the crosshairs.

He squeezed both controls, launching searing blazes of laser energy from all four cannons. The beams targeted on the bomber just before it could drop its proton explosives. Instead of destroying the homes of hundreds of Wookiees, the bomber became a brilliant ball of fire and smoke. The belch of detonations grew louder as the TIE fighter's own proton bombs fed into the eruption.

"Got one!" Jacen crowed.

Tenel Ka fired repeatedly until another pair of TIE fighters exploded in the air. "Two more," she said.

By now, additional Wookiee defenders had arrived to assume positions at the remaining guns. Jacen fired again and again, rotating his chair to aim at the rapidly moving targets. He blasted another TIE fighter out of the sky.

"Just like our practice runs in the *Millennium Falcon*," he said. "Only this time, hitting the targets is a lot more important than winning a contest with my sister."

"This is a fact," Tenel Ka said.

Another wing of TIE fighters swooped down, and Jacen shot wildly. So many Imperial targets, he thought, all of them bristling with lethal weaponry. . . . His quad-laser cannon spat beams of energy, but they all missed as the fighters spun evasive loops in the air.

"Oh, blaster bolts!" Jacen said.

Wookiees kept appearing, leaping off the vine pulley-lifts and rushing to their positions, although now there were more defenders than guns. Lowie and Sirra hurried over to Jacen and Tenel Ka, speaking loudly. Their grunts and growls overlapped, so that Em Teedee had difficulty translating both.

"One at a time, please!" the little droid said. "All right, I believe I understand the basics of what you're saying. Master Lowbacca and Mistress Sirrakuk have determined that a single-point defensive failure occurred in the traffic control tower for this facility. Somehow, all of the central command systems have been compromised. It appears that the attack is being guided from there."

Lowie roared a suggestion. "Oh dear," Em Teedee said. "Master Lowbacca suggests we would be well advised to go to the heart of the problem and leave these well-trained Wookiee gunners to continue the fight here. While I agree that it might be safer to move inside—I am skeptical about the wisdom of rushing into greater danger."

"Good idea, Lowie," Jacen said, ignoring Em Teedee's warnings. He fired the quad-laser one more time, almost offhandedly, and was astonished to see his quick shot destroy the side panel of another TIE fighter, which spun out of control and crashed to the treetops. "Hey, got another one," he said.

Barricaded in the traffic control tower, Zekk listened to outraged Wookiees pounding against the sealed door. A sizzling, melting sound worked its way into the background din as the Wookiees used high-intensity laser torches to slice through the armored metal. Their own well-constructed defenses worked against them, since they had intended Kashyyyk's command center to be impregnable. Slowly but surely, though, the Wookiees made headway, slicing through the door one centimeter at a time.

Using the security monitors, Zekk watched the hairy creatures out in the hall. With bestial rage one of them picked up a metal pipe and hammered at the door—to no effect, of course, because of the thick plating, but the Wookiee seemed satisfied just to be able to vent his fury.

Tamith Kai crossed her arms over her reptile-armored chest. "The noise level out there is most annoying," she said, then glared at the stormtrooper standing guard. Her violet eyes flashed with a twisted idea. "Why don't we trigger the locking mechanism and let the

Wookiees stumble inside. We can easily take care of the whole lot before they recover from their surprise."

Vonnda Ra chuckled. "That would be amusing to watch."

Before Zekk could voice an indignant protest that *he* was in command of this mission, the stormtrooper activated the door controls. The panel suddenly slid aside, shocking the Wookiee engineers who had been working to gain access. They howled.

The stormtrooper used his blaster rifle to mow them down in a few seconds, every one of them. Even encased in white armor, the stormtrooper's body language showed his pleasure. He keyed in the sequence to slam the heavy door shut again, leaving the fallen Wookiees out in the corridor.

"At last, peace and quiet," Tamith Kai said.

Overhead, TIE fighters and bombers continued to attack, dodging bursts of weapon fire from the tree facility's perimeter defenses. The reinforced dome overhead showed the battle in the skies. Several contingents of stormtrooper reinforcements had already landed.

Vonnda Ra worked at one of the computer stations, scanning security images. A minute later, she gave a gasp of surprised triumph. "Ah, I believe I've found them," she said. "The vermin were firing the perimeter guns, but now they're in the corridors. They seem to be making their way . . . ah! They're making their way here. Delusions of grandeur. That could prove quite convenient."

"Who?" Zekk said.

Vonnda Ra raised her eyebrows. "Why, those Jedi brats, of course. Had you forgotten your other goal for this mission?"

Zekk thought of Jacen and Jaina and their friends. "No, I didn't forget," he said. But he didn't want to confront the twins here, not in front of the evil Tamith Kai. This should have been his own private battle, the consequences of the choices *he* had made. "We'll meet them on the way. Ambush them. Lock down their location."

"Simple enough," Vonnda Ra said.

Reinforcing his position of command, Zekk turned sharply and issued brisk orders. "Tamith Kai, you will remain here and continue organizing the mission. Our primary goal is to get those computer systems for the Second Imperium. You—" he nodded toward the stormtrooper "—will stay here as guard. Vonnda Ra and I will take care of the young Jedi Knights."

Tamith Kai scowled at being ordered about, but Zekk rounded on her, his cape swirling. "Is that assignment beyond your capabilities, Tamith Kai?"

"Indeed not," she said. "Is yours? Just be certain you eliminate those brats."

When the stormtrooper unsealed the armored door again, Vonnda Ra followed Zekk, and they strode out into the corridor, stepping around motionless Wookiee engineers sprawled on the floor, heading toward a confrontation with Zekk's former friends.

Jacen rushed along, shoulder to shoulder with Lowie and Sirra. The interior corridors were full of smoke, debris, and noise. Glowpanels in the ceilings flickered off and on with energy fluctuations from the attack.

Jacen and Lowie drew their shimmering lightsabers and held them ready. Tenel Ka picked up a loose metal rod, a piece of destroyed pipe that had fallen from an overhead assembly, and loped along behind them, guarding the rear. She held the rod like a spear, as if hoping to find some enemy target.

Lowie and Sirra turned the corner in the corridor, and Jacen thought he recognized the route they had taken to the monolithic control tower during their visit with the Tour Droid. Suddenly, Lowie gave a surprised roar; Sirra bellowed in alarm. Tenel Ka brandished her long metal rod.

"Hey, it's Zekk!" Jacen shouted, skidding to a stop.

There in the corridor, as if waiting for them, stood the dark-haired scamp who for years had been a friend to Jacen and Jaina . . . who had taken them on excursions through Coruscant's abandoned building levels and dim alleys. Now the once-scruffy boy wore expensive leather armor and a crimson-lined black cape—and bore a scarlet-bladed lightsaber. He looked ominous.

Tenel Ka saw Zekk, too, and held her metal staff at the ready. In a flash of memory, Jacen thought of the warrior girl's initial meeting with Zekk, back on Coruscant: when the young man had dropped down from above to surprise them, Tenel Ka had whipped out her fibercord with blurring speed and lassoed him before he could jump out of the way.

Now, though, Tenel Ka had only one hand, and she did not choose to drop her long steel rod to grab for her rope, or her lightsaber.

For a moment Zekk's face seemed to open. His eyes grew round and uncertain. "Jacen," he said, "I—"

Tenel Ka glared at the Nightsister and spoke in a low, threatening voice, "I have your name, Vonnda Ra. I saw you try to lure others from the Singing Mountain Clan on Dathomir. In your encampment at the Great Canyon you chose me as a trainee for the Shadow Academy, but instead we rescued my friends—and defeated you utterly. We'll defeat you again."

The muscular Nightsister held up her clawlike hands. "Not this time, Jedi brats!" she said. "I shall enjoy destroying you."

Jacen felt her dark power crackle through the air, and he held his lightsaber high in defense. Fire-blue lightning bolts danced at Vonnda Ra's fingertips, burning through her body and sizzling behind her eyes.

She flicked her wrists to hurl her dark lightning at them—but Zekk shouldered the Nightsister to one side. The bolts of evil force flared past them like shadowy flames and scorched the wall plates.

Vonnda Ra glared at Zekk, but he snapped, "They are mine to deal with! *I* am in command here."

With a thundering sound of booted feet, a contingent of Imperial fighters charged down the corridor. Jacen looked up in alarm. Reinforcements had arrived—far more than he could hope to fight with his lightsaber, even with the help of Lowbacca, Sirra, and Tenel Ka.

Stormtroopers must have landed on the upper platforms, Jacen surmised. The Second Imperium apparently wanted something here at the fabrication facility. Judging from the alarms and explosions, the Imperials had already overrun most of the platforms.

Zekk stood waiting to battle the Jedi trainees, as if gathering up his courage and his anger, while the rebuffed Nightsister seethed with dark fury. The stormtroopers drew their weapons.

Jacen knew with sudden certainty that they could never win a face-to-face fight here. Tenel Ka pushed herself one step forward, brandishing her metal rod. "We must turn back," she said, darting a look at him over her shoulder.

"Good idea," Jacen said, casting a glance behind him.

"You, girl, are a traitor to Dathomir!" Vonnda Ra spat, just as Tenel Ka hurled the long pipe in her direction. The rod struck the Nightsister, knocking her sideways. Stormtroopers clattered toward them as Lowie and Sirra turned to charge back down the corridor.

"After them!" Zekk called, gesturing with one black-gloved hand.

The stormtroopers thundered in pursuit. Vonnda Ra cast the pipe aside. Patches of it were bent and red-hot where fire from within her fingers had super-heated the metal.

Sirra yelled something to her brother as they sprinted down the corridor, with Jacen and Tenel Ka right behind them. "Access hatch?" Em Teedee translated. "Escape? Yes, that sounds like an excellent idea. By all means, let us escape."

At an intersection of corridors, Sirra stopped beside a clearly marked floor panel. Reaching her long fingers down, she hooked the tiny ring-handles. With her powerful muscles, she hauled upward, pulling the heavy hatch free to reveal a trapdoor. She growled and gestured.

Without hesitation Lowie leaped into the hole, catching a strong vine that hung underneath. The tinny voice of the translating droid wailed, "But this leads to the underlevels of the forest! Master Lowbacca, we *can't* go down here. It's far too dangerous!"

Lowie merely grumbled and continued his descent. Tenel Ka followed next, hopping lightly over the edge, wrapping her muscular legs around a vine. Grasping it with her hand, she lowered herself into the darkness.

Jacen turned around just in time to see Zekk and Vonnda Ra rushing toward them, flanked by stormtroopers. "Down into the underworld, huh?" Jacen said, glancing at Sirrakuk. "Looks like you'll get an early chance to complete that risky adventure of yours."

Sirra growled her agreement. With that, both of them plunged over the lip of the trapdoor and descended into the murky, leafy depths below.

Scrambling downward into the tangled foliage, Jacen looked up through the dense branches to see the silhouetted figures of Zekk and Vonnda Ra conferring at the edge of the glowing patch of light. Jacen could hear their voices faintly as he fled deeper into the thick forest.

"We'll have to follow them," Zekk said.

"You should have allowed me to destroy them when I had the chance," the Nightsister snapped. "Now they will cause difficulties."

Zekk answered sharply. *"I* am in charge here. We'll do things my way." He turned and shouted to the stormtroopers. "Down into the forests. All of you."

Zekk, Vonnda Ra, and the stormtroopers plunged after their prey into the underworld of Kashyyyk.

14

BRAKISS PACED THE corridors of the Shadow Academy, like an inspector general ensuring that his troops were prepared for imminent combat. He glided along with silent footsteps. His robes whispered around him.

The Master of the Shadow Academy looked too clean, too handsome to be an ominous threat. And although command of the new Dark Jedi rested firmly in his hands, his mind was instead focused on resolving his own doubts.

Brakiss allowed a flicker of anger—*anger,* the heart of dark side power—to flash through him. His right fist clenched . . . then he dismissed the emotion. He must not lose control, he told himself, for therein lay a greater weakness. Now he must be strong.

Through his own work, he had created the armored space station as a Dark Jedi training center. He had done it all for the glory of his Great Leader, to help bring about the Second Imperium and restore the galaxy to order and firm paternal control. He had done so much work, risked so many things. . . .

And now the Emperor had snubbed him.

Since the secret Imperial transport had arrived at the Shadow Academy and the four scarlet-cloaked Imperial guards had taken Palpatine's sealed isolation chamber off to a restricted section, Brakiss had neither seen nor spoken to the Emperor, despite his many requests for an audience. He had been so honored to learn that the Great Leader would visit. . . .

But now Palpatine's presence threw all of his thoughts and plans into turmoil.

Brakiss glided along the curved corridors. The lights had been dimmed for the sleep cycle; most of the Dark Jedi students had sealed themselves inside their quarters for the evening. A small shift of stormtroopers continued their patrol duties.

Qorl had been successful in training new military recruits from the

Lost Ones gang on Coruscant. The TIE pilot had paid particular attention to the burly Norys, who had a knack for Imperial enforcement techniques—though the insolence Norys showed gave Brakiss cause for concern. Still, only rarely did stormtrooper trainees show such . . . enthusiasm.

As Brakiss drifted along the quiet corridors, he fleetingly wished he were wearing stormtrooper armor himself, so that his footsteps could make resounding, forceful clangs. But unfortunately, such a demonstration of pique would have been deemed unworthy of a Jedi superior.

Brakiss was a powerful man—or so he had thought, until the Emperor's entourage arrived. The red guards seemed to consider him the lowliest of servants. This was an unfair dismissal of all he had accomplished, he told himself. Perhaps the Emperor truly was ill; perhaps the Second Imperium was in greater danger than Brakiss had feared. He decided it would be best to speak directly to Palpatine, to see for himself.

He had been patient. He had been helpful. He had accommodated every whim passed along by the faceless Imperial guards—but now Brakiss needed answers.

Brakiss took a deep breath to center himself, to focus his thoughts to a razor edge of calm resolve. Propelled by his growing confidence, he turned about and made his way toward the isolated chambers of the Emperor and his followers.

Brakiss would not be turned away this time.

The section reserved for the Emperor's group seemed even dimmer than the rest of the Shadow Academy. The light had been polarized somehow, so that it contained a reddish tinge that made it difficult to see. The ambient temperature felt colder.

Two red guards stood posted at the intersection of the corridor. They towered over Brakiss as he approached, the folds of their scarlet robes gleaming in the reddish light as if they had been oiled. The guards carried force pikes, ominous-looking weapons that might simply be ornamental . . . but Brakiss did not want to test that theory.

"No intruders are allowed," one of the red guards said.

Brakiss stopped short. "I believe you are ill-informed. I am Brakiss, Master of the Shadow Academy."

"We are aware of your identity. No intruders beyond this point."

"I am not an intruder. This is my own station," he said, taking another bold step forward and trying to impart power to his words.

One of the guards shifted his force pike. "This station belongs to the *Emperor*. He holds the right to claim ownership of everything he considers valuable to his Second Imperium."

Following that thread of argument would do him no good, Brakiss decided. "I must speak with the Emperor," he said.

"That is impossible," the guard answered.

"Nothing is impossible," Brakiss countered.

"The Emperor sees no one."

"Then let me speak to him over the comm. I'm certain he will wish to see me once he and I have had a brief discussion."

"The Emperor has no desire for 'a brief discussion'—with you or anyone else."

Brakiss placed his hands on his hips. "And when did the Emperor delegate the authority to speak for him"—he spoke the words scornfully—"to his mere *guards?* By what right did you become his mouthpiece? I do not recognize your authority, *guard*. How do I know you're not holding him hostage? How do I know that he isn't ill or drugged?"

He crossed his arms over his robed chest. "I accept orders only from the Emperor. Now let me speak to him immediately, or I shall call forth all of my troops on this station and arrest you for mutiny against the Second Imperium."

The two red guards stood motionless. "It is unwise to threaten us," they said in unison.

Brakiss didn't back down. "It is unwise to ignore me," he replied.

"Very well," one guard said, and turned to a comm station on the wall. He pushed a button and, though Brakiss heard no words from beneath the armored helmet, the Emperor's voice instantly slid through the speakers, like sounds made of snakes.

"Brakiss, this is your Emperor. Your insolence annoys me."

"I merely wish to speak with you, my lord," he said, forcing his voice to remain steady. "You have not addressed the Shadow Academy or me since your arrival here. I am concerned for your personal well-being."

"Brakiss, you forget your place. You can do nothing to protect me that I cannot do myself—with ten times the power."

Brakiss felt his anger dwindling, but he clutched his pride for one last moment. "I have not forgotten my place, my lord. My place is as the Master of the Shadow Academy, to create an army of Dark Jedi for you and your Second Imperium. My place is *at your side*—not cast out and ignored like an insignificant bureaucrat."

Palpatine seemed to pause before snapping a reply through the speaker. "Do not forget, Brakiss, that when this station was constructed I saw to it that explosives were planted throughout the superstructure to ensure your obedience. I can destroy this Academy on a whim. Don't tempt me."

"I wouldn't dream of it, my lord," Brakiss said, feeling his anxiety grow. "But if I am to be part of your plans of conquest, I must be consulted. I must be permitted to give my input, because I alone can provide the valuable fighters you require to defeat the Rebels and their upstart new Jedi Knights."

The Emperor snapped, "You will learn of my plans when I wish you to learn of them! I require no advice from you or from any other. Perhaps you need to be reminded that you are merely an expendable servant. Do not demand to see me again. I will emerge from my quarters when it suits me."

With a click like the sound of a breaking bone, the comm unit switched off. Brakiss felt worse than ever. More insignificant, more confused.

The red Imperial guards stood firmly in their positions, holding their force pikes upright. "You will depart now," one of them said.

Without replying, Brakiss spun on his heel and marched in silence down the hollow, echoing corridors of his Shadow Academy.

15

TOO STUNNED AT first to move, Jaina hung on to the edge of the hangar bay doors on the platform high above the rest of the treetops. She stared down in unwilling fascination at the spot where Garowyn had fallen through the branches. Replaying the scene in her mind, still not quite able to believe what had happened, she saw the Nightsister falling . . . *falling.*

By the time Jaina managed to tear her gaze away, Chewbacca had retrieved the speeder bike and buzzed back up toward her. With an urgent sound in his voice, he pointed to the explosions and flickers of laser cannon fire in the distant fabrication facility. TIE fighters shot overhead, pummeling the residential areas with bright energy bolts.

Chewbacca gestured with a long hairy arm, pointing to the seat behind him on the speeder bike. Jaina gulped. Surely he didn't intend for *both* of them to ride that thing? The tiny vehicle was already wheezing and chugging under the Wookiee's considerable weight.

On the other hand, the two of them had walked to the hangar bay this morning, and they had no other vehicle to take them to the besieged fabrication facility—and they had to help. There was no time to call for a bantha. She hoped her brother and her friends were all right.

Chewbacca brought the speeder bike to an unsteady hover in front of the repair bay and motioned for her to get on. Jaina squelched her reservations and climbed on behind him. She found little room to sit, and her legs were still slick from spilled lubricant, so she threw her arms around Chewie's broad chest as far as they would go, threading her fingers through his thick fur to keep herself from sliding off.

With Jaina's added weight, the speeder bike sank. Chewbacca revved its engine, and they took off. Though their forward progress was faster than Jaina had expected, the vehicle continued to lose altitude until it barely skimmed over the bushy treetops. The engine sputtered. Jaina could feel the toes of her boots brushing against taller branches and sprigs of leaves. The wind in her hair blew the strands wildly in every direction.

Jaina yanked her foot up to avoid an upthrust bough, and nearly capsized the little speeder. But Chewbacca felt the change in balance and managed to compensate by shifting his weight in the other direction. Jaina clung to his fur and gratefully maneuvered herself back upright.

"Can't we go any faster?" she shouted into his fur-covered ear. Her heart pounded, and the sweat of fear evaporated in the cold breeze of their wild flight. The Wookiee roared back at her, clearly understanding the danger their friends might be facing.

When they reached the fabrication facility, Jaina could hardly believe her eyes. Grayish white smoke curled up from half a dozen different windows and skylights in the factory. Splintered and charred wroshyr branches lay scattered about like the broken playthings of a spoiled giant. Imperial fighters still flew in formation in the skies, but they dwindled in the distance, heading back to orbit.

"Is the attack over already?" Jaina asked in disbelief. Chewbacca echoed her surprise.

The Wookiee had a hard time controlling the laboring speeder bike as they landed, and both he and Jaina tumbled off. Not bothering to check their bruises, they picked themselves up and rushed to the closest entryway, calling for Jacen, Lowie, Tenel Ka, and Sirra.

The scene inside the factory was utter chaos. Frantic Wookiees rushed about bellowing orders, extinguishing small fires, righting toppled machinery, and helping injured or trapped friends. The smell of charred wood and singed fur stabbed at Jaina's nostrils. Pale chemical smoke stung her eyes, but most of the fires were already contained, and a fresh breeze blew in through the open windows to clear the fumes.

Chewbacca roared in recognition as he rushed to his sister Kallabow—Lowie and Sirra's mother. She was bent over another injured worker, tending his wounds. With nimble hands Kallabow had shaved the fur from around a bleeding cut and covered it with a coagulant bandage.

Lowie's mother looked up, blinking dazed eyes set within whorls of auburn fur, and she and Chewbacca engaged in a rapid, barking interchange. Jaina caught only parts of the conversation, but learned enough to know that the devastating raid was indeed over. The Imperials had struck with lightning speed, causing enormous damage to the outlying facilities—but their main objective had apparently been to raid the equipment stockpiles and steal computer components and encryption devices.

Jaina was reminded of Qorl's previous raid on the New Republic supply cruiser *Adamant*, when he had commandeered an entire shipment of hyperdrive cores and turbolaser batteries. The Second Imperium was definitely making plans for an all-out war—and soon.

Jaina bent down next to Kallabow. "Have you seen Lowie and Sirra? My brother Jacen, or maybe Tenel Ka?"

Lowie's mother rattled off a series of woofs, growls, and barks in a worried tone. She spread her arms to indicate the surrounding pandemonium, then gripped Jaina's shoulder, asking her to track down her children. Another Wookiee wailed in pain farther down the corridor; still dazed, Kallabow blinked wearily and moved past Jaina to help the victim to his feet.

"We've got to find them," Jaina said, and Chewbacca nodded vigorously.

Chewie made his way deeper into the damaged facility, assisting wherever he could and barking out phrases that were incomprehensible to Jaina. Never one to stand around wringing her hands in an emergency, Jaina helped to bind up minor wounds and put out small fires. Occasionally, she used the Force to help muscular Wookiees heave aside smashed equipment. Every time she asked about her brother and her friends, however, she received only confused answers.

Moment by moment, the cacophony around Jaina increased with a confusing mix of Wookiee yowls, barks, and growls. Oh, how she wished that Em Teedee were here to interpret all the nuances. Her head spun with confusion and disorientation, and she was relieved to see Chewbacca motion her over to help him tend a wounded engineer. Chewie greeted her with animated gestures and an excited bark.

"What did you find?" Jaina asked, biting her lower lip.

The injured engineer spoke, her voice just above a wheezing purr. Still unable to understand, Jaina turned to Chewbacca for an interpretation. The irony of the situation might have struck her as funny had the circumstances not been so serious.

Chewie explained slowly enough that Jaina could follow. The engineer had seen the two young Wookiees and two human visitors run down the corridor behind her. Not long afterward, she had noted some of the Imperial attackers in the same corridor—stormtroopers and humans in dark capes.

"Any way out in that direction?" Jaina asked hopefully. "Is it possible they escaped?"

The engineer shook her head. No exits, only maintenance trapdoors that opened to the dense and dangerous forests below.

Trapdoors.

Chewie finished binding the engineer's wounds, thanked her, and hurried off down the corridor she had indicated. Jaina skidded to a stop at the edge of a gaping hole blasted in the floor, where an access hatch had been ripped from its hinges. Chewbacca had to pull Jaina back physically to keep her from toppling over the brink. He growled, sniffing around the burned metal edges.

Jaina nodded. "Yeah, looks like the work of stormtroopers. They must've thought the trapdoors needed to be wider and did a little remodeling." She blew out a long, slow breath, trying to calm herself. "Lowie told us how dangerous it is down there. But I guess it didn't stop *them*."

Chewie opened an emergency locker on the wall. He yanked out two knapsacks filled with supplies and tossed one to Jaina. Then, with a barely audible growl, he pointed down at the hole in the floor.

"You're right, of course," Jaina said. "What are we waiting for?" She peered down into the inky darkness below.

"Your jungle," she said at last. "I guess you'd better lead."

16

DEEP INSIDE HIS hairy chest, Lowbacca felt his heart contract with primal fear. He had known since childhood the dangers of descending into the perilous, untamed forests of Kashyyyk. The darkened depths often proved deadly even to those who entered fully armed and trained.

Nobody went to the underlevels willingly . . . but now, with Zekk and Vonnda Ra and the stormtroopers pursuing them, Lowie knew the primeval forest was their only chance.

The last time he had ventured beneath the secure treetop cities had been to search out glossy fibers from the syren plant, from which he wove his prized belt. He had thought himself so brave to accomplish the task alone.

Sirra's friend Raaba had also gone by herself—because Lowie had. Despite her skills and courage, though, the dark-furred Wookiee female had never returned. But Lowie was not alone this time. He and his friends could fight together against whatever dangers the forest held.

Above and behind him, he heard the crashing of boots and the snapping of twigs as armored Imperials followed them, shining brilliant glowbeams into the dank, forever-night levels, startling exotic creatures that had never seen the light of day. A few random shots rang out as stormtroopers blasted forest animals. Burned leaves smoldered, then went out in a gasp of thick smoke.

Lowie and Sirra did their best to lead Jacen and Tenel Ka, using their darkness-adapted Wookiee vision to find broad, sturdy branches along the trunks of the wroshyr trees. Panting with the desperate effort, Lowie wheezed encouragement. The friends pressed on blindly, with no specific destination, knowing only that they had to keep going if they were to lose their pursuers in the maze of the forest underworld.

Em Teedee's round, yellow optical sensors shed a bright glow into the murk, the most illumination they could risk. "Do be careful of those branches, Master Lowbacca," the droid said as a twig scratched his outer casing. "I wouldn't want to break loose and fall. That happened to me once already, if you'll recall, and it was a frightfully unpleasant experience."

Lowie groaned, remembering the misadventure on Yavin 4. Losing the translating droid had caused other problems as well, since no one at the Jedi academy had understood Lowie's warnings that Jacen and Jaina had been captured by the TIE pilot Qorl.

Behind them, lightning shot through the darkness and branches crackled as the stormtroopers opened fire again. Lowie instinctively ducked, and Sirra dropped to a lower branch without bothering to test it for sturdiness. Streaks blazed across the thickets, erupting in fire and choking smoke.

"Hey, look out!" Jacen cried.

Tenel Ka grabbed on to a branch with her hand and swung down to Sirra's level. "This way!" she said. "It is safe."

Lowie leaped after her, one arm around Jacen's waist, then sprinted across the moss-covered boughs. Farther from the warm sunlight, each forest level had a different ecosystem made up of matted platforms of interlaced vines, branches that grew together, accumulations of mulch in which other plants—fungi, lichens, squirming flowers—flourished. Thousands of insects, reptiles, birds, and rodents fled at the sound of the intruders.

Lowie chuffed for the others to follow him. Racing along on his flat feet, he wrinkled his black nose and sniffed the odor-congested air. His nostrils tingled with a tantalizing, terrifying scent—a scent he had smelled before. Something that had nearly cost him his life.

In the lambent glow from Em Teedee's optical sensors, Lowie saw the wide-open maw of a syren plant, its glossy-yellow petals atop the blood-red stalk looked like a gaping mouth waiting for a meal. The plant had somehow taken root in a crook between two intergrown branches, and fed upon denizens of this forest level. The sparkling fibers that formed a plume at the carnivorous flower's center shone temptingly bright, while a delicious scent lured unsuspecting victims.

Beside him, Sirra also sniffed the air and spotted the deadly plant. She growled in anticipation, her patchwork-shaved fur standing on end. But Lowie put a hand on her arm, shook his head, then gripped her arm firmly. He could tell his sister wanted to secure the precious syren fibers and prove her bravery as soon as possible.

Sirra groaned in disappointment, but she clearly understood their priorities. Behind them, several levels up, the pursuing stormtroopers fired again, this time at some large creature crashing through the tree levels.

Far too dangerous. The Imperials were too close.

With a growl Sirra took the lead, and Lowie guided his friends behind her.

As she raced through the morass of branches, ducking her head to keep her red-gold braids from snagging on thorns or low-hanging limbs, Tenel Ka reveled in the calisthenics that pushed her body to its limits. But she would have preferred to do it without the threat of sudden death from the blaster of a stormtrooper.

Her reptilian armor covered only her torso, leaving her limbs unprotected from scratches and insect bites—but she did not allow such minor inconveniences to bother her.

As the companions ran deeper into the forest, Tenel Ka took care to maintain her balance and watched out for her friend Jacen. Though he was highly skilled in sensing strange life-forms, Jacen was not as physically capable as she was. This was the chase. The hunt. Here *she* was in her element.

But at the moment Tenel Ka was not the stalker, but the prey.

Her reflexes were sharpened by her inability to see through the forest shadows. Her lightsaber could have lit the way, but she didn't dare ignite it for fear of drawing attention to their position. At the moment her focus had to be on simply running.

All around, she detected looming dangers that grew worse, more foreboding, as they leapt from one level to the next, descending into thicker and thicker primeval wilderness. Tenel Ka sensed that the two Wookiees felt the increasing threat; Lowie and Sirra moved more cautiously, supporting each other as they used their night vision to choose a path.

At a broad, open intersection of wide branches, the Wookiees paused, panting for breath. Jacen slumped beside Tenel Ka, utterly exhausted. They knew they couldn't stop for long.

During the brief rest, Tenel Ka remained standing. She turned in a slow circle, granite-gray eyes narrowed, sharply attentive for movement, for predators lurking in the surrounding trees. Her Jedi senses detected no dangerous animals, only a tingling underlying threat that grew more and more powerful.

Just then, a leathery plant tentacle wrapped quickly around Tenel Ka's waist and drew itself snug. Thin thorns dug into her flesh through her reptilian armor. She cried out—and suddenly the air around them came alive with whipping, writhing vines from above.

Both Wookiees howled and thrashed. Jacen yelped. The thorny vines yanked him into the air, legs kicking, hands flailing. In an instant Tenel Ka snatched out her lightsaber and—ignoring the threat of revealing their position to the stormtroopers—ignited the glowing turquoise blade. Her arm swept sideways, severing the vines that grasped her waist.

Jacen yelled again and managed to get his lightsaber out, too. Swinging it above his head, he slashed through the vicious plant stems with a sizzling, wet sound. The spicy smell of burned sap cascaded into the air.

Lowbacca roared and ignited his Jedi weapon, striking left and right with the molten bronze blade. Hungry tentacles snaked toward him, eager to pull the Wookiee upward to where the knotted cluster of vines came together in a cavernous opening that emitted a sound like rocks grinding together, a slavering gullet ready to smash them into digestible pieces.

Two of the vines caught Sirrakuk and wrapped themselves tightly around her arms. She bared her Wookiee fangs and, bunching her powerful muscles, ripped the vines free of the central stem with brute force. The plant seemed not to notice; it went on thrashing its tentacles, and its open gullet continued to mash and grind.

Within moments, three flashing lightsabers sliced away the clinging tentacles and left only twitching stumps at the end of the voracious vine creature.

"We've escaped!" Em Teedee said. "Oh, how wonderful!"

"This is a fact," Tenel Ka agreed. She examined the red welts and oozing scratches she had received during the battle, then looked up toward the next level of branches. "But our lightsabers have attracted the enemy."

The others turned to follow her gaze. On the branches above them, completely surrounding the group, stood a contingent of fully armed stormtroopers, their blasters pointed down at the young Jedi Knights.

Jacen shut off the emerald beam of his lightsaber and squatted on the branch, breathing hard as he surveyed the encircling stormtroopers. In other circumstances, he would have found the underworld of Kashyyyk fascinating, filled as it was with insects and trees, ferns, vines, flowers, lizards—a million new pets for him to inspect, then set free. He found many of the life-forms to be incomprehensible, unlike anything he had ever experienced. Even now, with stormtroopers like pale statues above, blasters at the ready and aimed at him, Jacen could sense the hidden creatures around them.

Near one of the stormtroopers who stood on a decaying branch, Jacen noticed that a broad patch of bark lay wet and damp, like a mottled tongue wrapped around the tree. It was slick, glistening, moving on a cellular level.

Two more dark figures joined the gathered stormtroopers. The ominous Nightsister Vonnda Ra, with her hard muscles, broad shoulders, and glittering black body armor, stood next to Zekk, his dark hair neatly tied back with a thong at the nape of his neck, his swirling scarlet-lined cape undamaged by leaves or twigs. The stormtroopers shone glowrods down on the scene.

"You are trapped, Jedi brats," Vonnda Ra said. "It could be amusing to watch you grovel for your lives—but I can assure you it would do you no good."

"We do not intend to grovel," Tenel Ka said, and the Nightsister glared at the young warrior girl from Dathomir.

Jacen focused his concentration on the wide, mysterious slick patch wrapped around the branch. It seemed like a river of damp leather, and as he concentrated, he felt a dim awareness, a rudimentary brain that was more a cluster of reflexes. But reflexes were all Jacen needed right now.

"I'm sorry it has come to this," Zekk said, "but I owe my allegiance to the Second Imperium now, and you are my sworn enemies. I can no longer deny it. That was my choice." Despite his words, the expression on Zekk's high-cheekboned face and the disturbed look in his green eyes showed Jacen how troubled he truly was.

One of the stormtroopers moved sideways to get a clearer shot at them.

Jacen watched. *Just a little more, just a little more* . . .

Perhaps he sent out the thought with the Force, because the stormtrooper did indeed take one more step. His heavy, booted foot planted itself squarely on the wide wet patch.

Without warning, the creature reacted.

A slithering flap of wet, slimy meat in the form of a monstrous sluglike beast raised itself from its sleeping position. The motion knocked the stormtrooper completely off the branch, and he tumbled screaming into the depths of the forest.

With a thick slurping sound the enormous slug creature reared up and up and *up*, thrashing from side to side, knocking two other stormtroopers from their positions. The Imperial soldiers were thrown into pandemonium, shouting and shooting.

Jacen did his best to send a thought to the thing, identifying the white-armored guards as the enemy and planting the idea that Jacen, the two Wookiees, and Tenel Ka were the slow-witted creature's friends.

Stormtroopers opened fire on the monster, but the blasters did little more than annoy it. Branches crashed and snapped. Energy bolts ricocheted around in the forest as the slug creature continued its reflexive attack.

Jacen stood transfixed, fascinated with the battle and the havoc the beast had already caused. Zekk and Vonnda Ra shouted conflicting orders.

The next thing Jacen knew, Tenel Ka slammed him aside. A blaster bolt sizzled past him as she wrapped a vine around her arm, grasped his waist, and dove to a lower branch. The two Wookiees were already ahead of them in their headlong flight.

Making quick use of the diversion, the young Jedi Knights continued down, *down*—dropping all the way to the bottom levels of the forest.

17

THE FOREST DARKNESS was so thick Jaina could practically taste it. She followed the agile Chewbacca more by sound than by any other sense, finding herself relying more and more on the Force to guide her hands and feet. The air was cooler here below the canopy. Jaina shivered, though she doubted it was entirely because of the drop in temperature.

With his sharp Wookiee vision, Chewie led the way without hesitation. He barked an occasional warning about a patch of slippery moss or a weak branch. Neither made any great attempt to keep quiet: their one concern was to catch up with their friends before it was too late.

Gradually Jaina's eyesight adjusted enough that she could make out the shadowy forms of tree trunks, black against deep gray. It wasn't much to go by, but it helped. Chewbacca made a snuffling sound and gave a low woof of triumph.

"They came this direction?" she asked.

He yipped an affirmative. Their smells were here. He detected four . . . no, *five* of them, as well as a faint smell of metal. Jaina decided he must be picking up on Em Teedee. Chewie growled low in his throat, muttering about other smells too: plasteel, burned branches, the thunderstorm-smell of ozone from blaster discharges.

Jaina's heart skipped a beat. "Definitely sounds like the Nightsisters brought stormtroopers down here with them."

Chewbacca increased his speed, following the fresh trail. Once Jaina misjudged the spacing and almost fell between a pair of tree branches that were farther apart than she'd thought. "Chewie, I can barely see," she said.

With a chuff of understanding, the Wookiee stopped briefly, rummaged through the emergency pack he had taken from the fabrication facility, and pulled out a small mesh jar. Jaina recognized a phosflea lure. He broke the seal.

Moments later, as if the glowing specks had materialized directly from the air, the lure's surface was covered with tiny phosphorescent insects. Chewbacca fastened the lure to a strap around Jaina's waist. The "light" now shed a pinkish glow directly in front of her that swirled like a comet's tail as she moved along.

Chewbacca pointed below Jaina to a freshly broken branch and the burned scoring from weapon fire. The others had come this way.

"You're right," Jaina said. "I can feel them, not too far ahead."

The Wookiee helped her across the broad gap and they resumed their descent. Jaina climbed after him, watching handholds and footholds more carefully now as the glowing phosfleas lit her way. A feeling of dread mounted more strongly within her as they descended to each deeper level. She could feel the weight of the overlying forest pressing down on them.

Unseen predators bounded across leafy limbs, pursuing their quarries; the shriek of victims fallen in the endless hunt echoed through the thick labyrinth of branches. Smaller creatures chirped, buzzed, and chittered. None of them sounded friendly to her.

Jaina knew that her friends were good fighters, but she knew, too, that even Lowie, the strongest of all of them, feared the jungles of Kashyyyk. That alone was cause for worry, but the young Jedi Knights and Sirra had more to fear than the deadly plants and animals that populated the lowest levels of the forest.

Jaina could feel that something was about to happen. "No time to lose!" she urged. She picked up her pace. Chewbacca, sensing her urgency, did the same, barely taking time to rest his foot on one limb before bounding down to a lower branch.

In the distance Jaina heard a shout, a human voice that sounded loud and chilling, mixed with the wild noises. When she stopped to look in that direction, she saw flickers of light and heard the sizzle of blaster fire.

Just then, the rotting branch beneath her feet creaked and threatened to give way. In her haste, she had not bothered to check the branch before stepping on it. Chewbacca spun and reached out to pull her to safety on a thicker branch closer to the trunk. She scrambled for purchase.

But the whole side of the wroshyr tree must have been weakened by rot or disease, for at that moment the bough on which the large Wookiee stood gave way as well. Snapping and popping, the gnarled wood dropped out from beneath him.

Jaina watched, her mouth open in a silent scream, as Chewbacca plummeted, crashing into the darkness below.

18

EXHAUSTED, ZEKK STOOD with the lightsaber still gripped in his sweaty hand. He found it hard to breathe the thick, cloying air of the underworld.

The smoking carcass of the dead slug beast, now sliced in pieces, lay draped across the overspreading branches. Burned slime bubbled with a noxious stench. Small fires crackled from stray blaster bolts that had ignited portions of the dense foliage. The surviving stormtroopers shouted to each other over helmet comlinks, completing their damage assessment.

Vonnda Ra stood trembling, jaw set, face drawn, as if the fury she had unleashed to fight the monster had drained her somehow. The new Nightsisters were supposedly proof against the physically damaging effects of the evil powers they invoked, but the tremendous battle Vonnda Ra and Zekk and the stormtroopers had waged against the mindless slug had left her looking shriveled.

Zekk slumped against an upright tree trunk, feeling the soft squish of blue moss mixed with ichor from the slug creature.

Only four stormtroopers remained with their party. The slug beast had crushed the others or flung them into the unseen depths below. Chunks of the dead thing sloughed off the main branches, oozing down to where rodents and scavengers rustled through the darkness in a feeding frenzy.

Zekk heard a crash and a crackle of snapping twigs far behind them. Suddenly, with a tingle through his own Force senses, he knew that two others followed, attempting to catch them—and he identified one of the pursuers. In astonishment, he blinked his green eyes into the forest shadows, reaching out with the focused power of his senses.

"It's Jaina Solo," he said to Vonnda Ra. "Behind us. She's coming this way." He planted his black boots firmly on the branch. He had to choose, but he could not. With all of Brakiss's promises, he had never thought it would be so difficult.

Ahead Jacen, Lowbacca, Sirra, and Tenel Ka had succeeded in eluding Imperial pursuit so far—but Jaina, completely unaware, was heading straight toward them. He would have to confront her himself.

"We must split up," Zekk said. "I will go back alone and stop Jaina. The rest of you, continue after these others."

"Yes." Peering ahead into the forest maze, Vonnda Ra seethed. "I'll make them pay for what they've done to us!"

With a gesture of her clawed hand, the Nightsister and the remaining stormtroopers set off after the young Jedi Knights.

Though Jacen fought to stay within sight of his companions, this deep level of the forest had become so dark he felt as if he were swimming through a pool of ink. Finally, surprisingly, the depths began to shimmer with wonder. He noticed the cold illumination of phosphorescent organisms, glowing insects, pulsing fungi and lichens that threw heatless chemical light into the smothering darkness.

All around him in the branches and leaves he could see spangles like starlight, as if—instead of being deep within a dense forest—he stood on a sprawling plain under a clear night sky. Jacen found it breathtaking, and nudged Tenel Ka's warm arm to get her attention. The immensity of it overwhelmed him. He had never thought he'd experience something so wonderful down here.

As he and Tenel Ka stared upward, wordlessly sharing the experience, an unexpected volley of blaster shots streaked across the jungle like fireworks. A sparking white-hot globe of fire blazed toward them like a meteor—the stormtroopers had shot a dazzling flareball that spewed light in all directions.

The flareball crashed into the crook of a nearby tree and lodged there like a tiny sun, sputtering as it burned hot and bright. The flare sharpened the shadows and washed the humid air with garish light, stripping away the cloaking darkness.

Jacen saw to his dismay that four stormtroopers were standing on a single wide branch and aiming their weapons at the exhausted Jedi trainees, though the brilliant flareball had dazzled their eyes as well.

Tenel Ka shoved Jacen away from her. "Hide!" she said, and dashed off into the thick branches. Jacen ducked just as a blaster bolt sheared off a steaming chunk of wood above his head.

A rustling noise through the branches told him that Lowie and Sirra had also fled. He heard somebody else, but he could see only the four stormtroopers. He wondered if it could be Zekk . . . and he wondered if his dark-haired former friend would show them any mercy.

"Oh, blaster bolts," he said as another shot tore through the air too close to him. "Hah—no kidding," he muttered to himself.

In the strobing light he could discern only brilliant colors dancing before his aching eyes. Then he glimpsed the flickering movement of a slender figure suddenly sprouting a bright turquoise blade—Tenel Ka with her lightsaber . . . and she was just beneath the four stormtroopers!

The Imperial troopers saw her, too. They shouted excitedly and took aim—but too late.

With a single stroke, Tenel Ka slashed through the bough that supported the stormtroopers. Her rancor-tooth lightsaber flared, and sparks spat off in all directions as her blade severed the centuries-old tree branch.

Tenel Ka dove out of the way. Wood cracked, vines snapped, and leaves were torn asunder under the enormous weight of the surprised Imperial soldiers. They fired randomly, shouting in panicked bursts through their comlink helmets as the branch fell away, spilling them into the forest floor below. The four stormtroopers toppled to their deaths, blaster rifles still firing.

Looking fiercely satisfied, Tenel Ka deactivated her lightsaber and clipped it to her belt. Jacen, standing within her view, gave the warrior girl a round of silent applause.

Farther down, in the shelter of a curved and stunted tree, Lowbacca crouched close to his sister Sirra as the thick branch bearing the four hapless stormtroopers plummeted past them through the darkness. With his dark-adapted Wookiee eyes, he could see Sirra sniffing the air, waiting.

Sirra seemed preoccupied with testing the air and studying her surroundings. Then Lowie caught a twinge of scent—the frightening, tingling aroma of a syren plant, a large one, farther below.

With a quiet groan, he searched the area with his golden eyes until he saw the monstrous carnivorous flower in the thick underbrush of the ground level, its glossy yellow petals spread wide, its blood-red central stalk giving off a tempting scent. Sirra maneuvered herself until she was above the dangerous plant, then sought a safe way to get down to it.

Suddenly, Vonnda Ra leaped out of nowhere and slammed into Lowie, her hands crackling with evil lightning force. Jolts of searing electricity coursed through Lowie, and his fur began to smoke even as he staggered backward with a bellowing roar, stunned and disoriented.

In a blur of claws and teeth, Sirra leaped into the fray, flashing her ferocious Wookiee fangs. Her strong arms pushed Vonnda Ra away from her brother. The Nightsister turned on Sirra and released a bolt of her sizzling evil power.

Sirra cried out in pain and stumbled, then regathered her strength, launching off with powerful leg muscles into a full-body tackle of Vonnda Ra. Together, they went over the edge of the slippery, moss-covered branch and out into open air, tumbling and slashing.

Lowie shook himself and leaped into motion, rushing toward his sister. He reached out and caught the falling Nightsister's black cape, but the tough, slick fabric slipped through his fingers.

Sirra and Vonnda Ra fell.

Lowie howled in despair as the two combatants careened directly toward the waiting jaws of the syren plant.

Struggling as they dropped, Sirra managed to get on top. With an impact heavy enough to knock the wind out of a gundark, they crashed onto the broad, deadly petals. Vonnda Ra's back struck the soft sensitive tissues inside the syren plant's open maw first. Sirra instantly pushed herself up to her feet, but the huge petals squeezed together in a reflexive, hungry action.

Roaring, Lowie leaped off the high branch, frantic to do something. His attention fixed on the glossy petals as they contracted, folding around its two new victims. High above, Jacen and Tenel Ka yelled down to him.

Vonnda Ra squirmed as the plant's trap squeezed tighter. Lowie saw his sister's head disappear as the thick muscular petals swallowed her up. Only one arm with pattern-shaved fur extended from between the deadly flower's jaws.

Lowie reached the syren plant, then grasped the leathery petals with his clawed hands, pulling, straining. The roots of the plant squirmed, digging deeper into the forest loam.

Lowie didn't dare take out his lightsaber and slash the flower to pieces, because he knew that would kill his sister as surely as the plant would. He tugged, groaning, and the sealed petals peeled slightly apart. The syren plant made a gurgling, gasping sound. Sirra's hand still protruded from the opening, flexing and struggling, as if she were in great pain.

While Jacen grasped a vine and began to climb down, Tenel Ka dropped beside Lowie, one of her throwing knives in her hand. She stabbed at the leathery wall of the plant, but her knife could not penetrate the tough skin.

Then a burst of black lightning and static from within caused the plant to convulse. Its petals flapped open again, as if in a gasp of agony. Inside, Vonnda Ra struggled to her knees, teeth gritted together and eyes blazing with the Dark Force concentrated in her. Lowie took the opportunity to reach in and get a firm grasp on Sirra. He pulled.

Laboring for breath, the young Wookiee moved as rapidly as she could across the slippery, shifting petals. Tenel Ka grabbed for Sirra's outstretched arm, and pulled. The syren plant began to contract. Jacen gripped the edge of one waxy petal to slow its closing and murmured low, soothing words to the plant. Lowie braced himself and leaned back, dragging his sister away with all his strength. Her feet slipped free of the petals just as the syren plant clamped shut again—with Vonnda Ra still inside.

Its deceptively beautiful, fleshy yellow petals squeezed with viselike muscles, squashing its remaining prey. A few flashes of black lightning flickered from within the plant, and Vonnda Ra gave one last, muffled cry. The lumpy form caught in the folds of the flower struggled once, twice, then subsided into stillness.

Lowie held Sirra, knowing she might be injured and might need help to get back up to the higher levels. He noted with anguish the burned patches on his sister's fur where Vonnda Ra's power had singed her—yet to his amazement Sirra seemed happy, even delighted. She let out a roar of greeting.

Her eyes sparkled as she lifted her other arm up so he could see what she was clasping as if it were the greatest treasure she had ever held. During her ordeal inside the syren plant, before it had opened long enough for her to escape, Sirrakuk had managed to grasp a handful of the gossamer fibers with her trapped hand and yank them free.

She held up the silken strands in triumph, and Lowie barked with proud laughter. He embraced his sister and pounded her good-naturedly on the back with enough force to crack stormtrooper armor.

19

MOVING TO A stronger branch and gripping the tree trunk to ensure her balance, Jaina leaned over, anxiously peering into the forest depths where Chewbacca had tumbled. "Chewie!" she shouted.

She heard a Wookiee howl of pain rise toward her from the murky shadows below. He was still alive—and conscious—though she knew he must be injured.

Adjusting her grip on the vine-draped trunk of the wroshyr tree, Jaina bent over and cast the pale, pink light of the swirling phosfleas into the leaves below. As she had suspected, the light did not penetrate far enough for her to locate her friend. "Chewie, I'm here," Jaina yelled, using the Force to amplify her call. "Can you move? Can you climb back up here?"

She heard a far-off rustling and crackling of branches, then a loud yelp. Chewbacca groaned in dismay and then roared something about a fractured leg.

His words doused Jaina's sense of relief like an icy torrent of rain on a candle flame. A wave of weakness spun behind her eyes. Jaina clung to the tree, pressing her face against its rough bark.

Kashyyyk's jungle was dangerous enough for a healthy human with a full-grown Wookiee guide, but Jaina had no idea how to get *herself* out of the jungle—much less herself and an injured friend whom she'd undoubtedly have to carry. And then how could she help her brother and the others?

Meanwhile, she realized, Chewbacca's injury might even draw predators hoping for an easy kill.

The thought snapped Jaina out of her momentary weakness. She had to think; she had to help Chewie. She was in training to be a *Jedi Knight*—and this problem certainly couldn't be impossible to solve, she told herself. First things first. She had to get down to Chewbacca right away. She felt ashamed that she had wasted precious seconds with her panic.

"Chewie," she yelled again, "keep calling to me until I find you."

She would have to move quickly. She felt around for a sturdy vine, yanking one after another until she found a rough strand that would hold her weight. Pressing the toes of her boots against the tree trunk, Jaina lowered herself hand over hand, maneuvering around the splintered stumps of branches broken by the Wookiee's fall. "I'm coming," she said, as much to reassure herself as to comfort Chewie.

By the time she located the injured Wookiee, her feet ached, her palms burned, and every muscle in her body shook with weariness. She unstrapped the phosflea lamp from her waist and held it close to Chewbacca's body to get a better look at him. The fuzzy light swirled as she moved.

A quick examination of his injuries told Jaina that the news was grim. The minor scrapes, bruises, and cuts could be dealt with easily enough, but one leg was broken. Chewbacca would never be able to walk out of here.

Jaina knew she was not equal to the task of transporting a wounded Wookiee hundreds of meters up to the forest canopy, even if she used the Force. She had barely made it this far herself.

Besides that, her brother and the others still needed her help. Jaina didn't know what she could do for them.

She thought the problem over while she used a few of the meager emergency supplies from their packs to clean Chewie's wounds. He groaned and did his best to help her.

Clearly, Jaina had no choice but to abandon her search for the others. Jacen, Tenel Ka, and the two young Wookiees were still fleeing from the Imperials. Jaina was no tracker, and she had little chance of finding them down here.

But she and her twin brother had always shared an uncommonly close mental bond, just like the one their mother Leia shared with her twin Luke. Perhaps if she sent out a cry for help, Jacen might be able to find *her*.

Concentrating all of her mental effort, Jaina sent out a cry—*"Help me!"*—that rang through her mind like a mallet striking a cymbal.

Opening her eyes, Jaina checked the fracture in Chewbacca's leg again. The bone fragments had not torn through the skin, but the injury was still serious. Jaina raised her phosflea light high and looked about for any sturdy material she could use as a splint.

The pinkish glow fell on a pair of black boots. A familiar voice said, "Did you call for help?"

Jaina started and nearly fell off the branch. Growling, Chewbacca bared his fangs, though he could make no move to attack.

"Zekk—what are you doing here?" Trying to check her astonishment, Jaina stood and held the glowing light higher, but the leather-clad figure took a step backward, keeping his face partly in shadow.

"I had business here on Kashyyyk."

"*Imperial* business?" Jaina asked, and bit her lip as soon as she had said it. Her heart contracted painfully. "What's happened to you, Zekk? How could you stay with the Shadow Academy? I thought we were friends."

He ignored the question, and asked two of his own. "Why are *you* here, Jaina? Why couldn't you have stayed away? I don't want to hurt you."

Chewbacca voiced a snarl of warning at these words, though at the same time he hissed in pain from his injury.

"Then don't hurt me, Zekk," Jaina said reasonably. She took a step along the branch toward her former friend. "I'm no threat to you. I'm your friend. I *care* for you."

"Step back and stay out of my way," Zekk snapped. "It's already too late for the others."

Jaina flinched and shut her eyes, feeling the blood drain from her face. Could it be true? Had Zekk already killed Jacen, Lowie, Tenel Ka . . . even an innocent stranger like Sirra?

No, she decided at last, it couldn't be. She would have felt it. Her brother and her friends were still alive. They had to be. She couldn't believe that Zekk's heart had become so scorched and black that he could murder someone he had once called a friend.

In an effort to distract him, as she had done with Garowyn, Jaina tried her trick again. She used the Force to riffle the leaves in the branches surrounding him, as if a chill wind were blowing through the claustrophobic cage of the forest underlevels.

Zekk looked up, his green eyes bright even in the shadows. It took him only a moment to realize what she was doing. His pale lips curled in a smile, then he gestured with one hand. The wind picked up, the branches clacked together, and a storm of dislodged leaves and twigs whipped through the air with the force of a small tornado.

Jaina shut her eyes, shielding them and shrinking back from the whirlwind. Chewbacca yowled, but Zekk paid no attention to the Wookiee. "I'm not impressed with your tricks, Jaina," he said. "Don't play games with me."

Then, with a *whoosh,* a sizzling brightness stabbed through her eyelids. Jaina opened her eyes to see Zekk holding the weapon of a Jedi, his face lit by its pulsating scarlet glow. "Don't go for your lightsaber, Jaina," he warned.

She shook her head. "I won't raise a weapon against you, Zekk. And I don't believe you'd kill me either."

Zekk's face distorted with warring emotions. "Then stay away from the Jedi academy. If you ever get out of here, don't go back. The Second Imperium will soon target Yavin 4—and I will fight as a loyal warrior for my Emperor."

"Emperor? Zekk, you don't know what you're saying," Jaina pleaded.

"Stop treating me like I'm an ignorant street kid!" he snarled back. "You've always underestimated my abilities, denied me opportunities. But Lord Brakiss doesn't. He has shown me what I'm capable of." He tilted his head to look up into the dark nest of branches overhead, as if he could see the daylight far above.

"I've already sent a signal for a fast ship to pick me up. I believe our raid has been quite successful. Time for me to return to the Shadow Academy."

Zekk twitched his lightsaber from side to side as if shaking a finger in warning. "For the friendship we once had, I'll spare you this time, Jaina. But don't ever test my loyalties again."

With a harsh laugh, Zekk swept his lightsaber upward, releasing a storm of leaves and twigs that showered down on Chewie and Jaina, knocking the phosflea light from her hand. Jaina ducked and covered her head. She couldn't see.

A moment later Zekk was gone, his hollow laughter ringing behind him as he left them in darkness.

20

LEFT ALONE AGAIN, Jaina shouted once more through the Force as the deep forest sounds grew thicker, more threatening around her. Predators, hidden in the leafy branches, cautiously approached, attracted by Chewbacca's muffled sounds of pain. They sensed helpless victims, easy prey.

"We need help!" she called. Her words quickly died to silence in the jungle gloom.

Then a blaze of rainbow light shattered the shadows: a flash of turquoise, a streak of emerald green, a slash of molten bronze. Lightsabers, like hot machetes, chopped the underbrush aside. Jacen, Lowie, and Tenel Ka pushed their way forward, with Sirrakuk following close behind, grinning so widely her fangs flashed in the vibrant light.

Chewbacca bellowed a greeting, and Lowie and Sirra clambered up to help their uncle.

"Hey, Jaina!" Jacen called. "Are you all right?"

She wiped grimy tear streaks from her cheeks, still shaken from the confrontation with her former friend. "I'll survive," she said, then drew a deep breath. "Zekk was here. He said the Second Imperium is going to wipe out the Jedi academy, and that he was going to fight along with them."

Lowie growled, looking up from tending Chewbacca. Tenel Ka stood rigidly, holding her rancor-tooth lightsaber high. "Not if we can help it," she said.

Jaina indicated the injured Wookiee. "We have to get Chewie up and out of here. I think his leg is broken—nothing a medical droid and a few hours in a bacta tank can't fix. But if we don't get back up to the treetops, we're all going to be somebody's lunch."

Sirra growled in defiance. Now that she had succeeded in her dangerous quest against the syren plant, Lowie's sister looked as if she could take on the whole jungle by herself.

As the two strong Wookiees carefully eased their uncle to a standing position, Jacen and Tenel Ka did what they could to help, using the Force and their hands. Jaina took the lead along with Sirra, blazing a trail with her lightsaber.

Together, the companions made their way back up to the light.

21

THE CAMOUFLAGED ASSAULT shuttle hovered in the void of space, waiting for confirmation, until the Shadow Academy shut down its cloaking shields. The ominous spined ring of the Imperial training station shimmered into view just long enough for Zekk to give the order to dock. He was tense as the shuttle approached, unsure of the reception Brakiss would give him.

Beside him, in the command cockpit, Tamith Kai seethed silently, her wine-dark lips pressed together in a cold line, but she said nothing. Zekk had lost not only the team of stormtroopers directly under his command in the treetop city, but also two of her greatest Nightsister allies. Both Vonnda Ra and Garowyn were presumed dead in the depths of Kashyyyk's jungles.

Though Zekk had not been with either Nightsister when they had died or disappeared, Tamith Kai blamed him for the debacle, as she blamed him for the death of her prime student Vilas. Tamith Kai resented his presence—though presumably she and Zekk both worked toward the ultimate victory of the Second Imperium. All other losses, he felt, should simply be considered the price of their ultimate triumph.

But Tamith Kai was not pleased with how the young man had handled himself on Kashyyyk. And so, during their return from the fateful mission, Zekk kept to himself, avoiding direct contact with the Nightsister.

He brought the assault ship in, sitting in the command chair while other Imperial pilots handled the controls, guiding the craft into the Shadow Academy's open docking bay. As they entered, he saw another shuttle—an impressive Imperial transport surrounded by deadly force fields—and wondered what had happened during his absence.

The battered assault craft, with its precious cargo of stolen computer components, settled into place with what sounded like a mechanical sigh of relief. "We have landed, Lord Zekk," the pilot said.

The tactical officer studied the controls. "The Shadow Academy's cloaking device has been reactivated. The station is once again undetectable by Rebel sensors."

The hatches opened, and the crew began filing out. Stormtroopers marched up from the Shadow Academy's interior to surround the battered shuttle, ready to unload the stolen cargo as soon as Zekk released it.

Tamith Kai stood beside him in the cockpit; with a flick of her shoulder, she tossed her spined black cape back. Her long-nailed fingers balled into fists as she struggled to contain the fury within her. The electric fire in her violet eyes boiled like lava.

Zekk closed his dark-ringed emerald eyes and drew a deep breath to focus his thoughts, center his concentration. He let her anger wash over his mind and drain away. His greatest concern was Master Brakiss and how he would face him. His teacher had such high hopes for him, and he might be even more displeased than Tamith Kai. Contemplating the probable disappointment of his mentor hurt Zekk more than any display of rage by the continually bothersome Nightsister from Dathomir.

Squaring his shoulders, he straightened his padded leather armor and adjusted his crimson-lined black cape. He tossed his long dark hair behind him and turned toward the assault craft's hatch, making himself an imposing figure, ominous and menacing. He had learned such posturing from observing Tamith Kai herself, and it amused him to think he could use her own techniques of intimidation against her.

With the tall Nightsister following him, Zekk strode down the ramp like a conquering hero. Inside his heart, though, dread grew.

The sculpture-handsome teacher stood at the edge of the airlock bay, watching the proceedings. As Zekk emerged, Brakiss glided forward with smooth, even footsteps. His silvery robes clung around him like whispers.

Zekk held his chin high, looking into the open, clear gaze of Brakiss. The master of the Shadow Academy folded his hands in front of him. "Young Zekk, my Darkest Knight, you have returned from your first mission. Report. Were you successful?"

Zekk swallowed hard and gave his straight-forward account. "Unfortunately, Master Brakiss, our mission did not come off as smoothly as we had planned. During our battles at the fortified Wookiee facilities, we lost fourteen TIE fighters and bombers, as well as eleven ground assault troops.

"It is also my duty to report that we lost two of our Nightsister companions: Vonnda Ra in the lower levels of the forest, and Garowyn, who was apparently murdered when she tried to reclaim our *Shadow Chaser*."

Brakiss showed no reaction and waited. Finally he said, "But the computer components—the guidance and tactical systems? Did you succeed in obtaining the vital resources the Second Imperium requires?"

Zekk flinched. "Yes, Master Brakiss. All of the computer equipment is stored inside this assault transport, ready for distribution to the Second Imperium."

Brakiss clapped his hands together. "Excellent! Then your mission was a success, with acceptable losses of personnel. Those other . . . *inconveniences* are insignificant in our overall conflict. You have achieved our most important goal."

Tamith Kai's eyes widened with anger, and her normally pale face flushed a blotchy red. "Master Brakiss!" she hissed. "Zekk also claims to have removed those Jedi brats. But although Vonnda Ra accompanied him to this confrontation, Zekk returned alone . . . claiming victory."

Zekk stood rigid. "The young Jedi Knights are no longer a problem," he said. "This I swear."

Tamith Kai obviously didn't believe him. But Brakiss did, and that was all that counted.

Zekk didn't know how long he could keep up the charade. He had fallen to the dark side—and he had also protected his friends. The two seemed incompatible. Sooner or later, Brakiss would learn what he had done—and then Zekk would face an impossible choice. But, as always, no one else would make Zekk's choices for him . . . and no one else would face the consequences.

"The Second Imperium applauds your efforts, Zekk. The history of the galaxy will remember you as an instrumental fighter in our grand cause."

Zekk knew he should have felt better, prouder . . . but he could summon no emotion other than dread. And disappointment in himself. He was no longer sure of where his past decisions would lead him.

One of the stormtroopers standing in ranks within the hangar bay shifted uneasily. Zekk focused his attention on the burly trooper—instinctively identifying Norys. Qorl stood beside the bully, frowning in disapproval at his white-armored trainee. The leader of the Lost

Ones still bore a chip on his shoulder, resulting in a perpetually surly attitude.

Suddenly, the air in the huge docking bay shimmered. Zekk looked up as the other stormtroopers backed away. Beside him, Brakiss grew tense, almost fearful, but stood his ground against the projection.

An image formed in the air, a giant cowled head with yellow eyes and an age-ravaged face that emanated dark power. The visage of Emperor Palpatine was incredibly clear and focused, as if the transmission came from very close. Very close indeed.

"My subjects at the Shadow Academy," the Emperor's shuddering voice said, "my fellow fighters in the cause of the Second Imperium, I am pleased to learn of this successful mission! Through our various raids and by gathering the scattered remnants of my lost Imperial glory, we now have the might to move on to the next phase in our plan of conquest. The new hyperdrive cores and turbolaser batteries have already been installed in our secret battle fleet. I have commanded that the new computer components be incorporated immediately. We must strike again while the Rebels are still reeling."

Under the leather padding, Zekk felt a cold, damp shiver work its way down his back.

"It is our mission to remove the only real line of defense the Rebels have against us. Brakiss, you promised me an invincible fighting force of Dark Jedi Knights. The time has come to make use of them.

"Together, as our primary campaign, we shall attack and destroy Luke Skywalker's Jedi academy. Those light side Jedi will be crushed to dust beneath our feet.

"I command you all to move out. Set the Shadow Academy forces in motion. We must transport our station to the jungle moon of Yavin 4 without delay. Once we have eliminated the new Jedi Knights, the galaxy will be ours for the taking."

Zekk stood stunned. Brakiss stared at the fading image of the Emperor in amazement. Then, as if a power switch had been flicked on, all of the stormtroopers sprang into motion.

The Shadow Academy rushed to prepare for its greatest battle.

22

IN THE AFTERMATH of the devastating attack on the Wookiee computer fabrication facility, Jaina knew they could not afford to wait. Too much was at risk—and right now.

While the New Republic forces sent a few nearby ships filled with a complement of engineers and soldiers to help in reparation activities, Jaina and Lowie worked tirelessly with Chewbacca to complete repairs to the *Shadow Chaser*. The tall Wookiee still limped on his sore leg, but his injuries had mostly healed, and he didn't let a little stiffness slow him down.

Inside the crowded power-supply bulkhead of the *Shadow Chaser*, Jaina, the smallest of the workers, crammed herself deep into the tightest spaces, hooking up power leads and disconnecting diagnostics. All the replacement parts had been ready even before the Imperial attack on Kashyyyk, but now the sleek vessel needed to be reassembled.

"Power it up before I crawl back out of here," Jaina said. "All the circuits are grounded and shielded, but I want to make sure everything checks out before I fight my way into open air again."

Lowie grunted and flicked a power switch. He and Chewbacca simultaneously roared an affirmative.

Jaina heaved a sigh of relief. "Well, I'm glad the ship's functioning again," she said. "We have to get out of here and back to Yavin 4 before the attack comes. We need to be ready for the Shadow Academy." She swallowed. "We've all been training a long time for this."

Lowie roared in agreement, though he and Chewbacca and Sirra seemed somewhat saddened. Sirra growled a series of notes, and Em Teedee said, "Mistress Sirrakuk says that she will stay to help her people clean up and make repairs, but she understands that her brother Lowbacca must return to fight with the other Jedi. There are many Wookiees who can assist here on Kashyyyk, but there aren't many other Jedi Knights . . . and she is exceedingly proud that her brother is one of them."

Lowie rumbled his appreciation.

Em Teedee added, as an aside, "I do believe she's quite pleased with him."

Sirra patted her big brother on his hairy shoulder, then proudly ran one hand over her glossy new belt, woven from the strands of fiber she had harvested from the syren plant. Jaina knew that Sirra's personal opportunities were now wide open, possibilities for her life that had always been there . . . but that she would now be better able to take advantage of.

Jacen rushed aboard the *Shadow Chaser* carrying the small cage with his pet Ion and her babies. He cooed reassurances to the furry rodents.

Tenel Ka accompanied him, looking confident in her freshly polished reptilian armor. She had reworked all of her braids meticulously, brushing her hair out and plaiting it using the new one-handed technique Anakin Solo had developed for her. "We are prepared to depart," she said. "And we are ready to fight as true Jedi Knights."

Lowie roared with enthusiasm. Sirra embraced her big brother, and then each of the young Jedi Knights.

Chewbacca limped up the ramp and strapped himself into the *Shadow Chaser*'s pilot seat. Lowie slid into the seat behind his uncle, flipping on the controls and powering up the various subsystems. The two Wookiees barked a preflight checklist back and forth.

Sirrakuk slipped back out of the sleek ship and stood watching as the craft prepared to depart. Within moments the *Shadow Chaser* rose up on its repulsorlifts, bearing its message of warning to Luke Skywalker and his Jedi academy.

"We've just sent the alert to Yavin 4, but now we have to go," Jaina told her brother. "Uncle Luke is back from his scouting mission with Dad—but the Jedi academy is still in danger."

"I've got a bad feeling about this," Jacen agreed.

He held the small cage in his lap, still whispering soothing words. Tenel Ka sat beside Jacen, eager to go. She brushed her fingers over the weapons at her belt, anticipating the fight to come.

Chewbacca yowled a brief order to prepare for acceleration, then the *Shadow Chaser* leaped skyward. A few minutes later, they catapulted into hyperspace and left Kashyyyk behind.

They raced back to Yavin 4 at full speed, knowing they had to prepare for the greatest challenge of their lives.

The Shadow Academy was coming.

JEDI UNDER SIEGE

To Letha L. Burchard
a supporter, fan, and friend
who "knew us when" . . .

and is still speaking to us

Acknowledgments

The usual round of thanks to Lillie E. Mitchell, whose flying fingers transcribe our dictation and whose dedication to our characters and stories keeps our interest focused; Lucy Wilson, Sue Rostoni, and Allan Kausch at Lucasfilm for their above-and-beyond-the-call helpful suggestions and open minds; Ginjer Buchanan and the folks at Berkley/Boulevard for their wholehearted support and encouragement over the course of this entire series; and Jonathan MacGregor Cowan for being our most avid test reader and brainstormer.

1

IN THE UNCERTAIN predawn light, Jaina watched her uncle, Luke Skywalker, maneuver the *Shadow Chaser* into the Jedi academy's hangar bay at the base of the Great Temple. Her father, Han Solo, and Chewbacca had not even stayed long enough to perform that chore after the young Jedi Knights returned from the Wookiee homeworld of Kashyyyk.

With the Shadow Academy on the move, they had no time to lose.

Jaina found it hard to believe that barely two days earlier Kashyyyk had been under attack by Imperial forces led by none other than her friend Zekk, now a Dark Jedi in the service of the Second Imperium. When she'd confronted the dark-haired young man in the forest underlevels, he had warned her not to return to Yavin 4 because the Shadow Academy would soon attack.

Jaina had to believe the warning was a sign that Zekk still cared about her and her twin brother Jacen.

She and her friends had been back on Yavin 4 for only a few minutes. None of them had gotten much sleep on the swift hyperspace flight back, but they all ran on adrenaline. Jaina felt as if she would explode if she couldn't *do* something right away. So many preparations to make, so much to plan.

Standing beside her near the entrance to the hangar bay, Jacen gave her a nudge. When she glanced at him, his brandy-brown eyes looked straight into hers. "Hey, it'll be *okay*," he said. "Uncle Luke will know what to do. He's been through plenty of Imperial attacks."

"Sure, that makes me feel a lot better," she answered, not believing it for a minute.

As usual, Jacen resorted to one of his favorite weapons to get her mind off the battle that was sure to come. "Hey, want to hear a joke?"

"Yes, Jacen," said Tenel Ka, striding up to join them. "I believe humor could be of some use now." The warrior girl from Dathomir glistened with perspiration from having spent the last ten minutes running "to stretch her muscles" in an effort to work off her own tension.

"Okay, Jacen. Fire away," Jaina said, pretending to brace herself for the worst.

Tenel Ka pushed back her long, reddish-gold braids with one arm. Her left arm had been severed in a terrible accident during lightsaber training, and she refused to accept a synthetic replacement. She nodded to Jacen. "You may proceed with the joke."

"Okay, what time is it when an Imperial walker steps on your wrist chronometer?" Jacen raised his eyebrows, waiting. "Time to get a new chronometer!"

After a heartbeat of dead silence, Tenel Ka nodded and said in a serious voice, "Thank you, Jacen. Your humor was quite . . . adequate."

The warrior girl never cracked a smile, but Jaina thought she detected a twinkle in her friend's cool gray eyes. Jaina was still groaning in mock agony when Luke and the young Wookiee Lowbacca climbed out of the *Shadow Chaser*.

Deciding there wasn't a moment to lose, Jaina hurried over to them. Apparently Uncle Luke must have felt the same way—when Jacen and Tenel Ka trotted up behind Jaina, the Jedi Master began to speak without preamble.

"It'll take the Second Imperium some time to install the new computer components they stole for their fleet," Luke said. "We may have a few days yet, but I don't want to take any chances. Lowie—Tionne and Raynar went out to the temple on the lake for a training exercise. I'd like you to take your T-23 and go bring them back here. We all need to work together."

Lowie roared an acknowledgment and sprinted for the small skyhopper his uncle Chewbacca had given him. From the clip at Lowie's waist the miniaturized translating droid Em Teedee said, "Why certainly, sir. It would be Master Lowbacca's great pleasure to be of service. Consider it done." Reprimanding the little droid for its embellishments with an absent growl, the young Wookiee climbed into the small T-23 and closed the canopy.

Luke turned to the warrior girl from Dathomir. "Tenel Ka, gather as many students as you can and give them a crash course in ground combat against terrorist attacks. I'm not sure what strategies the Shadow Academy will use, but I can't think of anyone better to teach them about commando tactics than you."

"Yeah, she was great against those Bartokk assassins on Hapes," Jacen said.

JEDI UNDER SIEGE

Tenel Ka surprised Jaina by blushing pink before she gave a curt nod and sped off on her assignment.

"What about Jacen and me, Uncle Luke?" Jaina asked, bursting with impatience. "What should we do? We want to help."

"Now that the *Millennium Falcon* is gone, we need to get the new shield generators back up and running to protect us from an aerial attack. Come with me."

The primary equipment for the Jedi academy's new defensive shield generators was located in the jungle across the river, but the shields were controlled from the Comm Center. Han Solo had recently brought the components from Coruscant as a stopgap measure while the New Republic scrambled to assemble a major defense against the impending Imperial attack.

"Hey, should I send a message to Mom?" Jacen asked, sitting down at one of the consoles.

"Not until we know more," Luke answered. "Your dad and Chewie were going to contact her and explain everything once they were under way. Leia has her hands full mustering troops to station here as permanent protectors for the Jedi academy. At the moment, *we've* got to do everything we can to guard it ourselves.

"Meanwhile, Jacen, monitor all the communications bands. See if you can pick up any signals, especially ones that might be Imperial codes. Jaina, let's get those shield generators powered up and running."

"Already on it, Uncle Luke." Jaina grinned at him from the control station. "Shields are up and at full strength. Guess I should run a complete readiness check, though, just to make sure there are no gaps in our defenses."

Jacen put on a headset and began scanning through the various comm frequencies. No sooner had he begun than a loud crackle erupted from the earpiece, followed by a familiar voice.

"... requesting permission for landing and all that usual stuff. Here I come. *Lightning Rod* out."

"Hey, wait!" Jacen said into the voice pickup, on the verge of panic. "You can't do that—I mean, we have to drop our shields first. Give me a minute, Peckhum."

"Shields? What shields?" the old spacer's voice came back. "Me and the *Lightning Rod* been doin' the supply run to Yavin 4 for years now. Never had to worry about shields before."

"We'll meet you down at the landing pad and explain everything," Jacen said. "Hang on a minute."

"Am I going to need a code to get in?" Peckhum asked. "No one gave me any codes before I left Coruscant. Nobody told me about any shields."

Jacen looked up at Luke. "It's old Peckhum in the *Lightning Rod*," he said. "Does he need a code to get in?"

Luke shook his head and motioned for Jaina to drop the shields. Jaina bent over the control console, her lower lip caught between her teeth. After a minute she said, "There, that ought to do it. Shields lowered again."

For some reason, now that the shields were down Jacen felt a cold tingle of vulnerability run up the back of his neck. "Okay, Peckhum," he said, "you're clear to land. But make it quick, so we can power up again."

When the old spacer stepped out of his battered supply shuttle, he looked the same as every other time Jacen had seen him: pale skin, long lanky hair, grizzled cheeks, and rumpled flight suit.

"Come on, Peckhum," Jacen said. "I'll help you get the supplies inside. We need to hurry, before the Imperials get here."

"Imperials?" The spacer scratched his head. "Is that why you've got energy shields up? Are we under attack?"

"It's okay," Jacen said, impatient to get the *Lightning Rod* unloaded. "The shields are back up. You just can't see them."

The old spacer craned his neck to stare up into the misty white sky of the jungle moon. "And the attack?"

"Well, we heard a rumor—a pretty solid one." He hesitated. "From Zekk. He's the one who led the raid on the computer fabrication facility on Kashyyyk—and he warned Jaina that the Shadow Academy is on its way. We'd better get inside."

Old Peckhum looked at Jacen in alarm. The teenager Zekk had been like a son to him; they had lived together in the lower city levels on Coruscant . . . until Zekk had been kidnapped by the Shadow Academy.

As a familiar cold tingle crept up the back of Jacen's neck, Peckhum whispered, "Too late." He pointed into the sky. "They're already here."

2

FROM THE HIGHEST observation turret on the Shadow Academy, Brakiss—Master of all the new Dark Jedi—looked down at the insignificant green speck of the jungle moon. The devastating assault was about to begin, and before long Yavin 4 and its Jedi academy would be crushed under the might of the Second Imperium.

As it should be.

Through the winding metal corridors of the station, stormtroopers manned their battle stations, newly trained TIE pilots conducted preflight checks on their ships, and the eager Dark Jedi students prepared for their first major victory.

The ultimate battle would be a two-pronged assault led jointly by the most powerful of the new Nightsisters, Tamith Kai, and Brakiss's own protégé, dark-haired Zekk, whose enthusiasm to make something significant of his life had left him an easy target for conversion to the dark side.

Brakiss closed his eyes and drew a deep breath of the recycled air that rushed through the ventilation shafts. His silvery robes swirled around him.

Though he stood isolated here, he could sense the accelerating preparations affecting everyone in the spiked station; tensions mounted, as did hunger for battle. In the undercurrent of swirling thoughts, he clearly felt the troops' dedication to the Second Imperium's great leader, Emperor Palpatine. He also detected an undertone of anxiety over the coming attack, but this only made his lips curl upward. Fear would give an added edge to their fighting abilities, enough to make them cautious . . . but not enough to paralyze them.

Brakiss longed to see Luke Skywalker defeated. Years ago, he had infiltrated the Jedi academy as a student to absorb the methods the New Republic taught, then bring them back to the remnants of the Empire. But Brakiss hadn't been able to fool the Jedi Master. Instead,

Skywalker had tried to turn him away from his devotion, undermine his dedication to the Second Imperium. Skywalker had tried to "save" him—he thought with a sneer—and Brakiss had fled.

But because of his willingness to dabble in the dark side, Brakiss had by then learned enough to form his own Dark Jedi training center.

Now it would be a marvelous showdown.

Beside him, the air shimmered. Brakiss opened his calm, beatific eyes and sensed an ominous static surrounding the projection of the Emperor. The mysterious great leader of the Second Imperium hovered in front of him in holographic form, a cowled head as tall as Brakiss's entire body, a towering image with glittering yellow eyes and a wrinkled face pinched by shadows.

"I grow eager for my domination again, Brakiss," the Emperor said.

"And I am eager to give it to you, my master," Brakiss answered, bowing his head.

Accompanied by four of his powerful red Imperial guards, the Emperor himself had recently taken up residence on the Shadow Academy, arriving in a special armored shuttle. While the fearsome, scarlet-clad guards kept all prying eyes away, the Emperor remained sealed in an opaque isolation chamber. Palpatine had never spoken directly to his loyal Shadow Academy subjects, nor had he even conversed face-to-face with Brakiss. The Emperor had appeared only in holographic transmissions.

"We are ready to launch our strike, my Emperor," Brakiss said. He glanced up at the forbidding image. "My Dark Jedi guarantee you victory."

"Good—because I have no wish to wait further," the Emperor's image said. "The remainder of my newly constructed fleet has not yet arrived, though they shall be here within hours. My Imperial warships are presently being refitted with the computer systems stolen from Kashyyyk. My guards report that many vessels are ready to fight, and the rest will be finished shortly."

Brakiss bowed again, clasping his hands in front of him. "I understand, my lord. But let us withhold the military strike force for our next major assault on the more heavily guarded worlds of the Rebel Alliance. On Yavin 4, we have only a few weakling do-gooder Jedi to deal with. They should cause no problem for my Force-trained soldiers."

Inside his shadowy cowl, the Emperor looked skeptical. "Do not let your overconfidence betray you."

Brakiss continued speaking with greater passion. He let his feelings come to the fore, hoping to convince his great leader. "With this important strike on the Jedi academy, the Second Imperium becomes more than just an undisciplined band of pirates raiding equipment. We mean to retake the *galaxy,* my lord. This battle must be a battle of philosophies, of willpower. This is the *Imperial* way against the *Rebel* way—and so it should be my trainees against Skywalker's, Jedi versus Jedi. A shadow play, if you will, of darkness against light. We still intend to harass them with TIE fighter strikes from the air, but the main conflict will be direct and personal—as it must be! We can crush their very hearts, not merely breach their defenses."

Brakiss smiled, looking up to meet the glowing yellow eyes of the Emperor. "And when we defeat them utterly with the powers of the dark side, the remainder of the Rebels will scatter and hide, trembling at their own nightmares, as we recapture what is rightfully ours."

The Emperor's holographic face did something frighteningly unusual. The withered, puckered lips curled in a satisfied *smile.*

"Very well. It shall be as you request, Brakiss—Jedi against Jedi. You may begin your assault when ready."

3

THE SHADOW ACADEMY dropped its cloaking device, dissolving its shield of invisibility. As the spiked station appeared over Yavin 4, two specially equipped TIE fighters dropped out of its launching bay. Silently moving in tandem, they plunged into the misty atmosphere.

The fighters had been coated with a stealth hull plating to blur their sensor signatures, and the output from their high-powered twin ion engines had been damped. Their mission was to strike in secret, not to provide a show of force.

Commander Orvak swooped into the lead, while the second TIE fighter, flown by his subordinate Dareb, flanked him. Together, they shot around the small moon and skimmed lower into the atmosphere, spiraling entirely around the equator back to the coordinates of the ancient temple ruins where Skywalker had established his Jedi academy.

Orvak flew with the controls gripped in his black-gloved hands. He felt the quiet thrumming of the Imperial fighter's engines as if he were riding an untamed beast of burden. He piloted with careful concentration, dancing on the air currents, buffeted by thermal updrafts from the jungle below.

"Keep steady," he muttered to himself. This commando run would require the utmost precision and piloting skill. Along with a new batch of TIE fighter trainees chosen from the ranks of young stormtroopers, Orvak had completed the simulations over and over again en route to the Yavin system.

But this was the real thing. Now the Emperor was depending on him.

Massassi trees formed a chaotic carpet of green below. Gnarled branches thrust above the thick canopy like monster claws. Orvak glided in low, watching the wake of his passage disturb treetop creatures who fled from the blast of his hot exhaust.

His companion Dareb spoke over a tight line-of-sight beamed channel. The other pilot's words were encrypted and descrambled by a special coding system in Orvak's cockpit. "Long-range sensors are picking up the protective energy field," Dareb said. "The shield generators are right where our covert information said they would be."

"Target verified," Orvak acknowledged, speaking into the microphone built into his helmet. "Lord Brakiss, who endured some time here, knows much of the layout of the Jedi academy itself—if the Rebels haven't moved things around."

"Why would they?" Dareb said. "They're far too complacent, and we are about to show them their folly."

"Just don't show me *your* folly," Orvak said. "Enough chatter. Head for the target."

The invisible shields hovered like a protective umbrella over a section of jungle where a river sliced through the trees and an ancient-looking stone pyramid rose majestically. Orvak hoped that by the end of this day Skywalker's Great Temple would no longer be standing.

But before the Shadow Academy could begin the primary assault, Orvak and Dareb had to complete their preliminary mission: to knock out that shield generator and open the doors wide for a devastating attack.

Orvak checked his sensors. In the infrared and other portions of the electromagnetic spectrum, he could see the deadly ripples of the hovering force-field dome that protected the Jedi academy. Yet, because of the tall Massassi trees, the shield did not reach all the way to the ground, halting instead five meters above the treetops. Five meters—a shallow gap between foliage and sizzling energy, but wide enough for a crack pilot to negotiate. Here and there, a few upthrust branches were singed and blackened where they had intruded into the crackling energy dome.

"It'll be a tight squeeze," Orvak said. "Ready for it?"

"I feel like I could take on the whole Rebel Alliance by myself," Dareb said.

Orvak didn't acknowledge this display of overconfidence. "Closing in," he said.

He brought the stealth TIE fighter lower, just skimming the treetops. Leaves whispered beneath him, chattering and scratching against the wings of his ship. The air seemed to ripple in front of the fighter, a faint indication of the energy shield, and he hoped the sensors were correct.

"Stay on target," he said. "Once we get under the shields, our real work starts."

Just as they passed underneath the invisible boundary, Dareb swerved to one side to avoid an unexpected moss-covered branch that elbowed up only a meter above the canopy. The young pilot overcompensated and struck a corner of his square wing panel against another branch, which sent him tumbling.

"I can't hold it!" he shouted into the comm system. "I'm out of control!"

Dareb's TIE fighter pinwheeled up into the deadly force field and exploded as it hit the disintegrating wall. Intent on his mission, Orvak streaked onward, looking into the rear viewers to see the flaming debris of his partner tumbling out of the sky.

He clenched his teeth and drew a deep breath through the oxygen mask in his helmet. "We're all expendable," Orvak said, as if trying to convince himself. "Expendable. The mission is all-important. Dareb was my backup. So now it's up to me. Alone." He swallowed hard, knowing that now the Rebels must be aware of his covert mission.

Without pause, Orvak homed in on the isolated shield-generating station. The machinery looked like a set of tall disks half buried in the jungle underbrush, surrounded by a cleared maintenance area that provided just enough space for him to land his small Imperial fighter. Visible in the distance rose the great pyramid that housed Skywalker's Jedi academy.

He shut down the muffled twin ion engines and opened the cockpit door, heaving himself out. Reaching into the stowage compartment behind his pilot's seat, he retrieved the pack of supplies that contained all the explosives he would need for a full day's work. . . .

Orvak stepped on the squishing, plant-covered ground. The jungle brooded around him, chaotic and threatening. Overhead, he could hear the crackling hum of the energy shield that had destroyed his partner.

Compared with the clean, sterile Shadow Academy, Yavin 4 felt disgustingly *alive*. It swarmed with vermin, plants growing everywhere, little rodents, insects, strange biting creatures that moved in every direction and hid in every cranny.

He longed for the precise and spotless corridors of the Shadow Academy, where his boots could ring loud and clear on the cold, hard metal plates, where he could smell the recycled air flowing through the ventilators, where everything was regimented and in its rightful place . . . just as the Empire would be again after its victory over the Rebels. Orvak took comfort in his solid leather gloves and the helmet that protected him from infestation by the parasitic creatures of this uncivilized world.

Taking the pack that contained his demolition equipment, he

sprinted away from his TIE fighter toward the humming shield generator station. It hulked over him, powerful and unguarded. Doomed.

Although the shield generators were obviously new, vines, creepers, and ferns grew in tangled profusion close to the warm machinery. Orvak could see hacked ends and broken branches where someone had chopped away the foliage in an attempt to keep the access clear. The irresistible jungle, though, kept pressing its advantage. Orvak shook his head at the folly of these Rebels.

When he reached the pulsing station, Orvak hunched over and glanced from side to side, expecting Rebel defenders at any moment. Opening his pack, he withdrew two of his six high-powered thermal detonators, shaped charges he would place against the generator's power cells. These two explosives would be sufficient to take down the Jedi academy's shields.

He would save the rest of the explosives for the second part of his mission.

Orvak synchronized the timers. Then, removing his recalibrated compass and glancing at the coordinates he had programmed in, he ducked and fought his way through the underbrush toward his next target, which was some distance through the jungle and across a river.

The Great Temple.

He paused for only a moment, opaquing his blast goggles as the timers ran down to zero—and the explosive charges detonated.

The boom was deafening, and a pillar of fire rose to the sky, singeing the surrounding Massassi trees. Satisfied, Orvak congratulated himself on an excellent explosion. Most spectacular.

But the next one would be better yet.

4

WITH RAYNAR AND Tionne crowded in the back, Lowie piloted the T-23 skyhopper back toward the Jedi academy at full speed. As they skimmed along the treetops, Lowie explained the situation as best he could, with Em Teedee translating.

". . . and that is why Master Skywalker requested that Master Lowbacca retrieve you with such haste," the little droid finished.

"Well, well, well," Raynar said in a sour voice. "I suppose you think this is going to make you heroes for coming back to save the Jedi academy. I'm sure *I* could have managed quite nicely without your help. While you were off playing, I was here training with Tionne."

Lowie could tell by the blond-haired boy's tone of voice that he was none too pleased to be stuffed unceremoniously into the cramped rear seat, with his brightly colored robes tangled about him. Raynar's parents had once been minor royalty on Alderaan, before that planet was destroyed by the Death Star, and now they had made themselves into wealthy merchants. He was not accustomed to taking a backseat to anyone.

"No, Raynar," Tionne chided. The silvery-haired Jedi teacher blinked her alien mother-of-pearl eyes. "No one does as well alone against an enemy, and we must all work together to prepare. Without preparation, a battle is all but lost."

Raynar snorted, trying to straighten his robes. "Battle? We don't even know there's going to *be* a battle. Why should we believe the word of some traitor boy who's gone over to the dark side? He could just be lying to get us all worked up. He's probably laughing at us right now."

Lowie's growls rumbled louder than the engine of the T-23. "Master Lowbacca wishes to point out," Em Teedee said, "that for many years Zekk was a close friend to Master Jacen and Mistress Jaina."

Raynar pouted. "Then Jacen and Jaina Solo need to be more careful about the friends they choose."

"Sometimes," Tionne said in a firm voice, "the gap between friend and enemy is not as wide as you may think. Help often comes from unexpected sources."

Lowie wasn't sure why, but senses in the back of his mind urged him to go faster still. The small skyhopper shuddered and dipped as he pushed its engines to their limits, and then beyond. He flew in among the trees, below the deadly dome of the energy shield that protected the Jedi academy against an attack from the skies.

"Hey, watch out for that big branch!" Raynar yelped as Lowie swerved to one side. "Save the heroics for when the Shadow Academy shows up—*if* they come, that is." Lowie was pleased to sense, though, that Tionne not only remained calm, but actually approved of the way he piloted the little T-23.

Lowie looked up into the sky and understood why he had felt the sudden need to accelerate. He gave a sharp bark, pointing up at the ominous spiked ring shape barely visible as a silhouette through the film of the atmosphere. "Master Lowbacca says—oh dear!—it seems that the Shadow Academy has arrived!"

Raynar fell silent, finding nothing more to criticize about Lowie's piloting. Before long, a blade of piercing sound sliced through the silence, followed by several explosions. According to Lowie's sensors, the flickering energy shield above had failed. He growled out the news.

Without waiting for a translation, Tionne said, "We can still return to the Jedi academy, but we should leave the T-23 at the edge of the jungle. I have a feeling it's not safe to approach the temple landing field or the hangar bay. It's bound to be under attack." She sat up straight between the two young Jedi trainees. "It has already begun."

The Great Temple of the Massassi had stood nearly unchanged for thousands of years. The stone blocks in the walls and floors were as solid as they had been the day they were assembled. Even so, Jaina felt a vibration in the floor of the Jedi academy's control center. Warning lights flashed across the shield generator console.

"Something's wrong, Uncle Luke," Jaina said. "There's been an explosion out in the jungle . . . oh no! Our defensive shields are down!"

Luke stood behind the chair where Jacen sat at the communications controls. He nodded grimly to Jaina. "Can you get the shields back on line from here?"

She frantically flicked switches and checked connections, trying to bring the shields back up. She scanned the display screens and diagnostics, continually pushing buttons. "Don't think so," she replied. "Power's out. The entire generator might be gone."

Her brother Jacen blew out his breath and pushed back from the comm console. "I've got a bad feeling about this," he said, running fingers through his tousled brown curls. "I'll bet it's sabotage."

Luke caught Jaina's eyes, then Jacen's, and came to a decision. "I'm calling an all-hands meeting in five minutes. We may need to clear out the Great Temple, go into hiding in the jungles where we can deflect the assault. Send a message to your mother that we're under attack *now* and need those reinforcements right away. Then meet me in the grand audience chamber."

Jacen looked at his sister in a state of near panic. "My animals . . ." he said. "I *can't* leave them in their cages if the Jedi academy's under attack. They'll stand a better chance of surviving if they're free. And if Uncle Luke's going to evacuate all of the students—"

"Go ahead," Jaina said, waving him away. "Take care of your pets. I'll get a message to Mom."

Already running for the door, Jacen tossed a "Thank you" over his shoulder.

Jaina plopped down at the comm station, selected a transmission frequency, and tried to make a connection to Coruscant. She received no response, only dead static. With a sigh of disgust over the erratic behavior of the old equipment, Jaina tried a new frequency.

Still nothing.

Odd, she thought. Maybe the main comm screen wasn't working. She donned the headset and selected yet another frequency.

Static. She switched again. Stronger static, as if something had swallowed up her desperate signal. Soon the crackling hiss built to a crescendo squeal loud enough to set her teeth on edge. Jaina snatched the headset off her ears and tossed it down with a shudder.

"We're being jammed!"

Jaina checked the readouts on the communications console just to be sure. Their long-range transmissions were being blocked by the Shadow Academy.

She had to let Luke know right away.

In his chambers inside the ancient temple, Jacen lifted the latches and slid aside the doors to each cage that held his menagerie of unusual pets. He could see that Tionne had kept them well fed while he was gone on Kashyyyk. The near-invisible crystal snake with its iridescent scales glittered with languid satisfaction, but the family of purple jumping spiders in the adjoining cage bounced up and down in agitation.

"It's all right," Jacen sent the message with his mind. "Be calm. You'll be safe if you get to the jungle. Just get into the jungle."

One cage rattled with two clamoring stintarils, tree-dwelling rodents with protruding eyes and long jaws filled with sharp teeth. In another damp enclosure tiny swimming crabs peeked out of their mud nests. Pinkish mucous salamanders slid out of their water bowl, gradually taking a distinct form. Iridescent blue piranha-beetles swarmed against the tough wires of their cage, chewing and eager to be free.

He turned them loose one by one, carrying them to the window as carefully as he could, moving with a controlled urgency. Jacen had just set the last of his creatures free—his favorite, a stump lizard—when he heard a loud Wookiee roar, followed by the voice of Em Teedee.

"Oh, thank goodness, we're not alone in the temple after all."

Jacen turned to find Lowie, Em Teedee, Tionne, and Raynar standing in his doorway.

"Did the others leave without us?" Raynar asked with a look of forlorn worry on his face.

"Everyone's up in the grand audience chamber," Jacen said. "We need to get there as quickly as possible. Master Skywalker's giving his final instructions before the battle begins."

When the group stepped out of the turbolift into the grand audience chamber, Jaina was already there talking in a low voice with Luke and Tenel Ka while the other students sat in frightened silence.

A look of relief washed over Luke's face when he saw that Lowie had returned successfully from his mission. Tionne stretched out her hand toward Luke, and he gave it a brief squeeze.

"I'm glad you're safe," Luke said.

"What did Mom say?" Jacen asked his sister.

Jaina bit her lower lip, and Tenel Ka answered for her. "The Shadow Academy is jamming our transmissions. We were unable to send our distress signal."

Jacen felt the blood drain out of his face. How long would it be, then, until reinforcements arrived, if they couldn't even send a distress call?

Luke spoke in a loud voice, addressing the gathered Jedi students. "We can't rely on outside help to save us. We must fight this battle ourselves. I believe the Great Temple will be the initial target of attack. Tenel Ka has already briefed you on ground tactics, so we're going to move this battle to the jungle—where the territory will be new for the Shadow Academy's troops, but familiar to us. We'll fight them one-on-one.

"But we must evacuate the Jedi academy immediately."

5

FROM THE SHADOW Academy's crowded hangar bay, Zekk watched the final preparations for the attack. The frenzy of bustling troops, mixed with their brooding anger and lust for destruction, galvanized him. He felt as if the lines of Force around him had been set on fire.

The hub of the activity was an immense hovering battle platform that dominated the hangar bay. Constructed specifically for this most important assault on the Rebel Alliance, the movable tactical platform bristled with weaponry. Stormtroopers crawled over its armored surface, preparing to launch. Guided by the ominous Nightsister Tamith Kai, the platform would be the staging point for the ground combat, Jedi versus Jedi.

At the battle platform's helm she stood, eager for vengeance. Her long black cape slithered around her with a hissing sound, like snakes coming out to strike. Spines, taken from the carapace of a murderous giant insect, protruded from her shoulders. Her black hair curled around her head like ebony wires, writhing and crackling with dark powers, each strand seemingly alive and malevolent.

Tamith Kai's violet eyes burned as she ordered the stormtroopers to board the battle platform, gathering her inner power. Her onyx-scaled armor clung to her muscular, well-formed body. Her demeanor spoke of power and confidence—and a yearning for destruction.

Zekk tended to his own duties. He himself had been a target of Tamith Kai's suspicious thoughts. The Nightsister didn't trust him. She felt that his commitment to the dark side wasn't strong enough, that he was blinded by his former friendship with the Jedi twins, Jacen and Jaina Solo.

Zekk had been trained as the prize student of Lord Brakiss, and had defeated the Nightsister's own protégé Vilas in a duel to the death. By winning the duel, Zekk had gained the title of Darkest Knight. And Tamith Kai—perhaps because she was simply a sore loser, or perhaps because she sensed his flickering doubts—rarely let him out of her sight.

But Brakiss had given *him* command of the Shadow Academy's new Force-wielders who would be the vanguard of the battle to reclaim the galaxy. He himself would lead the Dark Jedi strike force, dropping like death from the skies to obliterate Master Skywalker's trainees.

Zekk drew a deep breath, smelled the metallic tang in the cold air. He heard coolants pumping, engines powering up, the clatter of stormtrooper armor, preparatory signals as systems were locked down. They were ready to launch.

Zekk turned to his group of Force-talented warriors. He wore his crimson-lined black cape and his leather armor; his lightsaber hung clipped at his side, waiting to be used. He had secured his long dark hair in a neat ponytail, and his emerald-green eyes flashed at those gathered around him.

"Feel the Force move through you," he said to the other trainees. They stood with their jaws set, their eyes alert, eager for battle. They had been trained for this.

He gestured to the waiting platform, and the Dark Jedi moved with a fluid motion as they entered the armored vessel. "We must strike the Jedi academy now, before we lose our element of surprise."

The TIE pilot's helmet fit perfectly on his gray-haired head. Along with the breathing mask, goggles, black flight suit, padded gloves, and heavy boots, the uniform seemed to transport Qorl back to a different time, a time when he had been much younger . . . a pilot for the first Empire.

Years ago, he had flown with his wing of TIE fighters from the original Death Star to attack the desperate fleet of Rebel X-wings. He had been shot down in combat, spiraling down to crash-land in the wilds of Yavin 4. When he had looked behind him, to his absolute horror and disbelief Qorl had watched the invincible Death Star blow up, leaving him stranded on the miserable little moon.

After recovering from his injuries, Qorl had lived like a hermit for over twenty years until four young Jedi trainees had stumbled upon him . . . setting in motion the events that had returned him to the Second Imperium.

And now, Qorl found himself boarding another TIE fighter, launching from another battle station—once more ready to defeat the Rebels. This time, though, he was sure it would end differently. This time the Empire would make no mistakes.

Qorl stood in front of his wing of twelve TIE fighters. Crowded into

JEDI UNDER SIEGE

the side of the launching bay, the small fighters would take off as soon as the battle platform descended. He turned to his troops, all of them unproven fighters, taken from the ranks of the most ambitious new stormtrooper trainees. The new pilots had never seen combat. They had only practiced, performing simulation after simulation—but he knew they were itching for a real fight. The pilots stood beside their ships, clothed in identical black flight suits and helmets.

One new pilot fidgeted with obvious eagerness, glancing toward his TIE fighter, studying the laser cannon turrets, anxious to be off. He finally stepped forward. The fighter removed his helmet and held it against his chest. Even before seeing the young man's wide face, though, Qorl knew it was the broad-shouldered Norys, former leader of the Lost Ones gang.

"Excuse me, sir—I have a suggestion," Norys said. "In light of my superior performance during the simulations, since I scored better than any of these others, I think I should be the one to lead this wing."

Qorl quelled his anger. "I . . . understand your reasons, Norys. You have done excellent work in your cross-training as a TIE pilot and stormtrooper. You are eager to learn and, presumably, to *serve* the Second Imperium. But I must turn down your request this time."

"On what basis?"

Sensing the challenge in the young man's voice, Qorl kept his answer firm and direct. "On the basis that Brakiss chose me to command this mission. If you prefer to not follow orders, however . . ." He shrugged, leaving the implication hanging in the air between them.

The boy was rude and so often insubordinate that if he hadn't shown such a true aptitude for weaponry and fighting skills, Qorl would certainly have left him behind. Too much was at stake in this mission to allow an overeager young man to botch things up.

Norys flushed. "I think *you* are afraid, Qorl. You're old and haven't flown a mission in years. You're leading the wing so you can hold us back to cover your own failures."

"That will be all," Qorl said in a voice that, although quiet, was so commanding that the air cracked with tension. "I give you the choice: say the word and I'll ground you from this mission, or hold your tongue and fight for your Emperor." At the moment Qorl didn't care what the surly young man chose. He would gladly take a smaller fighting wing if it was the only way to ensure that all his pilots were well disciplined.

Fuming, Norys struggled to keep silent and rammed the black helmet back onto his head.

Qorl spoke, more to divert attention from the outburst than for any other reason. "We have successfully jammed all signals from the Jedi academy. They are unable to call for reinforcements. Since no battleships are in orbit, the foolish Jedi Knights must have assumed that their own powers and their puny energy shield would be enough to thwart us.

"According to our monitoring systems, our first Imperial commando raid has already succeeded in removing their shields. The Jedi academy lies open and vulnerable to our attack.

"When Tamith Kai launches her battle platform to guide the military strike, Lord Zekk will take his Dark Jedi trainees and combat the Jedi Knights directly. Our wing will fly harassment strikes from the air. Although we are meant to cause considerable damage, our mission is to *support*, not to serve as the front line of attack. Is that understood?"

The pilots murmured their understanding. Qorl couldn't tell if Norys's voice had joined them.

"Very well. To your ships," he said.

His pilots scrambled into their cockpits, and Qorl settled in behind the pilot's controls of the lead TIE fighter. He drew a deep breath through the filtering mask, smelling the delicious and familiar chemical taint of the air from his tanks.

He smiled. It felt so good to be able to fly once again.

From the helm of the tactical battle platform Tamith Kai shouted, "Let us be off. We shall return victorious before this day is done!"

The great hangar bay doors opened, revealing the blackness of space shared with the emerald moon, behind which loomed the boiling orange cauldron of the gas giant Yavin. The moon looked insignificant against the panorama of the universe—but it was the Shadow Academy's target, destined to become the site of a furious battle and an Imperial victory.

Tamith Kai commanded the battle platform to rise up on its repulsorlifts and head out of the Shadow Academy. The military vessel appeared to be a large, flattened sailbarge with rounded corners, two levels high, with an upper command deck that would open to the air once they reached the atmosphere. Armed stormtroopers and ground assault forces filled the first level, while Zekk and his Dark Jedi took their positions in the bottom bay near the drop doors.

The battle platform descended through space toward the thin fingernail of atmosphere around the green moon. As the minutes passed, Zekk paced back and forth. He looked out the viewports and saw the ring station high overhead, dwindling as the battle platform increased speed toward Yavin 4.

"Packs ready?" he asked, adjusting the equipment strapped across his chest and back. His black cape hung over it, its scarlet inner lining flashing as he moved. His squad of Dark Jedi checked their weapons, scores of identical lightsabers manufactured aboard the Shadow Academy. The team members adjusted their repulsorpacks on their shoulders. One by one they declared their readiness.

The blackness of space was streaked with white haze as the battle platform plunged headfirst into the atmosphere. Zekk felt a buffeting vibration as the winds clawed the armored plates.

The hull heated up, and Zekk could sense the ionized scream of the shockwave through the air, but Tamith Kai piloted the battle platform expertly, without hesitation, directly toward their target.

The Nightsister's deep, hard voice came over the comm. "We're approaching target altitude. Zekk, prepare your Dark Jedi for departure. The air-drop doors will open in one standard minute."

Zekk clapped his gloved hands, ordering the Dark Jedi to stand in ranks. "The repulsorpacks will carry you," he said, "but use your Force abilities to guide your descent. We must strike directly. These are our sworn enemies, Luke Skywalker's Jedi Knights. The future of the galaxy hinges on our victory today."

Zekk fixed his penetrating gaze on each one of the trainees, trying to impart a fraction of his determination to them. They were valiant warriors, vowing to succeed in their quest.

But Zekk had not yet dealt with his own inner turmoil. He knew in his heart that Tamith Kai's doubts about his loyalty had a legitimate foundation—he *did* feel a longing friendship toward his dear friend Jaina Solo and her brother Jacen.

Deep in the forests of Kashyyyk he had warned Jaina to stay away from the Jedi academy. He did not want her to be part of this battle today. He did not want her to become a victim.

But he knew with equal certainty that the Jaina Solo he knew and cared for would never stay away to save herself and leave her friends to die. He dreaded the thought that she might be down there ready to fight against him.

Zekk was grateful to have his thoughts interrupted as the floor thumped and the drop-bay doors creaked open. A line of brighter air like a thin, toothless smile appeared at their feet and then yawned wide. The jungle treetops were visible below, punctuated by the protruding stone towers of ancient Massassi temples.

"All right, my Dark Jedi," Zekk shouted into the howling wind.

"The hour is ours. Depart!" Leading the charge, he dove into the sky, switched on his repulsorpack, and tumbled toward the unprotected Jedi academy.

Behind him the other Dark Jedi dropped from the battle platform one by one, falling like deadly birds of prey.

In flight Zekk ignited his lightsaber, holding it out like a glowing beacon. He glanced up to see the other assault troops similarly extending their blazing weapons, capes fluttering behind them.

Dark Jedi rained down from the sky.

6

THE SHRIEK OF twin ion engines ripped apart the relative quiet of the grand audience chamber. Tenel Ka's reflexes took over even before she recognized the source of the sound, and she found herself running in a crouch toward the closest window slit, with Jaina, Jacen, and Lowbacca right beside her. Through the slit in the stone wall, Tenel Ka saw TIE fighters on a strafing run—coming straight toward the Jedi academy!

"Master Skywalker, we are under attack," Tenel Ka shouted.

Luke Skywalker raised his voice to be heard throughout the chamber. "Everyone, stay in the jungles until the battle is over. Fight with all your skills and abilities. Remember your training . . . and may the Force be with you."

A series of hollow-sounding explosions punctuated his command. A loud *crack!* echoed through the chamber as a proton bomb struck the lowermost levels and dug a crater in the jungle soil outside the pyramid.

From where she stood, Tenel Ka observed the other Jedi trainees and judged that their reactions to Master Skywalker's orders were commendable. Several students gasped in surprise, and Tenel Ka could sense conflicting emotions—nervous anticipation, homesickness, trust in the Force, dread at the possibility of having to kill. But she caught no hint of confusion, panic, or denial.

Without waiting for further instructions, Jedi students streamed out of the grand audience chamber. Luke Skywalker dashed to the window where Tenel Ka's group stood and motioned for Peckhum to join them. The old spacer ducked as stone powder fell from the ceiling, shaken loose by the pounding from above.

The Jedi Master began issuing instructions immediately, and Tenel Ka marveled at how calm he seemed in the midst of the turmoil. "Jacen, take the *Shadow Chaser* into orbit. See if you can break through the jamming signal and send a message to your mother that we're under attack. Artoo-Detoo's down in the hangar bay already waiting with the ship. He's all the copilot you'll need."

Jaina, who loved to fly, was about to protest when Luke turned to her. "I need you to go across the river and check out the shield generator equipment. See if there's any chance of getting our defensive shields back up. Lowie, I want you and Tenel Ka—" The comlink clipped to Luke's belt interrupted him, signaling an urgent message.

Another explosion vibrated through the Great Temple, this one closer than the others. As soon as Luke switched on his comlink, Artoo-Detoo's alarmed bleeps and whistles issued from it.

"What's that, Artoo? Calm down," Luke said.

"If you would allow me, Master Skywalker," Em Teedee said, "I was able to parse your astromech droid's message and could provide a translation for you. I am fluent in over six forms of communic—"

"Thank you, Em Teedee," Luke Skywalker cut off the little droid's chatter, "that would be very helpful."

"Artoo-Detoo reports that—oh dear!—the front of the hangar bay has been hit. Rubble has completely sealed off the entrance. No ships can get in or out. The *Shadow Chaser* is trapped inside."

"Hey," Jacen said after a moment of thought, "Peckhum, what about the *Lightning Rod*? It's not sealed in."

Tenel Ka felt a frown crease her forehead at the thought of Jacen facing an Imperial attack in the rickety old cargo shuttle.

"The *Lightning Rod* doesn't have the *Shadow Chaser*'s quantum armor," Luke pointed out.

"Too dangerous," Jaina said.

"Hey, we're *all* in danger here," Jacen said in a low, firm voice. "And we have to get a message out."

"Sure, we could do it," old Peckhum said. "I've learned some pretty good evasive maneuvers in my day—enough to make it to orbit without gettin' blown up, I'd guess."

Just then Lowbacca gave a warning yelp and pointed toward the window slit. Hovering over the jungle in the distance was an ominous-looking construction, a giant weapon-studded tactical platform, like a deadly raft carrying enemy troops.

Tenel Ka felt a stab of recognition. "Tamith Kai is there; I can feel her," she said.

"It looks like she's directing the ground battle from up there," Luke said.

"Then we must disable that battle platform," Tenel Ka replied without a pause. "I volunteer. The Nightsister is mine."

Lowbacca barked a comment. "Master Lowbacca wishes to point

out that his T-23 is still out near the landing pad. Using the skyhopper, he and Mistress Tenel Ka could easily reach that platform within minutes."

Luke nodded. "We each have our missions. I'll do one last sweep of the pyramid to make sure no one was left behind. I'll see you all out at the rendezvous point in the jungle."

As the young Jedi Knights raced down the stairs inside the temple, Tenel Ka's mind already began moving ahead to the coming confrontation. Adrenaline pumped through her veins, and her mind was alert. She had been bred and trained for battle.

Although fighting with only one arm would present her with new challenges, she felt neither afraid nor overconfident. She was simply *ready*. A Jedi must always be ready, she knew. Master Skywalker and Tionne had trained them all well. Tenel Ka had her lightsaber and her Force skills. Together, she was certain, that was enough for her to defeat any enemy.

By the time they all reached the landing pad, Jaina had already split off from the group, plunging toward the river and the shield generator station. Tenel Ka was surprised to note that the old pilot Peckhum had kept up with them as he and Jacen sprinted toward the battered supply shuttle.

Dodging energy bolts from the TIE fighters that swooped overhead, Tenel Ka and Lowbacca scrambled into the T-23 skyhopper while Peckhum and Jacen boarded the *Lightning Rod*.

Watching Jacen run up the ramp into the *Lightning Rod*, Tenel Ka felt a tug at her emotions she could not explain, even to herself. Almost at the same moment, Jacen reappeared and stared at Tenel Ka with a serious expression. His face broke into a grin. "I'll tell you a joke when we get back—a good one this time." Then he was gone again.

As Lowie fired up the T-23's repulsorjets, Tenel Ka answered, though she knew he couldn't hear her, "Yes, my friend Jacen, I would like to hear your joke. When we all get back."

7

THE *LIGHTNING ROD*'s engines whined as the ship strained against gravity. Just after liftoff, the battered vessel gave a sharp jolt. Alarm bells went off inside Jacen's head. "We're hit!" he cried, not even bothering to check the readouts.

"Naw," old Peckhum answered. "*Lightning Rod*'s been doin' that ever since I switched out the power coupling to the rear repulsorjets. I guess I'll have to take a look at that again one of these days."

The knot of panic in Jacen's stomach eased a little—but only a little. "Maybe Jaina can help you with it later," he said.

An energy bolt streaked by as a TIE fighter sang past them on its descent toward the Jedi academy. "Hey, that was a close one!" Jacen said.

"Too close," Peckhum agreed. "Hang on, young Solo—I'm gonna try some evasive maneuvers."

Lowie focused his full concentration on getting the T-23 to cover. With his peripheral vision he could see other Jedi students dodging fire from TIE fighters as they sprinted for the safety of the trees. When they reached the edge of the forest, the young Wookiee pulled his skyhopper into a sharp climb.

The dense network of leafy branches had always signified protection to Lowie, and he longed for a few peaceful moments in the treetops. But no peace awaited Lowie and Tenel Ka up there. Not this time.

Lowie clenched the steering controls tightly and zigzagged the flight path across the treetops, trying to throw off any pursuers who might be on their track. Today trouble rained down on them from above, and he could flee to no safe height. His best bet lay in remaining in among the trees.

An energy bolt spat past the T-23 and sent up a plume of dirt and singed turf behind them. "Let the Force guide you, Lowbacca, my friend," Tenel Ka said from the passenger seat in back.

Lowie rumbled an acknowledgment and took a deep calming breath. He flew onward, letting the Force control his weaving and dodging. They headed toward the wide, greenish-brown river over which Tenel Ka and Lowbacca had seen the Nightsister's sinister battle platform. Even from half a kilometer away, they could see lances of laser fire shoot out from the armored vessel, incinerating trees along the banks.

Suddenly, Tenel Ka gave a shout of surprise. "Look. There!"

From the sky above a group of figures descended like swooping birds of prey—human forms. Dark Jedi dropped from the clouds in a dispersed attack pattern, light-sabers flashing as they controlled their direction with repulsorpacks.

A proximity alarm sounded the moment Lowbacca diverted his attention, and a laser cannon blast from a passing TIE fighter struck them. A jet of smoke and sparks spewed from the T-23's rear engines. The tiny skyhopper shimmied and bucked in the air. With a shriek of shearing metal, one of the attitude-control fins gave way.

"Oh my," Em Teedee wailed. "I can't bear to watch."

Lowie, reacting with the instinct of his Jedi training, wrestled with the controls. Directed by the Force, one of his sharp-clawed hands flew across the control panel, while his free hand guided their descent. Smoke poured into the cockpit, and the skyhopper sputtered and rocked. Without knowing quite how he did it, Lowie cut the rear engines and bled off their momentum into a steep upward climb. Then, letting the little ship fall back toward the treetops, he used one final burst from the repulsorjets to slow their descent—enough, he hoped.

The T-23 crashed onto the jungle canopy.

With every breath, Tenel Ka drew fire into her aching lungs. Nearby a Wookiee groaned, but she could not make sense of the growled words. She could see nothing.

"Mistress Tenel Ka!" A strident electronic voice broke into her foggy consciousness. "Master Lowbacca urgently requests your assistance removing the T-23's canopy."

Tenel Ka tried to look around. She saw only roiling, changing shapes of light and dark. The shifting patterns stung her eyes, and she squeezed them tightly shut.

A voice loud enough to wake a Jedi Master from a healing trance wailed in Tenel Ka's ears. "Oh, curse my sluggish processor, I'm too late. She's dead!"

Lowbacca bellowed a loud denial. At the same time, something reached out and gave her a sharp nudge.

"No," Tenel Ka managed to croak. "I'm alive."

Lowbacca gave a few crisp barks, and Tenel Ka found herself responding to his instructions even before Em Teedee could clarify, "Master Lowbacca asks you to push against the canopy with all your might whilst throwing your weight toward the port side—to the left, you know."

Tenel Ka knew. She pushed and rocked. Despite the choking clouds of smoke from the burning engines, she grew calm enough to let the Force flow through her.

Even through her closed eyelids, Tenel Ka could tell when Em Teedee switched on the bright yellow beams of his optical sensors to cut through the smoke. "It would seem," the little droid went on, "that the T-23's canopy is wedged against a tree branch. Oh, we're doomed!"

Then, just as the little droid finished his lament, the skyhopper's canopy popped free, and fresh air flooded the cockpit. Both Tenel Ka and Lowbacca stripped out of their crash webbing and scrambled free of the wreckage. As they moved away from the smoldering craft, panting for breath and waiting for their vision to clear, Tenel Ka's hand went automatically to her lightsaber to be sure it was still clipped firmly at her waist. It was.

"Oh dear," Em Teedee exclaimed in a tinny voice. "Now we'll most likely become lost in the jungle and captured by woolamanders. Do be careful, Master Lowbacca. I should hate to repeat that dreadful experience."

Balancing on a tree limb beside Tenel Ka, Lowbacca turned to gaze at the crashed T-23 and uttered a low, mournful note. Tenel Ka could see that his distress came not from the thought of jungle creatures, but from the loss of his beloved vehicle. The warrior girl understood loss. She reached out her single hand to touch Lowbacca's arm briefly and let the strength of the Force comfort him. Then, as one, they turned to seek out their destination: the giant battle platform—and the evil Nightsister.

To Tenel Ka's relief and surprise, Lowbacca had managed to crash-land barely two hundred meters from where the battle platform hovered above the crowns of the Massassi trees. Before she could speak, though, her Wookiee friend gave a low woof of warning and pointed downward toward cover.

JEDI UNDER SIEGE

Tenel Ka understood immediately and scrambled down into the leaves and branches until she was hidden. If they could see the giant battle platform, then they themselves could be seen. They would need to make their way to the battle platform *beneath* the rippling green leaves, like swimmers below the surface of an ocean.

With only one arm to help her balance and pull herself along, Tenel Ka had to trust the Force to place her feet securely at each step. She even welcomed Lowbacca's help when he offered it in crossing weak branches or broad gaps.

Tenel Ka wasn't sure why she felt compelled to speak. Perhaps it was the air of sadness that hung about her Wookiee friend. "We will spend many enjoyable days repairing your T-23, Lowbacca my friend—you, Jacen, Jaina, and I. After this battle is over."

The Wookiee stopped, looked at her quizzically for a moment, then chuffed with laughter. After a series of woofs, Em Teedee said, "Master Lowbacca adds that Master Jacen will most likely be delighted to have a captive audience to entertain with his jokes."

Tenel Ka felt her own spirits brighten at that thought, and they moved forward at a more rapid pace. Her mind focused on the goal of defeating the Second Imperium once and for all.

Suddenly, she felt a tingle run up her spine. "Halt!" she said. A TIE fighter swooped low across the leaves, rippling the canopy around them with its hot exhaust as it circled to inspect the crashed skyhopper. Lowbacca growled, and Tenel Ka held his arm to restrain him from any rash action. The Imperial ship circled again over the wreckage, as if looking for survivors. Tenel Ka hoped the pilot wouldn't blast the already-downed craft into a smoldering lump of slag and debris. After a tense moment, the enemy ship roared away in search of new prey.

She and Lowbacca pressed on through the trees toward where the battle platform waited.

It seemed like no time at all before Em Teedee said, "Unless my senses have become completely uncalibrated by the crash, we should be directly below the leading edge of the battle platform right now."

Lowbacca held out a hand, motioning for Tenel Ka to wait, and scrambled up a few branches to check their location. At his low bark of triumph, she climbed after him and pushed her head above the leafy canopy. There, hovering ten meters over the treetops, was the underside of the giant battle platform, massive and threatening, armored for assault, bristling with weapons.

"It should be a simple enough task to destroy it," Tenel Ka said.

The sounds of shouted orders and clomping booted feet carried down to them. Lowbacca pointed upward and then shrugged as if to say, What next? The platform was too high above the trees to make a jump, and they had no repulsorpacks of their own. Tenel Ka reached for the grappling hook and fibercord she kept at her belt.

"We'll have to climb for it," she said.

The platform hovered higher than Tenel Ka was accustomed to aiming, but the grappling hook caught firmly on the armored edge on her second throw. Tenel Ka tested her weight on the fibercord. The grappling hook did not budge. Then, wrapping her arm and her legs around the cord, she began to climb, using the Force to help levitate her when her single arm couldn't provide enough support.

Above on the platform waited Imperial stormtroopers, heavy armaments, and a Nightsister from Dathomir.

Tenel Ka swallowed hard. She knew that although the Force was with them, the *odds* definitely were not.

8

THE GREEN-BROWN RIVER that flowed sluggishly through the primeval forest was broad and powerful, yet outwardly calm. The current showed not the least bit of disturbance from the titanic struggle of good and evil taking place on Yavin 4.

The river hosted numerous life-forms: invisible plankton and carnivorous protozoans, water plants, trees that dangled sharp roots into the flow, and camouflaged predators that disguised themselves as innocuous parts of the landscape.

But as blaster shots rang out and the buzz of lightsabers droned through the jungle, other creatures moved in the thick branches over the river and in the water itself . . . creatures trained in using the Force.

Rounded reptilian snouts broke the surface of the murky river. Breathing slits rose up, nostrils flaring to draw in welcome oxygen. The three scaly creatures moved slowly enough that only slight ripples whispered across the water. Settling into position deep in the mud, they sniffed and lay in wait near the path at the river's edge.

Their enemies would come soon.

Moving stealthily yet radiating a supremely confident power, three of the Dark Jedi trainees from the Shadow Academy strode through the underbrush, hacking away the dense vines and branches with their lightsaber blades. They reached the riverbank and paused to consult with each other, still searching for their opponents.

"Skywalker's Jedi trainees are cowards," one said. "Why don't they come out and fight? They all hide in the jungle like terrified rodents."

"How can they not be afraid of us?" another one said. "They know the power of the dark side."

Consulting silently, with only a faint stream of bubble for communication, three of Luke Skywalker's reptilian Cha'a trainees lunged out of the river, spewing a stream of water at their enemies. They used the Force to summon a hammering flow of the river, a column of drenching wetness that reared up like a snake, then splashed down. The Dark Jedi lightsaber blades sizzled and steamed. The three Cha'a hissed and chattered with laughter as they summoned up more and more water.

The waterlogged Dark Jedi sputtered and thrashed from side to side as they attempted to summon up dark-side powers with which to strike back at their reptilian opponents.

Just then, from the dense shelter of the trees above, a trio of feathered avians left their perches and plunged down. They let out a high, fluting whistle of a battle cry.

The Dark Jedi were distracted for a moment, torn between two enemies. Then the avians landed on top of them, driving them to the ground and knocking them unconscious. The avians chirped and screeched in victory as the Cha'a hauled themselves dripping out of the river mud and slogged toward the three new captives.

Working together, Skywalker's alien Jedi trainees removed whiplike vines from the underbrush and lashed the arms and legs of their prisoners together. One of the Cha'a picked up the discarded Shadow Academy lightsabers, studied the poor construction and unimaginative workmanship. One by one, he tossed the tainted weapons into the river. They splashed, and sank without a trace.

Meanwhile, the avians crouched over the unconscious captives and used their Jedi powers to probe the minds of Brakiss's students. They added strong Force suggestions to make sure their enemies would continue to sleep for a long time. . . .

Tionne tossed her long silvery-white hair behind her to get it out of the way. She would need her vision unobstructed, with no distractions.

She looked at the other Jedi students with her gleaming mother-of-pearl eyes. Master Skywalker frequently entrusted her with training these students, and now Tionne would do battle. The Yavin 4 academy had often been a target of the forces of evil—but the true Jedi Knights had won before, and she had no doubt they would win again.

She and her students stood around the flat marble slab and broken columns of what had once been an open-air Massassi temple before it was swallowed up by the jungle. This was the place at which they had chosen to make their stand.

"Are you all ready?" Tionne said. "Remember what you have been taught. *There is no try.* We must succeed in defeating the warriors of the dark side."

Her students shouted their agreement, looking at her with eyes full of confidence in their abilities and her plan. One of the young women nodded to Tionne, took a deep breath, then ran off into the forest in search of the invading Dark Jedi. Within only moments the young woman cried out, shouting, challenging the trainees of the Shadow Academy.

Tionne heard a lightsaber sizzle. Branches fell . . . and then came the sound of footsteps crashing through the forest as her student hurried back toward the trap they had set. Tionne gestured silently for the others to prepare themselves.

"Come back here, Jedi vermin!" one of the enemy called, hidden by the thickets.

Four Dark Jedi came plunging through the jungles, bursting into the temple clearing where the panting student stood on the other side of a flat marble slab hanging above their heads. Tionne's student looked defeated.

The invaders stepped forward. "We will crush your mind with the dark side!" one said.

"Now!" Tionne shouted. From their shadowy hiding places, four of her special students reached out with the Force: in an unexpected, irresistible move, they snatched the four lightsabers from enemy hands. The Dark Jedi cried out in alarm and surprise at losing their weapons. Then Tionne and her students emerged from the underbrush and surrounded them.

"We don't need our lightsabers to defeat you. We can still flatten you with our power!" said the first overconfident opponent. "The power of the dark side!" All four of the enemy Jedi stood in a tight cluster, back to back, raising their hands.

"I wouldn't do that if I were you," Tionne said calmly, letting her pale lips show a brief smile. "You wouldn't want to distract us—a brief fluctuation in our concentration might become a *crushing* defeat for you."

She glanced upward. Her four students remained motionless with their eyes closed, focused on their task.

The Dark Jedi looked up and saw that the marble slab they had thought to be the ceiling of a crumbling temple was completely unsupported, a hovering rectangle of rock weighing many tons, balanced over their heads. It floated, held up by nothing but the power of the Force. Tionne's students maintained their concentration.

The Dark Jedi swallowed hard.

"You can try to escape if you like," Tionne said. "Maybe you have enough power to subdue all of us with enough left over to catch that block of stone before it falls down on your heads. Maybe." She shrugged. "It's your choice, of course. But I wouldn't risk it."

The four Dark Jedi exchanged glances, unable to find words. Finally, one by one, they lowered their clenched hands and surrendered.

Tionne heaved a quiet but heartfelt sigh of relief.

Another tree stood in the forest, short and stunted, with a thick trunk. Branches extended out in such a way that, if looked at in a certain light, it had an almost humanoid appearance: one of Master Skywalker's Jedi, a slow-moving, long-lived plantlike creature.

She often went out to spend days in the sunlight, using photosynthesis to drink in nourishment, absorbing minerals from the soil, water from the river, and carbon dioxide from the air.

She would spend all day, many days at a time, simply contemplating the Force and her place in the universe. Trees remained alive for a long time and did not rush into ill-considered action; yet at times such as this, she could manage to move fast enough. She understood the importance of protecting the Jedi academy.

She had entered into her training to understand the Force, vowing to defend the side of light—and here she found herself in a clear-cut battle against the Shadow Academy. Dark Jedi enemies coursed through the jungle, searching for victims, but Master Skywalker had taught all the trainees well. The light-side students would put up a good fight.

The treelike Jedi stood motionless, watching, sensing the jungle . . . and she knew her enemies would come to her. She had only to wait. Her roots dug deeper into the soil, drawing on it for greater energy. She felt the sap pulsing through her, boiling in her veins, allowing her to gain the speed for the unwavering action that she would require just this once . . . she hoped.

She had chosen her spot well, next to an ailing Massassi tree, tall with outspreading branches. Its trunk was nested with vines and dripping with parasitic shelf mushrooms that had tapped into its heartwood and begun devouring the great tree from within.

The Jedi could tell that this great-grandfather of a tree had lived for centuries and centuries. . . . It was the way of things, the cycle of the forest. As plants grew, they went to seed to bear their young, and then slowly decayed to warm organic matter and fertilized the forest for subsequent generations. She saw how the old Massassi tree leaned, observed the surrounding jungle . . . waited.

She reached out with the Force subtly, gently, so that even the adepts of the Dark Side would not know they were being manipulated. *"Come here,"* she thought, broadcasting it over and over again. At least one of them would catch the hint. They would think they had detected one of their light-side enemies—but it would be all the plant Jedi's doing.

After an indeterminate period—she did not measure time in small increments—she sensed a clumsy disturbance: two attackers from the Shadow Academy storming through the forest, as if the delicate ecosystem was no more than a nuisance that they would eradicate completely, given the chance.

The Jedi waited. She had to concentrate. She had to act at the right moment and not waste time thinking, or else her opportunity would pass.

Curled within one of her gnarled branches—a handlike appendage—was a knobby lightsaber built to accommodate her wooden grip.

The two Dark Jedi came into the clearing and stopped. "I see nothing here," said one. "Lord Brakiss would be ashamed of you. Lord Zekk would take away your lightsaber. The powers of the dark side are wasted on you."

"I tell you, I sensed it," said the other. He stepped forward, looking from side to side, studying the quiet jungle. His companion stood next to him, scowling.

At that moment the Jedi used all her stored reserves—and acted. She ignited the lightsaber and slashed sideways with her branch arm, like a bent sapling suddenly released to snap straight again.

"I am sorry, Grandfather Tree," she said—and her lightsaber blade cleaved through the trunk of the tottering old Massassi tree, severing it from the stump and letting the arms of gravity embrace it. Its wide-branched top leaned over and the tree crashed onto the two Dark Jedi intruders. They had time only to look up with a muffled outcry of surprise as a meteor of branches and vines smashed down upon them.

The Jedi deactivated her lightsaber, then felt a trembling through her entire wooden body. In one act, she had drained months and months of her energy reserves. She stretched her branches up toward the sunlight, dug her roots deeper.

It would take her a long time to recover from this day.

9

AFTER CROSSING THE river, Jaina fought her way through the jungle, seeking a suitable path through the thickest underbrush while keeping herself hidden from other attackers. Right now, the tangled forest was her ally, and she could use the cover to her advantage. She wasn't afraid to combat the Dark Jedi threatening the academy—but she had a vital mission in mind . . . something more to her tastes.

As long as the defensive energy shields remained down and the generator damaged, the entire area was vulnerable to repeated attacks from the skies. Luke Skywalker's trainees were defending themselves . . . but if Jaina could somehow repair the shield generator and get the protective force field up again, the new Jedi Knights could take care of these audacious enemies one at a time.

Jaina finally made her way to the clearing where her father and Chewbacca had recently installed the new energy shield generator. With only a glance she saw that the machinery was irreparable, despite her usual knack for fixing things.

Normally, she could make temporary repairs to get systems up and running again, at least for a while. But not in this case. An Imperial saboteur had used thermal detonators to wipe out the entire generating station. It was hopelessly ruined, a pile of shrapnel; no simple fixup would do.

Jaina's attention remained on the generator for only a moment, however. She caught her breath.

There in the clearing sat an Imperial TIE fighter in perfect condition.

Ever since Chewbacca had given Lowie the T-23 skyhopper, Jaina had longed for a vehicle of her own. That, in fact, had been the impetus behind her desire to repair the crashed TIE fighter the young Jedi Knights had found in the jungles—Qorl's TIE fighter.

She stopped and stared, frozen with excitement and apprehension. But other than the muffled noises of battle in the jungles and the distant shouts and blaster fire near the Great Temple, she heard no sound.

Jaina withdrew her lightsaber and pressed the power stud. The beam sprang outward, glowing an electric violet. Then she crept forward stealthily, ready to fight if the TIE pilot emerged with his blaster drawn. But she sensed no one else around, heard no noise from the craft.

"Hello?" Jaina called. "You'd better surrender if you're an Imperial!" She waited. "Uh, is anyone here?"

Only the simmering jungle noises answered her.

Moving forward, letting her eagerness take over, she ran to the abandoned TIE fighter. It was a sinister-looking ship: a rounded cockpit suspended between two flat hexagonal power arrays, twin ion engines that would propel the small fighter across space, a bank of deadly laser cannons.

Ideas and possibilities thundered through her mind. If she could pilot this ship into the enemy's midst, Jaina would be in disguise. She could slip in among them, and they wouldn't *know* she was actually an enemy . . . until it was too late.

Switching off her lightsaber again, Jaina opened the cockpit hatch and crawled inside. She had studied how TIE fighters worked when she and her friends had replaced the components of Qorl's crashed ship. She knew the buttons on the control panels, knew how the systems activated. Though the exiled old pilot had flown off in his ship before Jaina had had a chance to take it on a flight, she was confident she could handle the craft.

She settled into the pilot's seat, noting the oily scent of stale lubricants and the sour odors the Empire did not bother to remove. A rebreather mask hung next to a small life-support console. The cockpit walls closed around her like a protective shell, giving her little room to move, but all the controls were at her fingertips. Through the ship's front ports, she could see outside.

Jaina found the power switch and toggled it on, felt the engines' thrumming, systems gearing up, batteries charging. Control panel lights winked on in a brilliant flurry around her. She drew a deep breath, strapped herself in, and clutched the controls.

"All systems ready for takeoff," she whispered to herself. She glanced at the sky, looking for the black specks of other Imperial ships. "Okay, TIE fighters, prepare for some company!"

The Imperial craft raised up as Jaina worked the controls. Clearing the jungle treetops, she felt the exhilaration of actually flying. The ship seemed unbelievably quiet inside, until she realized that its noisier primary engines had been disengaged. This TIE fighter flew so quietly because it used only the lesser-powered engines. So *that* was how the enemy pilot had gotten under their shield unnoticed! No doubt the original systems remained intact, but the enemy commando had slipped in without the familiar howl of TIE engines.

All right then, Jaina thought—she could be silent and deadly as well. Finally skimming the treetops, she scanned around, acquiring targets. She shot forward, reveling in the thrill of flight, the landscape passing beneath her in a mottled green blur.

Up ahead she saw six TIE fighters flying in formation, firing down at the treetops, pounding the temple ruins, even structures that had never been used for training Jedi. The Palace of the Woolamander, an ancient ruin already nearly collapsed, was pummeled with brilliant streaks from laser cannons, though Jaina didn't believe any Jedi Knights had gone there.

She kept the Imperial comm channels on so she could hear the terse, gruff chatter as the TIE pilots discussed their overall plan, choosing targets, firing at moving figures sheltered by the thick Massassi trees.

Jaina kept her microphone off, though, as she joined the formation of TIE fighters, slipping in at the rear. Over the comm system she heard them acknowledge her arrival; rather than making them suspicious by speaking with a young woman's voice, she just clicked an okay over the microphone.

Then she powered up her laser cannons.

One of the TIE fighters broadcast, "Plenty of targets here for everybody. Let's cause some damage."

Jaina bit her lower lip and nodded. "Yes," she muttered to herself, "let's cause some damage."

She let her eyes fall partially closed and concentrated, feeling the Force. Despite the sensors and systems available in the TIE fighter, nothing could match heightened Jedi perceptions for enhancing her movements. She needed to target and fire and target again with lightning speed. She would have only one chance.

Jaina gripped the control stick of her weapons and focused on the aiming mechanisms, flying smoothly behind the unsuspecting Imperials. She had to disable them with one shot each. She couldn't risk repeated fire on a single target, because once she started shooting, they would be rather upset with her.

Jaina sought out the most vulnerable points: their engines and the joints that held the planar power arrays to their sides. If the TIE fighters turned side-on to her, she would blast the power arrays themselves—large targets, impossible to miss.

Giving herself a silent countdown, Jaina pointed her lasers at the closest ship. What am I waiting for? she asked herself.

Gritting her teeth, she fired a single shot, then swiveled the laser cannons, moving with hyperspeed, to target a second TIE fighter. Even before her second bolt struck the narrow joint next to the cockpit and sliced off the planar array, the first TIE fighter careened into a spin.

Jaina blasted again at the rear engine pods of the second ship. The TIE fighter exploded in front of her, momentarily blinding her, but she quickly averted her eyes. As she brought the laser cannons to bear on a third target, Jaina heard the TIE pilots shouting in outrage and panic. The formation began to split apart.

She didn't have much time.

The third TIE fighter turned toward her, and Jaina strafed across its surface, severing one of the planar arrays and striking the viewports in the cockpit. The third ship went down—but by now the remaining three Imperials had spun around and were headed straight toward her.

Jaina blinked as fiery bolts from their laser cannons shot past her. She put her TIE fighter into a spin. Now using the Force to anticipate the incoming weapons fire, just as her uncle Luke had used his lightsaber to deflect blaster bolts, she spun and turned and banked, then began to fly away at her fighter's top speed.

But the other three Imperial ships came howling after her, releasing a constant volley of laser fire, ignoring targets below now that they had acquired a single target . . . a traitor in their midst.

Jaina ducked and dodged, no longer enjoying the thrill of flight. She had a bad feeling about her impulsive attack. She streaked over the jungle, the three TIE fighters hot on her tail.

10

THE DIM FOREST floor near the Great Temple was familiar ground for Luke Skywalker and most of his Jedi trainees. Even with a battle of light and dark raging around him—or perhaps *because* of the battle—he found it soothing to be out in the wilds. The jungle itself was rich with life, and therefore rich in the Force that bound all life together.

Reaching down to confirm that his lightsaber was securely attached to his belt next to his comlink, Luke drew on the Force. He let it flow through him, let it show him the skirmishes all around him.

Alert to the emotions of his students, Luke reached out to bolster flagging confidence in one trainee, to warn another against an unexpected attack, to send encouragement to yet another who was growing tired.

An energy bolt from a TIE fighter sliced through the trees close by and set fire to the underbrush, forcing Luke to retreat behind a thicket to avoid choking fumes from the burning vegetation.

With his mind he searched for the center of the battle, the place where he could do the most good. Decades ago, when the Death Star had loomed over the jungle moon, his mission had been clear. The battle station's superlaser could turn an entire planet to rubble. Luke had had no doubt in his mind that the Empire's most powerful weapon must be destroyed. And with the Force to guide him, he had succeeded.

But today's battle was different—it had no focus. This time he had no superweapon to disable. The Jedi academy's long-range transmissions had been jammed, the defensive shields sabotaged. With Artoo-Detoo and the *Shadow Chaser* trapped in the Great Temple's hangar bay, Luke had no way of reaching orbit to fight the Shadow Academy directly.

The ground assault itself was directed from the giant battle platform that hovered over the treetops a few kilometers away, but Luke sensed that the military component of the attack was mere harassment.

TIE fighters had made direct attacks on the Great Temple—and yet *ground* forces and Dark Jedi had been sent to fight on a nearly even footing against Luke's students. With a different strategy, the Shadow Academy's victory would have been far easier—it almost seemed as if Brakiss *wanted* to do it the hard way.

Luke knew that must be the answer.

A loud incoming message signal on his comlink startled him. Students at the Yavin academy rarely carried comlinks, but the Jedi Master kept one at his side during times of turmoil so that he could be reached more easily. Even though the Shadow Academy had jammed long-range transmissions, local signals from Artoo could still get through.

Luke switched on the comlink. "Sit tight, Artoo. We'll be able to get you when the fighting's over." Before he could say more, a man's voice blared from the tiny speaker.

"—essage for Luke Skywalker. Repeat: this is a message for Luke Skywalker. If anyone can hear me, respond immediately."

Luke stared at the small device before replying, "Who is this?" But before he heard the answer, his Jedi senses told him the man's identity.

"You can call me *Master* Brakiss," the voice said. "Tell your teacher that I'm transmitting on all channels. He will want to speak to me."

"This is Luke Skywalker," he said. "If you have a message, Brakiss, you can give it directly to me." Luke's heart knocked painfully against his rib cage, though from surprise rather than fear.

A cultured laugh came over the comlink. "Well, my old teacher . . . the man I once called Master. This *is* a pleasure."

"What do you want, Brakiss?" Luke asked.

"A meeting," the smooth voice replied. "Just the two of us. On neutral ground. As equals. We didn't have a chance to finish our . . . conversation when you came to my Shadow Academy to rescue your Jedi brats."

Luke paused to consider. A meeting with Brakiss? Maybe this was the answer to the problem he had been trying to solve. After all, who was more central to this battle than the leader of the Shadow Academy himself? If Luke could reason with Brakiss, turn him away from the dark side, this battle could be won before too many lives were lost.

"Where, Brakiss? What neutral territory do you propose?"

"I think both your academy and mine are out of the question right now."

"Agreed."

"Away from the fighting, then. Across the river in the Temple of the Blue Leaf Cluster. But you must come alone."

"Will *you?*" Luke asked.

Brakiss gave a rich chuckle. "Of course. I have no need for reinforcements—and I know you are true to your word."

Luke paused to reassure himself that the Force was indeed guiding his actions. Both he and Brakiss were strong enough in the Force to sense any betrayal by the other.

"Very well, Brakiss. I'll meet you there. Alone. We can settle this once and for all."

11

"HEY, THAT WASN'T so hard," Jacen said, leaning forward in the copilot's chair of the *Lightning Rod*. The chair creaked, its padding bulging out through countless small rips and tears in the cushion. The engines rumbled and coughed and whined as the cargo shuttle finally broke free of the atmosphere.

"You had to say that, didn't you, boy?" Peckhum said as sensor alarms squealed on his control panel. Incoming enemy ships. Again. "We got TIE fighters coming, four of 'em. Looks like they were launched directly from the Shadow Academy."

Jacen swallowed, studying the pattern, and shook his head. "Oh, blaster bolts! We'd better transmit our distress message now before they get us. Otherwise help for the Jedi academy will come too late."

Peckhum looked over at him, his eyes red-rimmed, his haggard face serious. "You'll have to take care of that message yourself, Jacen. I'm gonna be mighty busy doing some fancy flying here—if she'll hold together." He patted the cockpit controls. "Sorry to do this to you, girl, but I didn't name you the *Lightning Rod* for nothing. Let's show these Imperials our stuff."

Jacen fumbled with the unfamiliar comm system, tuning frequencies and feeling completely inadequate. He wished his sister were here—*she* was the expert on these systems. She would know how to cut through the double-talk, the chatter, the Imperial transmission block.

He sent a subspace message blaring on all frequencies at the maximum levels of volume and power the *Lightning Rod* could spare and still keep her shields up.

"This is Jacen Solo," he said, then cleared his throat. He had no idea what to say, but he supposed the details didn't exactly matter. "Attention, New Republic. We have an emergency! This is Jacen Solo on Yavin 4, requesting immediate assistance. We are under attack by the Shadow Academy!"

"Repeat. Imperial fighters attacking the Jedi academy—request assistance immediately. Our shields are down. We've got ground battles taking place and air strikes from TIE fighters. We desperately need immediate assistance." He switched off the microphone, then looked over at Peckhum. "Hey, how'd I do?"

"Just fine, kid," Peckhum said, and lurched the ship to one side, going into a clockwise spin as the four TIE fighters roared past, belching fire from laser cannons. One shot struck the *Lightning Rod*'s lower shield, but the other bolts streamed harmlessly into space, intersecting the empty void where the cargo ship had been only a moment before.

"I used to be a pretty good flier in my day," Peckhum said. "And I still am . . . I think."

One TIE fighter broke away from the other three and spun in a tighter circle, firing repeatedly without taking the trouble to aim, spraying space with its deadly fire.

Peckhum dove down, skimming the atmosphere, so that the lower hull of the *Lightning Rod* grew hot. Then he bounced back into space again, turning about in a tight backward loop and heading up over the determined TIE fighter, which shot again and again. Sparks flew from the battered supply ship's control panels. Lights winked red on their system diagnostics.

"Uh, Peckhum? What do all those alarms mean?" Jacen said.

"It means our shields are failing."

"Don't you have any *weapons* on this ship?" Jacen scanned the panels, looking for any sort of targeting system, some firing controls.

Peckhum coughed and put the ship into a sharp dive toward Yavin 4. "This is a cargo ship, boy, and she's seen better days. I wasn't expecting to take her into battle, you know. Heck, I'm lucky the food-prep units still work."

The rest of the Imperial squadron zoomed away to continue the attack on the Jedi academy, but the one persistent TIE fighter came in again single-mindedly. This time he had them locked on target, so that most of his laser cannon blasts struck the *Lightning Rod*.

"This guy really wants to take us out," Jacen said.

Peckhum pushed his accelerators well beyond maximum safety levels. The *Lightning Rod* groaned and creaked as it rattled down through the atmosphere, buffeted by air turbulence.

Jacen was thrown from side to side. He grabbed the comm system again. "This is Jacen Solo with a personal distress this time. We are in deep trouble. Someone is on our tail. Request assistance. Please—can anyone out there help us?"

Peckhum looked over at him. "Nobody's going to get here in time."

Jacen remembered stories of how Luke Skywalker had been in a similar situation on the run down the Death Star trench, trying to send his proton torpedo through a small thermal exhaust port. His X-wing had been in Darth Vader's sights, unable to shake the TIE fighters and interceptors on his tail. Things had looked hopeless—and then Jacen's father, Han Solo, had appeared out of nowhere, saving the day.

But Jacen didn't think his father was anywhere close by now, and he couldn't imagine anyone else who might pop unexpectedly out of the skies to take care of the enemy. That was too much luck to hope for.

With a crackle of static over the comm system, a gruff and gloating voice spoke—but it wasn't any rescuer. "Well . . . Jacen Solo! You're one of those feisty Jedi brats we ran into down in the lower levels of Coruscant. Remember me—Norys? I was the leader of the Lost Ones gang. You stole that hawk-bat egg from us . . . and now I think we're about to even all the old scores. Hah!"

Jacen felt a shiver go down his spine as he remembered the broad-shouldered bully who had such an appetite for destruction. Norys continued.

"The little trash collector, Zekk, joined us in the Second Imperium, but *you* have made the wrong choice, boy. I just wanted you to know who was going to blast you to slag." The TIE pilot signed off, and continued the conversation with a volley of laser bolts.

"Well, I'm glad he picked such a fine time to contact us," Peckhum said, fighting with the controls, unable to fly an evasive pattern anymore. He worked with all his talent just to keep the *Lightning Rod* from falling apart in the sky. "I don't think we'll last much longer, and I'm sure that Norys kid would have hated to blow us up before he got a chance to say his little goodbye."

The engines of the *Lightning Rod* began to smoke. More alarms blared from the control panels. Behind them Norys's TIE fighter continued to fire mercilessly, pounding their hull, trying to crack open the battered cargo ship.

Jacen stared at the comm unit, but didn't think it would do any good to send out another distress signal.

The jungle treetops rushed by beneath them. Jacen looked wildly from side to side. "I don't suppose it would be a good time to tell a joke," he said.

Peckhum shook his head. "Don't feel much like laughing right now."

12

THE THICK BRANCHES of the damp and shadowy jungle closed around him, pressing in. It reminded Zekk of the murky lower levels of Coruscant. It felt almost like home.

He and his troops of Dark Jedi had fallen from the skies, buoyed by repulsorpacks. After coming to rest in the upper branches, they'd worked their way down to ground level and spread out to surround the fleeing Jedi trainees Master Skywalker had brainwashed into supporting Rebel philosophies.

Zekk knew little about politics. He understood only who his friends and supporters were—and who had betrayed him. Like Jacen and Jaina . . . especially Jaina. He had thought she was his friend, a close companion. Only later, after Brakiss had explained it, did Zekk understand what Jaina really thought of him, how easily she dismissed his Jedi potential and the possibility that he might be an equal to her and her high-born twin brother. But Zekk *did* have the potential, and he had proved it.

In spite of this, he hoped Jacen and Jaina would not fight him, because then he would have to demonstrate his power—and his loyalty to the Second Imperium. He remembered his first test against Tamith Kai's prize student Vilas, and Vilas had paid with his life.

In the upper branches of a tree overhead, one Dark Jedi fighter had become tangled. Zekk watched as the bright arc of a lightsaber blade slashed boughs out of the way, clearing a path for the fighter to descend to the lower levels.

Overhead a wing of TIE fighters roared across the skies, firing into the forest. The Dark Jedi spread out, looking for potential victims on their own. Zekk gathered three of the nearest fighters to his side and they marched along, crashing through the underbrush.

They reached the edge of the wide river, whose brown-green currents lapped quietly through the jungle, stirring overhanging fronds.

JEDI UNDER SIEGE

Farther downstream, closer to the tall Massassi temple ruins, he saw Tamith Kai's hovering battle platform.

Zekk stood beside his Dark Jedi companions on the riverbank. The other fighters exchanged glances and pointed skyward. Zekk nodded, knowing what they wished to do. "Yes," he said. "Let us conjure a storm, a great wind to knock the jungle flat and send these Jedi cowards scurrying."

He looked up into the clear blue skies and reached deep within his heart, finding a shadow of anger, the pain he had felt in his life. He knew how to use anger as a tool, a weapon. Zekk gathered the winds. Beside him, he felt the other dark-side warriors doing the same, drawing thunderheads until lumpy black clouds rolled in from the horizon.

The wind picked up and grew colder, charged with static electricity. Zekk's scarlet-lined cape rippled around him. Stray strands of his dark hair whipped around his face as the wind snatched them free of his ponytail. Flashing bolts of lightning skittered from one thunderhead to another. The rumble of noise drowned out even the sound of TIE fighters crisscrossing overhead.

Zekk smiled. Yes, a storm was coming, a victorious storm.

But as the clouds continued to swell, releasing a powerful weather energy, he heard sounds of repeated laser cannon fire and glanced to the sky, where another battle was taking place: a one-sided dogfight. A smoking ship careened overhead, pursued by a lone TIE fighter that shot its energy bolts again and again, mercilessly pummeling its prey.

Astonished, Zekk recognized the clunky patchwork form of the *Lightning Rod,* the cargo ship of his old friend Peckhum, the man with whom he had lived for many years.

Peckhum! They had been close companions, good friends despite how little they had in common. Too late, he remembered that the old spacer earned extra credits by making occasional supply runs to Skywalker's Jedi academy. Could it be that his old friend had been here on the jungle moon when this morning's attack began?

His heart sank, and a wrenching dismay filled his stomach. His concentration on the storm faltered.

In the backlash, winds whipped the trees closer to him, blowing back branches as the other Dark Jedi struggled to retain control of the gusting squall.

"No, Peckhum," Zekk said, looking up as he watched the TIE fighter blasting the hapless *Lightning Rod.* A small explosion flared on its hull, and Zekk knew that the battered supply ship had just lost its shields.

The *Lightning Rod* was going down—and there was nothing he could do about it.

He heard shouts of surprise next to him as the Dark Jedi Knights completely lost control of the gathering storm. The winds continued to snap branches and uproot saplings, then gradually dissipated as the dark-side warriors stopped manipulating the weather.

Their attention had been drawn to a young Jedi trainee they discovered in the underbrush—someone who had either been creeping up on them or simply hiding from Zekk's advance.

The boy scrambled out of the weeks, spiky pale hair blowing around his flushed face. His clothes and robes were so ridiculously garish—bright purples and golds and greens and reds—that they hurt Zekk's eyes. How could this young man have thought to hide while dressed like that?

The boy appeared frightened, but determined. He thrust his lower lip out and stood with his hands on his hips, his rainbow-colored robes rippling around him in the last vestiges of the angry wind.

"Very well, you give me no choice," the boy said, then cleared his throat. "I am Raynar, Jedi Knight . . . uh, in training. You will either surrender now—or force me to attack you."

Two of Zekk's companions laughed in wholehearted amusement, ignited their lightsabers, and stalked toward the trapped young man. Raynar stepped backward until he bumped against the rough trunk of a tree. He squeezed his eyes shut, struggling to concentrate. He held his breath until his face turned bright red, then purplish.

Zekk felt a slight invisible push as the boy attempted to use the Force to drive them back. The two lightsaber-bearing Dark Jedi seemed not even to notice.

Zekk found, though, that he had no stomach for outright slaughter. This boy seemed proud and brash, but there was something about him—an innocence . . .

Thinking quickly, before his two companions could drive in and make short work of Raynar, Zekk reached out with the Force, grabbed the boy by his bright robes, and yanked him off his feet. With a flick of his mind, he hurled Raynar over the heads of his companions, tossing him out into the river. Raynar yowled as he flew, then plunged belly-first into the thin, muddy waters.

The two Dark Jedi whirled, looking angrily at Zekk. Out in the water, Raynar splashed to the shallows, completely soaked in mud, his robes covered with river slime.

"It is a greater victory to utterly humiliate your enemy than simply

JEDI UNDER SIEGE

to kill him," Zekk said. "And we have humiliated this Jedi in a way he will never forget."

The dark warriors next to him chuckled at the observation, and Zekk knew he had defused their anger . . . for the moment, at least.

Then he looked longingly into the sky, hoping to spot any trace of the *Lightning Rod,* but he saw only a dissipating cloud of smoke overhead. He wished he could find some way to help his friend; would he be forced to count the loss of Peckhum as part of the cost of victory?

The wounded ship had passed out of sight to where the battle would reach its foregone conclusion. He was certain he would never see the *Lightning Rod* or Peckhum again.

13

QORL'S TIE FIGHTER flew low over the jungle, mapping out targets for the assault squadron. The rest of his fighter wing had their own orders, and they flew in their own attack patterns.

He doubted, though, that his student Norys would bother to follow orders once the battles actually started and laser shots began to fly. The bully would blunder from target to target like a mad gundark, likely to cause as much damage to the Imperial plans as he did to the Rebels.

Qorl felt cold inside, liquid dismay hardening to ice. He had expected to be exhilarated by flying and fighting again, piloting his own TIE fighter in battle for the Second Imperium.

Instead, he had only reservations and second thoughts. He dreaded the possibility that he had made a bad decision, and that the Second Imperium might have to pay the price.

Norys continued to be a great disappointment. When Qorl had selected the tough young man, he knew the bully's personality had hardened during years of harsh living, though he had lorded over the Lost Ones on Coruscant. The broad-shouldered boy had been dedicated, vowing to become an Imperial soldier because it gave him a feeling of power and confidence—exactly what the Second Imperium needed.

However, a loyal soldier was also required to obey orders. A servant of the Empire couldn't be a loose cannon, following his own wishes rather than the commands of his superiors. As he'd grown accustomed to his situation, Norys had become increasingly disrespectful, even insubordinate.

The bully was truly bloodthirsty, wanting simply to dominate, to cause pain, to achieve utter victory. He did not fight for the glory of the Second Imperium, or for bringing back the New Order—or for any sort of political goal. He fought simply to *fight*. And that was a deadly attitude, no matter which side he fought for.

JEDI UNDER SIEGE

Qorl circled, zeroing in on a raging forest fire that had been started by one of the TIE bombers, then streaked along the river to where Tamith Kai's battle platform hovered over the trees. Over his cockpit communication channel, Qorl heard a loud, desperate transmission on all bands—and recognized the voice.

"Attention, New Republic. We have an emergency! This is Jacen Solo on Yavin 4, requesting immediate assistance. We are under attack by the Shadow Academy!"

Qorl sat up, adjusted his black helmet, and flew steadily. He remembered the young twins who had helped fix his TIE fighter, the brother and sister who had been his prisoners around the campfire in the depths of the jungle. They had offered him friendship . . . and tried to turn him from his loyalty to the Second Imperium. But he had been indoctrinated too well.

Surrender is betrayal.

So Qorl had escaped and made his way to the Shadow Academy, where he had watched as the twins were brought in to be trained under the murderous tutelage of Tamith Kai and Brakiss. Qorl had been deeply disturbed by the violence of their instruction, the disregard for the lives of the fresh students.

No one had ever found out that Qorl had discreetly assisted the young friends in their escape as they fled the Shadow Academy. After that Qorl had privately done everything he could to atone for the indiscretion, making his raid on the Rebel convoy to steal hyperdrive cores and turbolaser batteries, then working hard to train Norys and the other new stormtroopers.

A smoking ship streaked overhead: a blaster-scarred and battered cargo transport. Qorl recognized the model of the ship, an unarmed carrier vessel of an old design. Its engines were sluggish, its shields not designed or reinforced for combat.

And now he saw that it was being pursued by a relentless TIE fighter.

Qorl was ashamed to see the TIE pilot waste shot after shot, although sheer luck allowed some of the laser bolts to strike the hull. It would be only a matter of time before the cargo ship exploded in midair.

Qorl tuned his cockpit comm systems to a direct channel with the other TIE fighter. "TIE pilot, identify yourself."

The gruff voice that responded came as no surprise to Qorl. "This is Norys, old man. Don't bother me—I've got a target in my sights."

He swallowed, but his throat remained dry. "Norys, you have already crippled the target. That cargo ship is not our main objective.

Your orders are to disable the Jedi academy. That ship won't be causing any more trouble for the Second Imperium."

"Leave off, old man," Norys said. "This is *my* kill, and I'm gonna score it."

Qorl tried to keep his anger in check. "We don't keep score, Norys. This assault is for the Second Imperium—not for your personal glory."

"Go stick your head up an exhaust tube," Norys said. "I'm not letting an old coward tell me what to do." Then the bully switched off his comm system and plunged after the burning cargo ship, firing with absolute abandon.

Qorl's disappointment turned to outrage. This young man's attitude flew in the face of everything admirable about the Empire. Qorl remembered his earlier TIE fighter training, how he and his fellow pilots had all worked together like a machine, precise well mannered, respectful, listening to orders—promoting the orderly lifestyle the Emperor had brought to the galaxy. *That* was worth fighting for.

But Norys did not represent such a philosophy. He didn't care.

The broadband comm signal came across his speakers again. "This is Jacen Solo with a personal distress this time. We are in deep trouble. Someone is on our tail. Request assistance. Please—can anyone out there help us?"

Qorl flew beneath the aerial dogfight just above the treetops, anguished inside. Jacen Solo was an honorable opponent. The boy had a strong heart, though he had fallen in with the Rebel band instead of the Second Imperium. But could the boy be blamed? After all, his mother was the Chief of State of the Rebel government.

Norys, however, *did* have a choice. The broad-shouldered boy knew what he had been trained for. He had adopted his Imperial uniform and his ship willingly . . . yet now he refused to play by the rules. Norys was no better than a ruthless, murderous bully.

The pursuing TIE fighter continued to fly in the slipstream of the crippled cargo vessel. Black smoke curled up from her engine pods, and Qorl observed the precise moment at which the shields failed.

Norys fired again, staining the hull with a slash of black blisters.

Qorl flicked on his own laser cannons and activated the targeting systems. The *Lightning Rod* would explode in a matter of seconds under Norys's continued assault. If it did, Qorl wouldn't be surprised if the bully continued to shoot the burning wreckage to make sure there were no survivors.

Disgust welled up within him. Switching off his comm system, he muttered, "Do I lose any honor by destroying someone who has no honor of his own?"

Qorl had studied every subsystem on the Imperial TIE fighters. He knew their weak points. Qorl knew how to destroy them.

He targeted Norys's reactor exhausts.

Ignoring his teacher entirely, Norys fired again. His lasers had fallen into a slower repeating rhythm now, as if he savored these last few moments.

The *Lightning Rod* lurched, in one last helpless attempt to dodge the laser fire.

Qorl closed in on Norys's ship.

And fired.

Norys's TIE fighter exploded in the air, annihilated so quickly and completely that the young bully didn't even have time to cry out in surprise.

Ashamed that his act had been a betrayal of the Second Imperium, Qorl made no attempt to contact the *Lightning Rod*. He simply changed course and swerved back toward the main battlefield, while the faltering *Lightning Rod* struggled to remain aloft . . . or at least to land without crashing too badly.

14

WHILE BATTLES RAGED above the Jedi academy and in the jungle around it, Imperial commando Orvak crept forward, intent on his mission.

He had left his TIE fighter behind in the wake of the explosions at the shield generator facility, but he would come back to it once he had finished here. For hours now, he had made his way secretly through the thick forest.

Several trees burned in the jungle nearby, sending up coils of putrid smoke from the wet vegetation. He heard blaster fire and shouts, the distant hum of lightsabers. He kept low and quiet, not willing to risk giving away his position.

Skywalker's Jedi had abandoned their Great Temple to engage in scattered skirmishes in the forests . . . leaving it open and unprotected for him to do his work.

Approaching the ancient edifice, still hidden by the jungle, Orvak saw black streaks on the thick stone—blaster scoring and scars from proton explosives dropped by TIE bombers. The ubiquitous vines that clung to the pyramid's sides had withered under the fire and fallen away in heaps. One close explosion had wrecked the temple's hangar bay door, preventing Skywalker's fleet of guardian ships from launching.

So, Orvak thought, after all these millennia, this ancient structure had finally been damaged. But it wasn't damaged enough. He would take care of the rest.

Moving carefully, ducking his helmeted head, he crept through the foliage, ripping up vines and uprooting ferns to clear the way until he finally emerged from the underbrush and stood behind the tall temple.

Above, TIE fighters streaked like birds of prey across the sky; Orvak looked up, silently urging them on.

To one side of the pyramid he saw a newly laid flagstone courtyard.

JEDI UNDER SIEGE

Across it, at the base of the stone structure, a darkened entrance stood open. Imagining what sort of fearful sorcerous exercises the Jedi students performed there, he stepped cautiously into the courtyard.

Already weeds had begun to push up between the flagstones. The jungle would no doubt reclaim its own within a matter of months after he destroyed the temple—and it would be good riddance to this place, he thought. By then he hoped either to be back on the Shadow Academy or perhaps promoted to officer rank on a Star Destroyer . . . if his mission today turned out well enough.

When the fighting became particularly loud, and proton bombs exploded in the jungle not far away, Orvak made his move. He rushed across the heavy flagstones to the dim doorway that led into the Rebels' secret temple.

He paused at the threshold for a moment, glad for his helmet in case poisonous vapors might seep out from the interior. Who knew what booby traps the Jedi sorcerers might have laid?

He used the sensors in his helmet to check for traps, but found none . . . which wasn't surprising, since the Shadow Academy's attack had been completely unexpected; the Jedi Knights had not had time to prepare.

Orvak entered the Massassi temple, shouldering his pack. He raced down the corridors, unfamiliar with the layout of the pyramid. He saw living quarters, large dining halls . . . nothing of significance that he could destroy.

He made his way down to the rubble-sealed hangar bay, where he thought he could plant his detonators to best effect and blow up all the Rebel starfighters. But when he emerged from the turbolift, he squinted in the dim lighting, unable to believe what he saw. Orvak found only a single, sleek-looking ship, all curves and angles. Nothing more. No fleet of spacecraft, no major defenses. He snorted in disbelief.

Suddenly, alarms squealed out from the hangar bay. Flashing red lights stabbed at his eyes. A small barrel-shaped droid hurtled toward him, whistling and screeching. Blue electric bolts sparked from a welding arm that protruded from its cylindrical torso.

Orvak slammed himself back into the turbolift, punching the controls to seal the doors. Could the Jedi have installed a force of assassin droids? Lethal, weapon-wielding machines that would never, *ever* miss?

But as the doors sealed shut and the turbolift whisked him upward, his last glimpse showed him that the attacker was simply a lone astromech droid trundling across the floor, sounding the standard alarms installed in its base. Apparently, however, no one remained in the temple to hear them.

He chuckled nervously. One astromech droid! It annoyed him when mere machines held too great a sense of their own importance. He no longer feared a trap.

Orvak had to find a different place for his purposes anyway. Someplace more special.

He finally located it on the highest level of the great pyramid.

Taking the turbolift to the top, and holding his blaster ready to shoot anyone who came out of the shadows, the Imperial commando stepped into the grand audience chamber.

Here, the walls were polished and inlaid with multicolored stones. At one end rose a great stage, from which Orvak could imagine the Rebels gave lectures to their students, handed medals to each other after victories in the war against the rightful rulers of the galaxy, perhaps even performed their disgusting rituals.

Yes, he thought. Perfect.

Moving quickly, heart pounding with the thrill of accomplishing the mission that had already cost the life of his companion Dareb, Orvak unslung his pack. He pulled off his black helmet to see better in the light that filtered through the temple skylights.

Smoke blackened the sky outside, like burnt paint brushed across the air. Distant sounds of the continuing attack echoed like ricochets inside the audience chamber. But he heard no one else nearby, no movement. The temple was empty, and he had the time to work.

Orvak strode up to the stage, his boots thumping on the stone floor. Yes, that would be the best place, a central location where the incredible blast could reflect from all sides. He yanked off his heavy gloves so that he could tinker with the fine electronic components.

Working cautiously, he removed his seven remaining high-powered detonators and linked them together. Then, he plugged all of the explosives into a central countdown timer and spread them out like the spokes of a wheel in the grand audience chamber.

Yes, it would be a fine explosion.

Ideally, when all the detonators went off simultaneously, the explosion would rip off the top of the temple like a volcano erupting. The shock wave would punch through the floor to the levels below and blast the walls outward. The entire pyramid would come tumbling down, no more than a pile of ancient rubble—as it deserved to be.

Orvak returned to the central unit and fiddled with the controls, kneeling on the polished surface of the stage. He thought with smug satisfaction that no more Rebels would ever lecture here. No future Jedi Knights would learn Rebel ways. This room would hold no more victory celebrations.

Soon it would all be gone.

Kneeling on the ground, Orvak keyed in the initiating code. All around the chamber, detonator lights winked green, ready to go, waiting for him to send the final command. Surveying his handiwork, he smiled and pressed the ACTIVATE button. The timer began to count down. Not much time left for the Jedi academy.

As he moved, resting his hand on the floor, Orvak caught a glimmer of motion out of the corner of his eye . . . something glittering and translucent, almost transparent; it had caught a reflection of the light somehow.

He pulled out his blaster, remaining in a protective crouch. "Who's there?" he called.

Then he saw it again, an iridescent sinuous shape slithering toward him across the stage. He lost sight of it once more.

Orvak fired his blaster, gouging holes in the floor around him. Streaks of energy bolts ricocheted around him. He flattened himself on the stage, afraid of return fire. He couldn't see the shimmering invisible thing anymore, and wondered what it could have been. Some sorcerer's trick, no doubt. He shouldn't have dropped his guard, but the Jedi would never get him.

Just then, Orvak felt needles of pain sting his hand. He looked down to see tiny droplets of blood welling from two punctures in his palm—and the triangle head of some kind of viper, a glassy crystalline snake!

"Hey!" he shouted.

Before he could lash out at it, the crystal snake dropped away from him and slithered toward a narrow crack in the wall. Orvak saw a last spangle of light, and then the serpent disappeared. . . .

But by now he was beyond caring, because a warm fog of sleepiness had begun to steal over him. The pain from the snakebite in his hand dulled to a throb, and Orvak thought drowsily that a long sleep could only make it better.

He collapsed into a deep slumber right beside the countdown timer.

The numbers ticked inexorably downward.

15

TENEL KA STOOD at the edge of the Imperial battle platform, her muscles tense, her body and reflexes ready to react.

She coiled her fibercord before returning it and the grappling hook to her belt. Then, with her single muscular arm, she held up her rancor-tooth lightsaber and ignited it. Beside her towered Lowbacca, ginger fur standing on end, dark lips peeled back to reveal fangs. The Wookiee used both hands to grip his clublike lightsaber with its molten bronze blade.

Surprised to see unexpected enemies, stormtroopers on the battle platform marched forward with blasters drawn, confident of their victory.

Em Teedee wailed. "Oh dear, Master Lowbacca—perhaps we should have planned this attack a bit more thoroughly."

Lowie snarled, but Tenel Ka stood tall, her confidence unshaken. "The Force is with us," she said. "This is a fact."

A single TIE bomber swooped overhead, dropping proton torpedoes into the forests. The sounds of blaster fire ricocheted around them.

On the raised command deck of the battle platform, the Nightsister Tamith Kai stood in her black cloak like a preening bird of prey. She turned, her midnight hair writhing around her head with static electricity, her wine-dark lips curled in a sneer. Tenel Ka and Lowie took three brave steps toward the waiting stormtroopers.

One of the white-armored soldiers, apparently nervous at seeing the two young Jedi Knights, fired his blaster—and Tenel Ka whipped her energy blade across to intersect the incoming energy bolt, deflecting it into the sky.

Then, by unspoken agreement, she and Lowie charged forward, yelling. They slashed with their lightsabers so furiously that though the stormtroopers sent out a volley of blaster fire, they were thrown into chaos. Lowie and Tenel Ka forced their way through them like a whirlwind.

On the command deck above, Tamith Kai strode forward to gaze down at the skirmish. "The girl is mine. I'll crush her heart myself," she said.

Tenel Ka slashed once more with her lightsaber, taking out another charging stormtrooper. She turned. Her heart thudded, but her breath came slow and even. Her muscles sang. She was prepared for this fight, sure of her physical abilities. This would be her best battle ever.

"That leaves all the other stormtroopers for you, Lowie," she said, springing up onto the command deck to meet her nemesis.

The young Wookiee roared his readiness, though Em Teedee did not sound quite as courageous. "Please be cautious, Master Lowbacca. It wouldn't be wise to get delusions of grandeur."

The stormtroopers pressed forward, fifteen against one gangly young Wookiee. Lowbacca didn't seem to think the odds were too bad.

Tenel Ka stood before the Nightsister, holding herself tall and proud, her turquoise lightsaber in front of her. She remembered the first time she had taken the evil woman by surprise and nearly crippled her. "So, how is your knee, Tamith Kai?"

The Nightsister's violet eyes flashed, and she shook her head mockingly. "Why not surrender now, weakling girl?" she said. "This is hardly a worthwhile test of my abilities. Ha! A one-armed child who dares to think she can be a threat to me."

"You talk too much," Tenel Ka said. "Or do you intend to use your foul breath as a weapon against me?"

"You have been around those twin Jedi brats too long," Tamith Kai said. "You've learned disrespect for your superiors." The Nightsister jabbed the air with her fingers and sent a bolt of blue-black lightning toward the warrior girl from Dathomir.

"I see no one here who is my superior," Tenel Ka said, intercepting the lightning bolts with her lightsaber blade. Then she used the Force to build her own positive thoughts and feelings, which she pulled around her like a shield. The Nightsister retreated a step, taken aback.

Down one level, Lowbacca slashed with his bronze lightsaber in one hand while picking up a white-armored figure with his other. He tossed the stormtrooper into three other attackers, knocking them all down. The Imperial soldiers were crowded too closely together to use their blasters. They seemed intent on taking down the angry Wookiee through the sheer force of their own numbers.

It was a big mistake.

Up on the command deck the Nightsister circled, eyeing her young quarry with amusement. Tenel Ka held her lightsaber steady, locking her granite-gray eyes on the violet irises of her opponent.

Overhead, TIE bombers swooped down, though the pilots seemed more interested in the duel on the battle platform than in their bombing runs.

The Nightsister curled her hands, and a ball of blue lightning crackled in each palm, gathering strength. Tenel Ka knew she had to use the Nightsister's moment of concentration for a quick surprise.

Tamith Kai stood near the edge of the upper command deck as Lowie and the stormtroopers continued to battle one level below her. The Nightsister raised her hands. Evil fire crackled at her fingertips, waiting to be released.

Tenel Ka feinted with her lightsaber and then, completely without warning, used the Force to reach forward like an outstretched hand. She nudged the Nightsister, pushing her just enough that she stumbled over the edge. With a wild shriek, Tamith Kai toppled backward. Bolts of blue lightning sprayed harmlessly into the sky and barely missed a heavily armored TIE bomber that swooped overhead.

The Nightsister crashed among the stormtroopers and Lowbacca, who snarled at her. Stormtroopers rushed the Wookiee, trying to drag him down, but Tamith Kai blindly released her anger, blasting them all away from her.

From the command deck Tenel Ka looked up toward the loud sound of an approaching engine—and saw a TIE bomber cruising in low, targeting its laser cannons on *her!* Brilliant shots streaked out, melting holes in the deck plating at her feet.

The warrior girl danced from one side to the other, using her attunement with the Force to second-guess where the bolts would strike. The high-powered weapons were too strong for her to deflect with a mere lightsaber. She stood all alone, unprotected—an easy target.

Grimly, she made up her mind. As the Imperial fighter roared overhead, Tenel Ka locked her lightsaber blade on, then carefully estimated the proper trajectory. Underhanded, she hurled her rancor-tooth weapon up at the craft.

She had spent a great deal of time practicing her aim, throwing spears and knives, striking her chosen target every time. But here the timing was rushed and the distance greater. Still, she never doubted her ability.

JEDI UNDER SIEGE

The TIE bomber arched upward, gaining altitude as it curved around for a final attack run.

Her lightsaber cartwheeled through the air and, with a blazing turquoise flash, struck the side of the TIE bomber. It did not slice off one of the power-array panels as she had hoped. Instead, the energy blade sheared off a stabilizer device and ripped open a hole in the bomber's hull. Her lightsaber passed completely through, then plunged downward into the jungle thickness below near the edge of the river.

Unable to articulate words, the Nightsister lunged back onto the command deck with a yowl of vengeful rage. Her black cape flapped like the wings of a raven swooping in for the kill. Tamith Kai's eyes blazed with violet fury.

Seeing the one-armed girl standing all alone without so much as a lightsaber, the Nightsister began to laugh. Her deep, guttural chuckle was filled with derision. "And now you are dis*armed*," Tamith Kai sneered, looking at the stump of Tenel Ka's arm. "You waste my time, child. Why don't you save us both some trouble and just lie down and die?"

Tenel Ka glared at the Nightsister coldly and moved a step forward, showing no sign of hesitation. "I may be disarmed," she said, "but I am *never* without a weapon."

With that, her left foot flashed out, swept around, and caught Tamith Kai just behind her heel. At the same time, Tenel Ka slammed her palm into the center of the Nightsister's chest and pushed forward, toppling her opponent to the deck.

She heard the stormtroopers shouting in panic—then overhead came the rattling whine of a TIE bomber in trouble. Tenel Ka flicked her glance up, and reacted instantly.

The TIE bomber she had struck with her lightsaber had managed to circle back—although its rear compartment was now in flames. Entirely out of control, wobbling and careening from side to side, the desperate craft came toward the battle platform.

Tenel Ka could vaguely sense the pilot's terror. He didn't know what to do and saw the platform as his last chance, a place where he might make an emergency landing. But Tenel Ka could tell from the speed of his descent and his total lack of maneuverability that a landing was impossible.

Seeing nothing but her own rage, the Nightsister lunged with one clawed hand to grab Tenel Ka's ankle. The dark woman didn't even notice the approaching danger.

Tenel Ka could waste no time fighting with her. She snatched her booted foot free and leaped over the black-clad Nightsister, landing among the stormtroopers next to Lowie.

The stormtroopers, though, had already seen the incoming TIE bomber and scrambled to clear the deck.

"Lowbacca, we must go now," Tenel Ka said, grabbing his hairy arm.

He roared, and Em Teedee chimed in. "Indeed. I believe that is a most sensible suggestion."

She and Lowbacca hurried to the edge of the hovering platform and looked down at the sluggish river below and the overhanging jungle trees.

Up on the command deck, Tamith Kai finally realized the impending danger as the TIE bomber came in, its engines building to a sputtering roar. The Nightsister screamed for the pilots inside the battle platform to start its repulsor engines and evade the impending crash.

They would never make it.

Lowie and Tenel Ka dove overboard, hoping for a safe place to land.

Behind them, the TIE bomber crashed into the Shadow Academy's battle platform and exploded in an instant. Its entire cargo of remaining explosives detonated along with the engines, blasting a hole entirely through the immense vessel.

Armored plates flew like metallic snowflakes in all directions. A gout of fire and smoke blasted into the sky, and the cumbersome battle platform plummeted, choking and rumbling.

The mass of unrecognizable wreckage exploded several more times as it plunged into the river. . . .

16

LASER BLASTS FROM the pursuing TIE fighters spanged against Jaina's stolen Imperial ship. One blast sizzled off a corner of the hexagonal power array, sending up a shower of sparks.

She fought to maintain control as her ship began to spin. She lost power, but still her ship flashed onward, propelled by its stealth drive. The silent engines had been made for covert action—not for all-out speed. Behind her, the furious TIE fighters closed the distance.

Jaina flew a frantic evasive action, up and down, diving toward the jungle treetops and then pulling up, hoping the Imperial pilots would make a mistake—slam into a tree branch or collide with each other or something.

No such luck.

The three pursuers had reached point-blank firing range, and Jaina had to take one last gamble. Using the mental speed given to her by Jedi training, she spun the TIE fighter about like a rotating ball, up and over, so that an instant later she headed not away from them, but straight *toward* them! The distance closed in a flash. Jaina had time for only a single shot.

And she didn't waste it.

The blast from her laser cannon ripped open the bottom of one of the TIE fighters, severing its controls, breaking the cockpit's airtight seal. The pilot fell through the hole and tumbled toward the jungle.

Jaina roared between the other two TIE fighters, heading as fast as she could in the opposite direction. They wheeled about, taking longer to complete a three-hundred-sixty-degree turn in the air, but within moments they were following again in hot pursuit.

Jaina flicked her gaze across the control panels, searching for anything that might help her, some secret weapon this TIE fighter might have. She doubted she would find anything that her pursuers couldn't counter.

Then her eyes fixed on a small button: TWIN ION ENGINE SHUNT.

Suddenly she realized this would add the TIE fighter's normal engines back to the low-powered stealth drive her fighter had been using.

Without hesitation, she toggled the button off, deactivating the shunt—and with a screech of power, her TIE fighter leaped forward. The roar of acceleration slammed her back against the seat, jolting her lips into a grimace. The ship pulled forward faster than anything Jaina had ever felt.

If she could gain enough of a lead and head straight up into orbit, if she could swing around the jungle moon out of visual range, she could cut her engines for a while and drift out into black space. The stealth coating on this ship's armor would be an enormous advantage. If she could just get out of sight, she could make her ship invisible . . . and she would be safe.

Making use of the ship's acceleration, working with her hands against the increased gravity from the thundering flight, Jaina tilted upward on a straight-line course through the atmosphere, up into space.

The remaining pair of Imperial fighters streaked after her. She didn't know if her acceleration allowed her to fly much faster than the TIE's normal power, but she knew she had to gain distance and use all of her wits.

The atmosphere thinned to a deeper purple, and then the midnight blue of space. To her dismay, she saw that the remaining TIE fighters had closed the distance again, not as much as before, but to within visual range. Her plan wouldn't work—she could never dodge them and disappear against the silent blackness. Her stealth armor would be useless now.

She wondered if she should fight them head-on again. There was a chance that she could take out both Imperial ships before they shot her down . . . but she doubted it.

She was done for.

Just at that moment of despair, Jaina saw a glimmering in the blackness as new ships emerged from hyperspace—reinforcements! New Republic warships! Her heart leaped. It was a small fleet, but well armed, ready to take on the Shadow Academy. Her brother's distress signal must have gotten through.

With a whoop of delight, Jaina adjusted course and shot like a projectile straight toward the fleet of Corellian gunships and corvettes, the quickest bunch the New Republic had been able to muster for the Jedi academy.

Her stolen TIE fighter vibrated as she pushed the acceleration far beyond the red lines. She was still losing power from her damaged side array. "Come on, come on," Jaina said, biting her lip. The ship had to last only a few moments longer. Just a few moments.

The front Corellian corvette loomed closer and closer. But the enemy TIE fighters clung right behind her, still shooting.

Jaina spun and dodged until finally she came into range of the New Republic ships. They began firing huge turbolaser bolts that streaked so close to her ship that the crackling beams dazzled her eyes.

It took Jaina a moment to realize that the gunships were shooting at *her!*

She quickly understood her folly. Here she was in an Imperial ship diving toward the fleet with two more TIE fighters right behind her, laser cannons blasting. It must have looked like all three craft were on some sort of a suicide run.

She grabbed the comm system, toggled it to an open channel, and broadcast at full power. "New Republic fleet—don't shoot, don't shoot! This is Jaina Solo. I've commandeered an Imperial fighter."

More ships appeared at the side, heavily armed hodgepodge vessels bearing the insignia of GemDiver Station, Lando Calrissian's Corusca-gem processing facility that orbited the gas giant Yavin.

"Jaina Solo?" Lando's voice came over the comm system. "Little lady, what are you doing out here?"

"Turning into space dust, if you guys don't take care of the two TIE fighters on my tail!"

Admiral Ackbar's voice broke in. "We're targeting now," he said. "Do not fear, Jaina Solo."

"I'm in the *front* one," she reminded him nervously. "Don't hit the wrong TIE fighter! Well, what are you waiting for?"

A flurry of turbolaser strikes lanced out around Jaina in a pattern so dense that space became a web of deadly weapons fire. Dozens of bolts shot from the Corellian gunships and Lando Calrissian's private fleet. Within moments the two TIE fighters were vaporized, and Jaina let out a long sigh of relief.

Sending a signal from the front Corellian corvette, Admiral Ackbar guided her to the forward docking bay. "Please come aboard, Jaina Solo," he said. "We will offer you sanctuary for the time being while we combat the Shadow Academy. We believe that is the best way to protect personnel on the surface."

"Sounds good to me," Jaina said. "But as soon as it's clear, I want to get back down to fight next to my brother and friends."

"If we do our job well," Ackbar said, "there won't be much of a fight left."

After docking, Jaina climbed out of the stolen TIE fighter, perspiring heavily and glad to be free of the Imperial ship. She no longer felt a great desire to fly one of the craft. Her first experience had been exciting, but not necessarily one she wanted to repeat.

Greeting some of the New Republic soldiers, Jaina quickly ran her fingers through her long, straight brown hair and then rushed to a turbolift. When she arrived on the bridge, she stood beside Admiral Ackbar and watched the fleet attack the ominous spiked station.

New Republic warships pummeled the Dark Jedi training center in orbit over Yavin 4. The Shadow Academy's powerful shields remained up, but the constant bombardment took its toll.

Lando Calrissian's ships swooped closer, adding their weapons fire. Under the combined onslaught, the Shadow Academy would surely be destroyed before long, Jaina thought.

Ackbar sent out a transmission. "Shadow Academy, prepare to surrender and be boarded."

Jaina didn't have time to relax, though. The Shadow Academy did not bother to answer, and one of the tactical officers suddenly shouted, "Admiral Ackbar, we're detecting a surge in hyperspace, off to starboard. It appears that an entire—"

As Jaina watched the viewscreen, a group of terrifying Imperial ships appeared, Star Destroyers that looked as if they had been hastily assembled and modified. Hasty or not, their weaponry was new and lethal.

"Where did *that* fleet come from?" Lando squawked over the comm channel.

Ship after Imperial ship arrived, an entire, fully armed fighting force that owed allegiance to the Second Imperium. Before even orienting themselves, the Imperial ships opened fire on the New Republic fleet.

"Shields up!" Admiral Ackbar ordered. He turned to Jaina, his round, fishy eyes swiveling in alarm. "It appears that we may experience some difficulty after all," he said.

17

LUKE SKYWALKER ARRIVED across the river at the Massassi ruin known as the Temple of the Blue Leaf Cluster, a tower of crumbling stone blocks. He came alone, hoping to negotiate but ready to fight.

This was the site Brakiss had chosen for their meeting, their confrontation . . . their *duel,* if it came to that.

Luke listened to the jungle noises: the chatter of creatures in the underbrush, birds in the vines overhead—and explosions from Imperial fighters in the sky. He hated to be here by himself when he could be beside his students, fighting with them to defeat the forces of the dark side.

But Luke had a greater calling, a more important one—to stop the leader of these Dark Jedi, a man who had once been Luke's own student.

Branches parted in a thicket beside the carved pillars of stone. A man stepped out, moving as if he were made of flowing quicksilver, a confident liquid shadow. His perfectly formed, sculpture-handsome face smiled. "So, Luke Skywalker, once my Jedi Master—you have come to surrender to me, I hope? To bow to my superior abilities?"

Luke did not return the smile. "I came to speak with you, as you requested."

"I'm afraid speaking won't be enough," Brakiss said. "You see my Shadow Academy overhead? The battle fleet of the Second Imperium has just arrived. You have no hope of victory, despite your meager reinforcements. Join us now and stop all this bloodshed. I know the power you could wield, Skywalker, if you ever let yourself touch the powers you have neglected to learn."

Luke shook his head. "Save it, Brakiss. Your words and your darkside temptations have no effect on me," he said. "You were once *my* student. You saw the light side, saw its capabilities for good—and yet you ran from it like a coward. But it's not too late. Come with me now. Together we can explore what remains of the brightness in your heart."

"There is no brightness in my heart," Brakiss said. "I did not come here to banter with you. If you won't be sensible and surrender, then I must defeat you and take the rest of your Jedi academy by force." He withdrew a lightsaber from the silvery sleeve of his robe. Long spikes like claws surrounded the energy blade that extended as he pushed the power button. Brakiss heaved a quick sigh. "This seems like such a waste of effort."

"I don't want to fight you," Luke said.

Brakiss shrugged. "As you wish. Then I'll cut you down where you stand. That makes it easier on me." He stepped forward and swung his blade.

Luke's reflexes kicked in at the last instant, and he leaped back, using a touch of the Force to add power to his spring. He landed with legs spread, crouching, and pulled his own lightsaber from the belt at his waist. "I will defend myself, Brakiss," he said, "but there is so much you could learn here at the Jedi academy."

Brakiss laughed mockingly. "And who's going to teach me—you? I no longer recognize you as a Master, Luke Skywalker. There is so much more that you yourself don't know. You think *I'm* weak because I left here before I completed my training? Who are you to talk? You were only partially trained yourself. A short time with Obi-Wan Kenobi before Darth Vader killed him, then a brief time with Master Yoda before you left him . . . you even came close to true greatness when you went to serve the resurrected Emperor—and you backed away. You've never completed *anything*."

"I don't deny it," Luke said, holding his lightsaber in a defensive position. Their blades clashed with a sizzling sound. Brakiss's lips drew back in a grimace as he lunged again, but Luke parried his attack.

"You taught that becoming a Jedi is a voyage of self-discovery," Brakiss said. "I have continued that self-discovery since I left here. I abandoned your teachings, but I found more, *much more*. My self-discovery has been vastly greater than your own, Luke Skywalker, because you have locked many important doors to yourself." He raised his eyebrows and his eyes glinted a challenge. "*I* have looked behind those doors."

"A person who willingly steps into mortal danger is not brave," Luke said, "but foolish."

"Then you are a fool," Brakiss said. He swept his lightsaber low, intending to slice off Luke's legs at the knees—but Luke lowered his blade in turn and went on the offensive, clashing, striking, driving his opponent back. The Dark Jedi's silvery robes fluttered around him like nightwings.

"You can't win, Brakiss," Luke said.

"Watch me," the Master of the Shadow Academy said. He attacked with greater fury, opening himself up to anger so that his viciousness grew as he struck again and again.

But Luke maintained his quiet center as he defended himself. "Feel the calm, Brakiss," he said. "Let gentleness flow through you . . . peaceful, soothing."

Brakiss merely laughed. His perfect blond hair was tangled and plastered to his head with perspiration. "Skywalker, how many times will you try to turn me? Even after I fled your teachings, you pursued me. Don't you know when you have lost?"

Luke said, "I remember our confrontation at that droid manufacturing facility on Telti. You could have joined me then—you still can now."

Brakiss dismissed that with a snort. "Those events meant nothing to me, a diversion until I found my true calling—forming the Shadow Academy."

"Maybe you need to look for a truer calling," Luke said. He slashed sideways to deflect Brakiss's lightsaber again.

Now Brakiss took a different tack, whirling around. Instead of striking at Luke, he slashed one of the tall temple pillars, a cylinder of marble etched with ancient Sith symbols and Massassi writings. Sparks flew from the blow, and the lightsaber sheared the column completely through. Gravity, clinging vines, and the overhanging stone made it unstable.

Luke dove out of the way as the pillar split in two. The front lintel of the Temple of the Blue Leaf Cluster tumbled down. Stones and branches crashed from side to side, broken stone flew in all directions—but Luke danced out of the way, avoiding injury.

"You seem quite light on your feet, Skywalker," Brakiss said.

"You seem quite destructive to ancient structures," Luke said. He scrambled over the new rubble, coughed in the settling dust, then clashed again with Brakiss. "Perhaps you should check on how your Dark Jedi are doing. My students have been defeating them quite consistently."

He heard the battle continuing in the jungles and longed to get back to his trainees. The meeting with his former student had been no more than a distraction; it was leading nowhere. "This has gone on long enough, Brakiss. You may either surrender or I'll defeat you directly, because I have work to do. I need to get back to defending my Jedi academy."

Brakiss showed the faintest glimmer of uncertainty in his normally calm and peaceful eyes when Luke drove in, this time intending to win. Luke struck again with the lightsaber, always maintaining his focus and drive, not letting anger take control, doing only what he wished to do.

The Master of the Shadow Academy defended himself, and Luke saw his chance to strike. He altered his aim just slightly, not striking the energy blade itself. He could have swung lower to take off the hand of his former student, much as Darth Vader had cut off Luke's own hand—but Luke didn't want to maim Brakiss in such a way. He needed only to ruin his weapon.

His lightsaber struck across the top of Brakiss's handle, just below the terminus of the energy beam and above the knuckles of the grip. The top two centimeters of the spiked-claw end of Brakiss's lightsaber sprayed off, sheared away in a smoking, molten mass.

Brakiss shrieked and dropped his sparkling lightsaber to the ground, where it lay useless, smoldering, no longer a weapon, simply a hunk of components . . . none of which worked.

The Master of the Shadow Academy held up his hands and staggered back. "Don't kill me, Skywalker! Please don't kill me!"

The terror on Brakiss's face seemed all out of proportion to the threat. Surely the shadow Jedi knew that Luke Skywalker was not the type to strike down an unarmed enemy in cold blood. Brakiss clutched at his silvery robe, fumbling with the fastenings.

Luke strode toward him, lightsaber extended. "You are my captive now, Brakiss. It's time for us to end this battle. Order your Dark Jedi to surrender."

Brakiss let his robes fall away, revealing a jumpsuit and repulsorpack. "No. I have other business to attend to," he said, and ignited the repulsorjets.

As Luke stared in astonishment, Brakiss rocketed skyward, flying high out of reach. The Dark Jedi instructor must have landed his ship somewhere nearby, Luke realized, and he would no doubt head directly back to the Shadow Academy.

In dismay, Luke watched his fallen student escape once more—defeated, but still capable of causing further damage.

The pain of loss flooded Luke's mind, as fresh as on the day Brakiss first fled the Jedi academy. "Brakiss, I've failed to save you again," he groaned.

The other man dwindled to a small point in the sky and disappeared.

18

IN SPACE, THE Second Imperium fleet fired their weapons.

Ackbar shouted, "All personnel, battle stations!" The Calamarian admiral gestured with his flippered hands. "Shields up! Prepare to return fire!"

The two front-most modified Star Destroyers lunged forward, their turbolaser batteries blazing. Brilliant green streaks sliced out, zeroing in on Ackbar's flagship.

Jaina stood beside the Calamarian admiral and squeezed her eyes shut as the blinding flashes shattered against their forward shields. "The Second Imperium must have been building their fleet in secret," she said. "Those ships look like the construction was rushed."

"But they are still deadly," Ackbar said, nodding solemnly. "Now I know why they stole those hyperdrive cores and turbolaser batteries when they attacked the *Adamant*." He turned to his communications systems, bellowing orders in his gravelly voice. "Shift target from the Shadow Academy. That training station is a lesser threat than the new battleships. Target the Imperial Star Destroyers."

The weapons officers working at their command stations called out in alarm and dismay, "Sir, our targeting locks won't match! Those ships are broadcasting friendly ID signals. We are unable to fire."

"What?" Ackbar said. "But we can *see* the Star Destroyers."

"I know, Admiral," the tactical officer shouted. "But our computers won't fire—they think those are New Republic ships. It's built into the programming."

Suddenly understanding, Jaina exclaimed, "They stole guidance and tactical computer systems during their raid on Kashyyyk! The Imperials must have installed them in their own ships just to confuse our weapons computers. We'll have to change our targeting locks, or else we won't be able to fire. The 'Identify Friend or Foe' fail-safe systems will prevent it."

Lando Calrissian had been listening on the open channel; his voice now boomed over the comm. "Since my ships from GemDiver Station use different computers, I guess the first round is up to us."

Lando's hodgepodge group of independent ships swept in on the Star Destroyers from all sides, firing a barrage of proton torpedoes at key points to dilute the overall shield strength.

"A little trick I picked up," Lando explained over the comm unit as Jaina stood beside Ackbar watching. "This whole thing reminds me of the battle of Tanaab." Then he gave a whoop of triumph as another volley of torpedoes detonated at once, two of them penetrating the shields and leaving a white-hot chain of flames along the side of one Star Destroyer. Lando's ships kept firing and firing, but now the Imperials began targeting the smaller craft, leaving Ackbar's vessels alone.

"Admiral," Jaina said, "if the Second Imperium is so clever that they can use our own computer systems to trick us, can't we turn the tables—use *our* computers against *them*?"

Ackbar turned his enormous round eyes on her. "What do you have in mind, Jaina Solo?"

She bit her lower lip, then drew a deep breath. The idea was crazy, but . . . "You're the supreme commander of the entire New Republic fleet. Isn't it programmed into the computers that they must accept some sort of override signal from you in cases of extreme emergency—like this one?"

Ackbar stared at her, his mouth gaping as if he needed a drink of water or a long breath of moist air. "By the Force, you're right, Jaina!"

"Well, what are we waiting for?" she said, rubbing her hands together. "Let's get reprogramming."

After destroying his own student Norys to rescue Jacen Solo, Qorl's insides felt deadened, as if the rest of his body had turned into a droid . . . just like his mechanical left arm.

After all his years of training and loyalty, he had betrayed the Second Imperium. Betrayed! He had allowed his heart to decide, rather than following blind obedience and cold ambition.

But young Jacen had been kind to him, had helped rescue him, had shown him warmth and friendship, though Qorl knew he had done nothing to deserve it. . . .

He had taken the twins prisoner, threatened their lives, forced them to repair his crashed TIE fighter so he could return to the Empire. Since then he had made small, secret gestures to repay them, such as when he'd cautiously helped them to escape the Shadow Academy. But killing his own student to protect them . . .

Qorl had committed a grave mistake by making decisions on his own. He should have known better. It wasn't his place to make decisions. He was a TIE pilot, a soldier of the Second Imperium. He helped instruct other pilots and stormtroopers. His allegiance was to the Emperor and his government. Soldiers didn't have the luxury of making up their own minds about which orders to follow and which ones to ignore.

His mind in turmoil, he took his TIE fighter up toward orbit. Most of his squadron had fallen out of formation, attacked or destroyed by unknown defenses on Yavin 4. He should return and report to his superiors. He would have to decide whether to surrender or confess what he had done . . . and face Lord Brakiss's retribution.

Qorl's jaw clenched. *Surrender is betrayal.* How could he be willing to do this? His ship's engines howled as he tore free of the atmosphere and headed straight toward the looming Shadow Academy station.

He saw with astonishment that he had stumbled into the middle of an enormous space battle.

New Republic warships had appeared unexpectedly, firing and firing upon the Shadow Academy. But then came the newly arrived fleet of Second Imperium ships, cobbled-together Star Destroyers, Imperial battle cruisers assembled from leftover pieces in reclaimed shipyards. The new fleet used the computer systems, hyperdrives, and turbolaser batteries that Qorl himself had helped to acquire.

But seeing the Second Imperium's ships filled him with a sense of dismay. The new fleet lacked the grandeur and impressive presence of the original Imperial armada. Qorl had flown on the Death Star, served as part of Grand Moff Tarkin's Imperial Starfleet.

This new fighting force looked somewhat . . . desperate—as if people whose dreams stretched far beyond their resources had leaped into the fray.

Qorl saw the Second Imperium ships pounding the Rebel rescue fleet—but as he watched, the tide turned and clusters of nondescript ships attacked the Star Destroyers.

Then the Star Destroyers' defensive shields suddenly and inexplicably went down, as if their own computers had switched them off. As if they had agreed to surrender!

Rebel battle cruisers fired into the opening at full strength, ripping great gashes in the hulls of the new Star Destroyers. What was going on? Why didn't his comrades reestablish their shields?

As Qorl flew toward them, frantic to do something to help with the fight, fresh TIE fighters streamed out of the Star Destroyers and began to pound the Rebel ships, though they seemed no more than tiny gnats against Ackbar's great fleet.

Qorl suddenly saw his chance to redeem himself. He had already been a traitor to his rescuers and friends and to the Second Imperium. No matter which choice he made, he would be cursed—he would never be able to live with either betrayal.

At the moment, though, Qorl could join the fight on the side of the Second Imperium and cause whatever damage he could . . . perhaps even die fighting. He was a TIE pilot. He had trained for this. Long ago, he had flown from the Death Star on a similar mission—and now he would make everything right again.

Qorl powered up his laser cannons, weapons that had last been fired against Norys's ship to stop the bully's murderous frenzy. Qorl could now use the weapons against his assigned targets: the Rebel Alliance.

His TIE fighter stormed into the fray from out of nowhere, firing on one of the Corellian gunships, leaving black scorch marks as he strafed along its side. Other TIE fighters joined him, flying in a barely recognizable attack pattern. These fleet members were obviously untrained, having spent very little time even in simulators. But the chaos served the new pilots well as the ships flew around each other, blasting and pummeling with no set goal but to cause damage.

The Rebel fleet responded with heavy turbolaser fire, lancing out in all directions. With a blinding glare, one of the Star Destroyers blew up, its command turret in flames. Another Star Destroyer went reeling, its defenses down; it turned in an attempt to limp away. The Rebel fleet pursued, all weapons blazing.

The Second Imperium was losing. *Losing!*

Qorl shot after the fleeing ships. Some of the TIE fighters sped off into space . . . though Qorl had no idea where they intended to go. Their flagships were destroyed and the Shadow Academy was under fire. Did they intend to give up?

"Surrender is betrayal," he muttered to himself—and flew directly into the Rebel flagship's line of fire.

Turbolaser bolts shot past, but Qorl dove forward, firing his insignificant laser cannons and diving down the gullet of the beast. He would never give up. This would be his final flash of glory.

The Rebels improved their aim—and the cross fire struck him. Qorl closed his eyes behind his TIE helmet, expecting to vanish in a bright puff of flame, a candle burning for his Emperor.

But the energy weapons had only managed to clip one of his engines and damage part of his power array.

Qorl's TIE fighter spun out of control, away from the battle fleet. Even in his crash restraints, he was thrown from side to side inside his tiny cockpit. Qorl held on, expecting his ship to explode at any moment . . . all the while careening farther and farther away from the continuing space battle.

Still spinning, he saw that gravity had caught him. He was crashing again, plummeting toward the jungle moon of Yavin. . . .

19

BRAKISS RACED HIS high-speed, one-person shuttle away from Yavin 4 and streaked back toward his precious Shadow Academy. He punched the coded controls that would automatically open the launch-bay doors and provide him clear passage back into the safety of the Imperial training station.

The space battle did not concern him. It was just one other event that had gone wrong today.

His heart still pounded from his lightsaber battle with Skywalker down at the temple ruins. His thoughts spun, filled with the resonating words of his former Master. Anger and despair swirled like an uncontrollable storm through his mind, through his emotions.

Every method he knew failed to bring his thoughts back to the cold, quiet levels he required to draw on his fullest powers. Brakiss even attempted to use some of the hated calming techniques Skywalker had shown him back in his incognito student days—but nothing worked.

Everything was crumbling. His grandiose plans, his carefully trained Dark Jedi, the troops of the Second Imperium—it all faltered here on the verge of what should have been his greatest triumph, the hammer blow that would shake the galaxy. The destruction of the Jedi academy should have been a simple victory.

The Emperor would destroy Brakiss for this failure, but for now he could think only that the Emperor himself remained their last hope. Their only hope. Brakiss would accept his punishment later; for now he needed to do everything in his power to bring about a victory.

He brought his shuttle to dock in the nearly empty bay of the Shadow Academy, where not long ago rows of TIE fighters and TIE bombers had prepared for battle. Tamith Kai had launched her armored battle platform, riding down from orbit with her stormtroopers and Zekk's squad of dark warriors. They had been proud, confident, sure of crushing the light-side Jedi. . . .

Brakiss climbed stiffly out of his shuttle, straightening his silvery robes, trying unsuccessfully to regain his dignity. Not wanting to be without a Jedi blade, he armed himself from a weapons alcove in the wall with another of the mass-produced lightsabers.

But *how* could he defend himself? He had seen Tamith Kai's battle platform plunge into the river, a flaming hulk of molten slag. Zekk's Dark Jedi had been routed, the TIE fighter squadrons mostly destroyed—and now Brakiss watched the Second Imperium's powerful new fleet being trounced by Rebel battleships that had appeared out of nowhere and had somehow deactivated the Imperial shields!

Brakiss strode out of the docking bay into the near-deserted Shadow Academy. All capable troops had been sent to the surface. Only a few command teams remained here to keep the Imperial station secure.

The sterile corridors should have been hosting a victory celebration, but instead the place seemed like a tomb, an abandoned derelict. The Emperor *must* find some way to save them, Brakiss told himself, to turn the tide of battle so that the Second Imperium could rule the galaxy after all.

Palpatine had cheated death not once, but twice. After he had perished the first time aboard the second Death Star during the battle of Endor, he had managed to resurrect himself, using hidden clones to prolong his life. And though all those clones had presumably been destroyed, thirteen years later the Emperor was once again back from the dead—without an explanation this time.

Any man who accomplished such feats could surely manage to wrest victory away from a hodgepodge gang of Rebels and criminals, couldn't he?

Holding his head up, trying to summon Imperial pride and hope, Brakiss marched down the steel-plated corridors toward the isolated section of the station. He had to see the Emperor, and he would not be turned away. The fate of the entire war hung on the next few moments!

Outside the sealed doorways stood two of the four scarlet-clad Imperial guards. They wore sinister, projectile-shaped helmets with only a narrow black slit through which they could see. The two guards stiffened, crossing their force pikes to deny him entry. Brakiss strode forward without hesitating. "Move aside," he said. "I must speak with the Emperor."

"He has requested not to be disturbed," said one of the guards.

"Disturbed?" Brakiss said, appalled to hear the words. "Our fleet is going down in defeat, our Dark Jedi are being captured. Our TIE

fighters are being shot down. Tamith Kai is killed. The Emperor should *already* be disturbed. Move aside. I must speak with him."

"The Emperor speaks with no one." They moved one step forward, holding out their weapons.

Brakiss felt fresh anger boiling within. It gave him strength. The power flowing in his veins tapped directly into the dark side of the Force. He could see why the Nightsister Tamith Kai had found the experience so exhilarating that she kept herself in a constant state of pent-up fury.

Brakiss had no patience for these meddling scarlet-clad obstacles. They were traitors to the Second Imperium—and he responded, letting the Force flow from deep within him.

His lightsaber dropped out of his billowing sleeve and fell firmly into his hand. His finger depressed the power button. A long rippling blade extended out, but Brakiss did not use it as a threat. He had grown tired of threats, of word games and diversions that prevented progress. He unleashed his anger.

"I have had enough of this!" He struck wildly from side to side. His anger narrowed his vision to a tunnel of black static that surrounded his two targets as they scrambled to use their force pikes against him. But Brakiss was a powerful Jedi. He knew the ways of the dark side, and the red Imperial guards had no chance against him.

In less than a second, Brakiss had struck both of them down.

He activated the sealed door mechanism. The security pass codes argued with him, so he used the Force to blow out the circuits. With his bare hands he wrenched the stubborn door aside, then strode into the Emperor's private chambers.

"My Emperor, you must help us," he called. The light around him was red and dim, hot. He blinked, finding it difficult to see—but found no one else around. "Emperor Palpatine!" he shouted. "The battle turns against us. The Rebels are defeating our troops. You must do something."

His words echoed back at him, but he heard nothing else: no response, no movement. He pushed on into another room, only to find it filled with a black-walled isolation chamber, its armored door sealed shut, its side panels held in place with heavy burnished rivets. This was the enclosed compartment the red guards had removed from the special Imperial shuttle. Bulky worker droids had lifted the heavy container out of the shuttle's hold and carried it here.

Brakiss knew the Emperor had secluded himself inside the chamber, protected from outside influences. Brakiss had feared that the

Emperor's health was failing, that Palpatine needed this special life-support environment just to survive.

But at the moment, Brakiss didn't care. He was tired of having doors shut in front of him. He, the Master of the Shadow Academy, one of the most important members of the Second Imperium, should not be brushed aside like some civil servant.

He pounded on the armored door. "My Emperor, I demand that you see me! You cannot let this defeat continue. You must use your powers to wrest a victory from the hands of our enemies."

He received no answer. His battering noises quickly faded into the thick, blood-colored light that filled the chamber. Brakiss's heart froze into a chunk of ice, like a lost comet from the fringes of a solar system.

If the Emperor had forsaken them, they were lost already. The battle had turned against the Second Imperium—and Brakiss had nothing more to lose.

He switched on his lightsaber again, held the thrumming weapon—and struck. The energy blade sparked and flared as it cut through the thick armor plating—nothing, not even Mandalorian iron or durasteel blast shielding, could resist the onslaught of a Jedi lightsaber.

He sliced through the hinges. Molten metal steamed and ran in silvery rivulets down the side of the door. He chopped again, hacking out an entrance, tearing open the wall like a labor droid dismantling a cargo container. He stepped aside as the thick chunk of armor plate fell to the deck with a deafening clang.

Brakiss stood waiting, frozen with indecision, as the smoke cleared. He held his lightsaber up . . . and finally stepped inside.

He stared in disbelief. He saw no Emperor, no plush living quarters, not even any complicated medical apparatus to keep the old ruler alive.

Instead, he found a sham.

A third red guard sat in a complex control chair surrounded on three sides by computer monitors and controls. Brakiss saw a library display of holographic videoclips taken over the course of the Emperor's career: the rise of Senator Palpatine, the New Order, early attempts to crush the Rebellion . . . recorded speeches, memos, practically every word Palpatine had spoken in public, plus many private messages. Powerful holographic generators assembled the clips, manufacturing lifelike three-dimensional images.

Brakiss stared in horror as it began to make sense to him.

The red guard lurched to his feet, scarlet robes flowing around him. "You may not enter here."

"Where is the Emperor?" Brakiss said, but as he looked around he already knew the answer. "There *is* no Emperor, is there? This has all been a hoax, a pitiful bid for power."

"Yes," the red guard said, "and you have played your part well. The Emperor did indeed die many years ago when his last clone was destroyed, but the Second Imperium needed a leader—and we, four of Palpatine's most loyal Imperial guards, decided to create that leader.

"We had all of the brilliant speeches and recordings the Emperor had made. We had his thoughts, his policies, his records. We knew we could make the Second Imperium work, but no one would have followed *us*. We had to give the people what they wanted, and they wanted their Emperor back—as you did. You were easy to fool, because you *wanted* to be fooled," the red guard said, nodding toward Brakiss.

The Master of the Shadow Academy stepped deeper into the chamber, his lightsaber glowing with deadly, cold fire. "You tricked us," he said, still in the grip of incredulous horror. "You tricked me—*me!* I was one of the Emperor's most dedicated servants, but I served a lie. There was never any chance for the Second Imperium, and now we are being destroyed here because of *you!* Because of poor planning. Because there is no dark heart to the Second Imperium."

Blinded by rage again, Brakiss flowed forward like an avenging angel, his lightsaber held high. The red guard staggered away from his controls, reaching into his scarlet robes to withdraw a weapon—but Brakiss didn't give him the chance.

He cut down the third Imperial guard, who fell smoking and lifeless onto the array of controls that had created the fake Emperor. The illusion had cheated Brakiss, and the Shadow Academy, and all his Dark Jedi . . . everyone who had devoted their lives to recreating the Empire.

"Now the Empire has truly fallen," he said, his voice hoarse and husky, his face haggard. He was no longer calm, like a statue, no longer a well-polished representative of perfection.

Hearing a noise outside the chopped-open door to the isolation chamber, Brakiss turned to see a flash of red—the fourth and final member of the group of charlatans. Brakiss moved slowly, feeling stiffness and pain, utterly discouraged—but he could not let this last one get away. His honor demanded that the deceivers pay. Brakiss rushed after him.

But the red guard had encountered his slaughtered companions outside and knew that Brakiss had seen all the video controls and holographic apparatus in the isolation chamber. The fourth guard, without hesitation, ran back the way he had come.

Brakiss realized with utter certainty that the glorious dream of a reborn Empire had already failed. His Dark Jedi had lost their battle down on Yavin 4. The Imperial fighters were being trounced—but he would *not* let this impostor, this traitor, escape alive. It would be Brakiss's final moment of vengeance.

With purposeful steps, Brakiss charged after the man. The red guard moved with astonishing speed, fleeing the restricted area and dashing down the empty corridors of the Shadow Academy. Brakiss ran, but the red guard knew exactly where he wanted to go. Exactly.

The last surviving Imperial guard reached the docking bay and dashed toward Brakiss's still-waiting high-speed shuttle.

Arriving at the docking bay door, Brakiss shouted, "Stop!" He held his lightsaber high, wishing he could use the Force to make the guard freeze in his tracks, to follow the command—but the charlatan did not hesitate. He dove into the lone shuttle, raised it on its repulsorlifts, and punched the code to release the magnetic atmosphere containment field.

Brakiss simmered with rage. He wondered if he could get to the Shadow Academy's weapons systems and blow the guard to frozen shards in the vacuum of space. But it would be too late for him.

He felt completely alone on the Shadow Academy. An utter failure. Everything he had tried had backfired on him. And this was the final insult: tricked by a . . . *guard.*

Unbidden, a memory came to Brakiss. When the Shadow Academy had been constructed—ostensibly under the guidance of Emperor Palpatine—as a fail-safe mechanism, enormous quantities of linked explosives had been implanted through the station's structure. That way, if Palpatine ever felt threatened by these new and powerful Dark Jedi Knights, he could trigger the detonation and destroy the Shadow Academy, no matter where it was.

Brakiss stood alone in the hangar bay, watching the tiny shuttle streak farther and farther away. It occurred to him that since there *was* no reborn Emperor, then the four red guards themselves must have kept the secret destruct codes.

As the escape ship fled from the Shadow Academy and the Yavin system, the last surviving guard acknowledged to himself that the military forces he left behind would be defeated utterly. With the success of the Rebel counterattack, there would likely be no Imperial survivors of this day's battles.

The guard had to preserve his secret and maintain the illusion that he and his partners had so carefully constructed as a way to restore themselves to power. He could not afford to leave the Shadow Academy intact if he hoped to cover his tracks. With luck, he might find a position among the many criminal elements insidiously working at the fringes of the New Republic.

The red guard sent a brief signal, carefully coded. He transmitted a dreaded phrase, a string of impulses, that he had hoped never to use.

Destruct.

As his tiny shuttle careened into hyperspace, the spiked ring of the Shadow Academy flowered into a fireball, an exploding blossom of flaming gases and debris.

20

AS HE PLODDED ahead, Zekk could barely see two meters in front of himself in the murk of Yavin 4's unfamiliar jungle. Dense underbrush tore at his hair and cape, and his breath came in ragged gasps. His ponytail had come entirely undone. Still Zekk pushed on. Occasionally he glanced back over his shoulder to see if any of Skywalker's Jedi trainees were pursuing him. He sensed no one following, but he couldn't be sure. Who knows? he thought. They might have light-side tricks he had never heard of, ways to keep him from sensing their presence.

He had seen many unexpected things today. Strange things. *Horrible* things. It hardly mattered that the winding path ahead was uncertain and difficult to see: he would have been blind to it anyway. His mind was partially numbed by the sights his eyes had witnessed today. Destruction, terror, failure . . . death.

Zekk's foot slipped on a patch of moldy, damp leaves, and he went down on one knee. Grabbing a low branch, he pulled himself back to his feet, then stood disoriented for a moment.

Which direction had he been heading? He knew he was going *toward* something . . . but he couldn't quite remember what. Finally some unconscious part of him remembered, and he set off again.

Suddenly, just ahead of him, a knee-high rodent sprang from the underbrush, its claws extended. Zekk's Jedi instincts automatically took over.

In one smooth movement Zekk withdrew his lightsaber and threw himself sideways out of the creature's path. His cheek split open as it smashed against the purplish-brown trunk of a Massassi tree; his thumb pressed the lightsaber's ignition stud at the same moment. Before Zekk could even blink or breathe, the blood-red blade sprang forth—and sliced through the rodent in mid-leap. With a shriek that broke off abruptly, the two smoking halves of the creature fell to the forest floor.

It reminded him of how he had killed Tamith Kai's student Vilas in the zero-gravity arena aboard the Shadow Academy station—not a memory that comforted him.

Blood trickled from the cut on Zekk's cheek, but the pain was too distant, too far away for him to feel. His ability with the Force had protected him just now—after all, he was a Dark Jedi. But what about his companions from the Second Imperium? What of *their* powers? Why had it all gone wrong? For today he had seen his Dark Jedi, one after another, lose their battles or be captured by Skywalker's trainees.

He had a terrible suspicion that only he remained.

Oh, the dark side had had its victories. The commando Orvak had obviously succeeded in destroying the shield generators and had no doubt moved on to the next step in his mission. And there had been other times during the day when Zekk had felt the Shadow Academy trainees achieve surges of victory. But each victory had been short-lived.

Brakiss, Tamith Kai, he, and his companions had all been so certain of a quick, decisive triumph. With their training in the dark side, they should have had no problem, Zekk told himself. Wasn't that what Brakiss had taught?

A few minutes later, Zekk emerged from the darkness into a broad clearing where the wide river ran sluggishly between the trees. His spirits rising ever so slightly, Zekk walked to the edge of the river and stooped to take a drink.

Despite the green color of the water, his reflection was clear. Sunken emerald eyes shadowed with dark circles gazed back at him from the rippling surface. Only the barest spark of his former confidence still lurked in his expression. Tangles of filthy dark hair framed a face as pale as the moon of his home planet Ennth. Blood still oozed from the wound on his face, contrasting nicely with the purpling bruises that surrounded it. It made him think of Brakiss and his finely chiseled features.

A wail of despair echoed through the young man's head, knocking him to his hands and knees in the mud of the riverbank. In a futile gesture, Zekk pressed his muddy hands over his ears. "Brakiss!" he screamed. "What went wrong?"

Hardly understanding what was happening, Zekk turned his face up toward the sky. For a split second he recognized the spiked ring of the Shadow Academy in low orbit above the jungle moon—

Then, without warning, the space station bloomed into a fireball high above him. Zekk's jaw went slack at the sight. He had not thought it possible to feel any more pain.

But he had been wrong.

Brakiss. The name whispered now in Zekk's mind. He knew that the Master had been aboard the Shadow Academy when it blew up. He could *feel* it. He had felt his teacher's despair—his mind crying out.

The silvery-robed Jedi had taken Zekk in when the young man had had no hope for his future and no purpose. Brakiss had trained Zekk, given him purpose, direction, position, and skills to be proud of. At the Shadow Academy Zekk had *belonged*. He had been its Darkest Knight.

Now what was left for him? All that he had trained for and lived for was gone. Pride, comrades, future . . . all gone. There was no doubt in Zekk's mind that the Second Imperium had been decisively defeated today, and now his mentor—the only man who had ever believed in Zekk—was dead.

No. Not the *only* man who had believed in Zekk. A fresh wave of anguish washed over Zekk at the thought. Old Peckhum had always believed in him, too. Zekk had promised never to do anything to hurt or disappoint the old spacer. Today, though, he had fought on the side of Peckhum's enemies. Despite all the faults that Zekk acknowledged he had, he had never in his life lied to old Peckhum.

Anger jolted through him—at himself, at having been forced to fight his friend, at having been forced to make such terrible choices. His muscles tightened until the tension inside seemed unbearable. With a cry of anguish he plunged his fingers deep into the mud. It was dark, slippery, treacherous. Yet this was what he had chosen: the darkness.

Today he had stood and watched as his comrades blasted the *Lightning Rod* out of the skies. For all he knew, the only other man who had ever believed in him might also now be dead. Zekk's hands clenched in the ooze and he jerked up fistfuls of mud and smeared it on his face. The mud stung his cut. Now he could feel pain again. But he didn't care. He deserved it.

He had failed them all—Brakiss, the other Dark Jedi warriors, old Peckhum . . . himself. Silent tears dropped unheeded from his eyes as he scooped up more and mud and rubbed it into his hands, his forearms, his neck. Dark mud.

This—*this* was what he had become. Darkness. He had chosen it, immersed himself in it. He was *stained* with it.

There could be no turning back for Zekk anymore. He had made his choices, and he was what he was: a Dark Jedi. That could not change now. Though his comrades were defeated or captured, and Brakiss dead, Zekk would never be able to cleanse himself for as long as he lived—however long that might be.

Not even Jaina and Jacen, if they were still alive, would be able to forgive him. Considering the space battles above, the destruction of the Shadow Academy, the attacks here on the ground, Zekk himself was responsible for a hundred or more deaths today. Maybe even Peckhum's. The twins would know that. They had never believed Zekk's decision to join the Shadow Academy was the right one, had never believed that he could become anything.

But he had made his choice and he had done his best. He had even warned Jaina on Kashyyyk not to return to Yavin 4, hoping to keep her away from the fighting, though he doubted she had listened.

He pushed himself to his feet and caught sight of his reflection again in the slow-moving water. His once-beautiful cape hung in tatters from his shoulders, its scarlet lining shredded. Mud covered his skin. And the sunken emerald eyes were now bleak and hopeless.

But he wasn't finished yet. It might not matter anymore what happened to him, but he still had choices. He would show the twins what he was made of. Turning, he headed along the riverbank toward the Great Temple.

Zekk still had one card left to play.

21

"DOWN THERE," JAINA said, pointing at the jungle clearing that Luke had chosen as a rendezvous point.

From the pilot's seat of his personal shuttle, Lando Calrissian grinned, flashing his beautiful white teeth. "Sure thing, little lady," he said. "I'll take 'er down. Looks like they're waiting for us. The fighting must be done."

As Lando brought the ship in for a landing, Jaina used Jedi techniques to relax, but it did her no good. Her muscles remained as tense as if she were still in the tiny TIE fighter flying for her life. For some reason, she just couldn't loosen up. For the first time, today, she had fought as a Jedi, with other Jedi, against the dark side.

It was what all her training had been about.

When Lando's shuttle touched down, Jaina wasted no time on formalities. She scrambled out of the ship as quickly as she could, ran to her uncle, and threw herself into his arms. "You made it. You're alive!" she said, feeling a surge of relief and jubilation.

"Luke, old buddy!" Lando said. "I came to offer you some help, but it looks like you've got things pretty well under control."

"We could still use your help, Lando," Luke replied. He hugged Jaina back and said soberly, "I'm afraid many of our number were not so lucky."

Realizing that she had no idea how the ground battle had gone, Jaina bit her lip and looked around wildly, hoping to spot Jacen, Lowie, and Tenel Ka.

What she saw shocked her. As far as she could tell, no student from the Jedi academy had escaped unscathed. Several trainees limped. Tionne's right arm hung in a sling and the hair on the right side of her head was singed. Others sported scratches and bruises, as well as more serious injuries.

Jaina stared in surprise when she saw Raynar, his face muddy and his bright clothing torn and covered with filth, moving among the wounded and offering assistance wherever he could. He seemed subdued.

When she noticed the patient Raynar was currently tending, she blanched and dashed over to where Tenel Ka lay, looking feverish and bleeding heavily from a nasty gash just above one gray eye. Another shallower wound ran along her thigh and ended at the knee.

Raynar was already tearing strips of cloth from his relatively clean inner robes. Jaina made a pad of the cloth and pressed it to Tenel Ka's head wound to stanch the flow of blood, while Raynar bandaged the leg cut.

Jaina looked around, still searching for Jacen. Only a few meters away, though she hadn't noticed him before, Lowie lay flat in the grass, moaning quietly and clutching his side.

Around the edges of the clearing, Tionne, Luke, and Lando helped the injured stragglers. There was still no sign of Jacen, though.

"Lowie, are you all right?" Jaina asked.

The Wookiee rumbled something noncommittal and waved a hand, as if to tell her to finish caring for Tenel Ka first.

"Oh, Mistress Jaina! Thank goodness you're here," Em Teedee cried. The little droid's voice sounded strange, and Jaina noticed that the speaker grille was bent. "You have simply no idea what the three of us have been through today. Master Lowbacca and Mistress Tenel Ka were forced to dive from the battle platform in order to avoid being blown up. Which was a good thing, since the battle platform crashed only moments later.

"When we fell to the trees, Master Lowbacca was able to catch himself, but Mistress Tenel Ka struck her head on a branch. She nearly fell all the way to the forest floor, but Master Lowbacca dove after her, caught her arm, and broke their fall by landing stomach-first on a wide limb. Oh, it was bravely done, I assure you, Mistress Jaina. I'm no medical droid, of course, but I'm afraid you'll find that Master Lowbacca has a dislocated shoulder and at least three broken ribs."

Raynar pressed a fresh compress over Tenel Ka's head wound and began winding a bandage around it to hold it in place. "You go ahead," he said, nodding toward Lowie. "I'll finish here."

When two more wounded Jedi students staggered into the clearing, Jaina looked up hopefully, but neither was Jacen. "Have you seen my brother?" she asked Raynar as she went to Lowie's side and knelt to examine his injuries. "He went in the *Lightning Rod* with old Peckhum to call for reinforcements. He should be back by now."

Raynar frowned and shook his head. "Well . . . well . . . I saw the supply shuttle—the *Lightning Rod*. I . . . think one of the TIE fighters hit it."

Jaina gasped. "Did they crash?"

Raynar looked away. "I don't know. The ship seemed to be going down, but . . ." He shrugged uncomfortably. "Anyway, it was hours ago."

Jaina bit her lower lip and closed her eyes, reaching out with the Force, searching for Jacen. "He's not dead," she said at last. "But that's all I can tell. Can't feel old Peckhum—don't have a link with him like I do with Jacen—but my brother's definitely out there somewhere."

A genuine smile broke out on Raynar's face. "Well, good," he said. "That's good."

"That's the last of them, I think," Lando said, striding up and kneeling beside Jaina. "How are you doing, Lowbacca, old buddy? You look like you've seen some hard action."

Lowie gave an *urff* of agreement.

"I think we got everybody who's in the neighborhood now," Lando said.

"We did find one more," Luke said, coming up to join them. He pointed toward the edge of the clearing, where Tionne was tending a treelike Jedi with a broken limb.

Jaina looked up at her uncle. "What about Jacen?"

"He's alive . . . ," Luke said slowly. "We don't know any more than that."

"Yes," said Jaina, "but where is he? Shouldn't we go look for him?"

"We need to get the injured back inside the Great Temple first," Luke said. "If old Peckhum and Jacen managed to get the *Lightning Rod* going, the first place they'd head is the landing field. They wouldn't be able to land in a small clearing like this."

Jaina's spirits brightened. It was true. She looked at Lowie. "Can you walk?" she asked.

Lowie groaned an affirmative reply.

"Master Lowbacca believes himself to be quite capable of perambulation with only minimal assistance," Em Teedee supplied.

"Okay then," Jaina said, "let's get back to the Jedi academy." She was anxious to see her brother again, eager to know that he was all right.

It was close to an hour later when the band of hobbling, limping Jedi trainees finally emerged from the jungle near the Great Temple's landing field. To Jaina's dismay, the flat patch of cleared ground stood empty.

"Don't worry, little lady," Lando said. "I'll help you look for them."

Jaina heaved a sigh and nodded. Even though she knew that Jacen was alive, she had a feeling of foreboding, of impending danger. "All right," Jaina said. "Let's get the wounded inside first. They'll be safe and protected in the temple. We'll have to take them in through the courtyard door, though. The hangar bay's blocked shut."

Crossing the landing field to the flagstone courtyard seemed to take longer than Jaina remembered it, but finally the entrance was only ten meters away. Seeing her goal so close, Jaina smiled and sped up.

Suddenly, a ragged figure lurched out of the shadowy doorway. His face was bloodied and bruised and covered with a thick layer of mud, but Jaina would have recognized him anywhere.

Zekk raised his chin proudly and stood barring the doorway.

"No one goes inside the temple," he said.

22

FACE-TO-FACE WITH HER old friend Zekk again, Jaina could find no words. Her breath refused to move in and out. It seemed to have frozen in her lungs like a chunk of winter. Her heart raced, and her palms grew sweaty.

Zekk didn't move.

Luke came forward to stand beside Jaina. On her other side, still partially supported by her, Lowie voiced a soft growl. And behind her, Jaina suddenly felt the presence of all the remaining Jedi trainees—people who had never met Zekk before today when he had led the attack against the Jedi academy. They saw him only as an enemy, without a glimmer of his being anything else.

Her eyes still fixed on Zekk's mud-covered face, Jaina said, "This is up to me, Uncle Luke. I need to handle this alone."

Luke hesitated for a moment. Jaina knew that her request was difficult for him. His voice held an undercurrent of warning when he spoke. "This isn't a broken machine that you can tinker with and fix."

"I know," she said softly. "I'm not sure he'll listen to me, but I know he won't listen to anyone else."

"I remember thinking the same thing," Luke said, "when I set out to turn Darth Vader back to the light side. It's a dangerous thing to attempt . . . and success is so rare." He sighed, as if thinking of Brakiss.

Jaina tore her eyes away from Zekk and turned to look at her uncle. "Please let me try," she said. Luke studied her for a long moment and then nodded.

Jaina focused her full attention on Zekk now, shutting out all other distractions as Luke took Lowie away across the courtyard. She drew strength from the Force, but was at a loss as to what to say to the young man.

Where did one start when talking to a Dark Jedi?

Zekk, she reminded herself. This was her friend. She took a step toward him and raised her voice, though only enough so he could hear. "The fighting's over now, Zekk. We just need to get inside to tend our wounded."

Zekk shuddered from an inner chill. He backed up a step and spread his arms across the temple entrance. "No. There'll be a lot more injuries if you don't stop where you are."

Jaina balked at the threat. She would need to try a different tack. Zekk's eyes darted from side to side, as if he were assessing the strength of the Jedi trainees, with their various wounds, wondering how many he could kill before they took him down.

"Let me be your friend again, Zekk," Jaina said. "I miss being your friend." He flinched as if he had been struck. "Let go of the dark side and come back to the light. Remember the fun we always had together, you and Jacen and I? Remember the time you salvaged that old slicer module and we tapped into the computers at the holographic zoo?"

Zekk nodded warily.

"We reprogrammed all of the animals to sing Corellian tavern songs," she went on. A wistful smile tugged at the corner of her mouth at the memory.

"We got caught," Zekk pointed out quietly. "And the zoo restored the original programming."

"Yes, but so many returning tourists requested it that a few months later the zoo added our singing animals as a separate exhibit." Jaina thought she saw some flicker of acknowledgment in his emerald eyes, but then they became hard as chips of green marble.

"We're not those children anymore, Jaina," he said. "We can't go back to the way it was before. You don't understand that, do you?" His gaze darted around the courtyard and he rubbed one hand across his forehead and eyes, smearing the mud there.

Jaina said, "All right, I *don't* understand. Explain it to me."

Zekk took a deep breath and began to pace in front of the dark doorway, like some wild creature trapped in an invisible cage. "There's no place where I belong anymore, Jaina. The Shadow Academy became my home. It's gone now—completely destroyed. Where can I go? The dark side is a part of me."

"No, Zekk," Jaina said. "You can give it up. Come back to the light."

Zekk laughed, a sound filled with anger and a touch of madness. He clawed at his cheek with one hand and held out his fingers so that she could see the mud there. A wound on his cheek seeped blood, but he seemed not to notice. "The dark side isn't like this mud," he said.

"You can't just wear it for a while and then scrape it away—wash it off like some child who has finished playing in the dirt."

Zekk wiped his hand on his tattered cape. "I'm a different person now than the uneducated street kid you knew on Coruscant. I don't belong there anymore. Where *could* I belong? I've been trained as a Dark Jedi." His expression turned bleak. "And now my teacher is dead, too. He taught me and believed in me, gave me skills and a purpose."

"Peckhum always believed in you, too," Jaina said in a gentle voice.

Zekk put a muddy hand to his matted hair, and a wild look came over him. "But he's dead, too—he must be. I saw the *Lightning Rod* go down."

Jaina felt as if she had been rammed in the stomach by a mad herdbeast. The *Lightning Rod* had crashed? Then Jacen could be badly injured.

"I failed my teacher Brakiss, and he's dead," Zekk said. He gestured as he spoke. "I led the Shadow Academy into battle, and all of my comrades were killed or captured. And if Peckhum's dead, then that's my fault too." Zekk's eyes looked glassy and feverish; his breathing was fast and shallow.

Jaina set her jaw in stubborn determination. "Well, Zekk, I don't want to see any more people die because of you. Just let me into the temple so we can take care of our wounded."

Zekk stopped pacing and whirled to look at her. "No! Stay back."

Jaina took a step forward. "Zekk, there's nothing left to fight about. What can you possibly hope to gain?"

Zekk shook his head. "You never did listen to my advice. You always thought you knew better." Despite his obvious agitation, Zekk's movements were eerily smooth as he drew his lightsaber from his belt and ignited the glowing red blade with a *snap-hiss*.

Then, in a move so instinctive that a moment later she couldn't even remember it, Jaina found her own lightsaber in her hand, its electric-violet beam humming and pulsating.

A feral grin spread across Zekk's face, almost as if he was glad that it had come to this.

"You see, Jaina," he said, taking a step toward her and twitching his energy blade from side to side, "once you let it in, the dark side is like a disease for which there's no cure." He lunged toward her, and their two blades met in a sizzling struggle of red against violet. "And the only way to remove the disease"—he lunged again and again and Jaina parried—"is to"—*thrust*—"cut"—*thrust*—"it"—*thrust*—"out!"

Jaina spun away and kept a wary eye on Zekk while she circled,

JEDI UNDER SIEGE

waiting for his next move. Out of the corner of her eye she could see Luke watching the battle with calm acceptance.

At that moment Jaina realized that she had been trying to force Zekk to turn to the light side. She had been trying to fix him. But she couldn't. It had to be *his* choice. She drew a deep breath, letting the Force flow through her, and backed away from Zekk.

"I won't fight you anymore, Zekk," she said, switching off her lightsaber and tossing it to the ground. "There's still good in you, but you'll have to decide which direction you want to go—starting now. It's your choice, so make the right one for you."

Surprise and anger and confusion chased each other across Zekk's face. "How do you know I won't kill you?"

From the corner of her eye, Jaina saw Lowie step forward as if to protect her, but Luke put a restraining hand on the Wookiee's shoulder.

Jaina shrugged. "I *don't* know that. But I won't fight you. Make your choice." Jaina pushed back her straight brown hair and looked directly into Zekk's eyes with calm assurance—not assurance that he wouldn't harm her, but assurance that she had done the right thing.

"Well, what are you waiting for?" she whispered.

With slow deliberation, Zekk raised his glowing red lightsaber over Jaina's head.

23

IMPERIAL COMMANDO ORVAK finally awoke, feeling thickheaded and groggy. He fought away nightmares that were filled with serpent fangs and invisible predators slipping out of cracks in the wall. When he shook his head, a wave of dizziness and nausea pounded through his skull.

Orvak couldn't remember where he was or what he was doing. The stone floor felt hard beneath his sprawled body. He had fallen in an uncomfortable position and apparently slept there for some time. His hand throbbed, and he saw two small wounds there—punctures—before his vision blurred and lost focus again.

He must have taken his gloves off, and his helmet. What had he been doing? Where was he?

He heard no other sounds of combat around the Jedi academy. What could be happening?

Then Orvak remembered creeping into the ancient temple, his important mission for the Second Imperium . . . and the invisible glistening snake that had struck at his hand. For some reason, its venom had knocked him unconscious.

He brought his hand close to his eyes, but clarity of focus continued to evade him. Some kind of poison . . . he had been drugged, but now he was coming out of it. Was he a captive of the Jedi sorcerers?

Orvak heaved himself to a sitting position, and the universe turned in giddy circles around his head. He clutched at the cool, smooth floor for support. He had come here to the temple to plant explosives, to wipe out the great stone pyramid. Then everyone would see the weakness of the Rebellion and its Jedi, and they would make room for the Second Imperium.

But something had gone wrong.

Now he heard something. A clicking. Shaking his head again, he looked in the direction of the strange sound. It came from the timing device across the stone platform from him—

Timing device!

He blinked and finally managed to bring his vision into focus. His eyes burned, but he could see the string of descending numbers on the clock display.

Twelve . . . eleven . . . ten . . .

He launched himself to his feet—but too quickly. Dizziness swept through him again and he fell into black oblivion.

Nine . . . eight . . .

24

THE BUZZING HUM of Zekk's lightsaber filled Jaina's ears as her former friend brought it slowly down toward her neck. "You never understood, Jaina. . . . You can't understand. You've always been so protected. The dark side is like a scar that's on the *in*side."

Zekk's eyes locked with hers. His hand remained steady, and he began speaking in a low voice, his words barely audible. "But these are scars that can't be healed," he went on. "You can try to cover them up"—*hum; buzz*—"but they're still there . . . underneath."

A swarm of angry insects buzzed near Jaina's right ear—but it was only the lightsaber, no longer above her head but continuing its excruciatingly slow descent.

Then, as if from a distance, Jaina heard new sounds: a crackle of static, and then a booming voice coming from a comlink.

"This is the *Lightning Rod,* callin' anyone who can hear me. Better clear everyone from the landing field real quick. We're comin' in. Oh, and if you got any of those energy shields back up, you better put 'em down now—we've had more'n our share of problems already today. My arm's broken, so the young Solo kid is flying—but our wings're clipped, and I'm not sure how maneuverable this baby is."

In that moment of delight and surprise, Zekk's lightsaber wavered and lifted away from her. A droning sound caught his attention, and Jaina glanced back over her shoulder to see the *Lightning Rod* coming into view above the treetops, sputtering and wheezing.

"Come on in, *Lightning Rod,*" Jaina heard Luke say into his comlink. "You're clear to land."

Zekk stared in amazement to see the battered old ship still intact, then shook his head. He reached out his free hand toward her. "Jaina, I didn't mean to—"

Just then, a concussive boom split the air, obliterating all other sounds. The ground vibrated beneath Jaina's feet, lurching with tremors and shock waves.

JEDI UNDER SIEGE 703

"Get down!" Zekk shouted.

She dove toward the courtyard wall and hit the ground, gasping at the jolt of pain that speared through her. She rolled, looking upward to see the gouts of smoke that erupted from a huge explosion inside the Great Temple. The crumbled remnants of massive stones tumbled down its sides in an avalanche.

Zekk ran for cover, too, but the hailstorm of rock moved faster than he could dodge. A large chunk of stone struck him in the head, while other fragments pummeled his body. As Jaina watched the dark-haired young man sink to the ground, it came to her in a flash: he had known.

Zekk had *known* the temple was going to blow up.

And he had saved them all.

25

OUT IN THE unexplored jungles of Yavin 4, on the far side of the moon from where Luke Skywalker had established his Jedi academy, the wrecked TIE fighter smoldered after the crash.

The cockpit hatch opened, and Qorl crawled out, coughing and wheezing. With a heave from his human arm, he raised his shoulders, then worked the rest of his body free. His droid arm sparked and sizzled from damage it had received in the crash.

Qorl felt no pain, though. He was still functioning on adrenaline as he hauled himself out of the ship. His legs were numb and stiff, but they still worked. He dropped down from his ruined TIE fighter, then staggered into the protection of the trees just in case the craft exploded.

Alone in the jungle, Qorl watched the TIE fighter smoke until he was confident that none of the engines would go critical. The wrecked ship gradually heaved its last sigh and died.

The damage to his craft was severe: its outer hull had been punctured by iron-hard Massassi tree branches, its two planar energy arrays ripped askew; one had even been broken off.

As he had flown in, pummeled by the Rebel forces, dodging turbolaser bolts until the fatal strike that had caused him to reel out of control, Qorl had seen the Star Destroyers defeated. While wrestling for control of his TIE fighter, he had watched the Shadow Academy explode behind him.

He knew now that all hope for the Second Imperium was gone. The Emperor himself had been aboard the Shadow Academy, as had Lord Brakiss. The remaining Dark Jedi fighters on the surface would no doubt be rounded up and taken to Rebel prisons.

Qorl had much to regret. Rather than let one of the Solo twins die, he had made the choice to sacrifice his twisted student Norys. That had been a betrayal, and he was ashamed of it. Surrender was also betrayal. . . .

But Qorl had never surrendered.

He found himself stranded in the jungle again. His ship was beyond repair. The Second Imperium was defeated. Qorl had no place to go, no orders to follow . . . no reason to do anything other than search for a new place to live.

Perhaps it was best this way.

He could make a nice home for himself here. He knew this jungle, the fruits that were good to eat, which animals were easiest to hunt. Qorl realized that, despite the glory of returning to the Second Imperium and fighting once more for his Emperor, he had enjoyed those years of solitude, the quiet peace of living alone in the jungle.

In fact, he decided that this fate was not so bad, after all.

Qorl trudged off into the jungle to search out a new home. This time, he intended to spend the rest of his life there.

26

THE MORNING AFTER the great battle on Yavin 4 dawned cool and clear. Within hours, the bright sunlight dispensed with the lingering tatters of lacy mist that clung to the rubble-strewn base of the Great Temple and to the trees around it. Overhead, the giant orange planet Yavin filled much of the sky.

Waiting with Lowie and Jacen on the landing field, Jaina marveled at the difference a night's rest and a good meal could make on her perspective. After Luke, Tionne, Lando, and a couple of GemDiver engineers had determined that the lower two levels of the Great Temple were structurally sound, the remaining trainees and staff had made their way back into the pyramid, retrieving an ecstatic Artoo-Detoo, who had been waiting below. Admiral Ackbar's transports had evacuated the most seriously injured students, while those with only minor wounds had been treated and returned to their own chambers in the temple.

Jaina felt fortunate—and a bit guilty—that she had emerged from the battles almost completely unscathed. She had a few cuts and bruises from where stones had hit her after the explosion, but that was all.

Jaina ran an appraising eye over her friend Lowbacca. His shoulder was back in position again, his arm supported by a wide cloth strap, his broken ribs wrapped. The Wookiee normally wore only his webbed belt made of syren plant fibers, so the sling and the thick white bandaging around his midriff seemed oddly out of place.

She heard a warble and bleep behind her, and turned to find Artoo and her uncle Luke coming across the landing field to join them. The Jedi Master's face held a look of serenity and determination, but his eyes showed a glint of humor.

"I think *I* looked even worse than that," Luke said without preamble, "after my encounter with the Wampa ice creature on Hoth."

"Yes, but Lowie's looking a lot better this morning," Jaina agreed.

Luke chuckled. "Actually, I was referring to the Great Temple itself."

Jaina turned to study the ancient Massassi pyramid. The topmost level had collapsed where the detonators had exploded, and part of the sides had slumped downward. The broken, jagged walls of the grand audience chamber could have been mistaken for crenellations atop the battlements of some ancient fortress.

"At first I thought we might have to move the academy to some other temple," Luke said, "but now . . . I'm not sure we need to."

"You mean we could rebuild it?" Jacen asked with a groan. "Great—more practice exercises, lifting rocks, balancing beams . . ."

Artoo-Detoo twittered and beeped, as if excited at the idea. Lowie rumbled thoughtfully, then growled in pain, holding his aching ribs.

"Yes," Luke said. "In one way or another we've all been hurt through our encounters with the dark side. I think rebuilding the Great Temple might be a part of healing each of our wounds."

"Like Zekk," Jaina murmured, feeling her heart contract painfully. "He needs a lot of healing."

"That reminds me, Uncle Luke," Jacen said, "what will you do with the Dark Jedi trainees we captured?"

"Tionne and I are working with them. We'll do our best to turn them back to the light side, but if it's not possible . . ." He spread his hands. "I'll have to discuss that with Leia, and—"

"Oh, Master Lowbacca, look!" Em Teedee interrupted from his clip at Lowie's waist. Jaina noticed that the tiny droid's speaker grille had been straightened and meticulously polished.

"Hey, they're back," Jacen cried.

Lando's shuttle, with Lowie's battered T-23 in tow, arrowed toward a corner of the landing field well away from the blaster-scarred hulk of the *Lightning Rod*.

Uttering a joyous howl, Lowie gave Em Teedee a grateful pat.

"Well, what are we waiting for?" Jaina asked as the shuttle and the T-23 touched down.

Jaina, Jacen, and Lowie hurried forward. By the time they reached it, the shuttle's landing ramp had extended, and Lando Calrissian strode down it with Tenel Ka on his arm. Lando's cape swirled behind him and he flashed his most charming grin. "Your friend here is quite a tough young lady," he said approvingly.

"This is a fact," she said, without the slightest trace of humor.

"I could have told you that," Jacen said. "Did you find it?"

Tenel Ka nodded, a satisfied look on her face. She pulled her arm free, plucked something from her belt, and held it out to show Jacen.

It was the rancor-tooth lightsaber that she had lost during her clash with Tamith Kai on the battle platform. "It was not as difficult to locate as I had feared," she said. "Perhaps because I knew the rancor whose tooth this was, I was able to sense its location."

Tenel Ka no longer appeared feverish, and Jaina was amused to note that the warrior girl had braided her red-gold hair carefully around her face so that her bandage looked like a primitive warband across her forehead.

"I've invited Tenel Ka to come and visit GemDiver Station, since she missed it last time," Lando said. "We have some good bacta tanks there that'll fix up that cut on her head no time. Lowbacca, looks like you could use a few days in one of our tanks, too."

Lowie barked his acceptance and a thank-you.

"Oh, that would be exceedingly kind of you, Master Calrissian," Em Teedee said. "Master Lowbacca is most anxious to complete his healing and begin repairs on his incapacitated vehicle."

"His little skyhopper ain't the only vehicle that's incapacitated."

Jaina jumped when Peckhum's loud voice boomed out behind her.

"I know just what he means, though. The boy and I can't wait to get started fixing the *Lightning Rod*. But I think Zekk is going to be laid-up here for a while recuperating." Old Peckhum stood by the damaged *Lightning Rod,* one hand on Zekk's shoulder, the other arm heavily bandaged.

Zekk's face was as pale as the dressing that wound around the base of his skull. His eyes seemed curiously empty, his face expressionless. He did not meet Jaina's gaze.

"I think you've got two more candidates for your bacta tank, Lando," Jaina said. "Can Jacen and I go along with them, Uncle Luke?"

Artoo-Detoo twittered.

"Oh, indeed! That's a marvelous idea," Em Teedee said.

"We promise not to get kidnapped this time," Jacen added with a lopsided Solo-style grin.

Luke chuckled. "All right, I think that would be good for all of you. You young Jedi Knights are stronger together. If you have some time away to heal, then you'll come back ready to help us rebuild . . . ready for a new beginning."

"Thanks, Uncle Luke," Jaina said.

"Jacen, my friend," Tenel Ka said. "Perhaps we had better leave soon. We do not want all of the injured students to come away with us and leave Master Skywalker here alone."

Jacen gave Tenel Ka a quizzical look. "What do you mean?" he said. "Why would you worry about that?"

"Because," Tenel Ka said solemnly, "a Jedi *must* have patients."

Jacen blinked at her, uncertainty written on his face. Then a shy grin lit Tenel Ka's face. It was the first time he had seen her smile so broadly.

"I don't believe it . . . ," Jacen began.

Jaina shook her head in wonder. "Sounded to me like she just told a joke."

"This is a fact!" Jacen said.

Lowie chuffed with delight. Jaina giggled.

Soon the entire clearing rang with laughter.

ABOUT THE AUTHORS

KEVIN J. ANDERSON and his wife, **REBECCA MOESTA,** have been involved in many STAR WARS projects. Together, they are writing the eleven volumes of the YOUNG JEDI KNIGHTS saga for young adults, as well as creating the JUNIOR JEDI KNIGHTS series for younger readers. Rebecca Moesta is also writing the second trilogy of JUNIOR JEDI KNIGHTS adventures.

Kevin J. Anderson is the author of the STAR WARS: JEDI ACADEMY trilogy, the novel *Darksaber,* and the comic series THE SITH WAR and THE GOLDEN AGE OF THE SITH for Dark Horse comics. He has written many other novels, including two based on *The X-Files* television show. He has edited three STAR WARS anthologies: *Tales from the Mos Eisley Cantina,* in which Rebecca Moesta has a story, *Tales from Jabba's Palace,* and the forthcoming *Tales of the Bounty Hunters.*